The Whiskey Promises Duet

A.R. THOMAS

Copyright © 2022 A. R. Thomas
The Whiskey Promises Duet

All Rights Reserved.
No part of this book may be reproduced or transmitted in any form or by any means, electronic or mechanical, including photocopying, recording, or by any other information storage and retrieval system without written permission of the author, except in the case of brief quotations embodied in critical articles and reviews.
This novel is entirely a work of fiction, all names, characters, places, and events are the products of the author's imagination, or are used fictitiously. Any resemblance to actual persons, living or dead, events or locations is entirely coincidental.
All rights reserved. Except as permitted under the UK Copyright, Designs and Patents Act 1988.
A.R Thomas asserts the moral rights to be identified as the author of this work.
A.R Thomas has no responsibility for the persistence or accuracy of URLs for external or third party Internet Websites referred to in this publication and does not guarantee that any content on such websites is, or will remain, accurate or appropriate.
Designations used by companies to distinguish their products are often claimed as trademarks. All brand names and product names used in this book and on its cover are trade names, services marks, trademarks and registered trademarks of their respective owners. The publishers and the book are not associated with any product or vendor mentioned in this book. None of the companies referenced within the book have endorsed the book.
First Edition.
Editing: Claire Allmendinger at BNW Editing
Cover Designs: Abigail Davies at Pink Elephant Designs
Formatting: Abigail Davies at Pink Elephant Designs
Proofreading: Katie Salt at KLS Publishing

Created with Vellum

Portrayal

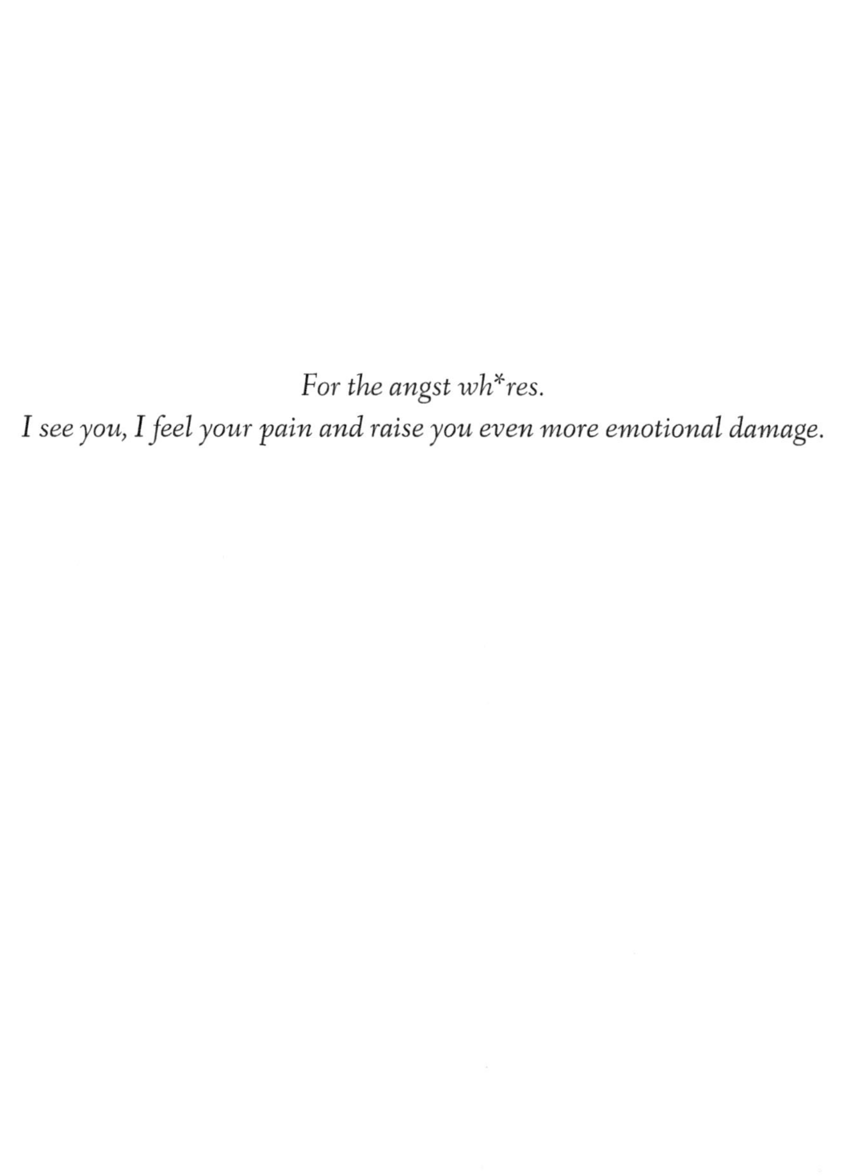

*For the angst wh*res.*
I see you, I feel your pain and raise you even more emotional damage.

Chapter One

I pack my photography gear in my boot and click it shut, then take a moment to re-pin my hair in the back windscreen, my grey eyes look dull in this light and the slight wind alerts me to a few wisps dangling free, I pin it into some semblance of professionalism, tutting when an errant strand slips my grasp repeatedly, Harriet my assistant comes out of the gallery with my handbag and coat slung over her arm. She shivers in the cold but plasters a smile on her face.

"Thanks, I will only be a few hours, any problems, ring me but I'm sure you'll be fine," I say around my hairgrip, already anticipating her wave of panic. Her eyes dart away, as though she's reading my thoughts.

"Okay, I'll contact Paco for you?" she holds my things out, blinking uncertainly through a fine fringe, as I take them with a smile and round my VW.

"Brilliant. I'll ring when I'm leaving." I'm not dressed appropriately for this meet, especially considering I'm taking photographs, my grey pencil skirt, silk blouse and tan high heels scream corporate cute, not comfy. I usually veer towards flats and trousers. I'm annoyed I gave in, but after the third call since yesterday, followed by another this morning, I figured it was better than enduring more calls until next week, plus I'm supposed to be going on a date later. I can make this outfit work if I run late.

Checking my reflection, I swipe some Vaseline over my lips and slide my sunglasses on, sheltering my misty gaze, I love autumn but the sun is a nightmare. I give Harriet a wave through the window and pull out into the steady stream of traffic, half listening to the radio and half following the robotic instructions from Google maps.

The Traffic is heavy and I'm conscious of the time, a horn blares beside me and I regret leaving as late as I did. Thankfully the further from the city I travel, the quieter my journey becomes.

Thirty minutes later, I find myself in one of London's most expensive areas, only the house poking above the treetops is nothing like the rest of the Georgian homes along this tree-lined, regal street. Blowing out a breath, I lean forward so I can look up through my windscreen at the unusual structure, it's set back in lush trees from the heavy wooden security gates. It's easily obscured by thick bark and dense leaves teasing any passerby with the slight flare of unusual edges and twinkling glass.

"Well this person certainly doesn't do things by half," I scoff, nor do they seem to like to conform, I have no doubt building this home here, in such a well sought out and pricey area has ruffled some seriously preened feathers. I clock an intercom ahead and the swiveling lens of a camera before the gates part showcasing a large circular, gravel drive. "Holy crap," I murmur, as the beautifully peculiar house opens up before me, like a rare flower. Wow!

It's a whole lot of glass, seamless wooden beams and apparently not for the private. Once you pass the towering gates and dense foliage that locks this place away— every inch of the house is visible, I would imagine from all directions? The light and bright design interrogates the outdoors with the interior. It's stunning in its simplicity, even if a little ostentatious.

I scan the build mentally snapping photos, all the while thinking, 'so this is what a commercial and domestic architect does,' it certainly puts my boxy flat to shame. I imagine it must pay very well— the house is extraordinary!

I put my car into first gear and cautiously enter, following the drive around to the left and parking next to a very sleek Mercedes, I chew my lip as I gawk at the house, I regret coming at this time of day, the sun is high and reflects off the upper glass, it's going to be hell to photograph.

Friday is supposed to be a little overcast, it would suit me better to shoot then, I suddenly feel a little trepidation at agreeing to this, landscape photography is my niche, I can haggle the weather aspect but I don't feel I will do this property justice.

Pushing my glasses into my hair I slip from my car and go to the boot, I'm hoisting my bag on my shoulder, when the large wooden door opens, a man in a three-piece suit with an expert quiff in his hair smiles over at me, I clunk the boot shut.

"Morning!" he calls, a little high pitched— I'm slightly envious of his ability to present himself. To say he looks good is an understatement. He gives a flamboyant waft of his arms when we meet halfway, "welcome Miss Spencer," he leans forward taking my upper arms in his hands and air kisses me, my eyes widen as I'm engulfed and doused in a sweet and refreshing aftershave.

I remain professional despite his over friendly attitude, "Oh Lily is fine, I take it you're Carl?" I hold my hand out with a knowing look to greet him, recognising his voice from the many phone calls.

He takes the lead and we make our way across the gravel drive towards the house, "That's right, we spoke on the phone, I'm Mr. Bennett's lackey," he laughs on a flap of his hand and enters the house on a subtle sashay, I follow, lifting my bag onto the nearest surface. "Can I get you a drink Lily?" I smile, as I follow him in, more at ease now we have met.

"A coffee please, white, one sugar." I reply a little absently, as I find myself lost in awe of this stunning house. It's not exactly my cup of tea but it is super luxurious, I have no doubt it was designed for a super-rich individual with eclectic tastes, I love how open and bright it is, everything is gleaming but in this location it's a little too open, I look through the expanse of glass trying to find a fault in the absurdly beautiful creation, I can't see any neighbouring homes from where I stand. It's been well thought out.

I feel completely out of my depth, I have never done this kind of shoot and seeing the level of expertise and wealth I've walked into, has my breath catching. I swallow my discomfort and force a professional smile on my face looking about for Carl.

"I'm afraid the man of the house is a little late." He offers from somewhere on the other side of the house, it's tastefully open plan, partially divided by heavy set wood or stone and at the centre raw slate stairs, I gawk at the ridiculous stair case, I could never manage something like that especially after a drink or two, I hope the new owners are teetotal.

I follow the sound of his voice, my heels clicking on the stone floor to find him occupied by a complicated looking coffee machine. With a deep frown, he presses a few buttons until it begins to hiss and grind at him. "One sugar?" He asks once the cup is filled with a rich liquid, it smells amazing!

"Yes, please. This place is incredible." Carl throws me a bright smile over his shoulder, obviously very proud of the work that's been done here. "I will need to take some shots and assess the glare, Friday is more overcast so it would suit me better, as you're aware— this isn't really my forte." I know I can adjust my camera but the subtle hint of clouds may make this place look less of a sweat box, walking to the far window, I look out across manicured lawns and an elevated patio leading over a pool.

"You say Mr. Bennett is late?" I find that a little unprofessional, considering he had Carl ring and ring the gallery, until I agreed to do the shoot. Seeing the immaculate, ultra-modern house, I imagine him to be a stuck-up arse with a general lack of respect for anyone. I sigh inwardly, regretting this more and more.

Real estate photography isn't my line of work, I have done the occasional wedding and odd family portrait, as favours to friends of friends, but running the gallery is my main source of income.

At least it should be, I'm barely cutting even though, so the odd wedding shoot helps. This is a wild card for me. I need the cash.

That is what brought me here, that *and* curiosity,

Carl joins me with two steaming cups, handing me mine, he looks out over the lawn. "I'm afraid so, he will be along shortly. Why don't you have a look around the property, get an idea of the angles and such. Megan from the magazine is coming by sometime before lunch, I think she wants Jace in a few shots." I don't follow— I definitely should have done a little research on Bennett and Klein, before I left the gallery.

"Jace?" I pull my head away from an unusual statue of some sort, it's beautiful and complex, I realise, belatedly, it's a water feature.

"Mr. Bennett." he elaborates, I nod in understanding as I blow on my coffee. I'm guessing Megan is interviewing the architect also.

"Can I ask why you personally requested me for this job, when there are far more established real estate photographers who would better fit the role?" my interest is certainly peaked now, the request is unusual and looking at the expertise presented before me, surely they have connections to prestigious photographers?

Carl smiles at me through the glass reflection. "We decided the last person we hired wasn't right for the job." He shrugs, although I see his face twist. "Jace wanted someone who had talent but no hidden agenda, plus we needed someone quick." What other agenda could someone have? Other than wanting to secure payment and a successful portfolio. Carl sighs, sensing my inner debate. "Mr. Bennett's creative eye is like gold dust." I frown a little because he still hasn't answered my question. I'm not surprised his business is a highly reputable one. The house is as big as a spaceship and looks like it should be placed strategically on some corner of the globe, overlooking clear waters and sandy beaches. It's spectacular.

"Everyone wants a bit of Jace," he states, on a sordid twist of his lips. His eyes hold mine and I feel as though he is trying to convey some hidden message. I nod in false understanding. Personally, I'm here for the money, and if the man himself is so highly rated it will do my portfolio good too.

Carl gives me a run through of the property and once I have finished my drink, I collect my camera and wander around the house, trying to gage the best angles, check room dimensions and get an idea on lighting. That in itself takes up a good hour or so, I can't help but wonder where the hell the architect is, as I'm assessing where to shoot from outside.

I've been in the garden for the last twenty minutes as Carl mentioned getting rear view images, only Harriet has been on the phone for what feels like a lifetime, rather than stand I have made myself at home in one of the oversized garden chairs that looks away from the house into the dense tree line, I left my coat inside and the bite of cold air is teasing its way under my clothes.

"But everything is fine otherwise?" she really does fret for no reason. I rub my forehead to repel the headache I can feel coming on from the constant doubt in her voice.

"Well yes, I just thought I should let you know." There is a clatter of noise down the line and she sighs. "So, is everything okay with the shoot?" I feel guilty for being irritated at her constant need to turn to me, I want someone who is confident enough to keep things running when I'm out with clients, this call could have waited until my return.

"Yes everything is okay, although I've got to go, the architect should be here in a minute, I appreciate you calling," I bite back the frustration caught up in my chest, "Harriet you are capable and resourceful, stop worrying," I coax nicely. I mean it too. She is riddled with self-doubt.

"Yes," she breaths softly, "yes I am." The words are for her benefit not mine.

"I'll be another hour, tops," I say, before ringing off. At least I should be, if the damn man of the house decides he wants to grace us with his presence.

I take a minute to flick through the images I already have and reason that a few, mainly the images taken from the east side of the house where the sun is less visible, are actually better than I expected. Thanks to the natural forest like wall.

Standing, I lift my camera and begin to take a few more, checking my footing as I move about to get clearer shots, the last thing I want is to take a unplanned dip in the pool with my camera in tow.

I try to focus less on the interior and capture the architectural elements of the whole building, but movement inside has me twisting to follow, I expect Carl but my mouth drops slowly at something else, *someone else.*

A tall, lean, athletic man, dressed in only dark jeans walks through one of the bedrooms, I stalk him with my camera, hand adjusting the focus so that I can sharpen his profile and get a better look.

Holy Shit!

He begins to turn my way, pulling a t-shirt over his head covering the clean-cut expanse of his chest and my whole body burns with embarrassment. I feel so ashamed of myself. I can't believe I was ogling some random guy! The architect?

I shakily lower my camera before looking back to the structure, disorientated. I don't think I have ever found a man so starkly handsome.

I stand immobile for what feels like forever before I walk back to the house on wooden, shaky legs, trying to formulate brain productivity, but my mind has gone blank.

What the hell is wrong with me, I frown as I make my way inside to find Carl tapping away on a laptop.

"You okay?" he asks, dropping his head to look over his glasses at me.

"Can I have some water please?" I mumble, robotically placing my camera on the side as he slips from the stool and lifts a chunky glass down.

"Ice?" he's looking at me with concerned eyes and I feel my cheeks heat. Maybe he caught me checking out the boss. Did he?

"Please," I croak. *Jesus I'm pathetic.*

"You look a little peculiar," Carl muses, as he holds out the glass for me to take, I feel peculiar, his steady gaze drifts over me, one hand on his hip and the other up by his shoulder as his shrewd eyes take in my dazed state, my gaze drifts to his, my eyes seeing yet my head still lost somewhere outside amongst the large potted plants. Imagining rippling muscles and a stark jawline!

"I ate early, I'm hungry." *Bloody hell Lily, get it together*! I place a hand on my stomach willing it to ease the frantic flutter of butterflies. It doesn't. I feel short-circuited.

I smooth my hands over my silk cream blouse and finish my water, when the evident sound of footsteps descending the stairs has me clutching my glass until my knuckles are white. I have the most insane bout of nervousness, which is crazy. He's just a guy!

Releasing a slow breath, I tell myself to snap out of it and turn with a smile that falls off my face when I'm confronted by a stunningly, handsome man. Definitely not, just some guy. *Holy shit!*

Holy, fucking shit!

Clearing my throat and forcing my eyes to move away from the whiskey hue of his eyes, I put the glass on the marble surface a little too hastily and it crashes unnaturally making me flinch. For a moment, I stare at the empty glass as I talk myself through how to breath normally. My hands are little shaky, so I drop them and force myself to turn back to him.

"Hello," I go for professional and sound anything but, *shit!* I mentally rush forward and introduce myself, "Lily Spencer, you must be Mr.—" Those eyes meet mine and I just about manage to blink. Slowly.

I stare up at him. Lost. He makes no move to fill the quiet, but holds my gaze. This is crazy, I can't think! Even the simplest of words have fled, taking my sanity and professionalism with them. I manage to swallow against the awkwardness that is starting to rise in me. I am experiencing firsthand how Harriet feels. I flick a look to Carl, who is watching us with an odd look on his face.

"Jace." My head snaps back around. Oh hell. That voice. He is wearing one of those tops that looks over worn and stretched yet this clings to every molecule of his masculine skin and I stare. Stare at his stark profile and strong build. He is not what I was expecting. Not at all.

I know I should probably say something, anything. But I can't, words fail me and the intense rich stare working its way down my body sends a rush of goose bumps over my flesh and lands with a thump in my groin. Swallowing nervously, I grab the glass, I need something to hold. I feel emotionally naked. And the heady stare working its way down my frame, is not helping!

"It's nice to meet you," he murmurs softly, deep eyes lock with mine and I smile awkwardly. I can't say I can agree, this is one of the most embarrassing moments of my life. Even worse than when I fell out my car prepping for a birthday shoot.

Turning abruptly, I walk to the fridge and get my own water, my mind at constant war with my womanhood, I catch Carl looking back between Mr. Bennett and myself a small smile playing around his mouth. His words come back to me now, *everyone wants a bit of Jace!*

Facing the fridge, I neck the water and give myself a pep talk. The icy water kicks me into gear and I place the glass in the sink with another clunk before I collect my camera off the side, "Has Carl explained that Friday will be better for me to shoot?" I'm glad he was late— I want to get out of here. He shoots an ill-disguised look of accusation at Carl, giving me the perfect glimpse at his tanned profile, dear fucking god!

"No, he didn't." He moves into the kitchen, his walk slow and confident as he watches me beneath heavy lashes. Oh...good...god!

I look to Carl who is biting the inside of his cheek, I'm so angry with myself for reacting to this man in such an obvious manner.

I have exceeded the normal requirements of embarrassment, heat hits my cheeks and I force my eyes to hold his to deny the obvious pink stain gracing my face.

"So, you're leaving?" He frowns, his eyes narrowed slightly, the expression highlights the true extent of his eyelashes. They are beyond perfect, dense, lengthy dark lashes. I lick my lips averting my gaze, before forcing confidence and professionalism into my voice.

"Yes." It comes out sharper than intended and Mr. Bennett lifts a brow in silent demand for an explanation. I stare wordlessly until I see the slight play around his mouth, it makes him seem less formidable and more arrogant. Cocky.

"The weather would suit me better." I waft my hand like a halo around my head, unsure which slab of endless glass to refer to. "There is a lot of glass. I have some pictures to work with and I can be here as early as eight." my voice wobbles the closer he gets, I know I should probably shake his hand as I leave but I daren't touch him.

He smells amazing, "Why not tomorrow?" he interjects, leaning a hip against the counter, is he for real he couldn't even make it *in* on time today!

"I have too many appointments tomorrow so I can't shift them, it will have to be Friday." What does he think I am, a lap dog!

He must! I'm practically panting at his mere presence. I'm a fucking joke.

I need to get out of here.

"Can I see the photos you've taken already?" Jace intercepts my path and leans across to take my camera out of my hand, my mind screams for me to find a reasonable excuse to disagree but my limp hand allows him to take it, he twists it over in his hand perplexed, his intelligent eyes hazed by curiosity,

"How do you work this thing?" he murmurs looking at it with a frown. I find his manner rude, and his lateness! Plus, I hate that I find him so attractive. Too attractive, his tall body and easy confidence adopts the room and my full attention. This has never happened, my head is always fixed on work when I'm with clients, not the impressive width of some random guys shoulders or his caramel eyes. *Fuck and shit!*

I pull it back and turn it on, thumbing through the pictures, eager to move things along and get out of here, my breath dances out on an unsynchronised rush at being so close to him.

"That one." He holds the camera. My hand caught below his. I have gone all wide-eyed and breathless, a reaction I'm not in the least accustomed too. Tingles start in my hand and taper down my spine before dancing to my womb, I grit my teeth and gasp softly at the contact. I faintly hear his sharp intake of breath and when I flick a look up, he is grinning down at me. I drown in embarrassment. I'm that transparent!

I flush beetroot red and will the ground to gape open and let me drop through.

Urgh, the arrogant prick!

"Too much reflection," I state with clenched teeth.

My heart has gone haywire, my legs shaky and awkward. Plus, the bang and fizz in my groin is an unwelcome distraction. Does he know?

I suspect a man as good looking and successful as him, knows exactly what he is doing, how he affects women. I'm sure even men recognise him as a formidable character.

The main door opens, giving me a brief reprieve from this man as his attention turns to a tall blonde woman walking in, her hair is up and wet at the ends suggesting she has dried it in a rush, she is grinning coyly at our host,

"Hi, sorry I'm late," she purrs and looks over Jace knowingly, intimately. It doesn't take a genius to work out why he was also late—Carl closes the lid on his laptop dragging my head back as he clears his throat, I suppose she is his girlfriend, she looks like a model.

"Lily, this is Megan. She's from In House magazine." He is ultra-professional and trying to deflect the evident frown off my face, splashing his extravagant personality all over the awkward atmosphere. It's a shame I can't match his enthusiasm.

Oh, I just bet she is! This is why he was late, because he was screwing her. I dislike him instantly. Or at least I want to. My head snaps round on an angry rush.

Their joint unprofessionalism riles me, my mouth pulls into a tight pinch, when I flick my eyes up Jace is watching me, face expressionless.

I feel anger dig her razor-sharp nails into my gut. This is a total waste of my time!

This time, it's me who raises a brow, my glare hard and direct. Yes Mr. Bennett, I'm pissed off. The twinkle in his eye darkens and he holds my look, hands tucked in his pockets whilst he breathes evenly, relishing in the situation.

"Right well, I'll see you Friday." I don't even greet her, I'm being ridiculously rude but I'm so cross. He persisted and demanded, through Carl, that I meet him today and the arrogant arse has the gall to turn up late, all in the name of a quick screw! I hope she was bloody worth it!

In fact, no I don't, I hope it was crap, awkward, boring sex!

Deep down, my intuition tells me this man is not capable of awkward or boring.

"You're going! But I thought we were getting some shots of Jace?" her big blue eyes widen in confusion and I smile sweetly.

"So, did I, I was asked to be here for eleven, it's now coming up to half one." her eyes slip to Jace involuntarily and I roll mine.

"Eight," I reiterate as I walk past her to my bag and begin stowing my things away. When I look back, she is glaring at me and Jace is just drowning me in that amber gaze. "If you're not here you can get someone else to do the shoot," I breath harshly, Jace's eyebrows shoot up but his lips twitch in amusement, it just irks me further that I've reacted so openly to this man, I walk past feeling heavy, amused eyes on me. God he is thriving off this! What a prick!

Carl has the decency to look embarrassed and follows me out the house, I forgo my boot and put my bags in the front seat, "Miss

Spencer, I'm very sorry." he looks at little flustered and I look at him from my window.

"Why are you apologising?" I'm boiling mad.

He looks taken back— looking to the house, then back to me, he frowns at me as though I'm stupid. "Well, because of Mr. Bennett's lateness," he says slowly.

"Well, Mr. Bennett has a mouth." I point out coldly, I close my eyes and remind myself this man has done nothing wrong, on a small sigh I force myself to inject genuine warmth into my voice "Thank you for meeting me." I start the engine up and it's all the indication he needs, to know this conversation is over.

Chapter Two

I drive back into Central London, full of so much anger at him for his devil may care attitude and at myself, mainly myself. Grinding my teeth, I try to forget how I made a spectacle of myself back there. I was pathetic. No man has ever done that to me.I called Harriet on my way back to the gallery, like promised, before calling Cass up. My trusty and closest friend, picks up on the first ring. "Lady you call at the most inconvenient of times." Her voice is tight and I frown at the road, what is she doing?

"How inconvenient because I need to vent?" I puff childlike.

She makes a soft grunting noise and my eyebrows fly up, "are you having sex!" I practically squeal down the hands free in mortification.

Her laugh is dirty and makes me smile despite my initial shock. "No, Marco, my personal trainer, is giving me a workout."

"Oh, is he now?" I drawl, I know all about Marco, Cass has been trying to get in his pants for weeks. She moans again and I know it's for his benefit, she's trying to make him snap. He will. They all do.

"What's up anyway?" I can imagine her bent double, as Marco watches her stretch inappropriately.

"New client. Fancy a drink later? I need a wine fix," I mutter, checking the road before I pull into more traffic.

"You mean you need to rant." She's laughing, which makes me laugh too.

"That also. I can meet you at the Waldorf for seven-thirty?"

"What about your date?" she wonders, her voice strained. I snort in response. I couldn't even consider it in the mood I'm in. Cass hums as though she is thinking it over, "Today is no good." No good for her lady garden, she means! "I can meet you tomorrow night? Oh, Marco," she purrs and I can't help but laugh, coughing at her brashness.

"Tomorrow is fine." It's not— I want to whine about Jace Bennett's work ethics and his beautiful eyes.

"Great, see you tomorrow," she chuckles, and I say goodbye before disconnecting the call, silently despairing at my friend.

Rather than heading straight back to the office like I promised, I find myself sat on a bench in Hyde Park, my phone in my hand as I debate calling Carl to pull out of the shoot.

My fingers grip the phone and I tilt my head back, letting the momentary burst of sun wash over my face and heat my skin. Clear blue sky greets me, as I think back on this morning. I don't want to see Jace again, but I know I have to— the money is too good to cut and run for the sake of some self-loving arrogant arse.

I smirk to myself, some arse though.

I cringe, thinking how ridiculous I acted back at the property, at least now I am a little prepared for what is to come on Friday. The anger still lurks, and I keep it knowing it is what will get me through the next forty-eight hours.

Carl isn't the only person I've considered cancelling with, my date with Mitch is about as appealing as sunburn. With Cass not being free later, I'm now veering towards the allure of my pyjamas and a bottle of wine over unknown company.

Sighing, I leave the park and head back to my car.

All this over some confident twat.

Harriet is chatting with a customer when I arrive back, we share a smile in greeting and I leave her to it, walking quickly down to my office at the back. It's nothing special but it's quiet, not sure that's what I need right now but I opt for it anyway.

I put all my things away, not giving much thought to where I place anything, I keep my camera in my hand and hook it up to my laptop, loading up the dozen or so images I snapped this morning.

Picture after picture of wooden beams and smear free endless glass litters my screen but only one has my full attention, I run the curser over the image watching it magnify as Jace's topless body takes precedence on my laptop. I stare at it for far too long. Too long to make sense, I almost believed I had imagined him, but there he is in all his tan, golden glory.

I hit delete before I can talk myself out of it.

When my phone chimes with a text from Mitch, I make my mind up.

Hey Lily, hope your day is going well, still up for tonight? Mitch x

My fingers fly over my phone as I type a response I can't change,

Hi, my day could be better, can we rearrange?

I sigh reluctantly, too tightly wound to go but feeling bad for cancelling at such short notice. It's a while before he replies but I don't bother opening it and work through the list of jobs noted in my diary. It's a needed distraction.

Harriet taps on my door lightly an hour or so later and hands me a few bills that arrived after I left this morning, along with my bank statement. "Thanks." I smile, as she backs out, closing the door. I blanch at the numbers, my head dropping in my hands. With the money I will make from the shoot and the event I have next month, I should finally be hitting even. Should be.

I process it on the spreadsheet and send a few emails, one to Carl confirming Friday's appointment before making myself and Harriet a coffee. She is sat at the desk out front, amongst all the art. "Hey." she smiles seeing me approach.

"Sorry I haven't gotten back to you about your holidays, that week is fine, I've logged it on the calendar."

"Oh, great thanks." I hand over her coffee and take the seat opposite her.

"I hope I haven't messed up any travel plans." I was supposed to get back to her last week.

"No, not at all." she sips her coffee, her other hand still cupping the mouse. "Do you mind if I give Faye a call?" she asks hopefully, a shimmer of excitement in her eyes. I shake my head in answer and watch her skip her way upstairs, her mobile clutched to her ear. As the gallery phone rings, she halts and looks back down at me from the wide iron staircase, but I shoo her away, picking it up myself.

"The Loft, Lily speaking, how can I help?" I greet breezily.

"Lily." A male voice rolls down the phone making me sit straighter, my breath catches and a pang of lust fires in my gut. Dammit. My anger sparks. *It's him!*

I go for indifference. "Yes speaking, how can I help?" My voice sounds shaky to my own ears and my swallow is too loud to disguise.

He chuckles and I grit my teeth, surely it's not natural that someone can cause such an array of emotion in another by simply breathing, I take what I need from the thought and tell myself it's because I don't like him and it has nothing to do with how wildly attractive he is.

Nothing. At. Fucking. All.

When I offer no recognition he sighs, "So that's how we're going to play it, huh?"

"I'm sorry, play what? Please, can I know who I'm speaking with?" I'm grinning now, happy with my efforts to play him at his own game.

"Jace Bennett," his gravelly voice is laced with amusement.

"Mr. Bennett, I'm assuming you're calling to confirm our rescheduled appointment, I emailed Carl, is Friday okay?" leaning forward I rest my elbows on the desk, more at ease now that I have the safety of a few miles and a phone between us.

"You're enjoying this," he states, certain in his observation.

"Excuse me?" I murmur, my lips twitching as I suppress a smile. He's much easier to handle this way.

"Lily let me take you out for dinner, I owe you an apology."

What the fuck!

I laugh incredulously, the absolute gall of him! "I think that's a little inappropriate, don't you?" I stand swiftly, unable to sit still any longer.

"No." He drops the word without an ounce of hesitation, no remorse just all male confidence.

"Well I do," I huff, feeling like this conversation is suddenly way out of my depth, I look to the door silently pleading a customer to walk through and give me a reason to end the call.

"Carl mentioned you were a little hesitant about shooting the build." God that makes me seem so naive and not professional at all. "I thought I could talk to you about the property, suggest some ideas about what I want from the shoot, in terms of marketing and so on, I'm offering an olive branch here, don't slap my wrist again." I have no doubt he is grinning ear to ear, I frown hard forcing my own mouth to stay firmly in a dissatisfied line. "I'll pick you up around seven?"

"I have a date." I blurt, the lie dashing off my tongue, I worry he will try to placate me into dining tomorrow evening, "and tomorrow evening is no good I have a meeting at the Waldorf, I'll see you Friday all being well." I can't believe I told him about my date. I'm having a serious case of brain to mouth malfunction. And I absolutely refuse to even acknowledge the little jig my womanhood is doing, at hearing his voice again.

He clears his throat and I hear the slam of a car door, "sure, have a good evening, Lily." my name is a rasp on his tongue, and I shiver, what the hell!

"You too," I murmur, disconnecting the call and breathing for the first time in a few minutes.

I'm utterly dreading Friday now.

Art has always been a huge love of mine, the sheer power of multiple emotions held in one form and perceived so differently to each individual, it's another form of oxygen to me. So it irks me now, that even being surrounded by all the art in the gallery, that I feel so despondent and agitated.

I have used all my willpower, to think of anything other than the man who I met yesterday. My thoughts of him have taken an unwanted priority in my mind and no swearing, staring at art, finances or online browsing have swayed its place. He has flummoxed me.

I find myself typing his name into Google and deleting it just as quick, I hate myself for caring because I don't care, not really, he has stupefied me, knocked me sideways and I'm still struggling to fathom what it *is* about him.

"Get a grip Lil," I mutter to myself and push away from my desk, Harriet is chatting away animatedly on the phone, it's nearing one so I make an impromptu decision to take her out to lunch, slipping my coat on I grab my bag and head out front.

Mitch is stood opposite the desk, I halt as I take in his sheepish look and realise Harriet was talking to him, my look of confusion turns to an awkward smile when I see him grin uncertainly at me. What's going on?

He's a nice guy, safe and I hate to say it, but boring, nothing like the likes of Jace Bennett, with his burning eyes and cocky grin.

"Mitch, Hi!" I try for enthusiastic, but I feel too deflated. I drag my high ponytail out from under my collar watching him uncertainly. My eyes meet Harriet's, who is also trying to not convey her unease at the situation.

He gives a nervous laugh, "Hi, I hope you don't mind me turning up here?" he rubs the back of his neck, no doubt sensing the awkwardness dancing in the air.

I inject warmth into my smile, "Of course not, is everything okay?" Harriet is smiling behind her hair and I try to keep my eyes upward so that I don't laugh, she knows me too well, I hate surprises, especially when it's not one you actually want.

His next words make her chuckle, which she covers with a cough, "Surprise," he grimaces, unsure whether he has made the right decision in coming here, his eyes are cautious and I know it has taken him a lot to build up the courage to do this. I flit a look to Harriet, silently asking her if she minds me going, my plan to close up and take her to lunch now on the back burner.

She nods and I give Mitch a false smile. "I will be an hour or so." I check my watch, already counting down to getting back here. His bland personality is painfully infectious. I can feel the life being sucked right out of me, at the mere prospect of spending the next hour together.

Harriet looks back up from the desk. "No problem, nice to see you Mitch." She is grinning stupidly up at him and he has no idea. Oh the poor sod.

He nods repeatedly, more to himself and then looks around baffled and in search of the exit. I wait awkwardly as he struggles to get himself together, before pointing at the door, all flustered.

"Okay, let's go." He breathes out a rush of air and my stomach sinks further. I shouldn't be so mean because he is a nice guy, subtly attractive, gentle, and I can imagine very affectionate, but I can't help but compare him to Jace Bennett and his driving confidence. I groan inwardly at my wayward thoughts and look back to Harriet with a pained expression, she stifles a laugh and waves us off.

"Have fun!" she whispers on a suppressed chuckle, I throw her a despairing look as I follow him out.

Mitch clasps his hands together and slips me a nervous look, I feel sorry for him and decide to take the lead. "So where are we headed?" I button up my thick coat.

He points the way we are walking. "There's a restaurant around the corner, Gustav's have you heard of it?" he can barely lift his head to meet my eyes.

I nod and smile. "Yes, Harriet and I go sometimes, the food is lovely." He flashes me a look of relief, and nods again his hands working frantically as we walk up the street. I ask about his work, knowing he is head of IT for a small firm, it was in his dating profile, something I'm now wishing Cass hadn't signed me up for.

After admitting any attempts to date were massive failures, I was momentarily convinced this was the way forward, real, genuine people looking for love. Call me old fashioned but I want to be swept off my feet and meet at random not through the click and tap of a computer. My mind instantly rushes forward with an image of Jace, topless, those blunt and smouldering eyes, his sexy smirk and cocky gait. I squash the thought and walk a little faster.

"I'm terrible with technology." I admit. "Harriet sorts any upgrades and I happily let her get on with it."

"If you want help with any of that, give me a call, I don't mind giving you a quick tutorial." Oh, how tantalising. I try to hide the look of inner horror, at the prospect.

"I'll keep it in mind," I mutter as Mitch pushes through the door and allows me through, it's instantly warmer in here and I take my coat off as we are escorted to a small table, looking out onto the street.

I'm barely seated when I say to the waiter, "Can I have a large class of white wine please?" Mitch's eyes fly to mine, I smile sweetly but see the look of unease at my eagerness to sink some alcohol.

"Ginger beer please," he adds, squinting at the menu.

The waiter looks to me. "Any preference of wine?"

"Pinot please, I always have the seafood platter here," I tell Mitch, "It's amazing." I hand my menu over, my decision made before we walked through the door.

The waiter leaves giving Mitch time to frown over his menu, I can't help but stare at the perspiration forming on his brow. I look away as he lifts his head. "I might have the risotto." He doesn't seem sure. Clearing his throat, he starts tapping his index finger on the table, as he swings his gaze everywhere but at me. He is kitted out in a plain shirt and one of those knitted vests. I'm not overly fashionable myself but given his age, he looks to be pushing sixty plus in the clothes department.

"Harriet likes that." I confirm he nods this over. "How long has she worked with you?" I inspect him. It's absurd that he is only a few years older than me, yet I feel he is twenty years my senior.

"For about a year now." My wine arrives and I take a healthy sip. "That's lovely thank you," Mitch's beer is placed down too.

"Are you ready to order?" The waiter holds out a small pad and I order my usual and Mitch sticks with the risotto.

"You both seem very different." He smiles, and I tilt my head.

"We both love art." I shrug.

"She seems fairly shy, I mean today she was a little more chatty." I sit back and frown.

"Have you been in before?" He blanches and I have my answer right there.

Because that's not creepy at all!

Dear god I picked a serial killer!

His face flushes and rightly so. "I popped in yesterday, I wanted to check we were still on for last night." I nod in understanding but

I'm pretty certain I never gave him my place of work, nor is it on my profile. It never occurred to me when he showed up earlier.

"She didn't mention it," I murmur, feeling completely spooked by his dedication to seeing our date through. I only recognised him from his dating profile, but now seeing the man in the flesh it is clear he hasn't been completely honest.

"Well, I said I'd text you." He wafts it off, as though his behaviour is normal. This is escalating way too fast. I'm not comfortable in his company at all.

"Well here I am." I shrug not sure what else to say. I decided last night I was going to let him down gently, but I'm crippled by the urgency to be upfront now, especially since he has stalker-ish tendencies. "Mitch, I have a confession."

His head lifts and he looks wary. "Okay." he smiles awkwardly,

"It was my friend who set up my dating profile, I'm not sure that I even want to date. I feel awful, but I wanted to be honest." He looks utterly gutted for a moment, but smiles to himself on a soft huff.

"Ah, it all makes sense now." He nods his head rapidly. Harriet's anxiety pales in comparison to his. He leans back in his chair and gives a little laugh, looking the most at ease I have ever seen him, He's definitely a serial killer.

"Oh, it does?" It's me now who looks around, slightly apprehensive in his next move— I feel Mitch is a nod short of a mental breakdown.

He throws his hands up on a short, sharp laugh of disbelief. "I honestly couldn't understand why a woman like you, would even *look* in my direction." His laugh lightens, and he shakes his head to himself.

"I'm really sorry." I wince, god I feel a total bitch. "Do you want to leave?" I ask, silently praying he will agree.

"God no, I said I was taking you out to lunch and I am," he huffs out a shaky breath. "To fake profiles and random lunches," he sniggers. Ouch.

"Well it's not a fake profile," I sigh, feeling the pinch of his accusation.

He offers me a blunt stare. God I'm going to murder Cass.

Our meals arrive and we manage to get though lunch with little difficulty, he even walks me back to the Gallery after. With an awkward hug he stiffly walks away, and I curse Cass under my breath.

As soon as I can I fire up my laptop, I log on to the dating site. Ignoring the flashing icons and messages awaiting me, I delete my profile and say goodbye to dating dramas. What a hellish few days.

I'm enjoying being single, I like the freedom of doing my own thing and not having to answer to anyone or compromising. It's selfish but after my last relationship I sorely need it.

Harriet and I manage to grab a quiet moment and sit out back in the brief sunshine pouring into the courtyard.

"So not a keeper then?" She asks, her face is full of mischief and when I slowly roll my head to look at her she bursts out laughing, I do too because there is little else I can do.

"He's a lovely person," I say, feeling guilty at having let it get as far as it did.

"He was a nervous wreck, when you walked out, I honestly think he was seeing wedding bells and everything." Harriet is clutching her chest, laughing heartily— I shudder at that thought.

"I swear Cass hates me, she is always trying to pair me with odd-bods, I mean Mitch was nice, but we had zilch in common and he had a weird nodding habit." I mimic him until we are both giggling loudly, Harriet's head is tilted back so far I worry she will tip back under the unkempt bush.

"Lucky escape then," she chuckles. "I have a date tomorrow, Faye has set me up with a work colleague." She looks dubious too, more so I assume after my lunchtime failure.

"Well." I sigh. "You never know, he could be your Mr. Right." I grin and stand, mentally hoping her date to go well. "I need to nip to the post office." I state, she nods then exaggerates it until we are both laughing once more. I don't think I could have lasted in a relationship with Mitch's constant nodding and nervous sweats!

The rest of my afternoon is caught up with errands, customers and sourcing new art before I leave to meet Cass.

Chapter Three

I've let my hair hang naturally and have added some gloss. I'm a little early, so I order a wine whilst I pick at the olives on the bar. I sort a few emails and track a package whilst I wait. Huffing out a sigh, I pop an olive in my mouth as Cass hops on a stool beside me.

"Well you sure are a happy little madam," she chirps, I clock the love bite on her neck and raise my brows at her but she keeps her gaze focused on the mirrored bar in front of us.

She orders a drink and turns then, giving me her full attention, I point to her neck and she grins slowly. "You first then me." She picks up her wine and takes a sip nodding to the waiter in thanks.

"That's what he said?" I say, grinning over my glass at her.

She flicks her hair over her shoulder on a laugh. "Would I ever?" I swallow the very blunt yes trying to be exorcised from my throat.

Shaking my head, I sigh and tell her about the shoot on Wednesday, leaving out the most crucial part. How attractive he is.

"And that's it?" She frowns, she knows me too well I nod around taking a healthy gulp of my wine. She tilts her head in response, so I know I haven't fooled her. I feel such an idiot. When her eyes narrow it tumbles out.

"He's arrogant and I don't want to have to go back there," I whine.

"Well considering he can't get out of bed by midday, I don't think you have anything to worry about." She points out, before popping an olive in her mouth and groaning in satisfaction.

"Fair point," I muse, he has gotten under my skin, and it's not just the lateness or the reasoning behind that. It's those eyes and his damn voice, that sexy smirk and sculpted body. Fuck!

Lifting my glass as the waiter passes, I ask for another drink. I shouldn't but the last tasted too good. "Are you going to tell me what really bothers you about him?" Cass asks, twirling her glass stem between her fingers.

My gaze lifts and she holds me with a pointed stare, I'm starting to feel as though I have overreacted to the whole thing, that he was a figment of my imagination and I made the whole thing up.

Back straight she lifts her hands and starts faffing with her blonde hair. "Spill," she says.

I groan loudly. "He's super-hot. I made such an idiot of myself." I cringe in my chair and look over at her.

"Ding, ding, ding." She taps her nail to her glass eliciting the sound of a tiny bell, "and there we have it." I scowl at her, and Cass leans in and hugs me.

"We have all made an idiot of ourselves in front of men, Lils, and the fact that he was up all night banging his hot magazine fold," she winks at me when my face twists in annoyance, "just pissed you off because he pushed so much for you to do the shoot."

It's un-professional!

"I know," I huff, "plus I cancelled on Mitch but he turned up at the Loft today." I say through gritted teeth, her eyes widen in horror.

"He did! He doesn't seem the type." She wrinkles her nose. "He seems a bit drippy." She looks apologetic, good. My afternoon has been crap.

"He was, we went for lunch, and I came clean. No more dating apps, no more men, I just want me time."

"With me," she drawls over her wine glass.

I grin. "Of course." I rest my elbow on the bar, propping my chin up. "Thanks," I murmur, glad she joined me for drinks— I needed the distraction of my friend. Let's face it— after tomorrow, I won't be seeing Jace Bennett again.

With the Waldorf being a few tubes stops from the gallery, I'm lucky I left my car there, because this wine is going down far too well. Two glasses turn to four and soon I'm giggling at the bar with Cass.

"Turns out Marco's main muscle, has a lot of catching up to do with the rest of his body." She pouts disappointed, I snort out a quiet laugh. "It's not funny, I don't think I can face him again." She rolls her eyes an olive centimeters from her mouth.

I give a little shake of my head. "You can't, he will know!" She is looking at me as if I have suddenly grown another head, she's awful!

"Oh, I already contacted another PT earlier, goodbye Marco," she sings, her eyes slip over my shoulder, to the group of men who invited us to join them for drinks not long after our second wine.

"I might take their invite up after all." She wiggles her eyebrows at me, devious as ever. We declined the invite in favour of our own company, but it seems Cass is regretting the decision already.

"What all of them!" I blurt, wine burning my nose.

Cass wafts her face, trying to salvage her makeup, and blows out a breath as she tries to diminish the bout of laughter. It seems like forever before we come down off our high and we move the conversation away from men. I'm in a blissful bubble, ignorant to yesterday's activities.

She starts to tell me about work. "I want you to photograph the next party." It's how we met with her being a party planner and me doing the odd shoot we hit it off and have been friends since.

"Pass my details to your client," I say absently. There is a flash of dark hair behind me and I react instantly. My head snaps up and I spin on my chair, as Jace Bennett casually saunters into the bar. Carl and another man join him. Spinning back around, I laugh in disbelief.

This. Cannot. Be. Happening.

This is ridiculous. I must be hallucinating. Surely, life wouldn't be so cruel!

Cass raises a brow at me, then her head snaps round too, my unusual behaviour forgotten.

"Oh, Jesus Christ, Lil three o'clock," she informs me on a girlish breath. "My ovaries just dry humped my tubes," she announces loudly, and I snort again. My thoughts exactly.

"Mmm hmm." I don't look. I don't even want to acknowledge him. In fact we should leave. "Shall we go?" It's a sick joke, I have never laid my eyes on this man before yesterday. Yet here he is!

In all fairness, this is only my second visit to the Waldorf, it may be a regular haunt for him.

"Hell fucking no, I'm not going." She spits indignantly, "Have you even looked? Lily *turn* your head." Her lips are pressed to my ear, fingers tips digging so deep they're chaffing my bones.

"Ouch!" I cry, I can't help but flick a look his way. It's instinctive, involuntary and annoying to say the least, his back is turned but as soon as his head inches this way, I pull my hair in my face and pick up my glass.

"Oh, thank the lord he's coming this way, now I can ogle up close," Cass purrs, I shrug and she nudges me. "Jeez, that guy really has pissed you off. You've become a man hater. I need to re-evaluate our friendship," she scoffs, over her now empty glass.

Oh, you have no idea!

He takes the space next to Cass, who has twisted to face him a flirtatious smile on her painted lips. I on the other hand sink lower in my seat, yet my eyes have latched onto his reflection in the mirror. He looks good, really damn good!

His dark mass of hair is roughly mussed and his inky lashes frame syrupy eyes. My stomach rolls as heat hits my pelvis, making me bite my lip in discomfort.

Gone are the worn jeans and casual top, here he stands modeling an expensive suit and making a mockery of every other man in here.

It takes him less than a few seconds to clock me— his eyes flare, those unusual ambers burning into mine. I groan because I still haven't recovered from our first meeting. I was reeling before but now I have been thrown back in the firing line and I can't escape.

His mouth widens slowly, he moves back rounding Cass and exploits an empty space so that he can lean against the bar next to me, I swallow as my eyes get drawn to him, with a frown he lifts a finger and tucks my hair behind my ear. "Lily," he breathes.

I melt. I've been rendered speechless, an un-consenting mute if you like.

"I owe you an apology." His voice is butter soft and I can't help but watch the way his lips move. His fingers are still caught in my hair and instead of pulling away and telling him to keep his hands to himself, like I should, I practically sway towards him. Wetting my lips as I do.

Something sharp stabs into my back and I jump in my seat, Cass leans past me her talon like nails appearing as she holds her hand out. "Cassandra Faraday, and you are?" She drawls her mouth fashioned into a flirtatious pout.

"Jace Bennett," he offers his hand, but his eyes stay on me. Holy shit those eyes are something else.

"Oh." My friend sits her butt back and sticks her tongue in her cheek as she looks over Jace.

Dropping to his haunches, so he is looking up at me Jace smiles. "How much you had to drink lady?" He smells amazing, fresh and earthy. He thinks I'm pissed— it's laughable because it's him I'm drunk on!

"Less than you're assuming." I force the words past my lips. My mouth feels dry, my face is inches from his and all I can do is gaze into those damn eyes. Jace runs his thumb over his lip and my eyes draw the same path, my own lips parting.

"About yesterday," he starts. Cass sniggers, bringing his head up. I cringe, knowing how blunt my friend is. I'm blushing before she speaks. Cass will have no qualms throwing me under the bus for a cheap jibe.

"How is centerfold?" She runs her tongue over her teeth and drops her gaze so she can stare him out. I've seen her do it a million times.

I silently will Jace to crack under her intense glare, but he smirks, meeting her challenging tone head-on. "You mean on a one to ten scale, or a generalisation of how she is post-sex?" He's shameful, and I want to dislike him. God, I really do want to dislike him.

Her smile is slow. "I like him," she states and hops off the stool. I don't. I'm gaping at his brashness. "I'm nipping to the ladies. Don't move, Lily." She pats my arm and as she passes, Jace says, "Is she always this bossy?"

"Yes," Cass and I both say in unison. I watch her leave and keep my eyes focused away from the man attacking my senses.

Jace takes her seat, unaffected by the sudden stiffness to my frame, I feel unease ripple over my nervous system. I don't want him to get comfortable. I want him to go away. Need him to.

I know she will be a while but I will take standing in the cold outside over sitting alone with this man. I don't trust myself around him.

"Would you like to join us for a drink?" he asks, his thick thighs stretched out in front so his foot brushes my ankle. I flinch at the contact and look everywhere but at him.

"No," I croak too quickly, Jace inclines his head at my abrupt reply. "No thank you." I add and shake my head, as I will the floor to swallow me up for the umpteenth time this week. One-way ticket to hell, *yes, please*!

Jesus, Lily, snap the hell out of it!

Slipping from the stool, I give him a tight smile as I put my coat on. "Goodnight." I know Cass told me not to move, but I'm not sitting here.

"You're leaving?" he chuckles, it antagonises me further, he knows damn well how much he affects me. I throw him a death stare and secure my coat around my narrow waist.

"Are you driving?" he asks, when the waiter brings over a glass of something strong. It's the same colour as his eyes and I can't help but stare up into them.

"No, I'll catch the tube." I feel a little tipsy but I haven't eaten since midday, so it has gone straight to my head, no wonder I'm falling all over him. I *am* pissed!

"Isn't it a bit late for that, you've obviously had a fair bit to drink?" A frown appears between his eyes and I stare at it. On a shrug I pick my bag up irritated he cares so much.

"Enjoy your evening." I look back to Carl and their friend, lifting my hand in acknowledgement, and muster the strength to walk out of the bar in a straight line, with the stomach-churning knowledge that he is watching.

I wait out in the foyer for Cass. My eyes defy me and slip to the bar bracketing the main reception. I can just about see Jace and he is looking straight at me. It's then that I remember telling him I would be here tonight. I'm astounded at this man's lack of principle.

He followed me! I shouldn't find that attractive, but I do.

Turning, I stand with my back to him and smile at the concierge. "Miss Spencer?" he asks, a little unsure.

"Yes?" I walk over, concerned. Where is Cass? I begin to worry something has happened to her. She's been a fair while now.

"Your friend asked me to relay a message," he says politely, arms braced behind his back.

"A message? What's going on? Is she alright?" My feet begin to take me towards the toilets.

"Oh yes, she says enjoy your evening." I stop and frown. *Enjoy my evening?*

She's gone? She's bloody left me here!

Turning, I look back to see Jace watching. I scowl at him, which makes him grin, and I raise a perfectly primed brow at this poor old man who has been left to deal with me.

"God, that woman is a pain in my arse!" I mutter under my breath. I could murder that bloody woman, she is such a conniving little cow! Pulling my phone from my pocket, I shoot a message to her,

I'm going to kill you! No kisses. I add the last bit for effect.

The concierge smiles sheepishly at me.

I make a noise between a grumble and a snort both are un-lady like. "Thank you for passing her message to me," I grate. I'm not thankful at all, in fact, if Cass was here, I'd kick her in the shin!

"You're welcome, Miss Spencer." He steps away and I grit my teeth in annoyance, today can take a flying leap off a cliff.

"Is there a problem?" That voice slips down my spine and caresses my body. I close my eyes and sigh, my shoulders drooping in defeat. I do not want to have to deal with him now, or tomorrow.

In fact, I wish he would evaporate.

When I open my eyes, Jace is hunched down in front of me, his beautiful eyes glowing like darkened sap. I mean seriously who has eyes like that. It's just wrong!

"Oh," I pull back a little and look away— I can't look in those eyes, or at his face without feeling as though I have been electrocuted. "No problem," I squeak. Dammit Cass!

"Where's your friend?" he mouths with a smile tugging at his lips, I roll my eyes at his insistent need to challenge this tension between us but smile tightly at him, studiously ignoring the cheekiness seeping through his overt sex appeal.

"She's in the bathroom," I lie.

"So that wasn't her who walked out of here a few minutes ago waving cheekily at me then?" His fingers find the loose curls of my hair so he can twiddle it, my eyes find his and this time I can't look away, *Oh god!*

He moves towards me and it's enough to gear me into action, I pull away and glare at him. He's a client!

I need to keep my wits about me but when confronted by this guy, I find myself two steps short of a lobotomy.

"I have to go." I walk away and push the door open before anyone can do it for me. The temperature has dropped and sneaks its way into my skin I pull my coat even tighter around me as a hand takes my arm halting me.

"Lily, it's freezing, you've had a drink. Let me drive you home." I know I shouldn't agree, every part of me tells me to sever any contact with this man but when he tucks my hair behind my ear and turns those hypnotic concerned eyes on me I find myself saying yes.

Jace lifts his hand and a few moments later a valet brings a throaty car up beside us, he opens the door and waits for me to secure my belt. I take my time before turning to look up at his stunning profile stood on the cold pavement. "You followed me here, why?" He eyes me for a minute and worries his bottom lip.

Yes, Mr. Bennett, caught red handed!

He stands to his full height. "I'm going to speak with Carl quickly." He nods back over his shoulder before closing the door, leaving me without an answer.

I'm not alone long. Within minutes, he is back and sliding in, the heating is turned on and he messes with the radio before indicating out. I give him my address and sink in the seat. I choose silence because I can't believe I'm sat in his car after yesterday. Plus, if he is refusing to give me an answer, I'm certainly not going to entertain his behaviour with small talk.

I shouldn't like this guy. In fact, he is the kind of man every woman wants but none can keep. Yet here I am, cushioned by his leather seats roaring through London as he flashes me an easy smile and golden eyes. The adrenaline rush I'm experiencing, has everything to do with him and not the car.

All I can think is that I've made a huge mistake.

Chapter Four

"So, am I forgiven yet?" Jace has his elbow resting on the window as he drives along, the thumb of his free hand brushing his lips— his smirk is a combination of sexy and annoying as hell. I hold on to the latter, I don't want to find him sexy.

His free hand drops and picks up mine, slowly he lifts it and traces his thumb over my matte plum fingernail, the delicate brush of his fingertips over mine causes my breath to catch. "You look so delicate." He observes openly. When I swallow it feels strained, how does he manage to be so cool and impassive all the time!

I ignore his odd remark and reply to his first comment. "I suppose it would be rude of me not to, considering you're giving me a lift home." Easing my hand free, I clasp them in my lap blowing out a steady stream of air.

"Take a left here." I point, my eyes flashing to his as he takes my hand, threading his fingers with mine and rests them on my knee.

"Good, I'd hate for us to get off on the wrong foot." It shocks me that he feels it's acceptable to be so familiar with me. I stiffen and stare at his long fingers, smooth and immaculate, just like his big glass house.

I can't breathe, let alone speak. I say nothing in reply.

"You suppose, but you don't want to." He smirks, attention fixed on the road. My own are pinned into big saucers of shock.

I press my lips together deterred by his direct approach, keeping my gaze firmly on the flash of lights and homes as we purr our way up the road. His hand is like a branding iron and no matter how much I push back in the seat it remains, I feel the heat of it work its way up to my groin and pool there. Finally, we turn another corner forcing him to remove his hand and shift gears, I sigh in silent relief.

I catch the small smirk tugging at his full lips and want to elbow him, for purposely making me feel a mess. Is he like this with all women?

I should find his arrogance a complete turn off, only my skin warms from the constant attention directed my way.

He accepts my silence for the remainder of the journey and for that I'm grateful even if the imprint of his hand is scolding the skin on my knee, it's awkwardly arousing and the raspy tease of *Kings of Leon*, does nothing to deflect the undercurrent of tension burning up between us.

Why I agreed to this is beyond me.

I want to blame it on Cass but know I could have got a taxi. *It's him!*

I can't help but flick the odd look at him through the curtain of my hair. His strong profile is focused ahead, sap eyes a perfect complement to his tanned skin, and his aftershave is delicious. Held in the confines of his car all I can smell is his fresh earthy scent.

When I shift in my seat our eyes meet and Jace swallows a smile. "I wouldn't mind some conversation." He jokes along with the lyrics, I drop a deadpan gaze at him but he's not easily dissuaded, instead he sings along. His lips twitch into a panty-dropping smile, as his own raspy voice fills the car, those whiskey eyes twinkle playfully and I melt all over again. My mouth tugs into a smile against my own will and Jace's eyes flash with satisfaction.

Damn him!

"You're damn pretty when you're not scowling." He muses with a deep smirk, I roll my eyes and count down the seconds until I can get away from him. It's hard to stay mad at someone when they look like Jace Bennett!

"Good job, you make me scowl a lot then," I quip, forcing my head to lock on the passing streets and away from the beautiful male relaxed next to me.

The elevated sanctuary of my apartment comes into view. I'm ready to bolt from the car, eagerly anticipating my escape. "This is me," I murmur, he signals and pulls over. For a second, I don't know what to say, the air has changed, become charged and for that reason I refuse to look at him. The man has heartbreaker wound around his lean body like a pole dancer. I get out before my fears become reality.

"Thanks!" I call, before the door thuds shut. I rush up the path glad to be free, sucking in large gulps of refreshing cold air when the sound of another door closing ricochets over my fleeting reprieve, I snap around to see Jace rounding his car.

No!

I stand immobile as he walks to me, eyes locked on mine. "What are you doing?" I ask a little harshly. "Go back to the car." I say stupidly.

Shaking his head he drops his gaze but it doesn't disguise the smile lighting up his handsome face, his hair drops forward and he runs a hand through it before looking to me with a stare so full of heat I stiffen. "Why Miss Spencer I wouldn't be a gentleman if I didn't see you to your door now, would I?" He takes the steps two at a time and leans against the entryway, eyes laughing down into mine.

I laugh freely for the first time since we met. "Oh you are no gentleman. And this doesn't qualify either." I motion between us, as my brow raises herself like a matron standing to attention. But he keeps on smiling— happy in the fact I'm affected by him.

The man is trouble, plus he is enjoying this far too much for my liking. His smug smirk and dancing eyes, slowly morph into something much more serious, just like in the car the air becomes oppressive.

"And what *would* qualify me?" He murmurs brushing forwards, his perfect face pulled into a serious frown. I back up and hit the wall until he is above me.

"Don't do this." My small hand hits the centre of his compact chest. The quick rise and fall of his thundering heartbeat makes me shudder. With those eyes holding mine, I can't look away.

I can't believe this man!

Or myself for that matter, He's *nearly* got me! Fuck.

He frowns a little, his expression mystified, "Lily," his voice groans and I see - I can't place my finger on it - desperate anguish in his eyes, eyes so perfectly framed by long dense lashes. Surely this is an act. I don't believe for a second, he is as taken with me as I am by him!

I can't look at him. "You need to leave." He sighs at my hesitant whisper and grants himself permission to run the soft pad of his finger over my bottom lip before dropping it at his side.

I lick my lips because my body is begging for this, crying out for him to lean in and kiss me. His eyes drop to my mouth and he takes my face in his hand ignoring my plea.

His thumb brushing again over the moist trail I just drew. "Please don't," I beg again, he tilts my face his way and pushes against the pathetic restraint I have on his chest, my fight dissolves and Jace closes the small distance between us, backing me up in the dark entryway of my modest flat.

I remind myself that only the other night he was with another woman, that I'm just number in a series of long accomplishments. But my body is begging for this. *He's so close.*

My eyes close as I try to find the resolve I so desperately need. "I can't let this happen." It comes out in a rush of indecisive air. "Stop." My fingers grip the crisp material of his shirt as I beg for self-control.

His lips instead graze my cheek and find their way to my ear where he pushes his nose into my hair and holds me for a second. My eyes remain closed as I enjoy the closeness of him.

I'm a weak woman and I hate myself for it.

"You've been on my mind all day." He confesses. It hits me straight in the gut, but it's heavily laced with unease.

"Jace please, you're a client." I force bored detachment into my voice.

"I won't be always, then what will you do Lily Spencer?" His hand is caught up at the nape of my neck, my hair trussed up in a handheld knot.

I find some will power hiding under all my lust and direct it at him. "Nothing, because this isn't happening."

When he pulls back, I drop his shirt from my fingers as I fight the urge to turn my head and find his mouth, instead I cross my arms over my chest. He looks at me, really looks at me all the while processing my words and seeing the resolve in my eyes, his own pull into a narrow frown and the fullness of his lips disappear into a straight line. "Goodnight Miss Spencer," he murmurs reluctantly.

His sudden turn surprises me, we both know had he kissed me I would have responded more than happily, even if my mind is screaming for me to run inside, my body is a girlish mass of pathetic hormones.

Jace takes the steps leisurely and points back at my door when he reaches his car. "Go on in Lily." I'm still riveted to the spot where he left me, like a damn idiot staring after him. Turning sharply, I key in the code and push open the door.

I can't deny myself, so I look back. *Damn, damn, damn!*

"See you in the morning," he says over the roof of his car, very much smug. I watch him fold his lean length into his car, before I shut the door and head up to my apartment, dazed and irritated.

I look like hell, I haven't slept a wink, last night has played a constant loop through my mind, I would love for today not to happen but I'll be dammed if I let a man, No, not a man, just one. *Jace Bennett* get the better of me. I'd watch hell freeze over before I let him throw me off my guard and call in with a poor excuse.

I pin my hair up and pull a stylish sweater over my skin-tight jeans, I find a chunky scarf to hoop over my head and slip my heeled ankle boots on, disregarding my favoured working flats.

Weak, Weak woman.

When I step out my apartment there is a steaming disposable cup and a croissant wrapped in a bag on the corridor floor, I know instantly that it's from Cass. I smile, despite her leaving me in a mess with Jace last night. I read the small note pinned to the bag with tired eyes.

Don't kill me yet, I need details of last night x

I laugh and take a sip of my guilt gift, I have had many of these over the years, the woman is a nightmare but I wouldn't change her for the world.

I fire her a text when I get in the car and dunk my croissant into my hot chocolate before I set off. I mess about with my music until I find what I'm looking for, it seems I have a new found love for *Kings of Leon.*

My heart begins to hammer away, as I pull up to the large wooden gates. Like before, they open and I'm confronted with an expectant Jace leaning against his low-slung car. He is dressed in similar attire as last night and I swallow against my dry throat. Parking up, I try to avoid the niggling feeling of eyes watching me. I brush the stray crumbs from me and mentally make a note to book my car in for a clean.

My door opens, making me jump, and I look up to see Jace resting his arms against my roof and door, the welcome scent of his manliness wafting up my nose. "Morning, gorgeous. Can I get your bags?"

"Another attempt at being a gentleman?" I ask, trying to hide my small smile. He's clever, a natural charmer.

"Is it working?" He straightens up to let me out. I grab my drink and pop it on my roof as he eyes me with an eager look. I want to ask him what it is he hopes to gain, but I already know the answer to that. I could ask why but that too implies I'm interested.

I mean, I am— I just don't want to be.

"No Megan?" I query, as I close my door and lift the boot. Jace scoops my bag up and grabs my drink with his free hand. He sniffs the small gap and smiles down at me cheekily before taking a swig.

My mouth drops open . . . the cheeky bugger!

He willingly crosses the line of professionally acceptable behaviour, blissfully ignorant at my shock. It's sort of adorable, if you like that kind of thing.

I tell myself I don't.

"Help yourself," I mutter on a scowl and pull it from his hand as we both make our way up to the house.

The gates sweep open once more and Megan swerves into the drive, her eyes bouncing between Jace and I, as she hurriedly parks up and flies from the car.

I smile politely, but I can't say I particularly like her. I wonder if she and Jace are an item when she walks straight to him and pecks him on the cheek, just short of his lips.

"Morning," she breathes. Her once-over does nothing to create a comfortable atmosphere between the two of us.

"Morning, Megan." I figure I should at least be professional, even if I acted like a crazy lady on Wednesday.

"Hi." She offers me hardly any of her time, as she struts in the house after Jace, cutting me up a little. I grit my teeth, unhappy in the knowledge I have to spend the best part of my day with her. And him.

"No Carl?" I ask when I see it's only us three.

"He has an appointment this morning but will be here after nine."

Jace places my camera bag on the kitchen island. Megan is already sat at an angle beside him, her leg brushing the back of his. "Okay, well, I'm going to get started, then we can do the shoot with you, Jace. Unless you have to be elsewhere, Megan?" I ask her, but her eyes are fixed on the lean, godly man now moving towards the coffee machine.

"Oh no, I'm Jace's for as long as he needs me." The double meaning doesn't go unmissed by either of us and I can't help the twitch of laughter when he pulls back in shock. Not his girlfriend then. I shouldn't feel an ounce of relief at this, but I do, and that makes me no better than the woman currently purring all around him.

Megan glares at me, but I feign innocence and lift my bag off the side. "I'm going to head upstairs and set up."

"Do you want a drink?" Jace asks. I lift my disposable cup and shake it but frown when I realise how light it is.

"How much did you drink?" The devil, I place it on the side as he laughs. "I'll have a coffee a little later," I say when he lifts a cup in offer once more. Megan slips off the stool. Her short skirt has ridden up, but she doesn't adjust it. In fact, she walks to Jace, complimenting his outfit on a low murmur. I choose not to stick around to hear their conversation and walk away. Like I should have last night!

Chapter Five

After half an hour or so, Carl appears, kitted out in a smart suit and fashionable thick, framed glasses. "Good morning!" he sings. I'm crouched on the floor, trying to get the perfect angle, looking and feeling less put together than he is.

"Oh, hi, give me a second," I mumble, checking through the lens once more before I stand. Carl holds out a coffee for me. "How's it coming along?" He sips his own coffee, trying to bite back a smirk. I can see the speculation in his eyes. He's dying to ask me about last night. I roll my eyes, because there is something very likeable and trusting about Carl. He grins and nudges me with his hip. "Oh, do tell," he teases.

"You know you and your boss have a problem with boundaries," I point out. I have only recently met these men, but they hurdle right over the term 'privacy'.

Looking over his glasses, he gives me a playful look. "Why do you think he hired me," he drawls and I laugh over my coffee, happy to have his company.

I shrug. "Nothing to tell, I'm afraid." It's the truth, in an around about way.

He nods this over before saying, "That would explain his mood after he came back." Well, shit!

I lift my free hand up in innocence. "Nothing to do with me," I state. "Did you have a nice evening?"

"Well," Carl huffs, pointing a finger at me. "You stole my personal bank, so I had to buy my own drink. He was supposed to be treating me and Rupert." He sniffs petulantly and I smile at his over-exaggerated body language.

"Sorry. Does Rupert work for Mr. Bennett also?" I wonder, taking myself back to my camera, placing my coffee on the sideboard.

The master bedroom is ultra-masculine and made up of neutral but grayish tones. The bed is a large low tan leather base with a high back headboard and is gorgeous. It's spotlighted by an unusual wire floor lamp and against the main wall is a giant black and white woodland picture. It's captivating. I have found myself studying it more than once. It's a clear representation of my own photography preference.

"Oh no, he would never get any work done!" Carl laughs at his own joke and holds his left hand up. "Rupert is my husband," he confirms as I click away.

"So, I really did mess your evening up? I'm so sorry." I stand and look around. I want the place to look a little lived-in. I see Carl has some papers tucked under his arm, pointing at them, I say, "Can I borrow those?"

Tilting his head, he frowns as he holds them out. Collecting up my coffee, I take it to the bedside table and place it there, then pull one corner of the quilt back and ruffle the thick duvet. I lay the papers on the covers, spreading them out a little but keeping them in order. When I turn back, I find Jace is leaning against the door frame, watching. Dropping my gaze, I turn back to the bed and bite my lip, my mind running through ideas. It requires a little something more. I look back to Carl, who is eyeing me curiously. My eyes fall to his glasses and I edge my way back to him. Hesitantly, I lift my hand to his glasses and slowly pull them off as he smiles at me. "Two seconds," I promise and lay them on the papers.

I stand for a minute or two, my mind whirring. "I need your suit jacket and shoes," I tell him, but Carl looks appalled.

"God no!" he exclaims. "This suit is new." He sniffs, as I laugh and walk confidently back over to him, ignoring Jace's slow smile. "Strip," I order, and Carl's eyes pop.

"You know I'm gay, right?" He smirks.

"I want your clothes, not your—" I point my finger in the direction of his groin and he laughs.

"Good to know." He eyes me for a minute, still indecisive.

"The jacket is going on the chair and the shoes by the window. Everywhere else feels more lived in," I tell him by way of explanation. He nods and starts undressing. I pick up the garments and arrange them just so.

Happy with how it looks, I proceed to take photos. When I stand, Carl picks up all his belongings and squeezes past Jace. "I would say shout if you need me, but I feel violated." He presses his lips together and I laugh.

Megan is nowhere to be seen, which puts me on edge. I begin to take my tripod down. "Everything alright?" Jace asks. I nod and hook my camera over my neck to secure it as I move to the next room. "For the en-suite, I think I will have to stand on a chair to get a higher scope," I say softly.

"Sure." Jace follows me in, with my tripod in his hand. "Do you need this?" he asks, lifting it up.

"No, not yet, but can you get me a chair, please?" There is a modern slipper bath and a double open-ended shower. The glass is as smear-free as the wraparound windows. It's stunning. There are no sideboards, only sinks jutting out from the wall. A leafy plant adds more colour, which is situated next to a chucky wooden wave chair. It's as low as the floor and adds character to the room. In fact, it's my favourite room in the house. I stand and soak it all in. I'm starting to appreciate the exposed elements of this property.

Jace comes back in with a chair and Megan on his heel. She lowers herself into the low seat as I place the chair in a corner. I go to climb up, but Jace grabs my wrist, halting me. "Whoa, Lily, I'm not having you falling off."

Rolling my eyes, I climb up, his hand feeling like a molten chain wrapped around my slim wrist. I wobble a little but place a hand on the wall to steady myself rather than grabbing at his wide shoulders.

"Okay, I'm up," I murmur, willing him to let go whilst lifting my camera up. Megan is still watching from the floor. I find it amusing that she feels threatened by me, especially since she has already had him. The thought makes my mouth sour.

Jace laughs, his hands slipping to my waist and making me suck in a breath. "Lily, you're not standing up there without support. Take your photo," he instructs roughly.

I grit my teeth, as his large hands span my waist, his finger burning into the curve of my arse. I'm annoyed the sun is on the other side of the house. I could use the excuse of shadows right about now. Blowing out an annoyed breath, I try to ignore his touch, but it's useless. It makes me feel agitated, and when Megan reclines back on the wave chair looking at her nails, I feel myself becoming angry. Sighing, I drop my camera and look at her, but she hasn't the faintest idea.

"Megan, can you get out of the shot, please?" Jace says. She swivels to look at him, her mouth forming into an embarrassed 'O' as she blushes, I feel sorry for her. She is following him around like a lost puppy.

"Close the door," he adds, ensuring she leaves us. I wish she would stay— I don't want to be alone with him.

"Sorry, how silly of me." As soon as she is up and out the door, I begin clicking away so I can get away from him. The clunk of the door shutting is deafening, so much so, that I flinch. Then it's just us.

I spend a moment gathering strength, and then I force myself to do my job. Using this vantage point to get different angles, I click away. I'm breathing nervously, my shaking hands trying to capture the perfect picture. Over the constant snap of photos, I can hear his uncoordinated breathing.

"Okay, thanks," I say, lowering my camera, expecting him to back up, but Jace uses his firmly placed hands to his advantage and lifts me with ease off the chair. I gasp and grip his biceps. Rather than placing me down to his side, I'm slid down his firm, hot, and very aroused body. My eyes shoot to his.

His nostrils flare and his eyes look like bulbs of fire, burning back at me.

It's calculated and has the very effect he wished for. His earthy scent winds its way around me and lures me into Megan mode. I'm all doe-eyed and aroused.

For a moment we are caught up in each other's stare. I feel utterly sucker-punched by this man— he is *that* handsome. I moan lightly when he sighs, at war with himself.

"Fuck," he groans harshly, before slamming his mouth against mine. The force makes me jolt back, causing the chair to scrape loudly on the tiled floor.

Moist lips brush against mine, their sensual stroke demanding a response. On a breathy moan, my eyes close against their own volition. My mind is lost to the moment, lost to the sexual tension pouring out of this man. I kiss him back and my hand drifts up his arm, across the wide bridge of his shoulders, and into his thick hair. As soon as his tongue sweeps against mine, a wave of heat blooms in my womb. I push him away in panic. He looks so shocked, his dark amber eyes lost in desire.

I'm shocked too. What the hell was I thinking? I wasn't. I can't. Not when I'm around this man. "No!" I cry softly. I'm so angry with myself for kissing him.

"You want this," he argues back, his hand goes to my hair and he pulls me close keeping the contact, his lips brush gently over mine. I want to relent. "Lily, it's not just me. I know you feel it too." I stare wide-eyed, lost for words, tortured and tempted by his close proximity. I manage to shake my head in denial, only to mutter another sigh when his mouth grazes over mine before his tongue dives right back in on a hot glide. Slowly, he pulls back so our lips barely touch.

"I don't."

"That's utter bollocks." His colourful language shouldn't shock me because I'm no princess but it does, he drops his head, shaking it lightly, before looking up at me through narrow eyes. "Me and you are going to happen," he delivers arrogantly.

"No." My disbelief at his behaviour is evident in my scathing laugh. "We are not going to happen." I brush past but Jace slips a hand around my waist, pulling me flush to his front. Lips fall to my ear, his rock-hard length burning its way through my clothes. "Lily you've been a mess since you met me, I feel the same." He groans brushing his lips behind my ear, I shudder but yank free.

"Jesus just stop will you, you're my fucking client!" I'm all het up and breathing heavily. I need to get out of here, before I give in and find myself pinned to his body once more. Every reasonable cell in my body is telling me to run out of here, but reasonable is slowly being swallowed up by an unforgettable kiss.

This is a fucking mess!

Jace smirks and it only pisses me off further. "If I was your *fucking* client, you wouldn't be telling me no." I reach the door and open it an inch before it's slammed shut. Jace turns me and his mouth slants over mine once more, it's a hard kiss, a statement of his desire. His tongue jams into my mouth drawing a groan from him and a sigh from me, he pulls back a few inches and looks as though he is ready to push me, until he sees me lift my chin to glare at him. I remind myself that the tension burning between us, is simply that, tension, it means nothing, not in the long run.

Only the other day was he prizing Megan out her knickers and I am in no way shape or form ready for another relationship.

"I'm walking out this door." My voice is uneven but as each word comes out, my walls come up. I try to detach myself completely and look through him, but when confronted by such a beautiful man who evokes a reaction in me that even I can't comprehend, it's hard. Really fucking hard.

"You're going to let me." I emphasise each word clearly. "I'll do the shoot. Alone. Then I'm leaving." I want to leave now. Fuck this man and his stupid arrogant, well-made arse!

Jace looks to the ceiling and blows out a stream of air, stepping back he holds his hands up before he clasps them behind his head. I can't help but slide my eyes over his stretched-out frame, his ruffled shirt has pulled up and the fitted trousers reveal tanned flesh and a trail of dark brown hair. "I'm sorry," the words are forced past his lips. There is no truth behind them.

"No, you're not," I scoff, his eyes drop to mine with a touch of annoyance, he works his lower lip between even teeth and all I can think is how perfect he is, *dammit!*

"Wednesday you *just* -" I hold my finger and thumb a fraction apart, "- about managed to untangled yourself from Megan in time for our appointment, I'm not interested in being the next woman on your list of accomplishments. If you have blue balls ask her to relieve them," I spit and whip the door open. I expect to find a sullen Megan, but the room is empty. Jace lets me go and as I walk through the oversized room, I contemplate walking out, I should. I owe this man nothing and he has overstepped the mark, by a long shot!

The last two hours I have been balanced on numb knees or perched in some obscure place to get the perfect picture, I tackled the outside photos and stopped for a quick coffee, mindful to avoid Jace. I'm propped up against the kitchen island looking over pictures with Carl, when my phone dances across the marble surface. Cass's name flashes on the screen. "I'm not talking to you," I say when I answer.

"Lil I'm your favourite person, without me your life would be boring. Plus, I can cook." She states smugly, I roll my eyes and catch Carl's look of laughter.

"My life is not boring," I scoff flicking to another photo.

"Well of course it isn't, I'm in it." Her throaty laugh pierces my ear. "So how is the superhuman?" She asks over the jingle of keys.

I look to Carl because he can hear everything— it's not hard anyone within a ten-mile radius could hear Cass she's loud all around.

"Superhuman?" I feign ignorance— she's a liability!

"Well there is no way on this planet that the man I left you with last night is even remotely human, god does not make them that good," she muses, Carl can't hold it together anymore he bursts into a fit of giggles all over the surface, glasses landing skew-whiff on the end of his nose. "Superhuman hearing too I believe," Cass notes, I can see her now smirking as she looks at her immaculate nails.

"No, that's not him," I laugh, as Carl tries to right himself. "I'm pretty busy at the moment, can we meet tomorrow, lunch?" I suggest. I don't want to talk about Jace in front of Carl or ever for that matter. In fact, after today, I will be Jace-free. I bite my lip remembering that blistering kiss.

Cass scoffs down the line pulling me back to the present. "Cocktails." She corrects, "Finnegan's, I'll come to you, we can get a taxi."

"Great," I agree on a smile, after the last few days I'm in need of a wine night.

"I'll be at yours at eight thirty, love you!" she rings off and Carl gives me his signature look over his glasses. "She's a bossy one," he comments kindly.

"Yes, she is." I smile, "She's a bugger." I turn my phone onto silent and slip it into my bag.

"Superhuman." Carl tries the word out, "Jace will appreciate that one," he sniggers, and I blush.

"You mean his engorged ego will," sarcasm drips like hot candle wax from my mouth and I regret the words instantly, I'm being unfair and rude. "Sorry," I sigh, "look I'd appreciate it if you didn't say anything, I just want to do my job and never see your boss again." I admit wearily refusing to meet Carls' eyes.

"I'm afraid to say it, but I don't believe this is the last time we will meet." Carl stands up to his full height, the look I throw him is all 'you want to bet' and he pats my shoulder as he rounds me to the coffee machine, checking his watch as he goes.

"Shall we do the final shoot?" He says, trying to gear the machine into action. "This bloody thing has a mind of its own, It nearly scolded my face last week," he remarks, my stomach has plummeted at the prospect of being around Jace again. Carl huffs and shakes the machine until it whirrs to life, "crush the beans and produce the goods," he growls. Any other time I'd find his theatrics funny, but I feel sick.

"Sure," I mumble, trying and failing to act indifferent.

I let Carl round everyone up, Megan walks from the extensive office with Jace following shortly after, her smile is smug and I can't help the deep ache in my gut, I've never considered myself a jealous woman, but the unwarranted rush of anger has my jaw setting.

It's enough to cement my decision to walk away from this man, despite the crazy reaction he brings out in me. No man has ever made me weak with desire. Instilled any envy into me, I always do everything with singlehanded drive and confidence.

Jace Bennett is nuclear.

I don't meet his eyes and busy myself with cleaning up my coffee cup. "I thought the office and the main living area would set a nice tone for the photo's?" My suggestion is quickly rebuffed by Megan.

"The bedroom is ultra-masculine and would pull in a wealth of consumers." Megan touches his arm, painted nails sliding around his bicep, as her red lips stretch into a sultry smile.

This woman is a joke— He's not a porn star!

I incline my head, I can see Carl's disapproval and I don't like her, so I say, "I thought I was capturing Jace's *architectural* talent?" I look to the man himself because as far as I'm concerned, he is paying me, not her.

Untangling his arm, he motions to the low and expensive looking arrangement of sofas and chairs. "The bedroom seems a little inappropriate." In the living room there is a rustic stonewall, with the smooth wood, abundance of glass and view of a well-maintained plush garden it ties in well. Whoever Jace hired to do the interior design, has impeccable taste.

"Just be natural," I tell Jace as he lowers himself to the wide square seat, he leans forward, his feet placed apart and rests clasped hands on his legs. His whiskey eyes burn through my lens and sends my heart into an unsteady beat.

Biting my lip, I slow my breathing and force my mind to concentrate, so I can take a series of photos, moving to get different angles but his eyes follow me everywhere, dark and sultry. His whole posture is coiled and ready to snap at any minute. It's so hard to relax when I feel as though any minute, he is going to push up and stalk towards me.

With my camera still to my face I point to a chair with a higher back. "Can you move to this chair?" Unfolding his delectable length, eyes trained on me, he straightens his suit jacket and takes up the whole chair. Hands poised to a temple, ankle hooked on his knee, I falter in what I'm doing. "Thanks," I croak. Carl whistles low and fans himself. Yes, the tension in this room is stifling. I feel suffocated by it.

I'm eager to get this over and done with. I'm desperate to leave and Carls open observation makes my cheeks heat. After a few more shots we move to the office and get a few of him reclined in a high back leather chair, eyes focused on a pen that he is twirling through his fingers. The last picture I ask him to lean against the window, this has one of the best views in my opinion. Hooking his ankles over one another and pushing his hands into his trousers I click away, breath abated. I feel so tense and awkward. Jace keeps flicking those sap-like eyes at me, their whiskey promise turning my brain to mush. As soon as I'm done I all but fly from the room.

I'm packing my bits up, eager to get away from him. "Right, I'll get the draft shots sent over to you and you can all pick which ones you like, as soon as you confirm them with me, I'll send them across." I zip my bag and hook it over my shoulder, Carl passes me my handbag as I scuttle past, I feel like a damn teen around Jace, Megan ignores me completely, but I say bye regardless. "It was nice meeting you all," I breathe and pull the door open. Jace follows me out.

"Lily." He is at my boot assisting me with my bag. "Can you look at me," he says softly.

I don't want to look at him— his eyes have fractured my resolve. If I have any chance at walking away from this man pain-free, I need to leave. Stepping back, I pull my boot down but he it doesn't budge, he's locked his arm holding the boot wide open and stopping me from escaping. I scowl up at him.

"Have dinner with me?" His deep voice is blended by both a demand and plea, his hand reaches to twine through my hair, but I push it away.

"No." I keep my eyes averted. In fact, the last two days will be burnt into my psyche forever. I know I won't forget him for a long time. I laugh at the absurdity of it. He has slipped his way underneath my skin and stored himself into my blood. He will be a part of me now.

This is ridiculous, I barely know him yet he affects me so much.

My pulse is banging away at an unhealthy pace, Jace places a finger on the hollow of my throat and my gaze is catapulted to his face, his eyes lift to mine from the treacherous spot. "You can drive out those gates but me and you are far from being done," he murmurs.

"You are such an arrogant arse," I growl, tugging the boot but find that it still won't move. My strength is nothing compared to his, physically or mentally it would seem, and I cannot believe I called my client an arse!

Jace shrugs, he isn't denying it. "If knowing you want me just as much as I want you makes me an *arrogant arse* then so be it." His statement is delivered on a casual, confident murmur, and his full and mischievous lips twist.

"I don't!" I deny forcefully.

"No? So those circles under your eyes aren't because of me?" He lets his smirk slip free once more and it's enough to snap me out of it.

I walk away leaving the boot up in the air, he can shut it. "I'll send the photos over tomorrow." I'm going. The quicker I finalise this contract the better.

The boot clunks shut but my door is held open in his hands as he fills the space between my door and frame. "Will you give it a rest!" I cry out.

His fingers take hold of my chin and he pulls my face to his, my knuckles are white on the wheel as we stare it out. Jace is breathing heavily, he looks harassed. Hell, I feel harassed! I'm worried he is going to kiss me.

"I'll fucking rock your world Lily, I won't stop until I have you," he declares.

I say nothing. I'm speechless. The guy is a fucking joke. He holds me for a few more seconds. "I will have you," he murmurs and drops my chin on a frustrated sigh. As soon as he steps back, I slam my door and in my haste wheel spin. I don't care about the wall of dust I leave behind.

Chapter Six

"So, are you going to tell me what's the matter?" Cass is propped up on my suede headboard, her bare legs crossed at the ankle. She is wearing a glitzy burgundy cocktail dress and has her blonde hair pinned to the side. She looks effortless and cute. If she wasn't my friend, I would secretly wish she were to get chewing gum stuck in her hair or something equally awful.

I can just about see her in the reflection of my mirror as I put my earrings in. I have gone for the smoky look, all sultry dark eyes, I glossed my lips and my hairdresser curled my hair this afternoon. "I'm fine." I'm not, I feel emotionally wrung out.

A pair of socks clips my cheek making me jump. Cass is grinning at my startled face. "Fine my arse, you have been a droopy mess all day. It's him isn't it?" Cass stands and makes her way over to stand behind me and fusses with my hair. I say nothing, but look up at her through my mirror.

She sighs, "Lil's, that man was smoking and not to mention, into you, a hell of a lot. Your chemistry was." She wiggles her brows on a laugh. "Look, you're stupid to say no." She gives me a pointed look, through the mirror. I haven't told her about our little make out session.

"He's a man whore," I spit sullenly— Cass shrugs and gives my hair a little tug as she moves around me. "Ouch!"

"So, what if he is? Have a night of fun. I'm not spending the next few weeks watching you mope around." Her accusation is met by a lift of my nose.

"I am not moping." I squirt a splash of perfume over myself and stand. "Which heels?" I have a tight beaded neckline dress on. Cass picks up some peep toe heels and drops them at my feet.

"Lily you're pathetic, it's shameful. In fact, seeing you like this, I have no idea what that man sees in you," she scoffs playfully, as my mouth drops open on a laugh.

Jace slips to the front of my mind and I feel deprived. A little lost.

"I like him." There I admitted it, fat lot of use that'll do me. Cass pulls me into a hug.

"I know." She rubs my back. "I've never seen you like this," she sighs.

"I don't want to feel like this. He's bad news," I say over her shoulder.

"Why, because he's good looking, single and successful?" Accusation rings in her voice, I'm being unfair, she has a point, I have pegged him as the entitled, playboy type and I don't even know him.

"Megan?" I point out.

She tusks at me on a shake of her head. "The guy is single and let's face it, she may as well have turned up naked. How was he supposed to know he'd meet you?" Cass dabs some of my gloss over her painted lips so they shimmer. She uses it to point at me, her other hand now occupied by wine. "You Lily Spencer are running out of excuses, Jesus do me and him both a favour and fuck him would you." She gives me a sly smile and I grab my lipgloss.

"You're vulgar." My comment is met by a wide smile.

"Why thank you," she clips, eyes burning with too many truths to my words, the woman is a literal nightmare. "Look, let's enjoy tonight because I wouldn't put it past him to turn up at the gallery on Monday." The thought hadn't crossed my mind before now, oh god!

We finish our drinks in time for the taxi and head straight to Finnegan's— it is owned by one of Cass exes and now close friend.

Sean Finnegan has dark hair and is damn attractive. He has a few freckles on his nose and bright blue eyes. When he sees us, he slips from behind the bar and pulls us into a hug. He's stocky and one of the nicest people I know.

"What do I owe this pleasure?" He grins, Irish accent sliding over the words, he pecks us both on the check, Cass thumb points to me. "This one is down in the dumps." I roll my eyes at her and ask Sean how he has been.

"Good thanks, let me get you both a drink and we can have a quick catch up." Cass leads us over to an empty table with huge armchairs.

"Sean looks good," I say, watching for a reaction from her. In all honesty, he is looking really good. His hair is a little longer than his usual buzzcut and he looks leaner.

Cass looks to the bar. "Yeah I guess he does." She watches him for a moment and turns back to me. "He smelt good too." She smirks, looking back to admire him walk over, her small hands adjusting her hair.

He has our drinks banked in his memory and takes a seat between us both. "So, who have I got to give a black eye to?" He jokes.

"No one." I waft his concern away and turn the conversation back to him. Cass mentioned he was opening a new bar, so I focus on that.

"I have a meeting with the bank, so nothing is set in stone yet." He gives me a trademark wink, as though he already has it in the bag.

"Well good luck." I mean it, the man has clawed his way up from a pretty rough upbringing, from what Cass has told me. I don't know the full story between these two and have never pushed it, but I see the tension building between them.

"I'm Irish, I don't need luck we are born with it." He tells me over his glass,

"You sound like an ad for L'Oréal," I scoff. Sean, ever the clown, shakes his head as though he has ample hair and it sets the mood for the rest of the night.

Within a few hours of us being there and Sean dropping a couple of shots on the table at regular intervals me and Cass are both more than tipsy, I'm laughing loudly at Cass's face from her tequila, when Sean wanders over again shaking his head in mock despair. "You girls better come back here before the night is out, so I can get you both home." His eyes linger on Cass and she smiles shyly up at him.

"We will," I giggle, blinking forcefully when I realise my vision is unfocused. I am the world's biggest lightweight. Alcohol is gliding its way through my body, a warm fuzzy burn tingling my skull and loosening my muscles. It's an addict's haven and I'm only too happy to dip my toe for a few hours just to forget the past week. I'm glad that I ditched my quiet night in for a night out with my friend.

"I'm going to get us some more drinks," she calls over the music as it turns up a notch— I nod sipping on the remainder of my gin. We've planned to go to a cocktail bar after here but I'm more pissed than I thought. Not that I mind. I need a good night to let my hair down and blow the cobwebs away or to get Jace out my head. I should probably eat something— soak the ridiculous amount of alcohol I have consumed already. I decide to mention that to her.

I'm watching Cass's progress at the bar when the strangest sensation rushes over me. I stiffen and look around for him, because my whole body is on high alert. An internal *uh oh* swirling around with the alcohol, it causes my breathing to alter. My glassy eyes work frantically over the crowded bar for a head of dark hair. Where are you?

When I see nothing, I relax on a sigh, but a waft of musky aftershave makes me shiver. Looking up over my shoulder, I'm suddenly faced with a pair of whiskey eyes. I follow his movements as he rounds my chair and blink rapidly as my alcohol fogged brain, blindly registers that Jace Bennett is now squatted in front of me, in fact my tiny foot is resting a breath short of his crotch.

I skate a look around the room, mindlessly seeking help. "Hi," I squeak.

He smiles slowly and I melt in my chair. "Hi yourself," he murmurs, his finger runs a path up my smooth shin. "Well lady you have outdone yourself, you look sensational." Those molten eyes trail from my ankle up to my face, his direct gaze implying he is already intimately familiar with my body.

"Oh." I can't speak. I can't believe he is here. My whole demeanour is on maximum guard but what surprises me more, it's the burst of happiness I feel. I'm so buggered.

"Oh," he parrots, his shoulders rise and fall in slow deep breaths and the look he rewards me with from below his lashes makes my thighs tighten.

Oh, good god! I'm so fucked, utterly and completely done for...

Jace cups my calf and runs his thumb back and forth. My knuckles have turned white as I stare wide-eyed at him.

Lips parted I watch his eyes dilute as he runs those remarkable eyes over me once more. "Lily, what am I to do with you?"

I moan, literally moan like a fucking idiot!

"You're stalking me," I accuse on a pained swallow, I search for Cass but his hand lifts to my chin and pulls me back to face him.

He's eyes are laughing at me. "I told you I wasn't giving up." I'm about to ask how he knew I was here then I remember my conversation with Cass, Carl must have told him, the sod!

My already boggled brain has hit a new level, I stutter, no words will come out, not the ones I want anyway.

"You make my head mushy," I complain, Jace laughs lightly, he leans in and presses a soft kiss to my mouth. "Good." He whispers, I'm stilled into shock. He just kissed me, like it was natural, and we aren't two . . . half-strangers? My alcohol fogged brain tries to categorise our level of friendship. If that's what you can even call it. Technically, he is still a paying client. Shit. I'm drunk.

"No not good," I say to myself on a frown. I laugh inwardly at the absurdity of this whole situation.

Jace keeps our lips close. "The problem is this is too good, I'm crazy for you," he murmurs, ambers smouldering into mine. "You're stunningly beautiful Lily, I want you." His fingers are rubbing soft circles to my calves, a gesture of reassurance. They're a pointless feat, especially since his eyes are silently speaking their own intentions, carnal intentions. My breath stutters out and fans back over my face, because he is so damn close. The heat of his chest emanates over my thigh due to his close proximity.

"This isn't a good idea," I croak, he brushes another soft kiss against my lips. His tongue darts out and finds mine. Oh god he's an incredible kisser. "Tell me does this feel bad?" He murmurs sexily.

"No." I sway his way as the last of my resolve evaporates in a drunken blur. Long fingers cup my face, cradling my neck as Jace takes advantage of my weakened defences. His kiss holds no softness but days of pent up lust. He doesn't rush though. Oh, he is taking his time, happy to finally be given the go-ahead to explore my mouth. As far as kisses go this one is movie worthy.

Somewhere deep inside is a girl shouting for me to walk away, but the claim of ownership being plundered on me wins.

Just one night, I promise myself!

I mentally enforce the words, one night and I will be Jace free. I have to be. Not enough time has passed for me to heal from my last relationship.

The clink of glasses catches our attention or rather Jace's, he pulls back and bites on his lip, Cass rests her elbow on the back of one of the chairs. "Oh hello, she wasn't expecting you until Monday." Jace looks back to me in confusion, as Cass winks at me over his head and my eyes find themselves appreciating the natural tan glow of his skin. "I got you gin, Lils, and you look like a whiskey drinker," she states, handing drinks to us both.

"You assume correctly," he laughs on a killer smile. "Thank you." Only when he stands, do I finally get a proper look at him. He's kitted out in worn jeans and a grey fitted tee, with his stubble and wayward hair he looks every inch the successful, confident male. A land of wisdom courts his eyes and the way he carries himself, excludes a quiet assurance that demands acknowledgment. He is a heady combination.

He leans across the table and says something to Cass, who nods and leans to his ear to say something back. Jace pulls a chair round and places it beside mine. He relaxes in the cushioned seat and takes my hand in his. What were they talking about?

Butterflies cause havoc with my stomach, for a moment I think it's the alcohol and fear I may be sick but it's him. My body has no control around him. Cass eyes me thoughtfully, conveying reassurance.

I reach for my glass, to keep my mind occupied on something other than his presence. My nerves get the better of me and my drink goes down too quick, Jace raises his brows at Cass. "You in a rush?" he muses, his smirk has me blushing and I look over to Cass who is nursing her drink now, watching us with unveiled excitement. I drag in a lungful of air.

My friend looks at me, her eyes pointedly telling me to relax. My head lolls back and I realise how drunk I am, frowning I decide I should get some fresh air and get up dropping Jace's hand. His presence is stifling, and I can't hold my liquor. "You okay Lil's?" Cass stands with me, I shrug and smile at her all goofy and drunk.

"I'm well and truly lubed," I slur. Jace throws his head back and laughs.

"Take note," Cass says to Jace. "This girl is a huge lightweight."

Before guiding me away, it's the little distance I need to mentally accept he is here.

I shake my head and roll my hips to *Bruno Mars* as he sings about being locked in heaven, Cass ushers me to the exit on a stumble. I'm on an emotional high, he's here, and I can't deny the fact that him tracking me down is massively hot.

The cool air hits me as soon as I step outside, I sidle past a group of smokers and Cass joins me. "Did you eat before you came out?"

Scrunching up my face I think back over my day and realise I haven't eaten since breakfast. "That would be a no," I laugh.

"Lily!" she scolds.

"I was busy," I whine. When I blink, I can barely see her. "I'm drunk." I whisper loudly. She swears and pulls me back inside the bar, I stumble only just managing to stay upright!

"I'm getting you a taxi home," she states, Jace is leaning against the bar and pulls me to his chest. I'm too pissed to argue, so I droop forward onto his toned body. Cass speaks to him briefly then disappears for a minute, and I lay flat to his chest enjoying the languid brush of his hand up and down my back. "As first dates go this was the quickest," he chuckles pressing a kiss to my head.

"We're not on a date," I mumble into his t-shirt. He smells amazing an intoxicating mix of fresh air and manliness!

Jace hunches down so our faces meet, taking my face in his hand he gives me a wink. "Just gives me an excuse to take you out another time." God he's gorgeous.

I grunt and yawn. "I want my bed." I'm already anticipating a monumental hangover.

Cass reappears with my belongings and hands them to Jace, they chat for a moment, but my ears are buzzing so I hardly can make out what they are saying. "Are you sure this is okay?" I hear through a fog of alcohol.

I'm trying to smile at my friend, but she pushes my face with her palm. "Bloody lightweight," she scoffs, I air kiss her but miss completely.

"Sorry Cass." I giggle, "You are a bad influence," I tell her, as her laugh penetrates my ears.

Leaning in she pats my shoulder, "Look Jace is going to take you home, he hasn't had anything to drink. He has our numbers. I will see you tomorrow." She pulls me in for a tight hug then thanks Jace. I'm too inebriated to argue.

"I'll text you when she's home." Capturing me by the nape, he directs me towards his car up the road.

He helps me get in. Squinting I manage to slot the buckle in, I rest my head against the leather, close my eyes and hum in satisfaction when the heating gets put on. I'm covered in a sheath of material absorbed in that earthy smell I love so much. "You smell good," I murmur, wriggling further into the seat on a yawn. When my heavy eyelids open Jace is smiling across at me. "Drunk you is very cute." With a gentle stroke to my hair, he sighs roughly and pulls away from the curb.

I hum in agreement, grinning blindly at his soft chuckle. "Drunk me likes you too."

Chapter Seven

My mouth is dry, uncomfortable. And I don't have to open my eyes to register the dull headache I have, groaning softly, I pull my knees up to my chest and push my face into the softest of pillows. Inhaling I get assaulted by the most perfect musky smell. I stay still, slowly breathing it in, drowning out the growing nausea— it's favorably therapeutic. In and out, in and out, I regulate my breathing and focus on that and not the delicate sensation in my stomach. I'm thoroughly regretting the amount of alcohol I had last night. How can people do this on a weekly basis!

Slowly I blink my eyes open, finding that I'm not at home, nothing I see is recognisable. Brushing my hair out my face, I lift onto my elbow gingerly, still trying to keep the sickness at bay and look around, it's dark still but the never-ending spread of windows allows for plenty of moonlight.

"Huh?" I'm a bit annoyed that I'm not in the comfort of my own bed. What the hell? I frown through the reflection of myself propped up in a huge bed. Hand clutched to my forehead. The possible shimmer of liquid reflects beyond the darkness. Water?

Where the hell am I?

I suppose now would be the time to start worrying but I think I may still be under the influence. Wriggling to sit up I find myself in only my underwear, I notice some bottled water and painkillers beside the bed, accompanied by a note.

Take these, Jace x

My heart thumps in my chest, Jace? I look about the room my, eyes drawn to the other half of the bed— it's empty but not unused.

My hand smoothes over the soft linen surrounding me. Where is he? Is this his house? Or another pet project he has in the pipeline?

I'm not left wondering for long. The sound of footsteps brings my achy head round when a boxer clad Jace strolls in carrying a glass of icy water, it clinks as he nears. But my eyes are lost on the sea of muscle on show. Our eyes meet and I feel utterly buggered.

How have I managed to say no to him? "There she is." Abandoning his water on the side he kneels across the bed and tucks my messy hair behind my ear. "How's the head?" He has the softest looking lips.

I scrunch my nose because all I can think is he is a breath away, practically naked, and I'm in his bed with panda eyes and a claggy mouth. Attractive I am not.

He works out. He *must*. His muscles ripple as he moves, flexing as he shifts on the big bed and growing taut when he settles himself before me. His eyes are content and focused on my knicker-clad body. All I can do is stare.

He, in himself, is a little tantric. I'm constantly aroused when he's around. My eyes have a mind of their own— I look over him, because to look anywhere else right now, would earn me a slap from the female race.

I stare wide-eyed and a little in awe of him, he has that V! When I finally manage to bring them back up and meet his, I find the natural whiskey hue has darkened.

"You're naked," I stutter. "My clothes." I blink up at him. But that look has me hooked. It affects me instantly, my lips part and I pant.

"Have some painkillers." Reaching over, so I get a front seat to that delectable smell, Jace pops some tablets out the packet and uncaps the water for me. I look about my surroundings trying to fathom our location.

"Thanks," I croak, pulling my knees up I rest my head against my hand, His smile is soft as he watches me swallow the tablets. Cass springs to mind and I'm swamped by guilt, "Cass?"

"She's fine, her friend made sure she got home safely, Sean I think she said." I nod, feeling myself getting shy. Hell, I'm undressed down to a miniscule assemble in Jace Bennett's bed.

I look about his room once more, I realise I'm definitely not at the house where I took photos, I try to figure out where I am but it's too dark and I'm still drunk.

"We're at my house," Jace says, taking the bottle off me and placing it on the side. "You fell asleep and I couldn't remember which street you lived on." Surely, Cass would have told him? His hand works through my hair, fingers moving to my chin to bring me to his face. "I could watch you sleep forever, but it has about killed me to do it." Smirking he finally leans in as his eyes search mine for approval, I say nothing and wait. Our breaths collide and Jace whispers, "don't stop me from fucking you Lily." It's both a statement and a plea. Bold to the core.

The bluntness of his statement has my body tingling, everywhere, in places that feel as though they were never quite touched in the right way. But are about to be!

My resolve is too frail, to deny anymore that I want him just as desperately. Not when his thick length is pushing its way out his boxers and he is declaring his intentions so brutally.

"Okay." I agree, Jace needs little more confirmation. I'm scooped up gently and rested on straining thighs as he brings our mouths together. His hand happily becomes lost in my messy hair, I sigh and attach myself to him.

Jace keeps a hand on my lower back, his finger sweeping back and forth against the lace of my underwear. For all his pushing, it surprises me that he goes slowly, his soft and gentle kisses lighting up my body. Wrapping my arms around his neck, I moan into his mouth when his tongue finds mine. I shudder and reach for his hair the soft strands brush against my fingers, so I tighten my grip and lose myself in him. He is the perfect mixture of hard and soft. He seems content to just kiss me, but with every stroke and tightening of his hand on my skin, I lose all restraint, wiggling my hips against him on a soft moan. His light smile doesn't go unmissed.

"You're teasing me," I scold on a whisper, Jace smiles, his eyes lit up all full of mischief. Unclipping my bra, he breaks contact to slip it free, holding me at arm's length, my neck firmly grasped. He sighs, "Lily, you blow me away." His hand runs up my hip and rounds to cup my breast.

"You're not too shabby yourself," I muse, my fingertips running lightly over the wide brush of his shoulders.

Jace dips his head failing to disguise a wide smirk. "I'm glad you approve." His free hand finds my nipple. Ever so slowly he draws a circle around the hardening peak. "You're beautiful." His eyes are drunk on me— it's a heady sensation. I enjoy the soft patterns he makes before he takes me in his mouth. His tongue lazily flicks over my nipple whilst his fingertips press harsh imprints on my flesh. Hard and soft. It feels exquisite.

My moan is all breathy and soft. I'm teased to within an inch of self-combustion, but it's still not enough. Gripping my barely covered arse, he rocks me against his erection until I'm clutching at his hair and panting, my hips now gyrating in rhythm with his unspoken demand.

"Jace," I beg, the hot swell building low in my stomach hurtles forwards but he pulls away. "Oh god." He takes my mouth in a bruising kiss and topples us back, "Please," I breathe, my womb feels heavy, achy.

He kisses me hard. "No going back now." His hand finds my neck in a gentle brush. "I've caught you and now I'm keeping you." My face twists with pleasure. "That okay with you?" he groans on sexy smile, I rub myself shamelessly against him desperate to feel more.

Jace works his way down my body, gentle fingertips caressing my sides, mouth working in tandem. "Yes," I don't know what I'm saying, I just want him. Yes, to keeping me tonight, yes to him sliding down my body with obvious intent, yes to all of my initial no's. I cannot recall one single moment before this, where I have craved a man so desperately.

His lips brush against my belly then in one movement he is hovering over me again, warm glassy eyes penetrating my arousal, he looks so serious. He taps my temple. "We'll revisit this conversation lady, I don't do fake promises." He whispers on a scornful, raised eyebrow.

I'm panting up at him, I don't know what to say back, but quite frankly I'd sell my kidney to get him to ease the ache. "I'm drunk, not insane." I smirk, or maybe I am, I did just agree to something, what that something was I'm not too sure.

Dropping a kiss on the end of my nose he disappears down my stomach once more until his mouth reaches the material of my tiny thong, his tongue dances across the lacy seam. "This is a useless piece of material," he muses, pulling the little strap so it snaps back making me flinch, I bite my lip a delighted smile brightening my face. *Oh god!*

Jace kisses through the material, his tongue wetting the lace and mixing with my arousal, he growls making me shudder. "Please." My hands are in his hair, my back arched, I'm a mess and he hasn't even touched me properly yet.

With a rough motion he drags the thong away, grabs my hips and lifts me to his slack mouth, his tongue darts in and laps at my wetness making my eyes rolls back on a pained moan. Jace is groaning in appreciation, the deep vibration of his approval adding to my pleasure, when his fingers press into me, he suckles at my clit until I'm shaking either side of his head and crying out in sweet agony.

Slipping off the edge of the bed, he drops his boxers and my mouth dries. My shock must have registered on my face, because he cuffs my ankle with his hand. "You're wet enough, we'll take it slow." Using the contact, he tugs me towards his towering body so that I yelp, he is smirking and I decide I love that smile. He's cheeky and roguish.

My grin reflects his own, biting my lip I watch as he takes his cock in his hand and lowers himself onto his knees, reaching to sheath himself— he takes his time and I watch his hands work the heavy muscle straining for me.

His look is carnal— his sexual confidence an aphrodisiac. "You're mine Lily." I find sentiment in his words, even though we are both running on lust.

"Kiss me," I whisper.

The kiss I'm given is so hot the hairs on my neck stand to attention and salute him. He's too good at this. My mind wanders momentarily, suspecting all the reasons why he is so experienced. It's an unwanted visual.

Blocking it out I drive my slender fingers drive into his messy hair where I hold him to my mouth and soak in the affection.

Every sense seems heightened around Jace, like my whole body truly woke up.

"Me and you beautiful." Jace snatches me up in his arms and takes my place on the bed, I'm elevated above him as our eyes meet, dark satisfaction burns into mine as he holds me locked in his gaze, the wide crown of his cock pressing at my entrance.

I can't look way. Any second now we're going to connect and Jace eagerly watches for my reaction.

Panting I finally sigh when the thick tip pushes for entry. Jace's jaw is slack, as he lowers me oh so slowly down his wide long shaft.

My moan is hauled from somewhere deep and my eyes widen at the pinch in my gut. "Let me in," he whispers. "Relax Lily." He gains a little more depth. "Oh, fuuuck." It's a guttural, broken plea as he grunts out his satisfaction and finally begins pushing himself in.

At first it feels like an intrusion, he's too big, "Jace." There's an edge of discomfort in my voice. My nails are biting into his skin but I hold his unwavering gaze finding comfort in his own pained expression, I'm not the only one struggling with this connection.

Jace pulls me to him so he can take my mouth in a slow kiss, designed to make me relax, I soften against him, my tongue tangling with his.

Only then does he lift me and impale me fully, our cries shatter off the glass, I grip wildly at his arms my face a mask of shock and pleasure.

Wide whiskey eyes burn brightly at me. "Fuck, fuck, fuck." Rolling his hips he lifts me and pulls me down harshly as he drives up, I reach to grasp hold of his hair as I try to maintain our kiss, his mouth is addictive, and the burning pleasure being forced on me is too much.

He is unforgiving, relentless and all I can do is hold on, my arms wrapped around his neck vice tight as he pounds away like a mad man. "Fuck Lily!" End is in sight but I don't want it yet, he feels incredible, sensing my nearing demise, Jace flips us prizing my hands from behind his neck he lifts them above my head, his breathing hard. "Fuck I knew it was going to be good, but this is so much more than what I imagined Lily." My eyes pop wide as he grinds into me. I quiver at the sensation my breath leaving in a loud rush.

The familiar ache is dancing a rapid tune in my womb, rolling and bunching together, building before it breaks and crashes through me.

"Oh, god," I wail. I'm losing control, desire is taking the lead, and any rational thoughts have taken the highroad.

"Dammit," he curses, as I clench and quiver around him,

He rocks high and holds himself deep within me, my moan is long and high. "Those noises are going to make me loose it, you feel fucking amazing," he rasps, his wet mouth connects with my moist skin, Jace nips and sucks at my neck and ear. "Did you know Lily?"

Know what? This? Him?

My eyes are locked with his. He looks at me awed. "It's almost painful I wanted it to be good but I had no idea we'd . . . I didn't expect this," his groan is guttural, lifting my hips I meet each pound of flesh on flesh. "Jace!" I cry.

No, I didn't expect this, *him*. Panic grips me but is quickly doused by desire. The heavy ache is back, more desperate than before, I whimper as it rolls from my roots to my toes and I black out, my cry of pleasure bursting through my lips.

Jace shouts and hammers away, roaring out an expletive as he reaches his own climax, he thrusts on, jerking above me.

His mouth finds mine and I manage to peel my eyes open in time for our dazed gazes to collide. I'm held close to preserve the level of intimacy as Jace brushes the damp hair from my face, he cups my cheeks in big hands and kisses me sweetly until my heart slows to a more calming pace. I feel sated and adored under his lust filled scrutiny.

I stroke weak hands down his damp back— we have something. I've never shared this kind of chemistry with anyone, I think, somewhat sober. Only, the admission is one I wish I could throw away. This is all too soon. I don't deserve this.

His kiss is contradictory to his frenzied speed a moment ago. I'm captive under his large body, his hips rocking back and forth as he draws all pleasure from me, it's sending a fizz of lust to spark up once more. But I don't think I can go again. In fact now he has given me a moment to think I yawn quietly.

Sliding out I'm lifted up the bed and tucked in, Pulling my arse back into his groin which surprisingly isn't as flaccid as I assumed it would be Jace wraps an arm around me and nuzzles my neck, I yawn and slip under.

A raspy voice brings my eyelids sluggishly back up, he tusks, "you didn't think that was it did you?" I don't know how long I've been out for, but my headache has subsided, my lethargy on the other hand, is refusing to let me fully rouse. "I'm offended," he teases.

The gentle prod of his arousal, demands I stay awake. I let out a shaky breath when he enters me in one swift thrust. "It's your own fault Lily, you feel too good." Cupping my breast he fucks me slowly, caressing the tender peak as his other hand disappears into the curls at the apex of my thighs. My sleepiness is no match for his sexual appetite, I wake instantly, heat sizzles across my skin and I groan softly, as I look back over my shoulder at the lean man wrapped around me like a blanket, he cups my chin and presses higher, eliciting a sharp gasp of pleasure as he places a deep kiss on my mouth.

"I imagined you here, in my bed," he groans against my mouth, his tongue a hot wave, his eyes are unblinking as he holds my face to look back at his, refusing to cut the connection.

He thrusts up and I sigh, "Mmm." He nips at my lip tugging it playfully and I let him, feeling the most sexually confident I ever have, his fingers are still rubbing over my clit, all the while he watches my face pull and pinch in pleasure.

"I pictured sinking into this perfect little body, over" *thrust*, "and over," *thrust!*

Oh my god! I blink at him astounded by the stark truth pouring out of his sexy mouth, my mind skips away at the thought of him here, imagining all what he wanted to do to me.

Any reservations go out the window as I spread my legs and arch my back to give him deeper access. Jace's light laugh makes me quiver. "See how good we are?" His soft murmur makes me moan. *Yes, we are. I like it too much!* Only, I refuse to vocalise my thoughts as much as he is doing.

So much for getting some sleep, I'm insatiable.

"Don't stop," I beg softly, my hips rocking in time with his, his hand lifts to my hair and using the grip as leverage he pushes me to my front, the hot swell of his chest presses into my back, I'm flat out and he drives deep once, twice before he hauls me to my hands and knees, the position causes me to jerk as he gains more depth. "Oh god Jace," I whine, the light traipsing of hair on his hard thighs presses roughly against my legs, his cock, feeling twice as big at this angle, draws a garbled whimper from me, the pressure in my womb is insane, his lips drop a kiss on my back.

"I need it hard," he states. His large erection is caressing my inner walls, but I don't have time to respond because his fingertips dig into my petite hips. On a loud bark, he slams into me, shunting me forwards on the big bed. Gripping the quilt, I go rigid to take the impact of his powerful drives. The repetitive pound is hitting me deep and right *there*. My eyes roll away in ecstasy.

Every internal part of me is sucking him in, gripping tight. "Let go Lily!"

"Jace!" My legs feel too weak to keep me up, and with the strong male slamming away behind me I choke out a series of pleas when my womb spirals out of control.

Sensing the tightness in my womb, he barks out a command, "Now Lily!" he strains over each hard thrust, we climax together in a combination of sweet ecstasy and harsh moans. It's painful in its intensity but perfect still.

I'm face first in a sea of cotton and tangled limbs, I'm pulsating and my body feels drugged. That was intense. Incredible.

Jace Bennett, is a miracle in the bedroom. His huge chest is cupping my back as he drags in large soft gulps of air. I'm twisted until I'm facing him, all too happy to be confronted by such a gorgeous male, I stare up into dark sap eyes as he wordlessly maneuvers my legs so he is in between them, my wrists are caught up and lifted either side of my face and slowly he lowers his beautiful face, smirk and all to place a long slow kiss on me.

This man can't be for real!

I feel, cherished, decadent and thoroughly desired. I'm still reeling as I drift off.

Chapter Eight

Light is painting the sky into a frosty glow— through my sleep-deprived eyes I can finally see my surroundings clearly. From the bank of windows, I admire a decking that juts over a small lake its dark waters resembling black glass, further on trees border the property like misshaped posts. The lawn is cut, but other than that everything is kept natural and a little wild. It's a breath of fresh air from the towering brick and smog of London.

I can hear Jace's soft snore, the heat of his close body and touch of his hand splaying over my stomach. Slowly easing free, I slip from below the covers and find the floor is heated beneath my bare feet, quietly I go to the toilet and on returning from the bathroom search for socks, pants and a t-shirt to wear. Rather than getting back under the quilt I tip toe through the house finding that, like the other house I photographed, this one is a giant glass box too. The house spans out in front of me, a large open living area leads off from the front door, an industrial dinning suite backs along a bank of windows overlooking the same view I could see from Jace's bedroom. It's not short of space and although the rooms all merge together, they each hold their own identity, set apart by strategically placed furniture. I pad my way into the ocean of space, further finding his office and, through a partition, a well-equipped gym.

Hanging over the low dark grey sofa is a heavy throw, I pick it up and wrap it around my small frame before managing to push one of the pivoting doors open and plonk myself on a heavily cushioned bucket chair outside.

It's pretty cold out, freezing in fact, but after the last twelve hours the cool, clear air is a refreshing change to the shock to my senses Jace has presented me with. There is a huge slab for a table and a fire pit. It's very earthy and rustic. I tuck the throw under my feet and enjoy the quiet. I wonder how far from London we are? It's so peaceful and still.

I want to regret last night but the man is a god. Fully equipped in the arts of sex, seduction and affection. Who knew being bathed at four a.m., with a fiend of a man, could be so much fun? I fiddled with the damp ends of my hair, recalling our bubbly encounter, a smile pulling at my tired face. Involuntary my eyes pull back to the house, I see Jace's form under the quilt and can only think of all the things we did.

Biting my lip, I sigh reluctantly, I don't want anything serious. Its scares me how I feel around him, He's pretty intense and I am still dealing with the fall out of my last break up.

I'm staring out at the murky water, lost in thought a little while later, when the revolving door pulls my head round, Jace is wrapped in his own blanket but his legs and chest are bare, he saunters to me with a sleepy smile and leans down to give me a kiss. My eyebrows rise because I was expecting some awkwardness.

"Hey beautiful," he murmurs against my mouth, his arms hooking below my legs to lift me so he can take my seat. I clutch at my throw to avoid any cold seeping in, "hey yourself," I hum against his mouth, Jace doesn't let up he pulls me close and renders me useless with the lazy flicks of his tongue.

He is in complete control again, driving the kiss forward at his leisurely pace, once he is content, he tucks my head into his shoulder, "this is my favorite place to sit."

"I can see why." I'd like to get some pictures, especially now the sun is still low, frost hasn't quite settled but mildew has claimed a lot of the surfaces so everywhere shimmers. "It's so pretty out here."

Arms tighten around my waist. "How long have you been out here, you're going to get ill?" Jace scolds, he pulls at my throw and see's that I'm in his clothes, his eyes flash with satisfaction, "my clothes drown you little lady." I resume my position against the flank of his chest, yawning. "Not too long."

He jostles me, the rigid length of his never tiring cock brushing my stomach, "maybe I should wake you up?"

Shaking my head, I yawn again, he has kept me up most of the night how can he look so fresh faced and gorgeous. "If the bags under my eyes get any bigger, Harrods will want a trade price."

Laughing lightly, he lifts my head up and drops a kiss on my nose. "You can tell Harrods you're mine." Those eyes cause havoc with my brain, not to mention his possessive declaration. Why does he say those things?

I offer a small smile but pull away, "have you lived here long?" My tact at changing the subject is awful but he doesn't comment.

"A year or so now, it was a private fishing lake, the owner died and his son put it up for sale."

"Oh, is there more than one lake?" I wonder sleepily, the tree line is fairly dense so I can't see past it, twisting I look back to the house, finding that I can see right through to the front drive where more trees cocoon the property.

"No there is a huge one through those trees." Jace points. "Another smaller one too, I suspect some fishermen still sneak in but they can't get up here." I nod at that and shiver, despite being wrapped in blankets and held close, it's still cold this morning.

"Let's get you in. I made coffee." I'm not given a chance to stand, as Jace carries me in and pads over to a large island central to the flash kitchen. It's toasty inside, but I keep the blanket when he sits me on a stool, Jace, on the other hand, slings his over a chair and gives me a mouth-watering view of his toned arse.

God, my ovaries can't take much more of this!

"What does the lady want for her breakfast?" He asks, head in the fridge, he pulls out some eggs and bacon, pops them on the side and walks round to the coffee machine and sets two cups in, I'm a few feet away and he takes the opportunity to come plant a kiss on me, "you smell like sex and it's driving me crazy," he hums against my mouth, his eyes are open and the deep whiskey depths pull me in.

I smile against his mouth. "Ah, so that's your excuse. There I was, thinking only I had an effect on you." I joke pushing at his shoulder. "Eggs no bacon please," I say, Jace is grinning at me, he walks backwards and my eyes drop to the heavy package trying to break free of his boxers, when I look up he gives me a wink. I melt on the spot, he flicks on the radio and the low sultry voice of a female singer fills the quiet.

Handing me my coffee, he makes us breakfast and takes a seat beside me, his hair is still a mess but his eyes are over-bright. I don't think he could look any better in that moment. "Thanks," I moan around the mouthful of poached egg on toast, his arm finds the nape of my neck, twisting my head to his he pulls me in,

"You're welcome beautiful." His lips find mine and deliver a toe-curling kiss. We eat mainly in silence, purely because I can't believe this is all happening.

"Are you able to drop me home, I have a busy day?" I don't but it's already past ten, I don't want to overstay my welcome.

Jace takes my pots and puts them in the sink, returning to me he twists my seat and pushes his way between my legs where he locks his arms either side of the kitchen island and smiles down at me, "I think I can manage that." I see the look of lust darkening his eyes and this time I close the distance myself, pressing my mouth to his, noting the look of dark satisfaction burning in his gaze.

It doesn't take long for him to resume control, his hands find the hem of his t-shirt so he can slowly lift it over my head, he takes my feet one at a time and pulls his socks off dropping them to the floor. His boxers that I have had to roll over at the hem to get them to stay up get pulled down swiftly, I lift my bum and rest my naked body on the throw covered seat, for a minute he looks over me, breath leaving his mouth in a rush, "you really are a special find, Miss Spencer."

"I'm glad you think so," I whisper smiling up through my lashes, his eyes have no filter and every carnal thought is shining down at me, "you look a little pained," my voice is cloud soft. Teasing.

"You make me feel pained," he groans, lifting my hands he wraps them around his neck and slips his waist further between my legs, "have dinner with me later?" Nose nudging my face, he doesn't let me answer because his mouth is brushing lazily against my parted lips, when his tongue dips out I'm lost.

Firm hands grasp my bum and lift me I coil myself around his tall frame enjoying the feel of his taut muscles as I'm carried through to his extensive shower. My moan is brought on by the grind of his arousal against my sensitive flesh. Jace sets the water to hot and walks us into the steamy spray. There is no foreplay, I'm kissed within an inch of my life, tormented with harsh grinds and with a desperate tug of my legs he enters me on a shout.

"Jesus Lily, I can't get enough of you." My hands are wound so brutally in his hair, that I know it must hurt but I feel violent with desire, legs wrapped tightly I cry into Jace's mouth as he pounds away. Our kisses are frenzied, my eyes wide and when he pulls out to the tip and drives in on a wild bark my nails rip down his neck, "you're perfect!" he grunts teeth bashing together with mine. My arousal is limitless with him, I'm hurtling forward, eyes rolling back, as my body begins to tighten, "no, Lily look at me baby, fuck I want to see them stars."

"Uh god." My head feels sluggish as I pull it back to his. The dark amber of his eyes have been counteracted by black, his pupils are dilated to the point of no return. Because of me. It's a crazy notion.

"Tell me, when we first met, did you want this." He bites on my lip,

"Yes!" I cry, I want to close my eyes but can't. "I'm going to come," I sob.

"Wait for me." Jace draws back rolls his hips and surges forwards, my climax snatches hold of the movement and I begin to whimper.

"Fucking wait for me Lily!" He shouts.

"I can't! Oh god Jace please." I'm desperate, I feel tormented. His hips do their magic and when he slams up his lips smash to mine, I taste blood, dragging my lip between his teeth he groans, "Now baby."

My whole-body pulses as we both let go, moaning deeply, our wet bodies sliding together. "You feel too good Lily," he pants, face lost in my hair, he may be softening but I still feel full and when his cock pushes up my breath catches.

"I could go back sleep," I admit, as I sag against him.

"Good I can keep you here all day then." Jace pecks my nose then pulls out and lowers me gently, now I really do feel deprived.

I watch him quietly as he reaches for some soap and begins to wash us both, focusing on soaping every inch of my body and then encouraging me to do his until we are doused in bubbles. Jace wraps big arms around me and kisses me, until I can barely breathe and am laughing under the dense spray,

"Let me wash your hair." It's not a question, I blink up at him through the heavy spray but he turns me and begins massaging shampoo into my long hair. I stand silently, constantly fighting the war in my mind, whilst he dotes the kind of attention on me, I desire from a man. He does his own and I enjoy seeing his wide chest pulled out as he lathers his hair up, I drop my gaze down to trim hips and his cock, flushing when I see him smirking, "out." He winks and pushes gently into the curve of my back, he tugs a snowy bath towel down and wraps me in the huge fluffy thing. I'm attacked by a sudden bout of panic. I could seriously fall for this man!

"Lily let me take you to dinner tonight?"

Stood in only a towel in his glass house I feel vulnerable all of a sudden, especially when he walks over, pressing a wooden slat in the wall and a row of clothes emerges. Posh sod.

"I can't." I need to process all this. I mean, as one-night stands go — not that I have had any others— this one tops any other sexual encounter I've had. Cass will be over the moon, as I haven't been involved with a guy since Adam.

"Can't or don't want to?" He asks, walking back to me, towel slung round his hips as he pulls a knitted jumper over his ridiculously toned body. The towel gets replaced by a pair of jeans slung over a chair. Just jeans, no boxers. He has no shame, and tucks his heavy cock into the denim and buttons them up. I watch every button conceal him and blush when his hand lifts my chin to his face and he raises a brow. "So, which is it?"

"Both." I mean to only think it but the word comes out anyway. He looks affronted, but I can't think straight. I need some space!

"I'll let you get dressed" is his reply. I don't know why he is walking away as he can see me from the kitchen area anyway. There is hardly any space for privacy in this house.

I hope no fishermen came up here, because they would have had one hell of a show last night. I groan inwardly and pick up my dress and bra as I pass on my way to the bathroom, with the wooden panel and steam, I determine that I'm pretty safe to get dressed in here.

I find him washing the kitchen down, he's domestic too. He is checking all my mental boxes. "I can't find my knickers." My blush seems to reflect back at me through the windows.

"They're in the wash," he mutters. "You ready?" He doesn't even look in my direction. Oh, he is so pissed.

I do the only thing I can do to focus my mind on something other than Jace and his remarkable ways, every time I think back to last night I mentally slap myself.

Wrapping my camera around my neck, I walk through Richmond Park. It's a little foggy and gives an eerie feel to the pictures I capture. I probably won't keep any of these, but it's a welcome distraction after last night's antics. I'm meeting Cass shortly for something to eat at hers but until then I enjoy the solitude. Bask in it because I have been on a sensory overload for the last few days, and even with the one thing I love held in my hand— I can't stop thinking about Jace Bennett.

I tell myself it's only sex, but even that doesn't shift the mood I'm in. I've known the man less than a week and he managed to get me into bed, scrap that, it was four days and I feel smutty. Not to mention our lack of contraception, the pill only accounts for so much. Sighing, I sit against a tree. I will want more if I continue down this path and long term, I don't think Jace will commit.

I sound ridiculous, I hardly know him!

I feel so frustrated and confused, since Adam, I haven't even looked at other men let alone considered the possibility of a relationship, I blame Jace. The man is a menace!

Frowning, I force the feelings away and head back to my car, my nose is cold and the sky is darkening, despite it being early still.

I text Cass, letting her know I will be half an hour tops and set off.

My loyal friend swings the door open wearing a huge grin and holding a glass of wine out for me. "Enter, enter!" I take the glass gladly and let her pull me into a hug, "Christ woman you're freezing!" She shivers against my well-padded body,

"You'd never know it was nearly winter," I laugh sarcastically propping myself against the wall as I take my shoes off, she tuts at me and pulls my coat off once I'm free of my shoes.

"It smells amazing." I walk through to the back and find a candle lit table with flowers. "Ah for me!" Cass swans in apron wrapped around her lithe frame.

"Always." Her grin is infectious, "how's the head?" We spoke this morning and I felt pretty worse for wear. Not to mention the impending regret working its way into my psyche.

"How's Sean?" I chuckle. The tension brewing between them for the past few months, has been gag worthy. Despite their history, apparently Cass fell for more than his lucky charms last night.

"It's that Irish accent." She pouts. I don't make any more Irish jokes, I bored her this morning with them all, shrugging I pull my knees up and rest my chin on them as I watch her lift a lid on a pot and sniff.

"Do you think you two could ever be more than friends?" I query, I hope so, and something gut deep, tells me Sean is good for her.

"I'm seeing him on Tuesday." She sighs, doubt in her usually confident voice. She has resigned herself to him being footloose and fancy, like before. They may have been together but they weren't exclusive. Cass doesn't hold it against him but Sean happily sought out other women whilst with her. In his defense she did say he could. Apparently reverse psychology doesn't always work.

"I don't want to get hurt," she mutters. Touché,

"It was years ago, you've changed, maybe he has too?" I reflect.

"Well since he opened Finnegan's he hasn't been dating anyone or so I'm told, and that was a year or more ago." Joining me at the decorated table her eyes twinkle, "and the superhuman, was he super good in bed?"

My blush burns brighter than the candles, I drop my gaze and laugh on a groan, "Cass the man would make you blush." I admit shyly,

She whistles low, "I knew it, he has this walk and look about him, it says I fuck like a world champion and make love like an angel." She grins over at me, doing a funny little shimmy.

My laugh is interrupted by a loud snort, with shocked looks we both fall over the table in fits of giggles. She's not far off the mark, the love part I can't comment but the man can fuck and fuck well he does.

I just don't want my heart fucked with.

Cass looks to the ceiling in a daze. "I was so in love with Sean." She admits finally. "We have this crazy chemistry." She blows out an unsteady breath, and after my Jace encounter, I feel I can empathise with her.

"I thought he was a fling, friends with benefits?" I sip my wine glad to be out of the cold.

"He was supposed to be, I agreed for reasons that were purely naive and cost me my heart." Her laugh is harsh, I'm worried this line of conversation will make her change her mind in giving him another chance but find myself questioning her further.

"You never said, you're always so-"

"Non-committal." She drawls flicking her blonde hair, she stands and shrugs, "Yes well being used as a piece of meat will do that to you," she laughs, like always she's brushing it off and takes life by the horns.

"Why did you never bring this up before, even after Adam you never told me?" Cass has always pushed me to open up, I feel as though I'm only just getting to know her.

"No point, it was done Sean had gone back to Ireland and I wanted to forget he ever happened." She looks out the window, where I see my confident friend lost in a sea of hurt.

"But you're seeing him Tuesday," I say brightly, picking up my wine and taking another healthy sip.

"Yep, after all this time he still has the power to make my stomach drop, and like you said we're different people." Her grin is over-bright, she is as scared at taking that next step as I am.

"Well I like him," I confess, I do, he has shown nothing but loyalty and genuine concern for us both, mainly it stems from him knowing Cass but I see how he looks at her. I smile over at her, excited at the prospect of her having an actual date and not just coaxing men between her thighs.

Cass starts serving up and we enjoy chatting about non-men related things over dinner. Mainly she tells me about work and I fill her in on the event I'm holding next month. It's the perfect end to an unexpectedly intense few days. I leave late and regret the amount of wine I have consumed this weekend.

Chapter Nine

I'm early getting up so take my time showering, I'm in the gallery all day and Harriet managed to book Paco in for eleven thirty, I have lunch ordered and plan on commissioning his art. I just hope he likes me, as much as I like his creative eye. There's something very refreshing about his desire to reveal and concentrate on controversial matters.

I choose a black pencil dress and match it with some court shoes, my hair is being more friendly today but I suspect that's because I had it cut over the weekend, I curl it and do my makeup before grabbing some breakfast and heading out the door at quarter to ten.

Harriet is already there— she walks towards me with a steaming mug of coffee as I enter. "You've had a delivery," she says, I'm not waiting for anything?

I frown in question but she points to a huge bouquet of flowers. "Oh wow," I laugh self-consciously. Couching down I pull the card from the artfully placed flowers,

I recognise the confident scrawl on the card from my short stay at Jace's.

Have dinner with me? Jace x

I can't resist smelling them— hidden beneath the fragrant petals I suppress a smile. It turns sad when I remind myself Jace isn't the kind of guy I want to invest my time in. Even if the sex is sheet clawing good!

I'm about to tell Harriet to get rid of them but find myself placing them on the low windowsill and thank her for my coffee.

"Secret admirer?" She pokes for information,

"Possible mistake," I grimace. "Can you check if Paco is still okay for eleven thirty?" I leave her with that job, taking the small card to my office and dropping it in my drawer.

My day goes by in a rush of catching up on emails and a successful meeting with Paco, who is far more modest than I expected, considering his creative interests.

I finalised the photos for Carl and sent them over before I left work on Friday. The photos they have chosen are my favourites of Jace. I'm staring at his image on my computer, grateful that I'm alone. The torrent of visuals from our night together plague me so much so, that I spend too much time looking at pictures of the man gazing back at my camera. There is unveiled lust in his eyes, a confident stance that reaches into me on deep level, I get the feeling that Jace is a force to be reckoned with, not just intimately but professionally.

Harriet has already left so I shut down and lock up.

As the day wore on, I decided it's best not to make contact with Jace. The flowers are a lovely touch and I should thank him, but I need a straight head about me and I don't have that around him.

My bag is a jingly mass of tan leather when I pick it up. Grabbing my keys, I forage for my phone as Jace's name flashes on the screen.

I know Cass gave him my number but I didn't know he had taken it upon himself to store his number in my phone? Biting my lip in guilt I disconnect the call and head to my car.

By Friday, the gallery is filled with the heady scent of flowers, each card signed by Jace, asking me out for dinner. Cass thinks I'm being a mean cow, but I know one night was all it was, all it can be.

Having done a little research, Jace has never had a serious relationship in his life, I can appreciate the big gesture and the girl at the flower shop is already half in love with him but I'm steering clear!

"No delivery today?" Harriet says over the top of her laptop.

I look up, glasses perched on my nose as I lean over my desk, it's nearly lunch and any Jace related deliveries have been first thing.

Shrugging I look to the window, as though that will miraculously bring the flowers to my door, "I guess not."

"Well whoever it is I don't think they will give up just yet." She smiles, I shrug and push my glasses back up as I look over some photos I snapped this week.

"What makes you say that?" I don't want to ask such questions but I can't subside the girlish part of me that adores all the effort with the flowers.

They are dotted everywhere, bouquets of light and pretty colours cuddled by fresh green leaves and all wrapped elegantly. Harriet had to buy two more vases to fit them all in, and yesterday we both went home with some.

"Because why all this." She holds her arms out. "Name a man that you know who goes to these lengths." She points a finger at me. "Any of your friends tell you that their men have dotted time and sent flowers daily?" His determination adds a certain amount of pressure on me.

I think on it for a minute but no, I have never known a man to do this. I feel guilty all of a sudden, these flowers can't have been cheap — all he is asking is that I join him for dinner. No sex, only food.

It's easy. I just have to not be...easy. Shit!

Harriet is watching me when I look back up. "Maybe give the guy a chance?" She pushes gently, her eyes soft and full of hope for me.

"Yeah," I say non-committal. I suppose the fact that he has given up isn't such a bad thing. This is what I wanted but now that the deliveries have stopped, I feel a bit deflated. I could laugh at myself—I'm acting like a crazy lady. And letting a guy continue to buy flowers repeatedly, when you have no intention of following through is really shitty, I feel shitty.

"Yeah," Harriet mimics, I pull a face at her and use my pencil to point. "Did Alfredo get back to you?"

"Not yet, do you still want a wrap from the deli?" She asks as she clicks away.

"Please," I hum. The door swishes open and a delivery guy walks in, flower free and carrying a thin parcel.

"Parcel for Miss Spencer?"

"That's me." I walk out from my desk and take the parcel. "Do you need a signature?" I ask as he hands over my delivery, Harriet looks at me expectantly, is it from him?

"No thanks, have a good day ladies!"

"And you." When he goes, Harriet breezes over.

"Oh open it!" She's bursting with excitement.

I tear the slim package open and find another envelope inside. The writing is different and I don't recognise it. Opening that one, I find a shiny card and my stomach drops when I see it's a birthday card.

"Bit early," Harriet laughs.

I know who has sent it and wish they hadn't. I flip the card open and read over the minimal message.

Happy Birthday - Dad and Joan x

Tears burn in my eyes, it's next weekend but thanks dad. I don't intend to reply in any way, there is no point. I haven't spoken with him in years.

I drop the card on the desk throwing Harriet a smile, I don't divulge my private life with anyone and my fallout with my Father isn't up for discussion.

When the door goes once more, Harriet and I both snap our heads up as a courier walks in carrying a large box. "Delivery for Miss Spencer?" seeing the matte black box I immediately know it's from him. Jace.

I hold my hand up because I know anything that leaves my mouth will be in a squeak that radiates on a frequency only dogs can hear.

Smiling he ambles over, he's a big guy. "Sign on the dotted line," his uniform is straining over big shoulders and the name Terry is wearing thin. My eyes latch onto the coffee foam stuck in his beard.

"Thanks," I say scrawling my name quickly.

Terry looks around and hands the parcel over, he clocks my card and all the flowers, "Happy Birthday!" He beams.

I open my mouth to correct him, but smile in thanks. The parcel is pretty big so I place it on the floor, waiting until Terry leaves us before I open it. Harriet is hopping from one foot to the other, her heels clicking a tap dance on the floor.

Sliding the lid away, I pull the tissue paper apart, on a bed of black silk is a card and a spattering of white rose petals.

"Oh, how romantic," Harriet coos. The word doesn't seem to fit Jace's profile, but this past week has shown me that he isn't at all as I predicted. Mr. Bennett has a soft side.

Scooping up a handful of petals I hand them to Harriet who is nearly hyperventilating with excitement. The card is heavy but when I open it, I realise it's the type of paper used.

Jace has good taste.

We are having dinner Lily! Be ready for 7:30, J x

. . .

Ah! Now that's more like Jace, sure he can be sweet if he wants to but he is a man who likes to get his own way, I make a mental note to remember how persevering he is when he wants something. I quickly remind myself I shouldn't, as I don't want to get caught up in anything serious.

Lifting the material, I raise my brows when the choker cocktail dress drops to hang in front of me. It's absolutely stunning.

"Oh wow, top marks for the mystery man!" Harriet sings, her eyes are so bright and full of childish love.

I smile broadly— the excitement that Jace has to offer is addictive. He is full of subtle surprises and makes me feel pretty damn special. I don't want to be sucked in and find myself in a mess, I have a strong feeling Jace has the power to hurt me, if I got in too deep. It's hard to admit but after the boring and disastrously crap relationship with Adam, the allure of fun is hard to resist and who better to rock my world that Jace Bennett? I'm still indecisive about him but figure I owe him at least dinner for all the trouble he has gone to.

Harriet and I work through the afternoon in a silent blur as we arrange art and contact other galleries, I should be looking into courier rates but get distracted worrying about seeing Jace later. Harriet sensing my mental absence suggests she lock up so I can get ready.

"Thanks, Sorry Harriet," I laugh, trying not to show my anxiety too much.

"Don't be, have a great night." She beams, despite my inner intellect screaming at me to book into a hotel for the night and hide out from the likes of Jace Bennett, I leave work a ball of doubtful, girlish excitement.

I stare at my phone for the longest time, with a groan of confusion I throw it on my bed and look at my reflection. I have the dress on, my hair is curled artfully and I have managed to master the smudged smoky eye again but I can't bring myself to actually go through with this.

I know why, Jace means something to me. Even after this short amount of time, tearing myself away from him is hard. I'm a glutton for punishment where he is concerned, I expect heartache in my future but the thrill and emotions he evokes are playing havoc with my usually sensible mind.

I dash for my phone and type a message out to him.

I'm not coming, Sorry Jace but I think we should call it quits, Take Care x

There done!

Letting out a sigh I kick off my heels and go to the fridge, my wine glass is already on the side so I add ice and top it back up. "Bottoms up," I murmur and take a large gulp.

The harsh sound of my ringtone screeches through to the kitchen, I jump as though I have been caught doing something I shouldn't and slosh wine over the side of the glass. "Oh fuck!" I know it's him. I ignore it and close my bedroom door, turn on the TV and find a music channel. *Hozier* flits on the screen and I put the volume up, as my ringtone goes at it again for round two.

"Give up," I whisper, begging my phone to stop ringing. Taking a seat on my sofa, I pull a throw over my feet and pick up a takeaway menu.

My phone chimes away again but I choose to block it out as I look over the menu, I'll order what I always order so it acts as a useless distraction technique. I drop it back on the side sighing helplessly.

I wait for ten minutes and finally relax when my phone remains silent. Leaning back on the sofa I flick through the channels sipping on my wine. I'm doing the right thing I remind myself over the nauseating reality of my life, Jace free.

I hate that he has made such an impact on me! And even more so because after Adam I made a pact to stay single and enjoy being me. To heal. I need to heal.

I was doing fine until Jace sauntered into my life, topless and smirking at me just so. The man knows he's trouble.

A series of loud bangs on my door sends me flying up to my feet. "Shit!" I cough through the face of wine.

"Lily! Open up!" He sounds desperate and pissed off! Oh shit!

My head flies to the door I can't believe he is here.

I don't want to open the door but I can't ignore him either. I'm drenched, the dress is splattered in wine and my hair looks dreadful. I pat my face with my forearm and stare at the door.

I jump when another bang rings through the place. "Open the door!" He shouts, I feel shit for standing him up.

I walk to the wooden barrier between us and rest my back against the joining wall, "Go away Jace," my voice sounds weak to my own ears.

"Not a chance Lily," his laugh is drowned out when he jostles the door.

"Please go away," I plead my eyes closing tightly.

"No!" He bangs the door once and I hear him sigh heavily. "Me and you are driving each other insane, you're in there hoping I will somehow find a way in, even though you're telling yourself asking me to go away is the right thing to do." I close my eyes again holding back a rush of tears, how does he do that, wheedle his way into my head?

"It *is* the right thing," I say forcefully, more to myself than him. I should be concerned yet I find his determination attractive.

"No," his laughter mocks me gently. "No it's not, the right thing is to let me in so I can spoil you, I want to see you in that dress," he says on a soft husk. "I want to see you out of it." I smile at the playful note in his voice. "I want to say a hell of a lot more but your neighbour is threatening to call the police," he adds impatiently.

What? I drag the door open worried that Mrs. Tufnell is sticking her lovely but unwanted nose in, only to get pushed back in with a pair of worried whiskey eyes trained on me.

Jace kicks the door shut with his foot and straightens his jacket. He looks hot and angry. I turn to mush. He is donned in jeans an open neck shirt and suit jacket, I mentally slap myself for my stupidity.

"You lied!" I snap.

"You stood me up," he snaps back, I open my mouth to say something but slam it shut, what can I say. It's the truth.

"It's for the best." I shrug and look away, I can't keep my eyes in his direction when he looks as good as he does, those deep sap irises burning up the room and his aftershave dancing through my veins. My glass is still in my hand but it's as good as empty, so I put it on the side.

"Bullshit Lily, we connect. There is something here between us."

"Sex!" I cry, so what? He can get that anywhere. I don't say that because I can't bear the thought of him tangled up with another woman.

I'm lying— it's more than that. What we have isn't only about sex, yes that plays a huge part, okay colossal I inwardly admit, our chemistry accounts for almost ninety percent of whatever this is, but I know that there's more. I can't say what, but it's *there*— I just can't give over the other ten percent of me to find out. Not after Adam.

"Oh, for fuck sake," he scoffs, "don't downplay it, have you ever felt like this before?" He's walking this way and I haven't a big enough place to evade him. I don't reply. It's easier than lying to him again.

When he is on me, he takes my hand, such a gentle gesture. Lifting it he places it on my chest, his own encasing mine. "Your heart is going crazy, you're thinking 'he's right'. You want me to fight to prove you wrong and beneath that, you're wondering how long before I get you out of that dress," his shaken voice brings my eyes to his, my lips part at the thought of us together, I bask in the silence as he searches my gaze. "You know I'm right Lily, I know *you* already, you want to know if you imagined how good it was, will it be better next time? You want me." He cups my face, his eyes daring me to defy him.

"You're going too fast, this is too fast." I choke on the words, I feel so emotional all of a sudden, I can't think around him. I simply soak into his presence and drift along with him. That's what scares me. I like control and with him I have none.

"I've wasted too much of my life on regret, to be dragging my feet now." Jace pulls me to him and cups my chin. "I don't want slow Lily, I want to hurtle along with you." Hurtle where?

"We don't even know each other," I argue reasonably, surely, he can understand that. This is *him* drunk on lust, nothing more. I pull my chin free and silently beg him to go.

I don't want to get hurt.

"I know how I feel won't change." He vows softly, his lips brush mine but I pull back.

"I can't do this Jace, I'm not ready for this." I plead for him to reason with me but he shakes his head.

"This is happening, I'm not going away." When his mouth brushes mine again my lips soften on impact. "Don't run from me anymore Lily."

My eyes close against the hot burn of tears. My heart is already in this. It was from the first moment. My problem is it never managed to heal from the last onslaught. I need him to slow down.

He must sense the last of my resolve diminish because he takes my face in warm hands and kisses me deeply. "You look stunning." He pulls back to take in my now crumpled state, he fingers the wet strands of hair.

"Wine," I mutter, Jace twists it around his finger so it becomes taut and brushes his thumb down my cheek. "You're too beautiful."

I roll my eyes but he tugs my hair playfully. "If I say you're beautiful then you're beautiful," he states, the twinkle is back in his eyes and I struggle to not melt at his feet. I'm stuck somewhere between lust, guilt and fear.

"Sorry, for dinner." I feel terrible about it. I let out a shaky breath and his lips drop gentle kisses over my face. "Lily relax and let us happen." He coaxes.

Dropping my head to his chest, I try to think for a second but the soft brush of his fingertips running up my thigh and hooking my knickers has me lost, everything about Jace is too much, he doesn't let up, doesn't give me time. He is the one hurtling us along— I don't think I will ever manage to catch up.

"I'm not sure I want this, if I did, I wouldn't fight you so much," I whisper. When he stiffens I will the words to be swallowed back up, the chemistry between us could burn up the sun. I can't trust myself enough to make the right choice. I've only been single for a few months and bam! Jace Bennett rockets into my life and rips the earth up from beneath me. I don't deserve the kind of happiness I know he could possibly offer.

His mouth finds mine is a harsh kiss, he's angry and I suppose I have hurt him, or bruised his ego at the very least. I'm hurting. This is what scares me, I barely know him and already I know it's going to emotionally suffocate me when he goes.

"Please go," I whisper around the attack of his mouth,

This isn't a passionate kiss, he's saying goodbye. My throat constricts painfully. I get swept up for what I promise myself will be the last time.

Jace powers us back and my shoulders crash into the wall, when his tongue sweeps in I knit my fingers in his hair and kiss him back. I mold to him and sigh when he grinds himself into me, taunting me with what I could have, what I will be missing. His nostrils flare angrily, as those damn eyes of his manage to pointedly convey, *look what you're giving up. Giving to someone else.*

"Lily, give m—"

"Dammit," I sob, covering my face with my hands, "that wasn't supposed to happen," I whisper.

Jace's lips press along my cheek and collarbone, he nudges his groin up groaning quietly and I gasp softly. "Fuck," I whisper in annoyance. I'm so mad with myself. Jace says nothing but keeps his face averted.

When he pulls away his jaw is set like stone. He looks desolate. Slipping away he steps back, leaving me shaken against the wall and panting. Finally, he looks at me with blank eyes and grinds his teeth together. He's angry with me, and himself maybe for chasing me all for nothing?

"I didn't want that to happen," I whisper, I know I did, but every moment more with him makes it every bit harder to say no. "I . . . you need to go."

He holds my tearful gaze with a deep, indecisive frown.

"God Jace please, go." The tears I have fought to keep at bay slip free, his eyes widen at my obvious distress, he drags a hand down his face, still panting. His teeth lock and I know he has finally relented, he swears under his breath whilst slanting an angry and frustrated look away.

With a gentle knock to my chin and a signature wink he clears his throat, "look after yourself Lily," His voice is thick with regret.

I feel the wind get knocked out of me.I want to stop him, I go to, but shut my mouth when he steps back, turns and walks out.

It's for the best.

I tell myself, before I sink to my sofa and force myself not to cry over a man I don't know.

Chapter Ten

Cass has exhausted all efforts to make me feel even half human but I have this ache in my gut that won't dislodge, she keeps telling me I made a mistake, maybe I did but men like Jace enjoy the chase, they play the game and reap the benefits before rolling the dice on a new challenge.

I should be thankful I got out so quickly.

"Lily, I love you, lady, but I'm calling an interven-thingy-some." She knocks my foot with her own as she moves to stand in front of me, hands on her hips, her blonde hair pinned on top of her head. She kicks me again.

"Even when you don't know how to pronounce it," I deadpan. She shrugs and blushes. I laugh at how hopeless she is at times.

"Whatever. You chose to walk away, so snap out of it. You didn't want him, now he's gone. It was your choice. So, move on." I hate how right she is, and love her honesty.

"Yeah, I know, sorry." She smiles widely and hops on the sofa, pulling me in for a hug. I go willingly. "Thanks."

"Anything for my favourite girl." She leans forwards and fills our glasses up. "Wine," she states and hands mine to me. If we drink much more, I will need new organs.

"It's your birthday this weekend. Let's go out for dinner, hit Finnegan's, and dance our little arses off." She chinks my glass and I smile genuinely for the first time in days. "Here's to us!" she sings,

"Here's to perfect friends and fake interven-thing-somes," I murmur and nudge her with my shoulder, laughing over my glass.

"You're a tit," she states.

"I know, but then, so are you," I reply honestly.

She sighs happily and wiggles her newly painted toes. I know things with her and Sean are good, she is seeing him later. I decide if I'm out this weekend I want a new outfit, it is my birthday after all. But for now I'm going to enjoy *Bridget Jones* and forget about all things Jace related.

Selfridges doesn't disappoint, I spend too long browsing at things I can't have before I finally settle on a low open back dress with long sleeves, it's fitted and I love it. I find a pair of sky-high patent heels and splurge out further, by buying myself some new lipstick.

I can't afford to buy any of this but this is retail therapy at its best.

"Hello," Carl steps up beside me, he looks immaculate as always, I instantly search for Jace but Carl lays a hand on my arm. "He's not here," he says softly, his eyes concerned. I feel stupid and find myself checking again anyway.

"Oh, I'm not bothered." I shrug and duck my head, as I look in my bag for my purse.

"If you say so," he remarks.

The sales girl is becoming impatient but I hold it up, "Found it!" I pay for my items and Carl walks with me. "How are you?" I ask trying to assemble my bags in an order that makes it's easier for me to carry, Carl sighs dramatically and takes a bag from me. "Thanks," I smile softly.

"Things are good," he states on a dip of his head, he fascinates me with how animated he is. He stops pulling up a dark sequin dress. "This would suit your complexion." He fingers the material and I lift my hand to run my fingers over the sequins.

"I'm not too sure," I say, it's nice but the kind of thing I'd expect to see Cass in, glass in hand, hair being swung about as she dances crazily on some poor man's table.

"He's a good guy," Carl says, as he drops the dress and looks over his glasses at me.

"I'm sure he is." I feel pressured to say something back, but I can see Carl isn't satisfied with my reply.

"I've never seen him like this before." Carl swings the gauntlet and makes me feel ten times worse. I swallow my unease and lift a different dress to look at.

"It's not that I don't like him Carl, I'm not ready to be swept off my feet so-" I can't think of the right words, Jace is a bit like a whirlwind.

"Violently," he offers. I laugh at his astute assessment. He has such a brutal and powerful effect on me. "You have some serious chemistry." He fans his face.

I choose to sidestep his direction of conversation and point to his bags. "Something for someone special?" I ask.

"You're translucent," He drawls, my blush is brighter than his salmon shirt but I shrug his comment off. "Watch for Rupert, he has been promoted," he gushes proudly.

"Oh wow, well done Rupert!" I smile Carl lifts the box and shows me, it's very ornate. "That's gorgeous," I stutter, shit Jace must pay very well.

"Nothing but the best for my man." His voice is full of pride, I can only recall what Rupert looks like from a distance. But I can't imagine Carl picking anyone who was unattractive, not that he seems shallow but he has an obsession with presentation.

"I'm sure he'll love it." My grin is as wide as his infectious excitement is.

Carl pouts and knocks my hips with his own. "Come on sexy lady, what's in the bags?"

"Oh." I pull out my dress. "It's my birthday Saturday so me and Cass are hitting the town, dinner, Finnegan's, the usual." I realise my mistake in telling him my whereabouts and clamp my lips shut.

He whistles long and low. "You'll look sensational in that." He rubs the material. "Oh yes, this will cling in all the right places." He winks at me, giving his perfect eyebrows a wiggle, my laugh carries.

Carl pulls my other bag. "Shoes I see, I love a good heel," he declares under his breath, he pulls my shoes out and gasps. "Oh, the luck of being a lady." He sounds deflated.

"Whoa, trust me being a girl has it's down sides." I point out fairly and he bites his lip, as he adores my shoe in his hand.

"I'm sure, how awful to have the likes of Jace Bennett, tripping all over himself, for you," he muses playfully.

"He is not!" I scorn. Taking my garments back I put them away and we walk towards the exit, I'm mindful to ask non-Jace related questions and figure Rupert is my best bet.

"How long have you been married?" Carl hooks his arm through mine, as we stop outside the food hall.

He seems off in his own world for a moment. "Four years now, but we have been together nine," he holds up his arm to check his own watch. "Bugger, I've got to go, I have an appointment."

"Oh okay, well it was nice seeing you." I smile Carl startles me with a sudden air kiss. "Have a great birthday. Sorry, I'm super late. Damn heels." He chortles, his eyes dancing.

"I'm sure I will." His smile is too big not to share in.

"See you soon and remember what I said." I frown and he tuts loudly, "He's a good man," he delivers before he breezes off, head held at an angle of superiority, his suit so precise and clean. I smile to myself wishing that things could be different— I like Carl.

Cass is late arriving at mine but when she finally does Sean is in tow, "hope you don't mind?" she pulls a face and holds a bottle of wine up.

"You said she knew!" Sean laughs disbelievingly, he shakes his head at me as I mouth, '*it's fine*'

"Come in." I open the door wide stepping out of the way for them to come through— Cass kisses my cheek and pushes the bottle into my hand.

"Happy birthday!" Cass sings.

Sean pulls out an exotic bouquet of flowers and leans in to kiss my cheek also. "Happy birthday, Lils. Had a good day?" He sidesteps and I close the door behind them.

"I'm not big on birthdays." I confess, Harriet had arranged for a breakfast to be delivered this morning at the gallery and we ate it out back wrapped in scarves and sipped steaming coffee, it was lovely but I'm ready to hit the wine, hard!

"Okay. That dress is going to break some hearts later," Cass chuckles pointing her finger at the offending item. "Damn girl."

I smile and give a twirl— it hits the dip in my back and reveals a hell of a lot of skin. "Voila." I grin holding my hands out. I love this dress but it's very revealing.

"Fucking hell!" Sean covers his eyes, Cass jabs his gut making him cough. "Shit Lily have some sympathy for the male race!" He argues, Cass rolls her eyes and I bite my lip feeling super self-conscious.

"I should change." I contemplate. Cass is smiling at Sean and I get the feeling she has put him up to this, being over nice, complementing me. Giving my confidence a boost.

"You look hot!" Cass grins. "Heart breaker coming through." She takes my hand raising it above her head and sashays past, her laugh is guttural and full of a confidence, I could never carry. "I wish a certain someone could see you about now, he'd swallow his own tongue." She clips my hip with her own, before giving Sean a cheeky wink.

My smile is a painful reminder of Jace— he would die on the spot or tackle me to the floor. I smirk inwardly at the thought.

There is a part of me that secretly wishes he will somehow be there. But like Cass said, I made a choice. "I need to grab my clutch," I say heading towards my room, I slip my heels on and grab it quickly. I look once more for my lipstick but I can't find it anywhere. I quickly apply a less racy one and walk out to find my friend all gooey eyed for Sean. "Love birds, thank you for my flowers and wine." I lean to smell the soft petals.

"You're welcome. Can we go, I'm starving?" Cass says holding her stomach.

She looks cute. Her hair is up for a change and pinned, and she has some leather-look jeans and a silk cami on. She's really down-played her looks. I frown because usually it's her pleading with me to wear less.

"I like your top," I say and she rolls her eyes at me, I fear there is more to her outfit than meets the eye, but with her choice of outfit I feel practically naked and we are going out for a meal. "Couldn't you have put a dress on, I feel like a hooker," I remark in her ear as I pass, pouting.

She gives me a sympathetic look saying, "honey no man could afford that arse, not even the superhuman." She slaps my bum and skips past me.

"Can we not talk about the superhuman?" I murmur, Sean wanders out looking completely lost by our conversation and sighs. "Only just realised you're in for a night of girl talk?" I jest.

"Yes, pass your key I'll lock up." I throw my key and, in a moment of self-doubt, grab my leather jacket to hide the expanse of skin I have on show. I let Cass lead me down the stairs. Sean has driven, so we head straight to the restaurant from here and plan to go on to Finnegan's.

After such a heavy meal I regret the tight dress. "Food baby." Cass prods my stomach as I rub it gingerly.

"I ate way too much," I complain, I feel ten times heavier and way too sleepy to party.

Sean is practically comatose in his chair. "Help me," he whispers, eyes pleading heavily with us.

Cass and I burst out laughing. "I figure the more I drink the less I will care." I knew I shouldn't have had dessert, but I need it to soak up the alcohol I plan to consume.

"Jesus you are out to get wasted." My friend notes. "Where has my boring, sensible friend gone?" She mocks.

"Oh, she's still here, just taking a nap though." I feign being asleep,

"You girls are weird." Sean strains, as he shifts in his chair. "I need to walk this off, I think I shifted a kidney."

"You big baby," I chuckle, "you both ready to go?" Hell after that meal, I'm ready to go bed.

We settle the bill and Sean drives us back to his bar, where he disappears out back and Cass rolls her eyes. "I bet you he has gone for a nap, the man can't handle his food." She tugs us both forward into an empty spot at the bar.

"I feel his pain." We get served fairly quick, Sean's employees recognise us so we put our order in and double up. I grin soaking up the atmosphere, this is what I needed, a crazy night with my friends. Total annihilation.

"I want to marry you," the deep slur comes from my left, both Cass and I look around to find a very drunk guy holding himself up at the bar. He squeezes my arm. "If I wasn't so pissed, I'd take you both out back." He grins and the group of men he is with laugh along, their own eyes glassy inebriated balls. One is squinting heavily and I pull back on a grimace. Yuck!

"Oh, how sweet, maybe I can hold your hair back whilst you're sick," Cass says in her most patronising voice and pats his head. His eyes cross as he attempts to register the insult and shifts on a grunt, so he can stand straight. "Greasy drunk," Cass sniffs at his shocked face.

"Bitch," he scoffs as Sean ambles past, apparently, he didn't need a nap after all. With the air shifting into more aggressive territory I'm glad he chose now to arrive.

"That bitch just so happens to be mine, and the other is celebrating, so if you want to keep drinking, apologise." We get a half arsed apology, I shrug it off whilst Cass smirks smugly at them, I don't want any trouble tonight. Cass thrives off it— she's a bloody nightmare!

I take my drink when Cass pushes it into my hand. Being sober around a room of drunks is hard work, but if you can't beat them, join them! We start moving through the heavy crowd, mindful of where we move, groups are muddled together slugging shots or dancing their way across the dance floor. This place is a bustling eatery in the day, serving some of my favourite food. It's a shame it's too far from work, else I would be here most days. We edge around a group of what Cass likes to call hyenas, a pack of women raised on hate. She shudders as we pass.

"Oh, you have got to be kidding me." Cass stops and I jostle into her, then Sean bumps into me. I expect her to turn to the group of desperate housewives only she is staring straight ahead.

"What? What is it?" I ask, I can't see past the heaving room of people. And over the music, I can only just hear her as it is.

Cass sidesteps and I find myself confronted by Adam. My mouth sours and fear erupts through me as the colour drains from my face. I step back enough that I can feel Sean, I grip what I can of his shirt around my clutch and stare at the guy who I shared my life with, not six months ago.

"Lily," he stutters. He looks over me and I stare not seeing any reason why I would have liked this man. He hurt me, both physically and emotionally. He caused me the kind of pain no person should suffer.

Adam coughs out a soft, nervous laugh. "You look amazing." When he lifts his hand to touch my arm, I flinch and slap his hand away. My skin crawls, tightening at the thought of his skin on mine, His head tilts and I see the hard sheen that I always hated. "That wasn't necessary. I can't touch you now?"

"No, you can't," I say shakily. Bile rises and I blink back the memories. This man is vermin. I wake everyday with the shadow of his actions around me, a cloak of pain worn by me alone. A cloak I have been trying to hang up, so I can move forward. I have been so close, was. Yet he is here and it all rushes back.

When Sean steps up and lays a hand on my shoulder, I let out a shaky breath I hadn't known I was holding in. Adam backs up as much as he can, holding his hands up he laughs. "What's with the bodyguard? I only wanted to wish you happy birthday." I'm not surprised he remembers, but it concerns me that he knew to look here, I look around quickly, desperately trying to find a way out but the crowd is too thick. He on the other hand is thinner than I remember. Adam is a good-looking guy with dark hair and pale blue eyes. He has a baby face but his innocence is skin deep.

"Well, you just did," Cass spits, her whole body is rigid with anger. "Goodnight, Adam." He looks to Cass, who is staring at him with a death glare. When he looks back, he actually looks a little forlorn. "I miss you, Lils."

"No, you miss having someone to hit!" Cass snaps.

"What the fuck!" Sean barks, I get shunted forwards as he moves to grab Adam. My drink sloshes over and drenches my new shoes, before Sean reaches him Adam darts away and pushes through the crowd causing a drink to smash as he rushes out the bar. I stare on helplessly as a thousand glances twist our way, they don't pay much attention and I exhale the breath I never managed to let go off. What was he doing here; he knows he's not allowed near me?

I knock back my drink. "Happy fucking Birthday," I sigh.

"Shit, Lily, if I'd known, I would have flattened him." Sean gives me a hug. I squeeze him back glad he was here.

"Yeah, I know." He leans over the bar and orders me a refill.

"Sorry," Cass huffs, she pulls me to a hug. "I want to snap the little twerp's neck." She squeezes me hard, emphasising her hatred for him. I laugh against her hair. I don't want him to ruin my night.

"We can save the murder mysteries for your birthday." I'm handed a new drink before Sean escorts us over to a more open area, I do a quick glance of the bar checking Adam has gone and mentally sigh in relief when I can't see him.

"I'll try get you ladies a table, place is packed tonight, I may need to work the bar for a bit," Sean says apologetically.

"Sure." Cass smiles. "As long as our drinks keep coming, I won't complain." She nudges me, trying to keep my mind from wandering a dark path.

Sean grins down at her. "Spoken like a true alcoholic." He presses a kiss to her mouth and I can't help but think of Jace, sucking in a deep breath I twist away from their intimate moment and find a guy watching me with his friends. He's no Jace but he's a looker, tall, dark eyes and a confident smile. He lifts his beer to his mouth and smiles at me, before slipping off his chair and walking my way.

Whoa confident much!

Chapter Eleven

With the place so busy it takes him some maneuvering but he seems determined, despite my heels I have to look up when he gets to me. "Hey I'm Travis." Travis has malteser eyes and a real cute smile.

"Lily." I flit a look to Cass but she is too busy with Sean.

"Well Lily you caught my eye the moment you walked in." He has an easy confidence that I can appreciate, but I'm not in the mood after my exchange with Adam.

"Why? Were you that bored?" I joke, Travis laughs and I feel myself start to relax, I can do innocent banter but I find myself stumped into shock when Jace walks in with both Carl and Rupert on his heel. His eyes sweep the bar once, twice. Then land on me, they flare and his jaw works slowly as he looks over me, and the company I'm keeping.

Travis looks over his shoulder. "Not another ex?" He laughs. I blush knowing my altercation with Adam didn't go unnoticed.

I drop my gaze and smile at Travis. "No, I . . . it's complicated." My eyes fall back in Jace's direction and I watch as women all around seem to stand at attention, like a mob of meerkats. My stomach drops, this is what I would be up against, an endless swarm of women. I find myself transfixed as I see them all straighten themselves out, check the flock for competition. It's laughable— does he have any idea of the silent commotion he is causing?

"So, is he your boyfriend or not?" Travis pulls on his beer again and shifts, so I can no longer see Jace. Calculated but for the best.

"No." It's the truth even if my reaction has me over thinking my decision to walk away. I sigh inwardly.

"Good, let me buy you a drink." Travis's voice filters off and my ears ring, until all I can hear is the unsteady chorus of my heartbeat.

How I feel around Jace, is how I would suspect a heroin addict to feel if they were strapped to a chair and someone laid a needle at their feet. I know I will only feel better when I have him. But the comedown is crushing. Travis waves a hand in my face, I blink and look up to see an odd expression on his face. "Excuse me," I murmur pushing away, I need some air.

Travis takes my wrist in his I look back at his concerned face. "Lily, do you want a drink, are you okay?"

"Sure, yeah." I pull away and walk down the steps towards the toilets I push my way out the fire exit thankful that no alarm goes off and suck in a lungful of air. I half expect Jace to follow me, and if I'm honest with myself, I want him too. But after five minutes I'm still alone out back. The wall chafes my skin but I close my eyes and rest my head against the cold bricks, I remind myself that I wanted this. However I wasn't expecting to bump into Jace any time soon, until a few weeks ago our paths never crossed and yet here he is, in Finnegan's.

"Lily?" Cass's voice echoes off the inside walls. "Lil!" I twist and pull the heavy door open to see my friends worried expression, "You okay?" She pulls me inside and rubs her arms. "Shit it's cold, I didn't know he was going to be here." She looks back over her shoulder as though he is on her heels, but he's not. It bothers me more than I care to admit, why is he here?

"I know." I sigh, she gets it and I love her for that.

"Do you want to leave?" I nod and follow her back into the bar, my eyes move instinctively towards the high back chairs where I find an uneasy looking Carl and plenty of women vying for Jace's attention. More annoyingly, he is all too happy to accommodate them. If he's trying to make me jealous it's working, I tell myself *this* only solidifies my reasons of why not to get involved with him— he's a serial flirt and a player. His eyes lift to mine and stop me in my tracks.

In that moment, it's only us— and all our pent-up tension. No matter how bad I think this man is for me, I want him desperately.

Cass pulls my arm and I follow, I'm ready to hit another bar but Travis walks our way. "Hey, I was worried you'd been sucked down the loo," he laughs. I muster a smile, as he holds out my drink in his hand. "Your friend, the guy at the bar, said you drink gin." He elaborates, he needn't have bothered I don't care where the alcohol comes from, as long as it keeps coming.

I nod in understanding and take the drink. "Thanks,"

He hands one to Cass too. "One drink and we leave," she says into my ear. I smile in agreement. Maybe we should start drinking elsewhere.

Cass edges us towards Travis's table where we are introduced to all his friends, names I barely recall. "Hi," I murmur lost in confusion as Cass says something sassy and makes them all laugh.

One guy leans over the table. "So, what brings you two out tonight?" *Coldplay* are setting the room into a frenzy of swaying bodies, any other night I would be on the dance floor but I feel useless, even to myself right now.

"It's Lily's birthday!" Cass calls back. I'm barely listening, my eyes keep finding their way back to Jace and this time I see a woman has perched herself on the arm of his chair, he is leaning in to her with his hand rested on her knee. I look away but find myself locked in Carl's gaze my mouth and stomach sour with jealousy, I barely lift my hand when I wave at him but he stands anyway.

Slowly, he makes his way over, looking every inch the elegant statue of colour. "Happy birthday," he kisses my cheek and rubs my arm.

I force a bright smile on my miserable face. "Thank you." How lovely.

"I have something for you." He lifts his brow and dips into his suit pocket.

"You do?" I frown. This night is full of surprises.

Carl hands me my lipstick and I laugh, "oh my god, my bag, you had it." I hold it up to Cass. "This is the lipstick I lost."

Her eyes flash with interest. "That would definitely look better on me." I roll my eyes and grin at Carl.

"Thank you."

"Well put it on." Carl smirks, he leans in and whispers in my ear. "You look sensational, my boss is having a fit over there." My eyes defy me, it's the worst form of torture, Jace reclined in a big chair, eyes wide with mischief, lips loose and head thrown back on a laugh.

"He looks pretty comfortable to me," I remark softly, even though it isn't warranted, I know that but I can't bear the thought of him with another woman.

"You think we're here for the atmosphere." Carl sniffs. "She's wasting her time, he's here for you." My heart soars but my gut drops.

I'm such a mess!

After our last conversation, I don't feel I can make the first move. I know I want him but I'm too afraid to get hurt, seeing Adam again was a stark reminder of why I am keeping my guard up. And Jace is the biggest temptation god could gift a woman.

Carl holds my clutch whilst I apply my lipstick I give my lips a smack and throw him a pout.

"Beautiful." It's Travis who says that, I blush as Carl gives me a wink and leaves me to it. "Have a great night Lily."

"And you, thanks Carl."

I track his movements and see Rupert fully when he stands to let his husband past, he is stockier then Carl and dressed in a three-piece suit and smarting a pretty impressive beard. It's not long, just well-trimmed and immaculate, like Carl is.

I'm halfway through my drink when one of Travis's friends brings shots to the table. Cass groans but I welcome the numbness alcohol offers. I drink mine before anyone else has lifted there's up and cough at the burn. "Shit!"

Travis pats my back. "Jeez girl." I down the remainder of my own glass to extinguish the burn. My stomach churns but I let it pass. I'm seeking absolution. I want to forget Jace, I drop my head to hide the look of distaste on my face from the shot and twist back to Travis who is smiling down at me, I return it, maybe I should go home with him. Take the high road like Jace, flirt with the first available person I see and fuck him out my mind. Forget him.

I have to because I know I can't handle someone like Jace.

He is watching, I can feel it and I can't hold back from the compulsion that notion has over me, our eyes meet and although some blonde number is drawling in his lap Jace rises, his destination obvious. Nothing else registers in my peripheral but the lean god zigzagging his way through the crowd.

He surprises me by standing on the opposite side of the table, capturing not only my attention, having him stood alongside the group of guys I can't help but compare how they lack so much in comparison. "Hello Lily." Arms resting on the heavy wood he smiles to Cass and turns amber eyes back on me.

"Hello." He looks good, so good, and given there are a heck of a lot of men around, all I can smell is his unique aftershave. I have no idea what it is, but odour de Jace has my womb drooling. I hate the silence that has dispersed over our table.

"How are you?" I ask tucking my hair behind my ear, I feel so awkward and self-conscious.

Jace clears his throat and frowns, I don't know why I asked how he is because he looks great and he seems happy enough, I appear to be the only one suffering and all at my own hands.

"I'm good, you look stunning, Happy Birthday." I can see down his shirt and my eyes feast on the smooth tan flesh I know is beneath, this table feels like a field of barbed wire, I want to go to him.

"Thanks." I flush, one of Travis's friends Henry cuts in. "Are we all ready to make tracks?" I know that was the plan, I should leave but I don't think I can walk away right now, not when Jace is mere feet away.

Travis nudges me getting my attention briefly. "Shall we go?"

"If that's what everyone wants to do," I answer absently, I look back and Jace has gone. I feel sick.

I have felt sick since he walked out my flat.

Gone is the pushy man who defies boundaries to get my attention. Jace is being painfully polite and I can't take it. I want the unconventional man back that was in my face constantly.

"Let's go!" Cass sings over the top, I know she's trying to keep me upbeat but I feel shit considering it's my birthday.

Emotion drowns me and I fear I may cry. "I'm going to nip to the ladies." I leave them to gather all their belongings together and despite my pathetic attempts to look for him I can't see Jace amongst the sea of people.

The girls' rest room is busy as usual but the queue is short so I manage to get in a cubicle quick, I lean against the cold partitioning wall and close my eyes, nothing about this evening has gone to plan. I phase out the chitchat of eager females, trying to snap out of the dark mood I'm now in. I admit defeat after a few minutes and exit the stall. I go to a free sink at the far end and wash my hands before I begin re-applying my lipstick. There is a small ruckus followed by a catcall of whistles, I roll my eyes but my inner nosy bitch pulls my head their way, Jace strides straight for me, eyes dark and full of intent.

I freeze, lipstick poised at my mouth as Jace, in all his dark hair and amber glory stalks towards me. He grabs my head in his hands and kisses me passionately. I'm wedged up against the wall Jace's hands drive into my hair as his hard body presses intimately into my own. He pulls back enough to break the connection. "Who is he?" he demands softly, I'm gripping the sink for support. Those damn eyes frantically searching mine for an answer.

My other hand is fisted in his top and the crazy rhythm of his heart mirrors my own, as it dances against my knuckles, my mouth dries and everything in me, drops to its knees.

He? It takes my alcohol-fogged brain a second to realise he means Travis. "No one." My frown is deep.

"You're mine Lily, I'm not the only one feeling this." Jace presses his forehead to mine. He sighs heavily and grips my face harshly. "This is what you want." He pleads with me to agree.

"Jace," I whisper, pleading too, that he will understand this is not about wanting him, that's a given, it's the intensity. He exhales and cups my face pulling it up to his. "This scares me." I admit, amber eyes burn up my heart as his lips move over mine. I give in and kiss him back slowly.

I have always maintained a level of control in my relationships, needed it because if life has taught me anything, it's that nothing lasts forever and words don't mean shit, not unless you can back them up. Adam was the biggest mistake of them all. He played me enough that I lowered my guard, thinking he was a nice guy only to find he was the worst out of a bad bunch.

Someone clears their throat and I blink to find Cass giving us a smug look. "You two want to join the party or you going to take my friend up against the wall in front of this lot?" She thrusts her thumb in the direction of appreciative women.

Jace grins at me and tilts his head considering it? The pervert!

"No!" I laugh, "Let me sort my lippy out."

Jace pulls my face to his. "You're perfect without it, plus I don't want to wear it every time I kiss you." he plucks it from my hand and slips it in his pocket. Bloody hell I only just got that back!

He looks over his reflection me bracketed by his arm, pushed up against the wall and uses his thumb to wipe the offending red from his mouth, his eyes dance in the reflection, before he gives me a wink. I'm breathing slowly as I try to regain some semblance of control.

Jace pushes himself up straight and grabs my hips twisting me away from the mirror and escorts me through his audience. "Ladies," he murmurs, receiving an entourage of wolf whistles and gob smacked faces.

Maybe this birthday isn't so bad after all?

We leave Finnegan's and head to a cocktail bar. Jace has his hand firmly in mine as we walk up the street. Henry and Travis disappear in the opposite direction with the rest of their friends. I waste no time feeling guilty. I don't get the chance, as I'm twisted into Jace's walking body so he can kiss me. "Every time we are apart you second guess this." He takes a handful of my arse and rolls his hips into mine. My eyes pop and I gasp into his mouth.

Oh.

"Because I'm not ready for a relationship," I admit breathlessly against the surge of heat rushing to my womb, she knows who is here.

His hips roll again and I gasp at the friction, how does he do that, make me weak with one touch? He groans holding me close, I absorb his heat, it's damn cold out but mostly I latch on, because to deny myself this feeling is absurd. I lean in running my hands up to hook around his neck, this close I can smell that earthy tone, heavily laced with way too much sex appeal.

When his tongue strokes mine I sigh, He is intoxicating and for that I'm afraid. I run my hands up to thread in his hair and Jace pulls back dropping his gaze, he brushes his lips over my cheek. "I've been in hell." Wrapping his hands around my face he scrunches his nose up on a groan. "God you're beautiful Lily." His hot palm moves so it is flat on the bare expanse of my back. "You feel so delicate, this dress is killing me Lily." It's killing me too I swear I'm going to get pneumonia, worst choice of dress to date!

"Come on!" Cass whines from the doorway, Sean is chatting

away to Rupert and Carl, my friend waves at the warmth of the bar. "Oh, look heat!" She remarks sarcastically, I roll my eyes.

"Your friend is annoyingly bossy." I laugh against the swell of his chest oh he has no idea. "Come on, you're shivering."

Rupert seems a bit stand-offish, I get the feeling he isn't a fan of Cass and he probably enjoys a smaller group but with us, he's been handed the sour deal. There is nothing quiet about Cass, especially since she's had a drink.

The bar is heaving and *Sean Paul* is breaking the room out into whoops of joy as people begin to dance. Cass orders us two pink cocktails, and everyone else waits for their drinks before we all find an empty table near the dance floor. Cass grabs my hand and pulls me from Jace's knee. "Sorry but this is my dancing partner." I'm hauled into the fray and swung out by a wild Cass. "Happy birthday!" She laughs, her arms are up above her and she is giving Sean 'come to bed' eyes.

"You slut," I joke, I love the girl but she is a crazy mess, she looks to Sean and beckons him over with a crook of her finger, Sean dives in for the challenge and rocks his way over, Cass wiggles her arse and I turn my back on them and dance by myself smirking when I hear her laugh happily. Some dance partner!

I'm not the only scantily dressed woman in here, so I don't feel too bad, although the dress has a habit of riding up. I'm tugging it down for the third time when thick arms circle my waist and Jace's mouth drops to my shoulder. "Lily, come home with me?" The distinctive outline of his arousal slots between the slope of my arse and he hisses. "All I can see is skin and those fucking dark grey eyes luring me to my death." Jace's agonised groan makes me laugh throatily. He chuckles deeply, as I drop my head back, turning so our mouths are close. The shots mixed with fresh air have sent me into a drunken stupor— my head is swimming.

"You scare me." I admit, His thumb brushes my mouth before my cheek is cupped, Jace sweeps his tongue out to meet mine, I'm held against his hard chest by a possessive hand on my lower stomach as he kisses me passionately. My heart is slamming away behind my breasts— will it always be like this with him, Uncontrollable lust?

I'm drunk on Jace and just drunk. I grin happily at him.

"You're coming home with me," he says firmly, eyes challenging me to argue, I know he hasn't had many relationships, knowing I may be the first woman who has ever truly caught his attention, gives me a naïve idealism that maybe this is meant to be, I want to hold onto that with every molecule of hope I can muster. Only deep down I know it's a futile attempt to romanticise this.

"I'm here aren't I?" He eyes me, not at all happy with how I've chosen to answer, on a huff he pecks my nose then spins me out on a squeal of shock, I'm laughing when he hauls me back and begins to dance with me. I'm not surprised the guy can dance— no man can move that well in the bedroom and not draw attention on the dance floor. He bites his lower lip and rolls our hips together, I get a direct slash of heat to my sex and begin to breathe heavily. Jace grips my slender neck in his hand and slants his mouth over mine.

Chapter Twelve

My moan is met by a harsh curse from Jace. I can't hold back the wide grin spreading over my face. "You're the most handsome man." I sigh cupping his jaw, like he has done me so many times, the rough chafe of hair prickles my skin and I shiver.

His mouth stretches into a slow wide smile. "Come with me." Holding my hand, Jace pulls me through the thick crowd, I grip tightly to his hand and bite my lip as I watch the confident, even strides he takes.

We pass down an occupied corridor my heels clacking an echo and push our way through a queue for the toilets. "What are you doing?" I ask but his grip tightens and I'm pulled further down. "Where are we going?" I'm breathless, curious and so damn aroused, the crowd thins and he turns a corner.

What's gotten into him?

We come to a disabled toilet with 'Out Of Order' on the door, Jace stops and tries the handle, it opens and I'm silently tugged in, the emergency light is the only visibility available and I'm thankful that it looks clean. I go in willingly noticing the seat of the toilet is off, which would explain why it is out of order. Dropping my wrist, he locks the door and stalks towards me. "Take off your knickers," his voice is strained, but I watch in both shock and excitement as he starts unbuttoning his fly.

Here?

Jace halts what he is doing, his wide chest is fluctuating unevenly and I can't hide what that does to me, his desire for me is tangible. He stares at me in the dim light. "Lily?" my eyes lift to meet his properly. I can hear the unsteady drum of my heart over the droning base. "Slip. Your. Knickers. Off." I stare, my heart skipping a beat as it hurtles forwards— I have never done anything like this before. "Now." He instructs softly, I nod trying to play catch up. I can do this.

Leaning on the wall for support I tug my knickers down and look up to find Jace with his cock out, he's rock hard and huge. I melt on a soft gasp. My eyes snap to his and back down as he works himself over.

"You like that?" He wants to know through lowered lashes, I nod and he shudders making me whimper, I'm desperate to have him in me. Taking my knickers, he shoves them in his pocket and slams his mouth to mine. "God, I need to fuck you," he gasps between rough kisses. My face twists in wracking lust.

"This is crazy," I gasp, some women need romance, I am one of those women but right now, holed up in this toilet with Jace panting over me, being fucked sounds perfect.

His lips brush mine harshly, before he grips my hair and cranes my neck to nip at my throat, picking me up he walks us to the wall, positions himself and surges upwards.

Holy Shit!

My eyes roll back as he enters in one velvet-like thrust, "Shit!" I squeak at the rough intrusion, as my fingernails dig into his jacket.

My dress is a roll of crinkled material around my neck as he gathers it and pushes it past my breasts. "You're so sexy," he breathes against my lips. I feel sexy— it makes me confident and allows me to enjoy this for what it is.

In the subdued light I see a flash of amber, I'm practically naked with my legs wrapped around his firm back as he stands fully clothed and takes me roughly up the wall. "God woman," he moans pounding away. I clutch tightly reveling in the feel of him, in this bulk of a man, thrusting his way between my thighs. Each pound delivered sends pleasure to ripple through my body, I scream softly as the feeling devours me utterly.

He withdraws, clenches his jaw and surges forwards. "Fuck you feel amazing." I moan my agreement, this does feel amazing, the lick of heat gathers in the base of my spine and twists its way up my neck, my womb surges alongside, chasing the feeling.

"Harder," I sob into his mouth, my greedy hips crashing down to join his harsh thrust. Jace kisses me on a growl, his eyes lock with mine, as he hauls me back down to create a more powerful impact, he watches in fascination as my mouth drops open on a silent cry, shuddering above him. He is shaking as his hips slam up drawing soft low gasps from me.

This connection we have, is real, so addictive. His hands are locked on my arse as he hammers away, until I'm a frenzied mess. Jace smirks subtly at my cries of pleasure. He halts, before alternating between slow deep drives and harsh slams into the most secret part of me.

"Oh god, now Jace, please!" I scream and double in on myself as sensation takes over. The raw sound of flesh on flesh echoes as he pounds on. Sweat taints his forehead, my cheek sticks to his, and I sob at the oncoming release ravaging my soul. "Don't stop, oh god." The ball of liquid heat that gathers in my womb, explodes and I cry out, sobbing as my orgasm begins to feel like a painful intrusion on my sanity!

"Again," he grunts.

What? No, I can't! My eyes widen, silently I try to convey my dismay, hard amber resolve has my thoughts retreating, Jace tightens his hold, it's both an encouragement and reassurance, his breath is exiting his plush lips is short sharp pants. "Again," he murmurs more to himself than me, but I hear him loud and clear.

Hips trapped between thick thighs and his hand cupping my arse Jace leans back and takes my jaw in his other hand his eyes drop to where we meet. "Fuuuuck." He slows as his eyes feast on the sight of us, when his eyes lift he looks feral. It's the biggest stimulant I have ever experienced.

My scalp feels infused with electricity and my whole body is dancing on the peripheral of satisfaction. "Jace, harder!" I want more, need more. I push against the restraint of his hand and slam my hips down to meet his,

"Lily!" he belts out, with his eyes blazing he smashes his mouth to mine, hostile hands grip me and hold my hips in place,

"Hard!" I scream. I can no longer feel my heart, it's slamming so wildly its affects have numbed me.

"Fuuuck!" His eyes are wild and so beautiful. His teeth graze my lip as he drives up with a force neither of us expects, and I splinter into another climax. Jace joins me growling low in his throat, he swivels his hips and hisses as he throbs deep inside, I clutch onto him, my body lax and too exhausted to deal with my unruly breathing.

Jace's weight cages me to the wall and his face hits my neck in a deep sigh, we stay like that for a while, still joined panting quietly. Slowly he pulls back and smiles at me, "I kind of like dirty bathroom sex with you." I sigh sheepishly, he looks around the toilet, displeasure pouring onto his face.

"You deserve better than being fucked in a public toilet." His lip curls in distaste,

"I like any sex I can get with you." My drunk admission makes him chuckle. "Well Lily if you didn't keep slipping through my fingers, I wouldn't feel like I had to take you in fear that it'll be the last time" he is smirking but it soon twists into something more deep.

I look away because I don't know how to answer, I keep telling him I'm not ready, yet here I am, legs wrapped around his waist, weakened by the lure of hot sex.

I'm in too deep already. I've been running for nothing, we are inevitable. No, the sex is inevitable. I correct myself because at this point, that's all I can offer.

"Let me clean you up." I feel the ache of loss when he slips out and wait for him to get something to clean between my thighs. He is knelt at my feet as he dabs me clean, my hand drops to his hair, I twiddle it through my fingers and Jace looks up at me.

It's such a pivotal moment for me, because I know I'm falling hard and fast for this man. I let my head loll backwards and close my eyes as Jace presses kisses to my navel and adjusts my dress to conceal my body. I'm not ready to fall in love.

"Come on beautiful." I wash my hands and Jace splashes his face before handing my knickers over for me to put back on. Snagging my dress, he tugs me forward and kisses me slowly, his body swaying to the seductive base carrying from the dance floor. "You're mine." He pecks my nose. "Happy birthday Lily." I fall completely. Only, my mind is already planning a strategic evacuation plan.

There is no denying where we have been, Cass is looking at me with her tongue in her cheek, her eyes are glassy and Sean is holding her up. "I'm taking Cass home, Carl and Rupert left, you guys want to share a taxi?"

"Yes please." I go to Cass and grin at her. "Wow lady you're pretty drunk there?"

"Well figured I needed to up my game after how pissed you were last time we were out," she sniggers, her voice slurring heavily.

Sean hitches her up. "Come on Cass." God we're both a mess when we're drunk, I feel bad for these guys, I laugh as we follow them out, Jace has my clutch in his hand and as soon as we hit the fresh air

Cass is vomiting, Sean is holding her up whilst Jace tries to flag down a cab, but with Cass in such a mess they refuse to take us.

Sean throws his hands up in frustration. "I hate this." He looks to me. "You girls have no idea how dangerous shit like this is." My friends slim body wretches and she is throwing up once again. I'm freezing and rub my arms as I try to comfort Cass.

"You're right, sorry, she needs some water." I pull her hair back and look to Sean, who is trying not to get angry at my friend's behaviour.

Jace is up the road on his phone. I don't know who he is talking to, but as soon as he hangs up, he walks back to us. "I've sorted us a lift."

I frown. How? I'm curious because apart from Carl and Rupert, Jace's life is a mystery to me. I don't question him, but remain wrapped in Jace's thick arms as Sean comforts my pale friend.

It's fifteen minutes before a blacked-out Range Rover pulls up. I expect some heavily tattooed mafia type to step out, but the petite blonde with bright blue eyes and an easy smile for Jace makes my back stiffen. Even Cass in her delicate state raises a brow at me. Who the fuck is that?

Jace steps around me and goes to her. I watch with discomfort as she flings her arms around his neck and kisses his cheek. "You owe me, Jace," she points out, prodding his chest with pink nails. She is stunning and super curvy. My inner self instantly hates her.

Dressed in skintight black jeans, a crop top that reveals her concave stomach, and hair that touches her arse, she looks exactly like the kind of woman I would expect Jace to go for. I begin to obsess about their history. Who is she?

"Thanks, Neve," he says before turning back to us. I shift uncomfortably and turn my gaze to Cass, who is two shades paler and cuddling into Sean. "I feel like I'm dying," she exaggerates.

"I put a bucket and wipes in the back," Neve says. I appreciate her forward thinking. She opens up the boot and grabs it all whilst Jace opens the back door for Sean to help Cass in.

"Sorry, guys." My friend's croaky voice is pathetic, and I laugh, telling her it's fine.

"Let's get you home, yeah?" I sound no better. My voice is husky and I know I'm bordering on slurring.

Neve is at the other side of the car and gives the bucket, wipes, and some water to Sean. "Thanks for this," he says.

"No worries." She smiles and her eyes lift to meet mine, mirroring my own questions. Jace turns back to me. "You okay? Not feeling sick?" His big hands cup my face. I shake my head as Neve hops in the driver's seat. With a quick peck on my lips, he helps me get in beside Sean, before buckling me in. "I can do my own seatbelt," I laugh.

"I know." He winks. I'm shut in and Jace takes up the seat in the front.

Neve puts the radio on and she and Jace chat quietly. With Cass slurring in the back, I can barely hear what they are saying. I want to tell her to shut up but know I will look like a desperate twit, so I opt to stare out the window instead, my mind racing with a million questions about little miss Barbie.

Sean and Cass are dropped off first and rather than take us back to mine, we head towards Jace's. I don't argue. I know deep down that geographically this evening would have ended differently had his friend not showed up. I wanted to go home. I'm pretty drunk and feeling the pinch of her presence, so I close my eyes and before I know it, Jace is coaxing me awake. The bitter air swirls in the car as he unclips my belt. "Lily, wrap your arms around me." The softness of his voice is at odds with his demanding personality. I smile to myself.

"Something funny, huh?" He's smiling too. Sliding my arms around his neck, I happily let him pull me from the car but wriggle until my feet hit the floor, resolute in my decision to keep this about sex. "Where did the bossy you go?" I challenge flirtatiously.

Neve is looking over her shoulder at us and I eye her curiously.

"Make sure you haven't left anything," she mutters. I scan the back seat, shrug, and thank her for the lift. "It's no problem. I'll see you Monday, Jace," she says casually.

I stagger off and squint my way to the front door. Jace is chuckling at me from behind as Neve drives off. "You naturally head to your left when you're drunk," he comments. I'm grinning when I get to the glass door and two arms cage me in, and my smile turns to a laugh as Jace begins kissing my neck. "In the summer, I'm going to make memories against this door with you."

"You sound so sure of yourself," I whisper, as both his hands wind around to cup my rib cage.

"With you, I'm the surest I'll ever be." The door clicks open and I step through, as Jace pushes the wide glass panel open. In my vulnerable state, it does nothing for my equilibrium. I stagger, but my wrist is caught up by his strong grip.

"Why do you say things like that?" I sigh. It needs to just be about sex.

The open-back beehive cabinets light up with a dozen or so spotlights as Jace fiddles with the remote. "Lily, I have accepted that no amount of time, will change the fact that you will always fight me on everything,"

"Again, you're so sure of this," I hum as I spin around on my drunken feet and drop down onto the squishy couch. "Heaven," I murmur. Jace shakes his head lightly and walks over with a grin on his face, his hand wraps around my slender ankle.

"You're here, aren't you?"

"I'm drunk." My eyes roll back and close, as the alcohol pulls me into semi unconsciousness. He is right I do fight him on everything.

"You wound me." I can hear the pout in his voice, I smile as his legs bracket mine and his weight holds me to the sofa. "Let's get you to bed, birthday girl." Soft lips brush over my chin and gently press to my lips. "Lily, give this a chance." His whisper is a calculated plea, and with a soft groan, his hips roll into mine and I can't fight the swell of heat in my groin.

"I don't want a relationship," I say, but the words sound alien to my own ears. It's bullshit. I want this man more than I have anyone else. I want him desperately, it has been my every waking thought since that first moment. It scares me so much, that I have been in fight or flight mode since we met.

My eyes feel so heavy but I drag them open to find those deep sap eyes, burning down into mine. My breath traps in my throat and I stare endlessly as my body adjusts to its new symbiotic state.

I merge when Jace is around.

"I won't share you." His lips dot over my cheek and down towards my ear as soft fingertips draw my dress up my thighs. "Seeing that guy drawling over you earlier, sent me crazy mad." I recall the feeling myself.

"Jace, you're being ridiculous." Hypnotic circles are being drawn over my hips, as I watch his somber look. "I'm not ready for this kind of relationship. This is too much, too fast."

"Why do I get the feeling that only applies to me?" He's right. I flush red and turn my head because I don't want to face this right now, I'm too drunk. Taking my wrists, he pushes them above my head. He sighs heavily and wriggles his wider body between my thighs. Happy with his positioning, he gently pumps his hips. It feels divine, but I try my damnedest to ignore the lick of fire in my groin.

"I think if some staid, corduroy, 'Y' front wearing pissant asked you to be his, you'd skip along." Despite the cocky grin, there is a note of seriousness in his voice. I burst out laughing and he chuckles, his eyes lit up like a brass object under intense light. "You're so fucking beautiful," he groans.

"Jace, I like you, but I think maybe we're better as friends," I slur falsely, laughing when he pulls back with a look of disgust on his face.

"No, Lily, you don't. You need to just let this be, you infuriating fucking woman," he growls against my lips, his hips swiveling once more. "You'll say yes to me."

"What does that even mean?" I roll my eyes and enjoy the gentle stroke of his hands over my legs. "I'm sleepy," I confess on a yawn. "Take me to bed."

"Make your mind up, woman. First, you want to be friends, then it's take me to bed. You're going to drive me nuts, Lily." He is grinning at the prospect, I smirk and lift my arms so I can wrap them around his neck.

"Better that you get out whilst you can then," I whisper.

"Maybe I should. I noticed a few grey hairs since I met you." He's perfectly flawed, in his inability to give me space. It's a heady feeling when someone pursues you so thoroughly. I know he won't walk away from me or let me him, I love that he is so determined to be with me. I refuse to admit it to him or myself. I'm still raw after Adam. I need more time to adjust.

He lifts me with ease and walks us though to his bedroom, perching me on the edge he takes my dress at the hem and drags it up my body so I'm sat in my underwear and heels. "Some wrinkles too," he sighs dramatically. "All this hassle for a woman who doesn't want me." Grabbing my heels, he pulls my legs up so I tip back on a short laugh. "I'm going to fuck you in these one day." I want that now, and I purposely wriggle so my thighs part.

"Not one day. Now." I drop my arms back over my head as my eyes roll shut and Jace laughs. God, I love that laugh, his smile, and those damn eyes own me. "See I do want you, I want you to make me come." I try to purr but it comes out on a thick slur. His laugh is deep and rough.

"Lily, you're wasted. As cute as it is, I don't want to get my leg over and you start snoring mid sex." I'm grinning, my eyes still closed, and sigh when he slips my heels off. I'm undressed fully by careful hands, then maneuvered under the quilt. "I need a quick shower. I have a surprise for you tomorrow," he hums and leaves after pressing his soft lips to mine. "Night, beautiful." I hum through my sleep-fogged brain.

"Tell me you're mine," he growls in my ear.

"You're mine," I chuckle. On a tut, he pulls my chin up and I only just manage to peel my eyes open. "Say it." His eyes are twinkly, but I can barely keep my own open. I yawn again and allow the alcohol to slip me into a semi slumber.

"I'm . . . you and me, hurtling," I whisper sleepily.

Chapter Thirteen

When I wake, everything rushes forward— the soft light huffs of breath beside me, the heavy smell of aftershave and sex. It's raining and the constant, unsynchronised tap on the glass draws my head that way. I close my eyes, drenched in self-hate. I don't know why I'm doing this to myself, or him. Is he really wanting more? Because I don't think I have more to give and sex is a poor excuse to meddle with someone's feelings, let alone my own.

I watch the even rise and fall of his chest, taking in his beautiful physique as I slowly edge my way out of his bed. I hold my breath, hoping not to trigger any movement from him. It doesn't— he lays flat on his back, a hand thrown over his perfect eyes, sleeping soundly. I need a wee, but I ignore the feeling and drag last night's clothes back on, bar my coat, which I can't find. Heels in my hand, I pass a stray t-shirt and slip that over my head. It takes me a while to work out how to unlock the door and when I do, I sigh in relief, knowing I'm moments away from being on my way out of here. I push against one end of the heavy door steeling another breath, when the suction sounds louder than an alarm in this silence. I check over my shoulder as I ease it shut, slide my feet back in my heels and begin to hobble my way over the gravel drive slipping my phone free as I go, I book an Uber and keep walking away from Jace's house.

By the time the Uber picks me up from the main road leading off the driveway, I'm soaked through and have ignored the two phone calls from Jace. I rush inside the warmth of the car and smile awkwardly at the old chap sat up front. "I'll pop the heating on," he says by way of hello.

"Thanks," I laugh, fingering the wet strands of hair stuck to my face as we head back down the road, towards the city. I look a mess and there is no mistaking I am doing the walk of shame.

"Bit far out, aren't you?" He says, adjusting the front console so that the draft of warm air powers through to the back.

"Crazy night." I shiver, I experience a wave of worry as I think of Cass, so I fire her a quick message. A voicemail flashes on my screen followed by a text alert, announcing I have a voicemail. "I know," I mutter, locking my phone and throwing it back inside my clutch. Closing my eyes, I rest my head against the seat and settle in for the journey. Sleep is taunting me, but I keep staring out the window to pass the time.

"Would you like some music on?"

I peel my eyes away from the passing fields and wild thoughts, and I register the plaque with his name on. "Yes, please, Malcolm." He smiles over his shoulder and with a nod, begins flicking through the radio stations, settling on something I have never heard before.

One song turns in to another and each passing moment has me battling the urge to check my phone, after it buzzes for a third time. I'm so lost in thought that I cry out as Malcolm swerves the car to the left when a black car flashes past. "Bloody idiot!" He hollers, his voice cracking with emotion.

"Oh my god, are you okay?" I'm clutching my chest, but the other hand is resting on his shoulder. My eyes latch on to the car powering away, overtaking yet another car ahead of us, and I recognise it instantly.

Jace.

I sit straighter as my heart leaps up my throat then hits my gut like a lead weight. Fuck!

"Are you okay?" I ask Malcolm again when he doesn't answer, squeezing his shoulder to gain an answer.

"Yes, yes, gave me a fright, that's all. Are you okay?" I drop my hand and sit back. I nod but say nothing. I'm trying to think of somewhere to go, but I have to go home. I want a shower. I need to change.

I need to face Jace fucking Bennett!

I close my eyes on an inaudible groan of frustration. I did get myself into this mess. I just don't know how to get out of it, how to get him to go away.

I debate on whether to call Cass, but she is all engines a go where Jace is concerned. Besides her, I have no one to call. I don't discuss my personal life with Harriet and have no desire to. Carl floats to mind, but I know from past experience, he is sure to drop me in it. Shit, shit, shit!

It's another ten minutes before we arrive outside my flat and Jace is there, arms crossed, arse flattened to the door of his car in the rain. He watches in amusement as Malcolm sidles up against the curb and lets the car idle as I unclip my belt. At first, he is oblivious, but then he clocks the sleek car pulled up across from us. He frowns and then it dawns on him. His eyes flash to mine in the rearview mirror and I wince. "Yeah, sorry." He grumbles, "You be safe, Miss." I nod and push open the door.

"I will, thanks." I have no doubt I'm physically safe with Jace, but emotionally I haven't a hope in hell at surviving him.

I straighten up and try to keep my head high but Jace is pushing his way off the car as I step past his bonnet intent only on getting to the main door and out of the rain.

"Hey!" He calls as if he is privy to some information I'm not. My shoulders tense, but I keep going, very much aware he is on my heel. "You look painstakingly familiar to the woman I had wrapped around me in bed last night." He says it loud enough for the couple crossing the path to stop and turn. I spin round, fury slapped across my face.

"Shut up!" I hiss, eyes flashing to see who else might be about. Jace reaches for me and I slap his hand away. "Fuck you, Bennett."

"You have and, as I recall, you seemed to enjoy every fucking second." He lowers so he is in my face, hands gripping my upper arms, slowing me down to a halt. "You can't even look me in the face," he huffs out a disbelieving laugh. "You want me. Admit it. What the hell are you running from?" He's super pissed, his face is tight around his eyes, and he keeps working his lip to no doubt stop him from saying some things he knows he may regret.

"No, we had fun, now I've had enough. Take a hint!" I spit,

"This whole act is boring the fuck out of me, Lily," he laughs lightly, completely unfazed by my anger. He drops my arms and I take the opportunity to keep walking to my door.

"Not an act," I state.

"So, I'm not the most handsome man then?" He goads. Clenching my fists, I try not to reply. My steps are even and determined, and when I reach my door and key my way in, Jace pushes his way in and I sigh, lost at what to do. "And I don't scare you?" He drops my admission insensitively between us. I growl and stomp towards my door, ignoring his chuckle. It's all geared to provoke me and I refuse to play his game.

I stop at my door and turn suddenly. He's surprised by my action and I can't help but take a small note of satisfaction from it.

"You know what? Yes, Jace, I do think you're incredibly handsome and, yes, you do scare me." I give a disbelieving laugh. "You got me, caught red-handed." I hold my hands up and see his face twist into a frown. "You're great in bed, is that what you want to hear?" I rub a hand over my face. "I honestly don't know what to say to you." I stare at his shoes and frown myself.

"You can stop lying to yourself for a start." His jibe is met with anger of my own.

"Maybe you should." I raise my gaze and lock it with his. There is no denying how angry he is— his neck is taut with tension and his eyes have darkened to molasses. "I told you, you're rushing me, that I'm not ready. Maybe back the fuck off and give me some time," I seethe.

"Time to what, think about how much sex we could be having?"

I swear in frustration. "I'm struggling to keep up here. All you talk about is sex, yet here you are, chasing me nearly off the road and pissing me off in a desperate bid for what, sex?"

He snaps back, "Off the road? What the fuck are you talking about?"

"The car you overtook, that swerved out your way, I was in it!" I shout, my face red and my hands shaking.

Two doors down, the door creaks open and I shove my key in and push my way into my flat. I drop my belongings on the floor, drag his t-shirt over my head, and sling it at his face. The second the material leaves my fingers, I swing the door shut and spin around, tears rushing forward.

The crash of the door hitting the inner wall makes me jump and I turn to find Jace striding in after me. He quietly closes the door and locks it.

"Please go." I drop to the couch and close my eyes, hiding my face in my hands, my elbows perched on my knees. My body jerks with pent-up emotion, dispersing into floods of tears. The sofa shifts and I brace myself for the impact of his touch. It's singular and has my breath shuddering.

"Why are you crying?" Thick fingers massage the back of my neck as I shake my head, too emotional to answer.

"Lily, I'm sorry about the car." His breath fans over my shoulder and I beg for something to make this stop. This feeling. The need. It's like an itch all over my skin, crawling through my scalp and dragging along my throat. It's as distracting as nausea but painfully addictive. I swallow harshly, trying to dislodge the achy pain.

"I want you to go, Jace," I whisper plea.

His voice is soft, patient. A gentle hand wraps protectively around my back. "Fuck, Lily, we both know you don't want that." Lips press to my hair and I shrug, trying to knock him off, but he is persistent. "I'm not leaving you like this."

"I'm not having sex with you," I huff, already feeling the burn of desire dancing its way along my body.

His chuckle doesn't piss me off as much as it should. He scoops me up and walks me through to the bathroom. There is no grand bathtub or walk-in shower. I'm seated on the toilet, where I choose to keep my face hidden.

"I'm not sure if you're hiding because you can't face me, or if it's because your makeup would scare a small child." I smirk, knowing my makeup is probably smudged and clotted in my lashes.

I don't reply, knowing his first assumption is far too close to the truth, to warrant a pointless excuse. He turns the tap on, testing it with his hand before he soaks a flannel and squats at my feet. I stare at the only thing in my eye line— his crotch.

My chin is cupped and lifted. I don't look at him but focus on something past his shoulder, a candleholder. With methodical, gentle stokes, he wipes my face clean.

"Thanks." I sniff. He is staring at me, but I studiously keep my eyes averted. He sighs and I inwardly frown. Why is he here? I'm a mess, an all-around emotional twat. Apart from the sex I'm every man's worst nightmare.

Tucking my hair behind my ear, he stands. "Have a shower, and I'll make you some breakfast." His attentive attitude has me flushing with guilt. I'm left alone with my faltering thoughts.

Why is he doing this?

I'm mechanical in my actions, subconsciously following orders as I flip on the water and strip down whilst it heats. The water is hot and sluices away the very last remnants of my makeup and the onset of a light hangover.

I'm none the wiser to what to do about Jace or how to deal with him, I suspect Cass would have a man like him by the balls, the tables a complete turn of events, I can barely get past the drugging lust. I hear of people succumbing to this kind of chemistry, how it doesn't last because there is nothing beyond it. The blind hope that there could ever be more snaps shut— I straighten my shoulders and feel resolution settle over me.

I half expect him to be sat on the toilet waiting for me but sigh in relief when I find he is nowhere in sight, slipping on my dressing gown I quickly towel dry my hair and drag it into a messy bun, I forgo makeup, the only cosmetic applied is moisturiser and Vaseline. I take a moment to stare at my reflection in the mirror. Gone is the glossy version. I look pale and tired. Last night has taken its toll on me.

Scrap that— the past year has torn away at me.

Stealing a breath, I leave the solitude of my bedroom and find Jace buttering some toast. Everything smells amazing. I spy a dish of bacon and eggs, and my smirk is self-indulgent even if a little sad.

I hover for a minute before making a coffee. He turns when I click the kettle on, and his eyes sweep over me. My appearance doesn't bother him. He winks and starts loading up the table. "Would you like a drink?" I say, following his movements. I can hash it out over breakfast with him, knock this thing on its head for real this time.

Happy with breakfast, he saunters over and winds the silk tie of my dressing gown around his finger, it unravels and so do my nerves, my breath rushes out and Jace blinks up at me from where his eyes were.

"I will never get tired of seeing you react to me." It's not said arrogantly but a simple statement of truth. He lifts his hands and, using both thumbs, parts the wrap on a long exhale of air and tucks it at either side of my breasts, his nails a smooth caress over my skin. "You hungry, beautiful?"

My hands lift to conceal my nakedness, but Jace takes my wrists in his, his thumbs running over my pulse. Satisfied with the erratic thrum, he leans down and places a kiss to my collarbone. I close my eyes in both pleasure and anger, and my rigid body is trying to fight off the feelings.

"Yes," I shudder as his tongue touches base, the soft pads of his thumbs running back and forth. I swallow a moan but another slips free.

He stands and I crane my neck to find his remarkable eyes. "Good, because I made bacon." I roll my eyes. He is smirking as he crosses my dressing gown and ties it securely at the front. He collects my coffee up and places it down before making himself one. I sit and wait for him to join me at my small table tucked away in the kitchen. Jace seems too big in here, my suitable flat dwarfs in size.

When he finally does join me, he doesn't hold back. "So, you want to tell me why you ran out on me this morning?" I pause with my cup midway, my gaze drops and I swallow the quick lump that develops whenever he puts me on the spot.

I shrug, there is so much I want to say but none of it sounds feasible when I'm about to declare it. Placing my cup down, I fill my plate on a sigh. "Honestly, I don't know."

"I think you do," he counters, following suit he starts placing food on his own plate. Looking completely at home in my kitchen, relaxed and painfully in control as usual. He must have showered before he came racing over, because his hair is damp at the tips and it makes it tilt ever so slightly hinting at the possibility of curls, with his long dense lashes and golden eyes the end result is gut wrenching. I fork a mouthful of food in whilst Jace sits opposite watching me closely.

"Okay, I don't want anything serious right now," I admit, pushing some food around my plate. "Which you know," I enforce. "And at the same time, I won't settle for anything less." My eyes meet his and I place my cutlery down when I feel my hands clam up. "This isn't me. I don't do the whole one-night stand—"

"That's not what this is," he grates, eyes hard.

I shrug again. "Fine, casual sex, it's not me. I've done it before and it didn't end well." I give him a tight grim smile. There are too many truths to my statement for it not to plague me.

"Okay." He accepts my words without argument, but he is expecting more from me, I can see it in the hard set of his eyes. Other than that, his whole manor is cool and calm as he bites into his breakfast, as though we have sat here a thousand times and will do a thousand times more.

"In fact, I've not long been out of a relationship." This gets his attention and his jaw ticks, but he says nothing, watchful, waiting. I swallow a quick sip of coffee. "I'm not ready because I haven't quite accepted the loss . . . of someone." It's not a complete lie. I suppose I lost some of myself when things went sour with Adam. I lost more than that, but I'm not about to admit that to him. "I guess I still have feelings," I say on a rush. There certainly is no love lost between Adam and me, but he doesn't need to know that. He takes it without reacting, his face a sturdy mask of stark masculinity.

When he says nothing and continues to eat his breakfast, I sit back defeated in my chair. Nothing seems to deter him. Silence settles over us and I sink into a mild food coma. Minutes tick by and I can feel myself becoming more and more skittish about what will happen when our pates are clean. I take my time chewing slowing, and prolonging the inevitable. Jace finishes up his meal and stands. I gulp in shock, nearly choking on my coffee. I stare up at him a mix of emotions on my face.

"I appreciate you being honest with me, Lily." When he drags his car keys from the counter and walks to the door, I hold my breath. He stares back at me wordlessly, before pulling the door open. I gasp lightly, fighting back the confused plea on my tongue. "I hope you find what it is you're looking for." His bitter tone suggests that I've given him cause to believe he isn't it, and his whole demeanor is taut and angry, even though he remains composed and polite. I watch on silently, mentally screaming to allow my guard down and let this man in, but I make no attempt to offer him that. Jace walks out of my apartment, leaving my door to thud shut with a resounding bang.

Chapter Fourteen

Cass is ready to un-friend me. I'm at home and she is on speaker phone. "I swear, you were dropped at birth!" She huffs. I chuckle, flicking through some files looking for an invoice.

"Your support is unwavering," I chirp, leaning my hip against the antique desk in my hallway.

"Friends don't support bad decisions," she scoffs mildly. I can see her scowling down the line at me, her poised face masked by a frown.

"Well, he certainly isn't a good one." I roll my eyes at her incessant need to push things forward with Jace. Surely, she can see why I'm hesitant.

"Yeah, you're right," she finally agrees, and I look over my shoulder at my mobile, her sudden change of tact taking all my attention, "Good looking, good dancer, good in bed." She lists them off. I open my mouth to argue, but she is on a roll. "And don't even *try* to deny the last point," she scoffs. "You were walking like Whoopi Goldberg in *Ghost*." A mental image runs through my mind and my face twists in amused disagreement.

"I was not!" God, she is so dramatic.

"Oh please, I'm not entertaining this anymore. You're in denial. Stay there if you want, but you're making a huge mistake."

"Well, he walked out, so it's done now. Can we not talk about Jace? I need your help with the gallery, that's why I rang." I'm quick to change the subject.

"Harriet sent me over the details, I have it covered, stop worrying." She sounds bored with me already.

"I will when you share it with me. You can't leave me in the dark. It's my gallery," I point out. I know she has everything under control. Cass is like a walking, talking calendar. I need the distraction.

"Will you relax? I'll be in tomorrow morning. You still have days. Stop panicking. This year will be different." She is all flippant and carefree.

"I hope so," I grunt, pulling at some paperwork but stuffing it back in when I see it's not the invoice I'm after.

"I know so, you guys have most covered anyway. I secured the wait staff and caterers, Harriet has received the RSVPs, and the place will be packed," she tells me in clipped bullet points.

"What about the flutes? Last year we were sh—"

She sounds exasperated when she says, "Got it covered. We can discuss this all tomorrow, you know, like we arranged." Her voice floats down the line, thick with sarcasm. My lips twitch and I roll my eyes at her again. She's so damn difficult. "I know you're rolling your eyes," she tuts as I push away from the desk, ready to deny her claim.

"Oh shit," she exclaims. "I've got to go."

"Okay, everything alright?" I collect up my mobile awaiting her reply.

"Yes, I have a delivery. Love ya. See you tomorrow," she says, hanging up abruptly.

"See you tomo—" She's gone. How charming!

I'm stressing like mad and I have no time to think of Jace Bennett. All thoughts are completely consumed with the event at the gallery this weekend. Grabbing up the paperwork I need, I lock up, taking a minute to think over my day. I have to call Alfredo to confirm the shipment arrived safely. I set a reminder in my diary and quickly rush to my car as the heavens open.

Harriet has the doors open wide for me as soon as I pull up, I regret my peep toes now, my feet are slipping inside the high suede pumps as I run with my umbrella into the gallery. "Why are you here so early?" I call over the heavy drum of water when Harriet yanks the door shut muffling the sounds of torrential rain.

"I knew you'd want to get ahead today so figured I'd get in and help." Harriet truly has a heart of gold, she worries far too much, but she is worth the strain. Her big blue eyes are scored lightly with eyeliner and her long blonde hair is twisted neatly, she naturally fidgets which I find cute and a sign of her constant anxiety, but she is an art whizz and an asset.

"Well, okay then, make sure you leave at one today. We have a quiet afternoon," I throw over my shoulder.

She looks startled. "Oh, are you sure? I don't mind." I head down the back to hang my coat up and plug my iPad in, then I return to the front desk.

"I know you don't, that's why you're going home early," I emphasise on a pointed look, as she grins.

"Great!"

Smiling I empty my bag, laying out my diary and phone, I check my watch. "The delivery is due in another hour, I'm going to sort a few emails." My diary is packed this morning, I have the security firm coming to check the alarm system, plus a lunch meet with Paco, I make a mental note to check the utility bills, we seem to be paying out more than usual. "Harriet, can you only order what we desperately need," I say absently, as I look over my never-ending list of jobs for this week. I'm always busy before an event. Bringing Paco onboard with his dramatic work is a bit of a risk. People will either love him or hate him. He is my marmite but I have a good eye for talent, plus the clientele in this area are all very artsy and self-indulgent.

Cass is always here to give a helping hand. She has emailed me specifics and scouted out the cheapest way for me to run the event. My last one wasn't such a hit and I felt the financial strain for most of last year.

Harriet drags me from my thoughts when she clinks a coffee on my desk. "We had a voicemail. Lina, she asks that you call her back. Do you think it's about the 'Shadow' Piece?"

"More than likely," I reply, boredom rolling off my tongue. I'm in a funk and it's not going unnoticed. I sense Harriet's curious appraisal, but throw her a tired smile, hoping it will appease her a little. "She is pushing for me to showcase it, but I don't think it will sell as well as the other painting." In fact, I know it won't, it's so different from her usual work. I can appreciate the beauty and hard work that's gone into it, but it doesn't fit for what I have in mind this weekend.

Harriet eyes me for a moment, thoughtful, and I elaborate further, "It doesn't tie well with the exhibition, and she needs to trust me," I say distracted, as I scan my emails.

"I agree," Harriet adds on a sigh. "It's a little dark and vulnerable, which I like but it will stick out like a sore thumb." She sips at her own coffee, I nod in agreement sharing a smile with her, professionally we click. And my observation seems to have settled her curious mind.

"Right, can you check supplies and double check all the bulbs, I can't be doing with one going last minute, the one nearest the door seems duller than the rest." Harriet looks over her shoulder at the offending object. "Yeah, sure." She hurries down the hall. I sit back and rub my temples.

I greet the delivery guy and arrange the artwork, FaceTiming with Alfredo once I catch a few minutes. His face comes into view, rough jaw of dark hair and deep brown eyes, his accent is very sexy. "Ah, there is my beautiful English rose. You're calling because you finally agreed to marry me, no?" He is smiling lightly at me. With a short laugh, I rest my chin on my hand. I have known Alfredo for three years now and he is an incurable flirt. He is classically handsome and I like him a lot. He has always respected my need to keep things professional but doesn't miss a chance to tease me.

"Bad news, I'm afraid," I huff dramatically.

"Bah, you only want me for my art!" There are no hard feelings between us.

"Would seem so." I laugh. "The shipment arrived safely, thank you."

"You are welcome, Lily. Did Marcie email you? I am coming to the exhibition. I have business in London this week. This is okay?" He is being polite, but he would turn up if I said no.

"Of course, it will be nice to see you." I smile.

"Perhaps seeing me in the flesh you will change your mind." He winks.

"I do hope you aren't going to actually be in the flesh," I say pointedly. "I have a reputation to uphold here, and I can't have naked Italians strolling about my gallery."

With a loud bark, he laughs. "English humour, you are a funny woman. Beauty, brains, the whole shebang. Tell me, how are you single?"

I blush and dip my gaze, my mind running straight for Jace.

Alfredo clutches his heart. "Ah, you have met someone," he assumes. "You wound me!" With an awkward laugh, I brush his comment off, neither confirming nor denying, only too happy when he is interrupted. "My appointment is here. I shall see you this weekend, Lily."

"Okay, bye," I manage to get out, as the back of his head morphs into a blurred object and the line goes dead.

I rush through the rest of my morning and meet Paco for lunch. It's his first event, so he is apprehensive. We go over the details and I reassure him to be his self. He is a likeable, creative, and intelligent person, so I think that in itself will help sell his work, there is something very appealing about his subdued intelligence.

He is a scrawny man with a short, unkempt beard and impressively long lashes. "I managed to get a suit cheap. It's navy." He informs me, wringing his hands together.

"You really are nervous, aren't you?" I smile sympathetically at him.

"Yes." He laughs. "I'm living on my friend's couch, I need the money. That sounds twisted, I know." He sighs. "I want my name out there, but at the moment I'm trying to just . . . " His shoulders drop when he admits softly, "Survive." His eyes meet mine with such gratitude. "Thank you for doing this, Lily."

"I admire your work. You're truly gifted. I'll be there all evening and Harriet too, so if you're feeling overwhelmed, come find one of us. It's not a huge formal event anyway." He nods picking up his coffee and taking a long swig. "Alfredo likes your work, and he will be there. His family own a huge collection of Italian artifacts and Contemporary art, so he is a good contact to have," I assure him, happy when I see him relax a little.

"Okay, great." He blows out a steady breath and checks his watch quickly. "I'm meeting my friend shortly, he's lending me some dress shoes, so I'll see you on Friday?" he says sheepishly.

"Okay, sure. I've got the bill covered anyway, stop worrying." With a forced smile, he finishes his drink, thanks me, and walks away. Once I have paid, I head back to my car. My phone rings from my bag and I'm thrust back into chaos.

Half an hour later, I'm stood out front in my coat talking with the window cleaner. "I can spruce this up if you like?" His gruff voice floats down to me on the street whilst he points to the words 'The Loft' holding court overhead of the door in chunky, brushed stainless steel. "No extra cost," he affirms.

"Oh, yes, please. Thanks, Clive." I finger a feral strand of hair away.

"No problem, lovey. Now, how about that tea?" He grins as a

splosh of water hits the path. It misses me, but only because I know what he is like.

"Coming right up!" I call. "Well, not up the ladder," I affirm, he laughs and I sweep past hearing Clive mutter about health and safety, reminding me to check our own insurance policy.

The whole week rushes by with a barrage of emails, phone calls, and last-minute trips to finalise everything for the gallery event. This time around I'm more prepaid, my confidence is back, and I'm anticipating the exhibition.

The Gallery has been closed all day and I insist on being here an hour before anyone else arrives, despite having spent the best part of the day here already, I want to double check everything is going according to plan.

The place is lit up and Harriet is stood talking to a small group of people dressed smartly in black. I'm carrying a huge bouquet of flowers that I intend to use to decorate the window. The whole place smells like polish and wildflowers, and the expected pang of nervousness is nowhere to be seen. Whilst she has everyone occupied, I drop my bouquet on the open desk and do a quick sweep of the room, checking lighting, further flower arrangements and ensuring toilet rolls are stocked, all the minor essentials.

Harriet is wearing a sheer deep purple gown and looks stunning, I tell her as much as I relocate the flowers down in the window and give her a quick hug.

"It isn't too much?" She blushes, straightening down her dress and wringing her hands together.

"God no, it's perfect. You look gorgeous, Hat." I smile brightly at her, she is probably nervous too it's her first exhibition with me. "Just remember, when you're talking to a prospective customer or even a gallery owner, think of it as talking to me." Her bright eyes flash to mine and I see my first glimpse of anxiety. "You can do this. There will be plenty of other people to occupy each other, so not everyone will speak with you." I rub her arm and she nods it over.

"It's silly, I do this every day." She wafts her hand up, looking annoyed with herself.

"It's not silly, it's on a different scale. But I trust you, Harriet, and attending an exhibition is not the same as hosting one." I can appreciate her worry, oddly I feel none myself.

"Thanks," she sighs.

I give her a quick hug before speaking with the servers, she has gone over most but I run through fire safety. "The alarms have all be serviced and tested so nothing should happen," I assure them, pointing out the fire exit. "The fire meet point is out the front, should anyone need medical attention, please find me."

Another huge bouquet of stunning lilies takes up a spot by the door and catches my eye mid-sentence.

Who are those from?

I falter in my speech, dragging my eyes back to the hired staff, one or two eye me suspiciously, I shake my thought away saying, "As Harriet has probably already informed you guests will be here within the next thirty minutes, artists and other gallery owners are in attendance, so keep their glasses filled and if you have any problems find me or Harriet." The anonymous flowers are an unwelcome distraction in my peripheral, anything else I was planning to say has been battered away by my curiosity, I sweep my gaze over their straight faces before asking, "Right that's it, any questions?" I silently will them to say no.

"No," they reply in unison and with a sharp nod I walk to the flowers, my heart picks up at the thought that Jace has offered another olive branch, but as I turn the card over in my hand, I see they are from Alfredo.

"Oh." This is very unexpected. How lovely. I chose not to think on the fact that he has never sent flowers before and accept the kind gesture.

Paco arrives shortly after and then guests begin to arrive in tandem, I try my upmost to welcome everyone on entry, introducing them to Paco and offering them champagne, I network with Paco my eyes lifting to locate Cass and Sean, forcing my eyes away I continue around the room until Alfredo himself intercepts me with open arms and a kiss to each cheek. "My rose, here she is. You have had a good turnout, well done!" He gushes and I blush at his over voiced compliment.

"Thank you, and for the flowers, they are beautiful." I introduce Paco to him when the sight of Jace striding through the front door stuns me into silence. My mouth turns down further when I see Neve hooked around his arm. My eyes fly to Cass's and she looks away in guilt. Pain clutches my chest and I swallow back a mouth full of regret.

Alfredo's voice pulls me back as I fight the urge to look for the tall, amber-eyed god standing in my premises. "You're welcome, and Paco, it's such a pleasure." His voice lilts, Paco is a nervous wreck but shakes his hand enthusiastically. "Lily has told me so much about you, your work is outstanding, the way you manipulate the light." Alfredo looks thoughtful and I smile reassuringly at Paco. "It's genius. I look forward to getting to know you better." He hands his card over.

Paco is speechless for a moment. "Wow, thank you. And you, Lily," he gushes, looking to me with such gratitude. "You have no idea how thankful I am." I nod, unable to do anything.

"You underestimate yourself, Paco. You're incredibly talented, so thank you," I tell him, my professional hat still on but nowhere as secure now Jace is here. Excusing myself, I walk over to Cass, who looks green around the gills. I can't see Jace anywhere and for the time being I'm glad.

"Please, *please,* tell me you had nothing to do with this?" I beg. Sean clears his throat and takes a hefty gulp of champagne whilst Cass stutters.

She rubs my arms hesitantly. "Hear me out, okay?" I shrug her off.

"*Cass!*" God, I'm so pissed at her right now. "Why tonight?" I scoff. "Of all nights, why?" If there was one night, I needed my wits about me, tonight was it!

"I didn't know he was going to bring the wannabe wife along," she grumbles, flicking hair out of her face. I snap back and deflate as it all sinks in. I nod. I have nothing more to say.

I don't think I can spend an evening buttering up the art community whilst Jace wanders around my gallery with his . . . I don't even know what she is to him, but the fact that he has brought her here, has pissed me off no end. Cass is a pretty astute person and although I'm ignoring her opinions on Jace, her observation on Neve hankers pretty well with my own.

I leave them, ignoring her plea as I walk away.

I eye the door multiple times. It's too much of a temptation. I want to escape, seek emotionless solitude. Only I refuse to give Jace the satisfaction of knowing I'm affected by his presence. Luckily, I spend the next hour inundated with questions about Paco and some of the more eclectic pieces. I make a quick sale and Harriet is at hand to take over, jotting down their details for me. The whole time my eyes are running around the room. To most unobserving eyes, I would look like a dedicated host, taking it all in, surveying the party. I'm not — I'm looking for him.

Since I can't see him, I suspect he is upstairs. There is a huge part of me that I am weighing in on constantly who wants me to go up, see them together and confirm my suspicions but the thought sours my stomach rotten and my feet stay firmly to the lower floor. Cass catches my eye, regret pulling at the corners of her usually smiling mouth, my shock has worn off and I manage to give her a soft smile, discreetly she points to the ceiling around her flute alerting me to Jace's whereabouts. Stiffly, I nod, my eyes betraying me and searching for him, but he is out of sight. Just not out of mind.

A waiter passes and I cause him to jump as I make a grab for a flute of champagne. I apologise and see Harriet giggling at me close by. I roll my eyes and she makes her way over. I sip gingerly aware I have eaten little all day.

Paco seems far more relaxed and is talking animatedly to a small group of people over by his selection of arts. "He's a hit." Harriet grins. The champagne has gone straight to her head, her eyes are glassy and she keeps smirking, I grin inwardly.

"He is," I sigh, pleased, my anxiety for him leaving me in one big rush. She giggles again and I shake my head.

"That hot guy is here," she states loudly, and I drop my head on a soft laugh. "I'm glad one of us is keeping level-headed," I murmur. She always gets gushy around Alfredo.

Harriet hiccups and her eyes widen. "Sorry." She isn't. Her shoulders are shaking, I can't help but join in.

"I can see that." She hides her face and I pat her shoulder. "I'm glad you're having a nice time."

"I got asked on date," she whisper shouts, and I cough out a laugh at her change in demeanor. It's then that Alfredo approaches me with a warm smile in tow and Harriet disappears, wiggling her eyebrows encouragingly. Slipping a hand on my lower back, he leans in and I stiffen. "So where is this man of yours?" He wonders. Startled, I recall my slip-up and mentally slap myself for my lie.

"Early days," I say by way of explanation, silently willing Jace to come do his macho alpha thing. My response isn't enough to satisfy Alfredo.

"So, it's not serious?" His deep-set, dark eyes watch me shrewdly and for the first time, I dabble with the possibility that his innocent flirting wasn't so innocent after all.

"I never said that." I shrug, giving him a pointed look before sipping on my champagne and giving myself a silent moment to gather my wits about me.

"But you didn't deny it." His leg brushes mine and I start to see our professional relationship being sucked down the drain.

"He had a prior engagement." I mentally chastise myself for lying. It's not in my nature, yet lately it seems I've been doing nothing but. I don't like the person I'm becoming. My heart thuds and I step back so his hand drops away.

"I flew over a thousand miles," he states arrogantly, smirking at my pouty face, his playful demeanor back.

"Oh, give over, you had a work commitment too." I roll my eyes and hide my scowl behind my glass. Alfredo checks his watch and shakes his head on a sigh, obviously sensing he has over-stepped the mark.

"Yes and no," he hums on an odd look. I can't bring myself to meet his eyes. "I've got to go." He looks as though he is going to say something more. Instead, he closes the distance and pecks my cheeks. "I will call you on Monday," he affirms.

"Okay, thank you for coming." I smile as he steps away.

"Anytime, Lily. Goodnight."

Chapter Fifteen

I neck the remaining liquid in my glass and deposit it on a moving tray, doing an extended walk around the room, for reasons I refuse to admit, before I walk towards the toilet. Seeing there is a short line, I bypass, smiling warmly at people as I head down to my office. There is a toilet out back, and I can be in and out in minutes.

Unlocking my office, I click the door shut and feeling my way to the toilet slip in and click on the small light. I take a moment to enjoy the solitude and drop my head in to my hands— this night is a fucking joke.

"Fuck," I growl, flushing the toilet and washing my hands. I have a few makeup items stashed in here so give my face a once over. The dress I have chosen is simple and elegant, it skims my curves and drops to the floor on one side in a long slither of cream silk, I swipe my lips with a deep red and sigh at my reflection, my eyes shutter and I force myself to gather any strength, to get through the rest of the night.

I swing the door open and come to a sharp stop when beyond the darkness a shadow reclines, feet hooked at the ankles, hands folded around each corner of my desk. “Hello, Lily.”

I step out from the toilet but lean against the frame, favouring its safety. I have to swallow before I reply, my nerves causing havoc with my ability to speak. “Jace.” It comes out on a soft croak. Clearing my throat, I look away.

“You look stunning.” His voice reaches me from where he sits and whispers around my body. I shiver and find myself caught up in his somber gaze.

“Don’t.” My hand cups my throat as emotion clogs there, I’m stuck here unable to move away, scared, knowing I will have to pass him to get away. His endless supply of control grates me, he doesn’t even blink but drowns me in that whiskey stare. Minutes pass before he chooses to respond and by that time, I'm a wreck.

“Don’t what?” he says on a subtle smile, pushing up from the heavy wood, the pressure makes it creak in protest and I stiffen as he walks my way, he stops at my feet, my back is pressed so hard into the door frame my shoulder blades are hugging the hard wood, he stares down at me, something close to satisfaction on his face. “Don't what, Lily?” His scent douses me and I close my eyes for a second, when I pull them open, his eyes are fixed on my turned down mouth.

“Why are you here?” I don't know what to do with myself, my limbs feel alien and for some obscure reason I finger the lapels of his jacket. My eyes take stock of what I’m doing but before I can pull away, my hand is covered. On a harsh sigh, he tugs me away from the wooden frame, cups my neck, and brushes a hard kiss over my mouth. I slap my palm into his shoulder pushing him away.

“I don’t think your date will appreciate you kissing me!” I snap.

He smirks. “Jealous?” Is that why he brought her, to antagonise me?

“Don’t be ridiculous,” I scoff. Jace lifts a finger and draws a soft line from the throbbing pulse in my neck, down between my breasts and stops short of my hips.

"Neve and I are networking. She works alongside me." I'm sure she does. I clear my throat and give him a fake smile.

"It's for work," he reaffirms. I nod and look away, my chin is clasped and my pouty face is pulled back to his. "You're asking me to go against every instinct I have with you," he growls.

I blink, struggling to keep up with the change in conversation. "I don—"

"Bullshit, you know." His eyes flash angrily at me, his grip tightens but it doesn't hurt. "Don't see you, don't touch you." His lips dance over mine. "Don't ask me to stay away any longer."

"You need to leave," I say on a strangled plea.

He allows me the luxury of a little room and steps back, but not enough that I can move."It may have slipped your notice, but there is a party going on and it's missing a host," I deliver in a clipped tone.

"And I'm missing a certain woman in my bed." I don't have time to think on that thought, a shaft of light streams into the room as Neve confidently pushes through. Her eyes drag over me with irritation, before they land on her target. "I'm bored and we have dinner reservations," she mutters sulkily. Without any respect for me or my office space, she walks around and plonks her tiny arse in my chair and drops her head to the side, looking at Jace. Her mouth pouts as she runs her tongue over her teeth, and my eyes flash at him.

What the fuck is this?

He sighs and I manage to side-step him moving away. I walk briskly to where she just came through and open the door, showing them both the exit. "Thanks for coming." I clear my throat, sounding anything but thankful.

"That was the plan." Neve gives me the once-over, and her comment makes me frown. Jace throws her a dark look. Taking her by the elbow, he steers her out, pressing a fleeting kiss to my cheek. I jolt in shock, but he is already starting down the hall.

"I don't get it," Neve huffs at him. "I've seen prettier."

My stomach drops and I blindly reach for the handle of the door, closing myself in the office. Darkness surrounds me and I shut my eyes on the hot burn of angry tears.

What a bitch!

I think about swinging the door open and firing off some smart retort, but Cass barrels in, her eyes wide with worry. I jump on a soft yelp as I get shunted forwards. Flicking the light switch, she runs her eyes all over me. "Fucking hell!" she exclaims, shoving a full glass of fizz in my hand.

"You owe me," I mutter shortly.

"I'm sorry, Lily. What did they want?" She hugs me quick and stands back, biting her lip. She knows she fucked up. Tonight, was not the night to push this.

They.

The term coils around my neck like a tight rope.

"Apparently, he wanted me back in his bed and I don't know what the fuck her deal is!" I shake my head and neck the glass in one movement, any concerns for my guests going straight out the window.

"That is her deal," she flicks my head. Squinting, I rub the sore spot. "She wants what you have." Her eyes go wide as she points out the obvious.

I fidget. "Well I don't actually—"

"But you could have!" Cass rubs her temples as though she is dealing with an errant child. "Do you know how infuriating your stubbornness is?" Her eyes bore into mine and I can see me heading for a grade 'A' telling-off. "Ten years from now," she starts, "you will be kicking yourself to the grave."

"That's a little brutal, I wasn't expecting to go so young." I'm smirking and her lips twitch but only briefly.

"Seventy years from now," she grates, "you will wonder what if." She points in my face, eyes holding false wisdom.

"No, I will be on some cruise necking free martinis," I say flippantly and pull the door open, leaving my friend to curse behind me. Staying in here to dissect the last few hours, will only bring on tears and too many unwanted thoughts.

I refuse to stew over Cass's words the following morning. I feel like shit for more reasons than one, my hangover is growling at me forcefully. I swallow another gulp of dark liquid trying to dispel my dry mouth and lethargy, but there's only one thing for this.

Grabbing my phone, I call Cass. She answers on the fourth ring, her words a thing of true friendship. "Café Mount?"

"Yes, please," I grumble.

"Give me thirty minutes and I'll pick you up." She sounds a little rough too.

"Love you!" She hangs up and I waste little time getting ready for breakfast. My crumpled yet still curled hair gets wrapped into a loose plait, and I drag on jeans, Converse, and my favourite jumper. Cass will be appalled to see me in last night's makeup, but I conceal my bags and plump my lips before collecting my coat and bag, in time for the honk of her car horn.

Her eyes hold the strain of one too many drinks and her lips look drier than the Sahara. My smile falls from my face and concern fills my grey eyes. "Sean and I had a fight, drunken shit."

"Are you guys okay?" I whisper, looking over my usually bubbly, bushy-tailed friend as she shrugs and her lip quivers. "Oh Cass!" I pull her into a tight hug and her sniff turns into a sob, I'm shocked. One hundred percent stumped by the sudden turn in her happy go lucky persona.

"I accused him of cheating. I found messages but apparently it was a work thing." She sniffs and shudders in my arms. I rub her back and wait whilst she wipes the stream of tears decorating her face away with her hands.

"So, you know this girl?" I poke gently and she nods on a hiccup.

"Sasha, she works the bar." She brings puffy eyes back to me. "Lily, she is always eyeing him up, sly touches." She grinds her teeth and I give her a sympathetic smile.

"Have you told her to back off?" Her hair loosens when she shakes her head.

"No, it's his work, his business, I can't go in, laying down the law." She sounds frustrated by that. I imagine if Sasha was a customer Cass wouldn't hesitate in giving her a mouth full of abuse.

"Has he told her to be a bit more professional?" I frown— surely, he would have picked up on this and had a word, boss to employee?

"Apparently, she is like it with everyone," she scoffs. I can imagine Cass went into this with mild insecurities after their past. She's certainly not one to overreact. Naturally, she is a bit dramatic, but she is level-headed and fair.

"And the messages?" I pry further.

"He said he would pick her up, and she was all 'I can't wait to see you again'. Again? What does that mean?" She spits, but I don't answer. Her tone suggests that wasn't a question but more of a dig.

"But it was work," I affirm, trying to reassure her. Surely, he wouldn't be so stupid?

"He says it was." She wraps her top around her hand to use it as an absorbent and pats under her eyes, pulling in a deep sigh.

"Do you believe him?" I ask hesitantly. They seem so happy together. Sean can't get enough of her!

"I want to." She nods quickly, pulling some Vaseline and concealer from her bag to transform her face. "He says he's going to talk to her."

"Well, that's good. She does seem a little over friendly," I say tactically, being the supportive friend.

She scoffs again. "I want to punch her every time I see her." I smirk at her harsh words and she grins when she clocks my cheeky grin. "Maybe we can line Neve and her up together," she quips and an honest laugh flies from my lips.

"She told Jace she had seen prettier." I frown, recalling the sting of her words.

"Bullshit." Ever the loyal friend, Cass gives me an, 'are you actually buying her shit' look. "Sounds like she is threatened," Cass scoffs.

"Maybe Sasha is, Sean was fair game until a few weeks ago, she probably feels this is her last chan-"

"She never had a chance!" Cass cuts me off harshly, before looking to me and softening her aggression with gentle flutters of her lashes, I laugh freely, seeing a hint of my friend rising from the ashes, feisty and brash.

She wafts her hands. "Anyway, I need food." The topic is done. I get the subtle message and keep my twitchy lips firmly shut.

Cass manages to wangle a space in her mini and we hop out the car showing forced enthusiasm, as we head for the warmth. "Hello, girls, not seen you in a while." The old boy who runs this place ambles past us, neither of us know his name and I'm sure he has told us a few times, I feel a pinch of guilt, in our defense we're usually too hung-over to retain the information.

"Being good has its downside." Cass explains our absence.

"Lesson learnt, I'd say," he says gruffly, tipping his head. "Be bad!" His face splits into a toothy grin and we both laugh. "Marty's working. He knows what ya like." He waves us in.

"Great!" I beam and head straight for an empty table nearest the window, we are intercepted before we sit and Marty jogs towards us, he is probably around our age and a beanpole of a guy.

"Rough night? Both in need of grease and coffee?" He sways on his heels watching us with over-bright eyes and the energy of a toddler. It's exhausting!

The word 'grease' makes my stomach churn, but I tell myself it's what I need. I nod and breathe through my nose, knowing everything is cooked to perfection here, hardly a drop of grease in sight. We slump into our awaiting chairs, eyes weighed down by last night's alcohol. It's not the worst hangover, but I feel pretty rough. I shouldn't have indulged in the lonely bottle of wine when I returned home.

"You'll make me sick!" Cass whines, rubbing her tummy gingerly, he pours us both water and I chug mine down quickly, washing the nausea away.

Marty gives a high pitch short laugh, he's not fooled. "Never, you're scarier than most rugby players I know."

Cass rolls her eyes. "Oh, now he tells us," she tuts and sighs over her glass, I smirk and ask for a Americano and another water, holding my glass out as icy liquid fills the chunky highball.

"You having the usual?" She wonders, Marty is leaning against a wooden post near our table, humoring us— we will both pick what we always have. A clean fry up, if there ever was such a thing, and two rounds of buttery toast.

I nod. "Yes, with extra toast and lots of butter."

"So, it's dripping off." Cass hums and hands our unread menus back, Marty chuckles and walks away with our order banked.

"Plans for the day?" I say sipping my water, I pick up a coaster and pull at the worn edge.

"I told Sean I wanted a day to myself, he has gone home, so nothing now," she laughs, but it sounds full of sadness.

"So, you're free?"

"All day." Cass injects fake happiness into her voice, she twirls her hair around her finger and swallows another sigh.

"Shopping?" I grin, her smile is slow and her eyes brighten— it's exactly the look I was hoping for.

"Can we pit stop before, we look awful," she grimaces at me, I don't blame her, my bags have bags and I feel as though my liver abandoned me in my sleep. I should learn to eat more before I drink.

"Yes," I laugh dryly, trying to avoid my reflection in the smear free glass, I'm a painful reminder of my inner angst— I look worn out, unkempt and sad. I blink away, shutting my feelings down and focusing on my friend looking lost on the other side of the table. "I think I have some of your clothes at mine anyway."

"Think? I made a drawer up," she laughs, so she did, I smirk at her and we both sink into silence until Marty arrives with our breakfast and coffee's.

"Delish!" Cass chirps, lifting her cutlery and arranging it over the plate before Marty even places it down.

"Thanks Marty." I grin waiting more patiently than my friend.

"No worries, I got to help Bert out back." Ah Bert, now I remember his name! Marty sticks his hands forcefully into his pockets and walks away, Cass is already chopping her way through the wide plate of food, I join in and we eat in silence, too food deprived to focus on one another.

Cass walks from my bathroom, her hair wrapped in a towel and fresh clothes on, I showered as soon as we got back and am finishing my makeup.

"I love that outfit!" Cass exclaims, I smile inwardly, my t-shirt dress was a special find and I have paired it with over the knee boots, it looks stunning against my subtle skin, I left my hair to dry naturally and tamed a few wild curls into a gypsy plait.

"Thanks, I have been waiting to wear it but the weather is horrible," I explain.

"Urgh, we're talking about the weather, how old of us." Cass throws herself back on my bed dramatically.

I scoff, "You're such a twat." I allow her the comfort of my dressing table and head off to make us both a tea, trying to ensure I don't go overboard with the alcohol. When I come back, Cass has adorned her face with my makeup and is drying her hair. I place her tea in front of her and go recline on the bed.

"You have a text from Sean," I say softly, the delicacy of the situation not lost on me.

"Okay." She shrugs, Cass is a hardball, she may ram feelings down my throat but she is just as good at shutting her own off.

"Just okay?" I ask, I catch a glimpse of her face and the hard set of a frown.

"Yes, just okay." She bronzes her cheeks and drags some daring lippy on.

I sigh at her dismissive attitude. "Cass, I don't want to put a spanner in the works-"

"Then don't!" She looks back at me and I shake my head, God the woman is a bugger, she is the first to point out my faults or make me deal with things, yet she is never prepared to deal with her own shit. "Sorry, I don't want to talk about it," she murmurs, I dip and peck her cheek and head off to sort the living room out, before we head out.

Cass finds me sorting a small bag, I check my reflection in the mirror by the front door and add some gloss. Her thickly lined eyes appear behind me. "Holy shit!" I grin. "Wow Cass, you look amazing!" She has gone all out.

"I know." She flicks her hair and gives me a shit-eating grin. "Goodbye savings!" She waggles her perfect brows and hugs my waist. "Ready to let loose?" She hums.

"Yep," it's like the old days, just us two. It's perfect.

We take her car and decide after we have shopped, to park it at the gallery before hitting the bars later on. We pile into the mini and Cass cranks up the radio, someone is singing about being driven crazy, I belt into song and begin shimmying in my seat, her neck dips back on a laugh and her voice joins mine.

"First stop Harvey Nicks!" She sings songs. "I want some sexy lingerie, new perfume and some killer heels!" Her grin is infectious.

"I need to top up my makeup, but lingerie sounds like a good idea." I relax back and she turns the volume down enough that we can still enjoy the music but talk comfortably. "That Basque you ordered the other month, I wonder if they do that in a nude?" I say, messing with the temperature.

"I'm sure they did, but the oyster would look amazing with your complexion." Her hands grip the wheel and her smile is big. "Thanks Lil." She throws me a quick smile before looking away, trying not to let her emotions get the better of her.

"Always, no more men talk, let's shop, drink and dance until our feet drop off." I can't wait, I can feel the buzz of excitement already, all the unease and anger racing to the surface, the disquiet that has been building up in me is burning for release. I'm about to give it the freedom it so desperately needs. *Kings of Leon* owns the station and I quickly lean forwards and flick it over.

"Hey!" Cass wails, "I love them!" She throws me an annoyed look.

I laugh at her pouty, childish face. "We don't like them," I say on a nod, my eyes pointedly conveying why, realisation dawns.

"Okay we don't like them," she mutters, I smirk and flick over until an artist we both like sends us into two wild ladies bouncing around in her car.

We reach Knightsbridge in no time and Cass finds us a small spot to park, we exit into the chilly air and move the conversation to her work, her client never did contact me?

"You got off lucky, they are a right pair! She is all the wedding is about me and he is already wondering why he popped the question, it's going to be a disaster!" It sounds like hell, I'm glad nothing arose from it.

"Who'd they hire?" I ask.

"Lucas."

"That's great, how is he?"

"Great, he has a daughter now." My head snaps up, he moves quick! Surely it wasn't serious?

"He does? When did that happen?" I'm genuinely intrigued, Cass and he fooled around for a little while last summer.

"Right after me, she's nearly five months." She's so la-de-da about the whole thing that I'm laughing inwardly already, how can she be so indifferent all the time.

"Hate to say it but that could have been you." I widen my eyes and wait for her reaction.

"I know, I had that thought when he first told me, he and his daughters' mother aren't together, her name is Lacey."

"Who the mother or the child?" I frown.

"Child, he never mentioned the woman's name," she says on a flick of her hand.

I don't particularly know Lucas, but I met him a few times when Cass would meet up with him, he didn't seem like the fatherly type. Before I can say as much Cass chimes in, "he is really smitten with her, has her most weekends, twice during the week, it's kind of cute." She smiles to herself and I groan inwardly, here we go!

"Kind of off limits," I remark gently, she gives me a, 'are you shitting me look' which I reciprocate. I know how this woman's mind works.

"You're playing man chess, Sean to E four, Lucas to D six." Her creamy complexion turns an envious shade of pink. She turns up her nose and walks a step ahead of me.

"You have never even played chess in your life," she spits, well and truly caught out. I know she is loyal to Sean but if she is feeling off kilter, she will be prepping a fallback for when the fall out happens. A fall out I suspect she has anticipated since she began the wobbly line with Sean.

A fall out that I hope doesn't arise.

Chapter Sixteen

Cass leads the way and we head straight for the lingerie department, her eagle eyes spotting exquisite garments all over, she scoops them all up giving me half to carry, we bundle into the changing rooms, Cass disappears behind a heavy curtain as do I and I begin peeling my clothes away.

"After this we hit the champagne bar, I'm feeling thirsty all of a sudden," she chortles. I model an extremely racy yet elegant bra and find myself smiling slowly, I have to buy this, only one person comes to mind and he would be insatiable if he was to see me in it, my eyes dim. I jump as Cass yanks the curtain back. "Ooh, Jace worthy." She wiggles her brows and I find her in a daring red assemble.

"That's cute." I untwist the strap.

"Oh please, I look fucking hot." Her smile is full of confidence once more. An older lady exits a changing cubicle and eyes us with distaste, stood in our underwear, chatting casually. "It will cost ya!" Cass quips laughing, when her prim face contorts further with disgust, I nudge her to behave, instead she whirls and gives her pert boobs a jiggle, I splutter out a laugh as the lady rushes out the dressing room.

"You should get it," I muse, slipping back behind my curtain and replacing the minimal bra with a more lacy full number, I try on a few more but settle with the first two. Cass's phone chimes loudly from the other side.

"Hello," she spits, there is no doubt it is Sean on the other line. "Well, obviously not at home." Her sarcasm makes me press my lips together, "I said I would speak to you tomorrow," she growls out a curse, leaving me to assume she has disconnected the call, I hold my breath and as expected, her phone blares through the changing rooms. It cuts off and then it's mine that begins dancing around the glass table I placed my handbag on.

"Is that him?" Boredom rings through the plush curtains.

"Yes." I stare at the screen for an age letting it ring off— he's not stupid he knows we will be together. My phone bleeps with a text.

Can let me know if she is safe? Sean x

I read it and despite knowing my friend would rather I ignore him, I know he cares for Cass, deeply. I honestly believe this is all a big misunderstanding and a hurdle they need to cross. I type a quick yes back, drop my phone into my bag and push free from the cubicle.

"What did he say?" Cass is reclining on a velvet chair, her hands free of garments, a saleswoman approaches and I give her my items, pointing out the ones I wish to keep.

"Asked if you were safe, I said yes." I drop my gaze and look for my purse. With our purchases now in our hands, we head to the makeup department, where I spend a lifetime trying to choose a new moisturiser and perfume.

Cass is growing impatient and I know it's because Sean has been in contact. She needs a different distraction. Shopping, although it has been a short trip, has served its purpose for her.

I give her a small smile. "Ready to head to The Loft?" I ask slipping around a rack of clothes, she yips a happy yes, it's sad to think she is having to force herself to have fun. I realise how it has been for her with me being so despondent about Jace, how hard she has tried, and how reluctant I have been, only half invested in her ideas.

"Great, let's get some cocktails. I'm parched." Her chuckle is music to my ears, as she hooks her arm through mine and tugs me towards the exit.

By the time we reach our destination Cass is back on board and brimming with excitement.

Multiple shots and cocktails later, both Cass and I are beyond caring. She is rocking her hips to the slow steady beat, lost to herself, and I'm all too happy to indulge. Her lips mime the words, serenading me about drinking someone away. I laugh, gently working my way towards her with fresh refills. She meets me and kisses my sweaty check. My hair is plastered to my face in unkempt strands, and she fingers it and tucks it behind my ear. "God we must look like riffraff," she slurs.

"You know you're looking at me when you say that, I might actually get a complex." I pout.

"We're too good looking for complexes." She grins wickedly.

"Good looking riffraff, is there such a thing?" She squints at my reply, the question seemingly too difficult for her alcohol infused mind, she groans in defeat and wafts my reply away and I chuckle.

"Piss off." Her eyes roll to the heavens and back. "Anyway, that hottie from the other week is here." She nods and points over my shoulder. Intrigued, I twist to find malteser eyes from Finnegan's. He's watching us and I'd guess by his relaxed demeanor that he's had eyes on us for some time. I acknowledge that without feeling, not even minimal elation at having a little attention, nothing, not a thing. It's a shame he is a nice guy, just not the right guy. I mentally laugh— I've been persuading myself that my right guy feels wrong.

God I'm a therapist's wet dream.

"Oh, it's Trent." I grin and give him a cheeky wave.

"Travis," Cass snorts into my neck. "It's Travis, who the hell is

Trent?" She splutters, my head lolls back on her shoulder and I laugh softly. I'm as bad as her.

"Don't know, don't care," I hum as she hooks an arm around my waist, trying to hold herself up.

"I'd say look sharp but you're sweating like an Olympic runner." She pushes my back with what little energy she has and Travis catches me as I stumble forward, my squeal caught up in his short laugh.

"Hey!" I yell, he flinches at my harsh welcome but smirks down at me.

"Heavy night huh?" His smile is still fixed in place and I lift my damp hair in explanation, it's drenched with sweat, I can't imagine I look good. Or at all like the professional gallery owner I feign to be.

"Heavy night," I murmur over exaggerating my blink, the alcohol making me sluggish. "Long day, heavy night." I nod to myself, affirming how ridiculously intoxicated I am, when I raise my drunken head to meet his deep eyes I see double, blinking I shake my limp hair and groan, clutching at my stomach.

"You're not going to be sick, are you?" There is no disgust, only concern, crouching down he lifts my chin and checks my face, I shake my head and try to disguise a yawn, when I look back to check on Cass I see a furious Sean striding through the club, Travis must have seen him too.

"*That* doesn't look good." He shouts, I groan out a curse pushing away from him.

"It could go one of two ways," I laugh sardonically, Cass is still dancing freely by herself, I manage to grab her arm and warn her of her impending doom, before Sean clocks us both. "Angry boyfriend, one o'clock." She scowls and twists his way, his eyes flare with heat and anger. I step back as he closes the space between himself and Cass, a comforting hand lands on my back and Travis pats my shoulder.

"I'm guessing this is one you should sit out," he says diplomatically. "Plus, I think you should sit before you fall," he jests.

"No shit," I splutter, seeing Sean look as angry as Jace has done me in the past. Travis scoops me onto a stool and I wobble on a short cry and clutch the sticky underside with a grimace, Travis centers me and asks for some water over my shoulder.

"Babe, you smell like a brewery." His laugh is low.

"You're too kind." I bat my lashes and he shakes his head, I squint over him and watch from afar. My fiery friend, oh so ready for this, brings up a perfectly manicured hand and points it straight at the looming frame of her boyfriend. Sean laughs and I cringe, waiting for my five-foot-nothing of a friend to explode. Instead, he grabs her neck and slams his mouth on hers.

"Oh, for god sake!" I huff. "Is that an unspoken code for men or something." Wobbling on the seat, I waft my hand in the general direction of Cass and her Sean.

"Code?" Travis is frowning as he wipes some of my hair off my face and looks over his shoulder, to the dance floor.

"Yes, the whole caveman act, silence them with a kiss?" I roll my eyes, then take a sip of my icy water— the sudden cooling to my sweaty body is bliss.

Travis chuckles. "Only when she is worth it." He inclines his head.

"Well then you obviously don't know Cass very well, I'm surprised she isn't still trying to tell him off." I huff and lean into him, too drunk to hold myself up fully.

Travis squints. "I believe she is." I lift my head and find that through the barrage of kisses being bestowed on her she is snapping out short, sharp, and no doubt harsh words. All being rebuffed by a playful smile and deep kisses. Personally, I think she has overreacted to the messages, Sasha is overstepping the mark, but I don't think Sean deserves to be punished so much. I hope they can reconcile.

Slowly she relents and softens into Sean, Travis and I mutter thankful words before laughing in unison. "You Lily, are a reoccurring surprise."

"Why, do you like your women sweaty and miserable?" I grin up at him and he laughs softly.

"You're not miserable babe, you're just stubborn. So, where is he?" The easy spoken question has pain shafting through my chest, I shrug and stir my drink with my finger, a warm hand pulls my chin up, deep, dark brown eyes hold mine, safe and comforting.

"If you tell me he has given you the boot, I will choke on my own tongue," he deadpans. I suck in a deep breath and shake my head. "See, stubborn." My lips twitch and he rubs my neck. "Ah you've been busting his balls, the poor fucker!" He's grinning wildly and I jab him in the stomach.

"It's not like that!" I defend myself, truth is I don't know what it is like, but whatever I am doing sure as hell isn't working, where Jace is concerned.

A figure appears behind Travis, I recognise him from the bar the other week, "Hey, birthday girl!" He swoops around and pulls me into a bear hug and I grab hold of Travis for support. I squeak and let him take my weight fully as I'm deposited on the uneven stool, they exchange a few words and Travis nods his head. I can't hear them and look around for Cass, I find them quickly and Sean signals me over, I walk away but not before Travis clasps my hand, I'm tugged back, his mouth drops to my ear and he sighs softly,

"If you want a lift home, I'm here, no funny business, just a lift okay." I look up and nod, why couldn't I fall for a guy like him. Not the likes of Jace Bennett with his unexplainable, emotional whiplash and controlling ways.

I stand watching Travis with his friends for a moment or two when Sean hooks an arm around my neck. "I'm taking you home, no arguing, and you're not going home with skinny legs."

"Skinny legs!" I chortle and snort, Travis actually has got skinny legs, well in comparison to Sean and Jace anyway. "God, unravel your frillies." I giggle and stagger past him and my subdued looking friend, I nudge her and she gives me a smile.

"You okay?" I mouth and she nods, I collect my bag and throw

Travis a wave goodbye, I hook arms with Cass as we exit into the biting cold.

"Holy crap," I whisper, the temperature has dropped. I huddle closer to Cass, desperate to share some of her body heat.

"Fuck," she chatters, my back goes rigid as the cold begins to seep in, through the chatter of teeth I barely hear Sean say my name, it's only when he takes my elbow in his hand, bringing me to a halt that I twist to look at him.

He looks sheepish all of a sudden, with my elbow still in his hand he rubs his neck with his free one. "Do me a favour," he sighs, his sudden unease so unusual that Cass steps forward. Is he angry that I didn't answer his call?

"What's wrong?" she whispers, my eyes are flitting from his to hers, then back to him, is this about skinny legs, I mean Trent . . . shit, Travis?

"Ah shit," he mumbles, he turns his gaze up the road and I follow as he says, "Give him a chance, Lil." My heart stutters to a stop and begins banging away heavily.

Him. Jace. He is leaning up against his car, a heavy coat around his bristling frame, he works his neck and I can tell it is taking every ounce of self-control for him to not walk to me.

"Sean, what's going on?" My eyes are on Jace, captured.

"He came to the bar." He clears his throat and knocks my chin back his way. "Not everyone is like your dad or Adam." My back stiffens and any other time I would throw Cass a vexed look for sharing such personal information but Sean holds me secure, my eyes though they drift back to the man waiting for me.

"We are all at risk of being hurt, difference is, you choose to hurt yourself before it's even begun." My shocked stare snaps back to his and he offers me a sympathetic smile, my chin wobbles briefly but I clear my own throat and find comfort in the knowledge that these two have displayed their full support, if everything goes south I know I'm in good hands.

"Aww Sean!" Cass coo's swooning further for him. Apparently, she has forgotten all about her hang up with the messages. Too used to squashing my feelings, I choose humor to show my thanks.

"So that's how you got her into bed." I drop a deadpan stare and he laughs loudly.

"That and a few other tricks." He quips as Cass walks into his arms.

"Sean is right." Cass smiles softly.

"About what, me or how he got you in bed?" I drawl, my eyes dart to the tall man watching intently a few meters up the dark road.

"Stop stalling," Cass snipes, before I can respond she looks up to Sean. "Take me home, I need feeding."

"Yes ma'am." He pecks her lips before tugging her away. "Goodnight, Lils." I barely muster a smile in return because my mind is occupied by someone else, I'm left standing watching them retreat, leaving me to make the one decision, I have been running full pelt from. Drawing in a deep breath I look back to find Jace still against his car, I was hoping he would have met me halfway, although I sense he is ensuring that this decision is wholly mine.

I've given him the run around that's for sure, sent us both into a tailspin and up on a high, before dropping him like a lead stone in a whirlpool and drawing in on myself.

I don't know who the hell I'm trying to kid. I'm falling in love with him. And it petrifies me completely.

He stares back at me down the street, watching, waiting. Silently willing me to walk his way, when I do, I shudder out a deep breath and swallow my nerves, forcing my drunken feet to take me to him.

There is no satisfied smile on his face or that trademark sparkle in his sap eyes, only burning lust and a touch of pain. Pain that I have caused. I swallow regretfully.

I stop in front of him and instinctively drop my gaze, too guilty to look at his face and claim blame for my actions. I open my mouth but swallow my words. When I lift my head, my eyes are swimming with tears and I manage a shrug of explanation for my behaviour.

Hands that were hooked in his coat slip free and pull me too him,

I fall forwards into his chest, my landing cushioned by his plush coat, my own arms go round his neck and just before our mouths touch he says quietly. "Thank fucking god Lily." I let out a soft sob, as he takes my mouth.

This is really happening— I'm throwing fear to the curb and jumping in feet first, ready to be hurtled along. I don't dwell on my guilt, it can wait for now. I mentally store it away for another moment, but not this one, I want to remember this exactly as it is. Skin to skin, breath-to-breath and deep whiskey eyes promising me the world.

Tenderness greets my tongue and I sink into the steady rhythm being set, the warm itch of a stray tear disappears down my face as I allow myself to accept what this is. This is real.

This is my nirvana.

"Don't ever do that to me again." He pleads, his eyes gentle but heavy with emotion, drawing in a sharp breath he holds me back so he can look down at me, his thumb catches the tear stain and he shakes his head. "Promise me Lily, I've been in hell." I nod my head, my movements jilted by the large hands cupping my face and the tangle of hair. My chin wobbles and I try my hardest to pull away to regain my composure but I'm held fast, glorious ambers flash at me. "I want it all, even those tears, don't hide from me anymore." I blink rapidly, holding the majority at bay but a defiant tear escapes and slips through my lashes, Jace dips and kisses it away, he holds his lips to my cheek, I feel his smile. "Admit you're crazy about me and I won't torment you about it for the rest of your life." He rasps.

I laugh out a sob, his intentions for us too beautiful. For some unfathomable reason this man wants me. He's chased me, wooed me, infuriated me and now he's caught me.

"So crazy," I croak out honestly, I look at his face, and melt when I see it stretched wide into a beaming grin.

I yelp as I'm suddenly turned and thrust up the car, my hands are flat to the cold metal but soon return to the brown mass crowning his gorgeous face, I moan low and adjust my position to allow him between my legs. He's rock hard and on a deliberate roll of his hips I gasp loudly. "I will take the tormenting now." I whisper plead. His lips tighten into a smile but he still kisses me thoroughly here in the cold, crisp air. My nose is no doubt the shade of the lipstick I'm still to reclaim back from this brute, with the privacy of his thick coat he shudders out a deep groan and runs his hand up my outer thigh, murmuring his approval when he hooks a deft finger around my damp knickers, he growls roughly. "I feel it's only fair that I inform you, that due to the inconvenience caused to myself as of late, I will be claiming this daily." He nips at my lips as thick lashed eyes pour into mine, then he slants a harsh kiss over my greedy mouth.

"Duly noted." I'm all breathless and pliable.

"Duly noted," he whispers, dropping a heavy-lidded gaze my way. His hands slip free and I'm slowly lifted away from the vehicle. Jace pulls the door wide and ushers me in, the door separates us as he motions me towards the warm sanctuary of his car on a soft wave of his hand. "Your man awaits."

"Still?" I exclaim. "The poor sod." I wince for affect and Jace coughs out a laugh.

"You owe me woman," he rolls out drily, watching as I lower myself unsteadily into his car and secure the belt through one eye. "And I will be accepting an advance for my troubles," he muses, I smirk softly as he holds my stare before swinging the door shut.

Chapter Seventeen

The drive is torturous and too long for my weakened nerves. Jace has put his foot down and we both sit in silence as the tension builds and builds, amping up our desire until it's leaking into the air, sending us crazed and edgy. I can practically taste his desire, it's *that* tangible. I shift in my chair and sap eyes flash to me knowingly, he doesn't speak but swallows deeply and tightens his grip on the wheel. I'm itching to relieve the feeling but can't bring myself to break the moment by saying anything.

I brace myself when we hit the end of his drive and his speed brings us to a slight skid. "Out Lily," he growls and I fumble for the handle, shuddering at his deep tone and the rush of icy air up my back as he exits the car, he's rounding the bonnet and I'm rushing to get out to meet him, I swing the door and groan when I'm jolted back, the seatbelt still wrapped around my front, I grasp at it, my eyes swinging between his and the clip.

"Jace," I plead for him to help me, ignoring his low chuckle, he drops to a fluid squat and unclips the buckle my breath is an uneven blow on his cheek. Slowly I lift my gaze and welcome the familiar pang in my groin.

My hand is taken with care and I'm eased to my feet, I wobble and remember how inebriated I am. I shake my hair away from my face and bring my chin up to look at him, he is smiling softly and I can't help but mirror it with my own, he leans in enough to knock the door shut then snags me up in his arms, rather than kiss me as I expected he begins to walk us to his home nestled in the dark, I drop my chin to his shoulder and watch his car slips into the night.

I clutch my legs tighter to hold myself up as he pushes his way in and presses a few buttons. A repetitive beep rings through the house and I lift my head in curiosity.

"New alarm system." He widens his eyes. "So I can keep track of your wandering arse," he quips, walking us straight to his bedroom. I'm wrapped delicately around him and allow myself to sink into his gaze.

"You know I could take offence to that, it may suggest my arse has begun to wander down south." I pout.

He laughs in response and shakes his head, squeezing the offending area, he groans and rocks his hips into mine. "No," he gasps. "Feels pretty damn fine to me."

Biting my lip, I close my eyes and let my head drop back slightly, a gentle, "oh." leaving my parched mouth.

"Oh indeed," he says gruffly, each step causing his hard shaft to gyrate against my sex, rather than drop me on the bed he takes to the mattress on his knees and topples on top of me, his mouth diving straight for mine. I hum happily and kiss him back, dipping my fingers into his hair and rocking my hips against his.

He draws back his jacket and it hits the floor with a muted thud, my clothes are removed quickly, my dress is gone in a fluid movement, my bra unclipped and flung over his shoulder, I whimper as his stubble runs across the sensitive peak and jolt when he dips to bite at my nipple. The slight sting is soothed by a soft wet kiss as he begins to remove my boots, then his fingers hook my knickers and I'm lifting my hips to allow him to remove them hassle free. "Jace, touch me," I beg, he grins and shakes his head, eyes bright with mischief and a haze I have become familiar with. Lust. Raw. Tangible lust.

My legs are hooked over his elbows and my arse is off the bed, I'm panting quietly, already clutching the quilt in preparation for the sensory overload.

"Are you finally read to hurtle along with me Lily?" He whispers, my eyes fly up to his. Hurtle? Yes please.

I flex my back in answer and cherish his smirk. "Admit defeat Lily, I've won you." his brow is raised and waiting for my agreement.

"No, I'm drunk and I don't want to say anything that can later be used in a court of law or bedroom floor." The words roll out of my dry, alcohol drenched mouth on a playful pout, I'm smirking and Jace has a shit eating grin on his face, his laughter is quiet but his amusement at my current state is plain as day. His beauty smacks me right in the chest and my heart gallops, leaving my feeling breathless.

"Kiss me," I flutter my lashes and wiggle my hips for good measure, he drops his chin so his lips are level with my ankle.

"Here?" he murmurs, dropping tiny kisses to my ankle bone then a little further, his mouth keeps moving, making gentle butterfly stroke kisses yet his eyes are on me, hot and heavy. "Or here?" His mouth connects with my knee and I bite my lip as a lick of heat greets my sex.

I groan, my head rolling away from him.

"Fucking hell Lily, you're so damn wet!" My eyes roll back to find his trained on my sex.

"Yes." I purr and wriggle. I want him *there.*

His groan is loaded with frustration, one minute he is there and the next he is gone, swiftly moving away from me, my head flies up and I rest on my elbows to watch him. "Where are you going?"

He cocks his head and blows out a stream of breath, his eyes betraying his actions and dropping to my naked form. "Nowhere." He swallows as his ambers drop to the dark place between my thighs. "Let me get you some water, then we can sleep." He strides off, purpose in every footfall and a light curse leaving his mouth.

What the hell!

Sleep? Since when do we just sleep? I'm still sat dumfound in his bed when he returns, the glass in his hand clinking like all those nights ago. Silently I watch him undress until he is gloriously naked and sporting a stutter worthy hard on. And he wants to sleep? He must clock my confused look because he begins to chuckle, softly.

"She's thinking," he muses, I watch him scoot round the side of the bed and drop the water on the bedside, I drag the quilt up covering my naked form and frown in annoyance. This is what he does— confuse the utter shit out of me, with his swing ball actions.

"Is this my punishment?" I swat his hand away, when he tucks a matted strand back from my face.

He laughs, knocking my hand back. "The opposite." He leans in and brushes his lips purposefully over mine. "This is me showing you the other side to us." My head jerks back and I'm staring up into those deep eyes.

"Other side?" I whisper, my eyes falling to the pull of his lips.

"Eyes up Lily." They do as they are bid, I ignore the small twitch of his lips. "Yes, the other side, there is no question we have chemistry." The finger that had tidied my hair is back but now it is running along my collarbone, he smiles to himself on a little shake of his head. "You make me pretty basic, with you my head is constantly in the gutter, I've never felt this *need* with anyone before," he confesses roughly, his forehead creases. "I crave that as much as I do you," he adds, his husky voice dropping to a more gravelly tone.

My hand is shaky when I cup his face. "And that's a bad thing because? I like this side of us," I whine hotly.

"Because you need more than sex, and I just need you." Dammit if the man didn't just cause my heart to seize in my chest, I let out a shudder of a breath and a strangled sigh, he lets me press my mouth to his but only so he can topple us back and hold me flat to the mattress. "The next time I'm inside you, it'll be when you're sober." He pecks my nose and rolls off, only to tuck me in his side.

I open my mouth to argue, but his hands swan round one to my breasts the other down below and his big body slots against mine as he says on a soft command. "Sleep."

I sleep late and let out a dull groan as I come round, my eyes pull tight before I can bring myself to open them and fully register how bad of a hangover I have, I push my face into the soft space under my arm and breathe in the smell of Jace, it's an achingly familiar comfort.

My mouth is dry and I attempt several swallows before I twist round and force my sensitive eyelids open, I'm not even all the way over when my arms snap to a stop, only then do I sense the tightness around my wrists I jiggle my arms feeling them locked together and strained above my head. "What the hell!" Blinking through what feels like a week's worth of makeup, I lift my head to find a tie hooked and twisted between my wrists before it disappears behind the cushions. "Jace?" I croak, my voice a quick reminder of how fragile I feel.

"Yes?" His voice is soft, cautious, my achy head lifts and I find him sat watching me from the wide chair. His hands are caught together and his elbows rested on his knees, gently he works his thumb back and forth over his lips. He looks mighty serious and that bothers me more than my current predicament.

"Jace?" I whisper, throwing a quick observation at my entrapped hands. When I lift my chin to look down my naked body, I find him fighting a perplexed smile.

I chew my lip in concern, seeing the turbulent storm rolling across his dark gaze, I tug my arms, huffing out a tired breath when I realise, I can't get free. "What's going on, what are you doing?" I whisper, not sure I'm ready for the answer.

"Well," he laughs playfully, I have a strange suspicion by asking I have played right into his hands, although I observe on a tilt of my head there's an edge of disbelief in his voice, as though he can't quite believe he has tied me to his bed. "It would seem as of late," he carries on, lifting his lithe frame from the chair and giving me a full frontal of his beautiful body, I drag my eyes over his thick thighs and narrow waist, I linger there too long and breathe low when his body reacts to mine, my eyes rise up his body slowly until I'm at his face. "As of late," he says around a cough getting my full attention. "I haven't had much luck with a certain woman, past experience has led me to believe that by night." He is hovering over the end of the bed and cuffs one of my ankles, tugging me as far as the tie will allow, I grunt softly at the tightness and pant as his eyes find their way to my thighs, I bite my lip and inch my legs apart for him, his grin is pure filth and he smirks up at me. "By night she is a willing participant, but by morning." He knocks my legs back together and cocks a brow. "Poof she is gone." He angles his head, looking at me with a lifted brow.

"Oh, how terrible for you," I gasp, my lips twitch but I manage to force them into a feigned O.

"I think so." A large hand smoothes over his flat stomach and my traitorous eyes follow the movement before I peel them away again. It's only as I'm staring up into his face that I recognise the dull, deep ache at the base of my skull. I frown and Jace drops his weight to a knee so he can lean in and take my chin in a choke-like hold. "You okay?" I blink trying to decipher the level of headache I'm dealing with. "Feeling sick?" I shake my head, no I don't, and it's more than I deserve, I have well and truly been burning the candle at both ends, plus a little more in the middle with this brute. I'm burnt out.

"Tired." I offer. "Slight headache." His hand roams, a smooth thumb glides over my lips and I kiss the soft pad before it moves across my cheek, wide fingers delve into my hair and he is nudging his way between my thighs.

With my hands locked above my head, I haven't much movement up top. I lift my chin silently, asking him to kiss me. Instead of closing my eyes when his face drifts down to mine, I lock my gaze with his own.

Keeping himself just out of reach, he smiles down at me, his golden gaze taking in every inch of my face. After last night's antics, I should feel self-conscious. I'm in no doubt that I look a mess.

"You feel it," he whispers, his fingers massaging that achy patch at the back of my head.

I drag in a deep breath through my nose, unlike before when he says such things to me, this time I hold his gaze. "Yes." I lick my lips. "I feel it." I feel him. His large hard frame pushing into my body, the gentle prod of his cock at my sex, my chin lifts off its own accord, silently begging for connection.

He drives in on a slow, deep thrust, my mouth drops open at the beautiful intrusion. "Tell me you're crazy for me Lily." The intense heat and pressure in my womb has my neck arching, I blindly register his rush of words, the brush of his tongue up my throat, before he is withdrawing and hurtling us forward on a sexy grunt. I grip the material tethered to the bed and bring my knees up to wrap around his waist. Jace's mouth slams to mine and we're kissing in a frenzy, his hips moving in slow, harsh drives.

Drawing out the strokes and savouring it all. His kiss slows mirroring his hips and I match him. "Harder," I moan as I sense the ache flourish in my womb, I want him to catch it and make me let go.

"Dammit Lily!" He rises to his hands and slams in hard, his eyes darkening with each thrust, his face is set in concentration as he hurtles us both along.

"Oh, god!" I cry as heat curls and licks in my womb, Jace is relentless pushing me higher up the bed. "Kiss me!" I know I must look desperate I can feel it in the set of my face, the burn of emotion in my eyes his mouth becomes more urgent on mine.

He grunts, "Yes." His hand takes both of mine and he slams up so hard my eyes fly open. Inexcusable, deep, harsh drives have me gasping loudly, lips parted I can't even manage a moan through the punishing blows. Jace is stretched above me, his arms kept high as he holds me secure to the bed.

"Oh please, now!" I shout as everything folds in and dances at the base of my spine, "Ja-!" I cry, I can't formulate a thought or word, the sensation is too much, too harsh, too perfect.

"You're close," he growls, his brows furrow as his eyes darken, turning more honey thick yet just as bright, my gaze is fixed on them, my hips rolling to meet each hit of his.

"Yes." I sound in pain, this is too much, a deep ache that I know will bloom and flow into the most exquisite pleasure. "Harder!" I want more.

"Fuck!" He snaps, rearing back and Slam! My mouth opens but nothing comes out. Sweat is dampening his hair into a slight curl, his shoulders glisten, and all I can see is pure perfection moving above me in measured, deep strokes. Our skin is touching almost everywhere from the rough brush of his legs against mine to the tight grip of his hands, and where I can't feel him I can smell him, that musky smell that I have craved since we first met.

My breathing becomes erratic and Jace's eyes watch me with intent. "Fuck Lily, together," he groans, rolling his hips out and slamming back in, his roar of pleasure tips me over the edge until I'm jerking gently below him and crying out my release.

Jace slams his mouth to mine catching my guttural wail, his tongue dashing in and swallowing it away, his own body pulsing above me as he swears against my lips. "So fucking crazy about you," he chokes out, dropping his weight to me and thrusting up to get the last bit of pleasure.

"Untie me," I whisper, I want to hold him. I expect him to move, but he uses his position to unravel the tie. When he realises it won't budge, he pushes back onto his heels in a fluid movement, pulling himself clean out, and I gasp at the sudden withdrawal of pressure.

"I need scissors," he states, quickly scooting me up the bed to relieve the tight pull on my wrists. I watch his arse retreat and sigh as my heartbeat hammers away in my chest— I swallow the dryness in my throat and force myself to take slow even breaths.

My hangover is an afterthought chased away by the man with the golden eyes. I smirk to myself. "Something funny?" The bed dips and Jace holds my hands still as he begins to cut through the expensive material.

"No, just happy," I murmur, Jace drops a look at me and smiles in return, as soon as the weight around my wrists disperses I wrap myself around him fully, arms, legs and push my body into his so our skin is flush. He hums out at deep sigh, the scissors clatter on the side and he rolls us so I am straddling his lap my cheek flush to his chest, I enjoy the languid strokes running back and forth along my back as I stare out the window, it's so serene and vastly beautiful, I imagine in the summer this places is cocooned in greenery and thick with flowers.

"What are you thinking?" his deep voice rumbles through his chest and mine absorbs it.

"How pretty it must be in the summer." Jace jostles me enough that I bring my head round and up onto my hand for support, he is watching me intently, his hair a dark mess on his gorgeous face.

"Soon enough you can see for yourself, are you hungry?" I smirk and peck his lips.

"Very." I grin.

"The lady is hungry," he comments, wrapping himself further around me to lift and remove me from the bed. He hits the floor with even, determined strides. I'm all too happy to be suspended in his arms and wrap myself around his athletic frame. Skin on skin.

My sigh is indulgent. I'm too embarrassed to consider why I fought this for so long. I watch his bed move further away, through into the living area where I briefly admire the low sofa arrangement and suspended fireplace. Circling the kitchen island, he walks us to the fridge and sweeps the door open, cool air wisps up my naked back and I thrust myself into Jace's body on a laugh.

He's already smirking, happy with this little stunt before he is sweeping his tongue into my mouth, I groan and cup his bristly face. "I'm hungry," I remind him, tugging on his hair, his hands are braced either side the open fridge, leaving me to hold myself afloat.

He bites my lower lip. "I have every intention of filling you up," he groans, lifting his gaze from my lip to my sparkling eyes.

"Food. I need actual food." I'm smiling happily at him— too close to fight the visceral reaction he has on me, I cup his jaw and kiss him hard. The coolness is making the hairs on my body stand up, I wiggle into him further, trying to draw heat, he kisses me slowly and pulls back on a contented sigh.

"I'm a lucky bastard," he murmurs, his hands run down to my arse so he can roll them over the small globes, which he does on a groan. "I honestly thought I had lost you, Lily." My gaze is a little sad and with a soft smile I bring my hand up to his face and peck his mouth.

"You've got me now." I whisper, my breath shudders out. "I hurt us, I'm sorry." My eyes are riveted on his stubble-adorned chin.

I'm a coward, I can't yet bring myself to look in his face and admit that. This is still so new. I want this. Him. Us. But first I need to take a few baby steps.

"We'll get to the bottom of that another time," he says soft but stern, there's no room for argument, he wants the grit and dirt, my past. I don't think I'm ready to lay myself bare just yet.

"I have my own questions," I say in response. Neve mainly. I give him a small lift of my brow suggesting as much but refuse to acknowledge it any more right now, I drop my head on his shoulder. "My butt is cold," I whine.

Silently he fills his hands with ingredients and drops them to the side, I'm placed carefully on the island, the cool marble making me flinch on a hiss.

"Cold, baby?" he smirks, pinching my nipple. My foot whips out to catch his naked arse as he strolls around to get tableware out.

"Want any help?" I ask shyly, very aware I'm sat butt naked in a house wrapped entirely in glass.

"No, do you want a jumper?" he is wielding a spatula in his hands and takes the opportunity to swat my naked flesh with it, I cry out and grasp my breast.

"An all in one suit preferably," I pout at him and he slaps his palm threatening worse.

"Never going to happen." He rebuffs and walks over to push his way in, he tugs me forwards and takes my nipple that I thrust into his mouth. "I need full access at all times." He sucks hard and I gasp. "It's detrimental to my health," he says around a mouthful of boob.

Laughing, I push him away. "Detrimental, my arse. Yes, to a jumper, please."

Big arms cover my goose freckled flesh. "Are you sure I don't keep you hot enough?"

"You're insatiable, you have a problem!" I yank the spatula and slap his peck.

"Playing dirty, Miss Spencer?" He leans in and licks the edge of my mouth.

"You wish."

"Oh, I do." He walks away, winking when my greedy eyes fall below his navel. I watch him back up with open appreciation and decide it's another thing I adore about him. His open masculinity and obvious comfort in his own skin.

Jace has pulled on a pair of boxers and holds out a thick hooded jumper, I pull it on and find myself swallowed whole by the garment. On a laugh Jace hooks the hood back and rolls the sleeves, dropping a kiss to my nose, he looks over me and says, "I hope your parents aren't going to be as hard to win over as you?" Hands wrap around by bum and he rests himself so he is level with my face, I swallow and run my fingers through his hair, flicking a look away.

"No, it's only me, so," I don't quite know how to finish that so I shrug as I add, "No." his eyes hold mine forever and he nods my words over, as though he is putting two and two together, possibly answering some questions of his own.

"Sorry to hear it," he murmurs on a sympathetic frown, he takes my hand and kisses my wrist, then my temple.

"It's okay." It is, my mum has been gone for nearly eight years now, I miss her, of course I do, but I have accepted that no amount of thoughts or heartfelt wishes will bring her back, and my father, well I prefer it this way.

"All the more reason to spoil you rotten." His smile is gentle. "Do you want bacon this time?" He rescues the discarded spatula and moves away, I had wanted to ask about his own parents but the quick turn of conversation has me holding my tongue, my mind though is running on all cylinders, I have no doubt he has his own skeletons.

"Yes please." I could sit and admire the view but slip off the surface and turn on the radio, it quiets my brain for now. "Where do you keep the coffee?" I wonder pulling a few cupboards open and coming up short, I need caffeine!

"Am I neglecting you?" He smirks and takes my hand, I grin and let myself be pulled along.

"That depends," I murmur.

"On what?" He pulls open a cupboard revealing a variation of coffees, Jace grabs the nearest and turns to me, awaiting a response.

"On whether we are talking about coffee or not?" I smirk.

"Lily your legs are still trembling." He is smug as hell. "You neglect to mention that." I roll my eyes and grab the coffee ignoring his deep laugh. I fill up the coffee machine and resume my place on the stool as Jace starts throwing things in a pan.

"Stay here tonight?" He keeps his face averted, his hands busy on his task but his shoulders are tense and I know that's because he is bracing himself for my excuse, my initial reaction hits my gut making me want to head home but I force it aside.

"Okay." Jace nods and I watch him visibly relax slipping from my seat I pad to him and wrap my arms around his waist, pressing my cheek to his warm back. "I need to pick some things up from home," I say, I press a kiss to his back, my fingers brushing across his taut stomach, hoping to dispel his unease. I've caused that and I feel shit for it.

"Sure, let me feed you then we can shower and head to the city." He lifts my hand and kisses the knuckle. "Lily," he says softly.

"Yes?" my cheek is firm to his back, his heart beat a constant source of calm, and with his lips grazing my skin I feel content.

"Always tell me how you're feeling, so I can fix it." I frown against the solid wall of muscle in front of me, I move in the hope seeing his face will help me gage his thoughts but he holds my hands, so I'm flush to him.

"What do you mean?"

"Don't run again." Big hands blanket mine, they shift so they are placed over the heavy drum of his heart. "Feel that?" His voice is a deep rumble, so serious and gentle in the same breath. He's the perfect mix of manliness. He is surprisingly passionate in and out of the bedroom, he isn't afraid to feel and that's what I struggle with. Feeling.

I force any habitual unease aside. "Yes." I flatten my hands, splaying my fingers so each thud vibrates through to my very fingertips, the steady drum a repetitive base in my ear. "I feel it." My chest is squished to his back and I know he must feel my own elevated heart rate.

"It's yours." It's a confession that makes my soul soar and my eyes prick with hot tears, I nod my head, jerkily trying to hold the tears at bay, he lets out a ragged breath and I want to look up in those eyes, but this moment is too prefect to alter, I stay still and dot kisses all over his back.

I know Jace has his own skeletons. We all do. Reluctantly I contemplate that Neve possibly knows them too and that is why they are close. Because they are more than colleagues, instinct tells me that much.

I'm not the jealous type, but that woman is like sandpaper to my skin, I don't trust her, or like her particularly. Her presence in my mind is sour and unwanted, I force her away and squeeze Jace a little harder, my hand drifts lower until it is brushing the top on his straining boxers. "And this?" I whisper, my tongue peeking out to meet his skin, my hand grazing the hard bulge.

"Yours, from the moment you flashed angry eyes at me." I grin against him and sigh. "Anything before you doesn't exist." He says quietly, his sigh is deep and long, but I figure that's because I'm working him through the thin barrier, "I'm going to burn your food," he drawls, I give him a final hard squeeze, drawing a deep groan before stepping away and collecting our coffees and hopping back on my stool, when I look up narrowed eyes are trained on me.

"I will get you back." He uses the spatula to enforce his words.

"I know." I state deliberately, "I can't wait." Jace's smile is slow and sexy. I bite my lip and drop my chin to my hand, as I lean and watch him from the comfort of the island.

He is quick to serve up, presenting me with a fluffy omelet. "This looks great," I muse forking some in my mouth, as soon as I swallow, I grin at him. "You're a really good cook," I say truthfully.

"It's an omelet," he says slowly, I turn my nose away.

"Yes, well, my omelets usually cement themselves to the pan," I mutter as an arm swoops around, hooking me at the neck, and I'm thrust into his face so he can kiss me on a smile.

"Please don't tell me I landed myself with a shitty cook?"

"You pig!" I laugh and kiss him hard. "I can cook," I whine, knowing full well I am usually too distracted and end up burning the contents of any pan.

"I think you're lying," he whispers.

The cheek of him, I refuse to admit my lack of culinary skills. "Think what you want, I can cook, and I can-"

"Fuck." Jace has a shit-eating grin on his face— I cough at his lack of tact and cover his mouth with my hand, ending any further obscenities from leaving his throat.

"Ever the romantic," I hum, my own eyes twinkling playfully, he nips at my finger and I snatch my hand away.

"Eat up, I'm ready for my payback." I press my lips together and my thighs. Me too.

We make our way up to my flat, as we stop at my door Jace runs his hand under my bum to my sex, I wince and his ambers dance with satisfaction, "When we get back, we can soak in the bath?" He offers by way of apology.

"Promise?"

"Deal." He winks and pushes us into my place. It's nice and

warm inside. "Do you want a drink?" I ask moving to the kitchen, Jace is hot on my heels.

"No." He stops me in my tracks and draws me back towards my bedroom. "No distractions get your things Lily."

"How is tea a distraction?" I scoff.

"When it keeps me from you all slippery and wet, it's a distraction," he states matter-of-factly, I roll my eyes to the back of my head and begin collecting up a few items for work tomorrow, I ask Jace to find me a bag and as he wanders off, I quickly put the lacy garment I purchased with Cass into my oversized handbag.

I'm unhooking a black knee length dress from my wardrobe when he returns, a large weekend bag in his hands, he opens it wide for me to roll my dress and place it in, I pick up some heels and drop them in too, I rush around the room collecting toiletries, perfume, underwear and a few pieces of jewelry.

"Anything else?" he smirks.

"Actually yes, I need my camera and some work files." I rise onto my toes and peck his lips as I pass.

"Meet me for lunch tomorrow?" He says as I wander back through to the living room.

"I have to check my diary but it shouldn't be a problem," I say absently as I grab a few files and my camera equipment, Jace is already waiting by the door, it occurs to me that I said I would already meet Cass.

"Actually, Tuesday would be better, Cass and I are having lunch."

"And I can't come because?"

"Because she will want to talk about you," I say openly. Jace laughs to himself and watches as I fill the last few things into my handbag. "I'm ready."

"Good, let's go."

"You're in a hurry!" I smirk, juggling my bags.

"Such a smart arse."

"You like my arse," I say over my shoulder on a purr.

"Oh, Miss Spencer I do, very much so." He closes the door and does a quick check of the hallway. "Especially when it's sky high and begging for my touch." I flush bright red, doing my own quick survey of the hall.

"Shush!" I garble embarrassed.

"Come on, I have a bath that needs some occupancy."

Chapter Eighteen

The sun is still trying to break through the clouds, it's dull and miserable outside, not that you would think so, given Cass is striding towards me with gym pants, a training bra and some form of a t-shirt that looks over stretched and showing way too much skin, winter attire it is not. Her hair is a nest of blonde curls on her head and she is carrying two coffee cups. "Morning!" She beams at me, it's past noon but I don't correct her. Two oiled up fitness enthusiasts jog past, one cranes his neck to check out my friend, his smile wider than the feet of the bench I'm currently sitting on, I give her a pointed look nodding my head for her to look over her shoulder, she does grinning wickedly at them, I haven't spoken to her since our spontaneous night out.

I clear my throat and eye her cautiously. "So?" I edge carefully, Cass drops down gracefully and thrusts my coffee into my hand, she groans in embarrassment.

"Please don't, I feel such a twat, I literally went from zero to psycho in ten seconds flat," she huffs back, so she is reclined on the cold bench.

"You weren't that bad." I muse nicely, I mean she was pretty crabby, she throws me an ill-disguised look, and I nod. "Okay you went kind of crazy." My lower lip pulls down at one side, and she snorts out a laugh.

"Stupid man still wants me." She shakes her head.

"Of course, he does. He loves you, Cass, and I think old insecurities rushed to the surface."

"Rushed. Ha!" She barks out. "More like chain-sawed their way out my skull." She mimics a knife-baring psycho and I throw my head back on a laugh.

"Sasha still alive, I hope," I say as I blow into my cup, the steam gloss's my face and Cass adjusts her position as if the mention of Sasha causes her discomfort.

"Unfortunately, although Sean put her straight, I mean she is a hard worker, she is never late, is always covering last minute." It's obvious she is repeating Sean. "I can't expect him to fire her, I want him too, but I couldn't ask that of him." She whines dramatically. "He has told her to back off."

"Well sounds as though things are okay?"

"Yes." She sighs reaffirming that to herself. "We spoke a lot about our previous relationship, his cheating, the girls, how that has caught up with me, he was pretty honest which I didn't like, *way* too much detail." She visibly shudders and I give her a sympathetic smile. "But I'm glad we are both finally on the same page." She smiles, slowly, knowingly and I frown.

"So definitely all good then?" I ask not too sure how to take her comments.

"Mmm-hmm." She glances at me sideways, her lips suppressing a wide smile and I incline my head.

"Okay what are you not telling me?" I twist, facing her full-on, and her face breaks out into a megawatt smile. Her excitement is tangible and I find myself smiling already.

"He wants us to move in together!" She squeals and sloshes her coffee over the side so that scolding water drenches her gym wear. "Oh shit, oww!" She stands quickly, her face twisted in discomfort.

"Oh fuck. Ow. Ow!" She is up in a flash pulling at her leggings trying to lessen the burn, I laugh until tears slip from my eyes. "Help me!" She laughs, but I can't I'm gone.

"I'm sorry are you okay?" I cough through my silent laughter.

"Fat lot of help you are!" She sniffs and sits back down, poised as ever.

"You think it's too soon?" Her fingers are still working the wet fabric.

"If you had only just met him probably, but you've known him years, there is so much history you're practically married as it is." I waft her concern away— she hums this over and smiles.

"You're right." Happy with herself, she relaxes next to me and sips her drink. The wind catches my hair, so I twist it tight and hold it still. "I know we aren't perfect, but what couple is. Plus, I would take a thousand fights with Sean over not having him at all," she states with conviction.

"I'm glad everything has worked out, Cass." I mean it, he is good for her.

"Well, enough about me. How is the superhuman?" She smirks at me over her cup and I grin slowly. "Ah, that good then?"

"It's only been a few hours." I laugh.

"Oh bollocks, you have been his since that first meet." She wiggles her perfect brows.

"I guess so." I smile, thinking back to seeing him first through my lens then in the flesh. I let out a long sigh. "I want this to be it," I say anxiously.

"I know, but no relationship is perfect all the time, so allow him his mistakes and you yours," she says, lifting her cup to take a swig.

"Shame you couldn't take that advice yourself last week." I laugh as she swats me, telling me to piss off.

"But I mean it, don't compare him to the other males in your life," she says, going as far as to point her expertly manicured finger in my face.

"I know, what works for others won't work for us and visa versa."

"Enjoy yourself but don't take any shit." She winks and we knock coffee cups. Cass leans back and looks out across the busy park. "Have you got a class later?" She wonders. Oh shit, I had forgotten about it, and I inwardly blame Jace for my mental absence.

"Yes, a one on one with Grant." I need to text Jace and let him know I will be late.

"How's it going?" She murmurs, her attention fixed on the wet fabric on her legs.

"Good. I feel so much better since starting, although after the other week, I feel a little off-kilter," I admit. Seeing Adam was like a heavy slap in the face with a wet plank of wood.

"Oh, I doubt Adam will show his face again. Sean has put a price on his head!" She snorts, but after hearing about Sean's past, I worry she isn't joking. When she sees my face, she laughs loudly. "It's a joke . . . well, sort of. Sean's staff know not to let him in." She wafts my concern away.

"Can he do that?" I chew at my nail.

"It's his bar, I don't see why not." She shrugs.

"I just meant, doesn't he need a legitimate reason to not let him in?"

"You have a restraining order on the guy, that's legit enough, Lil." I drop my gaze and frown down at my hands. And there it is, that vital nugget of information I can't quite bring myself to admit to Jace.

"We've got you covered, Lily." She rubs my back and I lift my head enough to smile at her. I believe her and Sean.

"Thanks." Her phone buzzes and she stands to retrieve it from god knows where.

"I got to go. Call me later so I know you're alright." She is looking down at me with a mix of sympathy and worry.

"I'm fine," I say.

"Well, you look green at the mention of you know who."

"He's not *Voldemort*." I laugh, thinking I'd rather have had a relationship with snake-face than Adam Burrows.

"He could have fooled me." She winks and I smile after her.

I head back to the Loft to find Harriet grinning like an idiot. "You okay?" I say, looking around at whatever has got her all in a fluster. She ducks behind the desk and lifts a bouquet of flowers.

"Oh, they're stunning," I say, moving over to read the pocket-size envelope propped in the leaves.

'2am is my favourite part of the day, the world is quiet and it is just us for a while.'

My heart stops and does that unusual thing where it shudders to a start again. I am so in love with this man. "You're all goofy happy!" Harriet sings. I laugh but keep my face averted. She is right— I'm euphoric and it's all because of one man and his gorgeous eyes.

I pick the flowers up and take them down to my office, thinking that two a.m. doesn't do the bags under my eyes any favours, but being made love to hard into the night certainly has its advantages. I place them carefully on my desk and dig around for my phone, firing a quick message to Jace.

I love my flowers. 2am is ours! I will be later than I said, about 8pm, L x

No sooner have I sent the message and put my phone down, it is dancing across my desk. Jace's name flashes on the screen, so I put him on loudspeaker. "You have a way with words, Mr. Bennett," I say by way of hello. I smile, thinking of his little note.

"You don't," he huffs. "Why will you be late?" I laugh inwardly and get more comfortable in my chair.

"I have a class at six-thirty. I completely forgot about it." I rifle through some papers but find myself reading his note again.

"Class?" he sounds perplexed.

"Yes, at the gym," I elaborate.

"Care to offer up any more information?" I laugh freely now. The man is a ticking time bomb.

"Why would I? It's the gym, I go every Monday." I sit back and take Jace off speaker as I hear Harriet headed down towards my office.

"So, you go to the gym on a Monday." He seems irritated by that fact.

"Is that a problem?" I question, smirking at his lack of appeal to my social life. Harriet slips in and places my coffee down along with some mail. I mouth 'thanks' as I hear Jace exit his car.

"Lots of sweaty men around you, now why would that bother me?" I can hear the note of laughter in his voice.

"It doesn't. I'm glad we cleared that up," I quip, all too happy with how this conversation has gone.

He groans so low I barely hear him. "Woman, you're going to send me grey." His laugh is deep and I can imagine him now checking his reflection for said grey hairs.

"I'll be at yours for eight. I'll grab some wine on the way."

"Be safe," he warns.

"I will. See you later." I grin into the receiver.

"Bye, beautiful," he murmurs, and I swoon to the floor and back again. I pick myself up enough to read through the mail and make a quick call to the bank. Harriet is nipping out on her lunch, so I head up front and sort through my emails.

"Do you want anything?" She asks.

"No, thanks." I offer her a quick smile and continue to sort through my junk mail.

I have a call scheduled with another gallery owner, Talia, at two-thirty. It's a while off yet, so I enjoy my coffee and watch the world pass by outside.

I jab twice and then throw an uppercut as my opponent and instructor, Grant, nods. "Good, good, again." I don't quit. I push myself until my body aches and I'm shaking, sweat trickling a soft pattern down my neck. I try not to watch the slow, steady tick of the clock when I'm being physically challenged. "Again, Lily!" He shouts, urging me to pull from my reserve and fight harder. Gritting my teeth through the exhausting strain, I force myself to jab, clip, and kick as instructed. My muscles are screaming at me to stop and my legs shake, but I keep going until I'm out of breath and nausea is tapping an unwelcome hand on my shoulder.

The gym is in an old warehouse. From the outside, it looks rundown and abandoned, but inside is a shock of modern workout machines and technology. After an hour of heavy training, Grant throws my water bottle at me and I only just manage to catch it. "You did good, Lily. Really pushed yourself." He nods, satisfied. "Have a drink, we'll stretch, then do a little cardio?" *Cardio? More?*

I nod because I can barely catch my breath, and I drop my head forwards between my legs whilst I try to allow my breathing to calm and centre myself. In . . . out, in . . . out, I breathe the mantra in and let go of it all as I breathe out.

I joined the gym after my break-up with Adam, needing a new form of focus. When they advertised self-defence classes, I was the first to sign up. Grant works alongside a group of instructors, but once a month I have a one-to-one, although this is my second this month. After bumping into my ex at Finnegan's, I realised how unprepared I am.

We do a little cardio and stretch, nothing heavy, just light exercise to bring my heartbeat back to normal. "So, he's back." Grant's taut arms are rested on the end of the treadmill as he points at me. "You know you can handle yourself. Don't let your initial reaction to him knock you down. It was always going to be a shock." Grant wipes his forehead and looks at me empathetically.

"I know. I wish I had smashed my palm into his nose," I growl. He hits the stop button and I slow until I'm standing on shaky legs. Never have I wished to see my ex so bad, even if it is to throat punch him!

"He is back for a reason, and not a good one. Be prepared, Lily, but don't get angry, remember that." With a deep breath, I let my frustration go. I know Grant is right, but the underlying tension at Adam's sudden appearance has trepidation lurking in my system.

"I'll be back next week," I tell him, hopping off.

"Sure thing." We walk towards the changing rooms and I grab my things up quickly, favouring a shower at Jace's rather than here, and leave. I thank Grant as I pass him on my way out.

"Bye, Lily!" I lift my towel as I go and walk straight into Jace kitted out in a dark suit.

"Oomph." I laugh, happily surprised, as he grabs at my arms to steady me. His eyes fly over my shoulder to Grant and the training room at the back.

"When you said class, I wasn't expecting this?" He frowns and chews his lip. "Why are you taking self-defence?" He takes my bag and hooks my towel over the top before swinging it onto his back.

I shrug, trying to avoid the topic. "It's sensible." I don't want Jace to see me as a victim and I certainly don't want to rehash my past, not with him. I want to move on and be done with it. Crazy to think only a few weeks ago I was running from this man, yet today I truly see a future with him.

He gives me a soft smile. "You've been holding out on me, Miss Spencer?" He ducks to press a soft kiss on my mouth and pulls back to eye me expectantly.

Oh, shit, here come the questions. "I have?" I know I have, but I'm not admitting that to him. Adam is in the past and he's staying in the past.

"Yes." His eyes darken and drop to my chest strapped tight in my gym clothes, then further to my leggings. "I expect more foul play in the future." His hand skims the side of my breast. I suck in a breath to disguise a moan as his finger runs over my pebbled nipple.

I hear his meaning loud and clear, though my smirk is hidden as I drop my chin and reposition myself so no one can see where his hand is. "Duly noted," I whisper.

He groans, pulling me close and dropping his mouth to mine. "You, Lily Spencer, are going to get me arrested for indecent exposure."

"Don't blame me. You chose to walk in here with your big cock begging to get free," I scoff into his mouth, his head drops back on a deep laugh. When he looks back, his eyes are molten and syrupy.

"I wasn't expecting the miniscule get-up." He twangs my leggings and I wrap my arms around his neck. Taking advantage, I nip his ear, causing him to growl low. "Lily," he warns.

"It's a gym. What did you expect, straight jackets and hazmat suits?" I scoff, pressing myself that bit too hard into his desperate groin.

"Now that's an idea." He flashes me a dark look. "We're leaving," he hisses. I'm turned quickly and kept at his front as he thrusts us out the main doors and to his car. I'm left to get in as he quickly gets behind the wheel, throwing my gym bag into the back. I strap myself in and relax back in the chair as he adjusts himself in the seat, throwing me a dirty look as the evidence of his discomfort outlines a huge bulge in his suit trousers. I stifle a laugh and look out the window into the street lit night. The cold air lingers for a minute and Jace drags off his jacket, handing it to me. "Put it on, it's cold." I do as I'm told, undoing my belt and replacing it just as quickly.

"How did you know which gym I go to?" It only occurred to me now that I never told him.

"Followed you." There is no shame in his statement.

"You don't trust me?" I know I don't believe those words because I would be angrier, but I'm intrigued.

"I do," he affirms. I'm certain he isn't completely sure why he followed me. He shrugs as he steers us around a corner. "I guess I wanted to know more about you." He speaks slowly, still mentally trying to fathom his actions.

"And?" I laugh lightly. "Do you know more about me?" I ask, as my eyes find his and they are dancing with pleasure.

"I think I'm getting there, just peeling the layers back, Miss Spencer," he quips on a low drawl. His eyes fall to my tight gym top, before he casts his eyes back to the road, leaving me feeling all hot and fuzzy.

Jace takes a call for most of the ride from some man called Viktor, but I zone out when they start chatting about port fees and landed costs. "Viktor, I'll call you first thing. Something's come up." My eyes fall to the offending object.

"Sure thing," he rings off and Jace swings the car down the gravel lane to his closeted home. I lick my lips and throw him a subtle look, but he is gripping the steering wheel as though his life depends on it. As soon as we hit the drive, he hits the brakes and he is out the door. I'm already unclipping my own belt and pushing free as he circles the bonnet, his eyes full of heated intent.

His hands are reaching for me as I swing the door shut and launch myself into his arms, our lips fusing and he is growling out a curse around my tongue. I envelope him and rub myself shamefully against his cock, moaning low when I get the kind of friction I require.

"Jace," I pant, willing him to rush us inside, but to my delight, he walks back a few paces, drops me to my feet, and spins me. I'm flattened to the heated bonnet. My toes barely holding me up as deft hands make quick work of my leggings and underwear. I suck in a lungful of air as it wisps around my bare skin and gasp when his mouth thrusts up between my thighs. My legs are dragged as far apart as they can go, and I push back as his tongue makes contact with my slick folds. "Oh god," I sob softly. Slowly, he drags his tongue from one point to the other and I buckle on a muted cry.

"Dammit, Lily," he growls, kissing over my cheeks. Every nerve ending rushes to join that one spot and it all drops away when he moves.

"No," I moan. His chuckle is deep, but he gives me what I want when his fingers replace his mouth. Gently, he glides his fingers in and out his tongue and mouth running over the sensitive spot below my hip.

"You smell incredible." He breaths harshly, twisting his fingers so my eyes flash wide and my legs lose consciousness. His teeth sink into my arse and my orgasm rushes up to meet it. I scream.

"Fucking, fuck, woman!" He grunts and then he is there, driving in on a harsh blow before pulling out to the tip and slamming back in.

"Yes!" I cry. I brace myself on the bonnet as Jace drives back in on a strangled moan.

"Ah, fuuuuck!" He chokes, and I can only silently agree. It feels incredible, silk on velvet, hard and soft, gentle and rough. He rolls in and draws out. This time, he pulls out and I whimper. "Get this off!" he snaps, dragging a trainer off and ripping my leggings away to free one leg. He hoists it up, resting my knee on the bonnet, and before I feel his cock, he drags his tongue along my sex on a deep satisfied groan. I gasp repeatedly for air and feel every ounce of moisture rush to that one place.

"I'm going to come," I confess, blinking into the dark.

"Good." With the kind of self-control I only wish I had, he runs the tip of his cock back and forth along my folds, breathing harshly, coating himself. "I love how snug you feel around me, Lily."

"Well, put it in then!" I snap, desperate to feel him choking my sex. His laugh is hoarse and smug as I thrust my arse back, yelping when he slaps it.

"As you wish." He drives in, making me shout louder. He's deep — so deep I can barely catch my breath through the punishing blows. I brace myself for each direct and levelled thrust. Jace is grunting through a series of curses and my moans drown out the slap of flesh. Everything gathers at one point and flashes before my eyes, so bright and all-consuming, and I'm crying out when Jace shouts loudly, "For fuck sake!"

Bright lights blind my vision and I blink dazed confusion away, as two head beams illuminate Jace's car and us. I jolt back in embarrassment and twist away from the bonnet so I'm hidden against the door. I begin dragging my leggings back on as Jace tucks himself away. "You okay?" Jace cups my face, but I yank away, eternally mortified by our sudden predicament.

"Who is it?" I whisper, both irritation and embarrassment evident in my voice.

"Neve." He sighs, and my eyes flash to his because the last time I was in the same vicinity as her, she insinuated I was unattractive. I'm not insecure by any means, but I refuse to be nice to her, nor can I be horrible. She means something to Jace, which I'm quickly realising I hate. Right now, I'm choosing the most logical option, one that doesn't consist of me slapping her smug face.

"Wonderful," I snap, dragging my tangled leggings back on and shoving my foot back in my shoe with unnecessary force. Her car door thuds shut and I flinch.

Jace sighs, softly saying, "Lily." It's a plea. He knows I have shut down. I'm not going to run, but I'm not standing here talking to her either. I wrap his suit jacket around me.

"Hi, Lily!" All I can offer her is a smile, which is insincere at best.

I refrain from going into a run when I head into his house. "If I knew you'd be putting on a show, I'd have bought popcorn." Her voice drags down my nerves like a scalpel.

"Cut it out, Neve," Jace spits. "What did you want?"

"Oh, we are grumpy. Did someone not finish?" She jeers in the most patronising voice. "Aren't you going to invite me in?" It's the first sign of irritation in her voice. I can hear her clearly from the entryway, which I imagine is her objective.

"Given your timing, I would say no." I mentally sag in relief.

"I always thought my timing was impeccable." She laughs

throatily and Jace clears his throat. Obviously annoyed at her juvenile antics, he is heading towards the house and me.

"Can this wait until tomorrow?" He sighs and the door clunks, vacuuming shut. Through the thick barrier of glass, I can't hear them, only see their mouths moving. Neve laughs at something, but it certainly seems condescending from the flash in her eyes. He shakes his head and she throws her hands up. As quickly as she arrived, she is storming down the steps and swinging her tiny arse into her spaceship of a car.

It's only then I realise my knickers are wedged to one hip, hanging from the top of my inside-out leggings. "Fucking great!" I spit and stomp to the bathroom, dragging my clothes away and flicking the shower on.

Chapter Nineteen

I want to call Cass and vent. I want to scream at that irritating blonde twig. But it's Jace who gets the brunt of my anger. His hands slide around my body and I go stiff. "Don't," I grate out as politely as possible.

"Seriously?" His hands drop from my body. "How was I to know she would turn up?" I ignore him and walk straight under the spray. He didn't, but that's not the problem, not entirely, not if I pull the layers back— I don't like her and I don't trust her.

I spin to face him. "You weren't!" I sound apologetic but still angry.

"So why the tantrum?" His words rattle me.

"What's the deal with her?" I ask. There, it's out. I eye him sceptically, irritated to find his own gaze is blank.

"I can't control what she does, Lily." His tone is softer now, but I'm stuck in the moment. I want details, anything to put the niggling feeling at rest.

"No, with you and her. You have history, so let's hear it." I throw my hands up and they slap back on my bare thighs. I must look awful with my hair plastered to my face and my makeup smudging my eyes.

He drags a hand through his hair, shaking his head at me, perplexed by the turn of events.

"You wanted me to tell you how I feel," I snap. I begin to wash my hair furiously as Jace's eyes widen at my vigorous movements.

"There is no history." His hands take mine and he takes over, washing the remnants away. I don't know why I allow him, I'm so cross.

"Bullshit." I drop my head. Did I actually expect anything different than the usual barrage of lies I have become accustomed to from men in my life? I laugh lightly to myself and look at him. "Okay," I say and turn away.

"Lily, she is just a friend." He squeezes my shoulder.

"That's not what I asked!" I robotically begin soaping myself and when his thumb rubs gently, I shrug him away. "Now would be the time to confess anything." My voice is strained as part of me wishes I'm wrong, completely and utterly wrong, while the other wills him to confess so I can deal and we can move forward.

His answer is to wrap his hands around me and pull me flush to his chest, where his lips drop to my neck. "Lily, I promise, she is a friend. She is protective."

"Possessive," I laugh, correcting him. His heat envelopes me, but I don't want to need it, even though I sag into his embrace.

"No, we have known each other for a long time, since kids. She is like a sister, nothing more." His hand pulls my face around, so I am looking into serious eyes. I'm twisted away from the water so that I'm facing him. He is still clothed and is completely drenched. Pushing me back, he holds me to the wall. His sincerity is shining through and I feel like a neurotic twit all of a sudden.

"Nothing more?" I ask, holding his gaze, asking a final time to offer up a confession if there is one. His smile is sympathetic.

"*Nothing,*" he says with meaning. "She will be the first to admit she is a bona fide bitch." He sighs apologetically. "I can't change her, but I can't kick her to the curb either." He swallows.

"I never asked you to," I mutter, blinking up at him.

"I know." His hands run across my face, clearing the water and hair so he can look at me properly. "Look, I've never been in a relationship before," he admits. "She is probably worried you're going to break my heart." He raises his brow and I give him a pointed look, to which he just grins. "You kind of gave me the runaround before. She's just checking your intentions are good."

"Well, I'm sure seeing me be fucked over your bonnet put her mind at rest," I scathe. Jace laughs and drops his head to my neck, and his hands slip to my arse so he can lift me up his body.

I drop my arms onto his shoulders. "I'm sorry, beautiful." He tilts his head to look up at my elevated position. Instead of replying, I peck his mouth.

"Maybe ask her to call ahead next time?" I still don't like the girl. In fact, I'm sure she is in love with Jace, and for that I feel a little sorry for her, but not enough to forgive her lacking personality.

"I'm hungry," I pout.

"So am I. I never quite finished my meal." He rolls his hips upwards and I take sympathy on him. I wriggle free and begin undoing his belt. My wet fingers work his trousers next. I struggle to pull them down his thick thighs, and with the added obstacle of the water, I'm out of breath by the time they hit the floor.

"Next time, enter naked," I huff, looking up past his impressive length into a dark, lusty gaze.

"Always." His breath is laboured, "Lily, you're killing me here." I grin at his fisted cock and on a smile, rise so my mouth is level with the glistening tip. "Open your mouth," he grates out slowly. He doesn't give me enough time to respond, already running the wide head along my lower lip. He hisses when I dip my tongue out. My hand covers his and I glide my fingers back and forth, hinting at a touch along the velvety skin.

I open my mouth enough to let my tongue free but not to let him in. He swears harshly, but I force my smile away. Jace is leaning one forearm on the wall, his head resting as he looks down at me. His shirt has plastered itself to his tan skin and his hair has darkened under the heavy spray. I drag my tongue over the tip, and as he closes his eyes, I take him fully in my mouth.

"Shit!" He barks, knees jolting and hips thrusting. I gag but breathe steadily through my nose. "Lily, I need it rough," he pleads. I want to argue that given the prolonged anticipation, he should be shooting his load already, but I figure my sass isn't welcome now. I relax my jaw and let him thrust into my mouth. "Fuck, fuck, fuck," he hisses, my head held fast in his free hand as the wide crown taps at the back of my throat and causes me to gag a few times. Each time, I manage to breathe it away and his movements become unsynchronised, clumsy, so I suck hard, anticipating his climax. He gasps and I look up to see his eyes wide and fixed on my mouth. He shouts my name, his eyes slamming shut as he empties himself down my throat. I swallow and swallow, until I can taste only him.

His chest is heaving, his breath ragged. I keep my lips locked around his cock and suck him gently whilst his hand massages my head and he pumps his hips, letting out a long drawn-out groan. I press a kiss to the tip and slowly rise so I'm bracketed by his body. Sleepy eyes find mine, followed by a smile. "Kiss me, woman."

"So impersonal," I pout, finding he is smirking at me. I press my mouth to his and Jace doesn't hold back. Instead, he sweeps his tongue into mine and groans deeply. He smells like fresh water and sex. I frame his face and enjoy the deepness of our kiss. He has a way of making me feel like every glide and press is personally designed with me in mind, as though this is about my pleasure, and not his, but in doing so, he finds his own.

I reach down to begin undoing the buttons of his ruined shirt, and Jace is kicking his clothes away before I have managed to get the soaked garment over his wide shoulders. It drops with a splat.

His palm rests over my chest. "Tell me," he rumbles through the water. I find inky lashes and whiskey eyes trained on me. His hand drops away as he leans in and presses his big body against mine, so we are skin to skin.

I sigh and wrap myself around him as much as I can. "I'm crazy for you." He lets go of his breath and drops a kiss to my shoulder.

"I've never felt this before." His chin is resting on my shoulder, his arms wrapped tighter than tight around my frame.

"Me either," I whisper.

"I knew though," he murmurs, turning to press a kiss to my neck.

"Knew what?" I run my fingers back and forth through his hair, enjoying the therapeutic feel against my skin.

"That I needed you. I was going out of my mind," he confesses, his big shoulders rising and falling on deep breaths. "I couldn't get why you kept running. I couldn't think fast enough of what to do, and every time I thought I had won you over, you pulled away."

"Never again," I declare softly. Jace pulls back and his amber gaze is full of such emotion, the wind gets sucked out of me.

He strokes his thumb over my lip and smiles. "I'm so lost in you, Lily Spencer." His eyes lift from my shocked mouth to my teary gaze. "Sometimes, I think this isn't real," he smirks.

"Of course, it's real." Nothing can knock the smile off my face as I press my mouth to his and push myself into him until we are nearly one.

"No, I mean . . . I think you're going to run or disappear and I'll be back to not knowing about you," he laughs nervously.

When I first laid eyes on Jace Bennett, I thought him an arrogant, cocksure arse, but the portrayal I have been gifted with, is so much more.

"I don't think that will happen. I doubt I could forget you either," I confess.

He sighs deep enough that his chest expands visibly. "I'll order in. I want you all to myself tonight," he says, between gentle flicks of his tongue.

"I suppose I can deal with that." I'm floating on happiness.

"Oh, you'll deal alright." He cups my face and kisses me hard, just once, his eyes dancing over my face, and he sighs. "We could stay in here and prune, but then we couldn't drink the wine I got." He smirks because it completely slipped my mind. I flash wide eyes at him. Oh bugger! "A forgetful little thing, aren't you?"

"It's you!" I pout. "You're the biggest distraction," I whine.

His eyes dance with satisfaction. "Good to know."

I run my fingers over the droplets pitter-pattering his skin and drop my lips to press a series of kisses from his shoulder to his ear, taking pleasure in the softness I find on such a hard, toned man. "Wash me," I ask quietly. He does, and we stand in silence as he quietly goes about his business.

"Come on," he finally says. His fingers twine with mine and I'm being pulled from the shower and twisted so he can wrap me in a heavy towel. "Turn around." I spin on my heel so I'm now facing away from him and he begins to towel dry my hair with care. I duck a smile into the fluffy towel, mentally elated at his attentiveness.

"Can we have Chinese?" I tilt my head back enough to meet his eyes over my shoulder, my hair being rubbed in between the fluffy sheet.

He winks and I turn away, happy with the result. Jace unhooks my towel and skates it over my skin, drying me fully. "Grab yourself a t-shirt. They are in the second drawer down." I head to the drawer and grab the first one I see, pulling it over my body, and begin finger-brushing my hair, too lazy to retrieve my brush from the bathroom. Jace comes up behind me and locks me in at the drawers. Reaching over to choose himself a top, he pecks my cheek. "Wine's in the fridge," he says and pats my bum, sending me on my way.

I head straight for the wine, hearing him on the phone ordering our dinner. I load my glass with wine and ice, fetching him a beer and heading over to the sofa and dropping down into it.

"I ordered a selection of dishes," he says, coming to join me. He takes the place beside me and repositions me, so I'm between his legs and lying back on his chest. He reaches for our drinks and flicks the TV on. Jace scrolls through until he finds a chilled song. Happy with his choice, he abandons the remote and drops his chin to my head. "I thought I could invite Carl and Rupert around next weekend. Interested?" He sounds casual, but I can tell by the tightening of his arm around my waist that he is expecting an excuse. I take a quick sip of my wine and lean to place it on the low coffee table before wriggling onto my front. Jace is looking down his nose at me, an amused smile working his mouth.

"I'm not going to run," I say, my eyes focusing on the collar of his polo shirt.

"Why can't you look me in the eye then?" It is true, I can't. I shrug, refusing to meet them now.

"Because I hurt you and I hate seeing it in your eyes," I whisper, clearing my throat and tracing the emblem on his top.

"Lily?" At the sound of my name, I drop my head to his chest and hide a smirk. "Look at me, Lily." Reluctantly, I lift my gaze but get no further than his mouth. "Eyes," he commands lightly, ambers burning down into mine. "Good girl," he hums. I scramble the little way up his chest and kiss him, but he lifts me back. "Don't do that." His eyes flick over my face and I blush in embarrassment. "Don't use intimacy to avoid shit. There isn't you or me— it's us. I know you're not going to run." He sighs, and I know that's a lie, but we wouldn't get anywhere if we both kept assuming the worst in each other. Truth be told, I've given him no other reason to believe me. "You didn't hurt me. I'm the happiest I've ever been," he tells me, running a finger down my cheek.

"Me too," I whisper, my eyes falling back to his lips. I want to kiss him but I hold back.

"Don't be shy." He grins as I flit my eyes to his and see the flare of happiness mixed with lust. "Kiss me, beautiful," he demands.

Jace's alarm wakes me early the next morning. It's barely daylight out and I groan in denial. I don't want to get up yet. I don't want to leave him or his bed. He chuckles and nuzzles my neck. I'm wrapped around him like twine, and with the added closeness comes the comforting smell of him. I sigh, contented, and draw him closer, pressing my body to his.

The contact has his cock hardening, and on a frustrated growl, he flips me on my back. Sleepy ambers glare at me accusingly. "I have an early morning appointment," he reminds me reluctantly.

"Yes, with me," I pout, rubbing myself shamefully against him. He circles my nose and mutters under his breath.

"Don't move," he strains, his face tight with discomfort. Ignoring him completely, I reach down and fist his erection.

"Lily," he warns. I huff and roll back.

"Honeymoon period over already?" I smirk.

"You cheeky shit!" He laughs, rolling back where he was and pressing my wrists into the mattress by my face. "I want nothing more than to sink my cock slowly into your tight pussy." My cheeks flame at his crass words. "I know you will be wet for me," he says thickly. I let my legs drop apart a bit more, encouraging him to follow up his words with actions. I nip at his chin and capture his mouth. His tongue sweeps aggressively inside and I moan on a high note. He grips my chin, holding me fast whilst he plunders my mouth. "Dammit, Lily." His eyes are hard, determined, but I can see the need to have me swallowing him whole. I hold his gaze, silently begging him to slide inside me, and when he doesn't move, I tilt my hips, but he curses and rolls off. He is up and out of the bed in seconds, putting space between us, his cock jutting out and taunting us both. He drags a hand over his face and goes to the bathroom, I suspect for a cold shower.

I'm too hot and bothered to go back to sleep. When the shower switches on, I climb out of bed and pull on the t-shirt I wore last night. It smells like sex and I grumble petulantly about how unfair he is being. I tip-toe my way through the house, unsure where the damn lights are, trying to use the outline of recognisable furniture as a guide to the kitchen, to make us coffee. Aggressive hands yank my hips back and I scream. Hauling me back, he swings me onto the sofa, dropping me on my back in the low cushioned surface. I can only just see the shadow of him above me as my legs are thrust apart and he steps between them. "Wet," he observes, eyes flashing at me through the dark. "This will be quick." He's pissed off . . . at me? Himself? God, I don't care.

I know how important this meeting is. It's a huge contract and I feel bad now for egging him on, but I don't apologise. I want this. I arch my back on a sexy moan. Without another word, he positions himself and thrusts up on a strangled cry. The wind gets chased out of me and I'm gasping as he withdraws and plunges back in. There are no soft touches, or gentle words like last night, no deep hard stares and knowing glances. Jace slams his fists into the sofa at either side my face and fucks me into the furniture, relishing my cries of pleasure.

No one has ever taken me with such selfishness, such greed. The thought alone has heat drenching my folds and he growls, picking up speed. "You're drenched." His body shudders in response and he works his neck. I'm crying his name as pleasure begs me to encourage him and pleas for him to stop all at once. "Come on, Lily!" he shouts. He is ready, his mouth is open, his big chest is dragging in air. He wants us to share it together. His hips slam away at a frenzied pace, and my orgasm is fierce in its approach as it rushes to the surface and catches me off guard, my back snapping up as it takes hold of me.

"Fuuuuck!" Jace is rampant between my thighs. He stills above me, his hands pulling down on my shoulder to keep himself deep. He pours into me, choking out a guttural groan.

I'm quiet for a moment, trying to catch my breath and recalculate my breathing. My hair is a mangled mess on my sweaty face. Tugging my lips to his, he kisses me roughly, rocking into me one last time. "Come shower with me, witch." His lips twitch at the last word and I'm laughing sleepily.

"Okay," I mumble and let him lift me to my feet. I follow him through to the shower and falter when I see no steam anywhere. I'm hauled up against his chest and he walks us straight under the freezing water. I scream and go rigid before trying to get free, but his arms tighten, keeping me tightly fixed to his chest under the freezing water.

Jace laughs and bites my shoulder. "That's for making me late!" He is laughing uncontrollably, at the frozen shock on my face and quickly douses us in heat.

I relax in his hold and jab him with my elbow. "That wasn't nice." My teeth are chattering, and he drops a self-satisfied look at me before he loosens his hold and lowers me at his feet. Happy with himself, he sets about washing himself and I do the same. I stand with my face to the spray for too long and pout when I blink the water away and find I'm alone.

Jace finds me wrapped in an abundance of towels. "I'm leaving. I need to get ahead if I'm going to meet you for lunch." He gives me a pointed look and I bite my lip.

"Okay, see you later." He drops a quick kiss on my lips and leaves me to continue getting ready. I don't have much here, so I drag my wet hair up and pull on any clothes of mine I can find. I quickly load my cosmetics into my bag and locate my phone and keys. It's only then that I realise my car is at the gallery.

"Shit!" I can't call Jace now, he has probably floored it to the city. I check the time, seeing it is creeping up to eight, and pull up Cass's number.

She is chirpier than me. "Morning!"

"I need a lift," I say in response.

"Oh, hello, Cass, how are you? Yes, I'm great, thanks!" Sarcasm drips from her tongue and I roll my eyes.

"Good, I'm glad you're okay." She scoffs at my reply and I laugh. "I'm at Jace's and I left my car at the gallery," I whine. She soon changes her attitude at the mention of his name.

"You're actually inviting me there?" Her tone is a playful warning. She is too nosey to pass up the opportunity.

"I have little choice, but yes." I laugh and drop down onto the arm of the sofa, running my finger over the velvet soft material.

"Send me his address," she squeaks in excitement.

"I love you!" I ring off and realise, I don't know his bloody address. I dash around the place, trying to find some paperwork, but the man is so organised he could rival Carl. I barrel into his office and start pulling open his drawers, finding everything and anything except a letter with his address on it. I sift through and stop when I see a photograph poking out. Gingerly, I pull it free and find myself looking at two kids, both around primary school age, and it takes a moment for me to register it is Jace and Neve. He is tall and scrawny, his hair is sticking out every which way, and his eyes are big and syrupy, a little sunken. He is pulling a face at the small girl beside him, and she is laughing, her blonde hair straggly and unkempt. They both look as though they have been rolling around in mud. I smile and accept he has in fact known her since they were kids. I estimate she is a similar age to me.

My phone vibrates in my hand and I quickly answer Cass. "I can't find his address," I admit.

"Oh, fucking hell, Lil, turn on your maps and find your location," she says as though I'm stupid. I tut her attitude away and cut her off, doing as she suggests and send her that instead.

A text comes through and I check it's from her.

Got it x

I make use of the time and do my makeup. Half an hour later, she is pulling up in her Mini and I head to the door to meet her gobsmacked face, as she walks up the wide steps to the wraparound.

"Well, shit the bed!" She coughs as I pivot the door open, letting her in. Her eyes flash to mine as she slips in out of the cold. "This place is massive." She laughs, walking around. "And very open." Her mouth turns down as she gives me a snooty pout.

"Tell me about it," I grimace.

"It's a good job it's out in the sticks, otheriwse people will be cancelling their porn subscription." She wiggles her eyebrows with seductive precision as I laugh and nudge her hip.

"Don't. Jace says fishermen still come up to the back lakes."

"Oh, how decadent, a spot of fishing and fuckery!" She teases, walking freely into the spacious entryway and further until she is central and can truly appreciate the view. "Holy fuck." Her laugh is one of disbelief.

"'I know." It's all I can say. This house is a hub of sanctuary, nestled away from the main road, surrounded by trees, and strategically placed hanging over a lake. A little more digging last night and I found that Jace had knocked down the toilet block and built his house over it and the car park. "Do you want a drink or do you need to get back?"

"Coffee," she says absently. She locates a stool and sits on it with a plop. "The superhuman is super rich."

"I guess." It is of little concern to me. I can appreciate the privileges that has to offer, but for me, Jace's passion for his work and his dedication sing to me on a far deeper level, than his money does. His passion is reserved for work and me because I have come to realise, he keeps himself pretty cut off. I mentally grin and join Cass, flicking the machine as I go.

"What's this?" She holds up a photo. "Shit, is this them?" I hate that she refers to them, well, as a 'them', but I don't pick her up on it.

"Found it looking for the address." I frown down at it, recalling Jace's words of reassurance. "Jace said they had known each other since kids, that Neve is protective of him."

"She's in love with him." Cass mirrors my own thoughts. Last night rushes back and so does my humiliation with it. I go into a torrent of ramblings as I make us coffee.

"No way!" She laughs. "Bet she got an eye full."

"God, I was mortified." I add sugar and milk, clunking them down before us. "She has this knack for making me want to be violent," I admit, thrusting away the offending visual of me diving over Jace's car to thwack her in the gob. I sigh instead, feeling deflated.

"Perhaps we should introduce her to Sasha," Cass grumbles.

"Still having trouble?" I wonder. Cass lifts her mug, blowing on it with as little enthusiasm she can muster, and shrugs half-heartedly.

"Sean hasn't mentioned anything, but I'm waiting for her to get brave again." I mull over her words, not sure what to say because I don't know Sasha enough to make a comment. In fact, I don't recall ever seeing her.

"Have I ever met her?"

"Not sober," she sniggers.

"Alright," I scoff. "You make me sound like an alcoholic."

"If the shoe fits," she jokes.

"You are always wearing my shoes," I drawl.

She shrugs in acceptance. "Like I said, if the shoe fits." I chortle and blow my own coffee, checking my watch as I take a sip.

"Have you much planned for today?"

She gives a shake of her head. "I'm scouting possible venues. You?"

"I have a fairly quiet day. I'm meeting Jace for lunch." My eyes momentarily drop to the photo again.

"I can't believe he lives here," she says, looking around again. "Don't get me wrong, I meet some social climbers, but this house is next level." She twists her neck, looking at the intricate tree-like beams inside. "Everything flows, I hardly feel like I'm inside."

"I think that's the idea." I laugh. Surely, she hasn't forgotten that he is an architect?

"God, you're such smart arse." She hums her approval when she takes a sip. "Coffee is good too." She inhales it appreciatively.

"When are you moving in with Sean?"

"Well, he practically lives at mine, but we are looking at getting somewhere near the bar." Her eyes are falling back to the photo and she checks her own watch, tutting at the time. "Better put that back," she says, finishing her drink. Good idea! I return it to the office and slide it back near the bottom before we head out.

Chapter Twenty

Cass drops me to the Gallery and I jump from her car straight to mine. I don't have much time, so I whip home and rush through my morning routine, before jumping back in my car and zipping back to work.

Harriet is pulling up and looks puzzled at my frantic state. "Everything okay?" I waft my hand and unlock the gallery, silencing the alarm as she follows me through the wide door.

"Car trouble."

"You should have called I would have opened up."

"I know, honestly it's fine, we have a quiet day." We both begin stowing our things away and I head down the back, popping into the kitchen to fill the kettle. My bag is vibrating its own tune so I answer it quickly without checking the ID.

"Hello?"

"Superhuman here," Jace drawls, smugness caressing his words.

"I'm going to kill Carl," I mutter, trying to disguise my smile.

"I just gave him a bonus!" He laughs. "Where are you?" He asks, when I begin clanking about.

"The Loft."

He sighs. "Shit, Lily, I'm sorry. I slipped out my meeting when I realised you had no car."

"It's okay, Cass picked me up," I reply dragging two cups down.

"Okay, I've got to go, I'll see you in a few hours."

"Okay," I hum.

"Take your knickers off before I arrive." His voice is honey over gravel and I can't possibly do that!

"Jace," I plead softly.

"Don't argue, I'll see you at one." He rings off before I can disagree. Well I'm not doing it. I'm at work! I continue to make Harriet and I a drink she joins me as I'm dropping the spoon in the sink.

"Oh thanks." She grins taking it and hugging the cup in her hands trying to absorb its warmth, it is cold in here I think on a shudder, I say as much and check the thermostat. "I've rearranged your meet with the magazine for when I'm back." She's on holiday next week so it's just me, myself and I.

I don't mind much, we have managed to work everything so that we can complete it before or pick up once she is back, I have no out of office appointments and despite being quiet today, we are busy all week.

Harriet spends the morning filing bills and other paperwork whilst I take a call from the bank and nip to the post office, when I get back I begin making arrangements to exhibit more of Paco's work, problem is I can't get hold of him, I have left two messages and called once again today. I mention it to Harriet who frowns. "How odd, I think we have the address of where he was last staying, perhaps they can pass a message on?" She offers, unsure of his sudden silence.

"Would you mind leaving a message, give my personal number and hopefully we can get him to pop in before you head on your holiday?"

"Sure." She loiters at my office and when I look up, I can see she wants to say something.

"Everything okay?" I ask sliding my glasses into my hair.

"Do you mind if I pop out this afternoon, I still have to grab some bits, I know its cheeky but we're so quiet?"

I laugh. "That's fine, don't fret." She visibly sags making me feel like a slave driver. "I'm going out for lunch at one, but as soon as I'm back head out."

Her smile is wide, relaxed until she registers my words. "Oh, I don't have that in the diary," she mumbles, throw off by my impromptu lunch.

"Last minute," I confirm, I check my watch seeing it is nearly ten to one now. "You going to be okay for an hour or two?"

"Of course, I need to finish up with the filing." She points over her shoulder at her work pile and I get up to follow her up front, she begins telling me about some of the bikinis she has purchased for her holiday, holding her hands up to mimic their shape.

"I like the mismatch ones," I say showing interest, truth be told I'm fretting over not having taken my own knickers off like commanded. "I can't remember the last time I had a holiday." That's not entirely true. I had a girls' trip with Cass, but prior to that was possibly when my mother was still alive, a last-ditch attempt to save their marriage. It was a lie. They were already dealing with divorce proceedings, the holiday had been for me, to give me one last family holiday or so my father claims, I'd have believed him if he hadn't of said it in such a way that it implied I had put him out.

My mother had died within a month of returning. He'd married less than six weeks later. I haven't spoken to him since.

"Yes, me and Faye have a few, I'm looking forward to some cocktails and sunshi—" The door swings open and Jace strolls right in. His eyes are fixed on me, and a small smirk pulls at his lips, brightening his ambers. My mind rushes back to the heavy dose of sofa sex this morning and I flush as his eyes glint with the same thoughts.

He nods a hello at Harriet who is riveted on the spot, her eyes widen at the minor interaction, Jace looks devastating in his charcoal suit and open neck shirt, I can see the affect it has on Harriet. Heat rushes to her face then recognition flares in her eyes. She shoots a look to me.

The exhibition. She looks between Jace and me her mind whirring back over the course of a few weeks, putting two and two together, all the flowers, my despondent moods, the shoot.

Jace only has one destination in mind. Me. He walks straight toward me and lifts my chin dipping his head to press a kiss to my mouth. "You look gorgeous," he breathes, then drops back for more, his tongue pushing past my lips, I feel his lips twitch then he is dotting a kiss on my cheek. "This dress is very short," he rumbles, his hand takes a measure, running down the flare of my hips to the hem brushing the middle of my thigh, he tuts softly. "I said to take them off."

"I need to get my bag," I murmur, face aflame as I see Harriet gawping at us, she blinks rapidly and swallows her own embarrassment down, I walk hurriedly down to my office, but force myself to slow trying to gain some control back, I hear Jace laugh lightly behind me and jump when I realise he is just a few short steps away. I rush into my office, looking for my phone so I can put it in my bag. "I will be super quick," I tell him, trying to hurry us out.

The door clicks shut and wide fingers brush over my hips. Jace takes the hem and drags it slowly over the curve of my arse and uses his strategically placed hands to push my chest towards the desk. "Ah, Lily, just look at you."

"Harriet—" I close my eyes as he runs a hand straight between my thighs and his palm cups my heated sex. "She will think we—"

"We don't care what Harriet thinks," he breathes into my ear as a deft finger brushes my damp knickers aside. Oh God. Oh God. Oh God.

"We don't?" I whimper as he runs it over my slick folds and around my needy clit.

"No, beautiful, we don't," he instructs. I flatten my hands on the desk and push back a little. "I told you to take these off." He sighs, disappointed, his lips running over my neck which are now pulled tight in a smile. He's enjoying this.

"You're early," I pant. From my position, I can just about see him standing tall behind me, devastating in his suit, his eyes downcast at my bare cheeks. He circles my flesh then presses both fingers into me. His face tightens in satisfaction and I gasp. "Oh God." My pussy clenches down on his fingers, soaking up the feel of him deep inside me.

"Greedy," he groans, pressing on his hand with his weight to gain maximum penetration his fingers roll then drive in and out, he begins a steady rhythm, rotating and curling his fingers, applying the right amount of pressure, his lips find my neck, his hand mimicking his cock, my hips gently rock with each precise thrust, Jace bites the taut skin making me yelp, pain wanes with pleasure and my eyes roll shut.

"You feel incredible, come on Lily." He coaxes, pressing his thumb to my clit and massaging with increased pressure. Oh hell!

"Ah!" My knees wobble and white-hot heat flares in my toes and rushes up my legs, I gasp and Jace groans roughly. "Lily let go," he whispers. My hand flies out and grasps his leg for support.

"Jace!" My whole body pulses from the inside, my climax reaching out to hold his fingers and, I don't know . . . shake them in gratitude, I think randomly. The thought makes me laugh inwardly, dousing out the small flourish of shame. God this is so unprofessional of me, I'm at work and Jace has me bent double my dress hugging my hips and his fingers knuckle deep in my sex. I have no self-control I think as I groan in disbelief, a light laugh tangled with it.

"Something funny?" he wonders, slipping his hand free, he readjusts my damp knickers and turns me carefully, his fingers brush his open lips, those fingers and his eyes sparkle with lust. I'm still pulsing, my eyes heavy and sated, he is waiting for an answer and cocks his head. His fingers disappear into his mouth where he sucks them clean on a pop!

"What was that for?" I ask shyly, my voice nearing a purr.

"Starters." He winks. "Off the al desko menu." He is laughing before he finishes his sentence.

I drop my head into his chest on a chuckle. "You're disgraceful," I chide playfully, I don't know what comes over me but I reach out for his hand, pulling his fingers to my face and sucking them into my mouth, his eyes widen and his nostrils flare.

"God you sexy, fucking woman," he growls and thrusts his hips heavily into mine, I feign innocence and blink up at him, dragging his fingers out my mouth with another pop, his lips smash to mine. Dueling, coercing, it's drugging.

Only when I begin to claw at Jace for kissing me into incoherence does he slow our kiss and pull himself away, "Your man wants to feed you." He readjusts his clothing, disguising the heavy bulge in his trousers.

"My man is a fiend," I mutter leaning back to grab my phone and bag, I secure it in my tan mini tote, and whip into the adjoining toilet checking my reflection.

"You look thoroughly fondled and sexy," he muses watching me from across the room as I look over myself and reapply my lipstick— I throw him a quick eye roll in complete disagreement with the latter. I look a bloody mess. Harriet is going to know the minute she sees me that I have been had by this man and if she didn't think it, I'm sure she heard us.

"This is so unprofessional," I grumble walking towards him.

"It's okay, I know the owner," he throws in, his face a mask of seriousness, I can't help but laugh, he stops me and hauls me in for a sweet kiss on my cheek. "Ready?" He grins and swings the door open, I slam a brave face on as I walk up front, Jace places his hand on my back and I take huge comfort in that, Harriet is sat at the desk, her face averted, eyes down. Shit she knows!

"I'll see you in a bit," I murmur, placing confidence in my voice, even though my cheeks look a similar shade to the red in one of the paintings.

She clears her throat nervously. "Okay sure." She barely looks up and I hurry out the door, Jace squeezing my side as we leave, he points to his car across the street.

I'm a meter up the road when I say. "She heard us!" I'm not angry, but embarrassed, I flash warning eyes at this brute and jab his hard stomach, taking pleasure when he coughs out a laugh.

"She definitely heard." And Jace couldn't be happier about it. I swat needy hands away, but he tugs me, twisting me so he can kiss me quick, and pulls me along to cross the road when the traffic eases up.

He holds open the door so I can get in safely, I grin up at him until I clock Adam's enraged face glaring at me through both car windows, I jolt in shock and shrink in my seat not before seeing him pin a death stained glare up at Jace and away. I press my pale face to the glass watching Adam ease his car up the road then back as Jace jogs around the bonnet joining me in the car, my eyes are fixed ahead on the Audi containing my ex. I can't forget the look of disgust and fury plastered across his face, why was he near my work? It worries me that he is popping up here and there. He knows he isn't allowed anywhere near me. I swallow a lump of bile and try to breathe evenly through my nose.

"You okay?" I blink and twist looking at Jace, I'm trying my hardest to shake off this feeling of dread but I know it's slathered on my face, my mouth is turned down and my eyes sad. I nod but he is having none of it, I haven't clipped my belt yet so he drags me over the middle, pulling me to straddle his lap, I say nothing and drop straight in for a tight embrace, wrapping my arms around his neck and wiggling so I'm flush to his body, I stick my nose right into the curve of his neck and drink him in. "Lil what's wrong?" He pulls me back, initially, I fight it but figure that looks too suspect, I let him put space between us so he can search my face, worry etched all over his, I sigh softly feeling the steady sense of safety ease back in with me being so close to him.

His hands cup my cold face. "You've gone so pale." His eyes search my face.

"I'm hungry," I say, my excuse is weak at best. "I feel a little sick."

My lips are dry and my throat rough. Liar, liar, he must see right through me.

His eyes turn even more astute, and he sweeps a look over my whole body. "Are you pregnant?" He says hastily.

"What!" I jolt back. "No!" What a ridiculous thing to say, I go to move but he holds me still.

"Okay, keep your knickers on," he huffs dramatically, smirking when he sees me eye roll him to heaven and back.

"Make your mind up. Off, on," I mutter, ducking to disguise my own smile.

"Off. Always," he remarks, rolling my hips over his groin and outstretched legs. "Kiss me." I drop forward and sweep my tongue straight into his waiting mouth thick arms circle my waist on a pleasant groan. "I'm taking you for Italian, is that okay?"

"That sounds great!"

"Good, hop back in your seat," he says pecking my nose and lifting me so I can untangle my legs.

The restaurant is an intimate, family run place nestled down a side street— it's a hidden gem. We are seated quickly and left to choose off the menu, Jace ordered us a bottle of wine to share and the waiter comes back within minutes of settling us at a secluded table, he smiles indirectly at us as he pours us both a glass and houses the wine in an ice bucket.

"May I suggest the specials board, we have some family delicacies."

We both dart a glance at the board and I eventually choose a seafood pasta dish even though my appetite left with Adam's Audi, Jace picks something from the menu, he lifts his glass and takes a sip. "How's your morning been?" His tone is soft, interested, but the glitter of satisfaction pinches around his eyes, he knows perfectly well how good my morning has been. He leans back in his chair, looking relaxed. My lips quirk and I trail my finger over the table edge.

"You're aroused," he comments, his eyes taking stock of my heavy lids, the soft swell of my moist lips and thundering pulse at the base of my neck, I swallow and his eyes darken, it's that connection, the deep buzz that raises it head whenever he is near and only intensifies when he hacks into my growing need for him, I wonder if it's unhealthy to have such a strong urge for another person? I feel my cheeks flush at his direct comment, of course I am, he was pleasuring me not twenty minutes ago, the sensitive purr is still clinging to me from my explosive orgasm, his voice is rough when he says, "tell me about your morning?" He shifts in his chair and tries to divert the conversation back onto safer ground, away from the electric pull we both find so hard to ignore, I can't quite shake it off.

I run through most my day, nothing much happened although I do mention about Paco. "Harriet is going to contact his friend." I frown worried.

"Perhaps he was busy when you called, up late, painting or something?" Jace offers, I nod trying to think through the rational possibilities, but strangely I have this sinking feeling in my gut. Jace's phone buzzes from in his suit jacket, he fishes it out and frowns down at the screen. "I need to take this," he mutters.

"Hope everything is okay?" I say as he pushes back from his chair, tucking it in quickly and closing the distance between us.

"Start without me." He drops a lingering kiss on my mouth and walks off, I pick up my wine, taking a healthy sip as our meals arrive the waiter looks momentarily alarmed.

"He's taking a call," I explain. "Please." I gesture for him to place the meals down and smile my thanks.

"A top-up?" He lifts the wine bottle, I raise my glass and he fills mine, dropping a similar measure into Jace's glass. "Enjoy your meal."

Seeing Adam has threatened my resolve. I'm halfway through my meal or at least my weak stomach feels it is when Jace returns, he looks agitated. "Are you okay?" I place my cutlery down, his jaw is held that bit tighter and his eyes are sporting a heavy dose of anger.

"Problem at the office."

"Do you want to leave?" I ask concerned.

"No, it's handled." He smiles at me and looks at his meal for the first time. "This looks good, how is yours?"

"Lovely." It's tasteless— I inwardly blame Adam's appearance for that but try to enjoy the now, with Jace.

"Good." He gives me a signature wink then lifts my hand, pressing a kiss to my thundering pulse, sensing the rapid beat his eyes flare to mine. "Lily, this is killing me," he admits on a soft rumble.

"Maybe we should stick to eating in?" I laugh, he lowers my hand but keeps our fingers entwined.

"Our health would be seriously affected," he murmurs, my cheeks heat and I swallow another laugh. "Although there are serious advantages at having you within touching distance."

"You're touching me now." I point out.

"Not where I want to." He smirks and I shake my head. Jace picks at his meal, chatting with me about his meeting and how he is finalising the contract tomorrow. "I have a few projects to finish up first, plus I had a buyer for the property you photographed."

"Oh wow, really? I thought that it was built with a client in mind?"

"No, I like to throw a random build into the mix, bit of a wild card," he says before forking some seafood into his mouth, My gaze drops to my own food and I twist some pasta onto my fork. "Are you sure you're okay, you seem pretty quiet?" Jace wonders between mouthfuls.

"I'm fine," I lie, I spend the remainder of our lunch feigning happiness, It's not until we are sat in the car that I inwardly admit it is easier for me to shut down and laugh things off than deal with how I'm actually feeling. I grin and laugh at Jace the entire way back, when he kisses me, I lean in as expected. It's not until he drives off that my face falls and I let out a heavy breath.

Harriet isn't at the front when I walk in but she soon appears above me, looking over the cast iron balustrade. "Hi, I'm just checking measurements, we have that shipment on Friday."

"Okay sure, thanks." I throw her a brittle smile, this day has taken a shitty turn I'm one grumpy lady.

"Are you okay?"

"Yes, go when you're ready," I offer another brief smile and head down the back to my office, very aware I look like a sour twat. Harriet mentions that she contacted Paco's friend whilst I was out, so I check my phone as she leaves, but I haven't had any calls. I tell Harriet to take the rest of the day off— in my despondent mood it's easier to be alone. The Adam related smack to my mental state has rattled me to no end. I'm feeling increasingly disturbed and rather than rationalize it all and talk myself around it, I allow it in. I'm not sure what I'd expect Jace to say if I confided in him, I'm sure he has a past of his own but after Neve's surprise visit and Cass's comments, mixed with the desperate fear of Adam lurking around, I'm an emotional mess by closing.

I already know Jace is home as he texted to let me know, before I left the gallery. I drive to his with pure intent. Today's activities not lost on me. The more I dwell on seeing Adam, I find myself fighting with my own inner angst. I'm losing some of my well-placed control. I need Jace. Confirmation he is as much mine, as I am his. That nothing is going to get in our way. I feel violent with need, so much so that I'm not clearly thinking, just feeling and I don't like it. I want it gone.

He is walking through the house his gaze fixed on his laptop as he places it on the kitchen island. I slip from my car and walk purposely to the house, my coat and bag already leaving my body. I push through the wide door and drop them at my feet, kicking my shoes off,

"Hey gorgeous!" Jace calls by way of greeting, I don't answer but continue to strip, deploying garments as I walk past the shelving unit, my breathing ragged, Jace lifts his face away from the screen and his hungry gaze instantly takes in my naked state.

I say nothing and walk with purpose to him, seeing my clear intent he slips from the stool as I near him, as soon as I'm close enough to touch him I slide my arms around his neck and his greedy hands are waiting as I swing myself up, wrapping my legs around his hips. I slam my mouth to his and revel in his deep groan— he doesn't question my sudden need, although I imagine his mind is a tornado of thoughts.

Wide fingers knead my arse before they roam up my back and tangle in my hair, the soft material of his suit glides over my nipples and I whimper focusing only on the sensation of him and not how I'm feeling. Jace walks us to the dining table and lays me down. I hiss as the cold, waxed wood welcomes my bare skin. He doesn't move his mouth away from mine but takes my hands and presses them above my head.

My eyes find his and unspoken words twist between us, he views me with a tinge of resigned sadness, I'm not handling this well, I wanted to deal with any past transgressions in a manner that would keep us both moving forward. I feel like I'm miles behind screaming to keep up, my eyes burn with the swell of tears, I want to forget this feeling. "Jace," I plead.

"Let me make myself clear." He swallows thickly. "I have no idea what is bringing all this on, but I will fix it, one day at a time." His eyes beg me to believe him, so wide and sincere the dark honey orbs full of heat and worry. "Just know that nothing will ever match this." My lips tremble at the sincerity in his words. "I'm crazy about you." He bends to kiss me. "You feel me?" He whispers, but he's not taking about the hard object pressing heatedly into my groin, he's talking about our connection, us. "I could live another life without you and my body would still never forget yours. Yours would never forget mine." His fingers tighten around my wrists and his lips take a happy jaunt along my jaw, I smile sheepishly at him, his words the most sensually, romantic coordination of letters I ever heard.

"Who taught you to speak like that?" I whisper, my heart altering to a steadier beat, my legs are hooked around his waist and keeping him close, where I like him.

His smile is slow and genuine. "You." Bright ambers flash a thousand thoughts at me, all reassuring and personal. It's a fact, I'm head over heels in love with this man.

"Crazy for you too," I manage on a cracked whisper. If only he knew what and who in my past was causing this meltdown. I'm wracked with guilt at allowing him to wade blind into this but I can't endure the ugly truth of Adam now, I don't want to tarnish this moment with such a violent one. I'm tight lipped as he carries me to bed.

Chapter Twenty-One

I wake before Jace the following morning and decide to surprise him with breakfast. I'm quiet as I begin pulling food from the fridge I place it all on the side and set the table with fresh juice, fruit and brew some coffee for us both. It's the smell that rouses him not the noise.

It's still not yet morning, not by Cass's standards anyway, sunlight is still lifting and the greyish, silver skyline is full of heavy clouds. I sense him before I see him and look over my shoulder to find him leaning against the wide end of the beehive bookcase, "Get ready to retract that statement Bennett." I grin over at his tousled state, given the early hour his eyes look bright, he smirks taking in the scene before him,

He runs a hand over his jaw, drawing my eyes to the shaded area, "I could get used to this," he warns me.

"What me cooking for you?" I wave a spatula at him and shimmy my hips, enjoying the flash of interest in his eyes at me wearing only a thin camisole and tiny briefs,

"You, half naked in my kitchen, daily." My eyes widen a little, isn't it a little soon for mentioning such things, I duck my head and the thought chases away my smile.

"Relax Lily, we're taking it slow." His voice is reassuringly soft, patient.

"Slowly hurtling?" My mouth twitches as he pads to me, a tight pair of boxers hugging him in the most heavenly way, I keep my back to him, trying to concentrate on whisking the eggs and not the lean god hovering behind me, possessive hands slip to thread at my waist, his chin drops to my shoulder and I get a whiff of his unique smell, I try to place it, it's a little exotic. I don't know what it is, but my womb bloody loves it!

"Yes, slowly hurtling baby, builds the anticipation," he tells me, squeezing a little tighter.

"To what?" I ask, he shrugs but keeps his chin secured to my bare shoulder, it's rough on my skin, and a complete contradiction to the gentle glide on his lips when they press on my neck before resuming his position.

"Whatever we want," he murmurs, his cock suddenly growing against my backside, I know what he wants.

"Is that so?"

"Sex is too simple for the kind of anticipation I'm after," he declares. "Something deeper." His husky statement is delivered around an open kiss to my neck. His tongue is warm, smooth, and I shudder.

I'm grinning like a fool already, "I like deeper."

"Oh, so do I, beautiful." I twist and hook my hands around his neck, the shadow of hair on his jaw chafing my forearms. I drop my head, examining this perfect specimen. "How do you manage to say such perfect things, then make them sound so basic?" I eye him with amusement.

"It's a gift." He drops a single kiss to my mouth, when he pulls away it's to inspect the worktop, "what's on the menu?"

"Scrambled egg," I state, "with a dash of lily of the valley," I mutter to myself, I flutter my lashes at him keeping up my bravado—

the poor man has no idea that I have the cooking ability of a toddler. That's why I have chosen something simple, even I can't mess this up!

"Sounds delicious," he murmurs, double-checking the ingredients,

"It will be, when you let me cook." I push at his taut stomach, eager to get it under way and spoil my man.

"Such a bossy little madam," He allows me the freedom to move around his kitchen but with his heavy gaze on me, I find myself distracted, I keep flicking a shy smile at him. He certainly isn't buying the innocent act, his smirk and amused eyes meeting mine each time.

"Baby you're burning the eggs," he states a few minutes later, pointing with his cup in my direction, and at the smoke protruding from the pan.

"No!" I whine, pulling a crispy edged, looking scrambled egg free and dumping it on his plate. I truly am crap at cooking. I know this, Cass constantly reminds me of it. I was stupid to think I could get through this unscathed. I swung the gauntlet on myself when I decided to make him breakfast.

I place it in front of him and take my place opposite him, my cheeks tinged red. He says nothing and tucks in, I spend most the time pushing my eggs around the plate, waiting for him to acknowledge how awful my culinary skills are. Instead he asks me my plans for the day. He has a meeting outside the city and rather than stay overnight he is driving back tonight.

"Why can't you stay here?" he questions me further, his cool gaze holding mine across the dark wood.

"Because you won't be here until late, I have things at home I need to sort," I tell him again, we already had this conversation last night. "It seems silly to cancel your hotel reservation for the sake of five hours," I manage a mouthful and regret it, the pungent taste of charred egg, attacking my taste buds violently. How on earth did he eat that?

"Fine, get a key cut and drop it to my office then, I'll meet you at yours." This is new?

Jace watches as I scrunch my face up and force myself to chew, I swallow and push the plate forward. "Don't you trust me?" I say, wondering why the complete upheaval of his plans.

"Don't say silly shit Lily, of course I do." His cutlery clatters in frustration.

"Then why?" he shrugs and stands, taking both our plates, I watch him empty the food waste into the bin and place the plates in the dishwasher, he is silent, I wonder what he is thinking but he turns before I can ask. "Come here."

I eye him for a moment, but his ambers hold on to me fast. He waits and I slowly slip from the chair and walk over to him. He makes no effort to move. Doesn't even lift his hands when I stop at his feet, "kiss me," he demands softly, I can't help the buzz of desire at his gentle command. As always, his lips are soft and welcoming, he opens his mouth enough to dip his tongue out and mine follows suits, a soft moan meeting in the middle, as soon as our tongues touch he deepens it pulling me in, then suddenly he cuts it short and runs a wide hand into my hair, keeping me still, "that is why," he breaths on a short laugh, "I don't want to spend a night in some random room, not when I have this." His eyes dim with heat, urging me to agree.

I could argue with him some more. It's one night. I'm not going to go far, and it seems ridiculous to travel all the way back rather than take it steady tomorrow, but I choose to keep quiet on that particular matter. "So, I'm driving back," he tells me, anticipating my argument. But I have none.

"I can get Harriet to drop you a key," I offer in reply, mentally running through my calendar.

"No, you can bring it, I have someone I want you to meet." He bends enough to lift me and I wrap my legs around his waist. He begins walking us through the house.

"A work colleague?" I fuss with his hair, trying to tame an errant curl.

"Sort of," he evades, he is at the edge of the bed when he says, "hold tight." I clutch onto him as we drop through the air a little squeak leaving me, we land with a bounce on the enormous white cloud of bedding.

"Can I tell you something?" He drops a kiss to the silk encasing my breast, I hum a yes and run my fingers into his hair when he nips at my nipple bringing it to life, he keeps his face averted when he says, "those eggs were by far the worst thing I ever ate." He begins to chuckle and I buck, trying to lift him off. Embarrassment engulfs me, but only because I know he is right.

"Go away!" I dissolve into a puddle of laughter, he lifts his face, his eyes wrinkled as he chokes out around his continuing laughter, "You weren't lying when you said Lily of the valley." Oh god he heard me! I buck him again, making him push me hard in to the bed.

"Piss off," I spit sullen, trying to cover my face when his deep laughter fills the place.

"I'm shocked, trying to poison me this soon into a relationship." He's killing himself, his shoulders shaking in silent tears, "Lily you're a fucking terrible cook," he delivers with a sympathetic kiss.

"I know." I pout as he pushes to his elbow, running a finger over my cheek.

"It's a shame, because you'd be a perfect ten, now you're a nine, five." He is grinning widely.

"You pig!" I slap his arm playfully, "kiss me sorry," I say breathless, his finger runs over my lips and is quickly followed by his mouth.

"Bring the key before you open up," he tells me between a bombardment of kisses, his kisses turn to licks and nips, his fingers dig into my side and I jolt on the bed.

"Jace!" I cry as he tickles me, into a writhing and squealing mess on the bed, He rolls off in laughter, I jab him with my elbow and wander to the loo giving him the finger as I go, I lower my bottoms and plop onto the seat, Jace follows me in and is trying to hold a smirk back when he flicks the shower on and drops his boxers, my mouth dries but I look away, turning my nose up and feigning indifference.

"Oh please, you're gagging to get in here," he is smug, as any man with his looks and physic would be, he even runs his hand down his front and fists his growing erection. Well if he wants to play dirty, so can I.

I sort myself out, flush the loo and wash my hands, annoyed that unlike at my flat, double use of the water doesn't send the shower ice cold. I flick a look over my shoulder at his naked body and walk out. Fighting the urge to rip my clothes off and lunge at him.

"Get in here!" he shouts, I hear his heavy footsteps and pick up speed on a giggle, I scream when I look over my shoulder and find he is closer than I thought, his eyes are bright with mischief, I run full pelt into the lounge, his own footsteps drowning out the sound of my small pitter-patter. I'm dragged high on a yelp of laughter, "sneaky little sod!" He flashes warning eyes at me, I use my grip to hoist myself up and let him haul me to the bathroom.

"So, demanding." I kiss him.

"I don't like these knickers," he grunts trying to drag them down my thighs, I wriggle free so I can stand, Jace is dropping to his knees and taking my briefs with him, he presses a kiss to my thigh and kneads my arse. "Hook your leg baby," he says already lifting it out the way, his tongue is a blink away from touching me when his phone blares through to the bathroom.

"Fucking kidding me!" he snaps, staring at my crotch for a minute before gently placing my leg back down on a mumble of irritation. "Someone is about to get fired," he sighs, I laugh and kiss him quick, "sorry beautiful." He doesn't return and I rush through washing my hair and body.

I tiptoe through the bedroom to find Jace securing a tie— the dark grey suit and bright strand of material around his neck make his eyes pop, "is everything okay?" I ask rubbing my hair dry with the towel.

His mouth is slightly parted, his tongue licking the curve of his lower lip as he watches his actions in the mirror. "Yes." It doesn't sound okay, his voice is tight. His eyes strained.

"Yesterday not quite as sorted as you hoped?" I don't mean to pry but I would like to think he could share some details of his work with me.

His laugh is scathing, "something like that." He drags his keys and phone off the side and pockets them, "bring the key Lily," he says stern but soft, I nod in reply, "I got to shoot." I'm sat on the edge of his bed when he walks to me, I lift my lips for a kiss but he swoops down to catch my ankles, hoists them up so I drop back and flips my towel open, he flicks a cheeky grin my way before dropping a delicate kiss on my sex, "until later," he murmurs.

"You tease!" I call after him, he lifts his arms up in defeat and walks out the door, I watch him head to his car in the rain and drive off down the gravel track.

Knowing I'm headed home for the night I collect up most my things and chose a simple black jumper, grey suit trousers and pair it with nude heels. My hair isn't playing ball and I put it down to the lack of products I have here, I can't wait to submerge myself in a huge bubble bath later. I make a mental note to pick up some wine and candles.

I drive straight to the city and get a key cut, the gentleman hands it over and I stare at it for a second, releasing the enormity of what I'm about to do. I've never given anyone a key, at least not because I simply wanted to.

I thank him and pay before nipping down the street to a cute boutique and picking a selection of fragrant candles. I load myself up and take everything to the boot. I'm keying in Jace's work address as I slip back into the car, the directions for Bennett & Klein loading. It's further than I first thought.

"Shit," I mutter, checking my mirrors before I pull out into the busy morning traffic and ring Harriet as I reach a set of traffic lights.

"Morning!" I crack a smile at the groggy tone in her voice.

"Hi, I'm running an errand, so don't be surprised if I'm not there when you turn up," I warn her, checking my wing mirror and indicating over as I'm instructed to take the next left.

"Oh, okay, I can open up if it helps?"

"No, I *should* be there, just thinking ahead," I muse.

"I'll grab us a caramel coffee on the way in," she tells me.

"Perfect, see you soon." I cut her off as the next series of instructions drones through my speakers.

The traffic is heavy and it takes me longer than expected to reach Jace's office. There is underground parking, so I zip down and pull into a bay, and take the lift up with a few business types to the main foyer. I step out into a vast marble reception— it's a bustling station of chatter and footsteps. Phones ring and laughter carries up, so all the sounds merge into a frenzy of collective noise. I'm suddenly very grateful for my little quiet gallery. Sidestepping a group of men donned in suits I head over to a walnut desk and find what I'm looking for, I quickly locate Jace's floor on the plaque and hop into another elevator. This one is heaving and we seem to hit every floor on the way up to Bennett & Klein. I busy myself on my phone wondering why I haven't heard anything from Paco's friend. I will probably need to give them a call again.

I finally arrive on Jace's floor and the elevator dings to a stop, the doors whoosh open and I step out with a group of people, someone grabs my wrist making me jump, I'm spun round quickly to find whiskey eyes laughing down at me. He was in there the whole time!

"Hey beautiful." He grins, Neve glides past barely offering me a smile.

"Why didn't you tell me you were in there?" I ask, smiling at her as she hands Jace a file and saunters off, her tiny body wrapped in a black pencil dress, it's very tight and very short. Her hair is curled artfully and she has the deepest shade of red on her full mouth. It doesn't seem very appropriate for work. I swing back round on a smile waiting for Jace to answer, curious at his actions.

"I like watching you," he says truthfully, he runs a finger over the frown line running between my eyes, "you pout when you concentrate."

"Uh, I hadn't realised I had bagged myself a stalker." I laugh, letting him pull me to his chest.

"You bet, come on Viktor is dying to meet you," he says and threads our fingers, I'm pulled along, past a large oval desk, "Good Morning Erin," Jace says curtly, the young girl blushes and her eyes widen when she cops a look of me, hand in hand with her boss.

I smile at her, "Hello," I'm breathless as Jace strides onwards, pulling me to keep up with him, my heels clicking on the marble floor.

"Good Morning," she murmurs.

"I'm going to snap my ankle," I grumble, yanking his arm back but Jace ignores me and grips my hand tighter, "If I don't break my ankle, I going to kick you for being such a brute," I can see the smirk pulling at his mouth and find I can't hide my own, as we pass through an open office space I manage to catch up with Jace. "Arse," I mutter and he coughs out a soft laugh, nodding politely as we pass, he drops in the odd 'Hello' or 'Morning' but keeps propelling us forward.

Carl swans out of the far office and as soon as he sees me, cries, "Lily!" He rushes down to meet us. "Oh, I love that outfit!" He coos.

Jace mutters, and pulls me behind him, "piss off Carl," he huffs when Carl slips round him and pulls me into a hug, I go willingly and manage to free my hand to hug him back.

"Did you get new glasses?" I ask, inspecting the larger frames on his perfectly groomed face, he holds a hand up to stop me.

"Urgh, don't," his face morphs into disgust, "Rupert stood on my McCartney's, I'm ready to divorce him." He rolls his eyes and Jace folds his arms, watching him with something close to annoyance.

"Can I have my woman back?" He growls, it's fake, Carl who has his back to Jace smiles slowly.

"No, I haven't finished my story," he pats my arm gaining my attention again, "so, now I'm stuck wearing these god-awful things, plus I have to work with this miserable arse." He thrusts a finger over his shoulder at Jace, who is smirking at me.

"Finished?" Amusement laces Jace's deep rumble and Carl flaps his hands over his shoulder and kisses my cheek.

"I don't know how you put up with him, must be those superhuman powers," he whispers, I throw him an affronted look for dropping me in it with Jace but he winks and sidles past walking away, before attacking another woman with an animated hug.

"So how do you put up with me?" Jace wants to know.

"Well, you can cook," I point out, he mules it over as he re-threads our hands nodding.

"Continue."

"You can fu-" I'm spun into his front and my mouth stalled by his own, I'm chuckling but he narrows his eyes at me.

"Miss Spencer you have a very dirty mouth on you," he admonishes, his lips fall to my ear, "I might need to punish you for your filth."

"Please do." I grin up at him. We walk past several more offices and two huge conference rooms before we get to his office, Jace pushes his way in smiling widely at me.

Chapter Twenty-Two

"Ah here she is!" A male voice booms, I shoot a look past Jace's arm, blinking at the large man with kind blue eyes and salt and pepper hair, his skin looks recently tanned and I deduce he has just returned from a long holiday. He is a stocky bloke and despite his age he looks physically fit. Unlike Jace he is wearing black jeans and a knitted grey top.

He wastes no time in getting to me, to look me over with animated interest, before flicking a bemused look to Jace, "You look confused," he tells me pulling his attention back to myself, I blink and open my mouth to say something, only to manage a baffled laugh.

"A little," I admit, "Lily Spencer." I offer my hand whilst I nervously tuck a stray strand behind my ear. He takes it whilst flicking to look at Jace.

"Viktor Klein," he informs, the names jump out and I mentally fumble with it before assuming Jace and Viktor are in business together, rather than shake my hand, he brings it to his mouth to drop a friendly peck on it.

"It's a pleasure Lily." He pats my hand in between his two and turns to Jace, "well boy," he sighs, dropping my hands and giving him a thud of a pat on the shoulder, "don't fuck this up." He grins, throwing me a playful wink. Boy? The sentiment, and it is exactly that, rings in my ears, there is a look on Viktor's aging face that is brimming with respect and pride as he looks over Jace, I would have guessed at a parental bond but there is no likeliness between the two. Maybe he is his uncle?

Jace laughs at the jibe and slings his arm around the old boy's shoulder, "think you have more important things to worry about than my life, how are you feeling?"

"Me!" He guffaws "I'm fine! I've been relaxing on a yacht for the past three weeks." He waves his concern away and winks to me, "ask the young lady, do I look unwell?" He lifts a white brow.

"Fit as a fiddle," I slot in. He genuinely looks in fantastic health. He has a warm glow to his skin which I know is from holidaying, but he seems well enough.

"You weren't six weeks ago!" Jace shifts and rubs the back of his neck, a gesture I have realized he does when he is holding himself back from saying or doing something.

"Nothing a holiday and some meds can't cure." He pats his own chest. "I'll be back in the office in no time."

"You retired," Jace drawls. Without thought, he pulls me to him and stares amused at the older man.

"Ah, so I did." His eyes hold too much mischief for a man who is unwell he shakes his head, "knew I shouldn't have retired, that explains the little wobble."

"You retired six years ago, you old goat. Pull the other one!" Jace calls him out on his lie, smiling fondly at the older man.

"The cheek of him," he looks to me, his blue eyes twinkling, "I've known this boy since he was a knobbly kneed teen, and this is the thanks I get, I'm an old goat because you made me one!" he coughs.

Jace laughs freely, and Viktor begins to take a seat on a plush white sofa cuddled by two armchairs against the wall. Jace's office is enormous and although it is one space, it is segregated into areas. Jace walks us over and I join them. I can see forever from the sofa, London sprawls out like a concrete labyrinth, not too far in the distance can I see the Thames weaving its grey snake like body through the stone landscape, I stare out for a moment thinking over what Viktor said, he has known Jace since he was a teen?

"So how did you two meet?" I ask innocently, although I can see from the hard shine in Jace's eyes that he knows I'm digging for information. He smirks and looks to Viktor, who is regarding Jace with sad eyes.

He points briefly to Jace. "When he was a teen, he would come to the site I was working on and draft up all these ideas, copy the architectural designs we were constructing, sneak in and check the foundations out. He was a pain in my arse," Viktor reminisces.

I laugh at the small insight I'm given. "So you always wanted to be an architect?" I ask. Jace relaxes back and gives Viktor an odd look. I cross my legs and turn to him, eager for more information.

"Yes," he says with conviction, like he knew from the moment he was old enough to consider his future that he was going to be an architect. "I wanted to create the perfect home," he adds. "I would sit and watch Viktor and the builders work after school, get ideas, create my own." He scratches his neck and I can tell he is feeling put on the spot.

"That's amazing," I breathe. "I was the same with photography." I pull a face. "Although I'm not a natural, so managing other people's art works better for me," I admit.

"Not a natural? You did see the images you took of the build for In House?" Viktor laughs, disbelievingly but kindly. "You captured the inner strength of the place and somehow managed to make the ugly box look like a fairy tale treehouse."

"Oh, you don't like the build?" I flick a look to Jace, who is wearing a huge grin.

"No, I've seen prettier sheds," Viktor barks out, I can't stop the gurgle of laughter and Jace doesn't seem to mind, he runs his hand along the back of the sofa and leisurely strokes my hair, when I send him a shy look he is watching me through hooded eyes.

"Viktor prefers something more refined," he murmurs.

"Yes, like a five-star hotel and waiter service," Viktor chirps. I'm enjoying their light-hearted banter so much, I don't realise the time until I turn and see it's been nearly an hour since I called Harriet.

"Oh God, sorry, I've got to get to work." I stand quickly and throw an apologetic look to both of them. "Viktor, it was lovely to meet you." They both stand as I move around the furniture, tucking my wayward hair as it drops in front of my face again.

"Likewise, Lily, it's a pleasure." He nods thoughtfully, giving Jace another secret smile.

"You'll have to visit the gallery if you're in my neck of the woods," I offer. Jace is watching me with quiet appreciation I give him a soft smile.

"I won't wait for that, lovey. I will bring Marie along. She's looking forward to meeting you." His hands drop into his trousers and his mouth widens.

"Oh?" I ask, intrigued, as I back away and check my handbag for my keys. Jace takes it from me and pulls them out in an instant. I throw him a smile and he winks in response.

"My wife, she has been pestering Jace," Viktor informs me.

"Of course." I mean it, and not only because I want to pick their brains about Jace Bennett. I gaze at him in his grey suit and carelessly styled hair— he is at least a head taller than Viktor, with his wide shoulders and lean frame. I can't help but ogle him. "I'll speak to you later," I say, feeling two pairs of eyes on me.

"I'm walking you down," Jace states. I open my mouth and see him staring at me hard, so I smile brightly and welcome the kiss to the cheek from Viktor.

"Bye, Viktor." I smile.

"Bye, lovey." Jace takes my hand and we walk back the way we came. I manage to leave, Neve and Carl free. As we pass the receptionist, Jace says, "If Carl asks for me, I'm walking Lily out." Her smile is professional, her eyes curious.

"Okay, Mr. Bennett. Bye, Lily."

"Bye, Erin," I manage as the doors swish shut. I don't know why, but I felt out of my depth in there. I'm breathless and wide eyed. Jace frowns at me and pulls me around. "You look stunning." My eyes flash to his with uncertainty. I put it down to being on Jace's turf—there are more critical eyes here. It's unnecessary and I'm hardly one to be insecure, but me meeting Viktor matters to Jace, and I could tell he wanted the older man to like me.

"Viktor's nice," I say quietly. "I didn't realise you were in business together," I mention, and he eyes me thoughtfully, knowing I'm still hedging at getting information.

"We're not. He's retired. I bought his half of the company." Jace picks up a strand of hair and twirls it before hooking it behind my ear.

"I like that you kept his name," I say, running my hands up his suit jacket and lacing them around his neck.

"He's done a lot for me. Plus, it has a nice ring to it." He always delivers some information, yet seems to be able to withhold all the details I actually want. We jolt to a stop, and unlike before, I come out straight into the underground parking. "Where did you park?" he says, slipping his hand in mine and walking out into the car park.

I nod, "Across that way. There were limited spaces."

"I know, I'm working on designing a high-rise parking lot, we're waiting for the contracts to come back and then we're good to go," he says casually.

"Man, of many talents," I muse, heading towards my car parked between two huge Range Rovers. "Oh God, my little VW looks pitiful squashed in there," I moan.

"You can always borrow my Merc," he says, following between the two hefty four by fours.

"Merc?" he doesn't drive a Merc, I frown heavily.

"I keep it here, it's better for longer journeys," he says by way of explanation, he points over to a sleek Merc back by the main elevator, my eyes light up. "That's a yes then," he laughs.

"Would you honestly let me drive it?" I suspect he is pulling a fast one on me.

"If you wanted to use it." I know I won't take him up on the offer, but I like that he has offered.

"Thanks. I'll see you later." I unlock my door and realise I haven't even given him the key. I rummage in my bag and realise I put it in my trousers. I pull it out. "I'll probably be asleep, so I'll put the latch on. I don't have any fancy alarm," I tease.

Jace is looking down at me his ambers shining like polished gold, "I don't have a new alarm system, it was already fitted but I hadn't set it," he confesses.

"Good, I thought you were actually going to keep me locked up in your big house," I grin.

"I will one day," he smirks, "kiss me woman." I don't wait to be asked twice, I lift up and let him press me into the curve of my car, he kisses me senseless, until I'm weak and gasping for air, "I need to go," I whisper.

"I know." he pecks my mouth again, "have a good day."

"I will."

"Sleep naked," he hums, diving in for one last kiss before he pulls away and puts space between us.

"Anything else?" I scoff.

"Chocolate sauce." He winks and I stare after him for a minute before I slip into my car and head to work. Not before making a quick pit stop at the supermarket, to grab the sauce.

Harriet has already opened up when I get there, I takes me an age to park my car, in the end I managed to find a spot around the corner, I rush in and see her sat at the desk. "Sorry, it took longer than I thought," I gush.

"Oh no it's fine." Harriet has a simple black dress and ankle boots on, her hair is down, and she looks really cute.

"God what did I do to deserve you," I say as I walk past, heading down to the back, Harriet follows my coffee in her hand.

"Should still be warm," she replies, pushing it into my hand.

"Great, Thanks, all okay, no answer messages?" I ask.

"Well, no but Paco's friend called." Harriet sounds a little dubious.

"Oh, he never called my mobile." I frown. "Did he want me to call him back?" I wonder, checking my reflection and adding another layer of gloss.

"Yes, Paco was in an accident," Harriet says slowly, I stop what I'm doing and look up at her, my face dropping in shock.

"Is he, he's not?" I can't even finish the sentence, I don't want to consider the possibility, she shakes her head and I visibly sag.

"No, although he is pretty banged up, Simon said he has been moved from intensive care to an ordinary ward now, he did leave all the details and his mobile if you wanted to contact him."

"That's awful, did he say how it happened?"

"Traffic accident, do you want me to arrange some flowers?" She says.

"Yes please, but deliver them here, I can take them in person," I say absently.

"Okay." She walks out and then comes back in, "I nearly forget, Adam dropped by and said." She pauses, trying to remember his message word for word, my heart has fallen into my shoes, *Adam was here!* "You would know who he was but as you weren't here said he would try and catch you another time."

I feel the colour drain from my face, Harriet must too because she looks like she just gave me an incurable disease. "Oh, sorry, was I supposed to call you?" She sounds worried, for herself. She should be Adam is dangerous.

I shake my head, "no," I manage to swallow the bile lodged in my throat, "if he comes back, don't let him in." She nods and I know she wants to ask me why but she doesn't and I could bloody hug her for it.

"Okay." The concern in her eyes warrants more details.

"He's not a nice person Hat, I don't want you alone with him." It's more than I'm willing to share but I worry for her too now. I know I should contact the police. I plan to but I want to go see Paco first.

"Okay," she nods, "if he comes in-"

"If he comes in and you can't get rid of him, leave." I know I'm worrying her, but Adam seems to have no concern for his own welfare and I know he doesn't give a flying shit about anyone else's. She bites her lip and runs her hands up and down her arms.

"You know if you ever want to talk, I'm a good listener and I won't gossip about you. I'm very professional and never discuss work with anyone unless it benefits us, or The Loft, I mean."

"I know, thank you Hat." I smile and sip my coffee, glad to be drinking something sugary. I need it to bring colour back in my cheeks. Harriet leaves me in my office and pulls the door too— I sit starting at the blank bit of wood my mind whirring with reasons as to why Adam would have the balls to stroll into my gallery, when I have a restraining order against him. I wonder if that was his intention the other week, when he spotted me with Jace, or if having seen me with Jace has brought on this sudden urge to break his order and risk further prosecution. His lack of concern for others or his future has me worried. I'm glad I agreed to take Jace a key this morning.

My day rushes ahead, I manage to grab a quick hour with Harriet at the end of the day to whip and see Paco who is sporting two black eyes, a broken arm, ribs and femur, he is napping so we don't stay long, Simon is sat with us and I can see Harriet bushing profusely at the attractive young man, his hair is dark and curling on top, it's that bit too long so it flops over his forehead, his eyes could give Jace's a run for their money, his lashes are as long and dense but where Jace has unusual amber eyes Simon has dark brown, with his pale complexion, angular jaw and dark hair, he looks like a model.

"Thanks for coming, it will mean a lot to Pac." He drags a hand through his hair attempting to move it but it drops back across his forehead, his eyes meet Harriet's and hold for longer than necessary, for that reason, I choose not to reply and let her take the lead, she eyes me and I give her a nudge by motioning with my head towards Simon.

"Oh, it's not a problem," she murmurs, "thank you for contacting us, we have been worried, I still can't believe it, I'm so glad he's going to be okay." She's all breathless and shy.

"Of course, Paco was so grateful for the recognition." He briefly looks to me, but his eyes naturally fall to the timid girl sat flicking nervous glances around, "he is keen to get back painting."

"As long as he rests up." I smile sympathetically— he looks so fragile all plastered up in that wide bed, "you'll keep us updated?" I ask standing, Harriet follows suit and Simon darts a look between her and me.

"Harriet is away next week, perhaps you can take her email too just in case I get tied up, that way one of us will have kept her in the loop," I drop in, seeing her eyes widen at my devious play. Simon jumps at the chance and I inwardly smirk. He pulls his phone out and Harriet stumbles over her work email address her eyes not quiet meeting his or mine.

"Great, I'll definitely let you know of any progress and I'll let him know you came to visit," he shoves his hands in his jeans.

"Thanks Simon, it was nice meeting you, despite the circumstances."

"You too." He replies, "both of you," he swings deep brown eyes to Harriet who goes red in the face— she manages an unsure smile before we leave the ward.

As soon as we hit the corridor, she covers her face. "How are you always so confident and effortless?" she asks, throwing me a pained look. "I made such an idiot of myself," she grumbles in frustration.

"No, you didn't. He liked you, and it was endearing." I rub her back, "trust me, he will be in touch." He's probably typing up a draft email as we speak.

She grins over at me, "thanks." I wink and hook arms with her.

"You're welcome, plus I'm not always confident, If it makes you feel better, Jace ties me in knots, when I first met him I barely managed the words Erm and huh," I scoff honestly.

Harriet throws her head back on a light laugh, "no you did not." She is so pretty when she is carefree and laughing comfortably, I wonder what caused her to be so shy.

"True story, I felt like my legs were wooden and my mouth went dry, he stupefies me." I look to her with a whimsical smile on my face, "even now, I catch myself lost for words."

"Well I'm not surprised," she states on a blush, I grin at her and sigh.

"And he can cook," I inform her.

"Oh jackpot, maybe you will eat more than beans on toast now." She pokes fun and I nudge her with my shoulder.

"I bet Simon will email you later or tomorrow, thanking you for coming," I predict.

"Do you think he will? What do I even say?" She goes wide-eyed and I can see panic slowly rising to the surface.

"Say you appreciate him keeping you in the loop and if he needs any help, you're more than happy to." I shimmy and she coughs out a laugh.

"I can't say that!"

"You can Hat, if you offer to help, you will see him again and if things happen let them." I give her a squeeze of encouragement.

"Is that what you did with Jace?" she enquires.

I snort out a laugh, "God no, I kept pushing him away, you've seen him, he is cocky and very intense, it scared me, it still does but I refuse to live life thinking what if."

"Thanks Lily." She sighs her mind elsewhere, I leave her to her thoughts and navigate our way out the hospital— we chose to take my car, to save having to park two. We hop in and I drive us back to The Loft. The traffic has multiplied since we arrived, so it takes me longer.

"I'd love to live in the country," Harriet mutters "City traffic is the worst."

"I wouldn't miss the traffic, but I love the energy of the city," I admit. Having the gallery has given me a little pod of peace in the city and Jace's home is a hub hidden on the outskirts. It's perfect. "Plus," I say looking over at her, "you wouldn't have met Mr Dark and Dishy." I wiggle my brows making her laugh.

"He was very handsome," she muses checking her own phone, "I'm a bit gutted I'm on holiday next week," her mumble makes me smile.

"I think he is too." Our laughter is cut short by the ringing of my phone, Jace's name flashes on the screen, I use my hands free and his husky voice rumbles through the speakers,

"Hey beautiful."

"Hi, you're on speaker and Harriet is in the car," I warn, my cheeks flushing Harriet presses her lips together and Jace chuckles, his deep voice like silk.

"And you think that would stop me?" He questions, I straighten in my seat, he wouldn't, surely?

"I'd like to think so," I counter, flicking a nervous look at Harriet who is trying her best to act unfazed.

"Oh, how very silly of you," he purrs.

"Please don't," I say, he goes quiet and I debate whether to cut the call.

"Don't do it," he is smirking, he knows me too well, "don't hang up!"

"I wasn't going to," I mutter.

"You were," he sighs, "it's a good job I like you Lily."

"It helps," I laugh.

"Hi Harriet," he says, she jumps and clears her throat.

"Hello."

"You ladies okay?" I suspect he is frowning, his voice has dropped an octave, it's after work and Harriet and I are in my car. I give him a quick rundown of Paco and our visit to the hospital.

"Glad he is okay, poor lad," he rumbles, I hear Neve's voice in the background, it grates on me instantly, and I hate that I'm suddenly glad he is travelling back tonight. "Lily, I need to get back. I'll see you later."

"Okay, bye." I cut the call and throw Harriet an eye roll at his antics.

"Is he always like that?" She shifts in her seat unsure whether she is crossing the line in asking me. I have always kept my private life exactly that, private. But Jace doesn't seem to care about any of that. In fact, he seems to be hell bent on stripping those barriers down and taking whatever, he wants. I know he would never divulge any personal information, but he likes to poke me and ruffle my well-placed professionalism.

"Pretty much." The traffic loosens and it's not much longer before we arrive back at the gallery, Harriet has chatted non-stop about her holiday next week.

"I think I have an adapter you can use," I tell her as she gets out the car, "I'll bring it tomorrow."

"Okay, night Lily." She beams from the door.

"Nigh Hat." I waste no time in heading home, I'm desperate for a bath.

Chapter Twenty-Three

The flat is cold so I flick the heater on and gear the thermostat up as high as it can go, there is a stack of bills but I pass them and head to the bathroom, turning the water on and praying I get hot water and not cold. "Thank god!" I sigh when warm water runs over my cold digits, I add bubbles and leave it to fill whilst I get myself a wine and pick at the wrinkled fruit on the side, I dispose of it before Jace arrives and check I have enough food for breakfast, I swing the fridge open and find an out of date yogurt and some wilting spinach, but I do have eggs and milk.

"That'll do," Jace is going to be mortified, although given I have spent the last few days at his he can hardly grumble, I should have made a pit stop at the shops but I refuse to leave the warmth of my flat now.

I spend the next half hour in soap suds, sipping my wine and listening to a playlist Cass put on my phone, I stay until my skin resembles the fruit in my kitchen and the water turns cold. It's past ten but I wrap myself in my dressing gown, towel up my hair and take my empty glass to be filled again, I light some candles and towel dry my hair as I turn on the TV, I fumble with the remote until I find something easy to watch and tuck myself up on the sofa. I miss Jace and it's such a foreign concept to me that laugh out loud. "Get a grip, woman." I blame him for spoiling me and always being so tactile. I hate to think I have become dependent on him being there. I irritate myself further when I check my phone to see if he has messaged me. I contemplate waiting up for him but take myself off to bed around half eleven, dialling the thermostat down before I brush and plait my hair and slide under the cool sheets.

My peaceful descent into cushioned warmth is broken, when cool hands run over my hip and around to lay flat and possessively on my stomach.

"Beautiful." It's a gentle attempt to rouse me. I know that voice. That smell. I smile in my sleepy state and roll draping a leg over his and my arms worm their way around his neck. Yes, I'm naked, as asked. His hands glide further round, curving the globe of my bare arse.

"Good girl."

I hum in agreement, suppressing a smile at his low chuckle, "What time is it?" I can't yet open my eyes. I'm too happy in my midnight slumber, surrounded by warmth, that exotic smell, and curious hands. But I desperately want to see those sap eyes that chase all rational thoughts away.

"Time for chocolate," he whispers, his nose brushing my cheek up so he can claim my mouth more accurately, "I'm going to smother your beautiful body in thick sauce and lick it all off." I'm grinning against his mouth.

"What if I just washed these sheets?" I pout, dragging my heavy lids open only to be attacked by his devilish grin, he rolls so he is weighing me down and regards me thoughtfully, his eyes assessing my face. How coherent I actually am. I'm becoming more alert by each passing second— he chews his lip and tilts his head.

"Lily I don't give a fuck if you're renting this room out to the queen we're still having" he spins the bottle his shrewd eyes squinting to read in the dark, "chocolate syrup sex." He grins and with that he lifts up until he is on his knees, the cool night air chases over my skin, I shiver as he flicks the lamp on and I find him fully naked, the sheet draped around his waist, he is sporting a thick hard on and a dirty smirk on his face. Slowly, he lifts the chocolate sauce and flips the lid, turning it to squeeze it out.

"You need to remove the film-" I gasp as dark brown sauce drizzles across my chest, Jace circles it from one breast to the next and I feel the sauce meet at my sternum before he drags it down to my navel, he rears back and squeezes the bottle hard so it pours over my sex.

I gasp as it seeps all over my crotch, "Jace," it's so cold, unlike his eyes which are full of heat and excitement. His eyes take on this faraway, blazing dazzle and it sucker punches my equilibrium every time.

"I bet your pussy is all soft and wet." He lifts the bottle, the sauce straining and thinning out but it doesn't stop, it slowly connects with his tanned skin and a dark trail runs up his abs and chest until he is putting it in his mouth, his neck taut as he tilts his head on a soft moan and drinks it.

Happy with his work he flicks the cap and drops it on the floor, "shall we see," he murmurs, "is my girl ready to be indulged?" He leans back so his hand can work its way up my thigh. I'm ready. My body is alive, every nerve ending rushing to the surface, desperate to meet his touch. He stops and my eyes fly to his with a silent plea. "Are you ready Lily?"

"Yes," I stutter, his fingers finding their mark, and with a gentle nudge, he pushes into my silky folds. "Ah." My head drops back and I zone in on everything south.

"Lily you're so responsive." I can't speak, his fingers are driving back in.

He is moving down my body with intent. "This is what I call

Lily's valley," he chuckles, and before I can rebuff him, his tongue dives straight in and I lose all thought. Jace brings me to the brink over and over until I'm sobbing for release. Only then does he lift me, and position himself. I slide down on a whimper, my dazed eyes finding comfort in his stark profile and satisfied syrupy gaze, I clutch on to him, the sauce acting as a lubricant so my breasts slide all over his chest, "god I missed you beautiful," he grunts, rolling his narrow hips and thrusting up on a slow and deep moan.

I nod, too over-sensitized to answer. Every time feels different, more deeper, fuller, passionate, or sensual. His gaze is locked on my face, and he can't quite bring himself to look elsewhere, in case he misses my eruption. My eyes close off their own violation, "you're close," he grunts arrogantly.

"Hmm, yes, yes." I drag my eyes open, the familiar sensation tingles along my spine, gathers in my toes and rushes up my legs.

"Now!" He snaps. Burying him-self so deep that I gasp for breath. So deep, I forget where I end and he begins. He climaxes loudly as he holds himself still and throbs inside me. My limbs are weak from his forceful drives. His soft hands run up my back, his muscle flexing gently inside me, reminding me we are still connected.

"I missed you too," I say quietly.

"Good." He grins into my neck, "let me take you for breakfast tomorrow."

Love flourishes inside me, driving me to squeeze him a little harder, "Okay." I agree.

"I should make plans with you post sex more often, you're far less stubborn." He cups my chin tilting my head so he can see me better, a smug lift to his mouth. Sweat has teased his hair into a slight curl.

"Don't get used to it," I quip.

"Wouldn't dream of it." He drags his finger over my chest and lifts a chocolate, coated finger sucking it into his mouth he sticks his tongue out showing the remnants now sitting on the soft flesh, I rise up and suck his tongue slowly. Jace draws his tongue back and pecks my mouth, "have I told you how crazy about you I am?"

"Not today," I whisper, he could tell me all day every day and I'd never grow tired of listening to this man shower me with sweet words, he is as charming as he is cocky.

"How rude of me." He frowns.

I check my nails, "I thought so," I mutter.

He knocks my chin and twists us so that his legs are off the bed, "Come shower with me." that certainly isn't a question.

"And if I said no?" I wonder.

"We sleep in this sticky bed." I wrinkle my nose, "my thoughts exactly. Let's bubble up."

"Bubble up?" I cough on a slight laugh.

"Yes, I wash you, you wash me, possibly a little sexy shower time." He wiggles his brows and bites his lip he looks utterly gorgeous.

"You're insatiable." He shrugs and stands taking us to the shower.

He flicks it on and checks it before stepping us under the hot spray and lowering me to my feet, I'm too sleepy to wash him how I really want or he deserves, I cling to his tall body and haphazardly sponge his skin not paying much attention to where I rub.

"Baby give me the sponge. I feel like you're giving me a demonstration of a sponge bath in my future retirement home." My shoulders jerk with a laugh and I hold the sponge up, not missing the state of his semi prodding my hip.

"Not sure your care givers will appreciate this fella," I cup his balls and flick a look upwards through the spurt of water, happy to see him grinning down at me.

He winks, "that's just for you."

"Glad to hear it." I drop my cheek back to his chest and enjoy the therapeutic patter of water on my skin.

Jace is gentleman enough to forgo shower sex, and whilst I'm drying my body, he changes my bed linen. I mentally sigh in relief when Jace picks me up and sits me between his legs he pats my hair dry and runs his fingers carefully through, getting any knots out.

"Don't ever cut your hair." His legs hooks over mine, keeping me locked in.

"It's more manageable longer," I tell him, I see his reflection in the mirror and realise he couldn't care less why it's long— just that it stays long, I smirk to myself.

"Pass me the dryer." He leans forward and holds his hand out for me to pass it to him. When I do, we fall into a comfortable silence, the dryer buzzing softly between us. I'm grateful for the extra warmth too.

As soon as he's done, I'm lifted and deposited in the bed. "I need to moisturise."

Jace tuts, but it's followed by a light smile. "Which tub?"

"White one, pink writing." I point although it is amongst all my other cosmetics, he must recognise it from being at his as he picks it up and hands it to me the lid already off, I scoop some out and massage it into my face, his hands find my legs and with the creamy glide I realise he is applying some for me, I should probably tell him this is face cream but I don't, "I can do it myself," I lift a brow but he is too busy watching what he is doing, in fact it is one of my favourite things about him, that he takes simple pleasure out of doing these things for me. He is very attentive. More so than I have ever experienced with any past relationship or I ever expected from him.

He drops a kiss to my smooth knee and winks up at me, "lie down beautiful." I go willingly.

"How was the meeting?" I mumble, my eyes already heavy.

"It went well, redesign for an apartment block, penthouses, upper class apartments, gym, pool, Neve secured the executive apartments, although he wants to go in a different direction with the penthouse suites." Jace wraps himself around me, his heavy limbs an added comfort.

"That's great, I'm glad." My voice sounds faraway to my own ears, I am as close as I can be my body draped all over his, "night," I croak.

"Night gorgeous."

"I can still smell that chocolate," I grumble lifting my hair to sniff for evidence of sauce, I find none, "I think it's in my pores," I scrunch my nose up at that, Jace shakes his head, my early morning moan a daily form of amusement. He looks fresh faced and displays the false belief that he has been up for hours, reality is it is barely half eight and I woke before him, yet I feel that my eyes haven't quite accepted it.

"Are you not hungry?" Jace leans and helps himself to a piece of bacon abandoned on my plate, I've eaten most but I'm not used to eating so early.

"That was a massive plate," I remind him, he thinks it over and shrugs before taking the sausage and toast for himself, I cough in disbelief.

"I'm a growing man." His tone is dead serious, but I can see the sparkle in his eyes.

"Well make sure a certain area doesn't take note of that fact, there's only so much muscle I can take." I shoot a pointed look over the table but he is chuckling quietly, his face focused on the food, he cuts into the sausage and lifts it to his mouth saying, "Carl said he can do Friday for dinner, think the weather is a bit warmer." He winks chewing heatedly.

"Okay, I'll ask Hat to lock up, do you want me to bring anything?" I push a few beans around my plate.

"Just yourself," Jace relaxes back in the chair opposite me, he looks too big at the dainty table. He drove us at high speed to a boutique cafe, it's adorable and quaint, there is hardly anybody here and the food is amazing. It's a shame I can't force myself to wake up enough to enjoy it properly.

"I'll pick up some wine," I tell him, not quite happy in taking only myself and nothing else.

"Bring enough things to stay for the weekend."

"I have work Saturday," I remind him, he dismisses my argument with a pointed look.

"I know," he replies unfazed as he rubs his taut stomach— I have no idea where he managed to put all that food, he hasn't even strained himself.

"Full?" He makes a face suggesting he could probably have more.

"We can order a coffee to go, there's a park up the road," he tells me standing, his mind made up. So, we're going for a walk. "It'll wake you up." I grunt in response and he nuzzles my neck, "it's a good job I like grumpy you."

The park is a leafy clearing in amongst one of London's most expensive areas. At the centre is a small pond and bandstand. Given the time of day, it's fairly empty apart from a man walking his dog and the odd runner. Jace links his hand with mine and we set a steady pace, or at least he does.

I'm grateful I'm wearing ankle boots and not stilettos because he strides off, me hurrying beside him. We walk around the park admiring the view, the sky is clear and the sun is warm to my skin, Jace points to a building poking free of a line of Georgian houses and tells me he and Viktor designed it, I show genuine interest asking what his inspiration was, I have seen his domestic designs but this is a black marble tower, it's striking and unusually pebble smooth, we talk as we walk me gradually getting more and more out of breath, and falling two steps behind.

"Little leg syndrome," I say breathlessly, he drops a smile at me and slows, revealing a knowing smirk on his face.

"Thug," I mutter, ignoring his widening smile, he is taking far too much pleasure from this, "little brutal at this early hour," I huff, placing my hand to my chest to slow my heart rate.

"After watching you work out, I know for a fact you can keep up." He tucks my hair away and lets his hand run to my neck, where he holds me fast.

"Yes, in gym gear. Plus, every step of yours is four for me," I object. He takes the opportunity to wind his hands around to cup my arse.

"A *walk* in the park," I point out wrapping my own hands around his waist, "did you list us for the marathon and not tell me," I tease.

"Now, that's an idea." He looks genuinely excited by the prospect.

I jolt back, "no! I was joking!"

"I know." He tugs me into his hard body, "but you could join me for a walk on the back lakes this weekend?" I'm intrigued to see what it looks like down there. I might even take my smaller camera.

I shrug, "okay." He smiles widely and I warm knowing that my simple gesture has satisfied him.

We walk the rest of the way round the pond and Jace heads towards the gate to his car. "We need to make morning rendezvous a thing," he tells me, stern but humorous.

"Oh, we do?" Ever the gentleman, he walks to my side and opens the door for me.

"Yes," he grins, I smile up at him and he dips to peck my nose, "I'll drop you at The Loft." I duck inside and fasten myself in, Jace joins me and settles himself in before driving me to work.

We arrive less than ten minutes later, the place is dark and looking less inviting now that grey clouds are clogging the sky.

"I'm seeing Cass tonight," I say remembering our plan to have a few drinks and catch up, just us two girls. His face drops, I shift in my seat and watch him closely, my mouth firmly shut.

"You never said," he grumbles, throwing a pissed off glare out the front window. When his eyes fall back to me, he is doing his damnedest to not show how annoyed he is.

After the rigmarole of last night, I should have anticipated this news was going to set him off. If he hadn't harped on about coming back to see me, I probably would have remembered to tell him!

"I forgot, it will be easier for me to stay at mine," I tuck my hair behind my ear and sigh when he grips the wheel hard. I don't understand this deep-rooted need to be with me always. He is being ridiculous, but I refrain from telling him so. It'd be like poking an angry bear. Instead, I chew on my lip, waiting for him to acknowledge he is overreacting. His jaw is set, accentuating his face, eyes hard and his mind is at work. I want to reassure him, but I only manage to sigh.

"I'll stay at yours then," he says attempting to thwart any further discussion— it's not what he wants, not truly. What he wants is me at his.

Why does he prefer to have me tucked away in the countryside with him? I have no problem with him being at mine, but the principle alone makes me sit straighter. Can I not have a night with my friend without having to put it past him first and navigate some bedtime deal?

"I'm seeing you tomorrow." I clear my throat when it comes out on a hoarse whisper, he swallows and I know some curse was choked down to fester in his gut, his shoulders rise and fall on a deep sigh, suggesting he doesn't find my need to challenge him endearing after all.

"And I can't see you tonight?"

"I don't want to argue," I murmur lifting my bag and fishing my keys out.

"We're not arguing, we're talking," he grates out and shifts in his seat, visibly agitated, "you just told me I'm not seeing you tonight, forgive me for being disappointed when I thought we had plans," we never had plans I do a quick mental check and tilt my head when I come up short as I assumed I would.

I snort, "to fuck," it's barely audible but Jace swings back to me, anger now bristling off his frame and eating up the interior of his sleek car.

His laugh is incredulous, "unbelievable," he shakes his head and turns the ignition on, "see you tomorrow then," his tone is short and crisp, it's me who rears back this time, is he really going to dismiss me?

"Okay." I don't sound okay, in fact I sound like tomorrow is a terrible idea I get out and look back at him sat rigid in his seat, when he turns to me the hard sheen in his eyes makes me feel ten times worse than what I currently do, I don't want to argue in fact I feel childish for pushing this when there was no need too, I could easily have let him stay at mine, deep down I wouldn't have expected anything different.

"Thanks for a perfect morning," he bites sarcastically, it hits me straight in the gut, he leans over and yanks the door shut, ending the conversation.

"Jace!" I call but he indicates out and pulls into the road, driving off up the street like he's in a promo for a race advert, his anger pouring from the exhaust.

I feel a complete bitch, he spent the entire night and morning pampering me and I reduced our relationship to its most basic level and insulted him. Again!

I don't even know how that happened. I stand dumbfound on the pavement for a moment before unlocking the gallery. I silence the alarm and wake the place up, flicking the lights on and gearing up the coffee machine, rows of art all stare back at me silently judging me in their own way, I sigh passing them all and drop my bags in my office. I follow my usual routine then head back up front and wonder upstairs to check everything is okay, the bell jingles and I check my watch surprised that Harriet is as early as she is.

Chapter Twenty-Four

"Hey Hat!" I call, walking to the farthest end of the upper viewing level and check through the fire exit door, looking down into the courtyard when she makes her way up to me, "shit, I forgot that adapter," I say turning, but find Jace stood a few steps short of the top of the stairs, his hands are wedged deep in his trouser pockets. My most favourite thing, his whiskey eyes are looking up at me through dense lashes.

"I thought you were Harriet," I say slowly, looking around the open space awkwardly.

"I know," he sighs, I clear my throat unsure how to tackle this, I want to go in head on because I acted like a child but his reaction set the precedence and I suspect his presence here means he is finally ready to admit that. We stand for what feels like an age.

"Why are you here?" I wonder, I fiddle with my hair a sure sign I'm nervous but Jace doesn't pick me up on it, instead he takes the last few steps and watches me from across the oak floor.

He keeps his hands safe in his pockets, "I came to tell you I hate arguing with you about just as much as I love fucking you." That entire statement resonates with the fact that he has never had a relationship. I drop my gaze momentarily but pick it back up when I hear him move towards me. I forget that this is new to him, that the art of compromise is foreign and not to his liking, he rushes on, "I'm not going to stand here and tell you I don't love that part of our relationship, I do." One hand slips free and dives into his own hair as he looks down his face to me, "I'd like to tell you I'd forgo sex for a few weeks and prove to you what this means to me." He runs his thumb over his lip his eyes are roaming all over my body.

I don't want that. Not now, not ever.

Reading my mind, he adds, "But I can't. You're barely a metre away from me in a tight as fuck dress and all I can think about is tearing it off so I can see your skin." He lets out a shudder of a breath, "I can't forgo it, and I won't." He elaborates further, his finger points straight at me. "Because that is me telling you *just* how crazy I am about you," I lick my lips and his eyes lock onto that one motion.

"I know this isn't just sex, I don't know why I said it. I was being crabby," I mutter and pick lint off my dress feeling guilty for being so difficult back in the car, Jace is crossing the floor, I lift my gaze and meet his head on, "I'm crazy about you too." He tugs me to his chest and drops a kiss on my lips, my eyes never waver from his, gone is the annoyance but it's replaced by another emotion.

"You're crabby because I don't want you to go out with Cass," he tells me. "You'll drink more than necessary and I hate to think of you in a bar with some seedy fuck trying his luck." I roll my eyes, but he pulls me back. "I'll pick you up at the end of the night." He tells me, deep serious eyes daring me to disagree.

This the real reason he is here, he's trying to control the situation and it gets my back up instantly, Jace must sense it too because his eyes flash across my face. He can't bear the thought of me out of his sight. I find it oddly romantic but the reality of it is staring me in the face with syrupy, churning eyes and a set jaw. If I give him an inch, he will take a mile. My 'yes' will stretch further than a lift, an excuse for an open invite to the entire evening. He would show up and slot himself into my night out. I decide to take a stance.

"I won't need a lift and I'll see you Friday," I reiterate, slowly, carefully and look up to find that impossibly dark mask back in place, "I'm sorry for what I said, I had a lovely morning it really was perfect, thank you." I press my mouth to his, and cool lips kiss me back, but it's half-hearted. I walk towards the stairs— aware he is following behind closely. He groans and I know it's because this dress hugs my arse like a glove.

"Are you wearing that out later?" I stop and look back up at him, he steps back gaining more height and takes in my entire outfit all over again, a closed but fretful look on his face.

"Probably," I say turning as I get to the bottom step, Jace manages to slide past me, I look up and he nods stiffly, kissing my forehead.

"I'll call you later." He barely looks at me and straightens out his suit jacket, reminding me how remarkable he looks, in his dark grey suit and open neck shirt, his aftershave is still as crisp and earthy as it was this morning. I want to invite him to stay at mine but press my lips together, as he strides out my gallery and jogs across the road.

I thrust the door open, wanting to make sure we are okay, but Harriet appears in my peripheral and I swing to grin at her instead. His eyes meet mine through the glass, but I snap around and walk away so that I don't cave.

"Was that Jace?" Harriet asks, her eyes swinging between me, and the now empty parking bay across the street.

"Yes, he dropped me here," I tell her, the distinctive smell of coffee has filled the gallery and like two slaves to sleep, we head for the kitchen, Hat gets down two cups and I fill them up.

"So, Simon emailed me." I grin at her. I knew it!

"I told you!" I point at her and lift my cup and warm my hands, Harriet does the same and leans into the counter, she has curled her hair today and been more confident with her makeup, I inwardly smile.

"It was creepy how on the mark you were," she says over the puff of steam rising between us.

"I could see he was into you." I take a place against the counter,

"Did you give him your number?" I hope she did, Simon was definitely keen.

She blushes all over, "I said I was out of the office next week and for him to update me by email or phone." She cringes which I find cute, she has no idea how pretty she is.

"I have a good feeling about this," I tell her, pushing up and walking to my office reluctantly, I know there is going to be a barrage of emails awaiting me. She follows me out.

"You look nice by the way," I say, she touches her hair, her cheeks pinching with colour.

"Thanks."

I was right in thinking I would be swamped with emails, I spend most my morning clearing the inbox and checking the bills, I sort any payments and rush to the deli to grab us both lunch, It's not too far a walk so I pull my coat on and stick my scarf in my bag in case I need it.

"I'll be back soon!" Harriet waves her hand out the kitchen and I shake my head, she is no doubt scoffing her face with the stash of Oreo's she keeps out back.

I round the corner and see Travis walking up the path on the opposite side of the road. I slow, deliberating what to do. I go to call him but frown as I decide to stay quiet. There is no harm in me talking to him but after mine and Jace's little spat this morning I don't want to add salt to the wound. I keep my head down and my pace slow. I can see the sign for the deli ahead, I figure if I can make it inside then I can go by unseen. He turns crossing the road directly in front of me, his face lights up, "Hey you!"

"Oh hey," I feign surprise.

"Oh hey," he mimics. I roll my eyes and he chuckles at my odd behaviour, no doubt putting two and two together and coming up with Jace. He wouldn't be wrong. He walks over and swings an arm around my shoulder with a familiarity that suggests we have been friends for a long time. "So, I take it you worked things out with . . . " he trails off,

"Jace," I sigh my mouth naturally widening at his name, he nods looking over me with a smirk.

"You got it bad!" He laughs, rubbing my hair. It's overly brotherly. I relax instantly and he must sense it because he chuckles. "I get it." He holds his hands up but returns it to hoop around my neck. "Besides, I'm pretty sure he would flatten me." I flash a smile at him and he drops his arm and sticks his hand in his trousers. I stop outside the deli and he points to the large blue door. "Is this where you were headed?"

I look back over my shoulder at the small line trailing from the counter, "Yes."

"Me too." Moving past me, he pulls open the door and waves me through. I curtsey and he laughs. "This is my Thursday dinner spot," he tells me as we join the queue.

"I work around the corner, I'm surprised I never bumped into you before," I say looking at the board, I always try to have something new, but I have probably sampled most things on the menu and my eyes linger on my favourite.

"Funny, we meet once and then I feel like I see you everywhere," he mumbles his tone indicating that is somehow a downer on his social life.

"I think you're stalking me," I say deadpan, his face morphs into shame.

"You got me, I mean I have nothing better to do with my day, working is a thing of the past, you are my priority now." My comment did come across a little self-obsessed. I blush and his face breaks out into a shit-eating grin.

"You're an ass," I mutter, finding my purse.

"No, let me get this." He pushes my hand back towards my bag.

I keep my purse firmly placed in my grip. "It's okay. I'm grabbing my assistant something anyway," I tell him. If it was only for me, I would possibly lean towards a free lunch.

"Oh, your assistant. Well, fuck me, posh socks." He turns his nose up at me and I shush him when a few people turn around. He is smirking, and I try not to laugh.

"Did you just shush me?" I flush. Yes, I did, but I'm not going to admit that, it makes me seem old, I scowl instead and shake my head denying it, he nudges me with his elbow and I crack a smile, It dawns on me why I feel so comfortable around him, he is more around my own age than Jace and he has an easy going manner that provokes the playful part of me, Jace does too, but it is always heavily tainted with the constant promise of sex.

Travis motions to his own wallet, silently conveying he has got the lunch covered, "So where do you work?" He asks politely.

I point haphazardly in the direction of The Loft, "At the gallery around the corner, I own it, The Loft," I say dropping my gaze even though my heart fills with pride.

"Shit really?" He moves us along the line. "That's impressive, Socks."

"Don't call me that," I huff. I'm not even wearing socks.

"No can do, it's my new nickname for you, posh socks." He does that stupid nose to the sky thing again, my eyes could rival his nose when I roll them and scoff at him.

"Piss off," I step up to the counter when the person in front moves aside to wait for theirs to be made up, I order Harriet her usual and run my eyes over the board once more, still debating my decision.

"She'll have the same," Jace's voice carries over my head and I startle, turning to see him shaking a foot or so behind me, his eyes are fixed on Travis and I shoot him an apologetic look, this pisses Jace off further and when Travis adds his order to mine and demands he is paying, Jace's jaw grinds down.

"Thanks," I say before turning to Jace. I scrutinise him silently and push onto my tip toes pressing my mouth to his, testing his level of anger, he pulls his eyes away from Travis for a brief second but as soon as I pull back he returns them, I swallow my unease as Travis nods to my overbearing boyfriend.

"Hey, man, how have you been?" He offers his hand and I don't seem to be the only one willing Jace to take it, the old lady behind him practically sags in her chair when Jace grasps Travis's equally large palm.

"Fancy seeing you," Jace grates, sending the atmosphere soaring through the roof once more, his eyes slip to mine and the emotion clouding his gaze is so misplaced I want to shout at him for his irrational behaviour.

"Funny you should say that me and Lily were just saying how in all the time we have come here that we have never bumped into each other before." Travis's voice seems fake to my own ears, he is nervous, and I don't blame him. Jace looks as though he is about to bust a vein, I give Travis his due he doesn't bulk at Jace's open hostility.

A mild and sarcastic laugh breaks free from Jace's lips, "funny that," he muses slowly.

I look up a deep frown on my face, "Did you follow me?" Jace bristles at my accusation and Travis tugs his hand free, tilting his head and eyeing Jace smugly, it riles him further, slowly he twists his head to me.

"That would suggest I don't trust you," he says quietly.

"Yes, it would," I hold his gaze, questioning him silently, the moment is broken when the man behind the counter calls to let me know my order is ready, Travis leans past me, his chest grazing my back and Jace audibly growls, I ignore him and thank Travis again, who flaws me a pair of wide, mocking malteaser eyes and an awkward grin, I want to laugh but I know it would send Jace through the roof.

"I'll walk you back," Jace mutters stepping aside so I can slip free, he purposely cuts Travis up and I flush with embarrassment. It's not okay and as soon as I'm out the door I turn to him my face set in an angry scowl.

"There's no need to be so rude!" I spit, Travis eyes me cautiously,

I can tell he is at war with himself, unsure whether to leave us or stick around.

Jace's brows snap together and he glares at me in the street, "when some prick thinks it's okay to wrap his arm around my partner." Jace throws a warning glance at Travis leant against the shop window, he shrugs not denying the accusation, "then I have every fucking right to be rude." His voice is so calm that I actually stiffen, it's worse than if he lost his temper and shouted, because I know I have hurt him.

Jace rubs the back of his neck and stares at me for the longest minute his jaw so tense, his teeth grate, "fuck this," he snaps and storms off down the street.

My heart plummets and I throw a panicked glance at Travis, who pushes off the glass in an instance. "You're a prick if you walk away!" Jace spins on his heel and storms at Travis.

"Jace, no!" I try to stand in his way, but Travis pulls me back. Jace has his fist clenched and I know he is about to punch him. This whole thing is flying out of control. "You're being ridiculous!" I cry helplessly.

"Chill out. I'm not interested. Anyway, she is all about you." Travis holds his hands up, I manage to push against Jace's chest halting him, he lowers his hand the little way it has risen and I drop my head forwards on a sigh, "we're friends. Nothing more," I plead for him to relax but his chest is heaving. I do the only thing I can think of and that is to kiss him.

His resilience is expected but the deprived and apparently unstable part of him isn't. For all his arrogance and success, this new side of him is an unpleasant revelation. I absolutely abhor violence. When his ambers drop to my grey's he must see all the questions swirling back up at him.

"We're leaving," he says against my mouth. I nod my agreement and flick a look at Travis.

"Take care, Socks," he mumbles, and Jace practically vibrates in my arms.

"Jace," Travis inclines his head. I sigh when Jace refuses to respond to him.

"Please don't be like that," I whisper, keeping his face fixed on mine.

"See you around," his smile is fake, his posture volatile. I wait for Travis to cross the road and head up the street, before I step away on an emotional sigh. This is beyond ridiculous. He followed me here. Has he been watching the gallery all morning?

Bloody hell, I certainly know how to pick them!

"I don't know what the fuck is going on with you," I start, I circle round him and make my way back to work, Jace follows, his laugh is short and scathing. I ignore him, throwing a disgusted look over my shoulder, "but I'm not the type of girl to sit around waiting on a man at home, I have friends, a business, a life," I seethe, Jace's strides have him propelling past me, he cuts me up and places a hand on my stomach stalling me from going any further.

"You let him touch you," he snaps.

"It was more of a brotherly hug!" I stamp my foot, painfully away I seem childish in doing so but I'm so damn angry with him, this whole situation is boiling out of control. "Why did you follow me?" He has the decency to look ashamed. When he rubs the back of his neck, I groan out a curse. Jaces throws a look to the sky, causing me to feel an ounce of sympathy for him. "Jace, why were you following me?" It's softer this time, sympathetic.

He shrugs, "I don't know." His eyes don't quite meet mine and I know he is lying, I sigh, it's bullshit, he knows exactly what he is doing!

"I wanted you to change your mind." He drops glassy ambers at me. "I don't like the thought of you out alone," he gruffly admits, I eye him pointedly, I won't be alone I will be with Cass.

"You realise that's *so* unhealthy," I say softly.

"I can't help how I feel, Lily." He works his neck and steps back from me, "I need to get back to the office, I'll walk you back to The Loft."

"You're giving me whiplash!" I fire angry eyes at him and pull my hand free when he tries to thread his with mine, he quickens his steps and secures our hands together.

"Back at you," he grates, "and I don't trust that little prick." He throws a disgruntled look over his shoulder at Travis's retreating back.

We walk in silence, all the while I'm trying to think of the right thing to say, I know I need to say something— it's just getting him to understand it. As soon as the gallery comes into sight everything comes out in a rush, "Jace, I love that you feel so deeply, you say some of the most perfect things to me, I could never change that about you."

He eyes me sceptically, rightly so— there is a big fat but coming up.

"*But* I don't want to be with someone who is going to micro-manage my entire life, that doesn't make me happy," I confess truthfully.

His jaw works and I can see the thoughts rattling around in his head, controlling it all makes him happy and I am taking away something that he needs, I hanker for control in a lot of things and I have given it over to Jace for the majority, but this, I need this slither of control.

"I want to believe you trust me, but you following me, trying to ensure we are never apart, doesn't feel like trust." I urge him to see that, perhaps he already knows.

"You'll run." It costs him everything to push those words past his straight lips.

"No, I won't, but I will fight you on this. I'm seeing Cass." I search his eyes for understanding. I find none.

His groan is full of unease, "not that long ago you told me you still had feelings for someone." He scoffs, my white lie, or a lie within the truth has come back to bite me on the arse, "Forgive me for feeling as though I'm putting myself on the line for some half arsed attempt back!"

I snap back at his cruel words, I'm not half arsed— I'm sensible, cautious.

Emotion creeps up and I feel my throat tighten, he takes my hand when he sees I'm close to tears, "Lily," he sighs apologetically, I tug my hand free and frown.

"I'm not going to run, I love being with you." My backward confession is worthy of a more sentimental moment, but it finds its way into this mess, "that's not easy for me to admit." I sound angry, I don't want to run but this side of Jace is distasteful, I don't like it. "But neither am I going to come running with every snap of your fingers." My voice grows. "And for the record I *hate* violence!" His eyes widen and I move back when he tries to take my hand.

"Lily." He sounds anxious, his eyes cautious. I know without a shadow of a doubt Jace is nothing like Adam. But the deep-rooted fear in me is yet to accept that.

"You were the one ready to walk away not ten minutes ago," I snap.

"That's bullshit and you know it," he says roughly. "I knew I would have lamped him if I stayed around!" He shouts, drawing Harriet out from the shop. Her eyes widen when she sees us, faces centimetres apart and caught up in a minor domestic.

"Oh sorry!" She flushes and rushes back inside, sensing my attention is momentarily elsewhere Jace takes it upon himself to slam his mouth to mine, my eyes snap wide and I find angry pools of whiskey burning down into mine, his hands are tight in my hair and he thrusts his tongue into my mouth on a soft groan, I couldn't refuse him if I tried, his tongue taunts me with delicious skill, his gaze is intense and demands a response.

"Don't ask me to explain how I feel, or why," he mutters on a sigh, his lips brushing across my swollen mouth, "I don't know what the fuck I'm doing, Lily." He presses a hard kiss to my mouth, "I only know you feel right to me and I don't want a day without that."

"Following me isn't okay," I whisper, my eyes soften but they plead with him to reason.

"Denying me isn't either," he states, I think he is joking, possibly trying to lighten the atmosphere, only my smirk slowly drops away when I find accusing eyes staring down at me.

"I'm not getting through to you, am I?" My shoulders drop in what he must mistake as defeat. I feel I have put myself in another unhealthy relationship one I have a heavy addiction too.

The truth is I don't actually know this man.

"Maybe it's you who doesn't understand," he points out. He's right about that.

"I have to get back to work," I tell him, it's evident I'm not going to be able to make him see sense. He is being totally unreasonable, I debate whether I should try and go about it another way, but I can't think clear for trying, not with him still bristling in front of me.

"You'll call me later." It's not a question.

"Sure," I sigh. Jace drops his gaze, reluctant to leave with things still shaky.

"I'm crazy about you, Lily," he whispers.

"I know," I mumble out the words. Unhappy with my response, he lifts my chin.

"Tell me you're crazy about me too, beautiful." His eyes are peering down into mine, and his lips are a whisper short of my own.

"I'm crazy about you too," just not crazy about his sudden personality transplant. I'm mentally voting for the old Jace to grace me with his presence.

Chapter Twenty-Five

"I can't get past that he *followed* you," Cass says, her big eyes reeling still, she sips some of her drink and shakes her head in concern, "I mean, has he been doing it since you first met?" She wonders her brow furrowed, "it's fucked up, in a hot way," she says more to herself.

"I don't know." I sigh sadly.

She puts her glass down, "I know what you're thinking but he isn't Adam." Her astute eyes meet mine with a touch of empathy.

"No, I know he's not." It's the one thing I have kept telling myself.

"*But*," Cass sighs, insinuating my idea of a happy ever after just go sucked down the drain, "there are a few warning signs there." She winces at me.

"I know." It's me who sighs this time, I wonder if I should try and talk to him about it. Although, I doubt, he will understand. He admitted he doesn't know what he is doing.

"Maybe you should come clean about Ada—"

"No." I cut her off and shift in my seat— the thought alone makes me come out in hives.

"Well then definitely question him, what the hell drives a man who is so confident, to act so out of character." He's controlling sure but this is something else, something deeper. She huffs sympathetically, "So have you spoken to him since lunch?" Cass holds her phone up and faffs with her hair in the blacked-out screen.

I look down at my dress and feel a pang of guilt, I decided to go home and change before I met Cass, this dress is worse than the first, Jace would have a fit. I reflect that is possibly why I am now sat in a cocktail bar at a high table with my back on show to the entire place. Defiance. Flaunting myself in front of him would be like poking an angry bear, this is the somewhat less insolent approach.

"Briefly," I tell her around nibbling the strawberry slanted onto the edge of my glass, we decided against Finnegan's purely because it was the most likely place Jace would look and after this morning I certainly wouldn't put it past him to seek me out. We have never been here before and it's further away than our regular haunts. Not only is it far more expensive, the interior looks like something fit for a multimillion-pound penthouse, sleek industrial surfaces, gleaming glass and subtle lighting. We look like we are floating above the clouds and amid the stars. The bar sits at the top of a staggering building, boasting a stunning roof garden.

"Did you tell him where you were?" Cass twirls her fingers around the stem.

"God, no, he'd be here already." I laugh, my sixth sense tells me his overbearing need to control everything is for his benefit and not mine, what's going on in that head of his?

"Don't give up on him, Lils," Cass pleads with me.

"I'm not." I sigh sounding resigned, although multiple alarms are ringing through my skull, "I know that no relationship is perfect but I wasn't expecting. *This*," I mutter. "I seem to attract nutters." My laugh is sad, I don't truly mean that, Jace is nothing like Adam.

"Either that or you're lady garden is toxic," Cass spits out on a laugh, I dip my finger in my drink and flick it at her. "Sends the men gaga!" She howls flapping her hand to stop the wine spray.

"Piss off!" I side eye her and look away before I also get a case of the giggles, she is too busy laughing to notice my disapproving scowl.

"He loves you though," Cass replies, her voice still carrying the tail end of her laugh, I keep my face forward and choose not to respond to her. He hasn't said as much and I don't want to lead myself into a false sense of security. Sure, I love him, I know I do but a huge part of me thinks Jace is simply running on lust. For all he says he is crazy about me. It's too soon to put label on his actions or his unvoiced feelings.

"I know you heard me." She jabs my ribs drawing my face her way, I raise my brow and she flicks it, "maybe he can't cope with how he feels. You said he has never been in a relationship before?" She says thoughtfully, still trying to work him out.

I shrug, "maybe." I don't know but something doesn't sit right with me, it never has.

"Maybe," she mimics, making me sound more like a child and feel more of an idiot.

"Can we talk about something else?" I ask, she collects up her drink and shrugs.

"Sure, how is Paco?" Her smile is wide and her interest genuine. She is a superstar of a friend.

We stay at Nexo for the next hour or so, drinking steadily and Cass tells me all about the wedding from hell she is organising. "It's a fucking shambles!" She drops her head in her hands, "Honestly, the groom is ready to flee, I can tell, and no matter how much everyone tells her to relax, she is hell bent on having the 'perfect' wedding." Cass air quotes.

I laugh, mentally praying for the husband. "Do you think he will show?" The wedding is less than a month away by the sounds of it he will be clamoring for any excuse to leave.

"I feel bad for him. When I met them both, they were so in love. He barely touches her now." She grimaces, "It's painful to watch."

"Maybe he should be straight with her," I say tentatively, easier said than done, I certainly haven't taken that approach with Jace.

"He is walking on egg shells at the moment." Cass shakes her head, someone catches her attention across the bar, a tall curvaceous woman with jet black hair. "Hey Zara!" Cass calls, she waves her hand and keeps her face in the other woman's direction but says to me, "Zara is amazing!" I hum in response, "honestly she came from nothing, like worse than Sean, she is a model now." Sean was as good as homeless but I can't see the polished and striking woman living like that. She looks like she was spoon-fed money and bathed in gold. The woman's face morph's into a jaw dropping smile, her bright teeth pop against her latte skin and post box red lipstick, "Well, fuck!" Cass coughs at the brick of a man at her back, his piercing eyes set on us before they drop to Zara's ass cuddled in a nude dress, he takes her wrist but she tugs free and he flashes her with a warning look, when his hand grips her neck through her hair I throw a look to Cass but relax when he smirks softly, there is no denying they are intimate with one another. Zara breaks free and moves around the bar to us, her companion follows her movement with night dark iris's, his attention briefly pulled away by a mountain of a man who takes a seat beside him. Both are dressed in expensive suits, their hefty watches look as though they could sink a ship. The larger of the two has a gold chain around his wrist, I cough into my drink thinking it looks thicker than my ankle, I duck my gaze when they catch me staring.

"Cassandra, how are you?" I realise that Zara is not as old as I had pegged her, she looks more mine and Cass's age, I blame it on the lighting and the exuberant amount of confidence she holds herself with. Her shoulder length black hair swishes as she twists in the seat to face us.

"Great, thanks, how are you? Your last campaign did well." I realise up close I recognise her from a few advertisements for high-end clothing and perfume.

"Yes, better than I hoped." She smiles and her eyes slip back to the dark-haired man watching her, he turns to his friend, who looks more of a bodyguard, and I catch the distinctive lines of a tattoo creeping up his neck and grazing the underside of his ear. Sensing my appraisal, his eyes pull my way, and they soon drop back to the dark-haired beauty perched on a stool beside Cass.

Cass leans back so I am in view, "This is my friend, Lily. Lily, this is Zara Reid." I naively contemplate leaning over to shake her hand, given she is way higher up the social ladder than me but I smile a hello instead.

"Your photography friend!" She beams at me, her eyes twinkling. I'm not unattractive by any means but this woman is undeniably stunning.

"Yes, that's me," I laugh, Cass grins proudly at me.

"She's amazing, she recently photographed for Bennett and Klein."

"They built this building," Zara informs me, I don't want to label her as being an airheaded model but she doesn't look the type to find such information worth her while, whether she anticipated my ill-mannered observation or not she points to the man staring deeply at her, "Callan owns Nexo," she says by way of explanation.

"Oh, really, small world, we tend to stick to the business district," I say around a sip. "Glad we didn't. This place is amazing." I look over the opulent room.

"Yes, it has its charm," she murmurs, her eyes betray her and fall to the man growing impatient, he motions with his head for her to come back to him. "Excuse me, ladies. It was nice to meet you, Lily," she murmurs, both Cass and I say our goodbyes as he motions for the bar tender who rushes over, he speaks quickly and points towards us, within a matter of minutes we have a highly priced bottle of champagne placed in front of us.

"Oh my God," Cass quietly sings.

I lift my glass in thanks and Cass follows suit, he inclines his head before standing and pressing his hand into Zara's back. He pushes her towards the exit, the security-looking guy a few paces behind. I see we aren't the only one's following their progress across the room.

I look to Cass once they have left. "Was it just me or was that—"

"Whoa, hot." She fans herself. I scoff at her typically male thought process. The lunatic is actually pressing ice to her throat. "Dear God, he was . . . wow!" God, if Sean were here, he'd slap her arse!

"Personally, I was going to say weird," I mutter. He was scary.

"Weirdly hot." She grins, she finishes her wine and picks up the big bottle of champagne, "he seems dangerous," Cass says, twisting the bottle and on a groan pushes at the cork, the bar tender rushes over.

"Ah, no, no, let me," he laughs nervously and directs it elsewhere, he pops it with a gentle bang, the liquid rushes out in a fizz of foamy bubbles, he inclines his head when Cass gives a soft whoop, he points to all the glassware decorating the ceiling of the central bar island we are occupying. "No smash glass," he says kindly.

"Of course," I reciprocate his smile and lift my glass to be filled, he tuts and takes our glasses away replacing them with new ones and pours us two fresh glasses. "Thank you." I blush.

"Enjoy." He bows away and I take a sip. It tastes like money and I laugh when Cass shoots me a shocked look.

"Holy shit!" She coughs.

"Liquid gold." I grin.

"Thank you, Callan. Thank you, Zara. Thank you for alcohol," she sings, I laugh and think back to what she said not long ago, before the bar tender rushed over.

"Do you think he is dangerous?" I'm intrigued. There was something very shifty about him.

"Did you not see the sketchy looking warrior hanging in the background?" she drawls.

"Hard not to," I muse. "This place looks too high end for it to be run dodgy," I say looking around the elevated seating area and explicitly expensive location.

"Doesn't mean he hasn't got other places less classy," she sniggers.

I think it over. "True, *there* was something about him. Did you see his tats?" I shudder, I like a well-made man, but the more I think of his cold stare, the more I want to get out of here.

"Bet Zara has." She chuckles, she necks half her glass on a soft hum.

"If he is dodgy, surely she can do better?" I reflect, taking a little more time with my own glass, I take another sip and I feel my phone buzz in my bag.

"Bet that's the superhuman." I know for a fact it is, he phoned me after work and did a crap job of trying to find out where I was headed for the evening, I roll my eyes and shift through my clutch for my phone.

You having a good night, where did you end up? J x

I don't open it but merely read it from the lock screen, I sigh and twist my phone to show Cass, she pulls a face, "let me check something," she says absently, she finds her own phone and dials Sean, putting it on loud speaker.

"Slave to a beautiful blonde," he answers on the second ring, I burst out laughing. "Fuck off, Lily," he chuckles.

"Hey, baby." Cass grins and mimics a whip, I shake my head and take another swig of my champagne, "has Jace been in?"

"Yes, he had that skinny blonde with him, seemed pretty stressed." Cass eyes me carefully, I grit my teeth hating that he is with Neve.

"Okay, I'll see you shortly." She eyes me sympathetically.

"You go someplace nice. Did you try that bar I suggested?" It's hard to hear him over the chatter of his bar.

"Yes, it's a hit, we're slurping champagne as I speak." She grins.

"Okay, great, we should try it. Love you, baby." His Irish accent lilts over the endearment and I swoon a little.

"Back at you!" She rings off and looks at me, waiting for me to flip but instead I fill my glass up and neck half the contents, "I don't want to cause a shit storm but I don't like that woman," Cass states her face pulling in disgust.

I incline my head and lift the bottle intent on filling both our glasses back up, but my annoyance gets the better of me and I place it down hastily. "You and me both," I mutter.

"Have you told him you don't trust her?" Cass gathers her hair to one side and fiddles with the end.

"He knows," I mutter.

"Urgh men," Cass scoffs. "More champagne?"

"Yes." I lift my glass and take a big swig, Cass follows suit and we are soon halfway through the hefty bottle.

Several glasses later and a shot of tequila it is nearing midnight, "how come we can never just have one drink," she slurs, I giggle and slip off the stool, the bar tender scoops up our empty glasses and begins wiping up the surface, "safe journey," he says in broken English.

"And you." I hiccup and push Cass towards the exit, we manage to get in the elevator and instantly it drops with a light whoosh.

Cass grabs hold of her stomach. "Oh God, that's not good." She holds onto my gaze with desperation, it's the only thing keeping her from losing all the alcohol we have consumed.

"Please, don't be sick," I whine, if she lets loose in here, I'm bound to go too. She doesn't respond, luckily we reach the bottom in record time and Cass rushes out gulping in lots of air, the concierge at the bottom steps back, I don't blame him she is three shades paler than when we arrived, she stops and closes her eyes breathing slowly.

"Urgh, I can't come here again," she grumbles rubbing her stomach tentatively.

"Do you want some fresh air?" I say softly, rubbing her back, she nods and looks at me through watery eyes.

"No more Nexo," she pouts, I laugh as we exit, she stumbles and I snort trying to hold her up, her foot slots between mine snagging me up and we both yelp as we go down in a tangle of drunken limbs, the ground scrapes at my body and I hiss feeling the throb of broken skin.

"Bloody hell, Cass!" I cry, pushing her head up, her eyes are closed and her mouth is pulled in a wide smile, I snort out a laugh, my wrist is all scraped up, "I'm bleeding," I whine, pushing at her to move but she doesn't. "You're a nightmare!" I laugh, she blinks her eyes open and lifts her gaze above me.

"Uh oh," she snickers, I twist when a shadow moves over our slumped bodies on the pavement, Jace is staring angrily down at us, his nostrils flare and I can't help the little bubble of laughter as it vibrates in my throat and leaves my mouth on a high cry, Cass throws her head back and laughs before burying her face in my stomach.

"Dog house here we come!" She chortles.

"Oh for fuck sake, get up!" He snaps, he pulls Cass up and holds her for a minute until she gets her balance, a little thank you leaves her mouth.

I flick a pair of angry eyes up at him, greys colliding with ambers. "Don't *even* fucking start, woman," he hisses. I'm lifted just as quickly until I'm stood up, and his eyes drag down my scarcely clothed body, "And what the fuck are you wearing?"

"A dress," I spit.

"You look as though you got it tattooed on, and your *arse* was showing," he growls. I tug at the material now halfway up my cheek, defiance shining up at him.

"God, lighten up!" I roll my eyes and Jace glares at me, Cass prods me and shakes her head, I lift my chin and walk across the street to his car parked haphazardly on the curb, my mouth feels dry and my heart is beating wildly in my chest.

"Sean's in the dog house too," Cass mutters, stomping after me. It doesn't take a genius to work out Sean gave Jace my whereabouts. She catches me up quickly. "I thought he was going to punch a hole in the ground." Cass shoots me a worried glance. "He's majorly pissed."

"Well, if that woman is in his car, he can fuck right off!" I seethe quietly, remembering Sean saying Jace and Neve were in Finnegan's earlier. As we get closer, my fractured vision slowly makes out the outline of a woman's long hair and my step falters.

I spin and find him fighting off a smug look. I was right. Did he bring her along on purpose to antagonise me? I scoff at his childish antics, and look him up and down, my irritation dive-bombing for repulsion. "I don't need this. I can't believe you," I spit furiously.

"Not cool," Cass winces at him.

"Neve was helping me look for you," he snarls. "She's my fucking friend, like *Travis* is yours." He takes my hand. How utterly juvenile! "So, get in the car and quit acting like a child." Me? A child! He snaps his eyes to Cass. "You too. I told Sean I would drop you home."

"No." I yank my arm free. "I don't think so." I eye him, feeling like I don't quite know this person, and what I do see, I don't like.

"Lily," he grates.

Cass steps in. "Jace, I think it is best you go." He laughs harshly as she points to the car. "Really?" she questions, driving home the absurdity of the situation.

"She's a friend," he grates slowly.

"Perhaps you should tell her that!" She has patronising down to a fine art and I could bloody hug her for it. How could he bring her?

He throws filthy ambers up to the sky, and when he drops them, he looks ready to rip us both a new one. "It's the anniversary of her parents' death. Forgive me for giving a shit." His tone is eerily calm. "Instead, she helped me search for Lily. I'd say that qualifies as being a good person." He slants a look of irritation at my friend, then one to me, daring us both to fight him on this. Why in the hell is he out looking for me!

I flinch at his tragic words, my own hurt dropping away. I too know the pain of losing a parent. I look at Cass, who winces sadly, both of us too compassionate to ignore the emotional bomb he just dropped. Wordlessly, I walk to the car and Cass follows. Jace drags the door open and we slide in quietly. Neve is sat up front but she says nothing and I can't quite bring myself to break the silence.

Jace drives us at an unusually calm speed and I wonder if it is because Neve's parents died in a car accident?

He drops her home first. "Thanks, Neve." He sounds apologetic.

"Sure." She doesn't spare us a minute of her time and walks up to a converted Georgian house. Gone is the bolshie, smart mouthed woman. Jace flicks a reproachful look in the back. I turn my head and keep it that way until we pull up outside Sean's. Cass leans and kisses my cheek before she unclips her belt.

"Thanks, Jace," her tone is quiet, regretful.

"No problem." Oh, it is a problem and every inch of his tense body suggests so.

"Ring if you need me, Lil," she murmurs.

"She won't need to," Jace rasps. Cass throws me a sympathetic glance. I sigh softly and turn to face out the window again, waiting for the car to pull into the traffic.

"Are you not getting in the front?" He asks, eyes meeting mine in the rearview mirror.

"Not if you're going to give me the third degree all the way back." His chin drops to his chest. He is fighting the urge to argue with me.

Chapter Twenty-Six

How did we go from blissfully happy to scratching each other's eyes out in a mere few hours?

He works his neck. "I won't." Strangely, I believe him. I stay seated for a minute but finally push up and scramble into the front. Jace is true to his word, so much so that he utters no words to me at all. We sit in an awkward silence for the entire journey— even when I realise, he is heading to his and not mine, I say nothing. I refuse to give him the satisfaction, although him admitting he was searching for me is not okay, I was out for a drink not kidnapped!

When we finally park up I get myself out, Jace is already walking towards the front door, he pushes his way in and flicks on the lights, I try to walk in a straight line and head straight for the bedroom ignoring his scowl, I perch on the edge of his bed and pull my heels off, my dress goes next, I slowly make my way to the bathroom and fill the sink with warm water, one of my hair ties is here so I drag my hair up and begin splashing my face, it chases away some of the alcohol. Sensing Jace I prepare myself for world war three and when I sluice the water from my face, he's stood behind me in his boxers, our eyes lock for a moment but I look away even though his mused hair and fiery gaze is enough to make me beg for forgiveness.

After he dumped Neve's bad news on me, I'm reluctant to push this or challenge him further. He is in the wrong, but deep down I know I could have handled it better. We're still trying to get to know one another.

All my toiletries are at mine so I have nothing to cleanse my face properly with or even a toothbrush, sensing my internal dilemma Jace steps forward and offers his, I mumble a thanks and make quick work of brushing my teeth and placing it back on the side, my mascara has underlined my eyes making the grey pop against my skin, I absently lift my hand and brush it away despite knowing traces will still linger.

Rather than back up, Jace stays at my back, I don't focus my attention on our reflection but I can see him battling his addiction to touching me, he drops his hands to the sink gripping it and his forehand rolls over my shoulders, he is at war with himself. Neither of us *wants* to give in, but the compulsion we have over each other is winning. I'm stiff between his strong arms, my face locked on the mirror but my eyes are distant. His desire wins.

He drops a hand from the basin and delicate fingers smooth themselves over my knickers, I let go of the breath I was holding it betrays me and turns into a sigh, his fingers brush the material aside and run the slippery length of me, I close my eyes and brace myself for the adept intrusion, it doesn't come. Jace spins me around and I gasp, clutching hold of the sink for support. I expect to find golden eyes burning down at me with lust and I do, but it's tainted fiercely with anger.

I want to say something but any words get chased away when he takes my knickers and rips them from my hips. His lips are so close they could be touching but he doesn't kiss me. He is panting as he lifts me and deposits my bare arse on the cold unit, I shudder on a gasp and reach for him, but he knocks my hand away and drags my bra down, the straps get caught around my arms and the cups dig into my stomach his face drops to the exposed flesh and he sucks a hardened peak into his hot mouth.

"Ah, God!" I hold tight to the sink, his hands massage my heavy breasts roughly, his teeth drag over the sensitive nub and I cry out but his hands soon become uncaring as he pushes my breasts high dragging his rough jaw over my skin and sucking my nipples, heat pools into my womb and I pull at his boxers desperate for connection. Jace growls and slaps my hand away, my eyes fly to his but the amber halo I love so much is unseen, there is no kindness in his eyes and it shocks me.

"Stop," I choke, I can't stand the distant glaze in his eyes.

Jace grips my neck and his mouth nips at my breast, I sob out a moan and go lax dropping back into the mirror with a thud, his fingers stay at my throat, his thumb is oddly soothing as he runs it back and forth over my pulse. His mouth though, his mouth is moving with intent to between my thighs, he lifts one leg over his shoulder and pushes up spreading me wide, his eyes take me in greedily and his tongue drives into me on a deep groan.

I grip at his messed hair and hold him to me. "Fuck!" I yelp, his teeth drag over my flesh and my eyes go wide when he does it again and again and again, "Jace!" I wail, my body arched and shaking, his actions are resentful.

He doesn't want to want me as much as he does. But he can't say no either.

His fingers press into me. "Goddammit, Lily! Come!" He thunders, pressing his face back into my folds and pleasuring me furiously, my orgasms spirals up wards and splinters through me, I drop his hair and sob loudly.

Jace stands and yanks his boxers down enough that he can free his cock. He has always been big, but he is pulsing and hard as rock, dragging my hips to the edge he positions himself and slams upwards.

"FUCK!" He roars, his eyes wild and his movements unsynchronised, unfeeling. I hate him for taking me like this, but I hate even more that I'm enjoying it. I don't want to enjoy this, I feel disgusted in myself, in him.

My hand flies out and cracks his cheek. He rears back, the shock knocking at his foggy brain. "You bastard!" I choke, my face twisting in distress for slapping him.

"You fucking hurt me!" He shouts, his hips piston into me with meticulous affect, I sob and hold onto the sink as he takes my hips and pounds away, he closes his eyes not wishing to bear witness to my tears, "FUCK!" he booms.

I know when I look into his lost eyes he doesn't want this but he can't stop either, his eyes clench tightly together and his head drops in defeat, he hates himself for this just as much as I do, I grip his hair harshly making him grunt in pain, I yank it because he is hurting me too, Jace smashes his mouth to mine.

He chokes out a rough groan and grips my hips hard enough to bruise, his eyes become lost on the darkest parts of us, I can't bring myself to look away from his strained frown, his mouth is lax and his hair drops forward. When amber eyes find mine I have the sudden urge to tell him I love him and hate him all at once, but his head rolls back on a gut deep groan, it's enough to hurtle me into another orgasm, I sob softly when it rolls through me and draws him deeper. With his head thrown back exposing the column of his neck Jace's hips jerk of their own volition, pumping me full, as he too gives into the pleasure.

He steps away and I sag against the wall. A low sob erupts into the room and it takes a moment for me to realise it came from me. I can't believe he took me like that. I feel dirty. Punished. Unloved.

This isn't the Jace I know. This whole day has been awful. I wish I could start it again and do it all different.

"Lily, I'm sorry." I slap his hand away, slipping off the side. My legs wobble beneath me, but I draw in breath and move past him, my vision blurred and shuttered.

"I . . . I was . . . that was . . . "

"Don't try and justify yourself, Jace," I spit. I'm a concoction of confusion and anger. I know I could have stopped him, and I should have, but I didn't and I don't understand why. It felt good, really good, but emotionally, not so much.

"Fuck." I hear him berate before his hand takes mine. I tug it free and he tries to pull me to him, but I won't go. I push at his chest, my eyes thick with tears.

"Jesus Jace, I can't do this, this is too much. Today has been . . . I don't even know you." I worry all the alcohol I've consumed is messing with my emotions, but I feel worryingly sober after that.

"No, wait!" Jace grabs at his hair when I slap his hand away again. "I'm sorry, so, so sorry. It just happened. I'm so fucking confused, Lily."

"You are?" I laugh. "You fucked me like a cheap hooker. I feel sick." I sniff.

"I didn't mean to make you feel like that. You hurt me," his voice softens and his own eyes drop with sadness.

"So, you thought you'd hurt me?" I snipe, wiping at my tear-stained cheek. God, I must look pathetic. His eyes scan my body looking for evidence of any physical damage. "Here," I whisper, roughly putting a finger to my chest. My lip wobbles and I drop onto the edge of the bed, and he drops down at my feet. "This isn't what I want, Jace." He turns away, dragging in a lungful of air. He can't look at me and my heart breaks for him. I start to wonder if Jace is more fragile than anyone realises. When he finally looks at me, he lifts a finger and runs it under my eye, removing a smear of makeup. I say nothing. He doesn't have words for what just happened, his quietness during sex suggests as much.

I'm so used to hearing passionate words raining down on me, sexy rasps of encouragement, and dirty groans that his aversion to speaking this time hits me on a cellular level. It reminds me of who I've become and who I'm not anymore. I refuse to accept anything less than what I deserve after Adam.

Before my mother died and my father remarried, I was carefree and confident. After her death and the pain of my father's quick marriage, I felt helpless, defeated, and so I emotionally armored myself to feel safe. Then Adam happened and I lost all faith and trust in other people. I mentally shake my spiraling thoughts away. I know Jace isn't like him, but he certainly isn't the cocky, confident man he portrays to be. Beneath his well-performed exterior is a man with a hell of a lot of emotions. A man I don't quite know. A man I don't think I trust, not this man anyway.

That niggling feeling is back and I know he has got skeletons in his closet just like I have. Skeletons I'm not going to like. Skeletons I don't want to know about.

I begin to gather up my belongings, quietly moving around the room all the while his eyes burn into my back. "Please don't leave." His deep voice is unusually soft.

"Jace, I can't do this."

"Lily, that will never happen again. I lose myself when I'm with you." His explanation makes me stiffen. I want it to go over my head and for me to not care, but I understand all too well what he means. If I wasn't as lost to him too in that moment, maybe we wouldn't both be feeling how we do now. I struggle with the notion that I'm to blame too.

"I need time to think, Jace." I can't look at him.

"So that's it, one mistake and we're done?" He scoffs.

"Seriously?" I whirl around. "I want some time to think. This isn't what I signed up for. You need to think what it is you want in a relationship because *that* isn't on offer!"

"I fucked up. That isn't what I want either." He pulls me to a stop and keeps my hand loose in his.

"Yet it happened!" My snap has his eyes widening. His hand drags through his hair and his mouth moves but I cut him off. "If this is part of what you have to offer, which apparently it is, then I'm done. I need to go, to think." I don't sound as resolute as I would like. My voice wavers off as a new wave of tears begins. I truly thought he was the one. I can't do this with him, not after Adam. "What just happened was not okay. I'm not okay." I hiccup. It's not only about the sex, this whole day has been a huge wake-up call.

I expect him to fight me into staying, but he takes my place on the bed, his head bent and eyes downcast. He leaves me to pack the little I have here and keeps quiet when I phone for a taxi. Some twisted part of me wants him to beg for forgiveness, but I suspect like me he is in shock by his actions. He wasn't lost. He was gone. He was somewhere else. Someone else.

We sit in separate parts of the house until my taxi arrives. He makes no move to stop me and I have no intention of looking back. I exit the house quickly and rush to the waiting car, my footsteps both eager but heavy. I'm indecisive. I want him to fight. I'm too scared to stay. My fear wins.

Compulsion has me looking back to the house. He's still there, head bent, looking as defeated and as gutted as I am.

"Drive, please," I instruct breathlessly. I can't witness his hurt as well as mine. I feel I'm making a huge mistake. Panic envelopes me and I grab the handle but stop myself. I was never ready for a man like Jace, not after Adam. I'm still picking up those pieces and now I've added whiskey coloured ones to the pile.

My tears come thick and fast, and the disgust I felt earlier returns tenfold. Maybe I'm more damaged after Adam than I previously thought. Maybe his abuse has left a mark on me, and now some dark part of me craves the brutality that Jace shocked us with.

Nausea whirls in my stomach, the idea repulses me, and I reject the possibility. I want to believe for my sake Jace isn't that kind of man. That thought alone has me looking back again. I can't see him. Not now.

The entire windowpane to his bedroom is a sheet of cracked glass, the once clear view marred by a frosted web of anger. His temper solidifies my decision, or at least that's what I tell myself as I sink lower into the seat, battling with the gut-deep churning ache at leaving him. The taxi crunches down the drive, taking me further away. I grit my eyes tight, trying to rid my mind of any memory of him.

No more hurtling.

No more two a.m.

No more Jace 'whiskey eyes' Bennett.

The End

Betrayal

Chapter One

I'm not sure which is worse, my hangover, or the ache in my chest. I feel terrible about last night. I've had too many hours to play it all over, and now that my mind isn't as distorted by alcohol, I'm not sure I made the right decision. I know I didn't.

If there is one thing I have learned about myself in the past few weeks, it's that I react the second I feel emotionally threatened. A by-product of Adam's actions, no doubt, and Jace Bennett just so happens to make me feel like I'm on the cusp of the most thrilling and terrifying moment of my life.

Jace's behaviour was far from okay, but if that is his worst, I'm getting off scot-free compared to my last relationship. I've chalked it up as one of those make or break moments. It nearly broke us. I just hope we can fix us.

I knew deep down there was more to him, just like there is with me. I laugh out loud into the quiet room. Hell, name me a person that hasn't got a few issues. I cover my face with my hands and rub at my tired eyes—they're gritty and sore.

"You're a mess, Lil," I grumble and roll over, staring at the window. It's not yet light outside, and the faint blush of the moon is pressing its way into the edges of my blind, and I roll back and blink in a huff. I've barely slept because my head is too consumed by yesterday's events. Not to mention the crushing fact that Jace hasn't contacted me. His words come back to me: *One mistake, and we're done*. The second I felt overwhelmed, I did the one thing he asked me not to do. Run.

Always running. I'm cross at myself for hightailing it out of there and for leaving him feeling as dejected and bewildered as I am. I doubt he will be having anyone over for dinner now that his bedroom looks like the hulk took a swing at it. That's going to cost him a small fortune. Maybe I should contact him and offer to pay for it? Maybe I should get my head checked, and I most definitely need to stop drinking!

I groan once more, unsure how to move forward with this mess. I pick up my phone and consider calling Cass, but I know I need to deal with this alone. Besides, she will be mad at me and accuse me of overthinking, overreacting.

Which I am now, analysing every word and second of yesterday until my brain is ready to evacuate and find a more suitable host. It's not yet five a.m., and my weak heart aches for Jace. I want him to cuddle me and tell me it is all going to be okay, but it's not. We're both on the edge of a cliff with a foot each in mid-air, free-falling into a relationship we have yet to understand because the stark truth is that we don't know each other. We've both been holding back, too consumed by lust. I open up his messages, tap the empty text box, and stop. I can no longer deny that with Jace, I feel like I'm on the periphery of something incredible.

What do I say? What if he doesn't want me back?

He probably thinks I'm an emotional loser.

I do too. I'm embarrassed at myself. I did a Cass: zero to psycho.

I try to tally the pros and cons of Jace Bennett. I'm not naïve enough to believe everything will be rose-tinted here on out, nor can I forgive his actions from last night, but I want to believe he is it for me. I've never, never in my life ever met a man like him, a man so all-encompassing, so consumed by another person that he is oblivious to the world and the silent riot he is causing around him—so consumed by me. He wants me, and not just with the partial indifference that I have witnessed in other relationships—he wants *me.*

Wants to know, learn, and love me.

How can anyone possibly say no to that?

One night is enough for me to know that I can't say no.

I won't. I refuse to let my fears crush what small amount of happiness I have felt in a long time.

I begin typing: 'Hey', then delete it because it sounds lame. "Hey, sorry I turned into a crazy lady." I say out loud and then snort before I drop my head back—what a mess.

Maybe I could start with something more direct. I chew my lip. 'I didn't deal well with last night. I'm sorry I didn't give us a chance to work it out.' I delete that too. Fuck!

Three dots appear. He's typing! I suck in a breath, and hot tears well up. Is he as cut up about this as I am?

Can't sleep? J x

This is it, my moment to bridge that gap. I know after one night of pain that I can't be without him. I miss The Hub. I miss hurtling. A vision of the splintered glass window shakes my resolve. It's his anger and his lack of control, not to mention his emotional abandonment in a moment that should have meant something—it's those things that have made me three-sixty into a massive ball of nerves.

I push my concern aside and mull over a response. I don't want to seem too keen because that would make me a pushover, and that's exactly what got me into a mess with Adam, but if I don't start fighting to gain control of my fears, I never will overcome them.

No. Too much going through my head. How's your hand . . . and the window? x

I chew my lip and sit up, rearranging my pillows while I wait for his reply. It takes him a little while, and when I do receive it, I smile sadly.

Hand is fine, heart, and lamp not doing too good. I miss you, beautiful x

I miss you too. I missed the man I knew, not so much, the one I met yesterday.

Last night is not something I want to go through again. I need to know why you did it? I'm sorry I left x

His reply is instant.

Lily, I can't stand myself for what happened. I hate what I have done. I don't want this to break us. Can I see you? We need to talk properly. Forgive me x

. . .

Has it broken us? I don't think so. Truly, deep down, I believe that we both are at fault. Somewhere between morning and night, we both made more than one wrong move. He went one way, and I went another, and we missed being able to reconnect in the middle. I'm staring at my phone when another message comes through.

Forgive me and come to dinner later. I miss hurtling with you x

I don't want to be the old Lily, the one that ran. Not any more. I contemplate my answer once more. I know yesterday I set a precedent for the day. I reduced our relationship to nothing more than sex when it is so much more than that. I pushed him further when I refused to meet him in the middle, then I went out and wore something inappropriate to provoke him further. Am I surprised he felt loopy with anger? I shouldn't be. With a sigh, I pull my knees up and stare back at his last few messages, scrolling through with a sad smile. This is the Jace I know.

I've really tried to separate my feelings and figure out what it was about last night that hurt me so much.

In fact, drunk me is a pain in the arse.

I know it wasn't the sex. That was incredible.

It was his emotional withdrawal. He was confused and angry and possibly more hurt than I realised, and he held all that in until he could no longer voice it. Instead, he acted on it, and it hit something deep within me. I felt used, nothing more than an object. I suspect many a woman has been subjected to that side of Jace, and I refuse to be that woman.

However, I refuse to give up on us. We have a connection, and I want to keep it. I'm not finished with my whiskey-eyed man and his two a.m. lovemaking. I want to hurtle too.

. . .

Can I think about it? x

It's a pointless reply. I know I will go. I will do anything to mend this between us, but until it is fixed, I don't much fancy pretending everything is okay to his friends.

Sure, can I see you today? Maybe we can grab a coffee? x

Light is peaking through the clouds when I finally push free of my bed, taking my phone with me. I head to the kitchen gingerly, my hangover is out in full force, and I feel terrible. I put the kettle on—coffee sounds great, now and later. I smile as my thumb runs over the letters quickly.

I can meet at around 2? x

I'm smirking as I wait for his response. I want to tell him I can meet him every hour on the hour. I really do miss him that much. Last night feels like an age ago.

Our favourite time sounds perfect. J x

Meet at Bobo's? x

It's neutral ground. It's either that or the deli, and after the mix up with Travis, I think this is the more suitable option. Jace agrees immediately, and I'm grateful to have managed to make a few baby steps between us. Feeling a little better than I have all night, I begin to get ready for work and make it to the office just before it opens.

Harriet swans in a few minutes late, but with two steaming coffee cups at the ready.

"Sorry, the queue this morning was horrendous," she calls. I grab my head, wincing at her high tone, and she pulls back when she sees me. "Good night?" She smirks.

"Cass is the worst influence. Do you have any painkillers?"

Harriet dives into her bag and pulls out a pack of tablets.

"I'm going to go and grab you some breakfast."

"Oh, you don't need to." I smile delicately, conscious not to make any sudden movements, but both my head and my stomach disagree.

"It might help soak the alcohol up." She screws up her face.

"Oh god, do I smell?" I smell my clothes and look at her in horror.

"Just a little of booze." She laughs. I drop my head in my hands on a deep groan. "So, breakfast?" she reiterates.

"Yes, please," I grumble.

"Great! I won't be long." She places my coffee down and takes hers with her to pick our breakfast up. As she heads out, I move to the front desk, praying that no one comes in because I must look a state and smell bad for Harriet to point it out. God, how unprofessional—I'm acting like a teenager!

I jump when the phone blares, clutching my head as the shrill ring fractures my skull. I clear my throat before I answer, "The Loft, Lily speaking, how can I help?"

No one replies, but the line stays open. I frown and press my ear into the receiver, trying to hear for anything on the other end. It's definitely connected.

"Hello?" I say it a bit louder. A scuff and the obvious sound of someone breathing come down the line. "Hello, can I help?"

The repetitive hum is too deep to be female.

"Jace?" I say softly, wondering if he has called me by mistake. The line goes dead, and I sit back, looking at the phone in my hand, willing it to tell me who it was. I decide to call back, but the automated voice tells me the caller withheld their number. Well, fat lot of use that is to me!

I figure if it is important, they will call back, but soon forget when Harriet returns with two breakfast rolls. They smell amazing. We wrap up, sitting out in the courtyard with the door wide open to keep an ear out for the bell.

"You are a lifesaver," I state, taking a seat.

"I know." She laughs, biting heartily into her roll. "So, you and Cass have a good night then?"

I grin and roll my eyes before I ask her if she knows Nexo. The club we went to last night.

"I've never heard of it." She shakes her head, tucking a stray strand before it gets caught in her food. "Any good?"

"If you have heaps of cash, sure," I snort. For some reason, I tell her about meeting Cass's friend and the free bottle we received.

"Ah, that's to blame for your hangover then?"

"Would seem so." I munch between answers and gulp the last bit of my coffee down. I already feel better, and with the painkillers working their way through my system, I'm ready to start my day. I stand and tell Hat I'm going to grab myself some water from the fridge, taking her rubbish with me.

"We're pretty quiet today. I need to do a post office run—we're running low on envelopes, and I forgot to order some," she tells me, taking a bottle I hand her. "Thanks," she adds.

"Can you grab me some highlighters?" I say as I remember I have that adapter I promised her. I hand it over, and she pops it into her own bag.

"Thanks."

"Okay, highlighters." She points at me, and she slips out, pulling her coat on as she goes. I watch her walk up the street briskly, a typical feminine grin on her face. Oh, she has got it bad for Simon!

My calls go from one to another, then another. Harriet returns while I'm still glued to the phone, chatting with the owner of Ebony Art.

"I will get it wrapped up and contact the courier this afternoon. If I schedule it for collection tomorrow, I can have it to you by Monday?" I suggest.

"Great, thanks, Lily."

"I'll email you the tracking number as soon as I've booked it in," I tell Stanley, checking the time. I'm ravenous.

"You're an angel!" he declares and briefly tells me about an exhibition he is having soon. Harriet walks in just as I'm putting the phone down, a pad and pen in her hand, a pen she is repetitively tapping against her notepad.

"The shadow piece is ready to be wrapped. Was he okay with the delivery times?" she asks, her methodical tapping never wavering. I don't believe she is aware she even does it.

"Fine." I shrug. "I don't think he was expecting us to move so quickly, so he's happy to have it as early as Monday," I confirm. I push my glasses up my nose and flit my eyes back to my screen to press send.

"Oh, good." She takes a seat opposite my desk. "I grabbed us some lunch, noticed you didn't have anything in the fridge."

"Harriet, I could cry. What the hell am I going to do without you next week?" I bury my head in my hands and moan softly, my hangover feeling more like a constant bruise.

She laughs and stands, and I lift my head and watch as she exits my office and returns with crusty baguettes and fruit pots.

"Make sure you give me your receipts," I tell her. I hold my hand out, and she drops a wrapped sandwich in my hand.

She sits with an amused look at the other side of my wide desk—a desk that not too long ago I was bent over, and my blush feels like a burn on my skin. I clear my throat to distract myself from my wandering thoughts.

"You're the best, Hat!" She really is.

Chapter Two

I arrive at Bobo's just before two o'clock. Jace isn't here yet, so I find a table near the back and pick up the menu. They have an array of drinks, each equally suitable to the décor in here. There are enough plants around to mistake this place as a registered forest. It smells like rain and foliage and gives the illusion of being outdoors. Each drink has some unusual organic ingredient that I haven't ever heard of, but luckily they sell coffee.

I sorely need coffee and lots of it, as my hangover is yet to leave me.

I'm rubbing at my temples when the chair opposite me gets dragged out softly. My eyes snap up, and there he is. His eyes are pinched tight, and his lips are pulled into a short smile. He looks to have run his fingers through his hair, leaving it in a ruffled mess on his gorgeous head. Even guilt-stricken and mussed, he is hot. Hot enough that his presence has caught a few women's eyes.

"Hey." He grips the chair but decides at the last minute to walk round to me.

"Hey," I whisper as he stops at my side. He cups my face, leans in, and places the most delicate of kisses on my cheek. Our eyes remain open, mine because I've missed this man, and I don't want to miss a second of his face. I just hope it's the same reason for him.

"You look nice." His voice is husky and accompanied by blazing eyes, and he holds my gaze as he walks back to take his seat.

"Thanks." I tuck my hair behind my ear and flick a look to the menu again.

"Harriet is leaving early, so I can't be too long," I say apologetically. He looks good, real good in his open-neck shirt and suit trousers. His sleeves are pushed back, and his face is coated with light stubble. He looks pretty damn fuckable. Damn this hot man and my weak flaming hormones. I force my gaze away and frown—why can't I be even marginally indifferent with him? I'm like a lovesick puppy. It's embarrassing.

"Okay, she's going away, isn't she?" His manner is relaxed, but I notice the set of his shoulders and the unease in his eyes.

"She leaves first thing. She's kept me fed all day. I drank too much last night and—" My eyes lift back to his. We stare at one another, and I let out a light sigh. I'm an emotional wreck. "I'm sorry I walked out," I confess quietly. I fight the compulsion to look around the room for people listening, but seeing the deep shine in his whiskey eyes keeps me rooted to his face.

"I'm sorry for what happened, Lily." His voice roughens. His face reddens. "It will never happen again. You have my word. I feel shit about last night."

"Me too." I chew my lip, and he reaches over and runs a thumb across my mouth.

He sighs roughly, and his hand clenches on the table as his eyes cast away before they come back, looking full of guilt and hope.

"Yesterday, I wasn't myself. Neve wasn't in a good place. I was worried about her, and you seemed hell-bent on . . . " his voice trails off. "This isn't just sex for me, Lily. Trust me, if it were, it would feel like last night every time." He holds my eyes, conveying how sincere he is. "You're holding back, but I'm not going anywhere. I want to be with you."

"I'm sorry. I was difficult." I was. There's no way to deny it.

"I just wanted to come home to you after all this shit with Neve," he confesses quietly. He drops back into the chair and rubs at his forehead, "I was angry: at you, Travis, and myself, and I took it out on you. I'm sorry." Big, apologetic eyes burn across the table. "It will *never* happen again. You have my word," he breathes out, reaching for me and holding my hand tight in his. I nod. I believe him.

"Please come to dinner later, beautiful?" He lets his hand fall away when the waiter approaches.

"Hi, good afternoon. Are you both ready to order?" The waiter's smile is warm, his pen poised.

"Two coffees, please," Jace replies absently. His eyes are still focused on me. The waiter puts his pen down, having no need for it, and steps away.

"What about your window?" I ask and fiddle with the menu, bending the corner nervously. I realise what I'm doing and quickly smooth the paper back out.

"It's being fixed as we speak. I won't even know they were there by the time I get back." Of course he won't. I imagine before me, his life was as smooth and calm as his big, glass, house.

Our drinks arrive, and Jace finally seems to relax in his chair.

"Can we forget yesterday happened?" He frowns. "I'm not excusing my behaviour, or yours," he says lightly, "but that's not what we're about. I'm trying really hard, Lily. I'm not used to feeling like this, and it fucked with my head." His admission is one I had already figured out, but it's nice to hear all the same.

"I'd like that. I'm sorry too." I just want him back. "Need me to bring anything?" My lips tug when his eyes spark, and his big shoulders drop, revealing the level of tension he is carrying. When he runs a hand through his hair, I reach to take the other one, holding it tight. He grins at me.

"Just yourself. Minus the attitude." His eyes bang with fire, and my jaw drops. The cheeky sod!

"You can't help yourself, can you?" I laugh. He shakes his head, and I catch the table of women behind, snatching glances at him.

"Missed you, witch."

"Brute," I counter, sipping my coffee to hide my smirk. He lifts my hand and kisses my palm.

"Crazy about you." His whisper is low, sweet, and at complete odds with the man I was faced with yesterday. His earlier comment is still swirling around my head like toxic smoke.

"You said if it was just sex," – I rub at my throat, not liking the images his comment triggered, – "you said it would always be like that. You've really never been in a relationship, have you?"

Jace leans forward and takes my hand.

"No." He shrugs and looks about the café. "Never wanted one. Then you came along, and I have no idea how to be in one. I just know I want to be with you all the time," he confesses on a little wink.

"So, you've always been like that with other women?" I hate the question. I want to swallow it back up, pay someone to infiltrate my mind, stamp on it, and set it on fire. Jace's eyes sadden.

"Don't do this to yourself. I can't deny I've been with other women before you." Remorseful eyes plead with me to drop this.

I really don't want to get into any of this, so I hold my hand up, halting him from saying any more. "I know, I never thought . . . I don't really want details, Jace, but—" What do I want? I feel shocked by his statement. I feel sorry for those women, I do. "You were just so vacant—there, but not," I whisper.

"Lily, please, if I could re-do yesterday, I would in a heartbeat. Vacant Jace is who I was before you. My head was going crazy. I felt sick with jealousy, and it was easier to just shut everything off. Forgive me?"

Finally, some truth. I nod over at him, my hands still caught up in his.

"At least we know how not to be with each other," I say softly as my eyes flick up to his, and he gives me a slow and uneasy smile.

"No more yesterdays," he affirms, lifting my hand to kiss my wrist.

"Does that mean you won't go out searching for me on a night out?" I ask sceptically. Who goes searching for their partner? Surely he can see how messed up that is?

"We weren't on good terms, and it was driving me mad. I needed to find you and put it to rest," he confesses shakily. His eyes drop from mine to where my hand is held in his—his ambers are so sad. "The house was pretty lonely last night." He pouts, running his fingers in lazy circles over my hand.

"It won't be later. Carl will be strutting around, I'm sure." I laugh. I wonder if he has said anything to his PA?

"He's looking forward to seeing you," Jace replies. So Carl doesn't know. Good. I'd hate to think they'd all been talking about us.

"It will be nice," I say, checking my watch. "I need to leave in a minute. Can we ask for the bill?"

"Sure, I'll drop you back at The Loft."

Harriet leaves around four, a little earlier than I initially agreed, but I'm happy for the solitude. I whip home and sort an overnight bag, just in case. I stopped off at the shop on my way and picked up some wine and a few things to make a tomato and mozzarella salad. I've changed out of my work clothes and swapped them up for some cut-off chinos, and an oversized off-the-shoulder jumper—the colours make my skin tone look a shade darker, thankfully. I sorely need some sun. I look pale and shattered. I pin my hair up and swipe some gloss over my lips before trying to conceal the bags under my eyes. I look cute and comfy, and with it only being Jace, Carl, and his husband, I don't feel I need to put too much effort into getting dressed up.

There is no part of me that regrets my decision to get back with Jace. Let's face it; we hardly split up. One night doesn't count, surely? I just wish I could learn to rationalise my feelings and emotions like I am doing now, rather than just reacting. It has done neither of us any good. One thing I know for sure is I am still getting to know myself again after Adam, and Jace and I are still trying to get to know one another. We are bound to have a few bumps in the road.

I'll admit Jace's confession has stuck with me all afternoon. I can't get over his previous behaviour with other women. It's evident he was only interested in sating his own needs—he was so emotionless and cut off. He really was a playboy, chasing tail for his own satisfaction and not at all concerned who he might hurt in the process. I'm surprised I haven't had to deal with a string of emotionally dissatisfied and horny women. The thought makes me smile, but then I frown. I don't condone his behaviour but a small part of me, deep down, likes to think only I have been given the privilege of his true self. It's a nice thought, even if unrealistic.

I only know his date of birth from my online search. We still haven't discussed our pasts or family. He knows it's just me, but we've never delved below the surface of why that is, and I am still to ask him about his own family. These things will take time and evolve when they need to. For the time being, I'm going to be happy knowing that he is as crazy about me as I am about him.

Chapter Three

I have felt the pinch of Jace's distance all afternoon. We haven't spoken since lunch, and he gave me the barest of kisses when he walked me back to The Loft. I continually brush it aside on the journey to his, but as soon as I turn into his drive, my tummy does a little flip, and not of excitement. I feel nervous. I mentally scold myself, but it only picks up as I get out of my car, so much so that my hands shake a little, and my skin pimples with unease. He looks up through the window, and instead of the usually sexy smirk, he looks more serious now, his strong features more harsh and striking.

I collect up the wine and food, leaving my bags for later. Seeing my hands full, Jace meets me at the door, slanting it open so I can slip through. I eye him cautiously, trying to gauge his mood, and my anxious swallow doesn't go unmissed.

His amber eyes drop to the huge platter of salad.

"I told you not to bring anything," he scolds. When they lift to mine, I give him an awkward smile.

"Annoying habit. I like to do the opposite of everything you say." I blush around the truth of that statement because I'm constantly, unintentionally testing him, trying to gauge whether he is in this for real or just hurtling me along for the ride.

He cups my neck, his thumb running along my jawline.

"Isn't that the bloody truth?" His eyes dance with humour, and his mouth quirks in that sexy way. I inwardly sag and smile genuinely for the first time all day, unable to fight the tension pushing and pulling between us he drops his mouth and kisses me. I'm unable to do anything other than allow him to nip and lick at my mouth on sexy little groans and bites, as my arms begin to ache with the constant weight of the wine and plate grasped in them. But I don't complain, not when his mouth is adoring me.

"You look gorgeous," – he pulls back and takes me in, his nostrils flaring, – "and you smell like we should have sex," he states on a soft hum. I laugh, grateful when he takes the food out of my hands and quickly places it on the side before pulling me flush to him. He is hard, and my soft, accommodating body melts into him. Without the restriction of the food and wine, he cups my arse and bends to take my mouth once again.

His mouth is divine.

"Oh," I hum as he sweeps his tongue with a long silky brush against mine.

He drags his mouth away and drops a soft kiss to my bare shoulder. I contemplate reaffirming my apology because I still feel like there is an undercurrent of tension, but he beats me to it as he lifts my chin and stares down at me.

"It's done, okay?" I nod, twisting away when a ball of emotion threatens to break my stoic expression. "Hey," he kisses my worry away, "you're my girl, Lily. Don't doubt this. We're bound to have a few hiccups."

"That felt more like indigestion," I complain.

"A stroke," he grumbles. I flash 'sorry' eyes to him, but he winks. "Come on, give me a hand." He threads his fingers with mine, and he lifts my salad off of the side. I collect up my wine again as we move into the house properly.

"Something smells amazing," I tell him. The air is laced with garlic and other delicious herbs.

"Other than yourself, you mean?" he jokes. As soon as our hands are free, I move into him, and anticipating my need for him, he opens his arms. I drop my nose into his chest, inhaling that heady smell.

"I'll make it right later," he tells me. I very belatedly realise it is always him making it right for me, second-guessing my feelings or my next move, always anticipating my needs. And I let him. I begrudgingly admit I've become selfish, and if yesterday has taught me anything, it's that Jace isn't the nonchalant man I thought he was. Below his confident, polished exterior, he is very complex.

I nod against his hard chest, biting at the taut flesh beneath his polo shirt and causing his wide flank to vibrate with a deep laugh.

"How was work?" He lifts me, placing me on the only spare surface. "I thought you wanted my help?" I raise a brow at him, but he shrugs.

"This is helping," he replies, as he lifts the lid on my dish and nods his approval. "I'm impressed."

"Don't hold your breath," I mutter. I have long since accepted I'm a terrible cook, and although something can look delicious to the eye, it can taste like utter dirt.

"I wasn't." He throws me a grin over his shoulder, laughing at my gaping mouth. There he goes again, the cheeky shit. I smile anyway, dipping my head before answering him.

"Work was long," I admit. "Harriet flies out tomorrow, so I have the run of the gallery all to myself," I slip in. His eyes move from his furious chopping and meet mine with a naughty twinkle.

"Good to know." He winks.

"Yes, I thought you'd appreciate the information." I drop my gaze and smile softly. This is what I love: the playful nature mixed in with Jace's strong sex drive and intensity. It's an addictive combination.

A little while later, I watch him over my glass of wine as he moves around the kitchen, pulling on his beer and throwing things together as he drops a peck or two on my mouth. James Bay is crooning softly in the background, and I sing quietly along to the tune and nibble at a bit of salad to my right. I feel the weight of his eyes on me and hold back a smile. Slipping off the side, I cast a look over my shoulder and find him watching me.

"Kiss me, Lily." The cutlery is placed on the side slowly, and he takes his time walking to where I stand.

"Your guests will be here soon," I tell him breathlessly. He shrugs and hooks his arm around my lower back, pulling me to him. I know where this is headed, and I need to stop it.

I peck his cheek and pull away, but he tightens his grip and slants his mouth over mine.

"Don't refuse me, Lily!" he growls and bites my cheek gently. I laugh, pulling free, but it only makes him nip me more: my nose, mouth, and chin. "You taste like watermelon," he groans.

"Get off," I pant, pushing his laughing chest away. He lets me go but slaps my arse as I pass, making me yelp. "Thug," I mutter, casting a glance over my shoulder at him. He shrugs and moves quickly, grabbing my jumper and tugging me back to him.

"What the fuck is that smell?" he moans into my neck, inhaling my body lotion. Laughing, I try to sidestep and duck underneath him. His eyes flash into mine, and I make a sudden dash away. "Get here!".

I cry out in laughter when he barrels after me.

"Shit!" I squeak as Jace pounces around my waist, sending me flying onto the sofa with him, I'm shrieking as I go down, but the sound of his deep laughter softens the high note of my pathetic scream. Thick knees straddle my back as he pushes my arms up and my jumper high. In the seclusion of the house, he presses into my back and licks my shoulder blade.

"Delicious," he purrs.

I squirm, trying to waft a hand out for help.

"No," he chuckles, "when everyone has gone, I'm going to fuck you on the table under the stars." My breath leaves me in a gigantic rush of aroused air. "Do you want that, Lily?" He grinds into my arse, and every nerve ending springs to life to greet him.

I close my eyes, mentally already at the table—a torrent of explicit images running through my mind.

"Yes," I whisper.

"Good, next time you wear that perfume, make sure you're naked." He jumps up and lifts me with him.

"It's lotion," I tell him breathlessly. This pleases him somehow. His lips quirk, and he tilts his head, and I'm not left wondering the cause of his satisfaction very long.

"I think a massage is on the cards." He grins.

I fling my arms around him and kiss him hard on the mouth.

"You're too good to me," I tell him. We're going to be okay. I just know it.

"You're worth it." His lips touch my nose before he steps away. "I've got to finish up." I watch him walk away and take the opportunity to nosey at his bookshelf, mainly lined with architecture books, along with unique ornaments and the odd photo. I'd never really paid much attention to it before, as he usually occupied my focus. There are only a handful of pictures: Jace on a building site, I'm assuming it's one of his builds. He looks younger, maybe early twenties, and one of him on a bike, looking even younger still.

None of him with any family.

The last picture is of his shoulders and head as he looks out over a shimmering sea. I don't want to know who took that picture, and asking may rattle the shaky foundation we're walking on, so I take myself back to the kitchen island and pull out a stool.

"Cavalry has arrived," Jace says. I lift my head to find Carl and Rupert pulling into the drive in a four-by-four. Carl is already waving at me through the windscreen. I lift my hand as Jace dries his hands quickly on a towel, then wanders to let them in. Carl swans right to me and kisses my cheek, scooping up the bottle of wine by my side.

"You look lovely," he says in passing, his attention solely fixed on pouring himself a large glass. He walks around Jace's kitchen with familiarity.

When he looks back at me, taking in my outfit, I shrug my shoulder.

"This jumper is actually really old." I laugh. I've had it since my teens, but it's been faithful, and I love it.

Rupert joins us with Jace on his heel, and he's carrying a bottle of wine too. I smile at him and feel myself flush with embarrassment. The last time I met him, I was very drunk, not to mention I was whisked off to the loo for hot sex by Jace Bennett.

"Lily." He nods, far more reserved than his flamboyant husband.

"Hello, Rupert, how are you?" I feel my skin heat under his appraisal. Jace sees my fleeting look of embarrassment and hooks an arm around my neck, slapping a very showy kiss on me. He then gives me a wicked grin, and I drop my head against his chest. "You quite finished?" I smirk.

"Never, woman." I eye roll at him and lean back into the counter as he steps away, knocking my chin in that endearing way.

Rupert is regarding me with both amusement and delight, and in reply to my question, he smirks, "Far less flustered than you are."

I grimace, dropping my head, but he surprises me by giving me a gentle cuddle.

"Don't be shy. You've done what every other woman has failed to do." He winks at me, and I slip a startled look at him, then to Carl, who is leaning over the counter, chin in his hand, earwigging. He wiggles his brow, mimics a whip movement, and nods at Jace.

"I can't whip up eggs, let alone a man into shape." I'm over-dramatic, sighing helplessly, and Rupert barks out a laugh.

Jace looks to the couple on his right.

"There is nothing wrong with my shape." He throws a wink at me.

"Well," I let the word drag, gaining his full attention. "Your head has got unforgivably big." I wince.

Jace moves quickly and snatches my arm, tugging me to him with a wide smile. His hand takes my neck and holds me so he can drop his lips to my ear.

"By the way I get you screaming, Miss Spencer, I think you rather like my big head." There is laughter in his whisper-soft words, and he nips my earlobe, making me jolt.

My eyes fly across the room, but Carl and his husband are caught up in their own conversation, so, knowing I'm safe from prying ears, I turn back, happy that we seem to finally be back to our normal, less argumentative selves, and whisper, "I think you need to remind me just how much I like it."

My eyes glitter into his, and when he smirks, slowly and widely, I rise swiftly and drop a kiss on his lower lip. He groans and adjusts himself, and I can't help the flutter of laughter in my throat.

"Let me cook," he grumbles.

"Be my guest."

He regards me softly, his big chest rising slowly, then he shakes his head and sends us all outside. The garden heater is pumping out steady warmth, and we have been lucky to get some sun most of the day. I grab a blanket anyway and slip outside with my wine and the guys, settling myself onto a wide bench seat.

The door is open, and the music carries out to us. Carl hums along, and I sip my drink, enjoying the purr of heat over my face.

Rupert sighs heavily.

"Thanks for the heads up," he says to Carl and jerks his head at the front of the house where Neve is hopping out of her oversized car. My eyes flash inside to see Jace is walking leisurely to the front door.

"I didn't know," Carl scoffs and pats my shoulder. "Brace yourself," he hums. It's the complete clarity I need to affirm that my suspicions about this woman aren't misplaced.

I lift my glass.

"Have we got anything stronger?" To my surprise, it is Rupert who stands.

"I'll grab some whiskey."

"Shot of cyanide?" I quip. His laugh makes me smile, and Carl is trying his hardest not to laugh.

"Oh, you are bad," he drawls.

"That was really harsh and horrible, but she is such a bitch to me," I admit. Carl looks at me long and hard. We say nothing but the mutually unspoken dislike for this woman meets between us.

"Watch yourself, Lily," he warns. I follow his gaze to find Neve lifting on her tiny-heeled toes and wrapping her arms around Jace's neck as she kisses his cheek, then rather than drop back, she keeps her hands hooked and laughs up into his face. I'm grateful his hands are on her waist, holding her at arm's length, and when his eyes slowly find me, his mouth is pinched in unease. I hold his stricken gaze for a minute too long.

I can't bear to see her sliding all over him, so I drop my gaze as I feel my stomach hollow out. When I drag them back up, Neve is wiping at her eyes and folding into him, resting her cheek over his peck. He rubs her back, and I remind myself she is going through a difficult time and that they are just friends. I want to believe I can trust him—she has known him a long time and having me around has fractured her place in his life. I try to see it from her side; that perhaps she is trying to find where that place is now and not much liking how the dynamics have changed.

We are all waiting, and despite her bolshie attitude, she seems reluctant to join us. Jace nods her through, but she flicks sad eyes at him, and to Rupert's obvious delight, she moves back toward the door with the intent to leave, but Jace captures her hand and pulls her through the house.

"Hey," Jace breathes. He quickly meets my eyes, but I drop them to my drink. "Neve is joining us." Rupert has his face fixed on his phone, but Carl manages a smile.

"Grab a drink," he says by way of hello. She pulls at Jace's arm, trying to get him to stay outside with her.

"Hi, Neve." I muster up the strength to speak to her. Jace winks at me, but I don't return it with my usual grin. Instead, my eyes find Carl and Jace leaves to fix up the last food bits.

"Still hungover?" She smirks and leans into the doorframe—not so sad after all?

"No, I feel fine. How are you?" I try to be polite and take her feelings into consideration, but she apparently doesn't care for mine.

"Oh, it's just you look ready for bed; are those your pyjamas?" she scoffs. "I have some concealer too, if you need any?" She makes to go for her purse, and I can't help but grind my teeth together.

"I think she looks stunning," Carl slips in, and I mentally thank him for having my back.

"You would," she huffs, her eyes running over my attire as mine do her. I don't want to care or compare, but she looks amazing. Tight jeans, strappy sandals that are in no way appropriate for this weather, and a tiny cami tucked in. She's cold, because well, her ample assets tell me so. Smirking, she flicks a look over her shoulder.

"Jacey, can I borrow a top. It's colder than I thought." Her eyes find mine, desperate for my reaction. I snort out a laugh and lift my drink, absolutely adamant that I won't play her childish games. I could go down the same route and throw myself at Jace, but since her arrival, I feel well and truly put out, and I hate that she pulls that emotion from me.

"Rupert, how is business? I never got to ask much about it the last time we spoke." I give him my full attention, trying to ignore the catty bitch glaring at me.

"Well, I wonder why that was?" he muses, locking his phone and laying it on the table. I open my mouth to respond and slam it shut as he sniggers and winks at me. "You filthy buggers," he titters. Neve rolls her eyes and wanders off into Jace's bedroom and returns a few minutes later, sheathed in one of his jumpers. When he joins us, his eyes soften.

"You may as well keep that; you always bloody wear it." He laughs at her around his beer, and she snuggles further into the heavy wool jumper as her eyes blaze into his, just like how mine do, and I feel every ounce of my body fighting against Jace's admission that they are just friends. I always follow my gut, and I can't help the deep, aching burn, telling me that he is lying about their relationship.

I know my hurt is starting to show on my face, but I try everything to keep smiling.

"Top up!" Carl sings, and I jump up with him, happy to busy myself elsewhere. I'm tempted to text Cass and get her to feign an emergency so I can hotfoot it out of here. Carl takes my hand and pulls me through the door, but Jace snags it into his own and holds me at his chest. His eyes search mine, and I smile at him.

"I can start to bring things out if you like?" My ability to act indifferent surprises even myself.

Jace says nothing but holds my hand in his and wraps his free arm around my neck, his bottle dangling down my back.

"Kiss me first." His deep, gravelly voice brings my eyes back to his. He knows I'm struggling with this. He releases my hand, but only so he can raise it to cup my chin and angle my mouth for his. His mouth moves past mine and rests on my cheek. "It means a lot that you're trying with her." I nod, a ripple of emotion drowning me because I don't want to try with her, but I know if I want to be with Jace, I have no choice but to accept she is in his life. He must sense my inner dilemma because he sighs. "She is like family, Lily," he says with deep regard for her.

"I know," I whisper. He's trying. That has to count for something. I want to confess my feelings for him, but I know my unease at her presence is the root of that need. It's not the right reason to admit I'm falling deeply in love with him.

Chapter Four

The past few hours have been as pleasant as having teeth pulled, so when my phone dings, it's the perfect distraction and seeing Cass's name is a godsend. I excuse myself and slip away, aware Jace has eyes on me.

"Everything okay?" I nod over my shoulder and leave him to Neve. When I get inside, I call Cass and wait impatiently for her to pick up.

"Hey, things all okay?" She's referring to last night. She must have been tied up all day with work if we're only just touching base now. I give her a quick rundown of the evening. I don't want to seem melodramatic, but I can't stand Neve. And I'm astute enough to know the feeling is mutual.

"Need a getaway?" she hums sympathetically. *Yes*!

I want nothing more than to leave, but I've had too many to drive, and Neve is sinking them like an alcoholic at a beer festival. I don't trust her. I rest my elbows on the counter and look out of the window facing the drive.

"Can't," I mumble. I pick at some salad on the side and pop a thin slice of cucumber in my mouth.

"Oh, hun, don't let her get to you. She wants to drive you away." Cass reinforces her words with meaning as a timer goes off in the background and makes me jump a little. She swears and clangs about on the other end of the phone.

"I know. It doesn't make it any easier to watch, though." My eyes drift outside. "She can't keep her hands off him," I mutter, "how can he sit there and allow it when he practically lamped a man for swinging his arm around me?" I vent quietly.

"If I knew that answer, I would have a penis," she chortles, and I bite my lip because I am struggling to find anything funny at this particular moment. Footsteps bring my head over my shoulder, and I twist away as Jace saunters in. His eyes seek me out with concern when he makes his way over.

"Got to go," I say in a rush, trying not to show my hurt, "love ya."

"Oh, okay, ring me if you're stuck!" She cuts the call, and I twist to find Jace leaning against the counter. I snap a bright smile on my face,

"Tell me we're okay?" He drops his head and looks up through his lashes, a bottle dangling from thick fingers, his cheeks stained. I would usually take some satisfaction after yesterday's argument, but Neve's snake ways are very unsettling.

I nod, enforcing my smile.

"We are." I shrug, and he inclines his head that bit further, questioning my reply.

"Okay, let me rephrase, are you okay?" His bottle lifts in my direction. He's pressing further because I am doing a piss-poor job at hiding my dislike for his friend.

"Yes, of course, why wouldn't I be?" I tilt my head, copying him. I wait patiently for him to openly acknowledge that Neve is a little too tactile, but he is picking at the label on his beer thoughtfully.

"You seem quiet." That's bullshit. Carl and Rupert aren't talking either—we haven't been given the chance! And when the occasion does arise, no one has anything to say in response to all Neve's childhood tales of her and Jace or his escapades. I'd rather spend an evening with Adam or go and hang out with my dad and his wife than hear about his sexual conquests.

"I'm good," I assure. I head back towards the door as Neve strides in, heading towards the bathroom. I lift to drop a kiss on his cheek as I go. I don't want to make this awkward for him, and I will if I play into Neve's hands.

It's selfish of me to want him all to myself, but it's the only feeling I experience when she is about. He holds me to him and frowns.

"It doesn't feel like you're okay." His syrupy eyes search mine, and I let them, but I know he won't find anything, not when he is so blind to Neve's deception.

He dips and pecks my nose.

"I want that smile back." I flash one—it's false, and I feel the strain of its lie right up in my scalp. He knows that me having to watch her fawn over him is no different from having Travis sling his arm around me. I really don't want to get into an argument, but I hate her touching him, and for the first time, I understand his hurt and jealousy regarding Travis. I imagine if Neve has always been tactile with him, it would seem odd for him to start telling her to stop. She will blame me, and he doesn't want any animosity between us.

Jamiroquai's '*You Give Me Something*' comes on, and Jace begins to move his hips in sexy little rolls.

"What are you doing?" I laugh nervously, seeing the glint of purpose in his gaze. Jace winks and mouths the words to me as he moves to the beat. He goes all Patrick Swayze on me and bites his lip —I swoon.

"*We,*" he emphasises, "are dancing." He spins me out, captures my wrist, and yanks me to his chest on a twirl. "To our song." His nostrils flare when my lotion wafts between us, and he licks his lips, causing me to go breathless and wide-eyed. He holds my hips flush to his and grinds them on a roll, and the first scrape of unease in me begins to flake away. "This reminds me of you," he says and spins me out. I go, laughing, and come back into his arms in a sharp tug. "Oooh," he laughs, encouraging me to roll my own hips along with his, our smiles chasing my worries away.

He sings on a soft husk into my ear, his hips rolling and swaying as he dances us outside. I brush my hands up his chest and thread them around his neck as he holds my hips, moving us together. I'm spun back out and pulled in so that my arse gets lodged in his groin. He grunts softly, and I laugh, my head lolling back. He pecks my cheek, anchoring me with thick arms, and when his hand slides down and bunches in at my hip, I twist around.

My face is flushed as happiness radiates off me, and his deep whiskey-gaze is sultry and honey soft.

"Ooh," he mimics the artist, biting his bottom lip and sending my illicit thoughts running wild. When I rise to capture his sinful mouth, he hauls me up, and my legs go willingly around his waist—the hot press of his thicker body between my thighs a delicious comfort. He groans into the kiss, grinning when Carl makes a retching sound.

"Piss off," he laughs, his face stuck on mine. I sigh in contentment, soul-deep happiness. This feeling. Right here. I need to keep that. This is what we have. Something deep. Real. I may not have a past with him, but I have a present. Neve can't compete with that. Jace runs his thumb along my lower lip, his hips swaying so gently it's hardly noticeable. His eyes follow the path of his fingers and lift to my grey eyes, no doubt full of dazzling emotion. He swallows, and his hand shakes a little against my mouth. "Don't look at me like that, Lily." His gruff tone is low enough for only our ears, and my grin is slow. I quickly cover the distance and kiss him again. He tastes like beer, and I hum happily.

"I'd kill for that smile," he tells me. I hold him tight, just a quick squeeze, but enough to reiterate to myself that it's me he is with, and her underhand play is not on his radar.

"I need a refill," I say, very much aware that all conversation has stopped, and the attention is on us. I'm wrapped around Jace like a vine—our chests flush, our groins finely cupped together. All too happy to keep the close proximity of us; he sits us together. Neve's eyes are downcast, and her nearly empty drink is being swirled in her dainty fingers. Despite all my efforts this evening to pull her into conversation or take an interest in what she finds worthy of Jace's attention, her eyes hold mine with nothing but cold regard.

"Get a room," Carl snorts.

"I have one," Jace grumbles before nipping at my neck with a loud groan. "You're in it." He lifts a brow to his assistant, who pouts and turns his face away on a slow lift of his chin, flapping a hand as though Jace's little revelation had just given him an unwanted visual.

Rupert bursts out laughing.

"Tink, you've gone all red!" Carl shakes his head dramatically, and a chorus of laughter fills the quiet.

"Tink?" I question, and Carl sends his husband a look that could kill.

"Yeah, as in Tinkerbell," Jace explains. "Neve, pass me that blanket." He holds out his hand for her to pass it. She is clearly reluctant and barely looks at him, her face pinched in tight annoyance. I don't allow myself to wonder about her any longer because Carl is bitching quietly to his husband.

"So why the nickname?" I ask. Carl rolls his eyes and brings his drink to his lips, taking a long, loud gulp.

"I used to get called a fairy at school." He shakes his head in amusement, and though his perfect quaff barely moves, his preened brows are accentuated when he raises them in some semblance of boredom. "Original," he muses.

I squeeze his knee, and he nudges my shoulder in a grateful gesture.

It's short-lived when I say, "Personally, I think you resemble a gazelle," while taking a swig of my wine.

"Oh, you cheeky blighter!" he slurs, scowling at me. Jace is silently laughing, and Rupert leans in.

"You actually do, the way you prance about and stick your snooty nose in the air." I lift my glass high in agreement.

"I hate you all!" Carl pouts. He doesn't at all. His eyes are glassy but full of laughter, and his lips soon spread into a wide smile. "I like the food, hate the company." He is sullen and laying on the theatrics for our benefit.

"Present company or my company: Bennett and Klein?" Jace chuckles, drawing another wave of laughs out—even Neve has lost her sour face and has joined in.

"No, I love BK." He acts offended—his mouth is in a practised pout, and his cheeks look even more gorgeous slanted just so.

"Just us then," I poke.

"Oh, piss off. You're all horrible." I dip for a hug, and he pecks my cheek. I lean back on a yawn, my head rolls, and rests on Jace's shoulder, and he takes the opportunity to rest his chin on the shelf my shoulder provides.

Curious hands knead my waist and slip under my jumper.

"Sleepy?" Hope fills his tone, and I don't suppress my grin.

I nod.

"Mmmm." He stiffens beneath me, and the long, delectable length of his impressive cock springs to life and nudges my arse.

"Mmm indeed." He's nuzzling my hair, and with our bodies sheathed by a blanket, his hand takes a leisurely journey up my thigh. I tense and feel him grin against my cheek, and it doesn't prevent him from reaching his target, as he cups me fully and applies just enough pressure to start a series of dull sparks in my sex.

I gasp lightly, and he shifts.

"Dammit, Lily," he grinds in my ear. I'm already chuckling at his frustrated state.

"What's going on?" Carl huffs, his pert nose heads up in the air as he tries to focus on us through drunk, thick-rimmed eyes.

"You lot need to go home—that's what's going on," Jace states and gives Carl a pointed look, as his PA screws his face up and grabs a full bottle of wine.

"I'm taking this!" He sniffs and winks at me. Rupert is the first to stand, but both Carl and Neve follow.

"Well, you certainly know when you have outstayed your welcome." Carl's voice rises, and he staggers across the decking and slams into the window, eliciting a resounding thud. "Oh, shit!" He laughs.

"Bloody hell!" Rupert scoffs. "You're a damn liability." He mouths a sorry to Jace, who is laughing quietly.

"And that's an expensive bottle, think yourself lucky!" Jace calls as his PA is led through the house.

"Thanks for the invite, Jace," Neve murmurs. She looks forlorn and sour. I offer her a smile, but it isn't reciprocated.

"No worries, see you Monday." She stays for a second longer, hoping for something—what that something is, I do not know—but when Jace makes no move to give her his attention, she forces her lips into a tight line and scowls at him. I feel him sigh, rather than hear, but don't question him. She will only become a problem if I make her one.

A loud crash rings through to us, and both Jace and I swing to find Carl's intoxicated frame clinging on to the kitchen unit at a funny angle, his legs spread like a newborn foal. My burst of laughter causes him to curse profusely, and when he finally gets back to his feet, he begins dancing out of Rupert's way every time he tries to take his elbow to steer him to the car.

"Fuck's sake, Carl, just get in the car!" Rupert snaps, trying to steer his husband out of the house.

"So bossy. Are you going to smack my arse?" Carl wiggles his brows, and Jace groans, rubbing his hand over his face.

"I did not wish to hear that," he chuckles to me. I'm giggling my head off. Neve wanders off through the house, her head down, posture sad.

I grab Jace's top.

"You promised me starry sex." My cheeks heat, my thighs tighten, and when I lick my lip, Jace grins slowly.

His voice rumbles out in a deep, lusty purr.

"Yes, I did." He picks me up in a swift movement. I watch the car head away from his home into the dark and sigh, glad to finally be alone. The pale glow of the heater fans us as he walks us to the other end of the table which is free of plates. I kick my shoes off as we go, hearing them drop to the ground with a thud.

"A little eager?" Jace muses, and my only form of answer comes in the removal of his top. He perches me on the table edge and lifts his arms up to help ease the material off. Both hands come up to cup my face, his thumbs positioning my chin just so. "God, you're fucking beautiful." His amber eyes gaze over my face.

"I like you too," I admit on a breathy laugh, staring at his muscled shoulders.

"Good!" My chinos are yanked down, and his glittering stare lands on my skimpy thong as he murmurs, "Perfect."

"That's the drink talking." I grin, running my hands up his taut stomach. He unbuttons his fly so I can just see the top of his groin and the thick muscle straining to get out. His breathing is shallow, and I watch him roll his lower lip in his mouth as he pushes his jeans lower, freeing himself fully.

I lay back and stare up as deft fingertips hook into my knickers and begin edging them down. The blanket of darkness above is scattered with the tiniest specs of lights. Each one blinks down at me as Jace begins to rain kisses along the inside of my thigh. I can't think of a better place to be with this man.

I wake with a start. Jace is already awake and resting on his elbow, looking down at me.

"Morning." His voice has that early morning husk, as though day hasn't broken it in yet: sexy and gruff.

I bite my lip, taking in his honey gaze and darkened jaw.

"Morning." My hand stretches beneath the quilt and connects

with toned flesh. "Can I stay here this weekend?" I ask, running fingers over his chest, focusing on his dark nipples. I'm taken by surprise when he rolls us quickly, and I find myself confronted by a gloriously fucked male with a beaming smile and sexy amber eyes staring back at me.

Last night was everything and more. Jace had made love to me and knocked every other moment out of the water.

"I've never had this kind of chemistry with someone else before," I admit, as I finger a stray curl of hair hanging over his tan forehead.

"I don't much fancy hearing about your previous conquests," he muses playfully as his hips jolt into me. I want to point out I was forced to endure that last night, but he is grinning openly at me, and I don't want to kill the moment. "In fact, I should have driven all thoughts of other men out your head."

My slim fingers run over the toned curve of his arse, and as he raises his brow, I direct them up his back and cup his face, bringing his mouth down to mine.

"You have."

Jace smirks, dropping to look at my mouth before eyeing me through heavy eyes.

"Good, because you're mine, Lily." His kiss is sweet and slow, and I'm so blissfully unaware of anything other than him. I blink in shock when I realise it's Saturday, and I have work!

"Oh, god, what's the time?" I try to push him off, but he stiffens, then drops on top of me, applying all of his weight. I grunt out a huff. "Jace, get off," I laugh, and he shakes his head.

"This is my happy place," he murmurs.

"I have work. I can't be late. Harriet isn't here." He grumbles and nips at my neck.

"I'm having words with your assistant when she's back. Does she not know she needs to work around my needs too?" He pouts up at me, and I laugh.

"No, I don't believe she got that memo."

"How selfish," he scoffs and leans to grab his phone. "Only eight forty." He frowns when his cock starts to stir to life.

"No!" I laugh. I need to get ready. He rolls us on a laugh and thrusts up, kissing me roughly. "Jace," I pant, "I have to get ready," I whine, sorely disappointed that I can't stay in bed with him. He drags himself away, and the constant tension in my womb objects as he rolls onto his side, biting my breast and groaning like any man would with his mouth full of nipple.

"You can stay this weekend," he tells me, dropping his chin to my wet skin.

Jace makes it to The Loft in record time. He parks against the curb and watches me to the door, moaning idly about my skin-tight trousers. I catch a look at his profile. He looks hot in his designer jumper and jeans, he's styled his hair, and sunglasses veil his unique eyes from the early morning glare.

Smirking at my open appraisal, he pulls his shades away, subconsciously knowing the effect they have on me.

"I'm taking you dancing," he says.

I stall at the door.

"Later?" I beam.

"Later." He winks. "I'll pick you up, and we can go collect some bits from yours."

"Okay." I can barely contain my excitement. His mouth stretches wide.

"Have a good day, baby." He replaces his shades, and I watch him fly off down the street.

I step back to get the door when I catch sight of a dark Audi parked up the road, and my heart clenches with fear. A figure sits with a hooded jacket and sunglasses on, and although I can't see his eyes, instinctively, I know he is looking straight at me. Anxiety unfurls like a dark liquid through my stomach, and I rush inside. My gut tells me it's Adam, but I have no proof, nothing other than the growing sense of fear. I head straight to the back, pulling my phone free as I watch the door in palpable fear. My breathing is erratic, and my heart sinks further when I remember I didn't lock the door behind me. I move to lock it but stop, needing the seclusion and comfort my office gives me. After an age, the car slowly rolls past, too slow to be anyone other than Adam. Tears form, but I refuse to let them fall. I stare at the figure looking through two panes of glass, and it's like he is here in the room with me. Vomit threatens to leave my body. *Go away!* I mentally scream at him.

The car moves on, and I sag in my seat, my body letting go of the air trapped in my throat. I need to contact the police this week. I have seen Adam on too many occasions for it to be a coincidence, plus he sought me out at Finnegan's and came to my work. That's a clear violation of his order.

After my minor incident this morning, my day goes quickly, and I even start to believe I overreacted to the Audi being outside The Loft. Harriet has emailed and updated me on Paco's progress, along with a few images of where she is staying.

Looks stunning—have a blast! x

I send the reply and eat some leftovers from the fridge, working straight through my lunch when I make two sales. I'm finalising all the details with the gentleman when the door pings and Travis walks in. Seeing I'm busy, he wanders around. I manage to hide my surprise, mentally debating whether to admit his visit to Jace. We hit a milestone yesterday. I don't want to take us back a few steps.

"If you come by on Monday, it will be all ready for you, Mr Charleston."

"Wonderful. I'll leave you to crack on." His look wanders to the lean back of the man casually wandering around the gallery.

"Thank you. Have a lovely afternoon." I close the door behind him, and hearing the ping, Travis turns.

"Hi, Lily." His hands slip into his jean pockets.

"Hi, you."

He laughs at that, and his eyes do a quick sweep of me.

"Everything okay?"

"Yes."

He nods, taking that information in.

"Good." His hand moves to his hair. "I just wanted to check." He looks to the street, almost expecting Jace to come barrelling in. "I'd hate to think I'd caused a problem."

Oh, he has no idea of all the shit Jace and I are tackling. There is a shit storm swirling between us.

"No, Jace and are I good. He's just a little protective," I admit shyly.

"Rightly so," he counters. I smile at his compliment. Travis looks around the place, clearly impressed, and he points to an abstract piece that I love. "I like this." He squints, trying to make head or tail of it. I press my lips together, trying not to laugh. "This structure." The word comes out slowly, unsure.

I snort.

"It depicts pain," I tell him, my own head tilting to find a commotion of colours all slanting to one point and being knotted together in an angsty ball. His head pulls back in disagreement.

"Oh!" He tries not to laugh. "I mean, I can see that." He clears his throat.

"You're a terrible liar," I tell him.

"I actually don't like it at all," he confesses sheepishly, as he pulls a regretful face at me.

I shrug on a smile.

"It isn't everyone's cup of tea."

"I'm definitely more of a Stella man myself." He puffs out his chest, and I laugh on a groan. Travis has this young, happy-go-lucky persona about him; one that I figure involves a lot of Stella.

"Well, I appreciate you popping in." I try to move things along, very much aware that the more time he is here, the more annoyed Jace will be.

His resigned sigh has me bracing myself.

"Look, Lil—" He casts a nervous look at me, and I mentally plead for him to just let it go. "You're obviously very beautiful—"

"Travis—" I wince, not happy to walk this road with him.

He laughs, holding his hand to his heart.

"Hear me out, okay?" I nod, and taking that as consent, he walks to me and stops at my feet. "But you being in love with someone else is a massive turn off." He holds his hands up and laughs at my expression. I instantly feel more relaxed. "Plus," he adds further, "you actually remind me of my sister." He visibly shudders.

"Oh god," I groan.

"Which," – he blows out a long breath, – "again, is a massive turn off."

"What exactly are you trying to say?" I try to help him out because he is stumbling his way through this, and it's painful to watch. I raise a curious brow at him, trying to lighten his tension.

"That if you need me, as a friend," he emphasises the last bit, and I smile at his cute offer, "I'm here, okay? If you need milk or a moan, or whatever—" He gestures with his hand.

"You don't need to do that," I tell him,

"I feel like I do. You're a nice person," he replies, "take my friendship." I study his sincere face and consider how silly it would be of me to decline.

"Okay." I breathe out slowly.

"That wasn't so hard, was it?" Laughing eyes meet mine.

"No."

He hands me a piece of paper with his number scrawled on it.

"Don't be a stranger." He dips to kiss my cheek, and I stiffen, purely because I feel I am betraying Jace.

"I won't." I finger the small slip of paper, conscious that he has already written it, and cares enough to turn up here and check on me.

“See you around, socks,” he grins, his honeycomb eyes full of humour.

“Oh, bugger off!” He pulls a prancy pose that has us both laughing, and then he is gone, sending a small wave through the window at me. I take the paper and drop it in my desk drawer. Other than Cass, I don’t really have any other friends, probably something I should begin to rectify.

Chapter Five

I relay my little interaction with Travis to Jace as we head away from The Loft, and he takes it better than expected, but I conclude that is because of the hell I had to endure yesterday by her royal vileness. He skims right over Travis, taking my word for it, although I omitted to tell him that he gave me his number.

"So you made a few sales?" His eyes are fixed ahead on the road.

"Yes." I lean back into the seat, more relaxed now that I have dealt with the Travis issue. "Two of my main pieces," I add.

"That's great, baby. Have you spoken to Harriet?" He flicks a look at me, then back to the congested road.

"Yes, she's enjoying herself in the sun." I sound envious. Jace knows and picks up my hand; the contrast of his tan skin to my paler complexion is embarrassing.

"Let me take you on holiday," he murmurs, lifting my hand and running his lips back and forth over the soft skin. My heart picks up. I can think of nothing better than sunning myself with Jace on some tropical island.

"Okay, yes!" I grin, excitement dancing in our eyes. "Abroad?" I confirm. He laughs and nods.

"I want to see you in a bikini." He wiggles his brows.

I don't want him to think I expect him to fund it—I'm definitely due a holiday.

"We can book it together," I state, conveying my meaning. "I have some savings."

"Let me take care of it." The notion doesn't sit well with me, and as though sensing my withdrawal at the idea, Jace bites my wrist. "Talk to me."

"Holidays aren't cheap," I murmur, shooting him an uneasy look. "I don't want you thinking I'm—"

"I don't," he cuts me off, refusing to even let me voice my inner debate. "That's why I'd like to treat you." We stop at traffic lights, and Jace takes the opportunity to lean and kiss me. "Let me treat you."

"I don't know—"

He checks the road and grabs my face. I hate the thought of not contributing to our first holiday; he squeezes another kiss in before we begin moving forward.

"A weekend, four days max," he negotiates. I search his eyes, sensing he really wants to do this. I sigh loudly, relenting slowly, and he grins knowingly.

"Okay," I nod, mentally talking myself into it.

"Think of all the starry beach sex we can have," he chuckles. I slap his thigh and realise I'm sitting up in the seat, full of excitement. His eyes roam over my loose blouse. "You better have a ton of bikinis, Lily."

"Ah, there's the real reason," I muse, "you have a bikini fetish you haven't told me about?"

"No, I have a Lily Spencer fetish."

I smile over at him. I very much have a Jace Bennett addiction too.

Jace pulls up outside my apartment block. He turns and raises a brow.

"You ready to get all sweaty and dirty with me?"

"At least buy a girl a drink first, jeez." I push free of the car and look back to find him now watching me over the roof.

"Won't a holiday do?" He pouts.

We both fly around the place, collecting things up for my stay this weekend.

"Would it be easier to stay here tonight?" I call to him from the living room. He is rifling through my clothes for a dress to wear later. I have stayed in the living room, hiding my amusement at his constant whining or disapproval at my wardrobe contents.

"What the fuck is that?" The clink of another hanger being forcefully replaced floats through to me, and I bite my lip. "Definitely not," he laughs shortly to himself, "too short, too hooker." His groan hits my sex. "Jesus, Lily, you got a secret past you want to tell me about?" I roll my eyes but walk to the door leading into my bedroom. Jace flings a red dress onto a pile of discarded dresses before he pulls out a strappy, silver slip dress and smiles to himself. His eyes lift, a hard sheen in them. "We're staying at mine," he tells me matter-of-factly. "Wear this."

"That shows my side boob."

"You don't have side boob," he spits, as though the possibility is ridiculous.

"No, I just meant, you can see the side of my boob," I warn him. His eyes darken and run over my body, already imagining me in the little dress. He lifts it, inspecting the material, and looks at my frame again, not entirely convinced by my admission.

"You'll wear it," he repeats softly, his tone light.

I scoff.

"I did warn you!" I tell him flippantly. I cross my arms. The material is deceptive and makes the dress look bigger than it is. The dress clings to my hips and tits, but falls away everywhere else, dropping low, either side of my ribs, giving a very ample view of my pert breasts. He will hate it.

He backs down a little.

"Try it on for me," he suggests.

"Oh no, Bennett." I laugh. "This is happening." I back away and leave him to ponder the shit he has just got himself into, and when I flick a look over my shoulder, he is advancing fast, a devious grin on his face, the material hanging limply in his grasp. I can see where this is going, and I wouldn't put it past him to pin me down and force it on. "We'll be late for dinner," I say breathlessly.

He laughs loudly.

"Dinner can be rearranged." He moves quickly, startling me, and I spin on a laugh and race off. I try to out-move him, but he vaults the sofa and grabs me up. "Gotcha!"

I squeal out a laugh and wrap myself around him.

"I could make you change your mind," he teases. "When you're all compliant and shaking," he groans, "I'll make you put it on."

"No, you won't." I dare to challenge him, lifting my chin, and my grey eyes clash with his own sparkling ambers, making him smirk.

"How so?"

He presses a very large erection to my groin and raises a brow.

"Because, when you see me in that dress later," – he knocks his cock into me again, and I swallow, trying to keep myself in check – "you'll thank me." I brush at his hair and peck his lips.

"Or kill you," he mutters. Oh, that too. He will love the dress but hate seeing me in it in public. He leans into me, so we slowly topple over the back of the sofa in a tangle of laughing arms and legs.

"I want a taste now." He sucks at my neck and grasps my breast roughly.

"No," I breathe. "No touching, not until later."

"Refusing me won't do you any favours in the long run. In fact, I vow not to hold back when I finally get in your damn knickers later." He growls and thrusts in warning.

"Oh, sounds like a challenge. Do you have something in mind?" I whisper. He is far more adventurous than any other lover I have had, more intense, playful, rough, and unforgiving.

"I don't have enough time to prepare." He sits back, looking away and mentally mulling it over.

"I swear, if I get back and find the place covered in clear sheets, torture devices, and a video camera, I will haunt you forever."

Jace barks out a laugh and slams his mouth to mine.

"Shut up." He nudges my nose with his. "But I do promise to make you scream," he admits. My breath leaves me on a shudder. I trust him with my body, but I also feel nervous because he has far more experience and control than I do.

"Better make sure you feed me first," I say pointedly.

Jace smiles and stares down at me and takes his time stringing it out, making me feel vulnerable and cherished all at once before he gives his head a disbelieving shake.

"I'm crazy about you, Lily Spencer."

"I'm crazy about you too." I lift my mouth and kiss him softly. "Now take me dancing." I'm rewarded with a disarming smile.

I managed to get Jace to agree to dinner at his. I opted for something light, as my dress isn't very forgiving, and I wouldn't be able to disguise the food baby. He has already changed and looks sharp since he has had a shave and styled his hair. I can still smell his aftershave in the bathroom as I apply my makeup. I keep checking the entryway, conscious there is no door. I want to surprise him.

I have curled my hair, gone all out with smokey eye makeup, making sure to really emphasise the silver to match my dress. This style always makes my eyes pop, so I keep my lips neutral and gloss them, staining my cheeks with a little highlighter. My lashes are dark and sultry against my fair skin, and staring at myself all dolled up, I smile. He is going to die on the spot. I have lost a little weight since I last wore this dress, and it skims over my curves, looking better than I remember. I have paired it with some strappy black high heels. I give myself a slow twirl and stop when I see Jace in my peripheral, staring at me.

"Ready?" I ask nonchalantly, trying hard to hide my smirk when his mouth drops open, and he drags unbelieving eyes down my frame.

"Ah, fuck, Lily," he pleads. His hand finds the back of his neck, and he massages it while he contemplates the mistake he made earlier.

"Something wrong?" I muse, leaning to apply more gloss in the long mirror, as I smack my lips together.

"You witch." I hear the smile in his tone and try not to let my own slip free. I keep my face as serious as I can and dust myself with my favourite perfume. I know Jace is getting a generous view of my side and breast as I flick my hair, checking my reflection. I feel the most confident I have in a long time, and it's partly down to the drooling man to my left.

"That's going to come away when we are dancing," he stutters. He walks to me and picks at the material. It doesn't budge, and I grin up at him.

"Titty tape," I purr. His anxiety lightens a little, but I can tell he doesn't want me to wear it. He moves back to the bedroom and rifles through my bag.

"Did you bring another dress?" he asks, pulling a pencil dress free and offering it up.

"That's for work. I'm wearing this," I tell him and walk past.

"Let's stay in." His voice sounds fretful. I can't help my shoulders shaking from suppressing a laugh.

"You're being ridiculous. I'm not changing."

He stops me, lightly running his hands down my side, they glide back up, and his thumbs brush my bare breasts. My big, enigmatic man is getting his knickers all in a twist over some little dress. It's priceless. Seeing my gleeful look, he grunts and rubs at his temples.

"I don't want you to wear that," he confesses, sullenly. I don't fully believe he wants me to change, but his little dramatics are making my confidence skip and glide ahead.

"And I don't want you thinking you can plan my wardrobe." I hold his stare, and his face hardens. I sense an argument coming on, and I almost relish it, knowing that is when he is at his most unforgiving, and when his stance widens and his flank rises with irritation, I drop a look beneath my lashes.

"You promised to take me dancing; stop stalling."

He tries the strappy material again, ensuring it won't slide off and offer anyone a free show of my nipple.

I wink and slip past, picking up my clutch and waiting impatiently by the door. He tips his head back and gives an over the top sigh.

"Please, Lord, make me patient, and do not let me punch anyone in the face for drooling over my girl." I bark out a laugh, loving his cheeky grin as I pull open the door and stare at his glittery gaze.

I am so in love with this man that my skin feels alive with electricity around him.

The club is in the city and high up above the rest of the bustling streets. We arrive late, and the place is full of energy. Jace laces his fingers with mine, and we walk to the bar.

"What do you want to drink, Lily?"

"A cocktail, please." I place myself beside him. This place is similar to Nexo, and it looks expensive in here. I'm so used to rocking up with Cass, club-hopping, and looking all sweaty and flushed that I feel out of sorts around such polished and glamorous people. I gawp at some celeb sitting in the VIP area and nudge Jace, who kisses my cheek with a laugh. I'm utterly terrible with names, but I know I have seen them on a reality TV show. He is gaining a lot of attention, women all pandering to his needs and laughing at something I'm sure isn't funny.

"Brent James, the guy is a prick," Jace enlightens me.

"Jealous, baby?" I pout. "Prancing on screen, yacht parties, and groupies not your thing?" He hooks an arm around my shoulders and pulls me in under his weight.

"No," he grumbles. "I like sassy photographers, and big, big—" His hand slips close to my boob. I raise my brow.

"—Buildings." He laughs. I scoff and look away from Mr James and his entourage.

"That bar I was in the other night, someone said you designed it," I drop in casually.

"Oh, Nexo, yeah, maybe don't go there again," he tells me. The bartender comes over, and Jace rolls off our order.

"Why?"

"The guy that owns it, he's dodgy." Jace is momentarily distracted when the bartender hands him his change.

"Who, Callan?" I say. This gets his attention, and he tilts his head.

"You've met him?" His face is tight with subdued dismay.

"He was there, with Zara Reid, the model." Jace's eyes widen, and Neve's words come back from the other night—she had suggested that Jace had dated a model.

"Is she the model?" I stutter.

Jace actually laughs.

"God, no, never met her in my life." I nod, and he pulls me to him. "It was some stupid, young fling that went to my head." He takes my chin and pecks my lips. "Honestly, I had forgotten about it until Neve mentioned it."

"How is Neve?" I steal myself for his reply. I know he has seen her because her car was gone when we got back earlier. He eyes me suspiciously.

"Do you really care?"

I refuse to lie, but I'm not heartless enough to ignore the grief she is battling.

"Not really, no, but you do, and that matters to me." I don't hide my dislike for her, but I'm not about to make his life awkward either. He smiles gently.

"She's okay." His fingers find the end of my hair. Our drinks get placed down, and Jace suggests we sit down in one of the booths. He has stuck to a soft drink because he is driving.

"If we had stayed at mine, we could have both had a drink," I tell him, sipping on my fruity beverage.

"I don't mind." He pecks my lips and twists to face me. "So, did you speak to Callan?" he questions further. I shake my head around my straw.

"He was all over Zara. Cass knows her somehow," I tell him. "He did give us a complimentary bottle of champagne though." I grin, and Jace grumbles. He lifts his glass.

"That explains why you were so wasted!" He smirks as he takes a sip.

"It was like liquid gold," I say. "I wasn't that bad." He sends me a pointed look and turns my hand over, revealing a series of grazes from mine and Cass's tumble.

"Need I say more?" His tone is soft but smug. I roll my eyes and lift my drink, ignoring his gloating grin.

Within an hour of us being there, things begin to pick up, and more people congregate on the dance floor. Jace has plied me with cocktails, and I'm eager to dance with him.

"I love this song." I grin, a little tipsy. He smirks, cupping my face, and kisses me sweetly.

"No slut dropping," he warns with a playful twist of his full mouth. I scrunch my nose up.

"I'm not a teen," I laugh, edging out of my seat and watching him stand to his full height. He hunkers down to cup my arse and kisses me.

"Thank fuck. I could be looking at a hefty lawsuit." He starts laughing, and my jaw drops. His hands fall away, and he holds his taut stomach until he gets himself under control, evidently finding it far funnier than I do. Eventually, it's his reaction that makes my mouth twist into a reluctant smile.

"Gross." I flap his hand away, but he anticipates it and snatches it midair, tugging me to him. When he drops his mouth to my neck, I sigh and run my hands to wrap them around his neck.

Latch by Disclosure is belting out, and I shimmy my hips to the beat.

"Show these stiffs how to move." He winks, encouraging me on to the open floor. I go on a strut and hear him chuckle behind me. His hand gropes my arse before I spin to face him, and he is there, rocking his own body to the beat. I wind my hips, and his eyes flash with a thousand filthy memories.

"Behave," he warns. I raise my arms, and he groans loudly, unaffected by the heavy crowd as he openly adjusts himself. "Lily, please?" I smirk and twist away, enjoying teasing him too much until I see the flash of unease he is feeling at my attire, and I dance into Jace and hold him to me.

"Keeping it PG," I coax him. He laughs over my shoulder, grinding into me.

"Good girl," – he kisses my hair – "we'll keep the slut drops for bedtime."

"Is that what you have planned?" I question over the music.

"I have many plans for us, Lily, many plans," he admits, sincere eyes meeting my more glassy ones. He lowers his head with a smile and kisses me thoroughly.

We dance through multiple songs, stopping only briefly for a drink now and then. My feet are achy, and my hair is sticking to the back of my neck. I'm more than tipsy, slurring, and I keep grinning—a sure sign I'm well and truly drunk. I fling my arms around his neck and plant a wet kiss over his mouth.

"Want to try that again?" he teases. I groan, vaguely aware I look a drunken mess while the rest of the women in here still look like a flock of exotic birds: prim and perfect. I head to the table and collect my clutch, using it to waft me, looking less and less lady-like by the second. It's another world. They all look as glossy as they did when they arrived; their makeup perfect—not a speck out of place. I do not have that level of dedication.

"Want to get a dirty kebab?" Jace whispers in my ear, and my head tilts on a husky laugh.

"You do say the most romantic things." I twist into him, latching on for support, as he leans back to look down at me. I'm blurry-eyed and sweaty from our dancing.

"Move in with me, Lily."

I snap my head back, squinting one eye to focus on him. He bursts out laughing, and I slap his chest.

"I'm drunk," I whine, "take me home." Rolling my forehead against his chest, I try to fight the ridiculous swirl of panic at his words. Plus, my dry mouth is pestering me for water, and each nervous swallow feels like I have sandpaper coating my throat.

"Is that a yes then?" He angles my head and keeps it in his view.

"That's . . . I'm drunk—ask me when I'm sober," I murmur, yawning. Deep in my subconscious, I'm screaming. He just asked me to move in with him, and my heart, gripping in fear, tells me I'm not ready to make such a big leap. If nothing else, the last few days have proved that I have a lot to learn about this man yet.

A lot, before I make such a huge step forwards.

I slip my hand into Jace's and wrap my other around his forearm as he heads us back to his car parked on the roadside. He puts the heating on full when I shudder in the large seat.

"Thanks." He drags a jacket from the back and hands it to me. I pull it on quickly and buckle myself in.

"I had the best night," I confess sleepily, pulling at the belt as I lean until I reach him and peck his cheek. "Thank you."

"You're welcome, beautiful." His fingers thread with mine so he can kiss my hand. "Hungry?"

"Very." A dirty kebab sounds perfect!

Chapter Six

"Baby, put your arm around my neck." I groan and lift my hand through closed eyes. I must have fallen asleep, and I want to stay in my slumber.

"I'm tired," I whisper.

"You're dribbling," he states. My eyes flash open and snap shut on a snort when I realise he is joking.

"Don't be mean." I pout at being pulled from the warmth of the car and thrust into the chilly night air. Jace swings me into his arms and kicks the door shut and lowers me, only so he can unlock the door. He pushes us into the warmth, and it's then that I see the place lit up with dozens of candles dotted all over the floor, petals decorate the large tiles, and his chin hits my shoulder ever so gently.

"Surprise."

I'm in shock. How did he?

"When did you? How?" I stutter.

"Carl," he admits, and I smile on a wobble.

"I don't know what to say." I don't. He is full of surprises, and other than the minor issue of Neve and his little meltdown over Travis, he treats me like a queen. I take in the flicker of tiny lights through watery eyes. I'm too drunk to fully appreciate this. Plus, the petal path is narrow; I can't walk in a straight line, let alone follow a petal-strewn path.

"Say I'm not the only one feeling this crazy connection." He swallows. I blink up at him. His nostrils are flared, and he's regarding me intensely, pleading as though he can't quite bear to hear anything other than what he is asking.

"I feel it." My confession brings swirling ambers to my parted lips, and his mouth tightens momentarily. Instinctively, I know I haven't quite said what he wants to hear. Is he digging for a confession of love?

"Jace I—" I swallow the words back, scared to utter them, and in turn, make myself vulnerable. "Kiss me," I breathe out, but instead, he pinches the rim of my dress in his fingers and begins lifting it slowly up my body. It resists at my breasts, and I bite my lip under the slip of material obscuring my view of him. "Tit tape," I remind him. "Not so sexy." I giggle, wishing I could see his face.

"Where is it?" he mutters, clearly frustrated by the minor obstacle. I can't move my arms because they are skyward, so I try to drag the dress away with my chin. "Urgh, just rip it off, it will come away with the—" Jace yanks it up, and I yelp falsely.

"Oh, shit!" He flings my dress away, and I find worried eyes inspecting my breast. I gurgle out a deep laugh.

"Got you!" I'm barely able to speak through my laughter. Jace grabs my face and kisses me hard. "That deserves being put across my knee." Our eyes are locked, as are our lips.

"Is that what you had in mind when I asked earlier?" I give my brows a little wiggle and tug at his belt. He clasps my hands and moves them away. Holding them still, he drops a kiss on my collarbone, down to my breasts, and sucks my nipple into his mouth. I moan and hold his head still, but he moves closer so that he is kneeling in front of me. His mouth and tongue petting my skin.

"You have the softest skin." He nips at my hip and pulls me so I'm perched on his widely stretched knees. Slowly, he lowers me back until I'm crushing the petals. Jace takes handfuls and sprinkles them over my body. The floor is warm, and I sigh when he slips a petal into my knickers.

"Jace, please—" My eyes flutter shut.

"Tell me what you want," he coaxes.

"You." I grin.

"Where?" Fingertips dance along the seam of my knickers.

"Everywhere." My own hands run to ease one ache, and I grope my breast, arching at the release of discomfort I offer myself.

"Fucking hell, Lily." He drags my hands back to my side and covers my breasts once more with both my hair and the rose petals; their smell is pungent and sweet, floral and fresh. With their waxy incense and Jace's male scent, I'm in ecstasy. I moan again, and he chuckles.

"It's painful, isn't it? That need. Imagine how hard it was for me when you kept running," he mutters. "I sat here, thinking about you constantly, imagining you naked in my bed." He is kneeling between my legs, looking all over my blushing skin. "God," he groans, lost in that thought. "I was so fucking desperate to taste you, Lily." My sex clenches, and his eyes flash when I squirm beneath him. "You kept running, and I fucking wanted to punish you for it." His hands tighten on my knees.

"Touch me," I purr.

"Don't move." He stands quickly and pulls his phone free. Swiping at his screen, he positions it so it's pointed at me.

"No, I am not displaying that in my gallery." I smirk.

"I'm going to get it printed on a canvas and place it over my bed." Oh, god, I hope not!

"Ha ha," I drawl.

"Come here." He leans down and lifts me to my heeled feet, the petals flutter away, and turning me, he covers my eyes and walks us through the house. He stops for a second, and I wonder what he is doing. I'm about to ask when the seductive sound of a raspy male voice floats through the speakers around the house. I'm pushed along further until Jace decides to stop. He pulls his hand away, revealing the wide bed, coated in petals and more candles glowing like mini beacons over the floor, but what really catches my eye is the blindfold resting on the pillow. I raise my gaze to his, burning over my shoulder. "Miss Spencer," he muses. I bite my lip and thread my fingers with his.

"Yes?" I fight off a nervous giggle.

"Get on the bed." He pushes me forward, and I go until his fingers drop away from mine. I crawl on to the low bed and feel it dip under his weight, and his lips drag over my arse.

"You're in a very playful mood tonight, and something tells me you wanted rough, but I can't give you rough tonight." He sounds remorseful. I'm not. I don't want rough, not when this is on offer. It's every girl's dream. I lie back on the bed, running my fingers into the plush petals.

"I can live with that." My lip disappears in between my teeth.

Jace is everything but rough. He is tender and patient; every thought, kiss, and thrust designed with me in mind. He makes love to me long into the night, exhausting us both. Saying everything we so desperately want to admit to each other but without uttering a single word.

I'm floating in euphoria when I get to work. I rush about my usual morning routine and make myself a coffee. The door chimes, and I stop stirring the dark liquid and call out Harriet's name. When she doesn't reply, I abandon my spoon and step out into the small hall leading to my office.

"Hat?" Thick hands grip my neck, turning my words into a gurgle, and lift me off the ground. I gasp and kick, desperate for air, my fingers scratching helplessly at the rope's tight clutch on my failing throat. Adam's furious eyes fill my terrified gaze, and I cry through the obstruction around my windpipe, thrashing at the restraint. Somehow, through sheer desperation, I manage to scream for help, and the sound rips from my lips, burning my throat and lungs in a high pitched horrifying scream.

"Lily!" The sharp shout splinters through my terrified mind. I jump up and blink through the fog, choking my subconscious. Fear has her dark claws in me, and it takes me a few seconds to fight the nightmare off.

I'm whimpering and shaking, my hands cupping my neck. I see Jace looking at me in panic, and it's an icy awakening to my fragile form.

I'm not at work—I'm here, in his bed, dreaming of my ex and his wicked hands.

"Oh god," I croak, as my arms push and kick at the quilt. I still feel restrained, choking on a fear nestled so deep into my psyche that I sob.

Warm hands drag me across the bed, but I push at him, desperate to get away.

"Get off," I beg. "Don't." I choke. His whole face is robbed of composure, and he looks horrified.

"Lil." His tone is softer, reassuring.

"Please. Just don't." I can't bring myself to look at him. "Just a minute." I stumble out of the bed and stagger to the bathroom, dragging in a lungful of air. "I need a minute," I tell him, beg him.

I feel sick with fear, embarrassment, and revulsion at Adam being so present in my mind. I remind myself it's just a nightmare, but it plagues me as I splash water in my face trying to chase it away. I'm slick with sweat. My legs are weak as I lean against the counter, allowing it to take my weight. I'm still a little drunk.

"Lily, talk to me," he coaxes.

I shake my head and cup more icy water, dowsing my face in it. Where the fuck did that nightmare come from? Why now?

"You're so pale. Please sit down." I can't meet his eyes in the mirror, but I expect his touch. His hands are gentle. He lifts me up and pulls me on his lap.

"Feel better?" I sag into his chest and nod. I know a million questions are going to come my way, so I force a laugh out, but it sounds fake to my own ears. Sighing, I look up at him, hoping that I have chased the look of dread out of my eyes.

"I don't know what that was," I huff on a short laugh. Jace is eyeing me with suspicion, and I don't blame him. I wouldn't believe the crap coming out of my mouth either. Cupping his face, I press my lips to his. I realise I'm shaking, but I hold my mouth against his. His tongue is gentle and soft, so at odds with his usually more aggressive manner.

"I'm cold," I say in the hope that he will take me back to bed. My voice is raspy and sore.

"Want to talk about it?" he presses. I shake my head and tuck myself into the crook of his neck, averting my face. Do I want to talk about it?

No. Not now. Not ever.

"Just a scary dream," I mumble, pulling at the ends of my hair. I force my shudder away. Jace stands with me in his arms, and I scrunch my eyes shut, dispelling the horrid dream away.

"Your heart is going like a piston." His observation gets ignored. The second my back hits the mattress, I burrow into the pillow and close my eyes, levelling out my erratic, shallow breathing. I can feel his eyes on me, and that alone has mine kept tightly shut.

Jace sighs.

"Night, beautiful." His fingers drift over my hair and rub my side gently.

I clear my throat.

"Night." His lips find my brow, and I stutter out a sigh and pray I can return to sleep.

I wake before Jace. His usually edgy self is face down and saturated in calm. I think I like him better asleep—I muse inwardly—when his eyes are not furiously watching everything I do. His body is relaxed, and my mind isn't pulverised into mush by his toxic eyes and sexy words.

Slipping free, I head to the toilet and wash before pulling some tight jeans and a hoody from my bag. I grab my underwear and converse before moving quietly through to the kitchen and getting dressed. My camera is out on the coffee table, so I scoop it up, find some paper, and write Jace a quick note before I slip out into the cool morning air.

The early morning sun is breaking through the dense tree line, making the branches look like widely spread fingers reaching to grasp for something that isn't there. I carefully make my way through the man-made path. I veer right and trudge my way down the bramble-lined decline. I'm going to regret all the scratches tearing up my ankles, but now, with the clean, fresh air filling my lungs and the glow of early morning touching my face, I don't care. It's too beautiful out here.

I need the crisp, clear air to rid my mind of last night's nightmare. I need the peace and distraction of photography, and I allow myself to soak into the silence. My tense body is relaxing in the comfort of my own company.

I walk for more than ten minutes, across an open field and towards more trees. Another lake sits nestled on the far side, and I am desperate to capture it first thing. Dew is seeping through my canvas shoes and soaking my toes, but I power on, my camera in my palm, and as soon as I round the wide trees, I lift the lens and begin snapping away, picturing the wild meadow in an eerie black and white landscape, just how it was last night. I cross along another path and kneel to get some of the water and tree reflection. When I stand and turn everything is set out before me, a vast craggy landscape. I focus on the scenery, adjusting my shutter speed, and getting the perfect image.

I spend an age taking photographs, sitting on my butt in damp grass, and flicking through the images. It is the perfect interruption after last night. I'd lain awake for ages after my nightmare, silently reliving it, over and over again, dissecting it and doubting myself. When Jace finally fell asleep, I let the hot tears fall. I haven't dreamt about Adam in a while, so I put it down to the numerous sightings of him and the undiluted fear I felt yesterday when I suspected it was him outside The Loft.

I hate that I'm slipping back into old ways and angry that I'm thinking about him again. I begin taking more photos until my stomach grumbles and forces me to head back up the track. I don't know how long I have been—time melts away when I'm taking pictures, and I become as immersed in the camera as I am Jace.

The only difference is, with my camera, I'm in control. That's what I need; a sliver of control because last night, I had none, and that petrifies me—even if it was just a twisted memory.

The sun is up, and so is Jace. I'm panting as I get to the top of the track and find him sitting in one of the deep chairs. My heart starts, and the familiar prickle graces my skin as I feast my eyes on wide shoulders encased in a heavy knit sweater and long, lean legs thrust into jeans. He hasn't shaved, and the darkness to his jaw adds another depth to him. He looks so sexy that I swallow a whimper. I'm so thankful he is in my life.

"Exploring, she says—" His husky voice is the sweetest sound to fill the air. I grin, oblivious to my state, and walk as quickly as I can until I'm in front of him. I flick an achy leg over his and straddle him, wrapping needy arms around his neck. My camera acts as a barrier, but our lips still manage to find one another. Large hands run up my back and cup the back of my head. "I missed you this morning," he manages to murmur between our lazy kiss.

"What time is it?"

"Just after ten. What time did you go out?" He frowns, wiping dirt from my cheek. I shrug. I hadn't bothered checking the time, but

I knew it was first thing. His eyes hold mine, and I know he is speculating about my meltdown.

"You're freezing." His hands rub therapeutically over my body, and his eyes come back up to mine, soft and worried. "Are you okay? That dream really shook you up." I cast my eyes away and nod reassuringly.

"I got some amazing shots." He sits back, and I begin thumbing through them on my camera. His sigh is so soft that I barely make it out. He isn't satisfied with me changing the subject or my decision to keep him at arm's length.

"You pout when you're concentrating." His thumb brushes across his pout, and I nip his finger and lift my camera to show him some of my favourites.

"That reflection is incredible." Unhooking the strap, he takes my camera and flicks forward. "I love this." I climbed up a branch to get that one. It's a snap of the lake, the craggy trees hooked over and pouring into the water like dehydrated men. It's eerie and stark in its beauty.

"Me too." He thumbs through more, stopping at one of a startled rabbit.

"You scared him." He smirks. I nod and point at the image.

"He has such sleek lines, look at his leg." I run my finger along the part I'm talking about. "He's so defined." My stomach gurgles again, and Jace frowns.

"You didn't eat him, did you?" His tone is laced with laughter, and I nudge him playfully.

"No, but I am starving," I admit.

"I already put the coffee on. I'll make us breakfast." He pecks my mouth and stands me on my feet.

"Great, I need a shower." I tug at my sodden knees.

"That can be arranged." He cups my neck and leads me to the kitchen. "Humour me and eat first." I don't argue. I'm enjoying his attention too much.

Jace leaves me to start the shower as I respond to a text from Carl.

I let him know I'm fine after our night in with Neve, and we arrange to meet on Tuesday evening.

Can't wait, plus that will help me tons as my car is in the garage x

Sure thing, I'll be at The Loft for 6! Cocktails here we come! C x

After breakfast, Jace rushes me to get dressed. The weather, although bright, is still cold. I make sure to wrap up, and he bundles me in the car, tight-lipped and with a mischievous glint in his eye.

"So you're really not going to tell me where it is you're taking me?" I ask after an hour in the car. This is the third time I have asked. I don't do well with surprises.

He laughs and squeezes my knee.

"Just a few more minutes." As promised, a few minutes later, we pull up at a large lake on the outskirts of London. "Viktor used to bring me here," he tells me. It's a small snippet of information about him, and I feel a glimmer of hope that he just might divulge more.

I follow him out of the car.

"I thought we could hire a boat, and I could row us around the lake." He holds his hand out for me to take, and I slip mine in his as he lowers his lips to my ear. "Then, when we are freezing cold, I have an excuse to get you in the bath." I laugh and keep pace as we head inside to arrange the hire.

The water is serene but dark, and all the greenery has lost its fresh summer colour and is musty and brown, each branch now visible without the shelter of leaves. The steady swoosh of the oars sweeping through the water fills the quiet. I'm tucked up in my life jacket, and

Jace looks like he is ready to burst out of his. It was quite comical watching him struggle into it.

"Stop," he smirks. "I've filled out since I last came here."

"You look like the action man I pestered my mother for because Ken just wasn't man enough for Barbie," I tell him with a soft laugh.

"Barbie? I can't imagine you with a doll?" He frowns through a smile, nudging my shoe with his large boot.

"It was a momentary slip-up. I usually was covered in mud in the garden or painting something," I admit, thinking back to a time when I was wild and doused in love.

"It's one of the things I like most about you," he remarks, his muscles rolling as he rows with a rhythmic flow. "You don't mind getting dirty."

"Your mind is filth," I tell him, enjoying his wide smile.

"Or yours is. I genuinely did mean that you're not afraid to get your hands dirty." I blush at my wayward thoughts. "And the fact that you look delicate and feminine while doing it . . . well—" He grins. "It's a huge turn on."

"You're looking pretty good yourself. If we gave you a man bun, you'd look Viking ready." I wink.

"Man bun!" He visibly shudders. "Not even if you paid me!" My feet are placed neatly between his widely spread knees. His, tucked into dark leather boots and faded jeans. He has a thick jumper and his parka jacket on again, the fur compliments the fading lighter tips, and his hair is getting darker now the sun has fled. He looks gorgeous. I'm going to miss those tips—they really bring out his eyes.

"What are you thinking?" he murmurs.

"Just how good looking you are." I smile. He grins back and lifts his chin, giving me a view of his full profile. "Shame that you're arrogant with it," I muse.

"You love my arrogance," he states, "but I probably should have made you bring your camera." He pulls at the oars, grunting as he powers us over the lake at a faster pace.

"No, it's fine. I love that it's just us." I stare out over the water. It's really peaceful.

"You do?" His head tilts, and those damn eyes flash with satisfaction.

"Yes." I breathe with a genuine smile. It's another pinpoint of solitude on the map, and I love it here, love the connection he has with it, and that he is sharing it with me.

"But you don't want to move in?" The softly spoken comment has me tensing up. I'm sitting on a boat in the middle of a lake with nowhere to flee. I realise my schoolgirl error and remind myself just how determined a man Jace is.

We're having this conversation. He's made sure of it.

It's somewhat calculated, but I can't help but admire his determination and creativity when it comes to getting what he wants.

"I never said that," I murmur, not quite meeting his eyes.

"You didn't say yes either—" He does that leg-nudge thing again, and I chew the inside of my cheek, feeling under a microscope all of a sudden.

"I know." I look away and stare at the blanket of water below us. "The idea of it is everything I want," I tell him softly, seeing the murky outline of his reflection in the dark water. He is leaning forward, elbows resting on wide knees, face set in a well-mastered look of calmness. He's not, though. I can feel the slight jitter of his knee bobbing continuously.

"So, what's the problem?" His voice is light, casual.

"Me," I admit, "the rational and sensible side of me is trying to keep me grounded." I huff out a nervous laugh.

"Well, can you tell her to piss off?" He laughs softly. I give him a look under my lashes and hold my smirk back.

"I just need a little more time. It's only been a month or so. Do you not feel it's too quick?" I dare to counteract.

He has stopped rowing, and we are bobbing away on the lake, the water lapping gently at the sides.

"No, I won't change my mind about you, so why lengthen the inevitable?"

"Just give me a few weeks. I need to look into the flat and where I stand with that," I reply, tucking my hair behind my ear.

It's not what he wants to hear, but it's a step in his direction.

"Sure." I relax a little and keep my face averted. "But," – my head pulls back his way quickly, – "I want you in before Christmas," he declares, "and I'm not taking no for an answer."

"And you think Cass is bossy—" I muse lightly.

"She is," he scoffs.

We spend a good hour on the lake, then walk around the surrounding path. Jace tells me about his latest project and what ideas he already has for another.

"Another wild card?"

"Yes, do you want to photograph it?" he slips in casually. I suspect he feels inclined to after the last shoot.

"Last time was a fluke. I won't be offended if you bring someone else on board." His fingers tighten in mine. The wind has picked up, so I have wrapped my scarf tightly around my neck. "You said Viktor used to bring you here?" I twist to look up at him, squinting my eyes against the dazzling sun.

"Yeah," he smiles, nostalgically. "He'd bring me here in the summer, just to get us out of the city to unwind. Marie would make us a picnic, and we'd hire a boat and fish—he would fish—I was never any good. When I bought the lakes, he was over the moon, not so much when I filled the top one partially in and built on it." He chuckles.

"Oh, does he fish on the back lakes?"

"Previously, but since he retired, he and Marie tend to holiday a lot. They never did that when he was working. He spent six days a week at the office, but Sundays were for Marie." He smiles to himself.

"And you?" I say quietly, not quite understanding their relationship. Their bond is deep—I see that much.

"Sometimes. They'd invite me over, or we'd come here, even took me to the zoo once." He clears his throat.

"Did you like it?" I used to love the zoo, mainly the elephants, but I keep this to myself in the hope that he keeps talking about himself.

"From what I remember, I was more bothered that I had time with them." He grabs a branch, pulling a stray leaf free and flicking it away. "They were my escape." His fingers knot tighter with mine.

"From what?"

"Life," he murmurs.

"What about your parents?" I ask. If he finds the question intrusive, he doesn't show it.

"Nothing to tell. It's just me." He means just him and Neve. Like me and my family drama, he doesn't wish to share, and I don't pry, even though I want to ask him. He quickly changes the subject and begins talking about possible holiday locations, and my mind is soon lost on the idea of sandy, half-naked Jace-filled beaches before we drive back and bathe together.

Chapter Seven

I find Jace bent over the bath, checking the temperature. He swirls his fingers in the bubbles, flicks the excess water off, and when he is happy with the heat, he takes his t-shirt and rips it off in the sexy way men do, one sleek tug over his head.

"Lily!" he shouts, and I laugh. He twists on a smirk and beckons me over with a jolt of his chin, his fingers working the buttons on his jeans.

"You're keen?" I raise my brow and begin shimming out of my jeans. I kick them aside and pull my top over my head so I'm left in my underwear.

"You judge me for wanting to have you all slippery and wet?"

"Never." I grin and walk to him. He is gloriously naked. His chest firm and toned, and his cock bobs as I near, causing me to bite my lip. "That for me?"

"All yours." He is fighting a smirk back, and as soon as I'm within arm's length, he tugs me to him and drops his mouth to take my own. He nibbles along my lower lip and groans lightly. "You ready to bubble up, Miss Spencer?"

"Sure am." He gives me a single deep kiss and then drops one to my shoulder as he undoes my bra. It falls away, and he takes a pew on the bath edge. I step between his legs, and his big hands run up my sides, his thumbs caressing my breasts.

"These damn breasts," he groans, leaning to pull a nipple into his mouth. I buckle and hold on tight for his onslaught. He is dragging my knickers down my legs as he moves to the other breast.

He nips, and I hiss, "Oh, god." I hold his head still and whimper when he sucks deeply, pulling my breast into his mouth. His hands are roaming, his fingers gently caressing my skin, over my back, and my thighs. His mouth keeps working, and then his hand is there, at the apex of my thighs. One stroke tells him all he needs to know. He kisses my sternum, then lifts me to straddle him. I grin at him, and then he is sliding us back with a splash!

Water careens over the sides and drenches the floor.

"Jace!" There is nothing elegant about our fall. We look like a pair of massacred mannequins, limbs all tangled and distorted. His big chest vibrates as he laughs deeply. "Mood killer." I pout.

"You're always in the mood, you nymphomaniac," he scoffs, tweaking my nipple.

"Ouch, and I am not! You are. You've always got a boner."

"Boner!" He throws his head back with a loud laugh.

"What?" I gawp. "What's so funny?"

"Oh, come on, Lil. You can do better than that." I scrunch my face up. Do better how? What does he mean? Jace is sprawled in his big bath, watching me intently. He bites his lip, and I feel the atmosphere shift. I squirm in his lap, and his eyes twinkle mischievously. "Talk dirty to me," he whispers. I watch him and see the way his eyes bloom at the thought. He chews his lip and runs a thumb over my cheek when it stains red. "Tell me what kind of things go through that mind of yours—what do you want me to do to you?"

Oh, god. I've never vocalised my desires to anyone, let alone someone who would more than happily bring them to life. My breathing shallows and I flick shy eyes up to him. He smiles softly.

"Tell me, Lily, what does your beautiful body need from me?"

"Touch me," I murmur.

"Where?" He moves me so I'm straddling him; his neck is relaxed over the edge, and I'm sitting with the cool air dancing over my bare skin.

I trail my finger down my chest, over my breast, and my lips press together, but he is still waiting. He wants words.

"Here," I tell him. His hand lifts, and he rolls his thumb over and over the hard nub. "Yes." I shift on his lap, but he keeps me still.

"Where else?" My eyes blink up to his, which are rich like fresh dark honey. My shaky finger moves down, right down to my sex. I'm panting.

"Here, I need you to touch me here," I tell him quietly. His stomach clenches, and he moves to accommodate my needs.

His fingers stop exactly where mine were. "Here?" He's still not right there. I want him there—inside me.

"Lower." I shift my stance, giving him more access.

"You've got to show me. Where do you want me?" My eyes flash. He wants me to touch myself. I swallow. I can do this—of course I can. I love this man. I trust him.

I move my fingers back and skim them over his. He lifts his head as my fingers slip over my sex. I bite my lip and watch him, watching me, watching right there. I press further, and my fingers slide in. A light gasp leaves my mouth, and he pushes my fingers in deeper.

"Fuck, Lily, fuck yourself for me, beautiful." His eyes have taken on a shade so dark that I can't see where his irises start and end.

"Oh, Jace." I do as he asks, massaging myself for him. My hips jolt, and he groans loudly.

"Come on, baby." He plucks at my nipple, and I gasp loudly. My hips move, and I work my fingers in and out. Heat rolls over my skin and my head lolls back. Oh, god, I'm close. "You look so hot, Lily. Give me those fingers." He growls. I'm too close to give up now, so I rub faster on a whimper. "Now!" He snatches my hand away and shoves my fingers in his mouth.

"Please?"

"Please what—what do you want?"

"Your fingers. I want to ride your fingers." I take his hand and wait for him to position them before I wriggle and lower myself down. I feel electric, needy, and alive. His thumb joins the assault, and I splinter, crying out and dropping forwards. My mouth collides with his. "Fuck me," I beg.

Jace manoeuvres us and pulls me down harshly. I latch my mouth to his as he sinks deeper.

"Oh, yes." I'm panting and moving my hips slamming down with every chance I get. "Harder, god, fuck me hard."

"I can't. This fucking bath isn't big enough." He growls and swings us both up and out. Most of the water has disappeared down the small drain in the floor, and Jace propels us to the bedroom. We don't get far before he spins us and presses me into the wall, lining himself up and thrusting deep. I bite his shoulder hard as each pound shakes me to my core.

"My god, you're dripping," he growls as he kisses me roughly. I whimper and moan as he slips out and walks us to the armchair in the corner. "Turn around!" he barks.

My shaky limbs just about hold me up as I'm thrust forward so I can grip the arms of the chair, then he is there, yanking my hips and roughly pushing in. He stalls, and I knock my arse backwards to gain friction.

"Jace!"

"What do you need?"

"Hard. God, so hard. Make me come." I quiver. Jace hammers away until I'm screaming out and doesn't stop until he roars out his own climax. I'm shaken and lax, and Jace is sprawled over my back—my face pressed into the seat of the chair.

"You're incredible." He presses a kiss to my shoulder, his big chest moving quickly against our sticky skin. "Come on." He lifts me gently, and we slip into bed. I wrap myself around him and sigh. I couldn't be any happier right now.

After a long day's work, I'm ready to get out of here. Carl sends me a text letting me know he is outside. With my car in the garage, it's the perfect solution. I'm in sensible hands, and I have a lift home. In fact, I'm thoroughly looking forward to our little dinner date.

I've made an appointment at the police station to follow up Adam's restraining order, and that I think he's been following me, and any anxiety I had over it, Grant helped disperse when he put me through a gruelling workout last night.

Despite all this looming in the background, I focus on the good—on Jace and moving this forward. I have evaded further questions to move in and tried to keep things with us ticking along. He needs to open up more if he wants me to even consider talking about sharing a home because each little snippet he offers just reminds me I don't know him much at all. It serves as another reminder that I, too, need to share my troubled past with him.

My phone pings again, another message from Carl telling me to hurry up. I roll my eyes and toss the paperwork I have to hand in the filing cabinet, locking it and dropping the key in my desk. My phone starts ringing as I'm scooping my bags up and dragging my coat on.

"You are so impatient." I laugh, clutching my phone to my ear with my shoulder.

"Yes, well, I need some fizz. Get your tiny heinie out here!" he huffs, childlike, down the line.

"I'm coming," I coax, turning the lights off and pulling the door shut. I'm juggling my keys, phone, and bag, all while listening to Carl whine about the disadvantages being presented to his liver. I don't see his car but notice a set of headlights just up the road, flaring up the darkened street.

"You up on the left?" I say with my hand stuck on the key in the door—damn thing won't lock.

"*You selfish bitch!*" The animalistic roar has me snapping around. Adam is powering towards me, his footsteps echoing as he runs full pelt at me. "*You don't get to be happy*!" The hate in his voice manages to spike through my petrified state. "*You ruined everything*!" he snarls before his fist slams straight into my jaw. The power knocks me back, slamming me into the window as pain shoots across my face. I cry out, and my phone flies out of my grasp and smashes against the concrete.

I stumble back, desperate to get away. Somehow, through the soul-shaking fear, instinct takes over, and I bring my fist up and crack him in the face, my small knuckles retracting against his hard cheek. Something snaps in my finger, and I yelp. Adam looks momentarily shocked, but his face contorts into an icy rage, and my cry for help gets tangled up in Adam's angry shout.

It's deafening and has me cowering away.

"YOU BITCH!" His face shakes—his gaunt skin blots red. He looks utterly terrifying.

I catch a blurred movement, then something heavy hits my head. The sound echoes through my skull in a sickening crunch. Pain splinters outwards in a sharp, furious wave, and I'm falling back.

The pained whisper seeps into my mind.

"No, I've never seen him before." It's followed by a deep sigh and a sniff. "I thought he was going to kill her."

Someone growls, and it's oddly comforting.

"You said he told her she doesn't get to be happy?"

"Yes, that she is selfish, and she ruined something." A weak sob echoes through my tender head. "Jace, I'm sorry. I could hear *everything* through my in-car speaker. I don't think I will ever forget that sound—" Every word sounds like I am listening to a recording on playback, through tiny earbuds with no speaker attached.

"Why isn't Cass answering?" The mention of my friend's name starts to kick my brain into first gear. Jace, I recognise his voice. It's full of anger. Worry. "Where is the nurse; why isn't she awake?"

"They said it's okay for her to sleep." That sounds like Carl.

"I need to see her," he snaps. "Fuck." I lay for a minute in my surreal state, and for some reason, Adam's face flashes in my mind!

I wince, and someone takes my hand.

"Baby? Look at me, are you okay?" His rushed whisper, so full of concern, makes me worry.

"She's sleeping. Let her rest," someone soothes.

"I need to see her eyes!" His voice is full of such panic, and he sighs, irritated and defeated. "You don't get it," he grates out, and pressure wraps around my palm.

"Jace, I get it. Calm down. She is okay." They aim to placate, but it's no use.

"Is she fuck!" The deep growl has me twisting away in pain, my head feeling every vibration of each deep syllable. "Lily, baby. It's Jace." Gentle hands take my chin with such delicacy that gingerly, I open my eyes. The lights feel like shards of glass, and I snatch my eyes shut. "Lily, let me see you. Come on, baby, look at me," he whispers, soft lips dancing over my hairline. I do as commanded, blinking against the bright lights.

Everything seems blurry around the edges for a minute, but I lock on to the intense ambers roaming over my face in worry. His face is pulled into a deep frown. When I finally focus on him, he sighs—his lips brush my mouth, and I wince.

"Sorry," he murmurs and moves his kisses a little further right. My whole face aches, and my head is pounding as though all the blood has rushed there and the pressure is about to make it pop!

"My head," I croak. I lift my hand, but I feel weak, so I drop it back down, wincing once more.

"Baby, you're in the hospital." My eyes whip to his. Hospital—but? I blink away, trying to catch up with my racing brain. Another image of Adam flashes in my mind, and my lip wobbles. "Shush . . . " I can't. A sob burns up my throat, chased by a stomach full of vomit.

"Shit! Carl, quick pass me that bowl." Jace thrusts it under my face as he pushes me up so I'm sitting. I heave until I'm dry retching—

until Adam's hateful, soulless eyes eat at any strength I have, and everything rushes back on a torturous wave of painful memories—distorted but lucid.

I sob gently as all my fears and worries break to the surface.

Only it isn't just vivid images of him outside the gallery. It's also him at my flat. I scrunch my eyes tightly, trying to deflect the image, but it stalks towards me like Adam did.

My lip bloody—my shoulder hunched over, protecting already-broken ribs and my stomach.

'Please, stop,' I beg, holding a hand up. My finger is at an odd angle, but all I can think is I need to protect my stomach. 'Stop,' I cry softly, sucking back another sob as I shake, my shoulders jerking with each painful inhale.

He bashes into the doorframe, and his eyes manage to latch onto me through the haze of alcohol.

'Fucking bitch,' he spits, but it's mangled with grief. He truly believes I have betrayed him. Guilt at my lack of love for him reduces me to silent sobs.

'Adam, please.' His eyes soften, and I back into the corner of the kitchen, watching him warily. 'I'm sorry,' I whisper, 'stop now . . . ' I request softly on a broken plea. His dark eyes roam over me, and his head drops, but he keeps walking towards me, and I brace myself against whatever else is to come. He wraps an arm around my neck, pulling me in for a kiss, and I let him, praying this is the end.

A heavy fist slams up into my stomach, my lungs exhaling in sharp pain.

'No!' I wheeze, dropping to the floor. My breath is no longer in my body, and a heavy boot slams into my stomach, again and again until I'm writhing in pain.

Tears rush down my face, blinding me as they mix with my makeup.

"Jesus, Lily, breathe. Just breathe." Jace pulls back, and I look around in shock, realising I'm not at home. I jolt back and scramble away as I look around for Adam, but he's not here. Carl is staring at me in complete disbelief.

"I'm getting a nurse," he says hurriedly, rushing out the room. I'm gasping for air, wheezing as it comes in and out too quickly, too much. My chest burns and my eyes blot a little. I'm still crying, and the mascara-laced tears irritate my eyes so much that I blink rapidly. My breathing hits a level that I can't control.

"Baby, calm down, shush, you're safe. I'm here." I push back against the bed, gasping for air as a nurse rushes in with another at her heel.

"Get back, please." She ushers Jace out of the way.

"You must be kidding!" He laughs, pulling me closer. I claw at the bed as a machine begins to beep wildly.

"Miss, you need to calm your breathing . . . " Multiple hands take mine but only feel like an added restraint. "Miss, I need you to relax." I can't. I can't breathe.

"Jace!" Carl snaps, and I gasp, my mouth opening and shutting like a stranded fish.

I can't breathe. *I can't.*

"Do something!" Jace roars. They ignore him, and one begins pulling liquid from a vial into a syringe. My visions blots and I go to scream, but any oxygen is drowning in my lungs, and my legs kick out in panic.

"I'm going to give you a sedative, Miss Spencer." I shake my head, moving away from them all. The sheets are moved back, and I look on in sheer panic. Carl has his hand plastered to his mouth, eyes wet with tears. It's as if my mind is holding on to every last detail, sucking it in, remembering it all, just in case it's my last image.

I gasp, short, painful pants, trying to breathe. Jace enters my blurring vision and cups my face; his mouth pulled down in heartache.

"Baby, I'm here. I love you—take little breaths," he says gently. I fix my stare on his face and sob a little. I love him too. But I feel like I'm going to die.

A sharp sting hits my hip. Wincing, I latch onto Jace, trying to tell him I love him. My eyes are wide with fear.

"I know, baby, I know," he says, dotting kisses over my face.

Chapter Eight

"She could have died!" I mentally flinch at the harsh words, my mind aching to get back to consciousness to defend myself and leave this nightmare, but I don't know how because I feel like I'm swimming in a slumberous void.

"I'm angry too. Jesus, had I known she hadn't gone to the police, I would have!" Cass's equally fierce voice breaks through my coma-like state.

"So he's broken the order, now what?"

"I don't know. I mean, she should have reported him being at the club. He knew it was her birthday, so he actively sought her out." Cass's voice feels like a sharp nail to my tender mind.

"Any other times?" Flashes of Adam float back and forth across my mind. My subconscious skips forward and offers up the information, even though I can't speak myself.

"She hasn't said so," Cass murmurs.

"But you think so?" Jace's question is uttered through what I imagine are gritted teeth.

"It seems likely, given he just attacked her." Her voice is scathing, and I will her to go easy on him. I don't know why because I'm dreading facing Jace's wrath when I'm less vacant.

A deep sigh halts their conversation.

"Fuck, I actually asked if she was pregnant the other week."

"Is she?" Cass seems both hopeful and concerned,

"No," he grumbles.

"You sound sad about that," Cass remarks. The bed dips, and my hand is taken. I attempt to grip back but can tell I haven't moved.

"Not now, Cass. I just want my girl back." There is a reprieve of silence, and the constant heavy thud in my brain lulls to a deep ache. "Did she suffer from nightmares at all?" His voice is gruff, tired, and I want to curl into him.

"Yes, why?" I mentally scream at Cass for opening her big mouth to him, but I can't do anything in this forced state of slumber.

A long, drawn-out sigh pulls at my guilt.

"She had one the other night; wouldn't talk about it, and I didn't want to push her." He curses. "Fuck, I should have. I knew something wasn't right."

"Jace, this isn't your fault. After everything he has done to her, do you really believe you talking to her would have stopped him from getting to her?"

"Yes. No. I don't know. She needs to wake up," he grumbles sadly.

I wake slowly, my eyes peeling back to find a row of worried faces. All four people rush towards me at once, but Jace makes it to me first, and soft lips brush my dry ones.

"Hey, beautiful," he croaks.

I open my mouth to reply, but a sharp sting attacks my lips. Lifting my fingers to my lips, I tentatively touch the sore area.

"You and I have got a lot of talking to do." It's a warning, spoken gently, but he is as serious as a disease. I eye him cautiously. Cass moves around the bed, and her face crumbles.

"I'm so mad at you," she sobs, wrapping her arms around me. Sean, Cass's boyfriend, winks at me, and I see Carl looking completely shattered at the end of the bed. Come to think of it, Jace looks exhausted too. I roll my eyes over him, seeing dark shadows under his eyes and a pale tinge under his usually drool-worthy tan. His ambers have lost that sparkle I love, and instead, they look murky and flat.

I sit still and take a mental inventory of the damage to my own body. I've felt pain before, bone-cracking, heart-breaking pain. This isn't like that.

I'm in pain. But it's mainly to my face—a dull, nauseating headache, throbbing to my mouth, and achy body. I do feel okay. Physically, I'm going to be okay.

"Water," I whisper before clearing my throat and avoiding the questioning glances. Carl whips off to find me a drink and Cass steps back to lean into Sean.

I could do with some painkillers, but I don't say that. The concerned and accusing looks have me holding my tongue. Carl follows a nurse, who comes over, clucking at me. She is a busty woman, and Sean's eyes widen when she walks in tits first, the rest of her eventually following. Cass slaps his arm, and I somehow manage a smile.

"How are you feeling, dear?" I eye the people around me and drop my gaze. "Never mind them, do you want something for the pain?" Her years of training have weighed me up in seconds.

"Please," I whisper. Jace growls, and I look at my fingers, knotted in my lap. I only then notice the tubing sticking out the back of my hand and the neat splint on my finger.

"The doctor will come round to speak with you shortly." She moves the drip aside and begins injecting an intravenous. My relief is almost instant. The drug soars through my bloodstream, and I relax back in the bed, nodding at her. She gives me a soft smile and eyes the big man bristling next to my bed.

Carl pours me a small glass of water, and I lift it shakily to my dry mouth. Cursing, Jace takes the glass and holds my chin, lifting the water and easing sips into my mouth. My eyes find his and he doesn't hold back the hurt swirling in the whiskey depths. I mentally shrink away and pull my head back when I've had enough. Jace plants his thick thigh on the bed and looks at me as though he has the world on his shoulder.

"Can you give us a few minutes?" he says over his shoulder, not making eye contact with them or me. Cass opens her mouth, but Sean pulls her back, and Carl gives me a sympathetic wince.

I'm in big, shitty trouble. I frown down at my hands and wait for him to speak.

"So your ex is a psycho—" he states, as his fingers move and tangle with mine. I stare at them but can't bring myself to raise my gaze. I feel an accusation ring in his voice and know from seeing the look of anger and sympathy that he is judging me for my lousy choice in men. His own pain is flickering there too. He is hurt that I never confided in him.

"He is sick," I say unevenly. I try to tug my hand away so I can twist it in my other. I know what Adam is, but there is a tinge of shame in me, and it's wormed its way so deep, riddling my mind with humiliation at having dated someone like that.

Jace's laugh is short.

"Don't defend the bastard." I drag my eyes up from my down-turned head and see the look of utter disbelief on his face. I want to tell him I'm not protecting Adam—I'm defending myself, but he has furious ambers pointed at me. "He," – he struggles over the words – "you miscarried," he stutters. "How can you defend him?"

"I'm not. I was there," I murmur, doesn't he understand I don't want to talk about Adam.

"Don't push me away, Lily." He moves up the bed and lifts me to him, kissing me gently. I wince at the sting on my lip, and he sighs. "I hate that I can't kiss you." His thumb glides with such softness over the sore part that I barely feel it. "I fucking hate that sick bastard," he spits. The mention of Adam has me stiffening.

"I just want to forget it happened." My sigh holds months' worth of inner exhaustion over the whole situation.

Jace shakes his head.

"I can't." He runs a hand over his face and clenches his fist so tightly all the colour drains. "Why didn't you report him to the police?" The look on his face says everything, but he holds back what he truly wants to say.

That I could have avoided this.

What can I say? He is right. I have been so caught up with work, and him, that I let it slide. It's feeble and irresponsible. I put myself at risk and others in danger; my lip wobbles, but I manage to make my tears subside.

He clears his throat.

"Has he contacted you at all?" His voice is tight, and I can see by the set of his face he already knows the answer, but it doesn't make it any easier to deliver.

"Yes. I have an appointment booked at the station to report him," I admit feebly.

His head snaps back like I've slapped him.

"Fucking hell, Lily," he chokes out, and I flinch in the bed, my head ringing like a church bell and guilt racking me into momentary silence. "When?" he demands.

"My birthday and the day you picked me up for lunch," I say hesitantly, my voice a scratchy whisper.

"Which lunch?" he huffs.

"Does it matter?" I wobble over the words, looking at him with sad eyes.

"What, he rang The Loft?" He is impatient for information.

"No, he beeped his horn when we went to the car," I whisper, remembering the look on Adam's face when he saw me with another man. Jace's eyes flare with recognition, then they narrow in concentration as he puts two and two together: my pale complexion that day, the sudden quietness. He nods, accepting the information.

"And that's it?" he clarifies. My eyes widen, and instantly he stands from the bed. "Are you fucking kidding me? How could you keep all this from me?" He rubs a hand over his neck, and I pull my legs up, watching him try to hold himself together. His self-control is slipping, and I feel helpless in the hospital bed.

"When?" he chokes.

"He came to the gallery the day I visited Paco. I wasn't there. Harriet spoke to him. Also, I had a prank type call—no one spoke, but I could hear someone." His jaw works, but I quietly go on, "I . . . I had an email in my junk mail. I haven't opened it. I think both were him."

"When?"

"I . . . it was . . . erm," I stutter, unsure what day it is. I know uttering those words is going to have Jace tipping over the edge. "What day is it?"

"Early hours of Thursday," he enlightens me in a deep growl. I've kept him in the dark. Refused him access to the most vulnerable part of me. I should have shared, opened up—that's what relationships are about, right?

"Yesterday, no Tuesday," I admit. "I think he was outside the gallery the other day. I can't be sure of that though." He drops down into the chair, and his head falls into his hands. Cass walks back in and looks at us both.

"Everything okay?" she asks carefully. My lip jitters and I drop my gaze away.

"Has Carl managed to get her phone working yet?" My man wants to know.

"Yes, it's pretty banged up though," Cass informs us both. I nod and look up through watery lashes as Jace stands. I'm surprised he hasn't hunted it down before now.

Cass slides in and walks to me, looking back as Jace storms out.

"He's pretty cut up," she says, stating the obvious. I'm trying to hold back the onset of heavy tears. "I had to tell him. I'm sorry." I just shrug and drop back into my pillow and close my eyes.

"I want this to end," I say tiredly. I yawn, and Cass climbs on the bed and snuggles into my side. I can't help it then, the tears leak through my lashes, hot, wet paths running down my face.

"Oh, hun, it's okay." Cass presses a kiss to my cheek.

"I feel exhausted," I sniff.

"You had a panic attack," she tells me. I frown into her hair, not recalling it but vaguely registering the lingering threat of sheer panic. I drop my tender head on her shoulder. "You need lots of rest," she tells me, her usually chirpy voice full of concern.

"What time is it?" I whisper, wishing it were Jace who was offering this level of concern.

"Coming up to eight." She yawns, and I wrap myself into her side and close my eyes. "I'll stay until you have gone to sleep." Her own voice is soft and sleepy.

"I'm sorry." My whisper is weak and full of hurt. After half an hour or so, a shaft of light pulls at the door, and a doctor strolls in, Jace right on his heel. The doctor gives Cass a warning look, and she slips off the bed, walking backward and giving me a dramatic eye roll. My lips twitch until pain radiates. I don't even want to ask what I look like.

"I'm Doctor Matterson," he introduces himself, collecting up my paperwork as he makes his way up the bed to me.

"Hello." My voice is far more assertive than I feel. I want to go home. I sit up, trying to seem alert and put together, but I struggle.

"How are you feeling?" he asks, looking at the paper and not me.

"My head still hurts, but the pain relief is helping." He nods and starts checking my vitals.

"Looks good," he says to himself, "any pain elsewhere?" My ribs hurt a bit, but I keep quiet.

I hold up the finger that is strapped securely. I know it's broken.

"I feel like I got hit in the face with a bat." I laugh it off, but Jace swings a set of disbelieving eyes at me, and I shrink into the bed. Apparently it's too soon for jokes.

"Yes, there is a fair bit of bruising coming out now. Your cut is minor, but the mouth is a sensitive area, so it probably feels worse than it is," he states, looking into my eyes and inspecting my head. His fingers graze over the achy area, the touch making it feel twice as sore. "These stitches are dissolvable," he informs me.

Stitches?

"Oh, will I have a scar?" I throw concerned eyes to Cass, lifting my hand to feel the area, but the doctor kindly knocks my hand away.

"It's in the hairline, easily disguised." His smile is genuine, fatherly. "Everything is looking good. I'm happy with your progress, and there is no reason why you can't be discharged within the next forty-eight hours. Should you experience a setback—" I frown at him, his hands are crossed at his stomach, paperwork held fast as he pivots on his heels a little, "—anxiety," he reminds me, making me flush, "your doctor can prescribe something to help."

He eyes me, waiting for a response. I nod, and he smiles happily.

"You have a good bump to your head, and I would like you to stay another night just for observation." I try to mentally calculate what he is saying, given that Jace said it's Thursday. So, home on Saturday? I'm frowning. "It is normal to have side effects with a mild concussion," he tells me. His pager beeps, and he checks his watch and pockets his pen in his chest. "I'll get the nurse to come and speak with you."

"What sort of side effects?" Jace asks, worry back in his tone.

"The nurse will be in to talk to you before Miss Spencer is discharged." He smiles. "If you're happy to take pain relief orally, I will ask someone to come and remove your cannula," he says, placing my paperwork at the end of the bed.

I nod.

"Thank you," I whisper.

As predicted by the consultant, I'm discharged on Saturday. Jace is almost carrying me out to his car.

"I can walk, you know," I mutter as he hurries me along, seeing his face set in a scowl and his eyes focused forwards.

"Don't test me, Lily," he warns, "besides, I like holding you." I look away, flushing when people walk past, eyeing us as I'm being escorted like a member of the royal family to the car park.

He deposits me by his sleek car and helps me in.

"I called the police," he informs me from above the car door, "they will be coming by sometime in the next few days to take a statement." His amber eyes drill holes into me, daring me to argue.

I give him an accommodating smile, and he shuts the door, closing me safely inside the car. I watch him stomp around the bonnet, and when he gets in, his lips are held in a straight line, and his face is pinched tightly.

He starts the car up and grips the wheel, his hands flexing as he stares ahead. He opens his mouth but then clamps it shut. He is struggling with this, and I feel terrible. Wordlessly, I climb over, moving his arm away to straddle his lap. Sad eyes lift to mine, and my heart aches for him.

"I'm sorry," I whisper. Jace drops his head away on a sigh, caught between wanting to love me and murder me all at once. I lift his prickly chin and press my mouth to his, careful not to hurt myself. I peck at his mouth, and he lets me, but to my annoyance, he stays still. His lips remain unresponsive and cause a deep ache in my chest. Softly, I dip my tongue out and try to chip away his anger. "Kiss me," I plead, dotting another kiss to his mouth, and when bottomless amber pools find my eyes, I swallow a ball of painful tears.

He frowns at me, his usually relaxed and beautiful face fixed into a scowl.

"Why didn't you tell me?" he spits on a dry whisper. "I don't understand how you could hide something like this—you knew you were in danger."

I sit frozen still on his lap as this big, confident man cracks in front of me.

I go to move, but Jace grips my hips, holding me still. He looks at me, really looks at me, and my heart breaks a little seeing how much I have truly hurt him. By withholding the truth, he doesn't think I trust him.

When he speaks, his voice holds so much emotion, and it's all rolled into one pained whisper.

"Don't ever, and I mean ever," – he sucks in a breath and stares at me, really punching home his meaning – "keep anything from me again. I thought he'd killed you."

I nod shakily, my sniffs of emotion not lost on him, but ignored all the same.

"I'm sorry," I croak. He cups my neck and pulls me down to his mouth.

I can't help but cry. I feel a wreck. His kiss is gentle but deep. It hurts my mouth, but I ignore the sting and fold into him on a sob.

"I love you, Lily, but we're supposed to be in this together. A couple." He breathes against my mouth. Those words—the ones I have been so desperate to hear, slip by, and I don't feel I deserve them. Jace's tongue rolls over mine in a deep groan, and I squirm in his lap. He laughs scathingly. "And that's a no," he grunts, lifting me back into my seat, "sex is off the cards for a while."

"What!" I whine. "Why?"

He throws me a pointed and irritated look.

"I'm not touching you when you're this fragile," he scoffs at me, implying I'm stupid for thinking otherwise.

"I can still have sex!" I tell him, finding his thought process abhorrent.

"I'm sure as shit not giving it to you, and you can get fucked if you think I'll let another man touch you," he laughs shortly.

"How can I get fucked, if you and other men are—"

"Lily!" he snaps quietly, his hands gripping so tightly I fear the steering wheel will snap. Okay, no more joke attempts.

"Sorry." I clip my belt in and keep my mouth shut. Jace sighs and rubs a hand down his exhausted face. He pulls out of the parking space, and we are quickly driving through the city and towards the outskirts. Despite how tired we are and the convenience of my place, he still favours his house.

"Cass is going to bring you some things round." I have no personal items with me, my phone has been confiscated, well, at least, I assume so, and my handbag is gone. I don't ask where any of it is.

We fall into silence, and I watch the world drift away as we head out of the city. It's at least forty minutes before we arrive at Jace's, and when we do, I'm nodding off.

He reaches over the console and coaxes me awake, gently brushing hair from my face.

"Lily? Wake up."

I blink across at him, sitting up slowly.

"Let me get your door," he says, exiting the car and walking around to me. When he closes the door and swings me up in his arms, I wordlessly allow him, although the quick motion makes my head swim, but I say nothing and rest my head on his shoulder, letting it pass. The doctor sent us home with pain relief and some information that Jace has folded neatly into his pocket.

Once inside, Jace walks us to his bedroom and rests me on the end of the bed. He leans over and pulls the quilt back, then drops down to take my ankle boots off, which get discarded to one side quickly. Leaning in, he takes the hem of my top, pulling it free from where I tucked it into my skirt. I lift my arms so he can pull it over my body, and deft fingers move round to my back so he can unclip my bra; easing it free, he drops it on the floor before he deals with the rest of my clothes. He rests a hand on my shoulder and gently pushes me back so I'm lying down. Air rushes out of my mouth, and I stare up at the intricate ceiling. He taps my hip, and I lift so he can pull my skirt down, then my knickers disappear.

"In you get," he instructs, holding the corner of the quilt up so I can slip underneath. I eye him suspiciously, but he looks back at me blankly. The cool sheets cause goosebumps to tidal wave along my skin. I rest back and watch as he tucks me in, but when he makes no demonstration to join me, I sit up.

"Aren't you joining me?" I ask, fearing I already know the answer.

"I have work to catch up on," he delivers, already walking away. I want to call him back, but don't. I know he is still struggling to process the last few days.

I swallow the 'I love you' rushing up my throat.

Chapter Nine

I've been awake for the last few minutes, but the comfort of Jace's bed has me staying put—that and the steady ache working its way through my skull. I can hear voices but can't make out any owners, other than Jace's anyway. The deep rumble is an auditory comfort.

Gingerly, I sit up, aware that the remnants of another nightmare are still plaguing my heart rate, and slowly, I push the quilt away. The cool air reminds me I'm naked, so using the throw to wrap myself up in, I tiptoe to the bathroom. Multiple sets of eyes swing my way from the sofas in the sprawling lounge—a lounge that now feels less inviting by each passing second. Why is she here?

"Lily." Jace is up and walking towards me with purpose. I dip my gaze and quietly go into the bathroom, dropping the throw and plopping down on the toilet. My mouth feels tight, and my fingers throb. He waltzes in. "Do you want a drink?" he says, leaning against the sink. I nod, and he turns away as soon as our eyes meet.

"Jace," I croak. My fingers naturally lift to rub at my mouth, and I watch as he slowly looks back at me. "I love you too." My lip wobbles over the whisper, and he swallows what I assume is a ball of emotion.

"I know. I just wish you had told me about Adam. I'm going to get you some water." He sighs. Is that it? No kiss, not even a hug?

I've really upset him. Busying myself by washing my hands, I wipe the tears away and try to lock my emotions up. I didn't know how to tell him. I still don't. I had only just felt able to breathe fully again from the constant knife-deep ache of loss when Jace ploughed into my life, dragging me to his bed and churning up all kinds of emotions I had never wanted to feel. I stare at my hands in the sink, coming to the painful realisation that I have felt so guilty for being happy—happy without the life that was ruthlessly taken from me. Adam doesn't just represent fear. He is the reason for my biggest loss: my baby.

I do want to be happy with Jace. When he returns, he silently hands me a pair of my pyjama shorts and a camisole. I smile softly at him, but his mouth is turned down.

I hate it. Hate the physical and emotional distance between us.

"How are you feeling?"

"Sore."

Jace lifts the camisole, and I weakly raise my arms to allow him to cover my top half. He points to the water, saying, "You need to keep hydrated." He looks so forlorn.

For the first time, I inspect my reflection. My face looks gaunt and pale, dark circles ring my eyes, and the neat but sore cut running along my hairline is longer than I thought. Precise stitches hook their way in and out of my skin, pulling the wound tight. My lip is swollen and bruised, and dark blood knots the skin in place. Slowly, I lift my fingers to test how painful it is, jumping when I hear him tut behind me.

Dropping my hand, I begin to slip my clothes on. I have to sit back down to pull the bottoms up. My body aches from the fall, but I ignore the stiffness of my limbs and force myself into the clothes.

"You're in pain," he states. I flick a look his way and respond with a simple shrug. My hair is a bloody mess, but I can't do much with it, so I twist it and let it drop down one side. "Your painkillers are by the bed," he tells me. Why is he being so distant?

Jace has laid out a jumper, so I slip it on and zip it up. I pick up the painkillers and swallow them quickly. The water hits my empty stomach, and I force a swallow to keep it from coming back up. I need something to eat. For the first time in a long time, I feel like I need my mum.

Closing my eyes, I lift my head and force my tears at bay.

The voices are louder now as I head towards them. Viktor, and a lady, I'm assuming is his wife, are sitting on the sofa, Neve opposite them. My eyes flash to Jace's, but he looks away with awkwardness pinching at his dark expression. There is no reason for her to be here, and he knows that.

Viktor stands and gives me a soft smile.

"Hello, lovey." He comes straight to me and wraps a loving arm around me. I have the sudden urge to sink into his embrace and sob. The need for a parent's love is too raw, and with both mine being absent, I'm emotionally clinging for anything, especially since Jace isn't offering. Viktor must sense that because he squeezes me gently. My breath leaves in a shudder, and I wipe my tears away. "Come on, love," he murmurs, "nasty bit of trouble you got yourself into." I step back, wrapping my arm around my waist, pulling at every last shred of energy I have to get through this, as my eyes meet Jace's, and he looks guiltily at me. Shame engulfs me. They must all know, and I can't bear the details of my relationship with Adam filtering through their minds. Do they know what he did to me before—how he robbed me of my child all those months ago?

My baby. Gone. Beaten from my body. She was mine. I don't want to share her. I'm not ready to give her up for other people's judgement. And despite knowing Jace is struggling and needs the comfort of his family, I can't help feeling angry that he's divulged my private life to them—to Neve.

Clearing my throat, I focus on him.

"How are you?" I ask brightly. He barks out a laugh, and I hold mine in to save me feeling the sting of pain—the irony of the situation is not lost on me.

"Surely I should ask you that?"

I waft him away, studiously keeping my gaze from seeking out my angry partner and his needy friend.

"Bruises heal." I keep my voice flat, but my face flinches at the rush of disjointed memories Adam has left me with.

"Hmmm, but the mind is a little more difficult," he says softly. My eyes lift to his, and I manage a shrug of indifference. I look at the woman sat rubbing Jace's knee. She is petite and polished, at complete odds with Viktor's rough and big exterior.

"Lily, this is my wife, Marie, and you've met Neve." My eyes betray me and slip to hers. She is avoiding looking at me at all costs. I'd prefer it if she avoided me even more, and left.

"Yes. Hello, Marie." I give her a little wave, my hand barely lifting, and the other, secure in the pocket of Jace's hoody, protecting my broken fingers.

Marie's eyes soften, and she has no hesitation in standing and covering the distance, gentle arms enveloping me.

"It's lovely to meet you," she soothes, rubbing at my back.

"Even under these circumstances?" I offer a weary smirk, fighting for the Lily I know best to come back.

"Well," she hums, "it would be awfully boring if we had just met for a coffee."

I laugh lightly, feeling at ease with her already. Both Viktor and herself have calming presences, and I feel no judgement from them, so maybe Jace didn't tell them everything after all?

"Are you hungry, love?" She rubs my arms lightly.

"Starving," I admit, slotting my other hand into the pocket.

Neve, never one to miss an opportunity, is holding Jace's hand and rubbing his back supportively. I feel my eyes glue to their entwined fingers, and my gut rolls with anxiety. When I look up, Jace stares at me. I lift my brow, and he slips his hand free. With any luck, he will ask her to leave.

I avert my gaze and look to the lineup of cars. I want to go home. I feel so out of sorts here. And with Jace's constant lack of affection, I feel hugely unwelcome. I know he is hurt, but I was the one who was attacked. I need the support from him. Why can't he give me that?

I rub my neck, easing the ache in my throat, and follow Marie towards the kitchen. I slow as dizziness taunts me, keeping my gaze forward and on the stools until I reach my destination.

"Let's see what the boy has got in here for you."

I hold the side, steadying myself.

"An abundance of bacon and eggs," I joke. Marie clucks, but it's motherly and a little nostalgic, I realise when I see the small pull of a smile on her face.

She opens up the fridge and begins rummaging through the contents.

"I can do that," I tell her, taking some cheese out of her hands. "I need to keep busy." I swallow, mentally recognising I feel jittery and exhausted. I stifle a yawn, and she rubs my arm.

"Let me, pet. You look ready to fall." My reply gets caught on my tongue when Marie gives me a stern look. I take a space on the stool and watch her because it's the only thing holding me back from looking at Jace.

I feel his presence at my back before I see him. He steps into my eye-line, and I can't help but think how stunning he looks. Wordlessly, he lifts my face and checks my lip and head.

"Do you know what time it is?" His voice is soft, but accusation burns in his eyes. I shake my head and pull my chin free. I can understand his sense of betrayal at my desire to keep him in the dark about my past, but he is really starting to piss me off. "Nearly three in the afternoon, Lily." My eyes widen. I had no idea it was that late. I search for a clock to clarify—I have slept for hours. His sigh is full of frustration once more.

"Oh, leave her be," Marie scolds, "poor girl has been through enough without you weighing in on her." She gives him a pointed look—the look of a mother. I would laugh if I didn't think it would hurt.

"I thought two o'clock was your favourite time of the day?" My voice is quiet, soft, and I look up hopefully, offering him a smile, but he chews his lip and stares at the tight cut on my forehead. "I'm sorry I didn't tell you," I whisper. Is that why he is being distant?

"Yeah, I know."

Marie fusses over me, and places a sandwich by my side with a steaming brew.

"Here you go love," Her hand rubs along my back.

"Thank you." I tuck my hair behind my ear and start to nibble at my sandwich when the distinctive sound of my phone blares through the room. Jace steps back from me then pulls it from his trousers, answering it.

"Hi, yeah, she's awake, just eating something." I can hear Cass on the other end. "Let her eat. She will call you later." There is a huff as long as the Nile before he cuts the call.

I eye him and hold my hand out.

"Can I have my phone back, please?" I could have spoken to her. She's my bloody friend, and I'm well enough to converse and be subject to his family's involvement. I raise my brow, becoming increasingly pissed off with his attitude. He returns my phone to his jeans and walks to his office—a decision that draws a scoff from me. What the hell is his problem?

Silence falls, and I roll my eyes, shoving a bigger bite in my mouth now my stomach feels more settled. I stare ahead for a moment before I slide down from the chair and follow him.

"Maybe give him a minute," Neve bites and looks me up and down. I'm glad when Marie sees the hostility burning across at me. I want to tell her to shove her opinion up her skinny arse, but I choose to keep my face neutral and walk off, ignoring the wave of dizziness.

I find Jace braced against the window, his head hung, and my phone gripped in his hand. He must sense me or see my reflection because he speaks.

"He hit you when you were down." He shakes his head, and I watch as his shoulders rise on an unsteady breath. "Did you know that?"

"No, and I'd rather not know." My hands slip to cover my stomach. I feel strangely exposed, knowing this information, hearing his pain. The stark fact that he can convey it so deeply through the window knocks me off-kilter that much more.

"Carl recorded the call. I heard him beating you. He would have killed you, Lily, if Carl hadn't driven at him." The vivid image he puts in my mind is as unwanted as the ones I already have stored there.

"Why are you telling me this? I've been through enough." He looks back over his shoulder, looking remorseful. "Why are you being so distant?"

"Why would you keep this all to yourself? Why put yourself and everyone at risk?" he asks, his voice rising.

I shrug because I don't know why I did. I just wanted to close the door on Adam, and I honestly didn't think he was capable of something like this. Obviously, now I know different.

I manage to keep my emotions from overflowing.

"I didn't want to bring him into our relationship." It's a feeble excuse, even if it's true.

"But he brought himself in, anyway. Lily, you should have gone to the police. He was in violation of his order. This whole thing could have been prevented," he vents—his tone quiet but harsh. My phone is gripped, knuckle-white-tightly in his palm.

I blink at the severity of his tone.

"I know that. I told you I was going to see the police. I had closed the door on it. I didn't want to have to be swept into it again. He hurt me." My voice wavers over a lump of burning tears.

I just wanted to immerse myself in the paradise that is Jace.

"You're just passing the hurt along." He quietly seethes, still struggling with my dismal decisions.

"You're being unfair. I haven't intentionally set out to hurt anyone. I made a mistake. Why are you making this harder for me?" I urge him to see this from my point of view.

"I nearly lost you, Lily."

"But I'm fine."

"YOU ARE NOT FINE!" he cries. My head snaps back, rattling with pain, and my tired, grey eyes spring open in shock. I suddenly feel conscious of the guests we have just metres away, all very much in listening distance. I draw breath to say something, but it sticks in my throat because anything I say in response will only fuel this further. We're both too emotional to deal with it properly. "You nearly died. I nearly lost you. I could have lost you," he croaks out.

"But you didn't. I appreciate you need your family here, but I'd like to call Cass back," I say softly, hoping to steer us down a calmer path. I want the comfort of my friend's voice. I'm feeling pretty outnumbered with his family here.

"Not happening, Lily." His grunt is one of both irritation and tiredness.

"That's not your decision to make." I sound far less confident than I hoped. I'll be damned if he thinks I will just roll over and let him dictate everything.

"Did you finish your sandwich?" he counteracts. I tut and walk to him with the intention of retrieving my phone from his pocket. As soon as I'm at his feet, my small hands ram into his narrow pocket, but he grips my fist, fast seizing all control. My phone isn't the only hard object I can feel against my palm. My surprised eyes lift to his, but he bats me away, hissing lightly. "That would just complicate things further." It would, but the constant buzz of electric heat we stir up in each other is dining out on all this tension. My hand is slowly retracted and empty. No phone.

"You're being ridiculous," I mutter. Is he scared I will leave if I speak to Cass?

"Can we save the domestic for later?" He sighs, holding me fully accountable.

"I hadn't realised me being attacked warranted *you* to spark a domestic, but thanks for being so supportive." I hiss and snatch my phone back. "You're angry at me for not telling you about Adam. I get it. You've made yourself *very* clear, Jace." I give a sardonic laugh and his cheeks flush. "You're treating me like shit, and quite frankly, I'm exhausted, so we can either be the couple you profess we are, or I'm going home." I raise my brow, and he sucks in a deep breath. "I need your support, not this." I begin to well up.

"Lily," he sighs apologetically.

"Why is Neve here?" I ask quietly.

"She came to see if you were okay?"

"Really?" I tilt my head. "Funny. She hasn't once asked me," I point out, and with that, I leave him in the office. I would rather not have our little spat dissected by his family. Everyone has made themselves busy, but I know they have all been hanging off every word. Marie looks slightly uncomfortable as I return to the kitchen and finish up my meal. I'm not hungry, but out of politeness, I polish it off. I expect it to give me a burst of energy, but instead, I yawn as another wave of sleepiness hangs over me. Jace, who is watching my every move like a hawk, stands and heads my way.

I stiffen, assuming he is ready to get into further discussion, so when he pushes between my thighs, I'm surprised. I let him because it's been so long since I felt the security of him. My hands get placed on his shoulders, and he lifts me. I go without complaint because any physical contact until now has been scarce.

Deep down, I want to push him away for his callousness earlier, but my exhaustion wins, and I drop my head on his shoulder and twist my body around his, keeping me secure. I don't know what I expect, but when he walks us to his bedroom, I stiffen.

"What are you doing?" I go to lift my head, but it feels heavier than all my other limbs.

"You need to rest," he grumbles.

"But I just woke up." I laugh and flush when it turns to another yawn. He shrugs, and my small hands grip tight to his shoulders.

"Your body needs to heal." That amber gaze scans over my face with only one intention, getting to the other side without maintaining prolonged eye contact.

"I won't sleep later."

"That's fine." I sigh and huff as I'm put down.

"It's not. I have loads to catch up on at the gallery." He pulls the quilt up and levels me with a hard stare.

"If you are even considering going into work, I will drag you straight back to the hospital," he growls.

"But I'm fine." I flop back in a huge grump, knowing deep down my attempt at negotiating with him is futile.

"Fine, is going for a run and coming back *unharmed,* Lily. Seventy-two hours ago, you were wired up on a drip, so you can take your tablets and go to fucking sleep, you stubborn pain in my arse." It's said hotly, but the beginning of a twinkle in his eyes tells me he is happy to finally have me where he wants me, with him, in his home—even if it is under sufferance.

I sleep for a few more hours and wake late in the evening. The house is quiet, dark, and it takes me a few moments to finally find the strength to push off the mattress. Sitting on the edge for a minute or two, I take a moment to just gather myself. I feel woozy and a bit sick. Putting it down to my lethargy, I go to stand, but my shaky legs mock me, and I slump back down. The familiar sound of the pivoting door sounds and Jace is rushing in.

"What's wrong?" His face is etched in worry, a deep frown line cutting into his forehead. I'm gripping the quilt to steady myself.

"I just feel really lightheaded." My lip wobbles and I damn it to hell for making me seem weak.

"That's it, we're going back to the hospital," he declares, quickly dragging some of my things together.

Whoa! I don't want to go back.

"Jace, just relax. It's probably a symptom of the concussion." I frown lightly at his panicked state.

"The registrar gave me a slip—you can go back in," he declares with a sharp point of his hand. The motion firmly telling me in one harsh swipe that we are going back.

If my head didn't hurt so much, I would roll my eyes.

"I don't think I nee—"

"You've got a concussion. You don't know what you want!" he snaps. I turn my head away and rest back on the bed, my eyes widening mockingly at his abrupt manner.

"Maybe call them and ask for some advice?" I say wisely.

"No. Don't move," he grumbles, storming off. Jeez, what a stress head!

Jace adds his charger to the small holdall and, with a determined look, sweeps me up, making my already wishy-washy head spin more.

"Urgh," I groan.

"Shit, sorry."

I wrap myself into him and press my face into his neck, feeling shakier and more out of sorts by the second. I feel as though if he placed me on my feet, my body would teeter off to the left. It's a horrible sensation and one that has my lip trembling.

An hour later, I'm propped up and drowsy in a hospital bed, with Jace firmly planted in the chair, his feet wide, elbows on knees, and a jumpy leg showcasing his impatience and worry. My hand is caught up in his and locked against his lips, the constant rock of his leg nursing me off to sleep.

"It'll be fine," I mumble.

He scoffs in complete disagreement with me. The nurse who had taken my vitals and escorted me into bed after Jace had carried me in, causing far more worry than necessary, has made a quick escape, and Jace is on the warpath, demanding, snapping, and looking ready to explode. Now it's a waiting game.

Chapter Ten

I'm coaxed awake by worried hands and find both Jace and the same consultant from the other night, each by one side of the bed.

"Hello, Lily."

"Hi," I rasp, my sleepiness making me seem far worse than I probably am. Jace has begun a short pace, keeping him close but also busy enough that he doesn't react to the doctor's obvious calmness that is at total odds with his tornado worry.

He picks up my paperwork and rifles through, scanning the notes and making some of his own, before replacing the clipboard and walking back to me, bringing a small light out from his pocket. I brace myself for the blinding shaft of light in my pupil and blink fuzzily afterward.

"All looks okay. Vitals are normal. Can you tell me how you have been feeling?"

"Achy, I feel stiff and sore, headache, really tired." He nods and smiles down at me.

"All extremely normal side effects of a head trauma."

Just as I thought.

"She's dizzy," Jace throws in.

"Only a little," I add, ignoring the dark glare being shot my way. I see the warning there. "Very dizzy," I admit softly. Jace nods, and I smile over at him, hoping it will calm him down.

"How is your balance?" the doctor inquires. I shrug, Jace has carried me everywhere, so I don't actually know, and I say as much.

"Right, let's get you up." The doctor smiles, pulling the sheet back to help me out, and Jace draws a breath to say something but slaps his lips shut. Gingerly, I stand, but my achy bones won't allow for much else. With my system full of painkillers, I hadn't really acknowledged the level of soreness in my side, and when I draw breath, it pulls, and a dull pain waves along my ribs. I grip the bed and lift my top, finding the edges of a black and purple bruise. My eyes shoot open in horror and rush to find Jace's pained ones burning back at me. He drags his face away, unable to look at my marred skin any longer, grinding his teeth loudly to stop the torrent of anger bursting free.

It hits me then like a bolt of lightning that all of his anger isn't directed at me but Adam. He's only angry that I didn't confide in him. This man wants it all with me. My heart and soul, and I have made sure to lock him out.

Dropping my top, I look back to find the consultant waiting for me to leave the safety of the bed.

"Just to the other side of the ward—" He points with the light down to the nurse's station, and I suck in a breath, wincing at the ache in my side, and begin small steps away from him. The first half-metre is uneventful, so I widen my stride and pick up speed. Dizziness washes over me, and I wobble, feeling that invisible force pulling me to the left. I grip the nearest side to steady myself, but as quick as it came, the dizziness is gone. Jace is already halfway to me, cursing to high heaven, but the doctor asks that he leave me to make the journey back alone. I do it without any further problem and perch on the bed, searching out the consultant with my eyes, and not Jace. "It's over as quick as it comes," I mumble. He nods and taps my paperwork with the pen tip.

"How regularly?" His pen is poised, ready to write my reply down.

"So far, it's after I have woken up."

"All the symptoms you are suffering are associated with the injury you have, but it may take a little longer to recover from some more than others. Plenty of rest, eat little and often if the wooziness is making you feel nauseous, and a stress-free environment." He angles his head Jace's way.

I nod, feeling silly for having wasted his time.

"So, another day in bed, then back to work?" I ask, hopefully. He shakes his head, laughing lightly.

"You have a stubborn one." He softens his earlier blow to Jace with a pointed remark about me, and Jace grunts and drops back into his seat.

"Doesn't she need a scan or anything?" He really isn't happy with this. I blanch at the thought and look back to the consultant, silently pleading with him to give me the all clear.

"No, we have ruled out a serious head injury, all vitals are good, and symptoms are to be expected." If he is irritated by Jace's constant argument, he doesn't show it.

"So, I can go home?" I question, rubbing at my sleepy eyes.

"Yes, remember, lots of rest. I would suggest sitting up for a short time before you try to walk after napping. What is it you do for a living?" he asks, scribbling something down quickly.

"I own a gallery," I say, picking at the fluff on my top—a gallery that needs my attention. I have no Harriet, and now I'm down. It couldn't get any worse!

"I suspect the dizziness will last a few days, but it could stick around for a week or two. As soon as you feel better, then you can resume working. Just take it slowly and let your body heal." I nod absently; my mind caught up on a different matter. No work?

It's late when we finally make it back to Jace's, and he demands I stay put until he has unloaded the car, but I'm slipping free before he makes it back to me. When he grips my waist, I wince.

"Ouch!"

"Sorry." His hands slip away and take mine. I grip tightly and let him lead me inside.

I catch sight of my reflection, and my nose scrunches in disgust. "I feel grubby," I whine. My hair is glistening, and not because it is glossy—my face is pale and bruised. I look a bloody mess.

"You can't wash your hair," Jace mutters, taking the opportunity to slide my hair aside so he can inspect my cut.

"I'm going to run a bath," I tell him. His wide fingers cup my cheek, and he regards me thoughtfully. Honey-thick ambers slowly roll across my face, lingering on both bruises and dropping fully to my lips. His dense lashes are really noteworthy from this angle, and his chest expands on a deep draw of breath. I expect him to say something, but instead, he lifts his gaze, and goddammit, my heart, and stomach jump and crash together in excitement. He's going to kiss me.

I do a little mental wave of joy and wait silently for him to close the distance. With every second that he doesn't, the tension swirls and knots until it's almost unbreakable. I suck in a shuddery breath and close my eyes because the thick swallow I just witnessed is a sure sign that Jace is finally weakening and will drop his mouth to mine.

"Look at me, Lily," he whispers. My dazed lids slip open, and it takes all of my energy to force my foggy brain to comply. "You want me to kiss you," he states softly.

Yes!

I nod, and my neck jerks a little against the brace of his hands.

"Yes, please." My breathing is all choppy and short. I want that kiss more than I need my next breath.

"Promise me; the truth, always." A shaky thumb drags over my lip, careful as it skims my healing cut.

"Always," I vow softly.

"Always." His lips do that little smug twitch thing that I have come to love so much, and my eyes shine into his, and I know, given some time, we are going to be okay.

I'm neck-deep in silky bubbles and swathed by a very aroused Jace. His thick arms circle my waist and keep me secure at his chest—my head is resting on his shoulder, and his full lips do a happy little jaunt down my jawline.

"Hmmm." I'm all slippery and content.

"We don't do this enough." His big chest vibrates beneath me. He's trying, but I can feel the tension locked in his chest.

"We did it last week." I laugh.

"See, not enough. There has been lots of sleep and naughtiness since then." His hands run down my arms, and he threads one through my uninjured hand. The other, fairly swollen still, is rested on the bath's edge, safe from the water.

"I'm not seeing much naughtiness as of late." I pout and make a cheeky roll of my hips. He grunts and grips my hip, stilling me.

"You're black and blue, plus if you pass out on me or throw up, I will be scarred for life." He tweaks my nipple, and I jerk under him with a little yelp.

"Your lack of desire is emotionally scarring me," I grumble, jabbing him with my elbow.

His hips thrust.

"Does that feel lacking to you?"

"Are you asking me or my vagina?" I thrust my nose in the air, and his deep laugh is as sexy as hell. I flip, sending water splashing over the edge in a mini tidal wave. My eyes widen, and my lips form a smile. He attacks my mouth, and I grin up at him, happy that he seems more relaxed and like his usual self again. I try to secure myself to him, but when I'm as slippery as I am, it's bloody difficult. He draws me up, and I take the opportunity to straddle him, rubbing myself shamelessly against him with a soft little purr. "Please," I whisper, nipping his ear and then his jaw. Stubble grazes my lip, and I purposely thrust my boobs in his face.

He curses me to next week and back, his erection knocking the back of my arse.

"Lily," he warns deeply. His palm glides up my chest until it splays over my heart, a sweet gesture but a calculated one. I'm being kept at arm's length. I pout but let it fall away into a smile, trying a manipulation of my own.

"Is that a yes?" I roll my hips on a feminine moan and angle myself,

Jace halts my movements and readjusts himself.

"That's a no," he grumbles and tucks away a lock of hair that has managed to get wet. I slump into his body and mumble my disquiet. "Just this once, don't fight me, beautiful. Let me look after you." He pecks my nose.

"I think you're secretly happy I'm here, in your home," I say, not quite meeting his eyes. My fingers are tracing a wet pattern over his wide chest.

"It's no secret, despite the circumstances, I'm fucking ecstatic I have you here." He lets out a short laugh, and I look up from my pattern drawing and see he is battling with smugness. "I might just manage to make you move in with me, after all." He adjusts himself as a shit-eating grin breaks out over his face.

"I suppose that depends," I murmur, enjoying the feel of him tense under me.

"On what?" His head rolls to the side a little as he looks at me down his nose. His lips are quirked, and his eyes shine back at me.

"Whether this drought will continue," I whine, jabbing him in the pec with my nail. He laughs and slowly pulls me back around so my butt is pressed into his groin.

"It's painful, isn't it?" He grunts, adjusting his hard frame behind me. His body ripples and nudges me in all the right places. But he is right; my need for him is all-consuming. It's an itch that can't be scratched, a pain that can't be eased, not unless he takes me to the special high that only he can deliver.

"More than my bruises," I quip. His fingers lift and splay, silently asking me to join. I press my delicate fingers in his, and he locks in.

"Move in with me, Lily," his broken plea is uttered into my ear softly, wide fingers splay against my stomach, and I encounter an unknown, weightless sensation of feeling perfectly safe.

"Okay." I stare at the window where I find our reflections latched together. Jace's eyes glitter with self-satisfied pleasure, and his chest does a big heave of relief.

"You have no idea how happy you just made me." His fingers run back and forth over my stomach.

I wiggle with happiness.

"I can guess." I shiver as the open air glides over my skin. We've been in here a while, and I'm starting to get a little cold.

He huffs.

"That's only a fraction of my happiness." His hand fists when it gets too close to my breasts, and I inwardly scream.

"A big fraction." I snigger. Slowly, I twist and crawl up his frame once more. Jace cups himself and keeps us separate. I laugh at this big man sprawled naked in the bath, cupping his family jewels from me.

"And to think I pegged Carl as the dramatic one," I mock, as his face bunches in annoyance.

"Kiss me, you damn tease." He drops his head back to look up at me, a slow smile on his face.

"As you wish." I grin and drop my mouth. His tongue is already protruding in anticipation. I dive right in. I've missed kissing him.

We soak for a little while longer; the water is becoming cooler by the second, but neither one of us complains. There is a calm silence between us, and all I sense is his low, comforting breaths and the reassuring swell of his chest against my back. My mind is serene; my posture completely relaxed. The pain in my body ebbs away with the knowledge that I'm safe, and there is nothing left unsaid between us. He knows my darkest secret, my worst, the ugly scab in my life, and he is still here, still ready to hurtle us to his world of happy.

His lips drop to my ear, and he presses his nose deep, inhaling on a rough grumble and sighing softly.

"Let's get dried off." He nudges me up and helps me out—the water sluices down my frame, and I see him turn away from the thick spattering of bruises.

"Thanks," I murmur. I move to get our towels and wrap myself up before handing another to him.

"I'm going to pop the oven on. Marie left us a lasagna on the side." I leave him to it, frowning, grouchy, and all together distracted. He is still trying to piece things together, evaluate and conquer it alone. He doesn't want to ask me the gory details because he thinks I don't want to talk about it, and he's right. I don't. But I will for him and only him. I refuse to revisit that place for myself alone, nor am I ready to broach it and initiate the conversation—Jace needs to come to me. He needs to be ready to hear it, and so far, neither one of us has wanted to taint our happy with my grim past.

By the time I've managed to dry off and get dressed, Jace is already dishing up our dinner. He nods towards the sofa as he walks towards me with my plate. I ease down and pull a face when he places it on my lap.

"What happened to it?" I frown, perplexed at the mushed up mess on my knee. Whatever it is, it certainly does not resemble lasagna.

"Nothing." His face is serious, and he ignores me further when I prod the remains of my dinner with a fork. I look at his meal. His is presented perfectly, a precise slab of meat, pasta, and sauce—it looks delicious, but mine, oh no, mine looks horrendous.

"Did the oven commit a hate crime?" Jace's head comes up, and he deadpans me.

"No, smart arse. I cut it up because of your hand," he tells me with a shake of his head. With what—a chainsaw? Jesus Christ, a toddler could have chopped this up neater.

"Thanks." I prod it about. "I guess." Choosing to ignore the scrambled state of my lasagna, I tuck in, finding that my mouth is still tight, but most of the pain has gone.

"You're welcome, I guess," Jace is smirking around his fork—his downcast eyes twinkling. "Here, let's watch this." He nods to the TV.

For a night, we do boring, normal, perfect-couple stuff. It's exactly what I need after the last few days.

"I didn't like that," I tell him a few hours later, lying in bed. I screamed through every jumpy part, shouted at the TV when anything bad transpired, and almost cried at the beginning. I hate real-life programs. I'd much rather watch something over the top and unbelievable.

"I'm never going to the cinema with you," he chuckles, pulling me closer. I'm slotted in, nice and warm, and his lips are lazily dragging across my temple. "If documentaries make you cry that much, I dread to think what a horror would do."

I grin into the darkness and sigh happily. We seem to be getting there—slow, steady steps, but we're making progress—moving toward that time when we were deliriously happy. I want that back—him back. Tonight has been what I needed. Calm normality.

"Lily?"

"Hmm?" I pull his hand up and rest my chin on it, closing my eyes.

"I need to know the truth. I can't cope with the possibilities running through my head." The rough and whispered statement makes me stiffen in his hold. He means Adam. He wants all the gory details.

Can I do that? Am I ready? I want to be for him. However, now that the moment is here, my heart shrivels into a tight ball, and acid builds in my throat.

I scrunch my eyes tightly, trying to recall all those horrible moments while detaching myself completely to give this man what he needs to move us both back to our happy place.

"Erm . . . okay." I swallow, my voice is shaky, unsure, but when his hands tighten, I relax. They are just words, I tell myself. Adam is gone. He can't get to me, and Jace is here—beautiful Jace Bennett, who I don't deserve, is here holding tightly onto me, onto us, and keeping us both afloat. I can do this. For him, I can do it. "What do you need to know?" I know I can't just get into it. I need some kind of platform to kick me off—a starting point. Anything but the usual horrid visual I conjure up whenever I think of that sick man.

"How did you meet?" Light circles are drawn on my stomach, a constant roll of reassurance and physical grounding. Is he just as worried I'm going to fall victim to another anxiety attack when I bring these memories forward?

"A bar." My throat catches as I recall the moment Adam Burrows approached me. It's there in my mind, just as vivid as the moment it happened. I recall my clothes, his, how everything smelt, and the song that was playing. My hatred for this man has hand picked every moment with him in it and turned it into a HD-ready, graphically perfected movie when really I should blur him out and make the ones I love and care about the main focus of my life and mind. "He came right up to me and professed his undying love. I just laughed." Hands tighten around me, and I frown at how ridiculous Adam was. "He'd had a drink, and I thought he was messing about." My eyes are slowly adjusting to the darkness now, and I can see Jace's outline in the big glass window. I feel his chin fall on my shoulder.

"But he wasn't?" His lips run back and forth, the light bristle of his beard breaking the surface of his skin.

"Looking back, he seemed to know a lot about me before we'd even got to know each other. He never admitted it, but I did wonder if he had been . . . you know—" I don't want to say it out loud because the thought is too creepy to comprehend.

"Do you think he'd been watching you?" Jace speaks the words so I don't have to.

"I guess. I have no proof of that," I admit, and I don't, just that gut-deep sickening churn that something wasn't quite right.

"But you started dating him?" The accusation I hear in Jace's voice stings, but I forgive him because I'm not really doing a good job of explaining all this.

"No." I laugh harshly, giving him a little jab. "It wasn't like that. We bumped into each other again before I agreed to go out for drinks with him. It wasn't until later that I started to wonder all about that, and by then, it was too late." I shrug.

"No alarm bells, then?"

"Not really. Just the odd comment about things I liked or did that I couldn't recall telling him. We'd go drinking, and I put it down to me being too drunk to remember." Does he really need to know more? The rest is fairly obvious. I shrug into the darkness, conveying there isn't much more to say, but he isn't sated.

"Was he physical a lot?" His voice is deep, low, and so quiet. He knows how hard this is. I shake my head.

"He never hit me, just grabbed me and would get really territorial, but we were only seeing each other. We weren't exclusive, and I thought it was a bit of fun. He started getting really needy, and demanding to know where I was, what I was doing, who I was with. A bit too obsessive, and I decided to call it quits. After I realised I was pregnant, he was over the moon. He wanted us to be a family, and I couldn't *not* give my child both parents, so we tried to make it work, but he knew it was just because of the baby. He became jealous. He would accuse me of cheating if I was late from work, commenting on my attire, asking who I had seen or spoke to in the day, and checking my phone. He just started to accuse me of anything, so I decided it was best to split, and he snapped."

We'd had a huge row. He'd accused me of everything possible, and I'd almost welcomed the accusations because anyone would have been better than him. Adam was blind with jealousy, sick with rage. The night he had beaten me had felt like hours. I'd been too scared to leave, afraid to stay. Our flat had become a prison, and every wall a cage to keep me in. I tried so hard not to think back to that night.

"He'd dragged me around the flat using my hair as a lead, and my knees were burnt from the carpet."

My eyes clamp tightly shut as thick tears pour over and coat my lashes. I shake my head.

"I just wanted him to stop, stop hurting me. He was drunk, sickly drunk. You know when you can smell it on their breath from a mile off?" I shudder, remembering that smell. It still turns my stomach now. "I thought I'd finally got through to him. I let my guard down," I say in a whisper. "He just kept punching my stomach, kicking me there when I was down."

"I'm so sorry, beautiful."

I'm crying softly now, little gentle hiccups into the night.

"A neighbour had called the cops, and they broke their way into the flat I was living in at the time. If they hadn't come, I don't think he would have stopped. By the time the police showed up, Adam had run off."

"Jesus, Lily. I'm so sorry, baby." He kisses my brow. "I'm so proud of you—of what you've achieved despite what he did to you."

"I really wanted to be a mum. I had accepted it by then. When I think about all he has done, there is this tiny part of me that is relieved my child would never know that their father was like that, and then I feel guilty for even thinking it," I admit with a pained croak.

"It's okay. There is nothing to feel guilty about. Anyone in their right mind would think the same."

"I feel guilty about you," I confess, sobbing softly.

"Why?" Jace turns me and pulls me into his chest. He smooths my hair back and looks down at me. "Don't say that, Lily—we're perfect."

"Because you make me happy, and I feel like I should have tried harder with Adam, for the baby. Maybe it would never have happened, and my baby wouldn't have died, but now I'm with you and so deliriously happy, and I don't know if I deserve to be." I bury my face in his chest. All these dormant feelings are rushing to the surface and hit me like a tidal wave. I sob and sob.

This evening feels like it is the quiet after the storm. My meltdown is cathartic. An emotional weight feels as if it's been lifted from my life. Jace holds me long into the night until I finally drift off.

Chapter Eleven

One week later . . .

Nothing and everything has changed. Jace is still keeping his distance physically, and Harriet is finally back. The Loft has been closed all week, bar the two occasions Cass managed to fit me in her diary so I could pick things up and let the cleaner in. The swelling in my face has all but gone, and I have managed to work my hair to cover the stitches. To any passer-by, I look normal, but I don't feel normal. I feel disjointed. Everyone is walking on eggshells around me, clearly worried I'm going to snap any second. It's enough to send the sanest of people crazy. What's worse is Jace hasn't touched me all week, he barely kisses me, and when he does, he prises me away to stop it from heating up. I want heat.

"So, how you doing, I mean really?" Cass says, sipping a coke up through a straw. We are at a small café, not one of our regulars, thankfully.

Shrugging, I lift my tea. I seem to have built a taste for it since Marie made me one—it's not as bitter.

"Honestly, I just want to move forward. I'm okay," I assure her. I just need things with Jace to be good, and I will feel heaps better. "Now, I know Adam is in custody, I can finally close that door and begin again with Jace." I meet her eye to cement how I feel.

"How is he?" She winces, knowing how hard it has been this past week between us. He's played the dutiful partner, but I can see the tension in him.

"Same," I murmur. "Do you think me staying with him is a bad idea?" I haven't admitted to Cass that I have moved in—I'm not sure why.

"No, it will all work out, Lily, trust in that." She rests her chin on her hand and winks at me over the table.

"But the timing," – shaking my head, I place my tea down and sigh – "it just doesn't feel like we are making progress." Maybe what we really need is space, not being thrust under each other's noses.

"Lily, Jace listened to the recording. You screamed for him, and he feels terrible for not being there." Her eyes soften but are equally tinged with sadness. I seem to be the only one happy to shut the door on the attack and move on. "Adam could have killed you, Lily," she points out slowly, cautiously.

"But he didn't." I grate with frustration. "I'm so desperate to forget it all and move on. I know you all care, but I need our," – I motion between us – "normal back." I stand, suddenly eager to get away. "I need to forget," I tell her. She nods and looks at me with concern, and I roll my eyes. "Cass, I'm fine." I sound anything but fine, and she holds my frustrated stare with a pointed one of her own. "Or at least I will be when Jace stops holding out on me." I laugh, forcing the conversation along. She cracks a smile, and I lean down and give her a hug. "Stop treating me like china. I'm really okay."

"Okay." She hugs me back and stays seated when my Uber pulls up. I wave to her as I hop in and send Carl a quick text. We have formed a tight bond since the attack. It's the only good thing to have come out of it because moving in with Jace isn't proving to be how I imagined it would be.

We seemed to have rocket-launched right over the honeymoon period and settled into our fiftieth anniversary within a week. It's dire, but I'm determined to change that. I made a quick but cautious dash to the shops before I met Cass, and my purchases are all wrapped elegantly in one of my bags. Happy with myself, I enjoy the ride back before I begin preparing dinner, my shopping hidden discreetly in our bedroom. I'm still suffering from the odd dizzy spell, so I've been mindful to take my time and rest when I can.

It's a little after eight when Jace pulls in. It's later than I thought he would be, but he has spent so much time with me this past week, he probably has a lot to catch up on.

"Hey!" I call, pouring myself a well-earned wine. It's the first one I have had since the attack.

"What are you drinking?" Jace grumbles, casting inspecting eyes over me.

I ignore his question.

"Hello to you, too," I quip. He smirks and walks straight over, looking immaculate in his suit. He left for work before I woke, so it's only now that I can fully appreciate it. "You look nice," I say.

"I know." He grins and pulls me to him. I'm doused in his perfect smell.

"Smell good too." I huff, pressing to kiss him, but he lifts his chin, ensuring he is just out of reach.

"What's in the glass?" He doesn't wait for my answer, just lifts it and sniffs before pouring it down the sink, all the while watching me with mischievous but serious ambers.

"Jace! I wanted that." I shoot annoyed eyes at him.

"Lily, you suffered a mild concussion a week ago." Just to hammer that home, he fingers my hair away from my face and inspects my cut. I tug my head away.

"Precisely. Mild. I feel fine." A little wobbly at times and my ribs are still sore, but all in all, I think I have recovered exceptionally well.

My fingers are still strapped up, but any pain has gone. They're just an inconvenience now.

"You still look pale," he offers up. I roll my eyes and lift quickly to kiss him. It's unexpected, but he lets me, so I keep my lips on his and cup his face. "I have to go out of town for a night," he informs between kisses.

"Okay, when?" I drop back to my feet and stir the pan.

"Tomorrow." I nod and check the pasta. "Smells good." His chin drops on my shoulder briefly so he can inspect the contents.

"I know." I throw a smirk over my shoulder. Jace is grinning too. "It'll be ready in a few, so you have time to change if you want?" I don't want him floating around while I'm cooking.

"Miss Spencer, are you trying to get me naked?" He backs away, his head tilted just so, and a playful grin on his full mouth.

"You have no idea." I laugh. He winks and wanders off—maybe I don't need my little plan after all. I feel deflated, but I'm too excited to throw it under the bus. I'll be damned if he seduces me first.

I plate our dinner up and take it to the table. "Looks great," Jace says, planting a kiss on my hairline. I set the table earlier, and even lit a few candles, but the constant twitch of his lips tells me he knows my game. I choose not to mention it and tuck in.

"I might see if Carl and Rupert fancy dinner tomorrow?" I know he won't like me being on my own, and I'm pulling at all the strings to soften him up.

"I'm sure they will." He clears his throat, and I drop a look at him.

"You already asked them, didn't you?" Unbelievable. I mentally shake my head at him.

He keeps his face averted and twists some spaghetti onto his fork.

"Well, Carl mentioned he was free . . . " He shrugs. He rests his hands on the table edges, giving off an air of importance and daring me to disagree. It's a constant push and pull between us.

"I'm not made of glass," I grumble as my fork prods unenthusiastically at my dinner.

He is grinning at me when he says, "Don't get all pissy." His fork lifts in my direction slightly before finding its way to his mouth, just as he says, "You suggested it too." He chews slowly, then pulls my hand up and dances a line of kisses along my wrist. "Rupert said he would cook so you can rest up."

I laugh.

"I've don't nothing but rest up—this is the first time I've cooked all week!"

"It's surprisingly good." He frowns. I'd be offended if I was in denial at my lack of culinary skills, but he is right—it is good.

"Marie taught me." That woman has been a saving grace this week; she has kept me occupied and been a constant support.

"What have you been up to today?" Jace has polished his meal off already, and I'm only halfway through. "Is there anymore?" he asks, already standing and taking his empty bowl to pile more in. I drop a smile and pick at my own dinner.

"Not much. Took some photos, met Cass, cleaned up, and used the gym," I say, not paying much attention to him because I know the last part will annoy him.

"The gym?" His bowl crashes down louder than expected. "Lily!" he sighs, "look at me." I throw a casual smile his way. "I don't think you should be doing anything too physical," he huffs.

"Evidently," I mutter, pushing a forkful of food in my mouth, stalling any further conversation for a few minutes. I hear his muted laughter, but I take little enjoyment out of it. I would never admit it to him, but I need sex. It's purely his fault. I never much cared for it, and now he is denying me. I feel like a loose cannon, and as far as working out goes, it's not like I put myself through a gruelling workout. I just did a quick walk, and I tell him as much when I finally swallow the mouthful. I don't tell him I tried to jog but found it too painful, not to mention how dizzy it made me feel.

"Maybe give it a little while longer, okay?" he tells me, doing that ultra-sweet thing and kissing my hair again. I have come to realise that it's his way of trying to be patient with me, buttering me up.

"I don't know. I felt great after it—" It's not exactly a lie. I did feel more energetic, but I did have a few dizzy spells, which had me holding the rails for constant support. I'm pushing myself to get better. I need to go back to work. I will go stir crazy otherwise.

Jace isn't fully convinced, and he side-eyes me and stands, taking both our bowls.

"Why don't you go and relax in the bath?" he suggests, rinsing the pots and filling the dishwasher. I grin inwardly and slip off my chair, heading for the bathroom on a quick walk. Running the bath is a perfect way to disguise the sound of tissue paper as I frantically tear it open and pull the nude waspie set on. The bruising to my ribs is still evident, but the once dark bluish stain looks yellower now. I cover the dark rings under my eyes and bronze my face to dispel the paleness that Jace mentioned. I gloss my lips and touch up the minimal mascara I put on earlier, rushing to do my right eye when I hear the distinctive sound of footsteps.

I quickly drop back to perch on the edge of the bath and cross my legs, supporting myself by stretching my arms wide. Jace strides through the bedroom and halts, his eyes widening at me.

"Hi." I allow my gaze to lift from his toes to his burning gaze, and when I stand, I take my time, knowing it will give maximum effect and silently hope any dizziness stays at bay.

"Where did you get that?" he swallows.

Lifting a hand, I trail it down the dainty bra strap and across my breast. My fingertips glide over the full mound, then hit the flat plain of my stomach. The waspie set stood out to me the moment I walked into the boutique earlier—the oyster shade and black lace complimenting my pale tone. Jace clears his throat, and I do a mini mental celebration.

"I picked it up earlier today, you like?" Of course he likes. The look on his face and the open adjusting of his groin tells me so.

"You know I do." He walks towards me but stops and leans against the open door frame. I tiptoe towards him, biting my lip to stop my self-satisfied grin from overpowering the seductive glance I'm trying to master.

"What are you going to do about it?" I whisper and lift to brush my mouth against his. His hands land softly on my hips, and he lets me pet his mouth.

"Nothing," he replies. I stop and pull back. He is joking, surely? My eyes search his and find nothing but resolution.

"You're not funny," I quip, rubbing up against him, reaching to cup him as I do. "That doesn't feel like nothing." I moan. He's hard as rock. I want him feverishly.

"Lily." His sigh is tense, frustrated, and he pushes my hand away, and then me, slowly. I blink in shock. *He's serious.* I don't expect the short, shocked laugh, but it flies out of my mouth, anyway.

"Okay." I step away and twist my back to him. Looking at him will only show the hurt. I scoff to myself and reach to unclip the bra before turning the taps off. I remove the rest of it and let it drop to the floor, and I have my leg halfway in the water when his hands slip around to my stomach.

His breath hits my cheek, then my ear.

"Lily, you look stunning, but it's only been a week. I need you to get better." His lips drop to my shoulder, and my eyes slam shut. I shrug him off. "Don't be mad. Let's soak in the ba—"

"I think I'll just have a quick wash," I murmur. I prise his hands free and keep hold of one as I step fully in, lowering myself into the thick bubbly water. Jace is crouched at the side in seconds.

"Lily, don't be like that."

I snap to look at him.

"Like what, hurt, frustrated? It's *sex*. I'm not asking you to perform surgery!" I spit before looking away. I cup some water and watch it drain through my fingers until it forms droplets. "Leave me alone, Jace." My sigh is weary.

"Don't be ridiculous," he mutters indignantly. "I'm not leaving, Lily. It's not a question of whether I'm attracted to you."

I scoff, shrugging him away.

"Could have fooled me!" What the hell is his problem?

"Seeing you unconscious in that bed." He sighs and cups the back of my neck, coaxing me to his face. "I can't get it out of my head," he whispers. My expression is sad, and I cup his face and push to my knees, pressing my mouth to his.

"I'm fine. I feel good," I plead for him to see that.

"But?" His hoarse voice sends a happy shiver down my spine.

"But, when I said yes to moving in, I thought it would be different." Jace pulls away, affronted, but I keep my hands tight, holding him close.

"Different how?" His eyes search mine with worry. His hair is ruffled and in need of a cut. His syrupy eyes are glinting under the light, and I can't help but stare at them—his colouring is beautiful.

"Honestly?" I frown, gnawing my lip.

"Always," he murmurs. His thumb glides over my lower lip, and I take a small leap of satisfaction that his eyes follow the trail.

"I was expecting us to celebrate," – my voice is low, teasing – "*a lot*." I stare up at him and sigh. "I want the old you back. I miss you touching me." I pout.

Jace wraps his hands around me so they dip below the surface.

"I don't want to hurt you," his admission is low—he means physically. I am a little sore, but we can be gentle. I want gentle.

"But you are." My mouth turns down, and I swallow the ache in my throat. I press his wet palm to my chest. "In here. I need you back, Jace." I drop my forehead to his and close my eyes. "We can be careful." I lean in and press my mouth to his. "Be gentle with me," I coax. I take his other hand and move them to my front so he can cup my wet breasts. His eyes drop to the bruise marring my skin. "Eyes up here, and don't stop touching me," I tell him. He smirks at me but looks hesitant. "Jace, please." I sound frustrated and dejected. "You say you want me better. This is what I need—this connection—us." I stare sincerely into his burning bronzes, and he regards me thoughtfully, his mouth pinching tightly.

In one quick move, he pulls me from the bath and walks me to the bedroom.

"I can give you gentle." His lips hover over mine before he softly sweeps his tongue in on a deep groan. I wrap my arms around his neck, keeping him as close as possible, and even when he lowers me, I take him with me, wrapping myself like a rope around his wide frame.

My body floods with heat, and every touch feels like the most static of electricity. Even when he grinds, then moves away, the buzz is still there. Jace's kiss is deep and slow. I'm so content with just that I don't realise his hand has moved until I feel his fingers *there*.

"You're soaking wet." His voice is all gravel.

"Yes." My thighs ache with the pressure I'm putting on them to keep them wide. "I need to feel you." I pant, lifting my hips to encourage his thick fingers inside.

"Fucking hell, Lily." Dark lust roams down my body.

"Now." I clasp his wrist, pushing his fingers in. They go deep, and my body goes lax. "Oh, god!" My eyes are fixed on his; the flare of his nostrils and the tense set of his shoulders tells me he is still unsure how much he should give—how much I can take. I don't allow him the chance to worry. I keep control of his wrist and work him in and out, and his deft fingers curl until I fly over the edge. "Oh, shit!"

"Lily, slow down," he breathes, averting his eyes from the slight jerking of my hips. When he slips his fingers free, I bring them to my mouth slowly, and when I open my mouth and slip them inside, his eyes widen, and he groans loudly. He moves to kneel on the bed and starts undoing his jeans, un-popping the buttons until he can reach and pull his thick cock free. "Put your legs on my left," he instructs softly, dropping a quick kiss on my thigh. I bend and pull my legs together on his left, and Jace leans against them, keeping me from moving. He takes my wrists and plants them on either side of my head. I expect him to kiss me, but he dips his head lower and pulls a nipple into his mouth, swirling his mouth around the stiff peak and sucking gently. "God, Lily, you're drenched."

"Should have fucked me sooner." I laugh lightly, jolting when he bites my nipple. His tongue does another swirl, then his wide head is pushing into my slick heat. My eyes widen, and any breath, ready to exhale, stalls, leaving on a long sigh when he sinks home.

"Oh, hell, you feel amazing, Lily," Jace pants gruffly. He lowers to take my mouth, and I let him, rolling my tongue against his as he slowly fucks me, driving in on long, slow, deep, deep thrusts. My arms remain strapped down by his hands, and my legs are trapped under his weight. I can't move, but I don't complain. I'm already tipping over the edge. "Fuck," he chokes around my tongue.

"Oh, don't stop." I'm pulsing around him.

"Jesus, Lily," Jace moans, quickening his pace. I'm sobbing quietly when he spills himself into me. "I love you, beautiful." He cups my head, thrusts in, and then stills.

I'm crying. I don't know why, but I'm thankful that Jace holds me tight and lets me hide my face in the crook of his neck.

"I'm sorry," he whispers, "you look so fragile. I couldn't bring myself to touch you. I thought I had lost you. I was just happy to be able to look at you." He pecks my neck as wide palms rub methodically over my bare back.

I nod stiffly into his shoulder.

"I love you too."

He winks.

"I know." He smiles. "I loved the lingerie," he tells me, prising me away so he can look at me properly. I lift my head, and he wipes a thumb under my eye. "Wear it for me when I get home?" he asks quietly.

My smile is soft and followed by a sniff.

"I don't know why I'm crying," I huff.

"Lily, you have been through a lot. I've probably not helped, and your emotions are all up in the air—plus you're coming, left, right, and centre." He smirks smugly. I nudge his shoulder and hide my face. "Hey, I'm not complaining." He laughs, dropping his head into my hair and nipping my ear. "I love you, beautiful."

"Even after I hurt you?" I ask him. We haven't really dealt with his disquiet head on.

"Even then. I was angry with him, and you took the brunt of that, forgive me?" He pouts playfully—his whiskey glaze full of sparkle and mischief.

"After those orgasms, it'd be rude of me not to." I grin, fiddling with his hair. He chuckles and kicks his trousers off. He is pulling his top over his head as I slip under the covers.

"It would be criminal." He snorts and pulls me back so I'm flush to his bare body. "Get some sleep, baby. You look exhausted."

Hearing him say those words unlocks something in me. I yawn on cue and let my eyes droop shut. The blanket of darkness and his arms are all I need to lure me under.

I wake to gentle Jace and have spent most of the day being indulged. Jace, who couldn't bring himself to touch me, is back to finding it hard not to. I don't complain as he is due to fly out this evening, so I make the most of being with him.

"Lily," he breathes hotly. His hands cup my cheek. "Beautiful, slow down." I'm straddling him on the sofa, my small hands holding fiercely to his shoulders as I ride him. I ignore his grunt and slam back down. My body shudders, and I drop my head back as I come.

"Ohhhh!" I cry. Jace takes my hips and rocks me slowly until I feel his cock thicken and pulse inside me. His groan is deep and sexy. Dropping forward, I cup his face, kissing him as he jerks beneath me. His forehead is damp with sweat, but I drop my own to it, panting quietly. "Oh god," I hum. He holds me still and dives his tongue in.

"I'm going to be late for my flight," he chastises. His hands do a quick sweep of my body, concentrating on my breasts, and he cups them so they spill out his hands. "Goddammit, Lily." I give my hips a little roll, laughing when he moans deeply.

"Shower with me?" I plead. His eyes burn up at me, and he shakes his head a little.

"You, Lily Spencer, are a damn witch." He grabs my arse, so I yelp.

"So you keep telling me." I pout, dropping to peck his mouth. "You have half an hour before you need to leave," I tell him. He was planning on a shower anyway until I waylaid him.

"What time are the guys getting here?" He shifts so he can stand and takes me with him.

"An hour or so," I huff. I'm looking forward to our night in, but I know I will miss Jace too. The water gets turned on, and Jace steps us under the spray. "I don't think I have ever been to Edinburgh," I tell him.

"It's pretty," he hums, pulling me for a quick but deep kiss. "I won't see much of it, just the hotel where the conference is held. I have a meeting afterward but will be back around two a.m." His voice takes on a lazy drawl.

"Oh, how convenient. Your favourite time." I bite his lip, and he twitches beneath me.

"Our," he corrects, "our favourite time." He gives me that trademark wink. "Right, get down." He lowers me and swats my arse. "I've got to get ready, baby." Jace washes himself, and I am mindful not to get my stitches too wet. They are dissolving already and leaving a red scar that is neat and fine. I exit before Jace and carefully wrap my head in a towel. His phone rings, so I yell through to him.

"Can you answer it!" he hollers. I check the caller ID and falter when I see it's Neve. I click connect.

"Hi, it's Lily. Jace is in the shower," I say as I answer, and she tsks.

"Can you ask him to just meet me at the airport? Something came up, and I don't need a lift," she utters the words quickly.

"Oh, oka—" The phone abruptly cuts out and leaves me open-mouthed and staring at the now blank screen. She's so damn rude! And she is going too? I don't have time for that to fully sink in because Jace saunters out naked and looking ready to model a calendar shoot. "Neve is going?" I whisper, annoyed.

"What's that?" He rubs his hair with a towel and walks to me. "Who was on the phone?"

"Neve," I say shortly, "you never said she was going with you." I give him accusing eyes, but he is oblivious—either that or he is really good at acting.

"I didn't?" He frowns. "I'm sure I did?" Jace inclines his head and pats his wet chest.

"No," I scoff lightly, "not a word." I punctuate the last part for effect, illustrating my annoyance.

"Well, it's for work." He casts his gaze my way quickly and belatedly realises my reservations before walking to me. His hands cup my face, and he drops his mouth to mine. "I love you. She is a friend and colleague. *It's work.*" My heart is pounding way too quickly, but I nod and force a smile because I don't want to cause an argument and him leave on a fight. But I really do not like the woman.

"Okay." He pecks my mouth before pulling some clothes on and checking he has his passport. I relay Neve's message.

"Oh, she say why?" He runs his lips across mine, not showing much interest in her call.

"No, that was it." I hold his gaze, suspecting that he avoided mentioning Neve because he knew I wouldn't be comfortable with it. I'm not.

"I've got to go. I'll call you later, okay?" My smile is fake, and he must see it because he pulls me back for a deep kiss. "I love you," he murmurs between sweeps of his tongue.

"Have a great trip," I murmur sullenly. He tilts his head, a light frown marring his otherwise perfect face. "Love you too." My voice is rougher than I expect, and his eyes flash with unease. He knows I'm not okay with this. Why would I be? It's so very obvious she is in love with him.

Chapter Twelve

Carl and Rupert arrive later than expected. They muscle in with bags of food, and Carl shakes a bottle of wine at me. I pull a face. Jace won't be happy about that.

"Oh, pfft, he's not here, and you look heaps better, a little pale, but that's lack of sun," he drawls, walking straight to kiss each of my cheeks. Rupert dumps the bags on the side and pecks my cheek.

"So, how's our favourite patient?" He rubs at my back and ignores my eye roll. "Carl is right. You do look pale. When did you last holiday?" Rupert hand-combs his beard and gives me a once over as he wanders back to the abandoned food.

"I don't even want to answer that." I think it was about three years ago, Cass and I booked a girls' break. There has been the odd spa day in between and days out, but I haven't touched sand or sea in what feels like forever.

"That bad?" he laughs.

"Jace did mention a holiday, but," – I point at my head – "this happened."

"Surely that's the perfect excuse to get away," Carl mentions. I think it over. It is, but I have been away from work for ages. I can't take more time off.

"I know what you're thinking." Rupert looks down his nose at me, a pointed gleam in his eye. "You are allowed to take time off. Besides, I think it would do your assistant some good." He winks. I know I've never mentioned Hat, but I can imagine Carl has. She is very timid at times, and my absence at the gallery has made her stand on her own two feet a bit more.

"Jace being away has been good for me. I have seen an aspect of the business I was never much involved in. It's been a good experience," Carl adds encouragingly.

"What my husband is saying is, if you could injure yourself more often, he'd appreciate it." Rupert half-laughs. Carl gawps, and I cough out a laugh.

"I'll keep that in mind." I'm grateful he is comfortable enough to make light of it; it's a refreshing change from all the concerned glances and hesitant comments.

"Rupert, that was awful!" Carl reprimands.

"A little bit funny," I defend, my cheeks heating. Carl tuts and wafts me away with an elegant flap of his hand.

"Look, if you want to sun it up, we can help out if need be," Carl says over his shoulder.

"I appreciate that." I leave it at that. I don't want to make plans just yet. Rupert is pulling items from the bags, so I walk over. "Need a hand?"

"Definitely not, go, put your feet up, have a look at what's on that monstrosity of a TV." I laugh at that because it is huge, like window-pane-huge. I do as I'm told and flick through until I find something neutral for us all and settle on a thriller. "I'm doing a stir-fry, so it won't take long," Rupert explains, and Carl saunters over with two glasses of white wine.

"He will never know." Carl winks, and I take the glass.

"Thanks." I sit back so I'm swallowed up by the array of cushions. Jace and I have spent most evenings strewn over this sofa, either watching some new series or listening to music. Most of our conversations involved Adam and my disaster of a relationship with him. It was never meant to be serious, more of a casual fling, just a little fun, but I fell pregnant, and my carefree life suddenly tipped on its arse, and before I knew it, Adam had moved in, and we were planning to buy a house for the sake of our child. I didn't love him, and he knew it, which only made it more difficult for him because he was utterly besotted with me. That soon turned to obsession, then aggression. Then loss.

I blamed myself for so long for causing his sickness—blamed myself because of my selfishness. If the attack gave me anything, it was closure.

I stare at the coffee table where a letter is tucked neatly in the concealed drawer. A letter Adam's parents wrote to me at The Loft, educating me on their son and his illness. Jace had curled himself around me as we snuggled on the sofa where he read it out to me, detailing how Adam was medicated before he met me, that he was impulsive and erratic in his behaviour, and informing me another girl had a restraining order against him. They had no idea that he'd beaten me and had expressed at length how truly sorry they were for the hurt he caused me and for my loss. I felt sorry for them.

I couldn't imagine the hardship of loving someone who was sick—how that must challenge them mentally and emotionally, and how exhausting and difficult it must be for them. Adam isn't just sick; he isn't a good person either—I knew that now. I no longer blamed myself.

Jace and I are in a good place, and the door to my past is firmly shut. I'm finally anticipating a future.

Carl holds out a pack of Maltesers, and I take a handful, popping one in my mouth.

"Mmm." Rupert is making the house smell like a Michelin-star restaurant. We eat on our knees watching the movie—Carl and Rupert either side of me. We don't talk much, and I like that. It's relaxed and easy.

My phone breaks the silence, and I just know it's him. Carl takes my bowl so I can stand and get my phone off the coffee table.

"Hey." I drop back down, and Carl deposits the bowl in my lap.

"Hey." Jace sounds harassed, distracted.

"Everything okay?" I pick at the food and pop a piece of marinated chicken into my mouth, chewing quietly.

"Yeah, you okay?" he grumbles. I frown, and Carl does too.

Neve's voice filters over the line. "What about single rooms?"

"You sure everything is alright?" I ask, forking the last bit of food into my mouth.

"There has been a mixup at the hotel, and they have overbooked," he tells me. I suppose it's due to the conference being held there. I've been subjected to similar situations, mainly with overseas travel.

"Oh, okay, can you not stay in another hotel?" I know it's costly, but surely that makes sense, and they can be refunded.

"Logistically, no. Neve is trying to sort it now." I press my lips together and keep any thoughts to myself. Unease settles like a lead weight in my gut.

"Okay, well, hopefully they can arrange something?" I say diplomatically.

"I'm sure they will. Everything okay then?" He tactfully changes the subject. I shoot Carl a tight smile but drop my eyes when he gives me a reserved look.

"Yes, just watching a movie," I reply, eyeing Carl again, who is eavesdropping openly. His ear is almost pressed to the back of my phone.

"You're not drinking, are you?" His voice is low and authoritative.

"Just a small glass," I wince, and Carl rolls his eyes.

"She is fine!" he calls, and I give him a grateful smile. Jace grunts down the phone, and I hear him snap at the receptionist about having separate rooms.

"I paid for two double rooms, not a twin!" he mutters crossly.

"It's says he—"

"Lily, I've got to go. I'll speak to you sometime tomorrow." My heart constricts at what is transpiring at the end of the line.

"Sure, okay." He cuts the call. I drop the phone on the sofa, and it disappears between Carl and me.

"You okay?" He heard everything, but I appreciate his politeness. Rupert collects up our bowls and wanders back over to the kitchen. If they are sharing a look at my expense, I don't notice. I'm too riddled with worry.

I shrug.

"Problem with the hotel. They overbooked," I tell him.

"Bullshit, I called yesterday to double-check: two double rooms." He looks confused and annoyed. "Let me call him." He is up and off. I leave him to it because my bruised brain can't cope with the thought of Neve and Jace sharing. Surely he wouldn't do that?

Five minutes later, Carl returns, looking peeved, and I can guess why.

"Ring to help and get told off." He drops down on the sofa like a child.

"The wine—" I grimace, and he rolls his head my way. I can see the annoyance there, but he doesn't express it fully: Jace should have more faith in him.

"Try living with him," I mutter, sipping on my wine.

"Rather not." He sniggers. "Working with him during this whole thing has been bad enough," he admits brazenly. I watch him over my glass, a little sorry for causing all this trouble. "He has been vile," he utters snootily.

"God, really?" Now I'm intrigued.

Carl twists so we are facing each other.

"He nearly fired someone yesterday, annnnd," he adds dramatically, stalling the gasp leaving my mouth, "he told Neve to fuck off."

Carl throws his head back and laughs. I do too. That little snippet of information just made my night.

"So did they sort the hotel out?" I wonder, trying not to sound whiny when I ask.

"I believe so. I just don't understand it. It was all confirmed. Jace said there were two reservations, so it's weird." I nod slowly in agreement. It is strange, but I can imagine with the conference being so big that a few wires have got crossed. As long as it's sorted, it's none of my business. I trust him, and that's enough for me.

We watch the remainder of the film in silence, and with the wine chasing its way through my system, I'm super sleepy. After I yawn for the tenth time, Rupert stands up.

"Right, bed!" he tells me. Carl and I burst out laughing—he sounds like a matron.

"Yes, Dad." I give him a poorly attempted salute.

"That was appalling," he drawls, picking a throw up to fold.

"Touchy," I mock. Carl is smothering a laugh—he has ingested a full bottle of wine and the majority of the first we opened.

"We'll lock up on our way out. You call us if you need anything," he says, giving me a sharp look as another yawn wracks my body.

"I feel like I'm being punished." I peek a look up at him and see his small smile.

"Just following the doctor's orders," he gloats, "ten on the dot." He taps his watch, and my eyes widen as Rupert fights a gloating smile. I come to the stinking realisation that my controlling boyfriend has actually given me a curfew. I open my mouth to say as much but slap it shut, far too embarrassed to utter the words. Mentally, I'm calling him every name under the sun!

Instead, I peck Rupert's cheek, and then Carls when he joins us.

"Thanks for coming over, guys, and for dinner. It was delicious." The anger growing in my body is causing me to shake inside.

"He cares," Rupert mouths. I nod and smile my way through them leaving, before heading to the bathroom on wooden legs.

The absolute bloody cheek of him—I'm not twelve!

When he gets back, things are bloody changing. What a control freak!

I hear the suction and click of the main door, and the engine starts up slowly a few moments later. I finish up in the bathroom and pick up my phone, sending him one short and annoyed message.

A fucking curfew!! I'm starting to think moving in was a very BAD idea!

I end it with an angry face and turn my phone off completely. Let him sweat, I think, pulling my clothes off and dragging the quilt back to get in. The bed smells dominantly of him, and it angers me further. It takes me an age to get to sleep. I'm too tightly wound.

I wake early after a broken night's sleep and groggily head straight for a shower. I'm going into work, even if it's just for the morning. Harriet has been a gem at holding the fort. I may have worked from Jace's and been in constant contact with her, but I need to be there. I miss it, and after last night's fiasco, I'm not sitting here any longer.

I pick a shirt and skirt combo and wash and dry my hair before moisturising and grabbing some breakfast. I spend the next hour picking at my breakfast, doing my makeup, and then my hair before I leave. It's bright but cold, so I whip back in for my coat, remembering to turn my phone on. It takes a minute or two to boot up, and when it does, I have over a dozen missed calls and messages. I ignore them all and lock up, setting the alarm before heading to my car.

I text Harriet to let her know I'm on my way in and that I will grab us both breakfast. I pit-stop to pick up some flowers and a card, writing a small message of thanks, and continue the rest of the journey listening to the radio. When my in-car speaker rings, and I check the caller ID, *it's him*. My heart does that quirky little jig.

I don't feel quite ready to speak to him. Only because I miss him, and I know I will give in too quickly. Silence is my best defence right now, and it's also my weapon. I cut the call, happy with my willpower.

Harriet arrives five minutes after me, and everything is ready and set up. She walks straight to me and gives me a hug. She never visited me at Jace's, but from what she explains, Jace was adamant I had my rest and assured her I was fine.

"He's a tough cookie." She giggles. I nod in agreement around my mouthful.

So fine that I can't drink, use the gym, or stay up past fucking ten p.m.!

I hide my irritation with a half-smile, and we take our seats out back and munch our way through our breakfast. "God, I missed the deli-brekkie." I groan in appreciation.

"I know. I couldn't get one without you—didn't feel right," Harriet tells me shyly. She is the cutest! The look I give her tells her as much.

"I got you some flowers to say thanks," I tell her. "I popped them in water in the kitchen." Harriet's surprised face pops up from behind the wide mug she is holding.

"You didn't have to do that." She gapes.

"I wanted to. I really appreciate all your help. It means a lot." I smile wildly, starting to feel more at ease now I'm back in the gallery.

"I'm just glad you're okay. I was so worried." Her eyes hold mine for a minute, that bit too long, and I know she wants me to open up to her, but I'm done talking about Adam. I'm done giving him space in my mind—in my life. He's had more of me than he deserves.

"Honestly, I'm fine," I say chirpily, "happy to be back at work." I casually change the direction of our conversation. If she suspects I'm skirting around the issue, she doesn't say so. I'm certain by the concern in her gaze that she still sees me as a victim.

"Oh, you said you were just in for this morning—are you back in full time?" she wonders.

I shrug.

"Well, I feel fine, so I don't see why not?" I look away when I catch her uneasy smile. It's enough to put me off my food. I finish up my coffee and head back inside. "Did those new pieces arrive? I might need your help to place them," I say. Harriet takes that as her cue to get up, but I stop her. "When you've finished and please don't feel you have to watch me. I'm not going to fall." She nods, but I can see the terror behind her bright eyes—anyone would think I'd undergone strenuous surgery or had a life-threatening illness.

I check the storage room out the back and find the new additions carefully wrapped. I bend to look through them and check the paperwork, but when I stand, dizziness washes over me, throwing me off-centre. I grip for the wall to steady myself, softly shouting out as I stagger to the side. Harriet rushes to me, my eyes slant shut, and I mentally berate her for choosing now to walk in, but I know it's not her I'm mad at. It's me.

I'm not accepting that I'm struggling. I've always prided myself on my independence, thrived on it. Now, I just feel like a hindrance. Weak.

"Oh, my god. Are you okay?" I blink slowly as my vision blots, and anxiety leaves a cold sweat over me.

My laugh is brittle.

"Stood up too quickly," I croak, but inside I'm feeling off-kilter, worried. Surely this isn't normal? I let out a few steadying breaths and close my eyes, only opening them when Hat rubs my arm gently.

"Maybe you should go home?" she suggests softly. "I know you want to be here, but I'd feel terrible if you passed out. You're really pale." She pulls a chair out for me to sit on, and I drop into it gingerly, very aware I still feel a little wobbly. My sigh is full of anger at myself.

"Do you want me to drive you home?" I lift to meet her sympathetic eyes and nod as I look away. I could strangle Adam. I feel myself becoming emotional and clear my throat as Harriet pulls me to her. "Hey, don't get upset. I know you feel fine, but your body probably still needs to heal." Her small hands glide up my back, and I stutter out a sigh.

"It's just so frustrating, and Jace is constantly hanging over me," I mutter, very much fed up. I shouldn't be discussing this with her.

"I can imagine, but everything is okay here, and it's not like you have left me in the lurch. I'm constantly calling you. I'm surprised I haven't pissed you off yet." She laughs, and I do too. Any other time, those calls would send me crazy, but I'm desperate to receive them at the moment.

"Sorry." I shake myself out of my mood and stand slowly. Harriet gathers my things, and I lock up as she goes to pull her car around the front. I give her Jace's address, and we spend the journey talking about her holiday—her checking on me every so often. Her small fists are knuckle-white with anxiety on the steering wheel. When we get to the main road, I instruct her to turn right down the gravel drive, and we crunch our way up the tree-made tunnel. When the house finally comes into view, she exclaims loudly and stalls her car.

"Bloody hell!" We both lurch forward in our seats, and I burst out laughing. Harriet's face is a picture of horrified embarrassment, "Oh my god. I'm so sorry." She covers her face, her shoulders shaking with silent laughter. I'm howling, tears pouring down my cheeks as I struggle to unclip the belt. I haven't laughed this hard in ages, and I sorely needed it.

"I can't believe you stalled," I wheeze. We're both shaking silently as laughter overtakes us, an invisible possession playing with our emotions. When I manage to calm myself and bring my breathing back to normal, I push free from the car. "If Jace had security cameras, I would watch that back." I chuckle loudly. Harriet scoffs and looks away, trying to disguise her smirk.

"I wasn't expecting," – her hands spread as widely as they can, with her still belted up in the car – "well this, I . . . it's—" She looks beyond, to the gleaming glass and smooth wooden house.

"I know." I bend to look through the open door at her. "It's pretty spectacular, isn't it?" My uncertain gaze looks at the structure with confusion. It's every girl's dream. I'm just not sure I can deal with the male owner's controlling manner.

"And then some," she states enthusiastically, as she checks her watch, "best get back." Her eyes find themselves taking in the house once more.

"Thanks, Hat," I say, tightening my coat.

"Anytime. I'll call you later to give you an update." I nod and close the door. I need to give her a raise. It's a crime not to. I've just been so wrapped up in, well, myself—an ugly trait that I can't shake. I've become selfish in my older years, over-cautious and caged, but I'm really trying to move my life forward with Jace. I just don't like being held back because it's what he thinks I need.

My phone is blaring at me from my tote. I know it's Jace, and despite my annoyance at him, I feel bad for causing him stress while he is at work. I key the code in for his door and push my way in as I answer.

"Hello," I sound miserable.

"There better be a good excuse for why you have ignored my calls, Lily!" he seethes. I follow suit, imagining him yanking at his tie in anger. His nostrils always flare, and a vein in his neck protrudes as though trying to break the surface to shout at me too.

"I didn't want to talk to you." My reply is forced through gritted teeth. I really thought I could go back to work, and that would be it. That once I crossed that final line, this whole ordeal would be over. Instead, it seems one thing follows another.

His short laugh is sarcastic.

"Forgive me for caring about you," he spits incredulously.

"Controlling me," I counteract. He growls, and I roll my eyes. "You made me look stupid!" I spit.

"I'm trying to look out for you," he snaps. His sigh floats off into another argument, but this time it's not at me, and I sit quietly as he snaps at Neve too. The fact that she is managing to grab his attention, despite him being on the phone to me during a spat, infuriates me further.

"You sound busy. I'll see you tomorrow," I say and cut the call before he can reply. When he rings back, I ignore it and send a message.

We'll talk when you get back.

I'm really not okay with all of this. It's beyond ridiculous. He calls twice more but soon realises I'm not entertaining his behaviour or being subjected to Neve; even if it is electronically. I hate the thought of her enjoying our little fight.

Instead of letting my mind churn up all my hurt and run with my negative thoughts, I find a chick flick, curl up on the sofa and spend the rest of the day emailing Harriet, texting Cass, and mooching through social media. By the time evening comes around, I'm bored to my bones and decide to run a bath. I give myself a full spa treatment and pamper myself until I'm in a natural, relaxed coma. I need little encouragement to get into bed, and as soon as my head hits the pillow, I'm gone.

I'm woken by the shrill sound of my phone ringing, but within moments of it starting and me coming around, it stops. I recognise the sound of the main door whooshing open, and Jace strides towards me with a look of worry on his face. With little regard to my sleepy state, he switches the light on, and I shrink under the intense blare.

"What the hell!" I croak, "Jace, turn it off!" The room goes black, and I hear his heavy footfall, feel the bed dip, and then he is there, hands nestled either side of my head.

"I thought you had gone home," he grumbles. Of course he did. I'm glad he can't see me roll my eyes. If he weren't weighing the quilt down, I'd kick him.

"I'm tired." It's hard for me to twist with his weight on the quilt, but I manage it *just* and turn away from him.

"Where's your car?" He rolls, so he is facing me and no longer trapping me. I blink through the darkness until slowly, my eyes adjust, and I see the outline of his remarkable face.

"At the gallery." My voice trails off in my yawn. "Go away. I'm angry with you." I pout, closing my eyes on him. He is still in his suit, smelling heavenly and looking sharp, with his hair styled and jaw trimmed to a shadow.

"Why is it at the gallery?" His whisper is a simple question, any accusation is completely gone, and he sounds cautious. He knows I'm seriously pissed off. I sigh into the blackness.

"I went to work but felt dizzy, so Harriet drove me home. You're right. I'm not fine. Happy now?" I sound like a spoilt brat, and a small part of me cringes at how melodramatic I'm being.

"No." Deft fingers brush into my hair. "Why didn't you call me?" He presses forward and finds my mouth. I tug away, fighting off the need to cement my mouth to his and let him make me feel better.

I give him my best, are you kidding me look.

"Because I'm mad at you, and you were miles away." I accentuate each word slowly, wanting to add, *with her!*

"Lily, look—"

"You gave me a fucking curfew, Jace, like a child!" I pull away and sit up. "Even if you were right about me not being one hundred percent, dictating my bedtime is embarrassing." I feel the sting of that now, and my eyes prick with tears. Sniffing, I push the pillows back so I'm more comfortable. But the fact that I'm still not okay is pulling at my emotions. Why aren't I better yet?

"Hey." He is sitting up too. The bedside lamp clicks on, and he is watching me carefully. He looks tired, his eyes heavy, and his jaw unshaved. "Lily, shit, I'm sorry. I didn't want them overstaying their welcome, or you staying up out of politeness, and you've been crashing before ten most days, anyway." I refuse to accept his valid point—I have been sleeping more.

"I want to go to sleep." I move to the other side. It's cold, but I close my eyes and will him to turn the light off. I'm too angry to have this conversation, and my reaction will be emotional and not rational.

"Did you mean what you said about moving in being a bad decision?" His hand slips around my waist, the light stays on, and I open my eyes to find him staring at me through the bank of windows. The glow makes his eyes look honey-thick, hypnotic, and his hair is flopping forward.

"You're trying to control me," I tell him slowly. "I don't like it." I punctuate the words. "I don't stop you from doing your own thing or tell you what you should be doing. I like you for you, not for how I could make you." I tilt my head to make my point, then close my eyes. I really am boiling mad.

"That's not what I'm doing." He is quiet, thoughtful. He may believe that now, but I know he is thinking it over. Good.

"Feels that way, and if it is that way, then yes, it's bad that I moved in. Good night." I wait for the light to dim, but it doesn't happen. Instead, his hand moves down and pushes between my legs. "Sex isn't going to fix this." I sound bored, petulant.

"You don't know that." His voice has dropped an octave, and his hands rotate in little circles. I feel sorry for him because he honestly believes this is the answer. Instead, I swing the quilt up and get out of bed with the intention of moving to a Jace-free zone. "I'm sleeping on the sofa," I grumble, but my head goes all wishy-washy, and I stumble into the glass with a short yelp. Jace jumps toward me and grabs me as I slide down the pane. The look on his face causes me to sob in a gurgle of fear.

"Fucking hell." He pulls me to his chest, and I stay for a minute, with him crouched down by me. "Come here." He pulls me up, and I go on a gulp of worried air. Jace walks us until he is sitting on the chair in the corner; my legs bent, either side of his. I drop onto his shoulder and lay my head there. "If you say you're fine, I will tan your arse." He grabs my arse for effect. My heart is thrumming crazily against my breastbone.

"But I do actually feel okay," I mumble into his shoulder. Jace's sigh is loud enough to wake our non-neighbours. I sit up slowly. "It's just if I stand too quickly." I cup his face and plead with him to hear what I am saying—plead with myself to believe it.

"And the tiredness?" he points out. I shrug. I guess my body is just healing. We aren't going to agree; that much is obvious. We eye each other for a minute, and I can see the genuine worry laced in his gaze. I can't do this now. I'm so confused about how I feel around him. I'm angry and scared, and I want him to hold me until I feel that undeniably serene wave of safety that I experience when he is close by.

"Take me to bed," I whisper, my thumb glides over his plush mouth.

"Bed-bed or the sofa?" He laughs, nipping my thumb.

"Piss off." I smirk reluctantly, still feeling the sting of his ridiculous curfew. I should tell him to get on the sofa where he can stick his curfew up his arse, and I make a similar comment as he takes us to bed.

Chapter Thirteen

Jace's alarm drags me out of my heavy sleep. He curses and turns it off, twisting to look at me. I blink groggily at him and pull the quilt over my head.

"Too early," I whine, stretching lazily.

"I know, sorry. I forgot to turn it off." His voice is riddled with tiredness too. He manoeuvres himself so he is under the quilt, and through the morning light, I can see his face well. "You're still mad at me." It's a statement, softly spoken and full of reluctant remorse.

"That all depends on how you choose to treat me, Jace." I don't want to nag him, but surely he must be able to see it from my point of view.

"Like a queen." His smile is small but sure.

"We'll see," I muse, wriggling into him for added warmth. I yawn into his chest and close my eyes. I know he planned to go into work later today due to his flight getting in so late, so he is happy to grab a few more hours and thrusts his leg between mine and hooks an arm over my waist.

"Let's have a lazy morning, and then later, if you're feeling up to it, we can go out for the afternoon," he suggests. His hand rolls up my bare back, and he pulls me tightly to him. I want to stay mad at him and tell him we are a team, but I know I haven't made things easy for him.

"What about work?" I nuzzle into him.

"I caught up on emails on the plane—we can grab dinner out?" It sounds perfect, but my eyes are too heavy, and my breathing is low and lazy, so I hum in agreement.

"I'm taking that as a yes," he muses. I manage a nod, and I'm fazing back out into a light but blissful sleep.

The wind whips at my hair, the air is bitter and cold, but Jace has his arm wrapped around my lower back, and I'm leaning into him. He arranged for us to go on a Thames night cruise. In all my years of living in London, I have never once stepped foot on a boat. Everywhere is lit up, threatening the oppressive darkness above. Below, the water laps and splashes at the boat as it chugs along. I expected there to be more people, but we are one of three couples. Jace pecks my hair.

"I'm stuffed," he complains for the third time. I grin and pull his other hand around my front. I'm sporting a food baby of my own.

"I love Gustav's. I've been with Hat," I tell him. I then proceed to enlighten him about my awful date with Mitch. "I honestly wanted to slap Cass." My laugh is throaty.

"Ah, so that's the man I was up against?" Jace has my hips and pulls them back into his hard groin, reminding me of how much male is enveloping me.

"Never," I scoff. "I cancelled, and he just showed up at The Loft," I tell him over my shoulder, "which meant he tracked me down. It was creepy." I shudder. Jace is silently laughing behind me. "What?" I snuggle into him and look out at the twinkle of city nightlife.

"You must think I'm a creep, then, because if you recall, I

followed you too." His smile is audible, even if I can't see his face.

"That's different." I grin, remembering how he just kept popping up in my life and dragging me off for wild sex. "I was attracted to you, too. Mitch looked like my old math teacher." I waft his silly remark away.

"Well, if he held any resemblance to mine, you have my deepest sympathy," Jace drawls, pulling a laugh from me. "Seriously, the man looked like a serial killer in a gilet," he informs me, and his chest vibrates with each laugh.

"Mitch had this nervous nod thing going on." I'm laughing hard now too. "He looked like one of those toys people stick in the back of their car. I couldn't help but compare him to you." I go a little breathless, making that admission. Jace grips my chin and tips my face to peck my lips, as his eyes stare into mine.

"You got off lucky then, I'd say." Jace brushes my hair back again to keep the wind from picking it up.

"You would. You won." I jab him lightly with my arm, smiling happily up at him.

"Yes, I did." He is painfully smug. "Besides, look at me," he drawls. "I'm definitely a Nobel prize." He surprises me further and flexes his free arm.

"God, you are so full of yourself," I scoff, but yes, he certainly is a prize. My prize. I never expected to be this happy. It wasn't on my agenda.

"Here." Jace hands me my camera again, and I take a few more pictures as we cruise up the river. A shadow falls over us, so we both look up to see one of the men sitting behind us smile in greeting. He points at my camera.

"Do you want me to take a photo of you both?" I grin widely.

"Yes, please." I give him a quick rundown of my camera, and he moves to the other side of the boat. The camera clicks away, and Jace and I smile broadly. Or at least I do. Jace bites at my neck and then pulls me in for a deep kiss. I laugh shyly. "Get off." I blush furiously, and our photographer smirks, handing it back over.

"Did you want a photo?" I offer, finding his partner smiling at him.

"Oh, no, thanks. We come on this regularly," he tells us and winks back at her, "we have dozens of pictures."

"Well, thank you." He leaves us, and we thumb through the photos. When we get to the one of Jace mauling me, he begins to grin widely.

"I like this," he breathes. His thumb dances over the screen, and he shoots me a hot look from below thick lashes. "I like me, when I'm with you." He swallows, slipping his hand below my coat to rest on my stomach.

"Ditto, minus curfews and wine control," I mutter around a cheeky laugh. I tuck myself back in, and Jace snorts out a gruff reply that gets lost in my hair when he sucks on my neck.

"Stop it!" I slap my hand over my neck, grinning. We sit in silence, enjoying the scenery. It's not much longer before we are back in the comfort of his flash car and flying back to his.

We share a shower, and Jace takes it upon himself to massage my shoulders. In fact, he is so painfully gentle and slow in his ministrations that I'm left in a state of delirious relaxation. He carries me back to his bed and lays me down, pecking my nose.

"You look drugged," he chokes out on a light laugh.

"I feel it." I grin, staring up at his slumberous eyes.

"Well, don't go to sleep. I have something to show you. Get some clothes on, or else we will never get anything done." He slaps my arse playfully and finds himself some clothes. When I make no intention to move, he pulls me out a t-shirt of his and flings it at me. I sit up and pull it on, forgoing underwear, and follow him to the lounge. I drop down on the sofa and flick the TV on, finding something uninteresting to have on as background noise. Jace collects his laptop and plonks himself ungracefully next to me. "These are in my top ten," he tells me, once his laptop has fired up, and he has logged into a site. He spins the computer, where a list of holiday villas stare back at me.

"Oh, wow." My finger moves on its own accord, and I open up the most viewed one, his favourite. I need my glasses for this, really. I lean over and pull open the small drawer under the coffee table and slip them on.

"Those fucking glasses are like Viagra." He pushes at his cock when it springs to life behind his work out trousers. I grin but lean to check the details of the villa, and he takes full advantage and hooks a finger in the neck of my shirt and pulls it to look down my top.

"Now, look up at me slowly," his instruction is soft, needy. I can't hide my smile, but I do it anyway, and he shakes his head.

"Fucking perfect." A wolfish smile splashes over his face before he attempts to tug the laptop free, but I hold it tightly.

"Not happening, Bennett. I want to look at these holidays," I tell him forcefully, and swat his hand away when it slides up my thigh. We'd already discussed that waiting until next year to go away was better, as the winter work rush was already upon us.

"Well, you could at least cross your legs. It's like being taunted with Pandora's box." He takes my ankles and yanks me to him. I squeak and grip the laptop to save it from falling, and his t-shirt rides up, leaving me exposed.

"Jace! Stop it." It's a false plea. I love his playful side.

Lifting my foot, he kisses my ankle.

"Never," he declares. I twist and lay my back against his chest. The laptop is covering my lap, and as I tug the t-shirt back into place, he mutters something about me being a spoilsport, but I ignore his childish jibe.

"This is your favourite?" I confirm. It is a little more than I expected to pay, but I can see the appeal. It is situated in a small fishing village on a hillside in Croatia.

"Yes." He points over my shoulder at the screen, instructing me to select the next photo. I do, and a stunning sea view covers the screen.

"Oh wow, this looks incredible," I gush, moving the cursor over the image to enlarge it. The coastal view is impossibly attractive, secluded, and dreamy.

"Let's go. They have availability throughout March." Jace hooks his feet over mine, so I'm trapped.

Biting my lip, I scan the price.

"I don't know. It's more than I thought," I tell him honestly.

"Lily, I've got it covered. I want to do this for you. It's a little way off yet, anyway." I suck in a deep breath, but he stops any words from coming out. "I know it's not going to be baking hot or a long time away, but it will be ours. Don't you just want to be tucked away with me on a little island?" Well, when he puts it like that. I mumble a reluctant yes. I feel his grin against my neck as he reaches to shut the top of the laptop down. "Good, because I already booked it." His chest vibrates with laughter when I snap around, almost jarring my neck in the process.

"Why am I not surprised?" I purse my lips, and he licks across the pouted seam. My lips relax into a smile.

"Lily Spencer, why didn't I find you sooner?" He poses the question for us both and goes quiet as he contemplates this himself. I shrug. I have no idea, but I'm glad we found each other, eventually.

He tugs the laptop away and flips me, crushing me to the sofa.

"You ready to be thoroughly loved?" His hips do a slow, hard roll, and my gasp gets lost around his tongue. "I think that was a yes." He grins.

I have felt the absence of the gallery. When I arrive on Tuesday morning after a weekend of relaxation with Jace, I'm feeling thoroughly refreshed. Harriet is waiting for me with a steaming mug. I've decided to take it slowly this week—every other day for half a day. Carl and Cass have both been popping in to help out when needed.

All the bruising has gone down, and I have managed to cover any yellowness with cosmetics. In fact, everything is perfect, as though all of my stars have aligned, and I'm now reaping the benefits. They do say things get worse before they get better, and with such a commanding man by my side, any discontent has abated.

"Morning!" I smile, laying my things down on the desk and taking the cup held out for me. "Thank you." Her eyes linger on the expertly disguised scar in my hairline, and she looks away when she knows I have caught her out. I know she still has questions, but I don't intend to discuss it. It's done. It's over, and everything in my life is perfect.

"I feel like I haven't seen you in months," I joke, blowing on my drink.

"I know. Are you sure you're okay?" The hesitant tone suggests she believes otherwise. "You worried me last time." Harriet moves a little closer, anticipating another wave of dizziness.

"Me too, but I'm feeling okay. I've just got to take it slowly. Let's get me up to speed. I'm sure there is something I have missed." I steer the conversation on to more neutral ground, trying to slip around her anxiety.

Harriet cups her drink and leans on the desk.

"Sure." She takes a quick sip and smiles with a heavy groan. "Is there anything better than coffee in the morning?" she states. My mind's eye flashes back to this morning and the amazing oral sex I was woken with.

I laugh and try some coffee, lifting my cup in fake agreement and swallowing the bitterness swirling around my mouth. Yes, there are better things than coffee, and they involve Jace Bennett, but I'm not about to share that with her. I swallow the dark liquid unwillingly.

"Any bills that need my immediate attention?" I question, slowly dropping down in the chair and looking out of the window at the steady traffic moving along the street.

"Oh, no. Jace sorted all that out." She frowns at me as though my accident left me with a dickey brain.

"Jace?" My cup stalls halfway.

"Yes, he was here all Wednesday—" Her voice trails off when she realises I am none the wiser. "I think he just wanted to ensure you had little to worry about." She grimaces at the tightness pressing in on my face. He never mentioned a thing to me.

"What else did he do?" I'm gobsmacked and angry. Should I be angry? I know he is only trying to help, but this is my business!

She blanches.

"He was just checking the finances and stuff like that," she whispers, her light eyes widen with guilt.

What!

"Harriet, why didn't you call me?" Her lip wobbles and I sigh inwardly. "It's not your fault," I smooth over, "but this isn't his business, and although you may find it highly romantic, I find it intrusive." She clears her throat with a nod. Shit, I feel like a massive bitch.

"I'm sorry." She bites her lip and looks away, causing guilt to shift through me.

"Don't be. I know how persuasive he can be," I mutter. "It's really not your fault," I assure her.

"I promise that will never happen again," she vows. "I really am sorry." Her fingers twist, reminding me of her age.

My smile is forced.

"I know. It's fine. Honestly." With that, I stand and head back to my office, simmering with anger.

As soon as I close the door, I pull my phone free and bring his name up, calling him.

"Hey, baby, missing me already?" He laughs. I wish I could respond with what he wants to hear,

"Why did you look through my finances?" It comes out sharper than intended, but I can't bear the thought of him snooping through the diabolical state of my finances when he has a booming business that rakes in god knows how much money. It's fair to say I am barely scraping the surface of even being in a stable situation. I merely keep my head afloat, and although the events and marketing pay off, I'm still not making much money.

"I was just managing the bills," he deflects.

"But you looked through my finances," I repeat, picking up a bill that is still sealed on my desk. No doubt a new one that will be another noose to my finances.

"What's yours is mine." His response makes me stiffen.

"Well, as you will have found, there isn't a lot for you to have," I spit, painfully embarrassed and thoroughly annoyed that he has been snooping through my life.

His laugh is light.

"I'm not after your money. A problem halved is a problem shared, beautiful. I thought we were in this together?" His voice drops in a question, reassuring and teasing me, all at once. I can hear the smile in his voice. I sigh and try to box away my misplaced feelings. "You're doing great with the gallery—on a steady roll. That's good. I'm really proud of you, baby." His genuine praise softens my hurt.

"Sorry," I'm remorseful and pliant.

"Good, you can show me just how much later," he quips. I can hear the steady tap of him on his computer.

"You're filthy," I mutter, hiding my reluctant grin.

"Just how you like me." He laughs heartily.

"Thank you for taking care of The Loft." I finally push past my pouting lips.

"Always. My appointment is here. I'll grab dinner on the way home. Love you, even when you're a grumpy, stubborn woman." He chuckles.

"Oh, you have a nerve! You need a word with your inner control freak," I splutter around an incredulous laugh.

"You like my inner control freak," he drawls. "And before you deny it, I think you should cast your mind back to Sunday night," he throws in.

"Sorry, can't, I have more important things to do. Like work," I quip, holding back a laugh, but my mind is already running back to re-encounter the loving but demanding session he bestowed on me.

"You're *there*. I made you cry," he gloats.

"Oh, look. I have another call coming in," I huff, happily irritated he can read me so well.

"That's my ego reminding you we're both right," he scoffs out on a deep chuckle. I burst out laughing. "I've got to go, gorgeous. See you tonight."

"See you later." I'm grinning wildly.

I give myself a moment to think before I throw myself into work. The coffee Harriet made is finally cool enough, so I sip it. I pull back and look at the cup before trying it again, and screw up my mouth in disgust. I have to force it down my throat because I refuse to spit it back in my cup.

"Hat!" I yell. I can hear her footsteps but continue shouting, anyway. "Did you get new coffee?" She enters with a perplexed look on her face, and she shakes her head, sniffing the cup as I push it away. "Perhaps it's gone off? It tastes weird." I frown at her, asking silently if she thinks so too.

"Oh, sorry, I can make you a new one?" She offers, picking it up and sniffing it.

"Oh no, thanks. I didn't mean for you to make a fresh one," I say. "Probably should stick to water. I still feel a bit groggy," I admit, and concern pulls at her mouth.

"Do you think you came back too early?" She looks ready to pass out herself.

"No." I laugh. "I was going crazy. I feel fine physically. It's just this tiredness and the on and off nausea, but that's mainly if I feel a little dizzy." Her eyes widen a fraction, and I regret opening up to her, especially when I know how anxious she is, anyway. "When I get up too quickly," I explain, in the hope that she will relax.

"Is that normal?" She makes herself comfy in the chair opposite mine.

"Apparently," I grunt out. I think I have been through enough without the consistent side effects. Surely it has to end soon?

"Well, just keep taking it slowly." She shrugs at me and takes my cup, sniffing it as she goes. It really did taste vile.

Chapter Fourteen

The next week follows a similar pattern. I have been taking it slowly at work and feel much better after seeing the doctor and being given the all clear. As far as my life goes, everything is how I want it to be. Things are good with Jace, and I'm enjoying how things have progressed between us. The dynamic has changed, and wc have so much to look forward to.

It's early, but I'm up with Jace and ready for work. It's hard to fall back to sleep when being woken up by such a brute. I have ignored his playful jibes all morning and spent the last ten minutes searching for my phone.

I finally find my phone in his office. I unplug it and quickly swipe on the notification on the lock screen until my eyes are pulled away by the paper strewn over the surface: planning permission, extension drawings, building contracts, and finalised plans all spring out at me. I shift through them, seeing an elaborate design. It takes me all of two seconds to realise it's The Hub. The roof is elevated and slanted out over one end—a huge bedroom consisting of an en-suite, walk-in wardrobe, and a balcony over the lake. A family bathroom, three spare bedrooms, and an open, higher lounge surround a galley landing and two-story windows, which bask in the stunning view. It looks like an exclusive mountain resort!

"Hey, beautiful, have you seen my keys?" Jace's rough morning voice pulls me around, the papers still in my hand.

"You're extending The Hub. Are you planning to sell after completion?" My eyes look back to the plans that have taken a lot of thought. I hope he isn't going to sell, but I see no reason to extend when it's only us two? The place is big as it is. I'm not sure I want to move to the city. I like the remoteness of this place. He wanders in, looking sharp in his suit.

"What's The Hub?" he asks, expertly tying his tie. My cheeks flush lightly because it has always been a silent endearment of mine.

I tuck my hair back.

"Here, this," I tell him, quickly hoping to skate over it, "why would you sell it? Is that why you're extending; to sell?" I whisper. I love this place. He's only just asked me to move in, so why would he move us out?

"The Hub," he whispers, his tone thoughtful. He smiles at me, his nostrils flaring with poorly disguised satisfaction. "I like that." He wanders to me slowly and takes my butt in his hands, tugging me close. I have to tilt my head to look up at him, and his bright eyes take in my face with a knowing but personal grin, a smile used only for me.

"Why are you extending?" I lift the papers, willing him to answer.

"For us. Why did you think I was selling?" He laughs at me with a shake of his head and pecks my cheek quickly before picking up a few more files. I lift the papers and stare at them, perplexed. In all honesty, I don't understand much of what I'm reading, but looking over it with my newfound knowledge, I don't know why I came to the conclusion I did. I suppose the extension seems too big for the two of us. It is too big. Selling is the next viable option.

"I don't know," I admit. "I guess I worried you were and then ran with it," I huff stupidly, placing them back on the desk.

"Well, worry no more: The Hub," he says slowly, smiling softly at me, "is ours." His lips do a happy dance along my jawline.

"I like The Hub." I lift my nose in the air and raise my arms so they hook around his neck. I want him back on my neck.

"I like it too, baby." That voice, the low one he uses, makes me shiver, and his eyes smile knowingly at me.

"That never gets old," he tells me, rubbing his hand lightly up my side, the files pressed into my back.

"I will, and then you won't find me attractive," I grumble playfully. He pulls back, affronted, but his eyes, those endless sap-coloured orbs, are gleaming.

"I'm older than you," he points out, thrusting his hips for good measure. "If anyone is at risk of being found less attractive first, it's me." He runs his nose along my cheek and inhales my perfume. His groin swells and hardens, and his throat rumbles with a deep groan as his teeth nip and dance along my jawline.

"I could never *not* find you attractive," I confess shyly, staring at his remarkable face.

"Same applies to you, woman. Now kiss me and tell me where my keys are." I press a soft one to his full lips as he sweeps his tongue in, and I sigh loudly, running my nails into his hair and holding him close.

On a defeated groan, he pulls away.

"You'll put me out of business soon." He chuckles, unhooking my arms. "Keys?" he reminds me, stepping away.

"Maybe in the book hive?" I suggest, not remembering where he placed them last night.

"Okay, I've got to shoot, have a big meeting with the construction company, and another with some hotel guy." He steps back and checks the files are all in one piece.

"So big, you can't recall his name." I laugh.

"Carl will update me." He winks, sending me an air kiss.

"Was that how it was with me?" I say sweetly. I even bat my lashes at him. Jace is already out of the office door, but he comes back and leans against the frame, arms spread wide so his chest expands through the space.

"It wouldn't have mattered how it was with you: one look and I was a goner." He grins through a lip-bitten stare.

I can't help but heckle him.

"Even with Megan?" I pout my lips, and he shudders.

His arms drop from the framework.

"God don't. I drank way too much and just thought" – he wafts his hand out – "fuck it," he spits, still unhappy with his poor decision.

"Literally," I drawl, shooting a flirtatious look up through my lashes, and battling the urge to laugh.

"Don't plague my mind. I'm happy thinking only of you." He comes back to me and reaches down to squeeze the full globes of my arse. I press into him, feeling and absorbing that natural sensation of safeness.

"Me too." I press up and kiss him. "Have a great day," I say, and running my fingers over his collar, I let him pull me on for a quick, deep toe-curling kiss.

"And you, baby. I'll grab Thai on the way home." His lips peck at my mouth between each word, and he hums his approval and powers me back, so I thud against the glass. His tongue dives in and sweeps through my mouth on an earthy groan.

"You'll be late!" I pant, not at all bothered if he actually is. I could stay locked in this lakeside hideaway forever.

"I'll miss you," he grumbles, unlocking our lips and dropping his eyes so his lashes shield them.

"I'll miss you too."

"Love you."

"Ditto." I grin, and he awards me with a wink before going to find his keys.

I'm beginning to depend on him and that physical connection only he can offer. He has lured me into a soul-deep lust and hazy, loved-up bubble. I'm swimming in relationship heaven. We're possibly cringe-worthy, but I'm too happy to give a shit.

Jace leaves me, and I study the extensive drawings. There is enough room for ten people to live here. I stare at the master bedroom plan for a long time. The walk-in sits adjacent to the bathroom and bedroom, but is open to both. I like that it is still its own room. It puts his already drool-worthy ensemble to shame. His current bedroom is being converted into a utility. The office and gym are staying, but the layout is changing slightly, and another room is labelled 'Lily'. I frown and look over more pictures, plans, and paper where he has jotted notes, but there is nothing to suggest what the room is for. I realise the time and grab my phone and bag, reluctantly cutting my snooping short.

My drive to work is eventful. It seems everyone is in a rush and lacking patience, and when I finally pull up outside The Loft, Harriet is walking up the street.

"Hey!" she calls.

"Traffic was a nightmare again. I can't get used to this commuting." I laugh tiredly. "I'm going to have to start leaving earlier," I grumble dramatically.

"I'm glad I can tube it some days," she tells me, meeting me at the door.

"So, how was the date?" I ask, pushing the key into the door. I still get an inner shudder from when Adam attacked me here. Harriet is on edge too, it seems. She checks over her shoulder, and we both push inside. Silly really, as Adam is paying the price of his actions.

"I really like him," she sighs, "he's funny and kind." She unzips her coat and fiddles with her hair.

"He seems to be rather taken with you, too," I respond. We both head out the back, and while I put my bags away, she is flicking the coffee machine on.

"He asked to take me out again," she calls through to me. I'm really happy for her. Simon seems such a good guy, the kind your parents want for you. Harriet had told me that he works in design for a large marketing firm.

"That's good. Have you arranged anything yet, or is it another surprise? Where did you go last night, by the way?" She never did mention where he took her.

"We went to a show at the theatre." Her face is full of excited disbelief. I slide my lunch into the fridge and make a cup of tea, all the while observing her girlish excitement.

"Anything good?" I mentally file it away to suggest to Jace.

Her face pulls at the side.

"Some artsy show. I didn't really understand what was going on half the time," she admits sheepishly. I laugh at her honesty. "It was captivating though." My lips pull a little. "A broken love story." She frowns, no doubt thinking back over the show. "It was very romantic," she muses thoughtfully.

"He definitely scored brownie points then?" I squeeze the tea bag out and dispose of it.

"Yes," she breathes. "And he kissed me," she blurts out, her cheeks flushing wildly. I pull back at the highness of her voice. "Is that bad?"

"It's a kiss," I reassure her, and she brushes her dress down. "And?" I coax more out of her. She sighs, and I grin, nudging her out of the way with my hip so I can make the coffee she has forgotten about. "I'm really happy for you, Hat."

"Me too," she squeaks, "just don't want to get my hopes up too much." She scrunches her nose up.

I nod: it's realistic and safe.

"Just take it slowly and enjoy," I tell her, not at all sure where my sudden wisdom has come from, as it left me high and dry where Jace was concerned.

Her phone pings, and she busies herself with that for a moment. "Your eleven has cancelled and wants to re-book next Thursday." I mentally run through my calendar.

"I have lunch booked with Alfredo. He is in London for a few days. Can she do three-thirty?" I ask around my cup.

"I'll check and let you know. Also, we are running out of coffee beans," she says, half distracted with her first task.

I wrinkle my nose.

"Well, that won't do." I laugh. "I can grab some tomorrow on my way in. Right, I need to call the bank," I excuse myself, heading back down to my office.

My day is slow, so Harriet and I decide to grab lunch together and head to the park, my camera in tow. I perch cross-legged on the bench, and between sips of my herbal tea, I lift my camera to take a few pictures. The lens opens up, and the object of my admiration tunnels in my vision. A tree is dipping down into the water, the branches reaching for the inky liquid. The leaves have admitted defeat and abandoned the bark, dropping free and floating like tiny boats. I catch a fish breaking the surface and smile as I pull the camera away and thumb through the images.

"You always photograph water," Harriet observes. I skip through my images until I find a similar one I captured when I was at Jace's.

"I know. I like it. It's calming, serene. I'm definitely a water baby." I laugh. I know Harriet is more drawn to sketching portraits, defining and toning with charcoal. She's good, and I have no shame in admitting she is better than me. But she isn't ready to share her talents just yet, and I won't push her. I know Alfredo would buy her work in a second. She is somehow able to capture the inner pain of her subject. Her creative eye brings it to the surface of the paper, in its most raw form. She has a real talent.

"Jace's house sits on a lake, as in literally sits over it." I laugh. "His bedroom drops away into it, and past the tree line are more lakes. It's stunning." I point to the image confirming the lakes.

"Wow, it's so vast," she gapes and holds up a muffin for me. I take it and pick at the fruit submerged in the fluffy sponge, murmuring my thanks to her. "I bet it's so peaceful at night when you're that far out." Where I pick at my muffin, she dives right in and takes a big bite.

"It is. I feel hundreds of miles away." I pop more cake in my mouth and pack my camera away before picking my tea back up.

"We should head back."

Work is just as slow in the afternoon. Harriet makes a sale, but I find myself stuck on the phone to the bank for the second time and then have to take a further call from the police following up on the attack. Cass calls to inform me she is coming round later, which I'm looking forward to.

By the time closing comes round, both Harriet and I are racing to get out of the door and home.

"You look shattered," she says, waiting with me while I lock up. She is constantly checking over her shoulder.

"He's not coming back," I tell her. She shifts nervously, and I feel bad. For my own selfish reasons, I have kept her in the dark, and left her to run the place alone, worried some psycho might turn up and do the same to her.

I swallow my pride and suck in a breath.

"The guy that attacked me was my ex, who I had a restraining order on. He broke that order, and he is now serving time. He isn't coming back, Harriet." She gapes at me and nods stiffly. She hasn't a clue what to say to me, and I don't blame her. It's a mess.

"I've put you through a lot, and I'm sorry," I apologise to her and clear my throat.

"No, I am. I didn't expect you to divulge such personal information, but I'm glad you did." I smile sympathetically at her. Anyone would think it was her who has the crazy ex. "I feel a lot more at ease," she says awkwardly. "I'll see you Monday?" she asks, deliberating over her mental calendar. We agreed I'd give tomorrow and Saturday a miss. I feel exhausted.

"Yep, have a great weekend. Any problems, call me." I watch her walk down the street before I head to my car.

Cass is already there when I pull up. She follows me in, we both kick our shoes off, and she grabs some wine. I collect two glasses and add ice before holding them out for her to fill, and we move to the sofas. I pull a fluffy blanket over my feet, ignoring the niggling dizziness hanging over me.

"So, you're living here then?" Cass side-eyes me as she sips on some wine. I stare at the glass and offer her a shrug.

"Not officially." That's a lie. I don't know why I feel so awkward telling her.

"So unofficially," she scoffs, "are you living here?" Her tone is verging on boredom.

"Jace wants me to," I whisper, filling my mouth with wine to avoid further questioning.

"And?" she urges me, shaking her wine midair as she tries to coax more information out of me.

"And what?" I mutter, not happy with this conversation.

She rolls her eyes.

"You're hard work." She kicks my foot. "Do you want to move in?"

"I've not been given much choice." That's not entirely true, but I honestly think he would have bullied me into living here.

"Lily, stop being so evasive," Cass groans at me, her patience gone. *"Do you* or do you *not* want to live here," she accentuates, giving me her best Cassandra Faraday glare—the once she reserves for when her patience has worn thin.

"Yes." I swallow the nerves that word brings to me. The rational side of me screams that it's too soon, but every other part of me is basking like a pampered cat at being so lavished on by Jace. Everything has slotted together so nicely. It's early days, but being under the same roof is nice, really nice. We are totally content.

"So where is he?" She looks around as though she's missed him somehow, which would be hard, given that we are sitting in a giant glass box.

"Gone to my flat to pick up more stuff. Also, he is working on an extension." I lift my glass and use my free hand to work the TV.

"This late? Hasn't he got minions for that?" I roll my eyes at her.

"For here. Says he wants to build up and put a balcony out over the lake." I'd spoken earlier with him about it. I managed to grab a few minutes after my lunch and between his meetings.

"Wow, he is certainly very serious about you being here."

"Is it a mistake?" I pick at my trousers.

Cass shakes her head.

"No. I think it would have happened eventually, and by eventually, I mean in the next three months." She laughs. "The man likes to move quickly. He knows you're a flight risk!" She gives me a pointed look.

"I am not!" I cough around my glass.

"Oh, hun, you so are, and now he gets it." She shrugs her dainty shoulders. "We should arrange a date night, all four of us." I rest back and grin at her.

"Sure, sounds good." My eyes glitter with excitement. I could use a night out.

"We can go to that Italian place you like," she suggests, kicking her feet up and sighing happily. It's the first time in a good few weeks that we have had some girl time together.

"Okay, I will mention it later." I can't see Jace disagreeing.

"How are you feeling?" Cass wonders, her eyes fixed on the screen.

"Good. I should be back to work full time on Monday. Jace is still watching me like a hawk," I confess.

"You don't still mean" – her eyes flip to my crotch – "I bet you're sealed up!" She visibly shudders.

My mouth drops open with a shocked laugh. I grab a pillow and clip her with it. "Cassandra Jane Faraday!" She is just awful.

"Don't hit me. Blame the hunk who won't hit the trunk!" She is a mess of snorting giggles.

"The trunk." My mouth pulls down at the side, but then I roll my

eyes at her and smirk. It's hard not to when she is laughing all over the sofa. "And everything in that area is fine. Honestly, things are going so well."

"Well, I'm glad," she tells me, shifting, so she sinks low into the sofa and is perched on a huge cushion. "You deserve to be happy." I knock her foot with mine in thanks, and we snuggle in to watch an episode of her latest TV obsession.

Chapter Fifteen

It's been our busiest Saturday to date, and Harriet and I have been run ragged.

"I cannot wait to get home and sink some wine," I tell her with a short laugh. She is smirking and drops down into the chair up front.

"Tell me about it. Where did all those people come from?" She closes her eyes and massages her temples. "Thank god it's the weekend."

"Got any plans?" I say, loading up my handbag.

"Sleep and more sleep. I'm still recovering from my holiday," she grumbles. "I think Faye was trying to kill me."

"Joke's on her then." I wink as I head down to my office to grab my phone. I'm tidying my desk and checking that I locked the back door when Harriet calls down to me.

"You have a guest!" On cue, the bell dings, and I poke my head round to have a look. It's Jace.

I hear his deep rumble as he says hello to Harriet, then he is on his way down to me.

"Hey, gorgeous."

"Hey, yourself. I thought you were seeing Viktor this afternoon?" Not that I mind that he is here.

"Change of plan. You ready? I have a surprise for you." He reaches me on the other side of the desk and pecks my lips. "You smell nice," he comments.

"Ditto." I grin and cup his face, giving him the kind of kiss I need after this morning.

"Don't start what you can't finish." He chuckles against my lips.

"You know I'm not a big fan of surprises," I admit, his face still in my hands.

"You will like this. Come on." He takes my hand, and Harriet waves us goodbye as she tightens her coat.

"See you Monday!"

"Bye, Hat." Jace watches while I set the alarm and lock up. I turn to look at him. "Is this why you demanded you drop me off today?"

"Pretty much."

"Well, Cass agreed to drop me home," I remind him.

"No, Cass agreed to go along with it. She knew I was coming for you."

"Ah, so you're in cahoots?"

"Cahoots?" He grins, then nods to the car. "No, Cass knew this surprise is what you need, so she did as she was told. You should probably take a leaf out of her book." The cheeky devil. I lift my brows and see his raise too. He is challenging me.

"Well, with the Cass I know, it's the kind of leaf you wouldn't want me to have."

"Why is it a marijuana leaf?" he asks, deadpan. I burst out laughing as I get in the car.

"So, are you going to tell me what this surprise is?"

"Nope."

"Not even a hint?"

"Nope." He starts the engine, and I buckle up.

"A clue?"

"Lily, it's not a surprise if I tell you anything."

"Can you not jus—"

"No." He laughs. "You're the worst at this." I smirk and relax as we head through the streets and out of London. Initially, I assume we are heading home, but it becomes apparent we aren't. I'm itching to ask, but I keep my lips firmly shut and settle in for the journey, however long that may be.

After an hour of steady driving, we roll into a sleepy village. It's picturesque with a cute stream and thatch-roofed homes. It's a million miles from any bustling city and exactly the kind of atmosphere I need after today and the last few weeks. The only information I was able to prise out of Jace was that we are staying somewhere overnight. We wind our way through the village until we are almost passing through, but then Jace takes the next turning, and I see a cottage tucked away between a few fields.

"Is this where we are staying?" I grin. It's perfect, cute sash windows and not a person in sight.

"Yes. The owner prepared lunch so we can snoop, eat, then I want you on your back." He gives me a devious wink, and I can't help but laugh at him.

"What if I want those things in a different order?"

"Back, eat, snoop?" he queries as we hit the drive and cruise under a huge willow tree. "Snoop, back, eat? Eat, back, snoop?" His voice is laced with amusement, and I roll my eyes as he comes to a stop out the front. I hop straight out. I definitely need to eat.

"Can we eat first?" I say as Jace pulls two cases out the back.

"Sure, the code for the key box is 1857: Eat, back, snoop it is," he says, loud enough for me to hear. I shake my head and get the key before letting us in. Jace gives my arse a squeeze as I hang my coat up. His hands wrap around my waist, and he sighs, dropping his chin to my shoulder.

"Surprise, beautiful."

"Thank you." He is so thoughtful that I could bloody cry. Emotion clogs my throat, but I keep it at bay.

"You deserve it, and, quite frankly, I needed it too." His lips brush my temple, then he is off carrying the cases with him. He does need this—we both do. It will be good for us both.

"Did you pack for me?" I ask as his wide frame disappears up a narrow flight of stairs.

"No, I value my life, and you don't seem the type to want to wear an all-in-one puffer coat." I laugh and look up at him, bunched up on the small staircase. "Cass came over this morning," he says, adjusting his stance to allow more room for his head. I swallow a smile.

"I'm going to check what lunch we have," I tell him. The hall is narrow like the stairs, but the rooms are spacious and cosy, typically farmhouse and quaint. It's really sweet and spotless. My man did well.

I open the fridge and find it stockpiled with fresh fruit and vegetables, some ready-made sandwiches, and a jug of cloudy apple juice. Perfect!

I hunt around for a few more bits and set us some places at the chunky table as Jace comes back downstairs. He grabs a handful of crisps and slings them into his mouth before pulling a face.

"Vegetable chips," I say, enjoying watching him chew them unhappily.

I pick one up and nibble it. I like them, but evidently, he would rather eat my burnt eggs again.

"Please tell me that sandwich isn't full of just salad?" He scoops me up, plopping me on the countertop, as he pushes his way between my thighs and cups my face, not allowing me any time to answer because his mouth is on mine: hot and hungry. We kiss, his hands massaging my arse and keeping me flush to his rigid length.

"Lunch," I pant.

"You ate a crisp," he whines. I burst out laughing, and he gives me a cheeky smile. "Are you really going to refuse me—refuse yourself?" Amber eyes blink up at me—glittering and full of fire. "I want to hurtle for a little while—hurtle right between these gorgeous legs and wake this sleepy village up." He grins, biting my lip. I groan and tilt my head, giving him access to my neck. "Is that a yes? Besides, it's nearly 2 p.m.. It'd be sinful not to fuck now."

I run my fingers through his hair.

"Why do I get the feeling you will say about anything to get me on my back right now?"

"This feeling?" He thrusts forwards, and I chuckle. "Lily, I have thought of nothing all morning except tasting in between your creamy thighs and sinking deep until I can't bloody think."

"Take me to bed," I demand. His eyes sparkle, and he sweeps me up, manoeuvring until we reach the bottom of the stairs.

"Fuck." He laughs. There is no way in hell we are getting up those stairs with me in his arms. I wriggle free and begin jogging up the stairs, eager to find the bedroom, but I'm hauled back and kissed roughly up the wall. I have a little height on Jace as I'm on the top step. His hands are frantic on my clothes, tugging me free until each item is flung haphazardly up or down the stairs, then his own are coming away, and his wide chest comes into view before he dips to drag a nipple into his mouth.

"I love these gorgeous breasts," he affirms, his gaze fixed to each pebbled breast. "So fucking sexy, Lily." He lifts me then, encouraging me to wrap my legs around his waist only so he can move us up a few more steps and bring me down on the top one. His lips find mine in a hard, crushing kiss. My hands are gliding into his hair to hold him at my mouth—he is an expert. No one kisses like Jace. His lips are full enough to cushion his assault—his tongue hot enough to have my limbs liquefying. When he pins my arms above my head and grinds into me, I'm a whimpering wreck.

"Jace, now, I want you in me now," I pant.

His chuckle has my eyes fluttering open, and as soon as they do, I'm lost in his ambers, where passion swirls like thick honey, pours into me, and sweetens my soul. God, this man.

"You want me, do you?" His head is tilted, and I know that look—he's teasing me. I jolt my hips. Yes! His hand slides down my arm, along the side of my body, then he is shifting to give himself access. I'm ready for him, and my legs open, welcoming him in.

"Yes, touch me, dammit!" I lift my mouth because I am craving our connection, but his fingers beat my mouth. His eyes watch mine vividly as he sinks his fingers deep inside me, and I choke out a sweet moan.

"Ah, Lily. God. If only you could see how beautiful you look, all blushed and sexy." His lips graze mine, then are gone again as his fingers begin pulsing in and out. I'm lost to the sensation, my arms still thrown above me as I rock my hips to his pace.

My limbs are shaking.

"You're too good at this. I'm going to come."

"So soon?" He grins, his hand tilts, and I jolt off the top step. Jace plants a hand on my stomach to keep me grounded. "Here's your sweet spot." He presses against my inner walls, and I cry out loudly. His fingers don't stop, and I'm choking out a plea as he works me to an orgasm. I always just felt he was super lucky in the sex department as his good looks were enough to get anyone off, but he really has learned my body. My orgasm comes soon after until I'm sobbing.

"Fuck me," I plead. He does, but with his mouth. Then he's dragging us both off to the bedroom.

A short while later, I lay with my arm slung over his chest, which is still beating furiously, as my own is. We don't move. Don't speak. That was delicious. My toes curl as my body still hums and pulses. Moaning happily, I rub against him and sigh as the after-effects roll over my skin. Jace rolls and cups me.

"You're throbbing," he growls sleepily.

"And starving." I laugh. I've really worked up an appetite. Grinning, he bites my neck and drags me into his chest, slinging his leg over mine.

"I can't move," he grumbles. "Let's stay here all afternoon."

"I need to eat. I need energy."

"You don't need energy. I have enough. Just lie there and let me take advantage."

"I'll be back in a minute with the food." I roll out from under him and give his butt an ogle before I wander downstairs and begin loading up a tray with our lunch.

Jace has barely moved an inch when I get back upstairs. I rest the tray on the ottoman at the end of the bed and peer around to find him snoozing lightly. I'm quiet so not to wake him. I pull on his discarded t-shirt and, taking a sandwich, I sit in the window seat. There are fields for miles and miles. A blanket of natural beauty as far as the eye can see. It's another thirty minutes before Jace begins to stir, and I have already eaten my way through my lunch and some of his. He rolls over and blinks at me, tucked up on the ledge.

"Morning." I grin and pop a bit of cheese in my mouth. Jace is still coming round. He looks about the room and then blinks forcefully, urging his brain to catch up with his eyes.

"Fuck. I fell asleep."

"You did."

"What's the time?"

"Nearly half three." I try to stifle the laugh rushing up my throat, but I can't help it. "You don't need energy. I've got enough," I mimic, and he laughs.

"I did. It's all been zapped out of my dick and into you. That's why you're still up," he tells me, patting the bed next to him.

"You're full of shit." I giggle.

"And you're full of sperm." He grins dirtily.

"Jace!" I choke out. "Gross." My nose wrinkles and I climb up the bed until I'm sprawled over him. He sighs, and I lay listening to his heart pump against my ear. My fingers are running circles over his taut flesh as his own become lost in my hair. On a gentle lift, he pulls my mouth to his and gives me another toe-curling kiss.

"I've booked us a table for dinner at seven." His lips peck my mouth one last time, then he's rolling us. He drags the quilt up and over our heads, our feet poking out of the bottom. "But what I really want is to stay in bed all day, making love to you."

"Then let's stay in bed," I reply, running my hands up his arms and hooking them around his neck. "There is plenty of food here."

He scoffs.

"Looks like you ate most of the lunch."

"I really was starving," I admit. I wrap my legs around his waist and fuse us together.

"No shit. I'm going to lose half a stone if we stay in!" I slap his arm, and he grins and drops, squashing me to the bed. Huffing out a groan, I adjust to his weight and sigh. I really can't believe how happy and content I am with this man. It feels good to have someone to enjoy my life with. I've been so focused on my own life for so long that it's good to share that focus and direct it on someone else. "I love you like I love two o'clock," I tell him, running my thumbs back and forth over his stubble. His lips find my thumb pad, and he kisses it.

"I love you too, gorgeous." I smile up at him. I never thought I would be sharing those words with another person. At first, I was too scared to, then after Adam, I didn't think I deserved to, but hearing them, saying them, has lifted the biggest weight off my shoulders.

"What are you thinking?"

"Just that I'm really lucky that you found me."

"Yes, you are." He grins and pecks my mouth before heaving us out of bed.

"Oh, the cheek, and are you not lucky?"

"I feel like I've got a horseshoe hooked around my cock." His grin is so devious, so playful that even though I want to be annoyed at his backhanded compliment, I just hold him tighter instead.

"Super lucky then."

"Go and start the shower. I'm going to eat my lunch, then I'll join you."

Jace has chosen a seafood restaurant not too far from the village we are staying in. We've finished our meal and opted to share a dessert, which looks like it would take a small army to defeat. Layer upon layer of chocolate cake and sauce sat between us both. I've stared at it for over a minute, and I know the moment it passes my lips, my appetite will be back, but I'm stuffed.

"Maybe we should ask for it to go?"

"I still can't believe this is for one person," Jace says dryly, "it's nearly a quarter of a cake." He shakes his head and grabs a waiter as they pass, asking them to box it up for us. We pay the bill, and Jace suggests we head to one of the local pubs.

"I did see a pub on the way here. It was just off the main road."

"Okay, we'll take a look. That cake may have to wait until tomorrow, gorgeous," Jace says, helping me into my coat. I throw a grin over my shoulder and slip my hand into his as we head out of the restaurant.

The air is cool, and the temperature has dropped. I shiver and welcome the warmth of the car as we set off to find the pub I noticed earlier. It's busier than we expect, but looks inviting nonetheless. It's very old-English and has low ceilings, so much so that Jace has to duck his way in and lean on the bar just to save his head from being squished.

"I think this place is for hobbit's only." I giggle at how ridiculous he looks bent over in his parka.

"I'm going to need a massage after all this." He winks. A woman comes over, frantically wiping the bar down. Her eyes flare when they register Jace fully, and she leans on the bar too, so they are inches apart.

"You are definitely not from around here," she hums thoughtfully. "I would remember if I had seen you before. What can I get you?" Jace twists, bringing me into view, and her pale cheeks heat. She is very pretty and very forward.

"Babe, do you just want a glass of wine or a bottle?"

"Just a glass?" I respond, allowing him to tug me into his chest. The woman looks a little put out that I'm there.

"Let's have a glass here." His head swings back to the bartender.

"Can we get a bottle to take out when we leave?" he asks, surprising me.

She tucks her hair behind her ears and distances herself from him.

"Of course, what wine will it be?"

"Pinot, please?"

"Medium?" Her tone is clipped and short, as though she really doesn't want to be conversing with me. Well, tough.

"Sure, thanks?" I side-eye Jace, who has also picked up on her tone. Jeez, what a psycho. I wonder if it's embarrassment, but she looks annoyed as hell with me.

"I'll have a lager. Any," Jace says, cutting over her when she starts to ask which lager he would prefer. We wait for our drinks before manoeuvring between the crowded pub to find a seat. We are lucky to get a place at the window seat, not too far from the open fire. We're sitting side by side, and Jace tugs me so my legs are crossed and into him, his hand on my thigh.

"You feeling relaxed yet beautiful?" Jace asks, sipping on his beer.

"Yes, relaxed and very full."

"Good."

"I'm just going to pop to the ladies," I tell him. The crowd is thick, so it takes me a little while to get through the throng. When I do, the bathroom is empty, so I'm in and out within minutes. Without the din of music, I'm able to just think for a second, and by the time I'm heading back to Jace, I'm suppressing a very mischievous smile.

Jace must sense it too, because he gives me a quizzical look.

"You okay?"

"Hi," I breathe softly. He smiles inquisitively as he watches me take a seat next to him. "You don't mind, do you?" I ask him. He's confused, and rightly so. I'm not acting myself at all. He shakes his head, and I smile seductively at him. "You are definitely not from around here. I would remember if I had seen you before." His eyes flare with understanding, and his mouth twists into a dark smile.

"Just passing through," he plays along.

"Lucky me." I bite my lip and give him a look from below my lashes.

"Jace." He holds his hand out, and my breath shudders out. Shit, we're doing this. I feel giddy and hot with excitement, and by the flare of his nostrils and the glint in those perfect damn eyes, he is enjoying this as much as me.

"Lily."

"Well, Lily, it's a pleasure to meet you."

"Likewise." I start to tuck my hair behind my ear but stop, realising that's a little too like myself. I shake my hair out and stare at him head on. "I hope you don't mind me being this forward?"

"Not at all."

"I saw you across the room and thought, that man is gorgeous." My eyes drop to his lips, and his tongue dips out, taunting me.

"Unfortunately, due to the overwhelming amount of OAPs in here, I wasn't lucky enough to catch sight of you until now. I'm glad you came over."

"You are. Why?" I ask, crossing my legs and picking up my wine from earlier. I swill the glass and look at him, conveying how much this is arousing me.

"Well, you are beautiful, obviously," he tells me, looking over me with interested eyes. "You smell delectable and," – he pauses and looks around the room before leaning in to brush his lips to my ear – "since you sat down, I have thought of nothing else but how you will feel under my tongue."

My breath stops, stutters, and then leaves in a long rush of air.

"Jace."

"Lily."

"I want you."

"I'm not that kind of guy," he tells me quickly.

My blush is bright, and I can't help but smirk. Oh, he so is.

"I think you are," I remark, resting back and sipping on my drink. Jace follows suit, and for a moment, we have a staring contest. The tension is palpable, heavy, and I'm enjoying this more than I thought.

"What gives you that impression?"

"Well, the fact that you told me you want to taste me," I say, deadpan. Jace laughs loudly.

"Touché. Minor slip-up."

"Nothing minor about that," I say, looking towards his groin area.

Jace frowns at me.

"Get back in character," he tells me, and I straighten my back. "Well then, Lily, my new drinking buddy, let me finish my drink, and we can get to know each other a little more," – he tilts his head and drops his eyes to my crotch – "intimately," he hums.

I lift my drink.

"Bottoms up." I wink and take a healthy gulp.

Chapter Sixteen

I wake with a start and roll slowly to find Jace flat out beside me. I smile and stare at his profile. The slight curl at the tip of his hair is becoming more prominent. His lips are slightly parted, and I take a moment to enjoy every cell of him, from the bristles around his jaw to the smooth expanse of his chest as it inflates on each inhale. I'm sure I'm very much biased, but he is stupidly handsome.

I lay still, just watching him, happy in the silence and early morning sun breaking through the flimsy curtains. My fingers reach out and rub along his collarbone as he exhales roughly, and his eyes press tightly together.

"Lily," he mumbles incoherently. I grin and hum, but he is still asleep. My fingers roam, tracing around his nipple and his pec.

Quickly, his hand snaps out and grabs me. I gasp and laugh as ambers burst with happiness into mine. He rolls us both and nuzzles into my neck.

"Morning." His voice has that sexy, deep, sleep-induced husk to it.

"Morning." I wrap myself around him, and we lay like that for a while, not really saying anything but just happy in our own company. When he finally rolls us again, it's out of the bed. I get scooped up with a huff, and Jace is stalking us both to the shower.

It's nothing like the shower at The Hub, but I huddle in and enjoy being pressed up against Jace.

"So, what's planned for the day? Do we need to head back soon?"

"Only if you want to?" He turns me around, and I reach up to hoop his neck.

"I'm happy to stay in here for a while."

"You couldn't get a sheet of paper between us, let alone an erection," he states grumpily.

"I don't want it between us. I want it in me. Stop making excuses, Bennett."

"I like bossy you. She's horny a lot."

"Regular me is horny too. You just don't give me a chance to show you." I grin because he always beats me to it.

Jace cracks a devious smile.

"Show me now." With a quick peck to his lips, I hoist myself up and reach to position him at my slick entrance. His eyes are rapt, his lips parted, and the second he pushes in, I drop my mouth to his for a drugging kiss.

God, this man is like nothing I have ever known.

It's late when Jace and I finally get back to The Hub. We stopped off at an upmarket restaurant on the way back for dinner. It was the perfect way to finish our romantic weekend away. The cottage was everything we both needed, a secluded spot, unreachable, and nothing but each other for company. Jace has been his constantly attentive self, and I feel thoroughly spoilt and loved by the time we pull up in the darkened gravel driveway.

"I'll get the bags. You go and open up," he tells me, unclipping my seat before he gets out. I smirk at that. It's the little things that he does that slip their way under my skin and make my heart swell. That and when he makes love to me like he has done the past twenty-four hours. He has made sure I feel utterly adored.

I make it to the door as Jace's boot clunks shut, and I push my way in and disarm the alarm before flicking some lights on. Jace follows me in and takes our things straight into the bedroom. We are back only minutes when car lights head down the driveway.

"Jace, someone is here," I shout through to him. I know I have agreed to live here, but I still feel it's really his house. It's nearing 9 p.m. who is visiting this late? The car parks up, and as soon as the lights dip, I see it's Neve. She hops out, slams the door, and comes up to the house with determined strides. She doesn't knock or wait to be invited in but storms inside with a face like thunder and drags her eyes down the length of me disdainfully.

"Where is he? Jace!" she shouts. He comes quickly, looking panicked, his eyes shooting to me, then her.

"Hey, Neve. What's up?" He looks on edge, and his welcome is forced. He shifts and leans against the doorframe, but he looks stiff, and I frown at him, unsure what is going on with him.

"Where the hell have you been? Why haven't you answered your phone?" she shouts, and my brows rise. Jeez, warpath much! Surely work can wait until tomorrow?

"I took Lily away for the weekend, and we didn't want to be disturbed," he mutters, dragging his hands through his hair.

She scoffs and looks back at me as though I'm dirt. She's not accusing him—she is accusing me, but of what, I have no idea.

"Of course, as long as Lily gets what she needs," she snipes, flicking her hair dramatically over her shoulder. God, she is such a damn drama queen.

My mouth drops, and Jace's brows snap together. He looks pissed at her, but before he can rebuff her, she holds her hand up.

"Well, while you were ensuring Lily wasn't disturbed, Viktor was having a stroke!" she snaps.

"What?" Jace and I are both in shock, and he has paled.

"Why the hell didn't you say that as soon as you came in?" Jace shouts.

"Because you never had any issues being disturbed before, and as of late, you've been putting others on the back burner. You needed a fucking wake-up call."

I ignore her comments and grab my bag. She is so wrong about me. I'm not making Jace put other priorities on the back burner. Am I?

"Is he okay?" I ask. Jace looks heartbroken.

"Hmm. He is still in hospital, under observation." She is looking at Jace the whole time, and he looks guilt-ridden and in shock. I walk to him and rub his arm.

"Jace, come on. Let's go to the hospital," I say, and he blinks and nods, stiff and confused. I pick up his keys from the side and look at Neve when he slips his hand in mine and mutters that he doesn't think he can drive. "That's fine. I'll get us there. Which hospital, Neve?" My heart is breaking for him.

"You can follow me. We've been trying to contact you since last night," she adds, making Jace drop his head in shame. I twist into him and take his head in my hands and lift up to press a kiss to his cheek. He shakes his head, and my heart twists painfully for him further. I've never seen him like this: so utterly crushed, bewildered, and lost.

"We didn't know. It wasn't malicious. He will understand that—they both will," I reassure.

He nods, but I can tell he doesn't quite believe me. Neve has planted a nasty seed, and she has done it with the blame firmly on me. I get in the car and quickly adjust the seat and mirrors. It's me who clips Jace in as he is in a complete daze. This has affected him deeply, and it hurts to see him in pain. I don't know how to fix it, but I will ensure I do, just like he has done for me so many times. I need to be the strength for us both now. If anyone has taught me how to support someone, it is this man with his steel backbone and attentiveness.

It's another forty-five minutes before we are at the hospital and on our way to Viktor's room. The hospital is a burrow of white sterile corridors and sick people. It has such a distinctive smell, both clean and dirty, like every tear of sadness and drop of blood has been swept away with sanitiser but yet still stains the place. It's the oddest combination.

I keep Jace's hand in mine, showing my support. I rub his arm every now and again as we move through the never-ending corridors. Jace hasn't said a word—his whole demeanour is of a wounded animal. It's worrying me that he has retracted within himself so much. I bite my lip and keep his hand in mine, squeezing it every now and then. As soon as we hit the lift, despite our hands being attached, Neve pulls him in for a hug. Her eyes are powering into me as his fingers slip from mine, and his head drops to her shoulder. Pain lances through me. I try to act unaffected, but the truth is my partner is seeking comfort from another woman—a woman who is very much in love with him, and I can't even vocalise my hurt because he is really struggling with Viktor's stroke.

I keep my gaze averted and watch the number on the lift change as it sweeps past one floor, then another. Jace has moved back, and part of me wants to snatch his hand back into mine, and the other half wants to slap him away. She speaks to him like shit, purposely stamps on his feelings, and manipulates his emotions, yet he turns to her as though she will make it all better. He wouldn't even hug me. My thoughts are spiralling. I mentally scream at myself that it's not about me, but I feel winded seeing him in her arms. She's gloating, a light but cruel smile pulling at her painted lips. It's only just dawned on me, but she looks impeccable as always: her blonde hair down her back in faultless waves, skin-tight jeans, and a cute little jumper.

We step out of the lift, and I see it then, the silent commotion they cause together. Men break necks looking at her, and women melt for him; and all the while, I'm quietly following behind like a starved teenager, desperate for his affections. I can't quit my thoughts, and I feel riddled with guilt for even letting it get to me when there is a man I respect and care for sick somewhere in this place.

We finally reach Viktor's room, and despite the hour, we are briefly allowed in to see him. The time of day hadn't crossed my mind at first, but luckily, the head nurse on his ward reluctantly lets us through when she sees how forlorn Jace is. Marie catches sight of us, and she comes up to Jace with a little hiccup. He wraps her in a bear hug and begins apologising profusely for going away for the weekend, and it makes me feel a ton worse for having taken all his time up this weekend. Am I really taking all his focus and allowing him to shun others?

I don't know who he was before we met, or who was important to him, who he spent time with, and when. I barely see his friends, and when I do, it's with him. I just thought this was his normal.

"Oh, come on, don't be silly, you deserved some time away. You work too much as it is. I can't remember the last time you took a holiday." Marie pats his back and then rubs his arm when he shoves his hands into his jean pockets.

"What's the latest?" Neve asks, leaning into Jace and keeping me back. Marie hasn't noticed me yet, and I don't speak up. I feel very much like an interloper at the moment, and Neve's brassy attitude always leaves me feeling a little brittle.

"No changes. He's overcome the worst. I think we will know more in the morning when he wakes up," she says. "His stats are good. I think he is just exhausted."

"Why don't you go home and get some rest. I can stay with him tonight," Jace offers.

"I do need to freshen up. I suppose he is stable. I haven't got a car," she mumbles, unsure what to do.

"Lily can drop you back," Neve says. Marie turns, and I smile from behind Jace.

"Oh, love. It's so good to see you."

"I'm so sorry, Marie. We feel awful for not checking our phones," I say. My voice catches briefly, and Marie gives me a hug.

"Enough. You two are as bad as each other," she chides, "but I will take that offer of a lift?" She looks at Jace, then me. I nod and smile, unsure where that leaves Neve in all of this.

"Sure, I can take you back."

"Great, let me just check in with Nurse Williams, then we can head off. I really appreciate this," she says. She looks tired, fraught, and pale. With that decided, Jace moves over to Viktor, who is fast asleep with an IV in his hand. I watch as he leans, drops his head to Viktor's, and mumbles something softly to him.

"He's got his boy here, so I know he is going to be alright," Marie whispers emotionally. I give her a quick squeeze before she goes to find Nurse Williams.

Neve, who seems all too happy to be here with Jace, takes a seat in the chair beside Viktor's bed, and I keep my face averted because I know it will show my hurt.

It's only moments before Marie is back, with Nurse Williams in tow. Nurse Williams makes it known only one person per patient is to stay on the ward, and I hide my smirk when Neve looks pissed.

"Of course, we're leaving shortly. Can I take your direct number?" I ask her.

"Why do you need that?" Neve asks, pulling her hair to one side before crossing her arms. Jeez, why is she always so snarky?

"Well, I'm assuming Marie hasn't got it either, so if Jace's phone dies, at least we can all keep in contact and up to date this way," I say slowly. Surely I'm not the only one who thought that? I look at Marie, who smiles in agreement.

"Oh." Why does it matter to her, anyway?

"Let me know if you need me to bring anything in for you tomorrow?" I say to Jace, pecking his cheek quickly and grabbing Marie's bag. I wonder if he has just realised we are going to be apart for the night. He takes my wrist and pulls me to him quickly.

"You don't mind?" he asks. Neve scoffs, and I go red, feeling like he is making true to her words.

"Of course I don't mind. It's usually you that has an issue with us being apart." I laugh gently, trying to clear the air and put Neve in her place, but his fragile mind takes the hit instead. His face falls, and he nods.

"I'll chat to you tomorrow then," he says.

I give him a soft smile and drop a kiss to his lips.

"I'll miss you—keep me updated," I say and step away, studiously avoiding looking at Neve and rubbing Marie's back as I follow her out.

Nurse Williams clears the room after us, ensuring Neve is exiting the ward too. I feel a little lighter, knowing he isn't with her, and I really shouldn't because this is about Viktor and his recovery.

"I feel terrible that we weren't there for you, Marie. Jace feels awful. He has hardly spoken since we found out." We all enter the lift together, and silence fills the small square metal tin of a car. I hate these things with a vengeance. I say as much, and Neve rolls her eyes, but Marie is happy for the distraction.

"I got trapped in one while I was on a school trip to France. We were between floors nine and ten. The air-con went out, and it took two hours for them to get the lifts working again. It was horrible," I say, laughing lightly.

"You kids must have been so scared."

I nod, thinking back to that time.

"And hot. A few of them stripped to their underwear. You should have seen the teacher's faces when the doors opened."

"I can imagine." Marie chuckles.

We come to a stop, and Neve smiles at Marie.

"I told Jace I would be back first thing, so if you need a hand with anything, let me know."

"Okay, thank you, Neve." Marie takes her bag from me and begins looking for a tissue as her eyes fill.

"Night, Neve," I say.

"Yeah, night." She waves over her shoulder dismissively. I refrain from running after her and yanking her stupidly long, perfect hair. I swallow my anger and give Marie a supportive smile. Both Marie and I are silent on the walk back to Jace's car. It's cold, and it only adds to the sadness lingering in us both. As soon as we are in and belted up, she sniffles, and her tears come thick and fast. I reach over and pull her into a hug, holding her as she weeps.

"Oh, I am being so silly. Sorry, love." She sighs thickly, straightening up to wipe her tears again.

"No, don't be. We're sorry we didn't get here sooner. We would have come home first thing."

"Well, how could you? I only told Neve an hour or so ago because I couldn't get hold of either Jace or you," she says, pulling another tissue free, unaware of the bomb she has just dropped.

"Right, of course. Sorry. I just thought you had been trying us all weekend."

"Oh, no. I didn't want to worry anyone. When I knew Vik was stable, I decided to call Jace, but that was only at six this evening. Jace had mentioned taking you away. I didn't want to ruin your holiday."

"Marie. Don't feel like you can't ever call us. Please do, no matter what. We'd prefer to know."

"Yes, love." She sniffles and settles in for the ride. I watch her closely as my mind is whirring. So Neve only just found out. I have to give it to her: I admire how quick she is, turning something so serious to her own advantage at the drop of a hat. This whole situation has made me realise how callous she is. I wonder if she knew we were away, and that's why she has made a scene. A tumble of random thoughts all cross my mind, but I don't think I will ever be able to align my mind with hers. There is a wickedness about Neve that has never sat well with me. I should be thankful I'm not capable of thinking like her.

It's another twenty minutes before we arrive at Marie and Viktor's house. Viktor's success in business shines through from the three-story townhouse in central London. The street lamp glows a spotlight on the cute and well-cared-for garden.

I see Marie up to the door. Her hand is shaking, so I help her in and find that their house is a stunning array of famous artwork and antique statues.

"Here, let me make you a drink. You take one sugar, right?" I ask, taking her bag and placing it on a gold studded armchair in the entryway.

"Please. I'm just going to grab a fleece. I'm a little cold." It is cold in here, but I think it's more that her adrenaline is wearing off, and she is a little in shock.

"Maybe pop the heating on too," I suggest and begin sorting her drink. I go about flicking the odd lamp on, drawing warmth from them before she comes down, makeup-free, and looking completely shattered. I follow her into the living room, which is just as tasteful as the rest of the house. "I didn't realise you were both art lovers?" I say, happy that we have that in common: that and our love for Jace.

"Oh, yes, we have a fair few pieces dotted around the place. Viktor and I would love to come to the gallery sometime."

"Well, you're both more than welcome. I do currently have a piece in at the moment that I think you would both like," I say. It would be perfect in their home. It's a landscape of Paris, and the colours are everything this house is: gold's, beiges, and a slight flare of red. Their home is truly beautiful, and probably the kind of home I would have aspired to have for myself had I not fallen for Jace and The Hub.

"We have been looking for a new piece in the hallway. We auctioned the previous one to a charity for domestic abuse," she murmurs, lost in thought.

"He will be okay, Marie. He is a formidable man."

"That he is."

"Would you like me to stay? I don't mind. I don't really feel comfortable leaving you alone?" I ask, sipping on my drink.

"Would you mind? I do feel a little shaky." Her admission is followed by more tears. Placing my cup down, I go to her and sit beside her as she weeps.

"Of course I don't mind. He will be okay. I have no doubt. Jace won't let anything happen to him." My voice is full of soft conviction. Jace would move heaven and earth for that man. I still don't know their story, and now is not the time to pry, but he loves Viktor and Marie.

"His health is declining, and this time he looked scared. I feel like his time is running out."

Oh, god, poor Marie, I can't imagine how worried she must feel, and I'm scared I'm not going to say the right thing. This brings back memories of how distraught Jace was when Adam attacked me.

"He won't leave you, Marie. I feel like your story still has plenty of pages to fill."

"What a lovely thing to say." She sniffs, and her delicate fingers dab her eyes.

"I know Jace has been worried about his health after the last scare. We will all have to be extra strict with him." I smile.

"He will hate that. He thinks he is indestructible."

"Hopefully, this is the wake-up call he needs." My reply is cut off when my phone rings. "That's probably Jace." I get up and fish my phone out as Marie tells me she is going to sort the spare room for me.

"Hey."

"Are you home yet?" His deep voice is quiet. I know he will be sitting beside Viktor in that dimly lit room, with all those machines beeping and assessing his vitals.

"No, I'm going to stay with Marie for the night. She broke down in the car and just now."

"I feel sick that she has been dealing with this alone," he confesses shakily. I know his head will be in his hands as he punishes himself.

"I did want to talk to you about that. I felt so bad seeing her cry like that, and I apologised again, saying we would have been there this morning, but she said she hadn't even contacted anyone until this evening, as she hadn't wanted to worry us." I deliver the news on a soft murmur, knowing he will either get angry at me for constantly putting up a wall with Neve, or he will direct it where it should be. At her.

"Is that so?" he scoffs. Oh, he is mad.

"I shouldn't have said anything, but I was just as shocked. She tried us at six this evening, then called Neve. I know she is your friend, Jace, but she purposely made you feel bad. She really doesn't like me, and I think this just goes to sh—"

"Lily." He sounds impatient. "I really don't want to get into a Neve hate-fest right now." Wow. I bite my lip and swallow the argument rushing up my throat. I know I don't like her, but I have always tried my hardest to be polite to her. Be welcoming. She is outright rude to me, and Jace never backs me up. My frustration at the undercurrent she is causing in our relationship is stewing, and I wish he would acknowledge her for what she is rather than making me put up with it. Is it because he thinks I'm weaker than her, give in quicker, or am easier to handle?

"Sorry. I shouldn't have said anything." I know Viktor is our priority, but surely he can see how twisted Neve is—why on earth would she do that?

"You should, but not now." He sounds so tired. I wish I could be there with him. He is hurting, and I can't help from here.

"Okay. How are you doing? Any news?" I ask, trying to change the subject.

"No changes. He is still asleep. The nurse is happy with how he is. They caught it just in time, and she doesn't think it will have affected his mobility or speech."

"That's good then."

"As soon as he wakes, we will know for sure."

"Do you need me to bring anything tomorrow? I know Neve is heading in, but I can grab you a change of clothes."

"No, don't worry. Neve is grabbing some bits I have at the office and bringing my laptop."

"Oh, okay." Why is she doing it? Surely that's my place as his girlfriend, or am I being possessive? I rub at my head, trying to dispel the on-coming headache. I feel like, no matter how long I am with Jace, she will always find a way to squeeze into a spot just between us.

He must hear or sense my withdrawal.

"It makes sense. You have the gallery, so Neve can drop my things off."

I clear my throat and close my eyes. It sounds reasonable, so why does my heart feel like it's being gnawed at?

"Yeah, sure." Marie comes back down and looks at me expectantly. "No changes," I tell her. "Marie is here. I will pass her over. Night, Jace." I give her the phone and stand quickly, taking out cups and washing them up.

I really don't want to be sharing him with Neve in any capacity. It's bad enough that she works with him, and I know how she feels about him: I see it in the ways he looks at him, how she speaks of him, and the misplaced anger at me for just being there. What hurts most is that he does still turn to her. I know relationships are new to him, but he would hate me to turn to another man for things. I know that much about Jace, so why can't he reciprocate and keep her at a distance?

Chapter Seventeen

I'm on my way to the gallery, feeling as though my heart is in a vice. Despite Jace's assurances, I feel guilty for carrying on as normal. A member of his family is unwell, and I need to be there for him. I make a decision and call Hat and tell her to take the morning off and that we will open up this afternoon.

"Are you sure you don't want me to open this morning? It's no bother."

"I feel bad if I ask that," I say. I don't want her thinking I am just dumping everything on her.

"Lily, honestly, it's for a few hours. I will be fine, and if I'm not, I can give you a call. Go and check on Viktor, and I will see you in a bit."

"Have I told you that you're a star?"

"Always. I'm happy to do it. See you later."

"Sure. See you." I make a quick dash to the shop to grab some lunch for everyone and head straight to the hospital. Being here, in this whitewashed place, gives me a sense of dread. I don't know whether it's because it reminds me of my attack or my mother's death, but the general sense of dread hoops around my neck and lies there, making me feel unsettled. I hurry to Viktor's room only to find it empty.

What the hell? Has he been discharged? No one said anything. I quickly head back to the ward reception and find Viktor has been moved to a private room. Of course he has. I take the lift up to the third floor and make my way along the corridors until I come to a private ward. There, a smiling nurse guides me to the room.

"Mr Klein is just through the doors on your right." I give her a nod of thanks and push inside. I stop short when I find Neve standing between Jace's knees, his head resting on her stomach. They jump apart, and I blink in shock. I open my mouth to say something, anything, when Marie comes in behind me.

"Hello, love, it's nice to see you here," she says, giving me a quick hug. I smile and drop my gaze to the floor. I really want to be imagining things, for my mind to be overactive, but none of this feels okay to me. I know they are friends, and I repeat that mantra over and over again as Marie gives me a little squeeze of thanks. Through it all, I somehow find my voice.

"I picked you all some lunch up for later. I know what hospital food is like." I keep my gaze fixed on the bag as I begin pulling things out. "Jace, I got you a BLT. Marie, I wasn't sure what you liked." I clear my throat, trying to disguise the emotion there. "Or you, Neve, so I just grabbed a few to choose from." I can feel the hot press of tears behind my eyes. I hate that he is seeking comfort from her. He hasn't even spoken to me this morning. I feel like I'm being made a mockery of.

"Lily, thank you. That's so kind." I lift my head and plaster a bright smile on my face. Marie takes over, looking in the bag. "This is great, thank you, love."

"Any update?" I ask, keeping my gaze averted from Jace. Neve is no longer between his legs but leaning against the wall. I feel like I caught them in a moment, and despite him being my partner, once again, it feels as if I'm the interloper—like I shouldn't be here. I don't actually feel as though I am wanted here. Jace hasn't said a word to me.

I decide to leave.

"No, he woke briefly, but not enough to gauge how he is." I nod when Marie speaks up.

"That's a good sign, though, that he is responsive. Well, I have to get to the gallery, so I'll probably call later." I throw a quick smile around the room, my eyes briefly landing on Jace's guilt-ridden ones.

"I'll walk you down." His voice rumbles roughly.

"No need." My smile is brittle, and he knows without a shadow of a doubt that I am not okay with this, and his guilty face only proves I'm right to feel off about it all. I know he will accuse me of being dramatic and selfish, and a part of me knows I am. This isn't about me, but I'm feeling really unhinged with her around, and I know deep in my gut that she isn't to be trusted. I step out of the room and begin walking quickly through the ward and out into the main corridor. I hear the door swing open behind me, and I know it's him. I head for the lifts and press the down button, my eyes stinging with pent-up emotion.

The lift pings, and I rush in as I hear my name being called. I'm alone in the lift, and I'm grateful no one witnesses me pressing the button furiously to close the doors. Jace's arm and body slides through the closing gap, and I stare at him, trying so hard not to show my hurt and confusion or my anger because I am feeling all that and then some. What is the damn deal with her?

"Hey, it's not what it looks like." He pulls me to him, and I go stiff and twist free.

"I'm not doing this," I tell him, "like you said, now is not the time." I remind him of his own words, and he gives a short laugh.

"Jesus, Lily. It's not the time. You're right. Yet you are still getting pissed any time she comes near me!" he snaps. "She is my friend."

"Okay."

"My . . . Viktor is laying in that bed, and you are getting pissed because I gave one of my longest friends a hug."

"No, Jace. I don't like it because she straight out lied to you yesterday to make you feel shit. It worked, and yet you're still seeking comfort from her and not me. You tell me to come to you always, yet you never turn to me. Ever. You go straight to her."

"It's a force of habit." He chews his lips, seeing I'm on the verge of tears.

"Well, enjoy your habit. I've got work to do."

"You are being so selfish!" he snaps, and I know he is right. Viktor is unwell, and I'm having a bad case of insecurity.

"I know!" I snap back. The lift pings to a stop, and a few people step in. Jace and I stand in silence all the way down until we are out and walking through the car park.

"So you admit you're selfish," he says to my back as I weave through the cars. I whirl on him so that we both come to a halt between vehicles.

"No, I admit at this moment, I am being selfish. Because even though I know there is a sick man in one of those beds, I still can't stand the sight of you in her arms. She's so damn rude to me, no matter how nice I am, yet it's me who is told to be patient, accept her, and try for you." I point at him.

"I know you try with her," he says quietly.

"She doesn't reciprocate. I endure her little digs, and I don't bite. I keep up appearances for you. But, yes, seeing you turn to her twice for comfort, when I am right there, is like being kicked in the heart with a hammer because she isn't just your friend. She is in love with you, Jace!"

"It's not like that," he grates out. His face twists in frustration.

"You're that blind to it. Jesus, Jace, wake up." I grind my teeth because he is either in denial or acting dumb, but neither makes me feel better.

"We have known each other since we were kids. Of course she loves me. We're as good as family. You're bein—"

"Do not say unreasonable or over the top because whether you claim friendship or not, a woman knows when someone else is trying to make a move."

"It was just a hug. It doesn't mean anything."

"It does to me, Jace. I will never expect you to walk away from her, even though the truth is screaming in your face, but I can't watch you give into her all of the time and placate her because it's easier to ask it of me than her."

Jace frowns.

"What? I don't give in to her."

"No? You ask me to try with her, to put up with her, but I don't see her trying. You have no idea how underhanded she can be when you're not there. You turn to her, and it's what she wants, and it hurts. It hurts me," I whisper. I feel stupidly emotional and completely ridiculous because even though I am hurting, Viktor is sick, and I have made this about me, and I hate that I have. "I'm going to work."

"Lily, can we talk, please? You know how I feel about you. She really is just a friend. I'm sorry." He tugs me, but I don't want to go to him. I just want to leave and call Cass.

"I need to go," I say.

"Lily, wait. I don't want you to go when you are upset."

"Answer me one thing. Why did you both jump apart when I walked in?"

"Because I knew you would be upset." He swallows. His eyes are tennis balling between mine, vividly watching for any reaction.

"Knew it, but still did it anyway. Nice. I'll speak to you later. I just want to get to work." My murmur is low and full of unease.

"Lily, if I caught you hugging Sean, I wouldn't act this way," he says as I back up.

"Sean isn't in love with me. You couldn't bear Travis coming near me, and that's because although I have only ever viewed him as a friend, you, as a man, could sense he was interested—to you, he was a threat." His jaw works. "It works like that for women too."

"I'm with you," he says resolutely.

"Well then, maybe stick that home to her a bit more. I know it probably hurts her that I'm suddenly around, and I'm sorry, but it doesn't sit well with me. I'm not okay with it. I try with her. I try so damn hard, Jace, and she barely looks at me—maybe she should learn to try," I say quietly.

A couple walks past us and looks at our little standoff. Heat rushes to my cheeks as they get in their car. I turn and begin to walk away to my car, which is a short distance away. I never wanted to have this conversation like this, or at all, and I feel so childish arguing about something that is so evident. This feeling has been there in the back of my mind ever since I met her, more so when I had to listen to her go on about all his conquests—and he let her. He never reins her in or tells her to be respectful. I blow out a deep breath and unlock my car as thick arms come round my waist.

"I'm sorry. I can see why you're upset, and I'm guilty. She is hard to handle, so it's easier to ask you to be accommodating. It's a shitty thing for me to do, and I'm sorry." He breathes roughly into my ear.

I could cry with relief. Finally.

I sag into his wide chest, chewing my lip before I twist into his arms.

"I don't want us to fight, Jace. I don't want to come between you and your friends, but even *they* have warned me about her." He frowns, and his cheeks heat. Yes, it's not just me being irrational. "You're hurting her because she is in love with you, Jace," I tell him softly. He blinks, unsure, and sighs, seemingly lost in thought. He really doesn't see it. I feel for him. How can he not notice?

"Give me a kiss," he murmurs, looking down at me. I search his eyes and find tiredness there. I feel awful for bringing this all up now. I lift and peck his mouth, but he has other ideas. He cups my face and sweeps his tongue in on a moan. "Last night was long. I missed you," he confesses between kisses.

"I missed you too. Are you staying again? If so, I think I'll stay at my apartment." I'm pressed into my car, but he soon shifts and looks down at me, annoyed.

"Why? The Hub is our home. Why go to the apartment?"

"It's closer if you need me." He smiles, and my heart does that stupid flip. Hot ambers burn down at me, and I bite my lip. It's that look—the one where I know all that is in his head is sex. He leans into me, and I feel it, the hot hard press of his arousal. His phone buzzes in his pocket, and Jace snaps back, pulling it free.

"He's awake!" he says, elation and fear rolling over his features and relief filling his glazed eyes.

"Go," I tell him, pushing him back to the hospital. "I'll call you when I get to work so you can update me," I say quietly.

"You're not coming back?" he asks on a frown, his tone baffled.

"I want to, but I'm not sure. I'm not family, so . . . " I know how strict hospital rules are, and rightly so.

"You're coming, Lily." He takes my hand, and we make quick work of the car park and hospital, rushing back to Viktor's room.

I find it odd that Neve is sitting outside in the corridor on a chair and wonder if I will be allowed in.

She stands as she sees us, and her eyes narrow at our clasped hands.

"Only fami—"

"We are family," Jace says brusquely. He pushes open the door and pulls me in. Jace's face crumples, but he doesn't shed a tear. He walks straight to Viktor, who looks beyond ecstatic that Jace is here, and gets pulled into a bear hug. "You're going to make me grey," Jace states. His tone is thick with emotion. I blink at Marie, who is already crying, and my own tears slip over.

"You silly bunch." Viktor laughs deeply. "I'm fine, look." He holds his arms out, showing just how okay he is. No sign of a slur or issues with mobility. He is so lucky. "My Marie acted so fast that this stroke practically ran away!" He laughs. He is overjoyed, maybe it's the dance with death that's making him so excited, but I'm surprised he is in such good spirits and so energetic.

"You had us all worried," I say. Jace grasps Viktor's hand, and Victor throws him a loving smile, pats his hand, and ruffles his hair.

"You not going to cry too?" His brow lifts as he directs his question to Jace.

"No, nice try." They both laugh, and I roll my eyes at Marie, who is trying to look busy, moving things about and neatening the bag at the end of Viktor's bed.

"Have they said much to you?" Jace asks.

"Stats are good. I'm in for observations tonight, but probably out tomorrow. It'll take more than that to ruin my retirement."

"You retired because of the first scare."

"Never, I just made you all think that. Right, who has some chocolate? I'm bloody starving!" he announces as the nurse walks back in.

"Chocolate will have to wait. Lunch is being served now, and we have ordered you the lentil casserole." Viktor's face sours, and Jace coughs on a laugh he is holding back.

"Now, do I look like a man that eats lentils?" He addresses the nurse, his voice playful.

"No, Mr Klein, but you also are out of other options as we ordered the lunches earlier, and that is all that is left."

"This damn stroke is becoming an inconvenience."

"Oh, only now it is?" I laugh, and the others laugh too.

"Now, I know they only let family in. Does this mean you have some news for me—good news?" He leans to check my ring finger, and I go bright red and garble.

"Not quite yet. I'm still getting her used to the idea of living with me," Jace admits with a wink. My whole chest fires with butterflies at his open response. I give Viktor and Marie a small smile and allow Jace to tuck my hand in his.

For the next hour, we chat about work and Viktor's discharge. Jace is collecting him so Marie can get things in order at home. Viktor starts to look sleepy, and Jace stands.

"Right, old man, you get some rest. I will be here tomorrow to take you home," he says, leaning to give him a quick cuddle. "No dying on me. I like you," Jace mutters, and Viktor chuckles.

"Shame, you're starting to piss me off; far too bossy."

Jace seems far lighter as we leave. Neve isn't waiting outside. I would have thought she would have wanted to know how he was since she has been here all morning.

The next few days follow the same pattern. Jace spends his days working from Viktor and Marie's, and I then join them for dinner. On the fourth day, I suggest they come to us for dinner.

"We'd love to have you over." I chance a look at Jace and see his eyes burning back at me. It's the first time I have openly acknowledged we are living together. "Of course, only if Viktor is feeling up to it. It will give Marie a break. It won't be strenuous—just here to ours," I say on a swallow after Marie declines.

"I will definitely have to help, or else we'll all be eating charred food." Jace winks at me, causing Viktor to laugh. I shrug on a chuckle.

"Look, I never said it would be a nice meal." My joke brings laughter all around.

"Let's do it. A change of scenery will do us some good, Marie, and like Lily says, it's not strenuous. I'm just going from one house to another." Marie is so frightened to let Viktor out of her sight, and I thought this would be a good way to lower her guard.

"I suppose so."

"I'll drive you both over and back again," Jace says, leaning back in his seat. His arms slings along the back of mine, where his fingertips trail up and down my back.

"Great, I will grab some bits for dinner tomorrow." I know for a fact that Viktor loves seafood, so I thought I could make a big risotto. I'm already planning my day tomorrow, so I can whip and grab all the bits.

"I'm looking forward to it." Viktor sighs. He still looks worn out, but he is so much better. I've become so attached to them both since being in Jace's life. They are both so selfless. I want to make sure I'm here for them as much as they were for me after Adam's attack. The one thing I have found odd, but I'm keeping studiously quiet about, is that Neve hasn't been on the scene. I recall Marie seeming shocked she was even at the hospital, and now Viktor is home, she hasn't even popped in one evening to check on him. I don't believe she was or is remotely concerned for Viktor. It was all about Jace—a way in. I really hope she isn't going to be a problem for us.

"Are you ready to head home?" Home. Those four letters make my chest flutter. It's silly to think how fast I ran from this man, and yet now we are living together. I don't think I have ever experienced this level of love for another person. My love for Jace isn't just face value. It goes so deep, deep to the bone, further still, to the furthest recesses of my mind and soul. He seems to be able to read me so well, to anticipate my needs, and always be a step ahead of me, and in return, I am determined to love him like he's never been loved before. I have no doubt in my mind that Jace hasn't had it easy. He never talks about his parents, and although I am desperate to ask, I can see he views both Viktor and Marie as that. I don't wish to offend him by suggesting otherwise.

"Yeah, sure. Are you sure you don't want help with the washing up?" I ask Marie, who is already picking up the odd pot.

"God, no, we'll see you tomorrow." We say our goodbyes, and Jace and I drive home in our own cars. He, of course, gets there far quicker than me—I've never known someone to drive so fast!

By the time I finally pull up, the house is lit up like a Christmas tree, and I know it will be a hell of a lot warmer than my car. I lock the door and head up the steps, surprised I can't see Jace with it being so bright. As soon as I push through, the lights all shut off with a loud whir. All the power is out. What the hell!

"Jace?" I shut the door and wait for his response, but nothing, not a single sound. Unease spreads over me, and although I will it not to, my heart begins to palpate with fear. "Jace, please don't mess with me. I never admitted it before, but I'm not a fan of the dark!" I say with an awkward laugh. I pull my phone out of my jacket and use the torch to look around the house. "Jace, this isn't funny! Where are you?" I sound annoyed, and I don't want to be, but after Adam, I feel so skittish in these situations.

"I'm right here," he breathes from behind me. What the hell? I jump and fall back into him.

"That's not funny," I whine.

"I know it's not. The power was out when I got back. I got it working for a few minutes, then nothing." He kisses my cheek. "I'd never let any harm come to you, anyway."

"Sorry. I got a little freaked out. So do you think it's a power cut then?"

"Yeah," he mutters as the lights flicker on. Jace grins. "Hopefully, it will stay on now. He's not coming back, you know." He means Adam, and I nod, biting my lip. "You're safe, Lily."

"Why would it go out? It's not stormy." I look around the house, looking for anything out of place.

"Hey, relax. Honestly, it's happened before. I think I share electric with the village over the fields. It's a few miles away, but if they are having work done, it will affect us too. It's probably been like it all day."

"Oh well, I hope it sorts itself out. Otherwise we won't be able to have Viktor and Marie round," I say, taking my coat off and kicking my shoes under the sideboard. "I hate these shoes. They kill my feet."

"Why wear them then?"

"They look nice," I retort as the lights shut off again, and I squeak in a panic. Jace's laughter carries. I feel his fingers, and then he is pulling me to him. "How am I supposed to get ready for Stanley's event?" I've been looking forward to this evening for weeks.

"Pack a bag, and we'll get ready at The Loft, and in the meantime, I'll get my electrician out." I grin happily at him in the dark. Perfect!

Chapter Eighteen

With Jace wanting to accompany me to Stanley Ebon's annual gallery event, I gave Harriet the night off so we have The Loft to ourselves. I've chosen a black wrap dress and nude heels, and I'm dithering about with what jewellery to wear when two hands move past my head, and a cold object trickles around my neck. My eyes fly to Jace, then to my neck in the mirror where he is holding a delicate necklace with a simple teardrop diamond in the centre. My fingers run the length on my neck, feeling the chain, before circling the diamond.

"I . . . Jace this is—"

"Does that mean you love it?" He clips it into place and drops his chins to my shoulder as his hands find my waist. "You look stunning."

"Yes, I love it, but why?" I don't understand why he has gifted me this.

"Because I love you, gorgeous, and I know I hurt you for turning to Neve." I chew my lip at his words. I don't want to say much more about it, as we've been over it all, and since then, I feel like he truly knows how out of place I feel when he allows her to barge her way between us. "I didn't want you to see me that way. I feel all these emotions with you that I can't contain, and honestly, I've never been like this. It makes me sound like a huge wuss." He laughs. I turn and kiss him.

"You're not a wuss."

"I know, but I'm always saying all these things that I would never have even thought of before, like how damn innocent your grey eyes are now. It brings me to my knees. See, wuss," he jokes.

"Well, you bring me to my knees too."

"I wish I did. I'd be feeling pretty damn happy right now."

I quip my brow and ignore his comment.

"Maybe later." I wink. Okay, so I didn't ignore him completely. "I like that you say those things to me."

"I know you do; that's why I say them. Is this dress new? It's a little revealing." He runs his finger down the low V created by the wrapped material.

"It's not. It just seems it now as the necklace is making you look there." He frowns and goes to remove the necklace. "Nope! I'm keeping it on. I love it. Honestly, Jace, it's beautiful." I kiss him again, and his smile turns lopsided. Cupping my face, he leans right in and gives me the kind of kiss that would win an award—the slow, tongue-curlingly-deep kind that sets me on fire. I come up panting, and he winks.

"No wandering off. I need every man to know that the sex on legs in the naughty black dress is mine." He pecks my lips and checks his own collar in the mirror over my head.

"I think I can do that."

Ebony Art is nothing like my sweet little Loft. It was originally an old swimming pool. I have been once or twice, and both times, I have been in awe of the space. Some of the original pool remains, running a narrow strip through the centre of the main gallery to make a tranquil water feature. Beyond this, walls of art and more rooms showcase some of the most renowned artists. It is easily one of the most exclusive galleries in London. Stanley Ebon is not what I would call a friend, but we call on each other from time to time to borrow art, so receiving his invite was a big surprise and the perfect time to network.

Jace and I arrive just before opening. He helps me out and threads his fingers with mine, giving them a possessive squeeze.

"I'm taking further precautions," he says on the last squeeze.

"Precautions. What do you mean?" We walk hand in hand across the road. The exterior is lit up like a beacon; soft purple lights make the black window sills seem both extravagant and mysterious. It's cleverly done. I know Stanley won't just make this about art; he will throw one of the biggest parties. I'm a few steps ahead of Jace, eager to get in and see the art, but Jace gently tugs me back, holds our hands up, and squeezes tighter for effect.

"Precautions. I knew at the first sign of art you'd be blinkered and wandering off. I'm keeping you locked in, witch. Our hands are not parting."

"What if I need the toilet?" I pout. He seems playful, so I enjoy this for what it is.

"Then I will stand outside until you are done. But our hands are one tonight." Conviction rolls from his mouth. He is being deadly serious; as much as his eyes are sparkling like crazy, he really is keeping me close by.

"What are you so bothered about?" I ask. He pulls back on a frown and looks around. Is there something he isn't telling me?

"Nothing, I just want to make sure I keep my gorgeous lady by my side all night. Is that too much to ask?" It's him who is pouting now. His amber eyes are like honey-coated diamonds, and I shake my head in a grin and lift to peck his mouth.

"Great, now I have lipstick face."

"This stuff was expensive. There is no way it is coming off," I tell him, encouraging us along the path, as he drops his mouth to my ear.

"Shame, I was looking forward to seeing that smudged on my cock later."

I gape at him, then bite my lip.

"I have a cheaper one," I tell him and giggle when he growls into my neck.

"Witch."

"Brute." Jace grins devilishly at me, and we head towards the entrance, where I slip the tickets from Jace's inner jacket pocket to hand them over. We are given champagne on entry. It's still early, but the inside is a hive of activity. Soft lighting throws an alluring glow over the artist's work. The photographs show pain, shame, hurt, angst, love, and happiness, all caught within a second but telling years of pain, and speaking days of hurt. The work is sensational. I head straight over to a piece that is shrouded in amber light—amber like Jace's eyes. The photograph is black and white and solely of the side of someone's face. They are crying, but also smiling. It's a beautiful picture.

"Look at how they have caught the light. Can you see how defined that tear is? It's genius," I turn to say and find Jace smiling down at me. "What?" I ask, sipping quickly on my flute of champagne.

"You go all glassy-eyed. It's nice to see."

"I love art," I say simply.

"I know. Do you like this?" He nods at the photograph.

"I do," I say quietly, turning back and staring at it. I'm looking at someone's deepest emotions on a big glossy print. Whoever captured this image caught this person's soul-deep happiness. Their love. It's shining from their eyes, reflected in their tears, and it's truly beautiful. Their smile isn't perfect, but it makes it all the more pure. "They don't even know they've been captured. They have no idea, but it's there for us all to see."

"I hope they know. Otherwise I think they'd find it intrusive," Jace says. An older man steps up beside us, wearing a suit and sporting an impressive goatee.

"My fiancée–she knew about the photo," he winks. "I asked her to marry me." He throws a gloating look at us. "As you can tell, she said yes."

"It's so beautiful; the light; what you've don—"

"Yes, that took some setting up. I needed the right light for this. I wanted to ensure I caught enough of her face that it would hold on to each curve, see here," he points, and Jace manoeuvres us to the side to allow him room, "she actually has a scar along her cheek, but the light disguises it. She thanked me for that, but I wanted the scar." As I look along the wall, I see they are all of his fiancé.

"She is my muse," he says, following my gaze.

"Berin Rhodes." He holds out his hand. I recognise the name instantly. I had tried to borrow a piece of his from Alfredo for my event, but it had been sold. He is big in the states.

"Lily Spencer." Jace briefly frees my hand so I can shake Berin's, then it's back in his.

"You own The Loft. You're a friend of Alfredo's," he says. Wow, I'm shocked. I didn't think this man would have come across my name.

"Yes, and this is Jace Bennett, my partner." Berin and Jace shake hands, and when Berin's fiancée appears, we fall into a steady conversation. I'm yet to see Stanley, but for the time being, I'm going to network and get my name out there too.

As the evening wears on, Jace and I walk around the room. Seeing Berin and Olivia from afar, they seem a really nice couple. I'm looking about the room for Stanley when a stocky man with white hair and a protruding belly comes straight to Jace, beaming.

"Ah, thank god. Another non-artsy male." He grins toothily at Jace, who seems to know this man.

"Sort of. This is Lily, my partner. She is a gallery owner, so it comes in the fine print that I'm quite partial to art these days. Roger, how are you?" Jace asks. Roger pats at his wide belly, sucking in short breaths. Jesus, he looks like he is going to keel over. I give Jace a worried glance.

"Good, good," he huffs. "Gwen is about somewhere. She will be happy to see you," he says breathlessly. I feel sorry for him. It's not that hot in here, but with his three-piece and weight, he must be stifling.

"I didn't realise you were both here," Jace says and frowns, looking around the room. I'm assuming Gwen is this man's wife, or maybe a friend? Jace must know them both. A decorative set of nails comes over Jace's shoulder as a stunning blonde woman circles him, all lowered lashes and a soft smile.

"Hello, Jace," she breathes, and I just know with every fibre of my being that they have slept together,

"Here she is. Lily, this is my wife, Gwen." Wife? So Jace slept with Roger's wife—his much younger wife? I hope it was before she decided to set her sights on Roger's failing figure. The man is at least twenty years her senior. I'm not one to judge anyone for their age gap, but when the man looks like he is close to a string of heart attacks and the woman is a stunning model of a female, I judge. I'm judging now, judging her for ogling Jace right in front of my face.

"I knew you would remember Jace." Roger looks at me. "Jace designed our new build," he says, I nod out of politeness, but Jace has gone stiff by my side.

"How could I forget?" Gwen replies on a purr, her eyes searching Jace's face heatedly. Roger can't be that dumb, surely?

"Nice to see you again." Jace's strained voice is anything but nice; he is not comfortable with this at all. "We're actually off to find Stanley. He is a friend of Lily's. Excuse us," he says, adjusting his clammy hand in mine and giving them a curt nod. He tugs me along, and I stare at the back of his head. I knew he had a past, and that it was probably colourful—but married women! It makes my throat sore, and my chest ache. I didn't expect that of him, and I'm judging *him* now too. I'm quiet as he pulls us along until we circle a big statue, and he can nudge me back behind a white gauze curtain.

"I know you are thinking the worst, and I deserve it. I was a stupid, selfish guy, and I hate that part of me. I'm not like that anymore. That was me before you, Lily." His eyes go from the floor to me, and he is pleading with me. "That was before, and it sickens me that I was so callous with women. Then you come along, and it's the biggest wake-up call. Like every curse I'd had to listen to before, every insult I had received from being such a . . . a dick came crashing down, and all I could think was no one had better have ever done that to her. How will she even like me if she knows?"

I can't formulate any words or take in what he is saying, so I blink away and pull in a soft breath.

"She's married, Jace," I whisper. Does he not care?

"I know, and it was wrong. It was over a year ago. She wouldn't leave me alone, and after a while, I just gave in because I didn't owe it to anyone not to. I didn't care for her or Roger. I still don't."

"I think I need to nip to the toilets," I say in a quiet croak. My murmur is met by a short hiss of pleas, but I gently tug free, place my champagne flute on the nearest tray, and walk quickly to the ladies. As soon as I'm inside and locked in a cubicle, I fire a quick message to Cass.

Can't talk but just had the pleasure of meeting one of Jace's conquests, and her husband! Oh, god, Cass, I feel sick ☹

Her response is almost immediate.

Well, shit!!! Was she a dog? Kidding. We all have a past. Sean cheated, and you still accept him. Jace loves you. Don't let this get too you, hun x

. . .

I chew over her response. She is right, of course, but it still stings. I suck in a breath and just let it all sink in. I'm really no good with conflict of any kind. I feel, and I run. It's like my body won't allow me to acknowledge it there and then. I need a little time to swallow it all and process.

I still don't like what Jace did, but the fact of the matter is I can't change it. It's done. I can't let it affect us. I have to move on from it.

Thanks x

I tap back quickly, hearing the outer door swing shut as Cass messages me to call her if I need to. I flush the loo so it doesn't seem odd that I was in the cubicle and push free, heading straight for the sinks, when someone leaning at the end of the vanity draws my gaze. Gwen. I count to three in my head, waiting for her little comment. Surely that's why she followed me in here.

"Trouble in paradise?" she asks with a smirk. Her blonde hair is twisted into an elegant knot on her twig neck, and her collarbone could scratch her own eyes out, let alone mine. She is willowy and top-heavy, but I refuse to react yet. She must have seen Jace pull me aside. I wash my hands and turn my head to see her sizing me up. Size away, love, it's me he wants. How pathetic. My mind screams 'gold digger'.

"Not at all. Personally, if I were you, I'd be more concerned with my own love life than that of others, unless, of course, you can't actually bring yourself to sleep with that unassuming man." I dry my hands, ignore her gaping mouth, and walk past, throwing her a wink.

I don't know who is more stupid for even entering into that relationship, him or her. "Try and enjoy your evening, Gwen. I know I will." I leave with a gloating smile on my face and swoop up another glass of champagne as Stanley comes over.

"Finally! I didn't think I was ever going to get the chance to speak to you. You look fantastic," he says, leaning to peck my cheeks. He is donning a three-piece suit and a ridiculous amount of aftershave, but Stanley always does go over the top.

"The gallery looks incredible. I forget how beautiful it is. The turnout has been brilliant. I hope one day I get this kind of interest," I tell him honestly.

"Half of them just want to say they have been here. You know what people are like; they want to indulge enough to gloat," he huffs. I wonder if he isn't doing as great as this event suggests. I give him a sympathetic smile as I rest my flute on my arm, cupping my waist. It can be a sting to your pride. I felt that after my first event.

"Well, you'll be sure to get some sales tonight."

"Oh, yes. I just wish the nosey riffraff would bugger off." He gives a wave to someone across the room and points to a painting above my shoulder as Jace walks over. His eyes narrow when he sees Gwen leaving the 'Ladies' with a scowl on her face. "This one, I love. It's very loud, but it softens each time I see it," he says.

Jace nods at him and pecks my brow, and leaning, he says, "Jace Bennett. I'm Lily's partner."

"Stanley Ebon. I recognise your name. Why do I recognise your name?" He pouts, then steals my champagne. "You don't mind, do you? I have an awfully dry throat from talking the ears off of everyone." He passes it back while looking at Jace.

"Maybe through Bennett and Klein."

"Yes, of course. You did some work over the road, the new roof for the museum."

"That's right. Viktor, my business partner, is a huge art fan. We came over here once or twice," Jace recalls. He adjusts his stance, and

I do a double-take for the third time this evening. He looks incredible in a suit. He never told me he had been here before.

Stanley taps his tooth.

"Yes, I remember him not being well when you brought him out. I'm sure I read that somewhere." Stanley is like the social centre of Earth and knows all the gossip, and Jace gives an awkward laugh.

"Yes, pretty much. He is doing well, thanks, enjoying retirement." He doesn't mention his recent health scare, so I keep my lips firmly shut.

Stanley looks at me.

"This one is a little diamond—nice to look at and tough as hell. She drives a hard bargain." I blush profusely at Stanley's observation of me and find Jace giving me a pointed smirk.

"Only when the need arises," I say in defence with a wide smile on my face.

"Of course." Stanley winks. "You look gorgeous in that dress. Oh, there's Edward Humphreys. Excuse me." He pecks my cheeks again and smiles at Jace before striding off with a wave on his way to someone else.

"I feel like if I put him and Carl in the same room, there would be one hell of a cat-fight." I laugh lightly and wiggle my foot in my heel. My toes are aching, and I'm done for the night. I've met one or two new people and swapped business cards. I think most are on their way to being drunk, so there is no need for me to stay.

Jace clears his throat and twists me so I'm facing him. His hands are placed on the outer globes of my bum.

"I noticed Gwen leave the toilets after you." He frowns down at me, furiously chewing his lip. I run my finger along it, halting him.

"I don't think she will be bothering us again," I say. He grins. His eyes sparkle, and his nostrils flare with a smile.

"You put her in her place?" he says lightly.

"I did." I press onto my toes and peck his lips.

"Indulge me. What did you say?" His eyes are dancing wildly.

This is turning him on. My cheeks flush, so I lean into his ear and repeat my short encounter with Gwen to Jace.

"Fuck me, Lily." He moves his head enough to slant his mouth over mine.

I'm breathless.

"I know. I felt so good afterward." I giggle, embarrassed that I staked my claim on him like that. I'm as red as my lipstick, and the champagne is going to my head. "Take me home."

"Gladly."

Chapter Nineteen

With Jace running late, I figure Thai is off the menu, so I decide to make a stir-fry. It's quick, and the most talentless of people could make it, so I should find it a breeze.

Flicking the radio on and pouring myself a glass of wine, I go about making dinner and flit about, tidying things away. We left it in a mess this morning, so I fold the throws and plump the cushions. When the sound of tyres on gravel brings my head up, I notice it's not Jace's car; it's Neve's.

I groan loudly and move back to the kitchen, checking my reflection as I do. I hate to admit that she makes me feel unkempt and awkward.

She doesn't knock and walks straight in. "He's not here," I say and hold a glass up in the way of an offer. She takes it from me with a tight smile and proceeds to find herself a different wine, as though I may have contaminated the freshly opened one. I'm being dramatic, but the woman makes me so mad.

"He might be awhile," I tell her. She has her back to me, her concentration fixed on pouring the wine.

"I can wait," she states in a manner that means; *I'm waiting*.

"I didn't realise he was expecting you. I only put enough on for the two of us." I don't want her to stay, but I say what I know: Jace would want me to be welcoming. Neve sips her wine and moves around the kitchen slowly. She eyes me and takes a seat on the stool at the island. Her long blonde hair is curled with an art I can't perfect, her face is contoured, and she looks like a model in her leather jeans, lace trim top, and sky-high heels.

"I heard cooking wasn't your forte," she muses. Her lips twitch, and I feel the jibe right down to my toes because it means Jace has been discussing me with her, and I don't like it.

"Oh, it's not. Thank god, it's not my culinary skills he's after," I quip. It's quite possibly the most juvenile thing I have said in a long while, but god, she pulls this unwanted nasty side of me right out. I want to claw her eyes out. I catch the tail end of an eye roll and force myself to grit my teeth.

"I'll give him a call if you like?" I pick up my phone with the very thought of doing that.

"Don't bother. He'll be here shortly," she says with utter conviction. Her finger runs the rim of her glass, and she gives me a forced smile. Oh, he will? He rang not long ago to tell me he was running late. I raise my brows a little at her pointed remark. She's probably tracking him on GPS, I think bitchily.

I turn away, refusing to show interest.

Sensing my dismissal, she lifts her glass and says as she places it back down, "It's Friday, and we usually had dinner before you moved yourself in. He leaves around six forty and will be here for quarter to eight." I stare ahead at the wall, wanting to tell her I was asked to move in, but it's very obvious she has made her mind up about me and vice versa. Nor do I tell her he is running late.

"How observant of you," I mutter. What is this girl trying to prove? "So, you do want dinner then?" I try for kind, but it comes out in a bored huff.

Her laugh is sarcastic—the thought of eating my food repugnant, no doubt.

"No!" She scowls bitchily.

"Okay." I frown at her but turn to stir the vegetables. Fed up of her company already, I turn the radio up a notch more, happy to drown her out.

"You don't like me." It's not a question, but a callous statement aimed at causing more tension.

"I could say the same to you." I keep my face averted and flick a look up the drive, eager to see the headlights of Jace's car, but darkness mocks me by allowing me to see her spiteful gaze.

"I suppose I don't blame you," she hums. I feel my shoulders stiffen but force myself to relax. Is she goading me?

"Okay." I don't allow her room to elaborate, but her brashness knows no bounds.

"Especially for a girl like you." Her choice of words niggles me more. As though she sees me as some naïve twit.

"Meaning?" This time I do bite. But I don't satisfy her with an eager look. Instead, I begin mixing ingredients to make a sauce. I'm putting no love into it and considering my cooking skills are nil-to-none, Jace has little luck of it tasting better than the underside of a shoe.

"You seem the jealous type. Maybe a little insecure." She makes no apology for highlighting her personal observations of me. I'm not that person, but with her, those attributes have reared their ugly head. I turn then and swig my wine, using it to point to her. For the first time since Jace asked me to move in with him, I really feel this is my home, and she is making me feel uncomfortable in it. It's another tally on the hate board for me.

"Yet, here *you* are, trying to make a point. Surely that says more about you than me?" Dipping my head, I regard her pointedly and let my words sink in. I refuse to be intimidated by her and figure enough is enough. "You want Jac—"

"I've had Jace," she cuts me off, her glass slamming down as she stares at me pointedly across the island. I don't mean to flinch, but her words hurt me.

I knew it! Deep down. God, I knew it, but having it clarified stings. I blink my pain aside and swallow. I want my voice to be confident when I reply. Sighing, I neck the rest of my wine.

"We all do things in our teens. It's just life." I shrug her off and decide to take it up with Jace himself. Now Neve has confirmed it, he better be ready to fight to win my trust back. He lied to me. It's not until I lift the spoon to stir the simmering sauce that I realise I'm shaking.

"I'd hardly call the conference our teens, or your exhibition, but who I am to argue. You clearly think you have won the unobtainable." She laughs, and I drop the spoon.

My exhibition? The conference? That was barely a week ago!

"You're lying," I whisper. Anger and shock collide in my stomach and attack my heart. I can't hide how much I'm shaking or the lack of colour in my face.

"Why would I?" She shrugs confidently. "I have nothing to gain from lying, and I figured you suspected, so all I have done is cement the truth. I don't have to like you to know you don't deserve to be lied to." She flicks her hair back over her shoulder and watches me. Her harsh but beautiful face is locked on mine.

God, while I was regimented to a curfew, he was with her! Sleeping with her!

I swallow dryly, still in shock that he could be so callous. My mind sinks further back to the night of the exhibition as I recall the events that unfolded: her obvious irritation at being there, and her sly words.

"Thanks for coming," I had said.

That was the idea. She was mocking me even then, knowing she would be trussed up in bed with him. I feel sick to the stomach. We weren't even a couple, not really, but the conference? I'd moved in then. I was asleep in his bed while he used work as an excuse to fuck her. Was the mess up with the rooms another taunt from them both?

I don't understand. Why would he chase me if he has been continuing an affair with her? My stomach flips in an aggressive roll. I look up through the fog of pain to find Neve battling a smug smile.

"I have to hand it to you, Lily, you really caught his attention for a while, but he always comes back." She bites her lip and swirls her wine as Jace's car ambles down the drive.

She is so utterly sure of herself that his presence doesn't cause her concern, and that in itself makes my stomach drop like a lead weight. She shows no fear or worry for herself because she knows she won't lose him. *He always comes back.*

I watch as he gets out of the car, and sickness spirals in my stomach. I leave the pan and walk quickly to the bedroom to collect my handbag. I search for my charger, but I can't see it through the build-up of hot tears. In a rush, I grab the small pile of makeup and forgo the rest of my stuff.

I can feel my heart running a mile in my chest. I can't think about what she has just told me. Not fully. I'm not ready to comprehend it. Every cell is repelling it. The overwhelming need to flee is the driving force in my choppy actions. I hear the deep rumble of his voice, and it makes my chest squeeze. As quick as I take my next breath, I tell myself I hate him.

Jace walks straight to me with a look of worry etched on his face, and that is all the confirmation I need. His lie is out.

"Lily, wait. I don't know what she has said—" I bash past him. "Lily, what's wrong?" When he grabs my wrist, I swing and slap him hard. I have the sudden urge to pummel my fists into his face, but I use his shock to snap my arm free.

What's wrong? He knows. His face told me that already.

"What the fuck did you say?" he yells at Neve, who is unaffected by his outburst. She lifts her wine and rolls her eyes at him.

"The truth. She would have found out sooner or later." She is looking at him with an abundance of irritation. She raises her glass to me like she has done me a favour. In some ways, she has.

I rush to the door, but he captures me around the waist.

"Lily, please. Let me explain. Fucking hell, don't run." I twist and slam my hands into his chest, giving myself a little distance when he staggers back in horror.

I'm clutching my things to my chest to stop me from hitting him again.

"I asked you!" I shout. "I gave you the opportunity to be honest." I hiccup as the first rush of sob-fuelled tears hit.

"Baby, don't cry. I'm sorry." He moves but sees me flinch, and it's enough to momentarily stall him.

"You lied to me!" I shout. "You were fucking her!" My lip gives way, and it all comes out in a broken sob. When my hand comes up a second time, he grabs it and pulls me to him. I've always abhorred violence, but my god, I want to hurt him.

"Lily, please. Don't leave. Talk to me." His usually heavy, syrupy eyes are wide with panic, and his face has lost some colour.

"Get the fuck off me!" My wrist is held tight, and I can't get free.

Neve looks utterly bored but watches us, nonetheless. I want to care that she is here witnessing it all, but I'm too damn hurt. Pride leaves me with one foul, brutal sweep of pain.

Jace swings a look at her.

"Why?" he snaps. "It wasn't your place." He's seething, and he looks to me with remorse, worry, and guilt plastered over every inch of his face, but I don't care for any of it. In fact, it's the first time I have looked at him and found him unattractive.

"Or yours apparently," she mutters, necking the last of the wine in her glass.

"Lily, it's not what you think," he says in a rush.

"No?" I laugh sarcastically, "So you haven't been fucking your *friend*." My tone is scolding, and my lip curls in disgust. "She's like family. Nothing happened," I mimic. "Fuck you!"

"It's not like that." He keeps me at his front and rubs a hand over his face. "It's . . . she's—" He's looking everywhere, even to her for help, and his mouth opens and closes, but he can't draw the words together to explain. It wouldn't matter. I'm done.

"What?" I scream. He made me feel as though I was irrational, but I knew it. Deep down, I knew something was off!

"Yes, Jace, what am I?" Neve laughs.

"Shut up, Neve. In fact, please leave." He motions to the door. God, he actually thinks I'm going to stay. After this! He is deluded.

"Don't bother," I tell her. "I'm going. Don't fucking chase me this time." When I look at Neve, she's smirking at me. "He can come back to you as much as he wants now!" She shakes her hair out and locks my stare.

Deep down, I know this is what she wants, but I can't see past that he cheated and lied to me. Lied and allowed me to second-guess myself about feeling uncomfortable and uneasy around her, even when I gave him the opportunity to come clean so we could deal with it and put it to rest, he chose to lie.

"The truth always," I spit, and his face falls again. "Just not for me though, right?" I don't even want him to answer that.

"Lily, please."

"Do you love her?" I ask, my voice breaking. It shouldn't matter. It's inconsequential now. It's over, and I can't trust him, or her for that matter.

"It's not the same." He sighs. "Stay, talk to me?" he pleads softly.

"You can't have us both," I croak. I hate myself for uttering those words with her so close to enjoy them because she knows she has won.

"Don't make me choose," he whispers, and his hand goes lax.

"So you do love her then." My arm drops away. Who is this man?

"Yes, but it's not—" I flee, pushing open the door.

"Lily!" he roars, and I rush down the steps and to my car, yanking the door free and locking myself in. The tears come thick and fast.

Jace is banging on the window, but he twists momentarily and shouts back at her, standing on the porch. I can't hear what is being said, not through the drum of my heart in my ears and the loud sobs wracking me.

I choke out a sob and turn as he repeatedly pulls at the door handle.

"You bastard!" I scream, "You fucking bastard!"

His eyes are wide with worry.

"Don't drive. Not like this. Fucking hell, Lily." He is still trying at the handle, the force creaking the door, and panic is etched all over his face. A face I don't ever wish to set eyes on again. I turn the engine over and begin to move, but he moves with me, keeping hold of the car. I speed off, and Jace swears loudly before I'm flying down the drive, sobbing uncontrollably.

I'm well above the speed limit, and on my empty stomach, the alcohol is dancing a chaotic race through my veins. I don't call Cass or head home. I avoid the obvious and take the route to the gallery. I park haphazardly around the back and enter through the rear entrance. Despite my blurry lashes, I force my way into The Loft, lock myself in, head in the dark to my office and open the safe, flicking through the contents until I find the business credit card. It's an impulse that crashed into my mind on the drive and one I won't back down from.

I don't want to be anywhere he can get to me, and I know with every bone in my body that he will chase me. He doesn't know how to let me go. Some twisted part of him won't let this be. Everything I just learned about him, I hate—how could he do this?

The sound of my name being called from the entrance of the gallery, accompanied by the rattle of the door, makes me jump. My heart is splintering wildly once again, and his pained voice snatches my heart and pumps a whole new level of anger around my shaken body.

I stand shielded behind my office door, sheltering me from the owner of a voice I have loved from the very moment it graced my ears, and eyes that hypnotise me into the most euphoric states—just a piece of wood hiding me from the cause of such deep-rooted pain. My hand lifts onto the handle, but I drop it and take a few shaky steps backward, my eyes blinking another wave of fresh tears loose.

I rush out of the back, thankful the door automatically locks, and weave through the small alleyway that backs on to the little courtyard. I check the car park before I step out under the streetlamp and rush to my car, a wobbly mess.

I waste no time in zipping out and taking the turning that pushes me further from him. I think back to all the times he has been late or not answered his phone, times I never paid much mind to, times that seem likely opportunities to continue his playboy lifestyle.

My naivety mocks me, and I feel a complete fool for thinking I could ever handle or keep a man like him—a man who has never committed to anyone but himself.

I brush my wrist along my tear-coated cheek and pick up speed. I drive right into the heart of the city so I'm swallowed up by traffic, and my car becomes nondescript and my location a mystery. My heart feels heavy, and the painful ache and dread bouncing around in my stomach aren't helping.

I hate that I so easily acknowledge that these feelings will walk with me for a very long time, feelings that will attack me in the dark of the night when I'm alone and at my most vulnerable. These feelings will latch themselves to earlier heartbreaks, coupling up and standing in force against me. My lip quivers and a low wail exits my dry lips.

I don't understand any of it. Not how he could even do it to me, let alone why. My wicked thoughts ride with me until I come upon a hotel with underground parking. My heart does another painful, sickening swoop when I think of how available she is to him at work or if it even stops with her. I beg the plaguing thoughts to leave me alone.

They don't. Not when I mumble my way through my booking or when I mindlessly trudge to my room. I push in and barely acknowledge the small interior. I'm tormented by too much emotion and so many rancid and sickening thoughts that I yank up a pillow and scream into it. The thick material I have pressed to my lips muffles the high wail. I scream until my voice cracks, and my chest is heaving. I scream until I'm rushing into the bathroom and vomiting. I scream until I'm sobbing, and sleep is the only temporary reprieve from my troubled mind.

I wake in the early hours and pace in the tiny room. It's too small, too unfamiliar, and the lure of my own place is too great to ignore. My phone is chocker with messages and missed calls from Jace and Cass. I turn it off, not willing or ready to deal with anyone—even the thought of having to converse with the hotel clerk when I check out gnaws at me. I just want to slip away unseen. I grab the little I have and step out into the corridor. The hotel is silent and empty—a physical representation of how I'm feeling. I'm happy to find the main reception desk unoccupied, so I slide my key on the top and leave.

I walk quickly to my apartment after I edge my way down the street, looking for any sign of Jace. I push the door open. It's dark and peaceful, but my head is a jumble of chaotic thoughts. I click the door shut, and it comes then, in a bone-curling, painful ache, and I discard my bag on the sideboard with a loud crash as I lean into the wall.

The first sob is quiet, low, but once it's out, it unfurls into a shudder of long, muted sobs. I want to hit something. I want this pain to end.

"Lily?"

I jump, choking on a scream. Jace stands, making himself visible, as the moonlight pulls him into view. My throat swells with pain, and I drop my head.

"Leave," I whisper as I realise I'm shaking like crazy. "*Get out,*" I repeat more forcefully, desperately. I can't bear to look at him, so I don't. I keep my head averted.

"Please. I need to explain." His voice cracks.

"GET OUT!" I grab the nearest thing and launch it at him. It smashes, and whatever it was echoes off the walls in a sharp crack, and my gaze turns narrow and cold.

He walks towards me, hands out,

"Hey, hey. Calm down." His hands are shaking. "Listen to me. I can explain. I need to explain," he croaks weakly.

"I don't want you to. Get out." I pull the door open wide and stare at him hard as tears run thick and fast down my cheek. "Thanks for coming." I push through gritted teeth. It takes a moment for my words to register, and when they do, his eyes widen, then sadden. He drops his head and takes a few steps toward the door, as he drags in a deep breath and runs a hand up the back of his neck.

"I never meant to hurt you." He stands in the doorway, and I see the key in his grasp. He is looking hopefully at me, obviously feeling that he has my attention, and he refuses to let the chance slip by. "Never," he says as he swallows thickly, his own lips shaking. "You need to know that." I can't keep my eyes on his, not when I feel this distressed and enraged.

"My key, please." I don't know where this strength is coming from because every molecule is screaming at me to run into his chest, yet my fingernails want to sink into his cheek. I hold my shaky hand out, and reluctantly he passes it over.

"Lily wai—"

"Goodbye, Jace." His mouth is flaying like a fish—his healthy tan now a pale sheen on his remarkable face: the face of a liar. He talks quickly, every word spoken with torment.

"I'm not going anywhere. I'm going to make this right." His hand is flat on the door, my chest heaves uncontrollably, and a mechanical laughs barks from my chest. He blinks, unsure of what to do or say next. "However long it takes, I'm not going without a fight. You need to listen to me. I don't know what Neve told y—" The very sound of her name makes me flinch, and I slam the door shut. It rattles on its hinges, and the brutal force makes even me jump.

The silence afterward is deafening. I just wish I could quiet my feelings too.

I stare at the door, every cell of anger running just under the top layer of my skin, crackling and spitting until it reaches my hands. My fingers curl, and I pound on the door with a sharp scream.

"I hate you!" I roar brokenly.

Chapter Twenty

Four Weeks Later . . .

Four long, painful weeks of sheer, gut-wrenching heartache. I feel it even in my skin. The pain is lingering in my veins and is being pumped around my system quicker than my own blood is.

It hurts. *God, it bloody hurts*. I know my eyes are reflecting the depth of my angst because no matter how widely I smile or upbeat I make my voice sound, everyone looks at me as though I'm about to break, but I think I already have.

Being in this much pain is exhausting. I can't sleep, and when I do, I'm attacked by vivid dreams of him. I wake in a sweat, and nothing seems to shift the crushing sensation in my gut. It's making me sick.

Another wave of nausea rolls through me, and I tense in bed, ready to fly to the toilet. I drag in a deep breath through my nose and slowly breathe it out. I blame it on the dreams—they're so real. As soon as I succumb to the exhaustion and finally allow sleep to win, I'm waking in a pool of sweat, shivering, and feeling sick to my stomach. The burn of whiskey eyes lingers in my mind, and in a groan of emotional pain, I twist, closing my eyes to rid the thought of him.

There has been no contact.

After the first week of him constantly turning up at The Loft, and Harriet politely telling him she would call the police—he stopped.

Stopped emailing. Stopped calling The Loft and me. Stopped contacting Cass. Nothing. He physically vanished from my life.

I don't know what that means, but I can't even think outside my own grief. The severing was so quick and final.

It's eating away at me—the lack of contact. I can feel the thick ball of hurt lodged in my throat. This time, when the nausea comes, it doesn't stop at my stomach; it races up my throat in a bitter, acidic roll, and coughing, I rush into the loo and drop to my knees as the poor amount of food I had managed to keep down disappears into the toilet.

I wipe at my mouth, but soon enough, I begin to heave once more and vomit until my stomach burns and aches. Nothing but my own organs remain, and I feel a sweaty, pathetic mess.

Resting my face against the wall, I close my eyes and sit for a minute. Slowly breathing in and out to rid the after-effects of the nausea.

I wish I were a fly on the wall: his wall. I want to take a small cell of satisfaction from knowing he is hurting as I am, but I don't believe someone who lacks morals like he does will have a hard time letting me go. If anything is hurting, it will be his pride. I can't imagine a woman has ever willingly chosen to leave him. Not that it matters. Neve will no doubt be occupying his time fully now.

I'm constantly at war with my gut instinct and the painful memories of him. I should have listened to my gut all along; something niggled the whole time, right from the first moment we laid eyes on each other.

My mind flies back to that first day when the deep, penetrating, syrupy gaze locked on me with a smirk of crude satisfaction. He knew how attractive women found him, and I was no different.

Or maybe I was.

Because I *was* stupid enough to let a man like Jace Bennett lull me into believing I was something to him. Stupid enough to move in with him, even though that same niggle weighed on me still.

Megan should have been enough of a deterrent. I tell myself I should be thankful the breakup happened so early on. It's my only hope of trying to build myself back up.

I tell myself it is for the best. I couldn't bear to think how hideous this would have all been if it had happened years down the line, or worse, if I had children with him. I know that pain too. I could never choose that pain for my child.

My stomach does another swirl of sickly unhappiness, and my eyes pop open as my hand lands on my sensitive belly—the sudden thought cruel yet undeniable.

No!

I heave again at the hideous and possible predicament, but throwing up doesn't make the fear of the indisputable any easier. Shakily, I stand and stare at my pale, tired expression. My mind flies over the torrent of painful memories and stops at my attack. I was sick after I was attacked, Jace had said. We'd had sex. A lot.

I shake my head as the unfair conclusion lands in my life, mocking me in silent laughter. No. This can't be happening. I think of anything to repel the unwelcome thought, but the seed has been planted, quite literally, I fear.

I brush my teeth and spit furiously into the sink, feeling sick with a different kind of dread. I move to my room and out into the living room, where my phone is charging. I know the local chemist is twenty-four hours, but I check the time regardless, pulling on a pair of jeans and an oversized jumper. I shove my feet in my shoes and grab my keys and purse. I have no makeup on, and I know for a fact, my hair looks matted on the left because I've sweated so much. By the time I get to the street, I have managed to drag it up into a scraggly bun, but I don't torture myself with checking my reflection. I must look as panicked as I feel desolate.

Chapter Twenty-One

I barely recall the drive, but at this early hour, I beat the rush. I head straight to the counter. If the assistant thinks I look dreadful, she doesn't show it. I ignore the ding of the bell sounding behind me and chew my lip. I just want to grab a test and get home. I'm fidgety and unsure when I meet her head on.

She looks fresh and clinical in her white pharmacist attire.

"Good morning. How can I help?" Her voice is bright and perky, at total odds with my own wobbly vocals.

"Oh, hello, a test, please." I shake my head, my thoughts a jumble. "A pregnancy test." I clear my throat and pray my eyes don't reflect my sheer terror at the prospect.

"Lily?" The deep whisper has me gasping, spinning, and tensing all at once, and I come face to face with Jace. I can't comprehend anything more, other than he is here, and I am purchasing a pregnancy test. My mouth drops open, and any colour that had refused to leave me during this hideous ordeal disintegrates on the spot. He followed me here. Does that mean he's been sitting and waiting outside my flat?

"We offer a free testing service if you like, Miss?" Jace's intense eyes go from me to the woman grasping a kit in her hand like a neon sign.

"It's not for me," I spit. "A friend," I explain. My poor heart is pumping wildly in my chest, and my stomach plummets and twists in a tight knot.

"Lily, can we talk?" he murmurs behind me.

"I have nothing to say to you," I whisper, my wide eyes holding the lady's as I spur her on. She must sense the tension because she is thrusting it in my hand as soon as I pay, and before I say thank you, I'm rushing to the door.

"Lily, please—"

His broken plea does nothing to me. I whirl on him in the street. It's quiet out, and the foggy sky represents my mood. I see him then. He looks worn out. Good.

"No!" I shout in his face, taking a step forward, and my hand swipes out and catches his shocked face. The sound is sharp and loud. The pleasant burn up my hand is oddly comforting, but it's quickly followed by the harsh sense of guilt at being so violent with him. "Stay the hell away from me," I screech, horrified by my actions.

"I can't." My handprint is pink and vivid on his cheek, and my palm tingles, reminding me I have sunk to a new low: Adam low.

"You can and you will," I scathe. I hate myself for hitting him, and I don't like who I'm becoming. I blame him for that too.

"Is that really for a friend? Cass?" His amber irises seem hopeful for anything to keep the connection between us. I'm silently praying there is no connection left, but dammit if my body isn't singing a happy song at his proximity.

"Yes." I hold his stare. The lie comes easily, and I even sound believable.

"Give me a chance." He swallows. Oh, he knows he is asking for the world right now.

"I did when I stupidly agreed to entertain this attraction." He reaches for me, and I slap his hand away.

"You still feel it," he shamelessly points out, even if his confident voice is husky with emotion.

"Yes, because it makes my skin crawl." He pulls back as though I've slapped him again.

"You don't mean that." His hand does that annoying thing I once found attractive, as it delves into his hair, and then he looks up through inky lashes, his head bent in defeat.

"I do. I hate that I even met you." I take a step back because I need the distance. My lip quivers, and my eyes fill. I can't look at him and not feel the crippling lust I have always been bombarded with.

"I love you. Don't cry." He is quick to close the distance, too quick, and as his hand takes my arm, and he pulls me to him, I jump and push free.

"Lily, please let me explain. I will do anything."

"Great, leave," I snap, "leave me alone." I sound hysterical. I look homeless. I haven't washed this morning, and makeup has become a chore I have chosen to forgo. "It's over," I spit.

I jump in my car and speed off. My eyes—like the magnet to him that they are—fly to the mirror where I watch him swear profusely, and punch his car, causing the alarm to flare up in a shrill scream.

I barely register the drive home. I just know that I can't do this alone. I'm sitting waiting impatiently for Cass to come over—the last ten minutes have been the longest of my life so far. My leg is jiggling about, my lip a worn chewed-up mess, and I have even bitten into my nails while I wait. My apartment door flies open, and Cass's face widens in shock. I'm guessing I look worse than I originally thought.

"No matter what, it will be okay," she tells me. Cass pulls me into a hug, and I go, but I'm a jittery mess. "Come on." She pushes me toward the bathroom.

I know my voice is going to break because I can feel the emotion hanging in there, "What if . . . " I can't bring myself to say it out loud. "Cass, I don't think I can have him in my life and never *have* him. I'll never be rid of her," I choke out.

"Let's do the test. You could be worrying over nothing," she coaxes diplomatically. She looks slightly unkempt, and I know I have got her out of bed.

"What if I'm not?" I swallow, the knot of anxiety getting bigger.

"Then I'm here, and Sean is here. We will always support you." I nod at the severe expression on her face. "You are stronger than you think," she tells me with a stern look.

Cass finds the tests on the side and begins unwrapping it all, and the crinkle of the cellophane makes it all seem so real suddenly.

"Oh, god." I'm shaking. This isn't what I want. Not now. Not after everything. Life can't be that cruel.

"Calm down." She nods to the empty seat. "Go on." I blink through wet lashes.

"Do you think he believed me?" I whisper, chewing my nail once more. Cass slaps my hand away from my mouth.

"I envy those nails. Don't ruin them." She huffs, then shrugs. "I don't know. He must have followed you there," she offers up. I'm too anxious to hear what she is saying. I take a deep breath and pull my jeans down, but just as my bum hits the seat, I stand.

"I don't want her in my child's life," I choke out. "She's crazy. What if they get together? My child will be subjected to that, *her*?" Cass pulls me in for a hug and holds me tight. I should feel some sort of awkwardness at my jeans being caught around my knees, but I don't.

"Then we fight." She brushes my hair and kisses my cheek. "Stop tormenting yourself. Let's find out; then we can deal." I nod and lower once more.

"Okay."

Cass passes me the stick, and I pee on it.

"How long does it take?" I say in a rush.

"Did you not read the back?" She rolls her eyes, already anticipating my answer.

"No," I mumble. Cass begins reading out loud.

"Can take a minute or two, plus for positive an—" I hold it up to her. She smiles at me softly, her eyes filling with happy yet sympathetic tears.

"Congratulations," she chokes, her face full of emotion.

Everything south of my eyebrows collapses. I drop the stick, bury my head in my hands, and sniff loudly.

"This isn't supposed to happen!" I sob angrily as gentle arms cup my body.

"I'm here every step of the way," she breathes. I hiccup and cry quietly.

It seems an age before I stand, and when Cass helps me up, my legs feel stiff from sitting in the same position for an extended period of time. Her voice has been a comfort, but I don't hear a word she says, not until she pulls my head up to hers and looks at me.

"Let me run you a bath." She swipes under my eye, removing the wetness coating my skin. I sniff and drag in a lungful of air.

I'm numb. Cass is sponging my back. My face is twisted away, pressed to my knee so all I can hear is the heavy thump of my own heartbeat. I've wrapped my ankles over each other and my arms around my knees. It's utterly pathetic.

"I hate seeing you like this." She is struggling to keep her own emotions in check, and her voice is thick with tears. My emotions are now at a standstill, in a permanent state of shock. There would have been a time when I would have been eager to see the mini Jaces running around with their whiskey eyes and dark hair. After losing my first pregnancy, I should be screaming with happiness, but I feel nothing. No elation. No sadness. I've opened up a void, and I'm stuck here. I no longer feel the crippling grief, but that's a relief I shouldn't celebrate. However, I am relieved to have the respite of being suffocated by such pain. I feel cold. Angry. Yes. That's the only thing I can feel: anger.

Anger at some higher power for laughing down on my misery and tossing more on the pile. I never wanted to become someone who pities themselves, but I do now.

"I want to be alone," I whisper. Her hand stills on my back, and I scrunch my eyes shut tightly. I love this woman infinitely but, right now, I want to scream into my pillow and hide, and I can't do that with her here.

"Let me call Harriet," she interjects thoughtfully.

I shake my head.

"No, I need to go in. I can't have more time off." I twist my face and look at her. Her pretty eyes are rimmed with tears, a sob creeps up my throat, and her comforting arms slip around my naked frame.

"Lily, I love you. You're so strong. I know this feels a cruel twist of fate—" Her hands tighten around my shoulders.

"Isn't it?" I sniff.

"Maybe this is what is supposed to happen. Maybe it's the slap in the face he needs?" she replies quietly. I shift, and the sound of water laps around us.

"I don't want her in my life. I can't," I croak.

"It wasn't all bad. I truly think he cares deeply for you. It doesn't add up, an—" She has the look of someone who knows they are going to hurt you by saying something, but believe you need to hear it anyway,

"Please don't say we weren't actually together. He lied repeatedly. Made me sit through dinner with her. He is a liar," I vent, "and the conference—explain that," I spit cruelly, knowing it's not her fault or place to bear the brunt of my anger.

"I know he lied. I just think he was scared of losing you. Have you actually heard him out? He's pretty torn up about it." She rubs my arm, urging me to see it from his side.

I scoff in disbelief.

"I can't believe you're defending him. They slept together at the conference." I sound bitter, incredulous.

She shushes me when my eyes widen.

"I'm not, not at all, but maybe this little bean is here to give you that strength. Maybe talking to him will help you move on." Cass adds, "Or—"

I shoot disbelieving eyes at her. I know that tone, and I am not getting back with him. Hell, no!

"You're hurting so much, though." She sniffs, holding me tighter again.

"I miss him." The one person who would have made me feel indestructible has reduced me to ashes. "But I can't forgive him." I shudder.

"I know. He isn't perfect, but I forgave Sean. You know about Neve now. The truth is out now," she tells me. I turn away, not ready to hear her words. "Don't be so quick to judge; you know better than anyone we all make mistakes, but they don't define us, Lily. I wouldn't trust her as far as I could throw her, but talk to him, hear his side. I don't think he would cheat on you. Did he admit to sleeping with her at the conference?"

"I want to be alone!" She doesn't deserve my curt reply, and I hear her sigh and flinch at the sound. I'm acting out of character, destructive and angry. The sensible and lost part of me is screaming for me to get it together. I don't.

"I love you, Lily Spencer, with all my heart, and if you can't pull it together for you or me, then do it for your baby." She leaves without a response from me.

I sit in silence, feeling the sting of her words after she has gone, and begrudgingly admit she is right. I have plonked my scrawny arse in a pit and wallowed for far too long.

I sit in the bath until I'm wrinkled and cold, and work forces me to get out and get ready. Any enjoyment at dressing has long left. I pull on a black dress and grab some underwear and stockings. I dry, straighten, and pull my hair into a severe ponytail and keep my makeup simple. I look pale and tired, but with the anger, I feel a sense of resilience wash over me.

I grab some fruit and crackers as I leave and head straight to work.

As soon as I turn the corner, I see Jace's car, and with a deep groan, I pull up in a free space and head straight to the door.

"Hi, Lily," he breathes softly.

"Leave me alone, Jace." I push through the door and silence the alarm, and he takes the opportunity to slip in.

"You look how I feel," he mumbles. I aim at him with unimpressed eyes. "I'm sorry." He scratches at his jaw.

"Thanks," I mutter, pulling the door wide open and gesturing for him to leave as I stare at him—actually, I stare through him. This anger is my strength; it's a shield, and I'm utilising it happily.

"I need to explain," he tells me adamantly. His golden gaze is sure and determined.

"No, you want to. It won't change my mind." I stare up at him and see the pain in his eyes, and it sparks more fire in my gut. "You want to know why?" I spit out.

His hand slips to the crown of his head, and he sighs softly at me, seeing none of the woman he knew.

"My father cheated on my mother. He lied to her, and he lied to me. She died in my teens, and her body was barely cold when he married his bit on the side." I speak the information emotionlessly, as though I'm reciting it from a book.

His back tenses, and he casts a worried look out to the street. Good.

"I'm sorry to hear that," he tells me.

"No more than I am, but do you want to hear the best bit?" I give a short laugh.

He holds my stare with uncertainty.

"I haven't spoken to him since." I step up so I am right in his face. "I cut him out. You are no different to him." I roll my angry gaze over him and disgust hangs off every word.

"I am," he whispers. Oh, I beg to differ.

"You came to my exhibition and professed your feelings for me, even though you were still shagging your mate, and then you left with her, to shag her some more, correct me if I'm wrong?" I lift my brow at him as I walk away, needing some distance.

"I can't." He shrugs, looking so miserable my heart lurches.

"I can't believe you were still sleeping with her. Why bother with me?" I hold my hand up when his lips move to reply. "Don't answer that. I can't forgive you. I don't want her in my life. I don't trust her, and if that means losing you, so be it. Now get out." I march to the door and swing it open again.

"Lily, please."

"You once told me she is family. That you can't cut her out." His eyes widen with worry. "I won't ever ask you to choose again. But *I* can make that choice, and I want out."

"Please—"

"What happened at the conference?" I search his gaze and see his eyes drop. He is on the doorstep, and I give him the filthiest look I possibly can. "Goodbye, Jace," I swing the door shut as he begins to tell me nothing happened.

I don't believe him. I lock myself in and walk away, ignoring the rattle of the door.

I'm shaking by the time he leaves. I rush to the back, but the tears I fear don't come. This anger has become my friend. I nibble at a cracker, flick on the coffee machine for Harriet and choose a fruit tea for myself, taking it to my office with me as my phone pings with an email.

It's Jace.

You will never know how truly sorry I am. I can't change the past, but I would wipe it clean if I'd known I would meet you. I love you always.

2 a.m. is lonely. I miss you. I miss who I was with you. I hope one day you can forgive me enough to allow me back in your life.

Yours always

Jace x

. . .

For some reason, my eyes lift to the window down the hall and out into the open gallery, to where he is staring at me through the window of his car. Slowly I stand and slam the door to my office shut on his hopeful whiskey eyes.

The next week drags. If Harriet is finding my despondent mood difficult, she hasn't said so. She also hasn't pried for information. There is no mistaking how utterly heartbroken I am, as sadness has left my face in a perpetual frown.

I have thrown myself into work. It's my solace. In fact, my need to block everything out is doing wonders for my business. I have landed multiple sales, began arranging another exhibition, and most evenings, to save me the pain of being home alone, I have made every effort to attend functions, building my rapport with other owners and artists. I'm burning myself into exhaustion, but my mind is busy, and that's what I need right now.

Harriet has put my lack of appetite in the mornings down to me being miserable. It's easier than admitting I got myself pregnant by my cheating ex.

Only Cass and Sean know my unsettling news. I still haven't quite come to terms with it. There is no doubt that I love this child. None whatsoever. I have felt glimmers of happiness at the news, but it is easily shadowed by the despair at what that means long term for me and my baby. Where will Jace and Neve come into it all?

I try my hardest to avoid those thoughts because the feelings that accompany them are hideously heart-wrenching. The level of hatred I feel towards Neve shocks me. I hate her for so many reasons that I no longer know where that hate starts and ends. It's so tangible that I can almost taste it, and with her being so close to Jace, those same feelings are factoring into my thoughts whenever I think of not just them, but him.

With my friends' unwavering support, I'm keeping as positive as possible and finding the odd time to do a little baby browsing. After my miscarriage, I'm doubtful about buying anything. I'm not usually so superstitious, but I can't bring myself to click buy.

I still can't get my head around everything that has happened these last few months, and the level of anger I feel inside is shockingly out of control. I know I won't ever get closure, not when there is a child involved, nor will I ever begin to understand Jace or Neve's mindset. Their depravity and callousness astounds and sickens me. I can't believe I dated someone like him.

Him and Adam. My taste in men is questionable, that's for sure. This whole ordeal has really knocked me sideways. I've questioned everything about myself. Who I am and what I want—those are things I can no longer answer, but the one thing I do know is that I want to be a mum. It's a less than comfortable situation, but it's my situation, and I get something good out of this.

Harriet knocks on my office door, and I jolt out of my thoughts. She's gone over her makeup and pinned her hair, so I know she is seeing Simon again tonight.

"I'm off now." She gives me a shy smile, and I grin at her from over my desk, being sure to throw my depressed frown off my pale face.

"Have a nice night. You look lovely," I say, shutting down my computer then stacking some files together to put in the cabinet. Her chiffon blouse and tight jeans make her look really willowy.

"Thanks. Need me to do anything before I go?" I shake my head and push back, collecting my bag up as I do.

"No, go and enjoy yourself. There is a piece of art in Lorton & Bouffe that I want to view. Did I send you the link?" I murmur while I place the files away.

"Yes, it will definitely fit in with the Capulet piece." I nod in agreement, stuffing my phone and glasses in my oversized tan bag. "I think it's really great that a percentage of sales will go to charity. I looked them up. It's such a good cause," Hat breathes passionately.

"Yes, it's a small company too, so I thought it'd be really beneficial." I swallow a lump of emotion. "I've contacted Maye, the founder, and she is thrilled. She is definitely coming to our exhibition," I say, moving through my office. I want my next exhibition to be about more than just me or art, I want it to make a difference, and Maye's charity is the perfect cause to plan an event for. No one needs to know it's personal to me. Cloud For You is a non-profit charity that offers support and counselling for parents who have suffered the loss of a child. Harriet falls into step beside me, and she smiles.

"That would be brilliant, really intimate."

"Also, I did want to ask you something. I know you're a little hesitant about putting your work out there, but maybe you could draw something in support of Cloud For You?" I stop and look back at her to see her working her lip into an absolute frenzy. "You're super talented, Hat, I'd love to showcase your work, and this is such an amazing charity. You have such an authentic and unique style. Just think about it, okay?" I rush to speak after seeing her anxiety spike. "No rush. Well, obviously the show is in a couple of weeks." I laugh lightly, and her shoulders relax a little. "It can be anonymous if you'd prefer; that in itself would pull everyone in. Don't stress yourself tonight. Go and enjoy yourself." I rub her arm.

"I'll do it," she blurts, and her quick rush of words shock me. I thought she'd be a little harder to win over.

"Really!" I grin widely and give her a hard squeeze. "Hat, this is great. I can't wait to see what you do." She is grinning like a fool too, and I know what the true cause of that smile and her newfound confidence is.

Simon.

Dating him has changed her. She has begun to see herself in a new light. One she likes. I remember the sentiment well. I felt indestructible when Jace came into my life. The unwavering attention heads straight to your core, and you begin to glow from the inside out, blossoming into a fresher, brighter version of yourself.

Only now I'm wilted and slowly drawing back in on myself.

"Lily? Are you okay?" My eyes snap up to find Harriet crouched with a frown.

I shake my head, knocking my thoughts back into line.

"Yeah, sorry." Rubbing my forehead, I blink away the hurt on my face. "Just got lost a little there."

She hugs me close, and I let her pull me in.

"I can cancel, and we can go to a movie or something?"

"God, no, don't be silly. I'll be fine. I'll get there. Sorry, I know I've been a miserable sod. You've been great," I mumble, faffing with my hair to hide my discomfort.

"You haven't been miserable, not really, just quiet, and it's okay," she adds quickly when my eyes find hers, "but I just want to say that I'm here if you need me." She blinks innocently at me,

"I know, thanks, Hat, but honestly, I'm okay." I lift her coat for her to put on, and she gives me a quick hug before she leaves. Once she has gone, I click the lights off and sit at the small desk up front, staring into the darkness. It's moments like this when I can't quite believe this is my life—all this hurt and pain I'm experiencing, and then other times, I feel a burst of optimism, a sense of hope, and it urges me to move on, look forward and appreciate the things I do have in life and what I have to look forward to. Pressing a hand to my stomach, I let out a long, deep sigh.

"I promise, I'm a fighter really," I say into the dark. "I won't let you down."

I've spent the last week or so keeping Cass at arm's length, and any contact has been purely through text. It's the coward's way, but I just need to come to terms with all this before her usually bossy self starts nit-picking at me again.

I have filled my time with sourcing other artwork, and I even go as far as to think about redesigning the gallery interior. Harriet is trying to keep up with my constant moods and changes in direction. She knows very little but has been a complete diamond.

I had an appointment with the doctor who confirmed my pregnancy. I'm due next summer, and I'm slowly coming round to the idea, but have ignored Cass's suggestion that I come clean with Jace. I can't bear to face him or allow myself to have anything to do with Neve either—I suspect she has got her clutches in him already.

She can have him, but she can fuck off if she thinks I will ever let her have anything to do with my child. For the first time, I feel a burst of happiness.

My stomach is slightly rounded. It's not visibly noticeable, but I can tell the changes when I get dressed: my favourite pair of grey work trousers won't zip up, so I find a cute dress that flares out and manage to disguise the small bump. I just look a little bloated.

I sit and do my makeup, picturing me perched here with a little girl or boy on my lap, their curious fingers reaching for all my brushes. I smile into the mirror, but my mouth turns down when I imagine what that would feel like if Jace were also here—how he would stroll in and lean to peck us both on the heads, telling us how perfect we are. I know I can do this on my own. I just never suspected I would have to.

I am holding on to him more than I should be, and after everything he has done, my heart is still pining for him. I make the quick decision to go to The Hub this weekend and collect the remainder of my things; that way, I can cut all ties completely.

I can meet him somewhere neutral like Bobo's and tell him about the baby after I've collected my belongings. Happy with myself, I rush through my morning routine and head to work.

Harriet has got the day off, and Cass mentioned she has a conference in York, so I do every little inconvenient job around The Loft I can think of to keep my mind busy.

Most of my morning is spent re-jigging the artwork and planning a solo exhibition for Paco, whose work has completely taken off. The harrowing and complexity of his vision is like canvas gold.

He could choose to exhibit his work with a more renowned gallery, but his loyalty is faultless, and even though he has been approached repeatedly, he has stuck with me, and I can't thank him enough.

I take a minute to make myself a tea and sit up front when my phone rings. It's Cass.

"Hey," I answer, blowing on the steaming mug. I check the paperwork in front of me and push my glasses back up when they slip down my nose.

"Hey, how you feeling?" Her tone suggests I will be feeling like crap.

"Really good." I'm breezy and chirpy because I do feel good. The hurt of losing Jace is still there, but it's more manageable now. It hasn't gone. I've just become accustomed to it.

"Oh." Her reply signifies her shock. "Okay, well, I'm glad. Any sickness?"

"Yes, but stocked up on ginger biscuits as they seem to help, and I moved the kettle into my room so I can make tea and not move." I laugh.

"God, are you that bad, still?" She vocally winces.

"It'll pass soon," I say hopefully.

"I've thought of another name," she squeaks out with excitement. Rolling my eyes, I sip on my tea—she has a new name every day. I enjoy hearing them, even if most of them are odd, and some most definitely have been made up.

"Morgan for a girl. Bryce for a boy." I wrinkle my nose, not happy with either. I have secretly fallen in love with the name Mila if I have a girl, but boy's names are still lost on me.

"Sean suggested you come round for dinner on Sunday?" she adds.

"Names, no. Sunday is good." I laugh.

"Oh, I love Bryce," she whines playfully.

"Well, call your child it then," I scoff.

"Maybe I will," she hums.

"Is this the part where you tell me you're pregnant?" I ask, knowing full well she will happily live her motherhood through me before she even considers having her own child.

"Oh, ha, ha. You are on form today!" She sounds sarcastic as hell, and I love that we are slowly getting back to our normal. It feels good.

"New me and all that," I quip.

"You're really feeling positive? Not just saying it?" she asks softly. "Because if you are, that's great, and if not, that's also okay," she slips in kindly.

"I'm getting there, just need a little more time, then I will, you know, tell him."

"Okay, good. He should know," she replies.

"I know." My sigh is long.

"We'll see you Sunday then?" I can hear someone in the background, so it's no surprise that she cuts our conversation short. "Got to go," she says.

"Okay. See ya!" I disconnect before she does and continue looking over my paperwork.

Chapter Twenty-Two

Driving here has cost me. I feel shaken and emotional, but what cuts me more is that when I amble down the driveway, mentally telling myself I can do this, and I need this to break that invisible chain linking me to this man, is that I find not just his car there but Neve's too. The house isn't lit up, but the flicker of low lights illuminates small fractions of the long building.

"Bastard." I'm shaking. My whole body is uncontrollably jittering. My legs feel useless, and my mind is now running frantically every which way as I contemplate having to not only face him but her too. He'd told me he would go out! When I messaged earlier to arrange a time to clear out my things, he promised he wouldn't be here.

Hot anger slams into my fragile mind, and I truly believe it is the only thing making me push forward. I refuse to allow them to intimidate me to this degree. It's the mouldy cherry on top of a very shit cake that gives me the fight to gain closure on this whole shit storm of a ride.

As I round the cars, the house opens up, and it comes into full view, but I don't care for that. All I can see is Jace, reclined on the sofa, his head back, and Neve straddling him in her underwear. My steps falter, and a sob flies from my throat in an agonised, low wail.

How could he, after everything?

I don't truly believe our passionate fling was all one-sided, but I don't recognise the man relaxing with this scrawny slut in his lap. This is the Jace I hate. The one I was scared to meet and give myself to. I should have listened to my gut.

I dash the tears away angrily and storm up to the house, pushing the door open. The cool night air whips and rolls through the toasty house and both sets of eyes pull to me. Neve's smug eyes twinkle in a hard glare, but Jace looks mortified. He lifts his head, but it drops back down.

"Li . . . Lily," he slurs, "what are you . . . " He is frowning in confusion at me, his voice thick and broken. I smell it then, the stench of alcohol. Bottles litter the table and lay on the floor, and the place stinks of smoke too. His head rolls my way, and his lip wobbles. "Lil."

I laugh sardonically.

"Don't bother. I'm not interested. I'm so glad I'm not caught up in this fucking disaster anymore," I spit. My stare drops to the spiteful little girl sitting on his knee because that's what she is—a child. No grown adult would be so purposefully juvenile and malicious!

My stare holds, and she doesn't like it. Good. Her back stiffens.

"What?" she snaps, flipping her hair and dropping into his crotch, making him grunt. Her lips quirk, but my attention is pulled to the man so intoxicated that he can barely lift his head or string a sentence together. Yet Neve is as sober as a nun. I narrow my eyes at her and smirk.

"You won." I shrug on a light, disbelieving laugh. "You won," I admit, looking no less broken than the man slumped in the chair. He really does look like shit. He hasn't shaved, for, well . . . I have no idea, but by the thick blanket of hair plastered on his face, I would say a good three weeks. I hadn't noticed before now, but each time I have seen him, he has had a chin full of hair, and his face has looked sharper, more angular—has he lost weight?

Neve smiles slowly. I reciprocate it.

"You won because I walked. Not because he chose you." I point to Jace, who is trying to lift her fragile weight off his clumsy frame, my name a difficult groan on his lips. "This is what you won." Neve drops her stare back to Jace, heaving to push her off.

"You won a man in love with another woman. Congratulations." I cough on a scathing laugh. I say what only he has said to me—it's not an assumption, maybe a lie from his lips, but I'm willing to use it to have the last word with Little Miss Barbie. Jace's face comes into view, and through the fog surrounding him, he blinks determination into his face.

"Fuc . . . get . . . of . . . f . . . " His slurring is a cause for concern. How much has he had to drink?

I shake my head, forcing my apprehension away; it's not my problem. But I can't help noticing how dreadful he looks: worn out, older, sallow.

I leave them both and feel the bloom of a tiny bud of satisfaction pressing through the fire of anger. They can have each other because karma is cruel, and they deserve nothing more than their own bitterness.

I begin pulling things from his drawers and fill a bag. There is a resounding crash that shakes the house, followed by his husky tone moaning in pain. I can't ignore it. I rush back to find Jace, staggering to his knees, his feet uncoordinated and weak, the coffee table on its side, and all the contents with it.

"Li . . . Lily!" he roars. I blink and rush back, trying to find my belongings, as heavy, clumsy footsteps thud and slide over the floor, followed by thick, drawn-out curses. He thuds into the doorframe, and my eyes flash up to find his. He chokes out a sob, and I truly glimpse a look at the effects of our breakup in his worn, red-rimmed, bristly face. "Li . . . Lily. I'm . . . sorr . . . fuck—" He shakes his head as if he can't find the words or even formulate them.

"You're absolutely wankered!" I spit and throw a t-shirt as a form of defence at him when he reaches for me. I see that he is fully clothed, unlike Neve, who is wearing a tiny scrap of material worthy of the bin.

"Not . . . wha . . . t . . . You . . . thin . . . k—" He shakes his head again, and I dare myself to meet his eyes. His pupils are painfully dilated. He makes to move but slides down the wooden arch, his hand reaching for me.

"Get away from me!" I mean to shout, but it comes out in a croaked whisper. What is wrong with him? He blinks sluggishly, and I watch his detached movements and the slow and almost alien way he moves to look at me. Jace lifts his hands, blinking at them, and swallows thickly—his head rolling as he fights a war against sleep.

He drags in a choppy and short breath.

"Don't . . . lea . . . Lily . . . Shi . . . it. I don't feel . . . good—" He looks like he is on drugs, and I pull back in disgust. His weary confusion and shortness of breath send a sinister thought crashing through my mind.

She wouldn't have. Surely?

He told me he wouldn't be here.

I sidestep him, flinching when his thick hand loosely and weakly cups my ankle. I move out of his hold, and he makes a murmured plea. The only form of comfort I offer him is my hand on his shoulder. I give it a little squeeze, and he chokes out a shuddery breath.

"Cra . . . zy bou . . . you—" he slurs thickly, and my eyes prick with hot tears.

Neve is bent, picking up the bottles, and I storm over, finding everything I hoped I wouldn't. I snatch the pillbox up off the floor and see the evidence of a powdery substance stuck to the rim of Jace's whiskey glass. I take that too, as she flies around. "Hey!" She moves to take it back.

"Those are mine!" she shouts, her blonde hair whipping around her like a sword.

"Then why the fuck are they in his system?" I scream, taking two steps forward so I'm in her face. She flinches, and on their own accord, my full hands come up, and I slam them into her chest. She cries out as she falls and lands with a thud on her skinny arse. "You sick bitch!" She blinks worriedly at me and looks around, possibly for something to help her or maybe hurt me.

"Don't bother." I knock an empty bottle towards her. "You just lost him. Anything else will just strengthen that decision. You need help, Neve. What the fuck is wrong with you?" I snap, staring at her with bewildered disgust. I cannot fathom any reason why someone could do or even think to do the harm she has.

"I love him!" she cries, her body jerking with loud sobs.

I grip the packet and thrust it at her face.

"This is not love!" I roar, and my throat constricts painfully. My chest is heaving, and my arms are shaking, and she sobs, but I couldn't care less for her pain, or her in general. I rush back and drop what's in my hands in the bag. I fall to Jace and lift his face. His head rolls, his eyes are closed, and his breath is hot with alcohol.

"Jace, can you hear me?" I gently shake his head. "Jace?"

"Mmm." His brow twitches, but his eyes remain closed. How much did he have to drink? How many tablets did she give him?

I start screaming for those answers, but Neve doesn't reply, and by the time I return to the living room, she is pulling on clothes. "How much has he had to drink? How many tablets did you give him?" She looks up but ignores me, unfazed about Jace's current state.

I stop and look at her as another thought leaps into my already shocked brain.

"Have you done this before?" She blanches, and I laugh in disbelief. "You're disgusting!" She is barbaric!

She actually has the audacity to scoff.

"No, I haven't. I thought it would help him sleep," she mutters, tying a little string behind her neck to cover her breasts.

"Surely the alcohol would have sufficed!" I snap.

She shrugs, making me see red.

"Those kinds of drugs shouldn't be mixed with alcohol. That can be fatal!" I cry. I should know, I was prescribed something similar after Adam and the baby. How stupid is she?

Her whole face drops.

"It was only two tablets, a small dose."

"But how much has he had to drink?" I scream. Talking to her is useless, and I'm in full panic mode now. I know I shouldn't lift him in my condition, but I coax him awake as much as I can. "I need you to stand," I huff, pushing my shoulder under his armpit and heaving him up. His face swims in confusion before he clocks me and gives me a toothy grin.

"Fuc . . . kin . . . bea . . . tiful—" Jace leans into the wall for support, and I manage to get him a few steps through the house when he drops down and crashes into the side. His arm waves out and takes the table's contents off with an ear-splitting crash. I jump, and Neve, for once, looks uncomfortable.

"Look what you've done!" I cry at her. Jace slumps into a chair, and when she comes over to him, my hand comes up like a stop sign. "Stay the fuck away from him. He'll never forgive you for this!" I'm shaking, lost in volatile seas. I know I could seriously hurt her, so I step back, my shoulders heaving uncontrollably in anger, and my breathing unsynchronised when I think of what I want to do to this woman.

"Now get the fuck out of this house!" I seethe. I stay rooted on the spot as she grabs her bag and runs out of the house.

It's a few minutes before I feel the light touch of his fingertips on my arm. I shrug him away, my fingers delving into my hair with agitation and worry. I look at him for a second. Do I call an ambulance? His breathing isn't normal. I pace, but my legs feel weak, and my body stiff. I'm still hiccupping through heavy tears that I hadn't known I was crying until I heard the light sob.

Jace is mumbling, so grabbing my phone, I call Cass, who answers on the first ring.

"Hey, girl, everything o—"

"I need you to come to Jace's," I sniff and sob.

"Oh, hell. What's happened?"

"Can you come?" His eyes are rolling in his heavy head.

"Yes. Shit. We'll be there soon." She shouts for Sean, and her breathing seems heavy with concern. "Lily, what's happened?"

"I . . . I . . . Neve. She's done something to him," I garble as I really take stock of that.

"We're leaving any second, okay?"

I nod and sniff loudly.

"Jace is in a mess," I warn.

"Okay, look, make yourself a tea, pop a sugar in it, and wait for us, okay?"

"Neve gave him a sedative," I say around choppy tears. "And he's been drinking."

"We're in the car. Maybe call 911 for advice?" It's logical. I should have called immediately—I feel a burst of nauseating guilt. I can't think straight.

"Okay," I stutter.

Everything after that seems to happen fast and in slow motion. Cass and Sean arrive at the same time as the ambulance. Cass runs to me as the paramedic follows Sean through, with another who hops out of the passenger side.

"I think he is unconscious," I sob, quickly walking back in to check on him again, lying lifeless on the floor.

"Do you know what he has taken?" The first asks. I barely look at their faces. I'm in such a wreck. I dither for a minute, then rush to the bag, pulling out the squashed box.

"Here." I drop it in their hand while the other is checking over Jace. "She said he had two," I whisper. Jace looks so vulnerable. I look away as they peel open his limp eyelids.

"Who did, Miss?" The paramedic kneels over him, attaching equipment quickly and calmly.

"Err, his friend," Cass scoffs, and Sean throws her a look, silently conveying she should keep her anger in check.

"He's been drinking, and he was staggering about, struggling to raise his head and slurring. He looked confused but tried to walk to me," I say in a rush, tucking my hair behind my ear. Cass encourages me to sit on the bed and murmurs to me something about a tea. I watch with blank worry as the paramedics start checking Jace over, each one stating vitals and noting them down. They talk directly to Sean, as I'm a nail-biting, pacing mess. I hear mentions of: 'stale alcohol smell, bottles aren't newly opened, small dosage sedative', everything sounds as though it is relevant, but my mind is still tinged with anger, and now guilt.

I can't believe Neve has done this. That stilts me into shock. Cass rushes to me with a drink. I take it, but any feeling has gone. I barely recall the sensation of it in my fingers.

"Why?" I say to my friend. "How could she?" I shake my head and blink a tear away. "She could have killed him," I sniff.

"He's going to be okay, Lily. They are taking him in."

To the hospital? The only thing that draws her attention to me crying is the shake of my shoulders, and she hushes me and pulls me in for a hug.

I watch through blurry eyes as Jace is moved to a stretcher and carried to the ambulance.

A few months ago, this man walked down slate steps into my life with a sexy smile. He chased me relentlessly, drove me crazy with pleasure, made me fall in love, and now I'm sitting, watching him be carried away on a stretcher, through an unkempt house, looking the most vulnerable I have ever witnessed. His unconscious head bobs lightly as he is carried with care through the wide living space and away from me.

I want my whiskey-eyed man back.

I wake to the light flutter of warm air on my skin. My lashes take the brunt as my eyes fight to open. On a groan, I drag a hand across my face to sate the tickle. Another stream of air attacks my lashes, and I squint my eyes open.

Deep, remorseful golden irises watch me thoughtfully, and for a minute, I lay completely still, the last few days filtering back with a sharp and painful stab to my brain. I blink, and Jace tilts his head, watching me closely. Our eyes meet, and I search his for more than emotion. He had me worried sick.

I rode with him in the ambulance; Cass and Sean followed behind as he was blue-lighted. He'd remained unconscious through triage, and afterward, when he was placed on a ward to recover, still victim to the drugs, unconscious and very un-Jace like, all suspected effects of the substance interaction, the paramedics and nurses had advised me.

It had been a long and tense twenty-four hours while he slept the sedatives off. His heart rate had been worryingly low, his blood pressure a state. Neve had been a pill short of overdosing him.

I'd been so wrapped up in my panic of losing him that I hadn't considered calling Viktor or Carl, and by the time I thought about it, Jace was coming round. He was groggy, hoarse, his face pale, and his eyes wore a sadness I knew all too well. But I couldn't sit with him. He hadn't wanted me to contact Viktor or Marie, so I didn't. I slunk away and contacted Carl—too raw to be in such close confines with him.

Yet here I am, giving his PA some respite and making sure he is okay. Deep down, I couldn't leave the hospital. I had stayed outside the ward, checking in with Carl, and watching him through the small pane of glass that allowed me a slight glimpse at Jace's bed. I couldn't leave then, and I can't leave now.

I'd like to say it's put it all into perspective for me, and in some ways, it has, but I can't forget what he did. I can't lose him either.

Slowly, I shuffle so I'm sitting up, and Jace props himself up on the coffee table, his legs spread either side of mine. He gives me a resounding sigh and leans back to regard me thoroughly. I fidget under his heavy gaze, but I can't look away.

"How are you, Lily?" His voice catches, and I bite my lip to hold in my emotion, shrugging as I tuck my hair away.

"I've been better," I admit. He nods and dips his head.

"I am sorry." His voice is low, deep, and scratchy, and his lips are dry. His eyes are dull, and his skin looks tired and dehydrated.

"Me too." My wobbly lip betrays me, and Jace scoots closer, pulling me into a hug. I resist at first, but he holds me gently but firmly to his chest, and as those thick arms engulf me, I relent. I scrunch my eyes tightly and press my face hard into his neck.

"I'm sorry for everything." His voice details a map of emotions. I can't speak, so I simply nod. He leans back, giving me room, and I'm glad. His touch makes my breath falter.

"I didn't know you had texted me," he whispers softly, holding his phone up in explanation.

I know that now. Neve must have planned the whole fucked up mess when I contacted him.

"I know." It all has painfully come to a head. She has manipulated everyone and put Jace in danger.

"I had no idea she . . . " He sighs and covers his face on a slow headshake. "I've known her my whole life. I'd never physically hurt her—I didn't think she was capable—" He looks away, lost in a sea of hurt.

"I understand," I tell him quietly. I may not have known Adam for years, but his capabilities were a painful slap to my sensibilities. "Some people are just wired differently," I murmur, rubbing my bare toes into the thick rug. "You see snippets, and you doubt them, but what really is the hardest part is accepting your own doubt. Because you know yourself better than you know them, and that's supposed to count for something, and when it doesn't," – I shrug out a deep sigh – "it's a real head fuck." I scoff harshly.

"I'm sorry." I reach my gaze up and find his remorse about the way he acted after Adam's attack filtering back at me. He thought the worst of me, but he didn't truly understand the situation.

"How are you feeling?" I stay where I am because standing would put me at closer quarters to him, and I'm not quite ready for that.

"Rough." His smile is soft and a little sad, and I'm not surprised—his body has been put through the mill. I dread to think how his liver is coping with all the alcohol he has consumed.

"I didn't tell Viktor, but he called this morning. He knows something has gone on. He sounded worried. I think you should call him back," I suggest. Jace eyes me for a moment before he takes my knees and tugs me closer.

"Don't!" I pull back, but he holds me tightly. "Jace," I plead for him to let me go. Instead, he leans in and drops his hands on either side of my face. When his eyes drop to my lips, I look away. He cups my chin slowly but purposefully, making me look at him.

"I fell in love with you that first night," he breathes. I shift, and his voice sounds desperate. "I couldn't believe I had finally got you back. I watched you sleep, and I knew you were different. I didn't know what to do about it. I was so scared I would fuck it up. I thought I finally had you, and then you ran anyway." His smile is nostalgic. "Always running," he murmurs, as his reminiscent smile turns into a sad smirk.

"You didn't do anything wrong," I finally admit. "I was as scared as you. I still am." I look at him with all my hurt swirling in my dark grey eyes. "I hate that you slept with her. But I hate it more that you lied." My damn lip trembles.

His eyes flare with guilt, his full lips flatten, and his hand runs over the back of his neck before finding my knee again.

"Lily, please?"

"I gave you a chance. I asked for you to confess. I knew in my gut, but I trusted you, and I fought with that self-doubt constantly. You made me doubt myself." My voice thickens. "I felt so unhinged with suspicion, then guilt over thinking that of you, and the whole time, you allowed me to believe it." He must have known. I stare at him, wordlessly letting my hurt slam him full force in the face.

"I'm sorry." He swallows. "I knew it would cost me you." He rattles my knee, physically urging me to see it from his side.

"You hurt me." I sniff.

"I know." He gives a despairing shrug of his big shoulders. "I'm sorry. If I could take it all back and change it, I would." Jace drops his lips to my ear. "I love you. Please forgive me?"

Surely, stepping back on this path would be stupid. Ludicrous. I remember Cass's words when she and Sean brought us back to Jace's from the hospital.

If you truly couldn't forgive him, you wouldn't be here. Deep down, you knew about her. You're angry that he lied, and that's fair enough, but you would have run if he'd confessed. He just didn't want to lose you. Let him make it right, Lily—no couple can surely go through any more drama than you two already have. Rebuild and let him love you.

"I give you my word, nothing happened at the conference. She messed with the bookings, and we shared a twin room," he says with utter conviction. "I was scared you wouldn't believe me after what she had told you."

"And that's it?" I whisper, finding his eyes and searching them for any signs of a lie.

He sighs.

"She tried to make something happen, but I told her whatever had happened in the past was done, that I was sorry, but I finally found someone I wanted to build a life with." He swallows thickly, his endless amber eyes pleading with me to forgive him.

"I can't ever forgive her," I say quietly. It's not an admission of forgiveness of him, but I see hope in his beautiful eyes. "This is so hard." I sniff.

"Lily . . . Stay here this weekend." I stiffen in his hold, but he keeps me in the cage of his arms. "Hear me out, please," he begs gently. "Twenty-four hours, give me that, and I will never ever let you down again," he promises. Holding my hands in his, he rubs little gentle circles across my skin.

I struggle to get free.

"I don't think it's a good idea." I know it's not. I'll sleep with him if I stay. I know my own weaknesses where this man is concerned.

"Perhaps not, but it's the only one I have, and I can't bear to watch you walk away again," he whispers.

"Jace," I sigh, sounding regretful. It's too much again, too quickly!

"Please, Lily. Just as friends." He drags his hand over his scrunched-up face as though us being friends is a foreign concept. "I'll sleep on the sofa, but I need to explain. I need to put this right. And if I can't, I need to know I tried my hardest." He swallows, his eyes big and hopeful. "This is still your home," he mumbles.

"It just hurts so much," I whisper. That tight, heavy ball in my stomach won't budge, and I know it won't for a good six months, as the guilt of my secret pregnancy is weighing on me too.

"Let me try to fix it. The truth." He swallows, and I look up through wet lashes. "You can ask me anything!" Full disclosure? I examine his eyes thoroughly. "I can't lose you again," he vows desperately.

"I'm not sure I'm ready to trust you," I tell him. He is asking for the world right now.

"Let me work on that," he states, "all I'm asking for is twenty-four hours." Shaky hands take mine and squeeze them softly, reassuringly.

"What, to change my mind?" I scoff and look away, giving my brain the small reprieve it needs from his intensely lost eyes. I'm at war with myself—am I being naïve again?

"I don't expect it to be that easy, but you still love me." There is no arrogance, just the simple, painful truth. I could spend forever denying that fact, but it's written on every cell in my body. "I just need you to know why." He sighs. "To remember why this is worth fighting for." I search his gaze and feel a twinge of fear at the prospect of him being out of my life.

"Is there anything else I should be worried about? Any more secrets?" I ask hesitantly.

"No, and I never wanted there to be Lily, but I realised how bad a mistake it was when I met you. I'm not proud." He admits gruffly, and his cheeks even flush a little. "Before you decide, I need you to know Neve no longer works for me. I contacted my lawyers first thing —she's gone." There is no remorse, just hard confirmation, and hope.

"Completely?"

"For good," he affirms with a light sigh and a sad smile on his face. In the space of a month, his entire life, like mine, has been tipped on its head!

"How do you feel about that?" I question quietly, knowing this can't be easy on him either.

He huffs out a tired laugh and tugs me closer by slipping his hands under my knees.

"Good and relieved. It's hard to admit how unhealthy someone is for you, even if they are just your friend, let alone someone who you have spent most of your life trying to protect," he mumbles regretfully.

"I'm sorry." I rub his hand supportively.

"Don't lie." He smirks, a tinge of sadness in his rough voice. "I don't blame you for being relieved too. I know you tried to accept her." He frowns with a shake of his head. I disliked her from the outset. I eye him sceptically because I think deep down, he knows that too.

"I do feel bad. She has had a tough time." I frown. "Losing her parents, that must have been hard on a child," I murmur, confused at her vile actions but trying to be supportive for him.

"Yes, but she can't use it to manipulate people like she has. Both you and I have lost our parents. That's how I met Neve—we were both in the system. My parents were addicts, and I was removed from their care when I was five." My eyes flash to his in shock.

"Oh, god, Jace. I had no idea!" My own loss seems so minimal compared to his. If he was in care, he was young, too young to lose his parents. My heart bleeds at the horrible thought.

"I know." He pulls me in for a hug, and this time I go willingly. He just opened his heart up to me, and the only way I can say thank you is to hug him back. "Come, walk with me. I'm not sure I can sit here, face to face, and discuss it." He swallows, and nodding, I slowly rise. He takes my hand with a soft smile. "Does this mean I get twenty-four hours?"

I nod slowly, still unsure.

"I'm not staying here though." My voice trips over the words, but I need him to know I can't just sweep everything under the carpet.

He sucks in a deep breath. I've met him halfway. He can't possibly ask for more.

"That means more than you will ever know, Lily." Jace stops at the door and looks down at me, and his hand runs along my jaw. "I love you, beautiful lady." I drop my gaze because it hurts too much to accept that right now. I open my mouth to tell him I'm not ready to go there yet with him, but he drops a finger to my lips. "Let me fix this."

Chapter Twenty-Three

We set off down the path on to the back lakes. The wind has dropped, so I'm grateful for the scarf Jace gave me.

"I can feel your mind whirring from here," he muses.

"I'm just a little stunned. I assumed, I mean, I knew Viktor wasn't your biological father, but—" I can't find the right words, and I feel a bit stupid for being so oblivious to what was right under my nose. "I don't know what I thought. He acts like you're family, and I just thought that maybe you and your parents had fallen out. I didn't want to push it because I never want to discuss my own family." I shrug, recalling Jace and Viktor's loving relationship—so at ease with one another—it was obvious they held a lot of pride and respect for each other.

"He is. Well, as good as. That's why I don't dwell on the past." Jace thrusts his hands into his pockets, and I follow suit because it's bloody freezing.

"If you're not ready to discuss it, I understand." I look up from around my scarf. It's heavy, but a warm weight around my neck.

"Sharing isn't my problem, Lily. I don't want you to think differently about me," he says ruefully.

"I won't. I think perhaps it will help me understand you and what went on with Neve." I glance his way as I utter her name. I hope it will help me lay it to rest.

"Even I don't understand that," he grunts. "I was already in the system when I met her, twelve, and in and out of foster homes. I couldn't settle. I didn't want what I'd had growing up—being around all those foster families didn't feel right. They weren't mine, not really, but nothing else felt right either. If I'm honest, it never has." His voice goes gravelly with emotion, and he drops a quick look at me before staring out across the murky lake. "Not until you. Meeting you, I felt sucker-punched." I bite my lip but refrain from interrupting him. "I still do, Lily."

"Me too," I croak. I clear my throat and follow him slowly down an incline. When we reach level ground, he continues. "Neve was six when she came to the care home, and for some reason, she latched onto me. At first, I didn't want to know, and I kept pushing her away and avoiding her, but she always found a way to keep close. I gave up and took her under my wing. It gave me purpose." He clears his throat, recalling darker days, days that I imagine are far worse than I can even comprehend.

"Do you think she will be okay?" I ask gently. As much as I believe in karma, I feel a sliver of sympathy for her. Living a life in the system can't be easy, and the one thing she ever loved, I took away from her.

"I don't know, but I did everything I could to keep her on the straight and narrow." He sighs, and we head towards the larger lake. Jace lifts a branch, and I duck under, waiting for him to meet me on the bramble-free side. His eyes hold mine when he stands tall. "I made mistakes too." He means her.

"None of us are perfect," I buffer his decisions.

"I know it won't make it easier to accept, but it never meant anything to me. I suppose that may be worse because it did to her, and I think I knew that deep down." He clears his throat. "I . . . " His face looks beaten with guilt. "I've never had to explain myself to Neve—it just was. As a matter of fact, I've never had to consider anyone else. It's allowed me to be selfish, and I was—very selfish." He clears his throat in discomfort. "I've no real family, so I guess she was my constant; family who wasn't actually family. There was no line to cross, and a lot of confused and hurt feelings that we both were trying to get through." Jace drops his head, frowning at his feet, still perplexed by his actions.

"You cared a lot for each other. I can imagine those lines can get muddied when there is no actual definitive restriction. You're not blood related," I offer my own excuses.

"It only really felt like a mistake when I met you. Before, I never cared because she was just always there, and we never spoke about it. It just was—" He shrugs with a loud sigh. "I've always felt beholden to her. She knows about my life, my past. Hell, she has lived it with me, but she has been this huge anchor around my neck that I could never shake. I couldn't move on fully, and at the same time, I couldn't just walk away and leave her in the deep end. I've seen the life she lived; *know it*. But I think her going is for the best." His head tilts back, and his gaze fixes up high as he comes to terms with everything that is changing in his life.

"Will you tell Viktor?" Or will he continue to protect her? He drops a look at me and pulls his hand free, taking mine in his after giving me a questioning look. I let him take it.

"Probably." He squeezes my hand. "I think he tolerated her for me; they were never very close." I nod and look away. We stand in silence, staring out over the sprawling view and countryside. So vast and raw. Even in our turmoil, we find a moment's peace to enjoy it.

"He and Marie can't wait to see you again," he muses softly. I recall both of their loving, worried glances. "Since meeting you, I have some serious competition." He smirks. "Marie is ready to whisk you off on a spa weekend!"

I never had that with my own mother. It would be nice, and I do miss her and Viktor.

Jace and I have our own demons to battle; with Neve thrown in the mix, it was like watching a volcano erupt from afar. But without her—maybe we stand a chance?

"I don't think this will be easy." I frown at our hands. His touch isn't the instant comfort it was, I feel a little awkward, and I hate that. I want the fire back. "But I do love you," I whisper. Jace turns me to him, his gaze sad, hopeful, and desperate. "Don't make me regret this, Jace Bennett," I warn him.

"Never," he vows. I tug my hand free and see his gaze drop at the loss of contact. I need this distance. I can't think clearly when he doesn't give me that little luxury of space.

"Let me hold you, just your hand. I won't ask for anything else, but I need to touch you, Lily. Let me have that." He takes my hand regardless.

"And what about what I want?" My brow lifts itself, and I watch him fail to hold a smirk back.

"It's standing right in front of you. I just need to make you remember, and to help you forget everything else." His mouth turns down a margin, and he tucks my hair when it gets caught up in the wind and wraps across my face. "Our love is fierce. I trust in that, and my instinct tells me this is what you need. No one loves you like I do. I know that love caused you pain, but you hurt me too, beautiful." I gasp lightly, wanting to defend myself, but something inside of me shuts me up. "You cut me off and assumed the worst of me."

I swallow the ache of pain in my throat. Yes, I did, and he is still here, trying to keep us connected, still fighting for me. Us.

"We heal together, and then we can carry on hurtling." He pecks my hand and tugs me along the lakeside. I don't answer because I'm still fighting the compulsion to flee. My heart is here, but my head is stuck between wanting to love him and wanting to run. And my stomach is a cage of butterflies. I know I need to confess to him. I look away before he sees my inner worry.

"Tell me about Viktor." I'm keeping the focus on him, for now.

"Well, he told you how we met. I used to break into the construction site, and after throwing me out multiple times, he took me on. I was still a kid, and he would walk me around and explain everything to me. I shared his passion. He told me to go to college, and he would hire me afterward. I couldn't afford it, but I refused to open up to them. Against all odds, college happened. I was determined to make something of myself, to get out of the hell I was living, but I knew even with all the effort I had put in, it wasn't enough. I was offered a place through a funded programme, and I wasn't about to let the opportunity go to waste. It wasn't until years later that Viktor admitted he had covered my schooling. I owe him everything." I listen further, without saying much. My mind is taking all this information in, but I'm also aware that I'm hiding a secret that could change everything.

I don't want it to push us further apart than we already are.

We are walking back up the incline when I stop, and Jace halts with me. I feel a rush of nervousness.

"I have something I need to tell you," I croak. My hands entwine together, and I puff out a breath, blowing the nausea away. My stomach is a rave of butterflies.

Worried eyes dance over me, and I rush on.

"I know you're going to be mad, and I want to say I'm sorry first and that I had every intention of telling you. I just wanted to get all my belongings first. I wanted to cut ties before I told you." I stumble over the words. We've never discussed children, and hearing the level of depravity of his own childhood, I worry he won't want his own children. What if this is what breaks us? I blanch at that thought.

"Lily, you're worrying me." Jace tugs me to him and rubs my arm, his own eyes looking fearful, desperate. I open my mouth once, twice, and then it just comes out, quickly and panicked.

"I lied to you. I'm . . . I'm pregnant," I whisper. My heart is galloping away in my chest, but the look of annoyance I expect, the anger, betrayal, doesn't come. Jace's face breaks out into a huge grin. He looks a little shocked but thrilled.

"You're sure?" he chokes out. His dazzling eyes search my face, and I nod with a hesitant smile. The elation that has been my own is finally ours. He pulls me to him and holds me close before I'm pushed back just as quickly. "How far gone?" His eyes drop to my stomach as though he can see through my skin at the little blip growing there.

I'm startled. I really was expecting him to be cross. After all, I withheld this information from him, lied at the chemist, and have kept him out of the loop since I found out. I search his gaze, looking to find anything other than deep amber joy burning back at me, but that's all I see, happiness.

"A few weeks. My due date is mid-June, the eighteenth," I confirm. Jace tugs at my coat and unzips it. The cold seeps in, but his warm eyes counteract any shivers. His hand presses to my stomach, and I laugh.

"I'm hardly showing." I brush him off, but his hand remains.

"I know this body," he announces, "and you do have a little added podge."

"Podge?" I scoff. "Thanks!" Typical male. I roll my eyes, but I can't lose the dopey grin I have.

Jace's is megawatt and contagious as his hand presses to the slight curve, a smile dancing over his lip.

"It's not a bump yet." He looks up at me, and I can't help but lift my hand into his tousled hair. "I won't let you down, Lily, I promise." His eyes drag up from my stomach.

I look away because I can't quite allow myself to believe him. We are quiet the rest of the way, and I leave him with his thoughts as we head inside. Jace offers me a coffee. He looks exhausted—his eyes dark and ringed. I ask for a tea and move to sit on the sofa, folding the blanket I left stranded and flipping it over the armrest as I tug my legs up, trying to keep warm. Jace lights the fire, and it creates a nice ambiance.

Once he makes the drinks, he comes over and sits next to me.

"How are you feeling?" I ask.

"Groggy, hungover." His cheeks flame, and he looks out of the window. "I don't usually hit the bottle so hard." His brows bunch together, a small sign of self-criticism.

"I know." I guess I don't, not really, just what I have seen, but he doesn't strike me as the binge-drinking type.

"I used to drink a fair bit, hit the bars—" he offers up hesitantly as his eyes latch to mine, watching for a reaction.

"Pick up women—" I slip in. I knew when we met that he was a serial player. His eyes held that mischievous light, and the way he carried himself was too cocksure. Not so much anymore.

"I had nothing much to live for and no one to disappoint. You can't disappoint yourself if you don't care." He swallows, and he looks at me. I offer him a sad little smile. I really had no idea this vulnerable man was hidden beneath all that arrogance.

"Not even Viktor or Marie; your business?" I sip my tea and wait for his reply. Jace takes his time answering. I imagine that laying out all his regrets is a bit like pressing salt into an open wound.

"They were keeping me afloat," he replies gruffly. It's obvious he's not okay with this line of conversation, but for me, he is putting himself through the discomfort.

"I see." There are far more demons in his closet than I ever allowed myself to believe.

"And now I'm scared that if I lose you, I'll become the person I was the other night." I shake my head. He isn't Neve.

"Jace, you won't," I tell him confidently. I may not know his backstory or who he was before me, but I know who he is when we are together. I owe him a big apology for being so quick to believe Neve's cruel words, even when I knew I couldn't trust her.

"How do you know?" He angles his head. His hand slips over my thigh, and he squeezes the slight muscle.

"Because you have a child to think of. That's what should be important to you now." My eyes hold his, and I try to convey what we need from him without actually speaking. I need to know that even if things between us don't work out, he is going to be the best dad he can be to our child. His head drops, and his lips get lost in the grip of his teeth, as big shoulders lift and drop with a deep sigh.

"But I don't have you," I feel a sliver of guilt at being so hard on him—all I see now is a lost boy, not a big, commanding man. I see a boy lost in a sea of hurt and more abandonment. I try to alleviate that worry for him.

"I never said no to us, but I can't just jump back into a relationship with you." His heavy head lifts, and I see that he is trying not to let his emotions take over his fragile composure. I finish my drink and stand.

"What are you doing?" He stands too, looking grief stricken. His eyes drop to my stomach, and his big palm rubs around his neck, a clear indication he is anxious and agitated.

"Going home. I need a shower and some time to think," I tell him softly.

"Lily, please." He takes my wrist, and his eyes slam shut. His fist is shaking, and it kills me to see him so torn up and vulnerable.

"If you're feeling up to it, we can grab breakfast tomorrow?" I suggest, hating how forlorn he looks. His eyes prise open, and I can see it is taking every smear of self-control to let me go. I put him at ease by saying, "I can't trust myself around you. I need to know we are doing the right thing for all of us." My hand instinctively goes to my stomach. I want the best for my baby, and I need to know he does too, and not just because it means he gets me back. Plus, I've been in this situation before, and it's bringing memories to the surface.

"Breakfast." He nods. "I can pick you up at nine-thirty?" he compromises, slowly letting my wrist go. He looks battered and tired.

"Only if you're feeling well. If not, we can grab lunch or dinner, either or?"

"All." He laughs faintly, and I share a smile with him.

"Don't force yourself. We need you better," I tell him, giving him a hard stare and reminding him of how difficult he was after my attack.

"I will be. I won't let you down," he states passionately on a low breath. I nod and step away.

"See you tomorrow." I give him an awkward smile. It's almost like we don't know each other anymore.

"Call me if you need anything," he blurts as I push through the heavy door. I look at him over my shoulder, finding him with his legs firmly apart and a determined gleam in his eye.

There is the man I know.

I wake to a message from Jace telling me he will be at mine for nine-thirty. I've slept later than expected and wait for the nausea to rattle my body. As usual it stays back, allowing me to believe I may have finally beaten it, but then it hits me with a violence I can't control. I push free of the quilt and dash to the toilet as everything pours out of me until my eyes sting, and I'm dragging in air through my nose noisily. Resting back, I close my eyes and sigh.

"You're going to make me rake thin." I smirk tiredly, rubbing my tender tummy. I'm pushing to my feet to brush my teeth when my phone begins dancing across my bedside table. I pad to my tiny bedroom and find Jace's name flashing up at me. He is probably in a panic because I didn't respond; he'll be going out of his mind.

"Hi." I aim for bright and airy, but my throat is still tickling from the burn of acid. I clear it and inwardly sigh when I hear him let out a long breath. Tucking my phone between my ear and shoulder, I recline on the bed as the nausea hangs around in my stomach.

"Hey, everything okay?" He goes for casual and indifferent, but I know him well enough to know he is fighting against the thoughts racing around his tense mind.

"Yes, sorry, I didn't respond. Morning sickness." I make light of it by laughing. I'm so used to it being a part of my daily routine, I don't account for his trepidation over it.

"Oh, shit, do you need me? I didn't even think—" he trails off and mutters lightly under his breath.

"No, but thanks." I sit on the edge of my bed and try to just breathe in and out at a pace that focuses my mind on that and not the turmoil my gut is in. "It will pass," I tell him.

"Have you suffered much?" he hums. The rush of wind at his end muddies the line, but I still hear his soft words. It's such a doubled-edged sword of a question, but I know that he is referring to my pregnancy.

"I'm sick most mornings," I admit, my stomach loosening up when my sickness finally disperses and allowing me the luxury of walking through to the kitchen to put the kettle on. "I think a lot of my dizziness was because of this little . . . " My words drift off.

I don't want to complain, but I feel pretty lousy most mornings. The sickness and dizziness are a small price to pay to eventually feel the weight of our baby in my arms, see the colour of their eyes, and kiss their soft skin.

"Brute." His voice slides down the line in a husky murmur. My eyes close, and a sad smile rolls over my face.

I laugh lightly, a soft tickle down the phone.

"Yes." Just like him.

"I don't know anything about babies," he admits. His thick voice sounds tired, and I imagine he has been up most of the night with my admission playing on a loop in that tragically beautiful head of his.

"That makes two of us," I add. With Adam, I had started to prepare for a child, recalling earlier memories of my mother and reading a few baby blogs, books, and surfing the net for little snippets of information, but it had all been locked up away with the devastation of losing my first pregnancy. "But I know not what to do." I mean my father, and I hope he can hear that in my tone and relate with his own loss and the rollercoaster that is Neve—all things that have taught us not what to do. "I just know I love this child more than I love myself, and I will do everything to keep him or her safe and healthy," I say with quiet conviction.

"I know you will. You're such a strong woman, Lily. I know you're in pain, and yet you've always kept one foot forward." His thick swallow drowns out my hum. "Your love outweighs your worry. It's one thing I adore about you." His guttural confession makes my eyes sting.

I frown against the phone pressed to my ear as the kettle hits a climax and whistles like a banshee. I step away and bite my lip.

"I don't know." I shrug like he is here and can see me. "I kept running," I muse, trying to lighten the deep conversation.

"To protect yourself, which given the last few weeks, would prove you were right to do so," he mutters regretfully.

"Jace, I don't want to keep going over the past. It won't do us any good." The mere thought of talking about everything again sends me mentally running for the hills. It is a little bit too raw. I've not had the chance to even come to terms with everything on my own. But it's always been like this with this man. Every time I feel I need the luxury of space and time to process everything, he just saunters in, dishes it up on an oversized plate, and before I have even finished that, he is tearing me from my underwear and muddling my brain even more.

"I know, but I don't want you to think I'm just brushing it aside, taking the easy road. You deserve more than that." He angles his voice, so it's demanding but soft—urging me to see it's all for my benefit.

"You do too," I whisper, gripping the phone tightly. I'm trying to forgive him. I won't forget, not for a while, but I can try to forgive. Seeing the level of Neve's manipulation and hearing Jace's past has given me cause to lie awake most of the night. I still haven't managed to pull myself out of the whirling emotions that have clouded me for the past few weeks. All I know for certain is that the thought of losing him for good, the fear of him leaving this world and me behind, is foremost in my mind. "I think our pasts have both been a burden, and we need to let it go. We were happy at one point. I want to get back to some semblance of that," I say, hoping I'm as genuine as I sound.

"You do?" His deep voice rushes out in a hopeful breath. "Lily, I fucking miss you so much beautiful." My heart constricts.

"Can we take it slowly?" I clear my throat and pull the phone away when I hear him clear the emotion from his own throat. "Everything has changed so much. I just need to know I'm doing the right thing, and I think you need to do that too." I'm trying to be as diplomatic as possible—he is still recovering from a pretty traumatic ordeal, yet he seems more bothered about me. Plus, I don't want to send him in an emotional tailspin by saying something that will hurt him.

"I am doing the right thing," he says with utter conviction, "my mind won't change. I'm not going anywhere." I can picture his passionate face at the end of the phone.

I open my mouth to tell him I just need to keep things on a more platonic note when there is a knock on the door. I jump and stand, as if that will help me to see who it is through the wall.

"One minute. Someone is at the door," I say distractedly.

"It's me," he breathes roughly.

"What?" I blurt, moving to the door. I quickly glance out of the window to find his car parked haphazardly outside.

"Let me in." I cut the call and open the door to find Jace freshly shaven. His face is looking brighter and healthier, and he is in a light knit jumper and jeans, a little smirk playing at his mouth. He lifts some flowers, and his eyes run all over me: my pyjama-clad body and fuzzy hair, as I've not even had the chance to grab a shower yet. He steps forward, and I step back.

"I'm not ready," I mutter, and his face breaks out into that trademark slow smile.

"I can see that." His eyes fall to my bare breasts under the small camisole top and drop further to my bare legs and light pink toes. I rub my eyes, trying to feel a bit more awake. I've still not even finished making myself a drink. "You look exhausted." Sympathy laces his husky voice. I duck my head when he moves completely into the room, and I close the door and watch him watching me. "Do you still feel sick?" His hand lifts, but he drops it before it finds my skin.

I shake my head and grab a thin and long cardigan hanging on the small hooks near my door. His eyes flash as I cover myself up.

"Why don't you grab a shower, and I'll make you a coffee?" He cups my upper arm, and I scrunch my nose up.

"No coffee." I make a face and find laughing eyes looking down at me.

"Okay, no coffee. What does my girl want?"

'My girl'. My heart aches and lurches. Ducking my head, I reel off what I want and head straight for the shower. By the time I'm out and pulling some clothes on, Jace is knocking on my bedroom door with my tea.

I feel awkward all of a sudden, and he furrows his brow and rubs at his neck.

"I'll wait for you to get ready." He nods back to the living room.

"No, it's fine." I give him the most genuine smile I can. I don't want him to feel uncomfortable around me, or me him. He drops down on the bed behind me and waits quietly while I do my makeup. I've hardly worn any this past month, so I don't go overboard, just enough to disguise the dark circles and to put some colour back in my cheeks.

"How's work been?" I ask him. Our eyes meet in the mirror, and I find syrupy orbs shining through the sheet of glass at me.

He shrugs.

"Okay, I guess. All okay with the gallery?" I offer a smile. I haven't been in much, and when I have been there, I have been lost in my own mind. Our conversation is so stilted and clumsy that I drop my gaze and try to think of something to say. It was never like this with us before. Maybe it's us trying to muddle our way through with the lack of physical contact. It's the one thing we always got right and possibly our biggest flaw because we couldn't keep our hands off each other. It was the driving force in our relationship.

It hits me like a lightning bolt then; we need to learn to love each other without the raging lust. I'm staring straight ahead, my face locked in thought, when Jace calls my name.

"Hey, where are you?" he says, pushing to sit closer to me. I blush and turn so we are facing one another.

"Why does this feel so awkward?" I huff, shooting him a regretful look.

"Because I'm not inside you," he drawls. His neck tilts back, and the thick column rolls as he swallows his own laughter down.

"I'm being serious," I moan, trying not to bend a little to his typical banter. He always knew when to be light-hearted or gravely serious, and both had me sighing internally and falling harder in love with him.

"So was I." His voice sounds deeper, and he keeps his face averted to save him the trouble of looking at me while not being able to react to his feelings. My cheeks heat more, and when he looks back, he catches the red flare with his thumb. "You still look so sad," he murmurs.

"Jace, don't. It's all just a lot to take in and re-learn," I mumble, standing up and moving away from him. "Let's grab breakfast," I say breezily. Maybe if we move out of the small confines of my apartment, the tension won't be so thick.

Chapter Twenty-Four

With my stomach being as fragile as it is, I stick to toast and fruit. Jace, on the other hand, ploughs through a full English breakfast, but I keep my thoughts to myself, happy to see him eat. He looks pretty worn out. Once I line my stomach, I find myself reaching over to pinch some bacon.

"Oh wow," I hum, chewing thoroughly.

"Do you want me to order you some? Are you feeling better?" He lifts my chin to check my face, and his touch tingles my skin.

"I feel loads better, but I'm okay. I find little and often helps," I tell him.

He is smiling sympathetically at me over the table and seems hesitant, but before I can ask him what's wrong, his hand delves into his hair, and I know he is deliberating saying something to me.

"Jace, just say it." I laugh, nibbling at the little amount of bacon left on his plate as he forks a mouthful in. His brow rises, and he looks surprised. "I know you want to say something," I tell him, picking up my water and taking a sip. When he swallows his food, he exhales softly.

"I don't want to upset you." He frowns, pushing food around his plate.

"Saying that makes me want to know more. I'm sure you won't upset me. You're annoying me by not saying it," I scoff light-heartedly, taking the remains of his bacon and biting into it.

"Okay, well, I wondered if, in your previous pregnancy, you suffered with morning sickness?" He clears his throat after voicing his concern awkwardly over the table to me.

The usual tinge of sadness that comes whenever I think or talk about that time is there. Still, I find myself smiling, enjoying being able to discuss the baby I never had without it circling back to Adam and my miscarriage.

"Yes," I reply quietly. "I was probably this far gone," I tell Jace. Something dark flashes in his eyes, but he takes my hand and urges me to talk to him. That one small gesture of silent comfort makes me feel brave enough to talk about it with him. "But I was just as sick. I had shut it all out of my mind, but now, things keep filtering back in, and I keep thinking, oh, I remember feeling like that or, my baby will be so many millimetres." I laugh lightly, and he shares a smile with me.

"I know you didn't find out what sex the baby was . . . before, I mean," – his hand squeezes mine – "do you want to this time?" I haven't thought about it. I've been too focused on keeping healthy and ensuring I go full term to even allow myself the luxury of that,

I shrug.

"Honestly, I haven't thought about it. I'm just so happy that I'm pregnant at all, but before, I had this gut-deep feeling I was having a girl—it was too early to find out, even after—" I trail off, frowning. I clear my throat and meet his gaze head on. "Do you want to know?" I ask him.

He scoots his chair closer and pulls my hand to his mouth.

"Lily, as long as I have you both, I'm happy. If we wait, I'm okay with that, and if you want to know, then I'd love to find out." I nod and slip my hand free. I don't want to break the moment, but my body is buzzing with addictive electricity. I can't think when he is this close, touching me, and looking at me like I'm the centre of his universe and then some. I know he is my world, but my life just exploded, and I'm still trying to work it all back in; find my own place again in this mess.

"I can't think." I rub the back of my neck and blow out a deep sigh, and when I lift my gaze, Jace is fighting a grin. "Don't look so smug," I drawl. He chuckles and leans back in his chair.

"It's just good to know I've not lost you; hurtling is my favourite thing." He leans forward and clasps his hands on the table, looking over me heavily.

"I thought I was your favourite thing," I respond lightly, "oh no wait, two a.m. is your favourite thing." I begin to laugh, enjoying being able to take a jibe at him. His lips quirk and pull into a bright smile.

"Anything to do with you is my favourite thing," he declares. His compulsion wins, and he leans over to tuck my hair behind my ear. I regard him from beneath my lashes, and when I look up fully, Jace is staring at me with such open appreciation that I blush. He smiles slowly.

"Hey, beautiful." He exhales deeply, and my lips twist in a soft smile.

Hey, to you, too.

His fingers twist and play with the ends of my wavy hair.

"I've missed this, us, you—" he tells me.

"I have too."

"Really?" His frown, although light, is still visible to me. He sounds so serious and unsure.

"Of course I have. None of this has been easy for me. I missed you the second I drove away. I'm glad we're talking," I confess shakily. "We need to, with this little one on the way." I pat my stomach, dropping to take in the small but evident bump now proudly protruding from my body.

Jace clears his throat.

"Yeah, of course," he says throatily. "We need to for the baby." He sits back, casting a perplexed look across the quiet café. My smile slips, and I stare off too, unsure what just happened.

We stumble through the rest of breakfast, hardly saying anything and leaving us both feeling more and more unnerved by the time we pay and leave. Jace, for the first time ever, seems to be completely lost in thought. I'm not sure what has changed all of a sudden, but he looks pretty sombre and far away.

"Thanks for breakfast." Rather than walk to Jace's car, I pass it and thread my fingers together because he seems distant. I lose my step when he isn't driving us forward.

"Where are you going?"

I throw a look over my shoulder and frown.

"I think I should go home." I tilt my head and try to keep my face neutral because I'm really starting to learn what losing my step around this man feels like. It's worse than after the attack, when I was irritated at him and his distance. It seems we are taking one step forward and two backward. This breakup has brought some serious inner turmoil to the surface, so maybe that's why we're struggling so much?

"You're running," he states, face plummeting and a small tick appearing in his jaw.

"No, stalling," I stutter. It's the truth, it's not goodbye but more good day. "Just stalling," I mumble.

"Lily, you're a terrible liar." He sighs hotly.

Yes, I am, but he seems to be finding this so much easier than me.

"You only got out of the hospital yesterday, and I'm still full of all these feelings." I press my hands to my chest. "Two days ago, I was still so angry at you, confused and lost, and then you were rushed to hospital and everything else that came after that—things I believed, that turned out to not be your fault—" I huff on a tremble of my lip. "One minute we're laughing, and the next we can barely string a sentence together." I frown at the ground, shoving my hands into my coat pocket to hide the fact that I want to knot them together, a sure sign I'm feeling anxious.

"Hey, don't get worked up, come here. We can sit and talk in the car where it's warm." Jace crosses the little space between us in two big, determined strides. He pulls me to him, and I go as stiff as a board. "You have every right to be angry at me. Hell, I was livid when all the shit with Adam went down. I get it, and I'm sorry, but I stuck by you even though I wanted to just stay hidden and get my frustration out alone. I couldn't look at you without seeing you beat up and unconscious or myself beating the living shit out of that arsehole." He kisses my hair, a small gesture, but I melt into him. "I'm not saying do it my way, but ignoring it won't work. We have too much riding on this. I won't lose you. I want us to be a family."

I look up to find him holding my heavy gaze with his own softer one.

"Let me take you home. We can talk. Work some things out."

"I just need some ti—"

"I'm not giving it to you. Time doesn't make things go away or easier to deal with. It drags it out. I may not deserve much from you, but I'm taking it, anyway. Please, get in the car." Jace takes my hand and pulls me back toward his car.

I know he's right. I run at the first sign of trouble, the tiniest slip of open confrontation or having to deal head on with my emotions. I'm a coward. I chose the easy option and not always the best one.

"We know the worst there is to know, so it can only get better from here," he tells me, settling me in the passenger seat. "You can't run, Lily, not anymore." The door clunks shut, and I stare at his retreating form, giving myself a good talking to.

The apartment is warm and cosy by the time we return. We remove our coats, and I find my boot slippers and grab us both some water. I've had enough tea to fill me up all day.

Jace is reclined on my small sofa, legs wide apart, and feet firmly placed. His arm is hooked over the edge, and his face is lost in a sea of thought as he stares out of the window. I stand and watch him for a moment, wishing I could crawl inside his head and pick through everything he has stored in there. I don't know him well enough anymore. I'm not sure I ever did. I thought shutting the door on our past would be the way forward, but an hour in his company and Jace has managed to flip it all back on its arse and demand we discuss it. He's right, of course. My way of dealing with things is to not deal with them. Not him, though. He wants to drag me down a bumpy road and is willing to hold my hand on the way.

He turns then, sensing I'm watching him, and I jump into action and cross the room, placing our waters down.

"Thanks." He scratches at his jaw and waits for me to take a seat. I opt to sit at the far end and pull my legs up, twisting so I'm facing him head on. I let out a short but deep sigh.

"Okay," I start, and his mouth kicks up at my attempt at being authoritative. I ignore him, of course. "I know I have something special with you," I start on a light mumble.

"You do," he replies, reinforcing my statement. His own body angles towards me, and he takes my ankle, cupping the slight limb in his large grasp. "Lily, I may have kept things from you, but my feelings were and are real."

I nod, pulling my sleeves over my hands and shoving them between my thighs.

"I don't like that you lied to me, but I understand why you did. I run when things get too much for me; it's a coping mechanism and not a good one." I blush. I'm very aware of my own downfalls, even if I don't like to admit them at the time.

"We can work on that, in time. I don't expect you to trust me because I ask you to. I lied to you, and I hurt you, and I let Neve hurt you. I know what she can be like, so I know it wasn't easy for you," he admits, ambers pouring heartfelt sincerity at me.

"I know you didn't cheat because we weren't even together, but—"

"We had been intimate, so it was wrong of me. I never set out that night to sleep with her," his confession is delivered with a soft plea, spoken gently to keep me grounded and not let me feel overwhelmed with jealousy and anger—to keep me from running. His thumb rubs therapeutically along my soft skin. "I was so angry with myself." His jaw ticks, giving me a small show of that anger now. "We left the gallery, and I got drunk. I just wanted you to want me back. I didn't know what I needed to do to make you feel the same way about me. I'd never felt like this before, so I didn't know how to handle it – or you. I just knew that I had never wanted to keep someone as much as I did you."

"I did want you back. I do," I correct myself when his face falls a little. "I was still dealing with stuff after Adam, and it was just a lot. You can be pretty intense." I laugh humourlessly.

"With you," he declares, "only with you, Lily." We share a tender look.

"Plus, I know that I judged you the same way as I did my dad, but I shouldn't have. You're not the same person. I'm sorry." I bite my lip, feeling shitty once again for being so callous with him.

"It's okay. I'm glad we are finally getting down to the gritty stuff." He gives me a lopsided smile, and I want to crawl in his lap and let him hold me. Instead, I snort. I don't like gritty; it gives me hives. "It's good for us to get it all out in the open. We need to if we want to make things work for us and baby Bennett." His smile is self-indulgent, and he rests his head back but keeps his face on me.

"Baby Bennett, huh?"

"It's got a nice ring to it." He grins, his eyes twinkling.

"Yeah, I guess it does," I muse.

Jace's hand grips my ankle a little harder.

"Come here." His instruction is gentle, and I watch the way his eyes burn and smoulder. I shake my head, but he tugs me anyway. "I just want to hold you, Lils, break down this wall between us." As soon as my torso is close enough, he scoops me up, turning me around, and pulls me back to his chest, and drops his chin on my shoulder. "Hey, beautiful," he sighs.

"Hello, brute." He chuckles at that, and my smile is at total odds with my rushing heartbeat.

His voice is thick when he speaks.

"I'm sorry for everything. I'm sorry I haven't been here for you with the baby."

"You didn't know."

"Because I fucked up." He squeezes me lovingly.

"We both did," I mutter, picking at the cuff of his jumper.

"You remember how it felt when you first met me?" he rumbles. Jace shifts his face and tucks my hair away before resting it back on my shoulder.

"Yes." I remember the blistering intensity of our first night together too. My breathing changes, and when Jace drops his nose into my hair, I know he is there with me too.

"Remember that, Lily, when you're feeling vulnerable or unsure, hold on to that if you can't hold on to me. I know right down to my bleak, shitty soul that I'm the right man for you. I know without a shadow of a doubt, you're my woman. It won't change for me. I know you. I know I'm good for you, and that's why I challenge you. So when you're feeling backed against a wall or ready to hightail it out of here, just remember who will be there to hold your hand on the other side," he affirms roughly, his breath a hot promise along my cheek.

My lip wobbles.

"You're going to make me cry." I shift to ease the emotional discomfort hanging out in my gut.

"I know you think you've cut yourself off from your dad, but did he ever really try to connect with you again after your mum died?"

I shake my head. I'd screamed at my father and yelled that I had never wanted to see him again, and he'd happily obliged. Over the last two years, I've started to receive cards, but the damage has been done. And my stubbornness has got her heels well and truly stuck in the ground.

"Everyone you have loved has gone. I know what that feels like. The new ones you meet along the way, you keep at a distance because if they go, you think it won't hurt so badly, but nothing can hurt more than the loss you're already carrying." I nod again, my tears spilling over my cheeks. "You're a loss I refuse to have; not until I'm grey and old and miserable." He laughs, and I do too, quickly dashing my tears away.

"I know you because I know me, and that's why we connect because you're the other half of me that was walking around lost too." Jace squeezes me and kisses my hair. "I love you, Lily. I love you with everything I have."

My voice feels thick before I even speak.

"I know," I say, "I love you, too."

"Let's take this slowly. We already know what works for us. Let's tackle what doesn't before we move forward." I'm giving Mitch a run for his money because all I can offer is a nod.

"Now, let's talk about this little surprise," – his palm lays flat on my stomach – "have you thought about names you like?"

I settle back and tell him everything, from how I found out to how much I initially struggled to come to terms with it and why I wanted to disconnect myself from him before I told him. How I love Mila for a girl but couldn't think of a boy's name because I would get lost thinking about him and how Cass has been shoving names down my throat left, right, and centre.

"But none that you like?"

I shake my head.

"What about you?" I tilt my head to try and meet his eye, and he grins and frowns, thinking it over.

"I was thinking of some last night. I like Leo for a boy and Luca and Finn. Marnie for a girl, Bella too." He clears his throat. "I actually like Bryce," he tells me, and I scrunch my nose up in disagreement. "Mila is nice," he adds around a chuckle. The distinctive vibration of his phone in his pockets has me scooting forward. He pulls it out and shakes his head tiredly. "Viktor, he keeps checking up on me," he says softly.

"He cares for you a lot,"

"I need to tell him the truth." His cheeks heat. I know he will go full bar and not hide anything, even if it means putting his own head on the chopping board to the man he respects the most.

"He loves you, Jace. I think it will mean a lot that you open up to him." I want to tell him he doesn't need to confide everything to him, but I know Jace has been carrying this around too long.

"Yeah, I know. I'm going to take this," Jace shifts me forward, allowing him the room to get up. He doesn't go far, just to the armchair where he fields a few questions and arranges to meet with him later. I get up as he hesitantly says, "There are a few things I think I need to tell you—"

I'm privy to the one-sided conversation, and when Jace says, "Yeah, yeah. I'm okay. Things are going well," I figure he has told them we are back on talking terms. I give him some privacy and slip off to my bedroom. I'd planned a day of cleaning, so I begin to potter, folding laundry and placing it away, all the while aware of the deep rumble of his voice. It soothes me from the other side of my apartment. After a few more minutes, it goes quiet, and I hear as he heads to my bedroom. He's hooked his fingers on to the doorframe and is watching me when I finally look up.

"I've got some things to take care of . . . before I see Viktor." He frowns, his gaze dipping to the floor. It's a Sunday; surely he can't mean work. My questioning look encourages the truth from him. "Carl needs to go over some things from the lawyer. Neve is kicking up a stink," he admits.

"Oh." I frown. How she has the audacity, I do not know. It makes me angry, but I hold it in.

"Do you need me to do anything? Give a statement about that night, or—" I shake my head, shocked she is still being difficult.

"I'm trying to keep things civilised. I massively underestimated her, and although I hold most of the cards, I don't want her doing something stupid." He clears his throat. I appreciate his honesty, but it bothers me that she is still affecting him.

"You don't mean . . . like hurt herself?" I whisper. He shrugs.

"I'll speak to you tonight?" I nod, and he hesitates before he drops a quick peck on my cheek. He grins, and with a wink, he is gone. I'm grinning at the empty corridor before I close myself in my apartment, feeling a bit lighter than I have done these past few weeks.

Lighter about us, but concerned about Neve's never-ending tactics.

Chapter Twenty-Five

Cass is rifling through my wardrobe as I finish applying the last of my makeup.

"I know I left it here," she mutters, yanking and stuffing items in and out. "It's the black, shimmery one, looks like oil?"

"No, I haven't seen it. Are you sure you didn't misplace it when you moved in with Sean?" Her arse is sticking out of my wardrobe, her head a concoction of clothing.

"No," she huffs amid the piles and piles of dresses.

"Well, I haven't seen it," I tell her.

"Yes!" she squeals and drags something out, holding it high. "Knew it!" I scrunch my face. I can't ever remember seeing it in there. "You need to sort this shit out. It's a jumble sale in there," she huffs and puffs, not bothering to pick up the clothes she has dumped on the floor. I eye the clothes, then her, and she grumbles before grabbing them all and shoving it all back in.

"And yet you still found that." I clip my earrings in and stand, slipping my feet into my ankle boots.

"How are you feeling?" She drops down onto my bed, the dress bunched up in her lap.

"Nervous still," I admit, "is that silly?" I look over my face, briefly checking my makeup.

She shakes her head in the mirror.

"I was like that with Sean, but you said the last few dates have been great, and he always ties you in knots. You two have this mad chemistry," she comments openly.

"Yeah, he does. That's why I wanted to take it slowly and not complicate it so much." I spritz myself and grab my jacket.

"If you don't feel ready now, you never will." Cass gives me a reproachful look, and I don't blame her. I have kept Jace at arm's length, not just because of what happened, but I needed to work on me and my trust issues, issues that sparked when my dad just upped and left at such a painful time in my life. Jace doesn't deserve the hurt my father caused. I want to give him the best version of me. Not a cracked one.

I reapply my lipstick and look back over my shoulder as I say, "I know. I miss him, and The Hub. I want us to be a family. I miss being around him. I want to go back to what we had before everything went south."

"Are you going to ask to move back in?" Her eyes go wide with excitement.

"Yes." I grin, I had wanted Jace to be the one to raise the question, but it will mean more to him if I ask. God, I really do miss him. This past month has been long, slow, and difficult, but so worth it. I've learned so much about him, and with every date, we are slowly getting back to being us.

She pleasantly shocks me by saying, "I'm really proud of you, Lily. You've had a shit year, but you're a different person now." She squeezes my hand.

"Thanks for always being there for me. I know I haven't been the easiest." I blush.

"I'm sure Jace will disagree." She cackles, moving away when I swat her for her underhand comment, cheeky bugger!

"Oh, ha, ha." I'm stifling a deep grin. "Can you lock up? I don't want to be late?" I lean to scoop up my bag and give her a quick kiss on the cheek.

Jace is parked out front, and his eyes widen when he sees me in wet-look jeans and a floaty top. I've paired it with leopard print boots and my leather jacket.

"I'm running out of clothes that fit." I laugh.

He exits the car and beats me to the passenger side.

"You look stunning," he compliments, pecking my cheek. I slip in a breathless thanks and check my reflection while he rounds the bonnet and gets back in. "We can go clothes shopping tomorrow. I'm free all day," he says roughly. His eyes flick up to me, and I smile.

"Sure, all my clothes are fitted, and this little bump is determined to be noticed." I rub the small swell and smile inwardly. I can't believe I'm finally going to be a mum.

Jace pulls back in surprise.

"Really, where on earth could they have got that characteristic from?" His brow is furrowed, and he is fighting a smile.

Shrugging, I pick at nothing on my trousers, a thoughtful smile playing around my mouth.

"His brute of a father?" Jace's eyes are twinkling like mad, and his chest rises on a deep contented sigh.

"That's right, baby. This little brute," – his hand splays over my small bump – "and I are going to drive you crazy. Lots of sleepless nights and late mornings." He grins.

"Got to let me move back in for that," I quip, fluffing my hair and feigning indifference. If Jace could read my body, he would see my heart clapping like a thousand hooves and my lungs expanding too fast. I'm a little breathless, so I clear my throat quietly to dislodge the ache there. When he doesn't say anything, I bring my head around to see he's smiling like an idiot.

"What?" I chuckle nervously.

"Lils, I've wanted to hear you say that for so long. I'd have moved you back in a month ago." He isn't belted up like me, so when he moves to cover the distance, I stay still. His big hand comes up, cups my face and neck, and his smiling face lowers on mine. I blink happily at him as soft lips glide over my parted mouth. "You've made my night. You know that, Miss Spencer?"

"I do," I whisper.

"Ah, two more words I want to hear very soon." I go still with shock. Is he?

He presses a deep kiss on me. Soft but firm lips attack my senses, falter my mind, and the rush of passion is so strong, I lose my train of thought. I kiss him heatedly as flashes of wedding dresses and wedding bells filter through my mind. Jace pulls back enough to allow himself to speak, and when he does, his voice is low and husky.

"I want you home. I'm missing out on all of this. I miss you," he says quickly.

"We have the scan on Monday," I remind him. I haven't kept him completely in the dark. I update him regularly, but I know he wants things to go back to how they were. I do too.

"I'll pick you up, ten-forty?" he questions, even though I know he has memorised any information I have given him.

"Yes, ten-forty."

He nods and flicks the volume setting up a notch on the steering wheel. I don't feel like I have thoroughly appeased him, and I know why. He has been busting his balls for me since we first met, and I have always maintained a level of control and kept myself at a distance by not vocalising how I feel, certainly not like he does. I know he enjoys that aspect as much as I do. Caring for me is second nature to him, a devoted chore that he perfects with every ounce of his being, but I need to reciprocate. This man deserves more than just me. He is entitled to the world, and I'm only giving him a small portion in return.

We travel for another twenty minutes before Jace pulls into a string-lit car park. The tyres crunch over the gravel until he comes to a stop between two four-by-fours.

"It looks very romantic." I smile.

"Yes, well, I'm trying to impress this stunning woman I'm crazy about."

"Oh, I think she will approve," I say, mildly disguising my grin, "possibly even earn you brownie points."

"I'll bank those and collect at a later date," he tells me on a wink and pushes free.

I'm already pushing the door open and have my feet out, but he rounds the car and meets me at the door, anyway. We're coddled between two vehicles. Jace keeps his face bent down so we're eye-to-eye.

"Thank you for bringing me here." That earns a soft smile.

I reach for his cheek, and his eyes fall on me. I smile, lifting to my toes and pressing a gentle kiss to his mouth. His eyes are brighter than a thousand fireflies.

"I've missed you, pretty lady," he says against my lips, his hands now resting on my hips.

I stutter out a deep breath.

"I need you to know I appreciate everything you have done for me—do for me," I add with conviction. "The way you love me never gets old. In fact, it makes me a bit selfish." I blush, but he grins and pecks my lips quickly, allowing me to carry on. "I want everything with you, a family, The Hub. I miss you more than you know. I want to ring you and tell you things all the time," I say breathlessly.

"Then why don't you?" He takes my face and keeps our eyes locked.

"Things have changed so much. It's not just about us anymore, and I needed to know us was just as important as having this baby."

"Jesus, Lily, without you or us, there wouldn't be a baby, and I can't wait to share it all with you. I need you back. I miss you." He searches my gaze before he dips and kisses me. "I want us to be a family. I'm ready when you are. I can't wait for you to come home."

I nod.

"I'm ready. I want to come home. Kiss me again," I whisper on a soft laugh when he smiles boyishly at me.

We have crossed a non-physical threshold. Jace is being more tactile, and neither of us seem as tense. I think we both were unsure when to make the next move, and more importantly, who would do it. But now that we have, I feel ecstatic. We are heading out of the city when he turns.

"I need to show you something," he says breathlessly, his mouth pulling into a smile, "it's a surprise, but I know you will love it."

"Are we going to yours?" I ask, looking for any familiar landmarks.

"Ours." He throws me a wink. "It's ours, Lily."

"Sorry, it's just, does this feel weird to you?" I laugh nervously. "Like the first time we met?"

"Good weird though." He grins. "There has been this gaping hole between us. I'm so glad we've begun to close that gap. I don't want to wave you goodbye, Lily. I want to wake up with you." He looks my way quickly before resuming watching the road. I lean over and rub his knee.

"I want that too, Jace." His smile is wide but hesitant. "Maybe I can stay the night, then move my things back over the next few weeks?" I croak quietly. He nods but keeps his lips closed as we turn off the main road and along the single track to his. As soon as the trees open up, I gasp. The whole house looks new. It's two stories high and boasting a slanted roof and balcony. It looks more incredible than I imagined. "Oh, wow. Jace, this is amazing!" He stops, and I'm out of the car. The site is lit up, but no workmen are around.

"I asked that they keep the lights on. I wanted to show you." He takes my hand. "Come inside. It's better than I pictured it," he says, drawing me towards the house. The ground floor is covered in dust sheets. "Where have you been sleeping?" I whisper, seeing a framed photo of us placed on the book hive. Jace drops his chin to my shoulder. "Hotels or the office."

"Oh," I murmur, my gaze fixed on the wide, happy smiles in the picture. The river cruise. We move along the hive, and another picture greets me, the cruise again. I'm laughing, and he is kissing me wildly. My cheeks are flushed, but our eyes are dazzling.

"I love that picture, Lily." Firm hands envelop my waist.

"Me too." That is the 'us' we both want back.

He shows me around the house. I recognise the layout from the extensive drawings I'd seen. All the wall foundations are in place with new bathroom suites, and furnishings are waiting to go in. Upstairs is still incomplete, but equipped with three spare bedrooms and a family bathroom. Jace explains that the electrics and plumbing need to be fitted. I stop at one door and find the word 'Pea' written on a sticky note and placed centrally.

"Pea?" I query, pushing in without an answer. I gawp when I find a kitted out nursery with stunning baby furnishings. The cot looks ornate, and there is a matching dresser and changing unit. Everything is covered in dust sheets, not that it's necessary as the room is spotless.

"I could hardly write 'Podge', now could I?" His chuckle falters when he sees my teary eyes.

"If you don't like anything, we can change it," he assures me, coming up behind me.

"No," I blubber, wiping my eyes, "I love it, Jace." I walk in, running my hand over the cot. It's already made up, and a blanket is hanging over one side, protected by clear packaging.

Thick arms wrap around my waist.

"The utility is just being fitted. I changed my mind about the units," he tells me, but I shake my head. I know I will love that too. He has really good taste.

"Just one thing was missing," he says regretfully, "you. I'm so glad you want to come home, Lily."

Twisting, I wrap my arms around his neck and press a quick kiss on him. My eyes pull back to the pretty room.

"I am too, but it looks like we won't be home for a little while." I laugh. Why didn't he say he was sleeping elsewhere? I feel terrible and say as much.

He shrugs.

"Does it matter? I'm not going to be anymore." He tugs me to him. "You're lucky you broached moving back because I was about ready to tan your arse." He laughs, nudging his groin into mine.

I give him a sassy smile.

"If I'd known that, I'd have kept my mouth shut." I move out of his grasp when he laughs throatily.

On a shaky sigh, Jace says, "Lily, there's something I need to ask you." His sombre tone makes me slow my movements. He sounds worryingly serious.

"What's that?" I twist to find him on one knee. I gape and slap my mouth shut. My heart is slamming away crazily but joyfully in my chest. A single, delicate, and petite ring is nestled snugly in a velvet box, with an ornate and vintage diamond glinting up at me.

"Be my wife, Lily Spencer? Be my family? Say yes so we can have everything that was taken away from us. Marry me, Lily." I'm so shocked, and he looks a little stunned too before he rushes on. I reason that he probably didn't plan on asking me tonight, and maybe his emotions got the better of him. "Fuck, this isn't how I planned it, but you want to come home, and now you're here, and I feel so fucking alive again, beautiful."

His gaze is glittering, excitement and fear swirling in those amber orbs, as he runs an agitated hand through his hair.

"It may seem too soon, but after living a solitary life, it always feels I was cheated out of meeting you. I waited too long for you. I want to marry the woman I love and bring lots of little Bennetts into the world." He stands and takes my face—my shock, stretching into a wide smile. "Dammit, Lily, I want to see that smile every morning, and I want all of your laughter. I want to see your achievements and share mine with you. I want all my memories to be of you. Us!" He motions to my swollen stomach. "Marry me, Lily Spencer?"

I sob out a yes, and wrap my arms around his neck as he kisses me swiftly, deeply, and passionately. I hold on to him with everything I have, and he sighs out a shuddery breath.

"I wondered what it would feel like with your stomach pressed up against me," he murmurs. "I love that our little baby is cocooned inside you. I honestly never thought I'd ever have anything like this. Thank you, beautiful."

He cups my jaw and kisses me before lifting my hand and sliding the ring onto my finger.

"I planned to wait until we were settled, but I can't wait anymore, Lily. We're missing out on too much. I want to hurtle with you. I want to feel breathless and free." He sighs, kissing me deeply: slow and delicious. Jace cups the back of my head and holds me to him as he devours me at a leisurely pace. He pecks my lips slowly, pulling away before he pulls on my lower lip. "I can never thank you enough for giving me another chance. I don't deserve you."

"Jace, you deserve more than you know. I love you. Thank you for taking a chance on me and showing me what love is." I find his empathetic, loving eyes on mine. "It's more than I ever expected. It's something I never thought I could have either, and I wouldn't change our story for anything. I love you. Kiss me."

He holds me for a while, standing in the nursery before murmuring about showing me around the rest of the house. With it primarily being open plan, it doesn't take us long to move around the spacious and contemporary structure. After twenty minutes, Jace is pulling me eagerly to a door back up on the upper level. I give him a quizzical frown.

"What's in there?"

"It's yours. Have a look." I eye him, seeing his anxious smile and excited eyes. I shrug and walk past him, curious to see what is behind the heavy door. My hand is on the handle, the grip reminding me of the token of fierce love now wrapped around my finger. My gaze drops to the ring, and I smile before I glance back at him. He is grinning like a child, and shaking my head, I push in and stop short of the threshold.

I'm speechless, utterly moved by this man's continuous desire to please me on all levels.

"Jace, I . . . "

"Do you like it?" Thick hands span my waist, cupping my swollen belly, as his chin finds a home on my shoulder. He sighs when I sag back into him.

"I love it," I whisper, and my eyes take in the unfinished darkroom. I'd mentioned once how I was forever hidden in one of these at university. It's perfect. "Thank you," I whisper.

"You're welcome, baby. It won't be much longer now, another few months, and it should be completed."

"That soon?" It still looks in disarray. Jace steers me out of my mini haven, and we descend the stairs.

"Hopefully, unless we have any sudden complications, but most of the foundations were in place. I made sure to include those on my first build. We're lucky to have had a fairly dry winter. The tree coverage also helps." He's in business mode, and I laugh inwardly.

"When did this all begin?" I ask as we head back to the car.

"The day I was discharged from hospital. I knew that I had to build this for you. I wanted to win you back," he hums.

"By building me a house?" I smirk when Jace pulls me to a stop and cups my arse.

"No, beautiful, I wanted to build you a home." Leaving me no time to respond, he pecks my nose, then dips lower for my lips. "I've been pushing it forward. The contractors have been here most weekends and evenings too. That's how it's happened so fast." Weeks, that's how long it's taken. The outer shell is already showing the promise of our future.

"It's amazing. I can't believe the transformation, just from adding another floor."

"Because I pre-empted wanting to extend in the future, I have saved myself and the builders a lot of time," he comments.

"I can't wait to see it finished," I tell him, getting into the car. We drive back, chatting animatedly about plans for the garden. Jace is against a pond now we're expecting. I love all the water, and I say as much, and we argue lightly about the pros and cons with a little one in the house.

It's not long before we are pulling up outside my flat. He meets me out the front and holds my hand up to the main door. He begins to smile, and I clock it, grinning too. He looks mischievous.

"What?" I ask, nudging his hip with my own.

"Remember when I dropped you here that night and followed you to the door?"

"Oh, the gentleman act?" I scoff playfully.

"If you recall, I was!" I'm back in the dark doorway and pushed into the corner, barricaded by this big man and his knowing smile.

"Not for long." I laugh.

His eyes drop to my lips being chewed.

"I wanted to kiss you badly, then," he husks.

"Why didn't you?" I never understood why he pulled away.

"I felt electric. I wanted to keep that feeling, and I thought you wouldn't do the shoot," he admits ruefully.

"I wouldn't have done it," I tell him honestly, sharing in his glittering happiness. My reaction scared me too much. If he'd have kissed me, I'd have cut the contract.

"This should have been our first kiss," he murmurs, his face holding that same quizzical desire from that first night. For a moment, I'm thrown back to a time when I didn't know this man, to a time when *we* weren't written, to *that* moment. His lips are a crushed bruise on mine, and I reciprocate with intent, humming my happiness.

"Are you not going to invite me up for coffee?" He wiggles his brows, making me snort, and patting my arse cheeks, he follows me up. When we get in, Cass has cleaned the place up. I make a mental note to get some flowers to thank her. I take my jacket off, and Jace takes it from me, hanging his and mine up. He then offers to make me a drink.

"Oh, a tea please, decaf," I say as I find something uninteresting on the TV, and he joins me with two steaming cups. We sit down and chat for hours. There isn't a worry between us. Everything is out in the open, and we have only the future to look forward to. Jace lifts my hand and inspects my ring before he threads his own hand with mine. The ring is as delicate as it feels alien on my finger, a foreign weight I haven't yet become accustomed to but love already.

"Here's to hurtling," he whispers in my ear. I turn and cup his face with my free hand to cement his toast with a kiss.

I would hurtle to the end of the earth and back again with this whiskey-eyed man.

Hurtle to my forever after.

The End.

Epilogue

They say the way to a man's heart is through his belly. They must not have accounted for me in that saying; the way to mine is through my soul. The way to mine is with Lily Spencer.

I've had the honour of having her in my life for the past three years, her big grey eyes and teasing smile, framed by long thick hair—hair thick enough to wind around my wrist. My nostrils flare when I think of how damn lucky I am to have a woman like her by my side, she's a witch, all fluttering eyelashes, and passion personified, and she simply floors me.

Everything has changed for us—for the better. My life is a dream. I have my stunning wife and gorgeous little boy. I gaze at his chubby cheeks and open mouth as he snoozes in the car, and my hands tighten on the wheel, knowing he will be out for a while, and I will have my wife all to myself for a few rare quiet minutes.

Hell, if someone had told me a few years ago, I was going to be a smitten, loved-up family man, I'd have laughed in their face and possibly fucked their wife for good measure.

I can't shake the guilt of the frivolous past I have lived, but I know for a fact it's what makes me love my girl so hard.

She's that little bit of heaven I never knew existed.

A bit of heaven I'm damn addicted to.

We've fought our battles, and although we lost each other along the way, we're stronger than ever, fiercer. I'm a better version of me than I ever knew possible. I have the world at my feet and the absolute love of my life holding my hand.

Everything I hadn't even known I was working towards is within these twenty-four acres. Safe and hidden away in our little Hub. I crunch down the driveway and smirk. Not so little.

Luca murmurs in his sleep.

"We're home, little man. Where's your Mumma bear?" I muse quietly, looking up at the display of windows, trying to find my anchor. One perk of this design is I can see everything the minute I turn the bend and hit the open driveway. The house is a wide glass display of luxurious homeliness. Lily really has got good taste. I mean, she picked me, so anything after that is a given. My eyes flick to the mirror where honey-thick irises look back at me. My eyes are her undoing, and I thank whatever higher power gave them to me before I exit the car and unclip Luca from his seat. He is out for the count, looking as angelic as possible, and a movement in the house pulls my head that way, to her. She is moving quickly through the top landing with a frown that has me kicking the door shut—that and the fact she hasn't noticed me.

Something is up.

I'm frowning deeply as I head to the door and use my shoulder to pivot my way in. Luca sniffles and presses his face into my chest, murmuring in his sleep. I can't hold back my smile because even when he is asleep, he seeks me out. He's a daddy's boy, that's for sure.

I take the stairs two at a time, my lean legs eating up the space, and I'm quickly pushing my way into Luca's room. I grab the remote on the small shelf and press the blinds into place before I secure him in his toddler bed and slowly peel his tiny shoes off. His breath huffs out, followed by a small snore, and grinning, I drop and press a kiss to his feather-soft skin.

"Love you, brute," I whisper and walk backward, watching to make sure he stays asleep. I'm pressing his stair gate into place when I hear the toilet flush in our en-suite.

I find Lily pacing as her grey eyes stare at something in her hands.

"Hey, what's up?" I ask softly. She jumps, and her wide eyes flash to mine as her cheeks pinch red. My eyes drop to the thing in her hand, and she holds it up guiltily.

"I'm late," she says and walks straight to me, biting her lip in a giddy smile when my mouth pulls into a shit-eating grin.

"Too fucking right," I huff. We've been trying for months. Her hands are shaking, so I scoop her up, my heart swelling with satisfaction when her soft laugh floats through the room.

"Where's Luca?" she murmurs.

"Fast asleep. You should have waited for me." I pout and peck her mouth to stop her gnawing furiously on her lush lips.

"Sorry." She blinks uncertainly up at me. "I've felt nervous all day. I really want this one to be positive," she tells me.

I take us to our enormous bed and sit with her in my lap, the pregnancy test clasped tightly in her small hand.

"Let me have it," I demand gently. As soon as I relieve her of the test, her hands knot, and I smile sympathetically at her. "Lily, we already have perfect—anything more will be a bonus," I say gently. "A perfect bonus," I tell her, and she drives her hands into my hair to save her from twisting them together. She kneels up and presses her mouth to mine.

"I know, I know," she whispers, her forehead touching mine. Her endless cloud-grey eyes shut, and I know she is trying to prepare herself for the same disappointment we've shared with each test, all the while keeping beautifully positive. Lily's constant light shines through at me always—she's the bravest person I know. "I just want to give you lots of little Bennetts," she hums, trying to keep her emotions in check. "It will be ready," she says in a rush of air. We both drop our gazes, foreheads still in contact. I twist the test over, and a sob leaves her mouth.

Happiness flourishes through me like an uncontrollable tidal wave, crashing through my heart and making it burst with pride and joy.

"Another bear cub!" I grin, seeing her eyes shine with tears. She sniffs back another sob, and I slant my mouth over hers, my own eyes stinging with unshed tears.

Delicate fingers cup my bristly face. Her vulnerability is her biggest strength, and she feels everything just as deeply as I do. Only once I won her back did I truly begin to learn who this woman was, learn who I was. We're a force. A dream. We have the kind of love that captures the attention of others—this undeniable bond that even now baffles and awes me.

I'm her safest place, and in return, she has given me the kind of life I spent my years feeling I wasn't worthy of. I'm indestructible with her at my side. I laugh into her mouth as she pushes at my suit jacket.

"Kiss me," she demands, as teeth rip at my lip and she forces me back, her tongue delving in to attack my own. I roll her and push her hands high and hold her still.

"Lily," I say on a rough husk, "beautiful. I don't want to do anything to jeopardise this. Let's get in with the specialist first." I search her eyes, and she shutters her pain. After Luca, we lost a baby, and it has been a challenge to conceive since then. Luca is a miracle.

Adam caused some damage, and birthing Luca took its toll on my girl. Until now, we have been met with repetitive disappointment.

"Me either," she breathes, her chest rising harshly below her shirt. "Just hold me." Her eyes flicker between each of mine. "I just want to feel you." Her low whisper sends a thump of love to roll through my chest, and nodding, I swaddle her face with my big hands and lower my mouth to kiss my wife in the way she deserves.

I strip us both down to our underwear and pull her to me so we are skin to skin, lips touching, her inky, damp lashes bringing a self-indulgent smile to my face.

"Don't be scared," I tell her. Lily's gaze drops away, but she brings it back, showing me how resilient she is.

"I don't want to be—" Her sigh is resigned, but her beautiful eyes shine with childish hope. "I am scared," she confesses shakily.

I dip and press my forehead to hers, breathing deeply. My life centres around this woman, and it kills me to know she is feeling such a mix of potent feelings. "I know. Let me go and give the hospital a call, then we can have a lazy afternoon. I'll make a carpet picnic, and we can slob with our little man."

Sighing, she smiles at me, and I wink and peck her mouth.

"I'm crazy about you."

"You're just crazy," she mutters and twists on a roll when I pinch her toned arse. Her yelp has me laughing.

"Damn witch,"

"Brute!" she calls when I saunter off. I lift my finger, telling her to be quiet when a little cough sounds from Luca's room. She is slipping from the big bed and walking towards me with the confidence of a woman who knows she has her man by the balls. My eyes roam freely over her body, and when she reaches my side, she looks up at me, mouthing, 'Crazy for you,' as she slips past and pushes her way into Luca's room—his baby voice calling for her.

I wake slowly. My eyes remain closed, but I can hear the soft huff of Lily beside me. It's the first night in months that she has slept solidly. Prying my lids open, I lie still and take her in. She's so fucking beautiful. Her skin has got a healthy glow to it from our recent holiday, and she looks the most relaxed she has in months. I'm ready to book another just so I can whisk my family away and have them all to myself again. I need to clear it with the specialist, but we should definitely celebrate.

Another baby. Viktor and Marie are going to be thrilled.

We're booked to go to the clinic in two days, and that has allowed us both to relax a little. I can't bear to watch her smile through another heartbreak. I want to give this woman the moon and the stars, but the universe keeps intervening, and I feel like it's my karma for how selfish I was just a few short years ago.

I stare at her with the world on my shoulders, silently pleading to an unknown force to give my girl everything she wishes for. I reach to touch her, but stop. She needs to sleep. She's putting too much pressure on herself to give me what she deems the perfect family. I'd love more children, of course I would, but I am also ecstatic with the family I have now. I slide out of the bed and sit on the end, yawning.

"Daddy!" Luca calls. I lift my head to see his cheeky little face grinning at me from the gated doorway down the hall. I push up and walk quickly to him, kissing his head as I lift him over the gate.

"How's my favourite little man?" I ask, running my hand through his curly mop.

"Sam! Sam!" he chants.

"It's like that, is it? I only love you endlessly and give you the world, but you want Fireman Sam." I lift my brow, and his legs kick excitedly. "You got a kiss for me?" I grin at his sleepy face, as his lips pucker, and I smack a kiss on him. "Shall we make Mummy some pancakes?" I ask.

"Pa-cakes!" he squeals, gritting his teeth and shaking with excitement.

"You're crazy," I say and take us both downstairs, dragging a throw off the sofa and shaking it out on the floor. I place Luca down, who begins pulling cushions down so he can lie on them. I need to get him a beanbag, I think, watching him struggle to gain his balance on the uneven surface.

"Sam, Daddy!"

Lily comes down half an hour later. She scoops Luca up and covers him with kisses.

"Why didn't you wake me?" She carries him over to me and

drops him on the countertop, leaning into him and blowing raspberries on his rounded belly. A gurgled squeal erupts from his little mouth, and we both flinch at the sound.

"You needed it." I nip her shoulder and kiss her mouth when she turns into me.

"Luca, kiss!" His small lips pucker, and his cheeks blow out like a puffer fish, and chuckling, I give my little brute what he wants.

"Resting for two now," – I wink – "maybe we will have a little Mila after all." I sigh hopefully. Luca wriggles to get free as his favourite theme tune comes on. Lily lowers him, and I pull her to me, happy to have her to myself for a second.

"There's only one thing that makes me hornier than you do." I kiss along her jaw.

"Oh, really, should I be worried?" She laughs, her brow slanting up high. I drag my teeth along her chin and move to grab her breast through the thin material of her top.

"Pregnant you, makes me crazy horny," I admit. "It will all be fine," I add, when I see a look of trepidation pass through her clear gaze. Despite our struggles, we try to keep grounded and not let the grief swallow us up. It's out of our control, but how we act and treat each other, regardless of those trials, is what keeps us striving.

Her smile is small.

"Well, I'm not spending a lifetime pregnant so you can walk around with a stiffy," Lily blurts on a soft laugh.

"Stiffy!" Luca sings.

I snap my eyes to Lily, who looks appalled. I double over in a belly laugh.

"Oh my god, no that's not funny," she whines.

"Stiffy!" Luca giggles, seeing how the mere word has brought tears of laughter to my eyes. Luca sings the words over and over in a toddler-fuelled mumble, and I shake and roll my hips to the words, grabbing Lily and thrusting my hips into her bottom.

"Don't encourage him," she chastises, trying to pull away from the hot press of my cock burning into her arse.

"Who Luca or my very hard co-"

"No!" She laughs, slapping her hand over my mouth and stopping me from uttering that word. I nibble her ear, then sigh and drop my chin to her shoulder, and my chest expands on a deep contented sigh. "Could life get more perfect? Look at him," I muse as we watch Luca, who has his little chubby knees bent whilst he bops to his favourite program. He thrusts his little hand in the air. "Stiffy!" he chants.

Lily's head drops back on my shoulder in a groan that quickly turns into a happy laugh, and she shakes her head in agreement—it doesn't get more perfect than this.

"Hurtling with you both has been the most fun I've ever had," I tell her, turning her so I can look at my beautiful girl. I smooth her hair back and observe my wife's gorgeous face with slow appreciation. "I love you like crazy, Lily Bennett," I declare on a rush, and I do wholeheartedly and with every fibre of my being. She is exquisite. Perfection, and somehow, she is mine.

"Back at you, my brute," she murmurs, dropping forward to seal it with a kiss.

Acknowledgments

Firstly I wish to thank my friends who pushed me to chase my dream, My book buddies who read Whiskey promises when it was a pitiful draft and told me to write more. My son, who forever tells me to never give up, you, my poodle, are an angel.

When I first started writing this series, I didn't think I'd ever finish. I also wrote it as one book, Portrayal, one humongous book, which I had to split in two, and that's how Betrayal came about. It's an extension of my love for Jace and Lily. The story I thought would never end. I'm still gutted I had to write those two words: The End. However, I had other characters wanting my attention, and so I gave it to them.

Thank you so much for reading!

More By This Author

Escape The Light
Mybook.to/Escapethelight

About the Author

A. R. Thomas is an indie author from England. She lives with her son, and when she's not screaming from the sidelines at his latest sporting event, she is usually lost to the thought of a book. She manages to make the most innocent of things sound dirty; it's both a gift and a curse, but thankfully her friends encourage her.

If you would like to connect with A. R. Thomas, she would be thrilled to hear from you.
Facebook: AR Thomas
Instagram: arthomasauthor